Regency RAKES

2 Glittering Regency Romances

TALLIE'S KNIGHT
by Anne Gracie

THE PROPERTY OF A GENTLEMAN
by Helen Dickson

THE Regency RAKES

A further collection from some of Mills & Boon
Historical Romance's most popular authors

THE
Regency
RAKES

by
Anne Gracie & Helen Dickson

MILLS & BOON®

First published in Great Britain 2003 by
Harlequin Mills & Boon Limited,
Eton House, 18-24 Paradise Road,
Richmond, Surrey TW9 1SR

THE REGENCY RAKES © Harlequin Books S.A. 2003

The publisher acknowledges the copyright holders of the individual works as follows:

Tallie's Knight © Anne Gracie 2000
The Property of a Gentleman © Helen Dickson 1998

ISBN 0 263 83668 1

138-0903

Printed and bound in Spain
by Litografia Rosés S.A., Barcelona

TALLIE'S KNIGHT
by
Anne Gracie

Anne Gracie was born in Australia but spent her youth on the move, living in Scotland, Malaysia, Greece and different parts of Australia before escaping her parents and settling down. *Gallant Waif* was a finalist in the Romance Writers of America's Best First Book competition. Anne lives in Melbourne, in a small wooden house which she will one day renovate. You can contact Anne Gracie via her website at www.annegracie.com. She would love to hear from you.

Also by Anne Gracie
in Mills & Boon Historical Romance™:

GALLANT WAIF
AN HONOURABLE THIEF
THE VIRTUOUS WIDOW
(within **Regency Brides** short story collection)

Prologue

Yorkshire, February 1803

'My lord, I...I am sure that Mr Freddie—'

'Mr *Freddie*?' Lord d'Arenville's disapproving voice interrupted the maidservant. She flushed, smoothing her hands nervously down her starched white apron.

'Er...Reverend Winstanley, I mean, sir. He won't keep you waiting long, sir, 'tis just that—'

'There is no need to explain,' Lord d'Arenville coldly informed her. 'I've no doubt Reverend Winstanley will come as soon as he is able. I shall wait.' His hard grey gaze came to rest on a nearby watercolour. It was a clear dismissal. The maid backed hurriedly out of the parlour, turned and almost ran down the corridor.

Magnus, Lord d'Arenville, glanced around the room, observing its inelegant proportions and the worn and shabby furniture. A single poky window allowed an inadequate amount of light into the room. He strolled over to it, looked out and frowned. The window overlooked the graveyard, providing the occupants of the house with a depressing prospect of mortality.

Lord, how unutterably dreary, Magnus thought, seating himself on a worn, uncomfortable settee. Did all vicars live this way? He didn't think so, but he couldn't be certain, not having lived the sort of life that brought him into intimacy with the clergy. Quite the contrary, in fact. And had not his oldest friend, Freddie Winstanley, donned the ecclesiastical dog collar, Magnus would be languishing in blissful ignorance still.

Magnus sighed. Bored, stale and unaccountably restless, he'd decided on the spur of the moment to drive all the way up to Yorkshire to visit Freddie, whom he'd not seen for years. And now, having arrived, he was wondering if he'd done the right thing, calling unannounced at the cramped and shabby vicarage.

A faint giggle interrupted his musings. Magnus frowned and looked around. There was no one in sight. The giggle came again. Magnus frowned. He did not care to be made fun of.

'Who is there?'

'Huwwo, man.' The voice came, slightly muffled, from a slight bulge in the curtains. As he looked, the curtains parted and a mischievous little face peeked out at him.

Magnus blinked. It was a child, a very small child—a female, he decided after a moment. He'd never actually met a child this size before, and though he was wholly unacquainted with infant fashions it seemed to him that the child looked more female than otherwise. It had dark curly hair and big brown pansy eyes. And it was certainly looking at him in that acquisitive way that so many females had.

He glanced towards the doorway, hoping someone would come and fetch the child back to where it belonged.

'Huwwo, man,' the moppet repeated sternly.

Magnus raised an eyebrow. Clearly he was expected to answer. How the devil did one address children anyway?

'How do you do?' he said after a moment.

At that, she smiled, and launched herself towards him in an unsteady rush. Horrified, Magnus froze. Contrary to all his expectations she crossed the room without coming to grief, landing at his knee. Grinning up at him, she clutched his immaculate buckskins in two damp, chubby fists. Magnus flinched. His valet would have a fit. The child's hands were certain to be grubby. And sticky. Magnus might know nothing at all about children, but he was somehow sure about that.

'Up, man.' The moppet held up her arms in clear expectation of being picked up.

Magnus frowned down at her, trusting that his hitherto unchallenged ability to rid himself of unwanted feminine attention would be just as effective on this diminutive specimen.

The moppet frowned back at him.

Magnus allowed his frown to deepen to a glare.

The moppet glared back. 'Up, man,' she repeated, thumping a tiny fist on his knee.

Magnus cast a hunted glance towards the doorway, still quite appallingly empty.

The small sticky fist tugged his arm. 'Up!' she demanded again.

'No, thank you,' said Magnus in his most freezingly polite voice. Lord, would no one come and rescue him?

The big eyes widened and the small rosebud mouth drooped. The lower lip trembled, displaying to Magnus's jaundiced eye all the unmistakable signs of a female about to burst into noisy, blackmailing tears. They certainly started young. No wonder they were so good at it by the time they grew up.

The little face crumpled.

Oh, Lord, thought Magnus despairingly. There was no help for it—he would have to pick her up. Gingerly he reached out, lifting her carefully by the waist until she was at eye-level with him. Her little feet dangled and she regarded him solemnly.

She reached out a pair of chubby, dimpled arms. 'Cudd'w!'

Again, her demand was unmistakable. Cautiously he brought her closer, until suddenly she wrapped her arms around his neck in a strong little grip that surprised him. In seconds she had herself comfortably ensconced on his lap, leaning back against one of his arms, busily ruining his neckcloth. It had only taken him half an hour to achieve its perfection, Magnus told himself wryly.

She chattered to him nonstop in a confiding flow, a mixture

of English and incomprehensible gibberish, pausing every now and then to ask what sounded like a question. Magnus found himself replying. Lord, if anyone saw him now, he would never live it down. But he had no choice—he didn't want to see that little face crumple again.

Once she stopped in the middle of what seemed an especially involved tale and looked up at him, scrutinising his face in a most particular fashion. Magnus felt faintly apprehensive, wondering what she might do. She reached up and traced the long, vertical groove in his right cheek with a small, soft finger.

'What's dis?'

He didn't know what to say. A wrinkle? A crease? A long dimple? No one had ever before had the temerity to refer to it. 'Er...it's my cheek.'

She traced the groove once more, thoughtfully, then took his chin in one hand, turned his head, and traced the matching line down his other cheek. Then carefully, solemnly, she traced both at the same time. She stared at him for a moment, then, smiling, returned to her story, reaching up every now and then to trace a tiny finger down the crease in his cheek.

Gradually her steady chatter dwindled and the curly little head began to nod. Abruptly she yawned and snuggled herself more firmly into the crook of his arms. 'Nigh-nigh,' she murmured, and suddenly he felt the small body relax totally against him.

She was asleep. Sound asleep—right there in his arms.

For a moment Magnus froze, wondering what to do, then slowly he began to breathe again. He knew himself to be a powerful man—both physically and in worldly terms—but never in his life had he been entrusted with the warm weight of a sleeping child. It was an awesome responsibility.

He sat there frozen for some twenty minutes, until a faint commotion sounded in the hall. A pretty young woman glanced in, a harried expression on her face. Freddie's wife. Joan. Jane. Or was it Jenny? Magnus was fairly sure he recognised her from the wedding. She opened her mouth to speak, and then saw the small sleeping figure in his arms.

'Oh, thank heavens!' she exclaimed. 'We've been looking everywhere for her.'

She turned and called to someone in the hallway. 'Martha, run and tell Mr Freddie that we've found her.'

She turned back to Magnus. 'I'm so sorry, Lord d'Arenville. We thought she'd got out into the garden and we've all been outside searching. Has she been a shocking nuisance?'

Magnus bethought himself of his ruined neckcloth and his no longer immaculate buckskins. His arm had a cramp from being unable to move and he had a nasty suspicion that there was a damp spot on his coat from where the little moppet had nuzzled his sleeve as she slept.

'Not at all,' he said slowly. 'It's been a pleasure.'

And, to his great surprise, Magnus realised he meant it.

Chapter One

London, February 1803

'I want you to help me find a wife, Tish.'

'Oh, certainly. Whose wife are you after?' responded Laetitia flippantly, trying to cover her surprise. It was not like her self-sufficient cousin Magnus to ask help of anyone.

His chill grey stare bit into her. 'I meant a bride. I find my own amours, thank you,' said Magnus stiffly.

'A *bride*? You? I don't believe it, Magnus! You've hardly even talked to a respectable female in years—'

'Which is why I require your assistance now. I wish the marriage to take place as soon as possible.'

'As soon as possible? Heavens! You will have the matchmaking mamas in a tizzy!' Laetitia sat back in her chair and regarded her cousin with faintly malicious amusement, elegantly pencilled eyebrows raised in mock surprise. 'The impregnable Lord d'Arenville, on the scramble for a bride?' Her rather hard blue eyes narrowed suddenly. 'May I ask what has brought this on? I mean, seeking a bride is unexceptional enough—you will have to set up your nursery some time soon—but such unseemly haste suggests… There is no…ah…*financial* necessity for this marriage, is there, Magnus?'

Magnus frowned repressively. 'Do not be ridiculous, Tish. No, it is as you have suggested—I have decided to set up my nursery. I want children.'

'Heirs, you mean, Magnus. Sons are what you need. You wouldn't want a string of girls, would you?'

Magnus didn't reply. A string of girls didn't sound at all bad, he thought. Little girls with big clear eyes, ruining his neckcloths while telling him long, incomprehensible stories. But sons would be good, too, he thought, recalling Freddie's sturdy-legged boy, Sam.

The issue of getting an heir was, in fact, the last thing on his mind, even though he was the last of a very distinguished name. Until his journey to Yorkshire it had been a matter of perfect indifference to Magnus if his name and title ended with him. They had, after all, brought him nothing but misery throughout his childhood and youth.

However, far easier to let society believe that d'Arenville required an heir than that a small, sticky moppet had found an unexpected chink in his armour. It was ridiculous, Magnus had told himself a thousand times. He didn't *need* anything. Or anyone. He never had and he never would. He'd learned that lesson very young.

But the chink remained. As did the memory of a sleeping, trustful child in his arms. And a soft little finger curiously tracing a line down his cheek.

It was a pity he'd had to ask Laetitia's assistance. He'd never liked her, and saw her only as often as duty or coincidence demanded. But someone had to introduce him to an eligible girl, damn it! If he wanted children he had to endure the distasteful rigmarole of acquiring a wife, and Laetitia could help expedite the matter with the least fuss and bother.

He returned to the point of issue. 'You will assist me, Tish?'

'What exactly did you have in mind? Almack's? Balls, routs and morning calls?' She laughed. 'I must confess, I cannot imagine you doing the pretty, with all the fond mamas looking on, but it will be worth it, if only for the entertainment.'

He shuddered inwardly at the picture she conjured up, but

his face remained impassive and faintly disdainful. 'No, not quite. I thought a house party might do the trick.'

'A house party?' She shuddered delicately. 'I loathe the country at this time of year.'

Magnus shrugged. 'It needn't be for long. A week or so will do.'

'A week!' Laetitia almost shrieked. 'A week to court a bride! Lord, the *ton* will never stop talking about it.'

Magnus clenched his jaw. If there had been any other way he would have walked out then and there. But his cousin was a young, apparently respectable, society matron—exactly what he required. No one else could so easily introduce him to eligible young ladies. And she could help him circumvent the tedium of the dreaded marriage mart—courting under the eyes of hundreds. He shuddered inwardly again. Laetitia might be a shallow featherbrain with a taste for malicious gossip, and he disliked having to ask for her assistance in anything, but she was all he had.

'Will you do it?' he repeated.

Laetitia's delicately painted features took on a calculating look. Magnus was familiar with the expression; he usually encountered it on the faces of less respectable females, though he'd first learnt it from his mother. He relaxed. This aspect of the female of the species was one he knew how to deal with.

'It might be awkward for me to get away—the Season may not have started, but we have numerous engagements...' She glanced meaningfully at the over-mantel mirror, the gilt frame of which bore half a dozen engraved invitations.

'And to organise a house party at Manningham at such short notice...' She sighed. 'Well, it is a great deal of work, and I would have to take on extra help, you know...and George might not like it, for it will be very expens—'

'I will cover all expenses, of course,' Magnus interrupted. 'And I'll make it worth your while, too, Laetitia. Would diamonds make it any easier to forgo your balls and routs for a week or two?'

Laetitia pursed her lips, annoyed at his bluntness but unable to resist the bait. 'What—?'

'Necklace, earrings and bracelet.' His cold grey eyes met hers with cynical indifference. Laetitia bridled at his cool certainty.

'Oh, Magnus, how vulgar you are. As if I would wish to be paid for assisting my dearest cous—'

'Then you don't want the diamonds?'

'No, no, no. I didn't say that. Naturally, if you care to present me with some small token…'

'Good, then it's decided. You invite half a dozen girls—'

'—and their mamas.'

A faint grimace disturbed the cool impassivity of his expression. 'I suppose so. Anyway, you invite them, and I'll choose one.'

Laetitia shuddered delicately. 'So cold-blooded, Magnus. No wonder they call you The Ic—'

His freezing look cut her off in midsentence. He stood up to leave.

'You cannot intend to leave yet, surely?' said Laetitia.

He regarded her in faint puzzlement. 'Why not? It is all decided, is it not?'

'But *which* girls do you want me to invite?' she demanded through her teeth.

Magnus looked at her with blank surprise. He shrugged. 'Damn it, Tish, I don't know. That's your job.' He walked towards the door.

'I don't believe it! You want *me* to choose your bride for you?' she shrieked shrilly.

Faint irritation appeared in his eyes. 'No, I'll choose her from the girls you pick out. Lord, Tish, haven't you got it straight yet? What else have we been talking about for the last fifteen minutes?'

Laetitia stared at him in stupefaction. He was picking out a bride with no more care than he would take to buy a horse. Less, actually. Magnus was very particular about his horse-flesh.

'Are… I mean, do you have any special requirements?' she said at last.

Magnus sat down again. He had not really thought past the idea of children, but it was a fair request, he supposed. He thought for a moment. 'She must be sound, of course…with good bloodlines, naturally. Umm…good teeth, reasonably intelligent, but with a placid temperament…and wide enough hips—for childbearing, you know. I think that about covers it.'

Laetitia gritted her teeth. 'We are talking about a lady, are we not? Or are you only after a brood mare?'

Magnus ignored her sarcasm. He shrugged. 'More or less, I suppose. I have little interest in the dam, only the offspring.'

'Do you not even care what she looks like?'

'Not particularly. Although I suppose I'd prefer someone good-looking, at least passably so. But *not* beautiful. A beautiful wife would be too much trouble.' His lips twitched sardonically. 'I've known too many beautiful wives not to realise what a temptation they are—to others.'

His subtle reference was not lost on Laetitia, and to her annoyance she found herself flushing slightly under his ironic gaze. She would have liked to fling his request in his even white teeth. However, a diamond necklace, earrings and a bracelet were not to be looked in the mouth.

Even if Lord d'Arenville's bride was.

'I'll do my best,' she said sourly.

The black knight reached down, caught her around the waist and lifted her onto his gallant charger, up and away, out of reach of the slavering wolves snapping at her heels.

'Begone you vicious curs!' he shouted in a thrillingly deep, manly voice. 'This tender morsel is not for you!' His arms tightened around her, protectively, tenderly, possessively. 'Hold on, my pretty one, I have you safe now,' he murmured in her ear, his warm breath stirring the curls at her nape. 'And now I have you, Tallie, my little love, I'll never let you

go.' Clasping her hard against his broad, strong chest, he lowered his mouth to hers…

'Miss? Miss Tallie? Are you all right?'

Tallie jerked out of her reverie with a start. The buttons she had been sorting spilled out over the table and she scrabbled hurriedly to retrieve them. Brooks, her cousin's elderly butler, and Mrs Wilmot, the housekeeper, were bending over her, concerned.

'Oh, yes, yes, perfectly,' Tallie, blushing, hastened to assure them. 'I was in a silly daze—miles away, I'm afraid. Was there something you wanted?'

Brooks proffered a letter on a silver tray. 'A letter, Miss Tallie. From the mistress.'

Tallie smiled. Brooks still behaved as if he were in charge of the grand London mansion, instead of stuck away in the country house belonging to Tallie's cousin Laetitia. Tallie took the letter from the tray and thanked him. Dear Brooks—as if she were the lady of the house, receiving correspondence in the parlour, instead of a poor relation, dreaming foolish dreams over a jar of old buttons. She broke open the wafer and began to read.

'Oh, no!' Tallie closed her eyes as a sudden surge of bitterness rushed through her. She had assumed that with Christmas over, and Laetitia and George returned to Town, she and the children would be left in peace for several months at least.

'What is it, Miss Tallie? Bad news?'

'No, no—or at least nothing tragic, at any rate.' Tallie hastened to reassure the elderly housekeeper. She glanced across at Brooks, and explained.

'Cousin Laetitia writes to say she is holding a house party here. We are to make all the arrangements for the accommodation and entertainment of six or seven young ladies and their mothers, possibly a number of fathers also. Five or six other gentlemen may be invited, too; she is not yet decided. And there is to be a ball at the end of two weeks.' Tallie looked at Brooks and Mrs Wilmot, shook her head in mild disbelief, and took a deep drink of the tea grown cold at her elbow.

Mrs Wilmot had been counting. 'Accommodation and entertainment for up to twenty-five or six of the gentry, and almost twice that number of servants if we just count on a valet or maidservant for each gentleman or lady. Lawks, Miss Tallie, I don't know how we'll ever manage. When is this house party to be, did she say?'

Tallie nodded, a look of dire foreboding in her eyes. 'The guests will start arriving on Tuesday next. Cousin Laetitia will come the day before, to make sure everything is in order.'

'Tuesday next? Tuesday next! Lord, miss, whatever shall we do? Arrangements for sixty or more people to stay, arriving on Tuesday next! We will never manage it! Never.'

Tallie took a deep breath. 'Yes, we will, Mrs Wilmot. We have no choice—you know that. However, my cousin has, for once, considered the extra work it will entail for you both and all the other servants.'

'And for you, Miss Tallie,' added Brooks.

She smiled. She knew he meant well, but it was not a comforting thought that even her cousin's servants regarded her as one of them, even if they did call her Miss Tallie. She continued.

'I am empowered to hire as much extra help as we need, and no expense spared, though I am to keep strict accounts of all expenditure.'

'No expense spar—' In a less dignified person, Brooks's expression would have been likened to a gaping fish.

Tallie attempted to keep a straight face. The prospect of Cousin Laetitia showing enough consideration for her servants to hire extra help was surprising enough, but for her *not* to consider expense would astound any who knew her.

'No, for she says the house party is for her cousin Lord d'Arenville's benefit, and he is to pay for everything, which is why I am to keep accounts.'

'Ahh.' Brooks shut his mouth and looked wise.

'Lord d'Arenville? Lawks, what would he want with a house party full of young ladies—oh, I see.' Mrs Wilmot nodded in sudden comprehension. 'Courting.'

'I beg your pardon?' said Tallie, puzzled.

'He's courting. Lord d'Arenville. One of those young ladies must be his intended, and he wishes some time with her before he pops the question. He'll probably announce it at the ball.'

'Well, well, so that's it. A courting couple in the old house once again.' Brooks's face creased in a sentimental smile.

'Lord, Mr Brooks, you're a born romantic if ever I saw one,' said Mrs Wilmot. 'I can no more see that Lord d'Arenville lost in love's young dream than I can see me flying through the air on one of me own sponge cakes!'

Tallie stifled a giggle at the image conjured up. 'And why is that, Mrs Wilmot?' she asked.

'Why?' Mrs Wilmot turned to Tallie in surprise. 'Oh, yes, you've never met him, have you, dearie? I keep forgetting, you're related to the other side of madam's family. Well, you've not missed out on much—a cold fish if ever I saw one, that Lord d'Arenville. They call him The Icicle, you know. Not a drop of warm blood in his body, if you ask me.'

'But I thought all you females thought him so handsome,' began Brooks. 'He had you all in such a tizz—'

'Handsome is as handsome does, I always say,' said the housekeeper darkly. 'And though he may be as handsome as a statue of one of them Greek gods, he's about as warm and lively as a statue, too!' She shook her head and pursed her lips disapprovingly.

Intrigued though she was, Tallie knew she should not encourage gossip about her cousin's guests. And they had more than enough to do without wasting time in idle speculation. Or even idol speculation, she giggled silently, thinking of the Greek god.

'Well, then,' she said, 'it is fortunate that we need not concern ourselves with Lord d'Arenville except to spend his money and present him with a reckoning. And if we need not worry about expense, the servants may be billeted in the village. I suppose we should begin to make a list of what needs to be done.' She glanced at the clock on the mantel. 'I am expected back in the nursery in half an hour, so we will need to hurry.'

Later that evening, as she walked slowly out of the nursery, leaving her three charges yawning sleepily in their beds, their loving goodnight kisses still damp on her cheeks, Tallie decided she would have to take herself more firmly under control. She could not go on in this fashion.

The degree of resentment she'd felt this morning had shocked her. And it was not Laetitia's thoughtlessness Tallie resented, but the mere fact that she was coming home.

It was very wrong of her to feel like that; Tallie knew it. She ought to feel grateful to Laetitia for the many things she had done for her—giving her a home, letting her look after her children… And it was Laetitia's home, Laetitia's children. Laetitia was entitled to visit whenever she wished.

The problem lay with Tallie. As it always did. With her foolish pretences and silly, childish make-believe. It was getting out of hand, pretending, day after day, that these three adorable children were hers. And that their father, a dashing and romantic if somewhat hazy figure, was away on some splendid adventure, fighting pirates, perhaps, or exploring some mysterious new land. She had dreamed so often of how he would arrive home on his coal-black steed, bringing exotic gifts for her and the children. And when they had put the children to bed he would take her in his arms and kiss her tenderly and tell her she was his pretty one, his love, his little darling…

No. It had to stop. She was no one's pretty one, no one's darling. The children's father was bluff, stodgy George, who drank too much and pinched Tallie's bottom whenever she was forgetful enough to pass within reach. He never came near the children except at Christmas, when he would give them each a shilling or two and pat them on the head. And their mother was Laetitia, beautiful, selfish, charming Laetitia, ornament of the London *ton*.

Tallie Robinson was nothing—a distant cousin with not a

penny to her name; a plain, ordinary girl with nothing to recommend her; a girl who ought to be grateful to be given a home in the country and three lovely children to look after.

There would never be a dashing knight or handsome prince, she told herself savagely. The best hope she had was that a kind gentleman farmer might want her. A widower, probably, with children who needed mothering and who would notice her in church. He would look at her plain brown hair and her plain brown eyes and her plain, sensible clothes and decide she would do. He would not mind that her nose was pointy, and marred by a dozen or so freckles—which *no* amount of lemon juice or buttermilk would shift. He would not care that one of her front teeth was slightly crooked, nor that she used to bite her nails to the quick.

Tallie looked down at her hands and smiled with pride at her smooth, elegant nails. That was one defect, at least, she had conquered since she left school. Her kindly gentleman farmer would be proud... Drat it—she was doing it again. Weaving fantasies with the slenderest of threads. Wasting time when there were a thousand and one things to be done to prepare for Cousin Laetitia's house party. Tallie hurried downstairs.

The Russian Prince cracked his whip over the arched necks of his beautiful grey horses, urging them to even greater speed. The curricle swayed dangerously, but the Prince paid no heed—he was in pursuit of the vile kidnappers... No! Lord d'Arenville was not a prince, Tallie told herself sternly. She patted her hair into place and smoothed her hands down her skirts. He was real. And he was here to be with his intended bride. He was *not* to appear in any of her silly fantasies.

But Mrs Wilmot was right—he certainly was handsome. Tallie waited for her cousin to call her forward and introduce her to the guest of honour. He had arrived only minutes before, clad in a caped driving coat and curly brimmed beaver, sweeping up the drive in a smart curricle drawn by two exquisitely matched greys. Tallie knew nothing at all about horses, but even she could tell his equipage and the greys were something out of the ordinary.

She'd watched him alight, springing lightly down from the curricle, tossing the reins to his groom and stepping forward to inspect his sweating horses before turning to greet his hosts. And thus, his priorities, Tallie told herself ironically—horses before people. Definitely *not* a prince.

He was terribly handsome, though. Dark hair, thick and springy, short cropped against a well-shaped head. A cleanly chiselled face, hard in its austerity, a long, straight nose, and firm, unsmiling, finely moulded lips. His jaw was also long, squaring off at the chin in a blunt, uncompromising fashion. He was tall, with long, hard horseman's legs and a spare frame. And once he'd removed his greatcoat she could see that the broad shoulders were not a result of padding, but of well-developed musculature. A sportsman, not a dandy... *A pirate king*... No! A haughty guest of her haughty cousin.

Tallie watched him greet Laetitia—a light bow, a raised brow and a mere touch of lips to hand. No more than politeness dictated. He was not one of her...*cicisbeos*, then. Tallie heaved a sigh of relief. It was not to be one of *those* house parties. Good. She hated it when her cousin used Tallie and the children to cover up what she called her 'little flirtations'.

Laetitia turned to introduce him to those of the staff whose names he might need—the butler, the housekeeper and so on. Tallie watched him, noting the way his heavy-lidded grey eyes flickered indifferently over Brooks and Mrs Wilmot.

'And this is a distant cousin of mine, Miss Thalia Robinson, who resides here and keeps an eye on things for me.' *Insignificant poor relation who hangs on my sleeve, depending on my charity,* said her tone, dismissively.

Tallie smiled and curtsied. The cold grey eyes rested on her for a bare half-second and moved on. Tallie flinched, knowing that in a single glance Lord d'Arenville had noticed the freckles, the pointy nose *and* the crooked tooth, and despised her. He hadn't even glanced at her nice nails. *No gallant knight,*

he, but a cruel count, coldly plotting the heroine's downfa—
Enough!

Tallie watched his progression into the house with rueful disappointment. Mrs Wilmot was right. The man acted as if he expected the whole world to fall at his feet, while he would not so much as notice if it crumbled to dust right under his long, aristocratic nose! She wondered which of the young ladies was his intended. She had not taken to any of them, but she could not imagine anyone wishing to wed this arrogant Icicle.

'Thalia!' Her cousin sounded annoyed. Tallie hurried inside.

'You called, Cousin Laetitia?' She did not allow herself to look at Lord d'Arenville, although she was very aware of him standing close by.

'I thought I made myself clear!' Her cousin gestured crossly.

Tallie looked upwards and repressed a grin. Three small heads were poking through the railings in complete defiance of the orders which Laetitia had issued to the nursery. Children were neither to be seen nor heard during the house party.

'I'll see to it at once, Cousin.'

'Your children, Tish?' His voice was deep and resonant. In a warmer-natured man it could be very appealing, thought Tallie irrelevantly as she gathered her skirts to run up the stairs.

'Do they not wish to come down?' he added.

Tallie paused and looked at him in surprise. The Icicle was interested in her cousin's children? No, for he seemed wholly engrossed in removing a speck of fluff from his sleeve.

'No, they do not,' said Laetitia quickly. 'It is high time they went to bed, and it is one of Thalia's little duties to see that they do so. Thalia! If you please!'

Tallie ran quickly up the stairs, biting her lip to prevent the retort she knew would escape if she stayed a moment longer. Time they were in bed, indeed! At five o'clock in the afternoon? And *one* of her little duties? Amongst the other hundred or so her cousin daily required of her in exchange for bed and board. She reached the second landing where two little girls and a boy were sitting. Watched by two pairs of eyes, she lifted up the toddler, took the other little girl by the hand and headed for the nursery, the small boy jumping and hopping on ahead.

'Now, Magnus,' said Laetitia, 'Brooks will show you to your room, and you can prepare yourself to meet my other guests in the drawing room at about six. Brooks, have hot water sent to his lordship's room immediately. And…brandy, Magnus? Or would you prefer a cup of tea?'

'A refreshment tray has already been sent up, madam, with hot tea and coffee, sandwiches *and* brandy,' said Brooks. 'And the hot water is awaiting his lordship.'

'Oh, er, good. Well-done, Brooks,' said Laetitia.

'Miss Tallie saw to it all, madam. She does the same for all the guests,' said Brooks, hiding a smile. Just another of her *little duties*. He felt the cold gaze of Lord d'Arenville on him and his face pokered up into its usual butlerish impassivity.

'If you would care to follow me, your lordship. Madam has put you in the Blue Room, as usual.'

'Thalia, you must dine at table this evening. That wretch Jimmy Fairfax has brought two friends with him and we have a shortage of ladies. And did you tell Cook that we must have goose as well as the capons? I have no time to discuss the menu with her so you must check it. And see that the extra guests have beds made up for them. I am utterly exhausted and need to repose myself before dinner. Lord, I hope Magnus is grateful for the efforts I am making on his behalf. I shall be glad when it's all over.'

Tallie mentally agreed. The last ten days had been exhausting and frustrating, and she was counting the hours until the guests departed. Still, she flattered herself that everything was going off quite smoothly.

This was, however, one order she felt unable to carry out. 'I have nothing to wear to dinner, Cousin.'

'Lord, girl, as if anyone will care what you wear. No one

will take any notice of you—you are just there to make up the numbers. Any old thing will do.'

'I have only one evening dress, Cousin, the one you gave me several years ago, and as you must know it does not fit me.'

'Then alter it, for heaven's sake! Or wear a shawl or something over it. I cannot be expected to think of everything! Now leave me at once, for if I do not get some peace and quiet I fear I will have the headache by dinnertime.'

'Yes, Cousin,' Tallie murmured between her teeth. It went very much against the grain to submit so tamely to her cousin's rudeness, but poverty had taught her to take a more pragmatic view. In the short term, it was unbearable to be treated in this fashion. On the other hand, Laetitia was rarely here, and for most of the year at Manningham there were just Tallie and the children and servants. In truth, she told herself severely, she had a delightful life. An orphan with not a penny to her name ought to be grateful to have a roof over her head. That she didn't *feel* grateful was, no doubt, a deficiency of character.

Tallie hurried downstairs. She consulted with Cook about the menu, Mrs Wilmot about the arrangements for the unexpected guests and Brooks about the wines for dinner, then hurried back upstairs to see to her dress.

Ten minutes later she was in despair. Laetitia was a smaller woman than she, with a dainty, sylphlike figure. The pale green muslin gown was designed to sweep low across the bosom and shoulders and fall loosely from a high waistline. On Tallie the deeply scooped neckline clung, causing her bosom to bulge embarrassingly. The waist was too tight and her ankles were scandalously revealed. Tallie went to her wardrobe and glanced through it again, desperately hoping that by some magical process an alternative would present itself. Two winter day dresses, two summer day dresses, all rather worn and out of date. She sighed and returned gloomily to the green muslin.

She was no needlewoman, and even if she were she could

not make larger that which was too small in the first place.
After some experimentation she managed to fill in the neckline
with a piece of old lace, so that it covered her decently at
least, even if it was still too tight. She tacked a frill along the
hem. It looked quite ridiculous, she knew, but at least it covered her ankles.

Finally she draped herself in a large paisley shawl to disguise the tightness of the dress. It would surely suffice to get
her through dinner. She glanced at herself in the glass and
closed her eyes in momentary mortification. The green colour
did bring interesting highlights to her brown hair and eyes,
and her curly hair was neat for once, but—she looked a perfect
quiz! Still, she told herself bracingly, Laetitia was right. No
one would take any notice of her. She was just an extra female—the poor relation—and she would slip away the moment dinner was over. In any case, she didn't like her cousin's
guests, so what did it matter what they thought of her? Taking
a deep breath, she headed downstairs to check on the arrangements for dinner.

Magnus took another sip of armagnac and wondered how
much longer he could endure the girlish flutterings going on
around him. His temper was on a knife-edge and he had no
one to blame but himself. The house party had been a disaster.

Ten days of the unalleviated company of high-bred young
women would have been bad enough—he'd nerved himself
for that ordeal. But he should have realised that Laetitia would
select a gaggle of young ladies most like herself—spoiled,
vain, vapid and silly. Magnus was almost rigid with boredom.

And exasperation—for he'd hoped to observe the young
ladies unobtrusively, make a discreet selection and quietly arrange a marriage. Ha! What a joke! His wretched cousin had
about as much discretion as a parrot! That had been made plain
to Magnus within days, when he'd realised he was being
hunted—with all the subtlety of a pack of hounds in full pursuit.

Creamy bosoms were made to heave and quiver under his

nose at every opportunity. Well-turned ankles flashed from
modest concealment. And every time he entered a room eyelashes batted so feverishly there was almost a draught. He'd
been treated to displays of virtuosity on harp, pianoforte and
flute, had folios of watercolours thrust under his nose, his
expert inspection bashfully solicited. His superior masculine
opinion had been sought and deferred to on every topic under
the sun and his every reluctant pronouncement greeted with
sighs, sycophantic titters and syrupy admiration.

They accosted him morning, noon and night—in the garden,
in the drawing room, in the breakfast parlour—even, once,
behind the stables, where a man had a right to expect some
peace and quiet. But it was no use—eligible misses lurked,
apparently, in every corner of the estate.

Yet, despite his overwhelming aversion to the task in hand,
Magnus was still determined to select a wife. The house party
had convinced him it was best to get the deed over with as
soon as possible. Any courtship was bound to be appalling to
a man of his solitary tastes, he reasoned, and if he did not
choose now, he would only prolong the process. And this collection of girls seemed no different from any others currently
on the marriage mart.

The trouble was, Magnus could not imagine any of them as
mother to his children. Not one had two thoughts to rub together; each seemed completely devoted to fashion, gossip and
male flattery—not necessarily in that order. And, like Laetitia,
they despised rural life.

That was a problem. He had somehow assumed his wife
would live at d'Arenville with the children. Though why he
should expect his wife to live in the country when few women
of his acquaintance did so, Magnus could not imagine. His
own mother certainly had not. She hadn't been able to bear
the country. But then he didn't want a wife like his mother.

Freddie's wife lived, seemingly content, all year round in
the wilds of Yorkshire with her husband and children. The
children's obvious happiness had made a profound impression
on Magnus—his own parents had been virtual strangers who

had descended on his home at infrequent intervals, their visits the bane of his youthful existence.

But Freddie's wife truly seemed to love her children. Magnus's own mother had appeared to love Magnus—in company. So Freddie's wife could have been fudging it, but Magnus didn't think so. Freddie's wife also seemed to love Freddie. But Freddie was, Magnus knew, a lovable person.

It was not the same for Magnus. He had clearly been an unlovable child. And was therefore not a lovable man. But he would do everything in his power to ensure his children had the chance to be lovable. And therefore to be loved.

Magnus glanced around the room again. He supposed it was possible that some of these frivolous girls would settle into motherhood, but it was difficult to believe, especially with the example of his cousin before him.

'Oh, it is such a delightfully mild evening,' cried Laetitia. 'Let us stroll on the terrace before dinner. Come Magnus, as my guest of honour, you shall escort the lady of your choice.'

A dozen feminine gazes turned his way. There was an expectant hush. Magnus silently cursed his cousin for trying to force his hand. Clearly she wished the house party concluded so that she could return to Town and the myriad entertainments there. Magnus smiled. He danced to no female's tune.

'Then, as a good guest, I must look to the care of my charming hostess,' he responded lightly. 'Cousin, shall we?' He took her arm, allowing her no choice, and they stepped through the French doors onto the terrace. The other guests followed.

Tallie trailed awkwardly in their wake. She felt most uncomfortable. Several of the young ladies had eyed her gown, whispering and tittering with careless amusement. Their mothers had totally ignored her and two of the gentlemen guests had made improper suggestions. The guests had taken their tone from Laetitia—Tallie was an unconsidered encumbrance, little better than a servant, and in the current mood of thwarted ambition she was a convenient target.

Tallie was angry, but told herself sternly that there was little point in expressing her feelings—they would be gone soon, and she would be left in peace again with the children and Brooks and Mrs Wilmot. It should be simple enough for her to ignore the spite of a few ill-bred aristocrats.

The pale young marquise held her chin high, ignoring the vile insults flung at her by the ignorant canaille, as the tumbrel rolled onwards. She was dressed in rags, her lovely gowns stolen by the prison guards, but her dignity was unimpaired…

Tallie slipped unobtrusively to the edge of the terrace and looked out over the stone balustrade to the closely scythed sweep of lawn and the woods beyond. It was a truly lovely view…

'Aaargh! Get down, you filthy beast!' Laetitia's screeches pierced the air. 'Get it off me, someone! Aaargh!'

Tallie hurried to see what had occurred. She wriggled between some of the gathered guests and let out an exclamation of distress.

Her cousin's small son, Georgie, had obviously escaped from the nursery and gone adventuring with the puppy that Tallie had given him several weeks before. He stood in front of his mother, a ragged bunch of snowdrops held pathetically out towards her. His shoes and nankeen pantaloons were covered in mud, as was the puppy. It was the cause of the trouble—muddy pawprints marred Laetitia's new jonquil silk gown.

Laetitia, unused to dogs, screeched and backed away, hysterically flapping her fan at the pup, who seemed to think it a delightful game. He leaped up, yapping in excitement, attempting to catch the fan in his jaws, liberally spattering the exquisite gown in the process.

Tallie was still attempting to wriggle through the press of guests when Lord d'Arenville grabbed the pup and handed him by the scruff of its neck to the little boy. Tallie reached the child just as his mother's tirade broke over him.

'How *dare* you bring that filthy beast near me, you wicked boy! Do you see what it has done? This gown is *ruined*! Ruined, I tell you!'

The small face whitened in distress. Mutely Georgie offered

the wilting bunch of snowdrops. Laetitia dashed them impatiently from his hands.

'Do not try to turn me up sweet, Georgie! See what you have done? *Look* at this dress! Worn for the *first* time today, from the *finest* of London's modistes, and costing the *earth*! Ruined! And why? Because a *wicked boy* brought a filthy animal into a *civilised gathering*! Who gave you permission to leave the nursery? I left the *strictest* orders. You will be punished for such disobedience! And the animal is clearly dangerous! It must be shot *at once*! Someone call for a groom—'

The little boy's face paled further. His small body shook in fright at the venom in his mother's voice. His face puckered in fear and distress and he clutched the puppy tightly to his chest. It whimpered and scrabbled for release.

Magnus watched, tense in a way he hadn't been since he himself was a small boy. He fought the sensation. His eyes darkened with sympathy and remembrance as he observed the frightened child and his puppy. He felt for the boy, but it was not his place to interfere with a mother disciplining her child. And anyway, he supposed it was how it had to be. It was certainly how his own childhood had been.

It would be hard for the boy to lose his beloved pup, but it was probably better for Georgie that he learn to toughen up now, rather than later. Pets were invariably used as hostage to one's good behaviour. Once the boy learnt not to care so much, his life would be easier. Magnus had certainly found it so...although the learning had been very hard... Three pets had died for his disobedience by the time he was eight. The last a liquid-eyed setter bitch by the name of Polly.

Polly, his constant companion and his best friend. But Magnus had taken her out hunting one day instead of finishing his Greek translations and his father had destroyed Polly to teach his son a lesson in responsibility.

Magnus had learned his lesson well.

By the age of eight Magnus had learned not to become attached to pets.

Or to anything else.

'I am sorry for the unfortunate accident, Cousin.' It was the shabby little poor relation. Magnus watched as she interposed her body between the cowering small boy and his infuriated mother, her calm voice a contrast to Laetitia's high-pitched ranting.

'*You* are sorry?' Laetitia continued. 'Yes, I'll make sure of that! The children are in *your* charge, so how was it that this child was allowed to escape from the nursery? I gave strict instructions…'

Magnus leaned back against a large stone urn, folded his arms and coolly observed the scene. He noted the way the dowdy little cousin used her body to shield the child, protecting him from his own mother. It was an interesting manoeuvre—for a poor relation.

The little boy pressed into her skirts, the muddy pup still in his arms. Magnus watched as the girl's hand came to rest unobtrusively on the nape of the child's neck. She stroked him with small, soothing movements. Magnus noticed the little boy relax under her ministrations, saw his shivers die away. After a few moments Georgie leaned trustfully into the curve of her hip, resting his head against her. She held him more fully against her body, all the time keeping her cousin's rage focused on herself. Her words were apologetic, her body subtly defiant.

Fascinating, thought Magnus. Did the girl not realise what she risked by defying her cousin? And all to protect a child who was not even her own.

'The accident was my fault, Cousin,' she said. 'You must not be angry with poor Georgie, here, for he had my permission to be out of the nursery—'

The little boy's start of surprise was not lost on Magnus.

'And I am sorry for the soiling of your gown. However, I cannot allow you to have the puppy destroyed—'

'*You?* You cannot—' spluttered Laetitia.

'No, for the pup belongs neither to Georgie nor to you.'

The child stared up at the girl. Her hand soothed him, and she continued. 'The pup is mine. He…it was a gift from…

from the Rector, and I cannot allow you to destroy a gift because of a little high spirits...'

'You cannot *allow*—' Laetitia gasped in indignation.

'Yes, puppies will be puppies, and small boys and puppies seem to attract each other, don't they? Which is why I was so very grateful to Georgie here.' She turned a warm smile on the small boy.

'Grateful?' Laetitia was astounded. Georgie looked puzzled. Magnus was intrigued.

'Yes, very grateful indeed, for I have been too busy lately to exercise the puppy, and so Georgie has taken over that duty for me, have you not, Georgie dear?'

She nodded encouragingly down at him and, bemused, Georgie nodded back.

'Yes, so any damage the puppy has done to your gown you must lay at my door.'

'But—'

The girl was not paying attention. She bent down to the child. 'Now, Georgie, I think you and my puppy have had enough excitement for one night, but would you do one more thing for me, please?'

He nodded.

'Would you please return, er...Rover—'

'Satan,' Georgie corrected her.

Her eyes brimmed with amusement, but she continued with commendable control. 'Yes, of course, Satan. Would you please take, er, Satan, to the kennels and wash the mud off him for me? You see, I am dressed for dinner, and ladies must not go to the kennels in their best gown.'

Her words had the unfortunate effect of drawing all attention to her 'best gown'. There were a few sniggers, which she ignored with a raised chin. Georgie, however, stared at her, stricken.

'What is it, love?' she said.

Guiltily, he extended a grubby finger and pointed at the mud which now streaked her dress, liberally deposited by himself and the squirming puppy in his arms. She glanced down and laughed, a warm peal of unconcern.

'Don't worry about it, my dear, it will brush off when the mud is dry.' She ruffled his hair affectionately and said in a low voice, 'Now for heaven's sake take that wretched pup and get it and yourself cleaned up before any other accidents happen.'

Relieved, the small boy ran off, his puppy clutched to his chest.

'You'll not get off so easily—' began Laetitia, incensed.

'Do you think it is quite safe for you to be out in the night air in a damp and muddy dress, Cousin?' interrupted Tallie solicitously. 'I would not want you to take a chill, and you know you are extremely susceptible…'

With a stamp and a flounce of jonquil silk Laetitia left the terrace, calling petulantly for her maid to be sent to her at once. The guests drifted in after her, and Brooks began to circulate with a silver tray.

Tallie bent down and gathered up Georgie's scattered flowers. She straightened a few bent stems, gathered the shawl more tightly around her shoulders and stepped towards the French doors, then noticed Lord d'Arenville, who had remained on the terrace.

His expression was unreadable, his grey heavy-lidded eyes observing her dispassionately. The hard gaze made her shiver. Horrid man, she thought. Waiting to see if there is any more entertainment to be had. She raised her chin in cool disdain, and marched past him without saying a word.

Chapter Two

'Well, Magnus, how do you like my candidates? Any take your fancy?'

Tallie froze. Partway into writing the events of the day into her diary, she'd run out of ink. She'd slipped down the servants' stair to the library, secure in the belief that the guests were all in the ballroom, dancing, or playing cards in the nearby anteroom. Concentrating on the tricky task of refilling her inkwell, she hadn't heard her cousin and Lord d'Arenville enter the library. She glanced around, but they were hidden from her view by the heavy velvet curtains pulled partly across the alcove where she was seated.

She stood up to announce her presence, but paused, recalling the shabby dress she wore. If she emerged, she would have to leave by the public route, enduring further sniggers and taunts. She'd had enough of that at dinner. Laetitia, still furious about the way Tallie had confronted her over Georgie and the puppy, had encouraged her guests to bait Tallie even more spitefully than before, and Tallie could endure no more of it.

Lord d'Arenville spoke. 'You know perfectly well, Tish, that my fancy does not run to society virgins. I am seeking a wife, not pursuing a fancy.'

Tallie swallowed, embarrassed. This was a terribly private conversation. No one would thank her for having heard that. Perhaps she should try to slip out through the French doors onto the terrace. She edged quietly towards them. Stealthily she slid the bolt back and turned the handle, but it didn't budge—the catch was stuck.

'Well, dearest coz, which one has the teeth, the hips and the placid temperament you require for the mother of your heirs? They all have impeccable bloodlines, be assured of that.'

Tallie gasped at Laetitia's effrontery and waited for Lord d'Arenville to give her a smart set-down for speaking of his intended bride with such disrespect. It was far too late to declare her presence now, and besides, she was fascinated. She edged back behind the curtains and wrestled half-heartedly with the door catch.

'As far as those requirements are concerned, most of your candidates would do, although Miss Kingsley is too narrow-hipped to be suitable.'

Tallie's jaw dropped. Requirements? Candidates? Those young women out there had been assembled as *candidates*? Miss Kingsley eliminated because of her *hips*? Laetitia hadn't been joking when she'd referred to teeth, hips, placidity and bloodlines!

Tallie was disgusted. What sort of man would choose a wife so coldly and dispassionately? No wonder he was called The Icicle. Mrs Wilmot was right—he was as handsome as a Greek statue but he obviously had a heart of stone to match. Tallie passionately hoped he would select Miss Fyffe-Temple as his bride.

Miss Fyffe-Temple was one of the prettiest of the young lady guests and the sweetest-spoken—in company. In truth she was a nasty-tempered, spiteful little harpy, who took her temper out on the servants, making impossible demands in a shrill voice, and pinching and hitting the younger maids in the most vicious fashion. The below-stairs members of the household had quickly labelled her Miss Foul-Temper, and in Tallie's opinion that made her a perfect wife for the great Lord d'Arenville!

'Actually, I have come to see, on reflection, that my requirements were rather inadequate,' said Lord d'Arenville.

Perhaps she was too hasty in judging him, Tallie thought. She did tend to make snap judgements, and was often forced to own the fault when she was later proved wrong.

'Strong hocks, perhaps, Magnus?' Laetitia had clearly imbibed rather more champagne than was ladylike. 'Do you want to check their withers? Get them to jump over a few logs? Put them at a fence or two? Or ask if they are fond of oats? I believe Miss Carnegie has Scottish blood—she will certainly be fond of oats. The Scots, I believe, live on little else.'

Tallie shoved her fist against her mouth to stop herself from laughing out loud. Heavens! To think she would be in such sympathy with Cousin Laetitia.

'Very funny, Tish,' said Lord d'Arenville dryly. 'I have no interest in the culinary preferences of anyone north of the border, nor do I wish to concern myself with any additional physical characteristics of the young ladies you selected for me.'

Tallie's eyes widened. *Laetitia* had selected the young ladies? Did he simply expect to choose one? Without the bother of courtship? What an insufferable man! To be so puffed up in his own conceit that he need not consider the feelings of any young lady, assuming she would be flattered enough by his offer!

Well, if a spineless ninny was what he wanted, she hoped he would choose The Honourable Miss Aldercott. Already she showed what Tallie considered to be a very sinister preference for gauzy drapery and sonnets about Death and Lost Love. The Honourable Miss Aldercott had fainted five times so far, had had the vapours twice and made recourse to her vinaigrette a dozen times a day. With any luck, thought Tallie viciously, Lord d'Arenville would think The Honourable Miss Aldercott charmingly fragile—then find himself leg-shackled to a clinging, lachrymose watering-pot for the rest of his life!

'So, Magnus, what other criteria do you have for the mother of your heirs?'

'It has occurred to me that most of your candidates are rather spoiled and used to being indulged.'

'Well, naturally they are a little petted, but that is only to be expected...'

'You miss my point, Tish. Most of these young ladies have found it an almost intolerable hardship to come to the country.'

'Well, of course they have, Magnus!' Laetitia snapped acerbically. 'Any woman would. Who in their right mind would moulder away in the country when they could have all the delightful exhilaration of London society? Is that your latest requirement?'

'Yes, actually—it is. I wish the mother of my children to reside with the children, and London is no place for a child.'

'What rubbish!'

'You know it's true, Tish, for you yourself keep your children here in the country all year round.'

'Yes, Magnus, *the children* live here all year round, not me. And that is the difference. Why, I would go into a decline if I were buried here for an entire year!'

'And the children—do they not miss their mother's care?'

Tallie had to stifle another laugh at that. Laetitia, a doting mother! The children would love her if she would let them. As it was, they tiptoed around on their best behaviour during their mother's visits, hoping to avoid her criticisms and sharp temper and heaving sighs of wistful relief when she left.

'Naturally I spend as much time as I can with my darlings, but I have my needs also, Magnus. And I have responsibilities as George's wife, and *they* take place in London, which is no fault of mine. But you need not think I neglect my children, for I leave them in the best of care.'

'Yes, I've noticed that.' Lord d'Arenville's voice was thoughtful. 'Your sturdy little cousin.'

Sturdy! How dared he? Sturdy? Tallie was mortally insulted. She might not be as sylphlike as Laetitia, but she was *not* sturdy!

'You're wandering off the point, Magnus.'

Sturdy! Insensitive beast!

'Would you say that any of these young ladies would be willing to live for, say, ten years in the country?'

'Ten years?' Laetitia's voice rose to a horrified screech. '*No* sane woman would agree to that! She would die, rather! Why on earth would you wish to immure *anyone* in the country for ten years, anyway?'

There was a short silence. Tallie craned to hear, but there was nothing. Suddenly Laetitia laughed—a hard, cynical laugh.

'Good God, you want a nun, not a wife, don't you?' She laughed again. 'Your father tried that, if you recall, and stuck to it for all of six months, while your mother cuckolded him with every groom, stableboy and tenant farmer in the district. And serve him right, say I. No, you couldn't possibly think that isolating a wife in the country would ensure her fidelity, not after that.' She laughed again. 'And if you have any doubts on the matter, dearest coz, ask George.'

Lord d'Arenville said stiffly, 'My decision is nothing to do with either you or my mother. It is simply that my bride must not mind spending my children's growing years at my country seat with them.'

'Well, I wish you'd told me earlier,' said Laetitia, 'for I wouldn't have bothered wasting everyone's time with this ridiculous charade. I am very angry with you, Magnus. I should have realised you were not serious about wanting a bride—'

'I am quite serious.'

'Well, you certainly won't find one here who could accept—'

'But I have.'

'You've what?' Laetitia sounded flabbergasted. 'Don't tell me one has agreed to your outrageous terms, Magnus! Oh, I cannot believe it. Who is she? No—do not tell me—let me guess. Lady Helen…no, she is positively addicted to Almack's. And it could not possibly be Miss Blakeney—no one so *à la mode* would agree to be buried in the country for ten years. Oh, I give up Magnus, who is she?'

There was a long pause. Tallie waited with bated breath.

Truly, she could imagine no young lady agreeing to such inhuman terms. It was a shame his mother had behaved so shockingly, but not all women were like his mother and Laetitia, and why should an innocent wife be punished for the things they had done?

Ten years in the country indeed! And would Lord d'Arenville confine himself similarly to the restrictions of country life? Tallie almost snorted out loud. Of course he would not! It was only his poor wife who would be shut away from society, breeding his heirs like a good little brood mare.

'Well, Magnus, don't keep me waiting all day,' said Laetitia impatiently. 'Which bride have you chosen?'

Tallie leaned against the doorhandle, eager to hear his answer.

'I have decided to wed—'

Suddenly the catch gave, and Tallie tumbled out into the night, missing his reply. Fearful that her eavesdropping would be discovered, she pushed the door shut and slipped away. A little irritated to be denied the juicy morsel of gossip, she hurried towards the kitchen. Which unfortunate young lady had Lord d'Arenville chosen for his bride? She would find out soon enough, she supposed. Whoever it was, Tallie did not envy her. However, it was nothing to do with her, except that his choice would signal the end of the house party. All the unpleasant guests would return to London, the children would be released from their unnatural curfew and she would return to the peaceful life she had led before. Tallie almost skipped with joy at the prospect.

When Tallie came down to breakfast the next morning she was surprised to find many of her cousin's guests already arisen. She paused on the threshold, feeling dowdy and unwelcome. Still, she decided, this was her home, and she had every right to her breakfast. Chin held high, she entered the breakfast room.

A sudden hush fell. Tallie ignored it. No doubt they were preparing to make sport of her yet again—the dress she wore was even shabbier than yesterday's. She went to the sideboard and inspected the selection of breakfast dishes, uncomfortably aware of hostile eyes boring into her back. After a moment, the buzz of conversation resumed. From time to time a low-voiced comment reached her ears as she slowly filled her plate.

'...done rather well for herself.'

'...but, my dear, one wonders what precisely she *did* to ensure...'

They were talking of Lord d'Arenville's bride, Tallie thought. He must have announced his betrothal at the ball. That would explain why so many had come down to breakfast. No doubt those who had not been chosen wished to make an early start on the journey back to Town.

'And, of course, poor Tish is utterly furious.'

'Naturally, my dear. Would not you be? After all she's done for her, and now this! The very ingratitude...'

'Trapped, undoubtedly.'

'Oh, undoubtedly!'

Tallie wondered which of the young ladies Lord d'Arenville had chosen. It had to be either Miss Blakeney or Lady Helen Beresford—they were the only two young ladies not at breakfast. That explained why she could sense such an atmosphere of hostility in the room—failed candidates seething with frustration and anger. Tallie tried to close her ears to the vehement mutterings. It would be a relief when Lord d'Arenville, Laetitia and all their horrid friends had gone back to London.

'Thrusting little baggage. A man of honour...no choice.'

'And that dress last evening—positively indecent!'

'No other word for it.'

Tallie began to eat her breakfast, though her appetite had quite vanished. Her cousin's friends were quite unbearable.

'More coffee, Miss Tallie?' murmured Brooks at her ear.

A friendly face at last. 'Oh, yes, please, Brooks.' Tallie beamed up at him and held her cup out for him to refill.

As Brooks poured, Miss Fyffe-Temple, one of Tallie's neighbours, roughly jogged his elbow. Hot coffee boiled over Tallie's hand and arm. She leapt up with a shriek of pain.

'Oh, Miss Tallie!' exclaimed Brooks, horrified.

'How very clumsy of me, to be sure,' purred Miss Fyffe-Temple. 'What a nasty red mark it has made. I do hope it won't leave a scar.'

'Yes, it's quite disgustingly red and ugly. Is it terribly painful?' Miss Carnegie added.

'Oh, how horrid…I think I'm going to faint,' exclaimed The Honourable Miss Aldercott. The others immediately gathered around Miss Aldercott, cooing with pretty concern.

Blinking back tears, Tallie ran from the room and headed for the scullery. She plunged her arm in a pitcher of cold water and breathed a sigh of relief as the pain immediately began to ebb. After a few moments she withdrew it and blew lightly on the reddened skin. It was quite painful, but she didn't think it was too serious a burn. But why had Miss Fyffe-Temple done it? Tallie hadn't missed the gleam of spiteful satisfaction in her eyes as she had made her mocking apology.

'Are you all right, Miss Tallie?' It was Brooks, his kindly old face furrowed with anxiety. 'I am so sorry, my dear.'

'It is not serious, Brooks, truly,' Tallie reassured him. 'It gave me more of a fright, really. It hardly hurts at all.'

'I don't know how it happened. She… My arm just slipped.'

Tallie laid a hand on his arm. 'It's all right; I know whose fault it is, Brooks. The thing I don't understand is why.'

Brooks stared for a moment, then suddenly looked awkward. 'I think you'd best speak to your cousin, miss,' he said. 'She's still abed, but I have no doubt she's expecting you.'

Tallie frowned. 'I shall go up to her, then, as soon as I have put some butter and a piece of gauze over this burn,' she said slowly. Judging from Brooks's expression, something was amiss. She could not think what it was. No doubt her cousin would enlighten her.

'*Me?*' Tallie's voice squeaked. She stared at her cousin, her jaw dropping in amazement. The effects of her indulgences the night before had kept Laetitia in bed, and from the sounds of things she was still inebriated. Or demented.

'Me?' repeated Tallie, stunned. 'How can you possibly say such a thing, Cousin? He does not even know my name.'

'Ha!' spat Laetitia, holding her delicate head. 'I'll wager he *knows* you in other ways, you hussy! In the Biblical sense! Why else would he choose a wretched little nobody?'

Tallie gasped, first in shock and then in swelling outrage. It was one thing to be asked to swallow such a Banbury tale— Lord d'Arenville wishing to wed Tallie Robinson, indeed! But to be accused of immorality! She was not entirely sure what knowing 'in the Biblical sense' meant, but she was very certain it was immoral. Tallie was furious. She might be poor. She might be an orphan, shabbily dressed and forced to live on other's generosity. But she was *not* immoral.

'Firstly, let me tell you, Cousin,' Tallie said heatedly, '*no* man has known me in the Biblical sense, and I am shocked that you could even suggest such a thing! Secondly, I cannot help but believe you must have made an error about Lord d'Arenville's intentions. Perhaps you misheard him.'

'I did not,' snapped Laetitia. 'Do you think I would imagine such an appalling thing?'

Tallie gritted her teeth. Imagination indeed! She could imagine no member of the aristocracy, let alone the arrogant Lord d'Arenville, choosing his cousin's poor relation for his bride.

'But I have not exchanged even *one word* with his lordship,' exclaimed Tallie.

'I do not believe—' shrilled Laetitia, holding her head.

'Cousin! I promise you.' Tallie tried to keep her voice calm, despite her frustration. Her cousin was very angry.

'Do not lie, girl! He told me himself he had chosen you.'

A small, cold knot of fear lodged in Tallie's stomach. She had never seen Laetitia this furious before, and she knew her cousin well. There was a hard, ruthless streak in Laetitia. This foolish misunderstanding—the result of too much champagne, no doubt, or perhaps a jest on Lord d'Arenville's part—could have dire consequences for herself.

'Well, either you misheard him, Cousin, or else he is playing a nasty joke on you. Yes, that's it—it must surely be a jest.' People like her cousin's friends were always playing tricks on some poor unfortunate. The joke this time might be on Laetitia, but Tallie was the poor unfortunate.

'Jest?' Laetitia snorted. 'Magnus does not jest—not about marriage.'

'Perhaps you took a little too much champagne, Cousin, and did not realise he was hoaxing you,' Tallie suggested tentatively.

'Nonsense! I know what I heard!' said Laetitia, but her tone belied the words. It was clear that she was starting to entertain doubts. Tallie felt a trickle of relief.

'I will speak to his lordship, shall I, and clear the matter up once and for all?' Tallie rose to her feet. It just had to be some trick Lord d'Arenville was playing on Laetitia. Tallie was not amused. His little joke had already got her scalded by boiling coffee, and now it threatened her position in Laetitia's household. But would His High-and-Mightiness think of that? Not he!

He who had been given everything his heart desired, ever since he was born—it would not occur to him that some people existed on a fine line between survival and destitution. All that stood between Tallie and abject poverty was her cousin's good will, and no careless jest was about to jeopardise that! Lord Look-Down-His-Nose would soon learn that one person at least was not prepared to have her life wrecked for a mere lordly whim!

She found him in the downstairs parlour, idly leafing through a freshly ironed newspaper, lately arrived from London. Fortunately he was alone for a change.

'Lord d'Arenville,' she began, shutting the door firmly behind her. 'I have just been speaking with my cousin Laetitia, and she seems to be under the impression that you...'

He laid the paper courteously aside, stood up and came towards her. Tallie's voice dwindled away. Heavens, but he was so very tall. She'd noticed it earlier, of course, but now, when he was standing so close, looming over her...

'Ah, Miss Robinson. Good morning. Is it not a pleasant day? Will you be seated?'

Miss Robinson? He remembered her name? She could have sworn he hadn't taken a whit of notice of her the day they were introduced. Or since.

'Er, thank you.' Tallie allowed herself to be led to a low divan. He drew up a chair opposite, a look of faint enquiry lifting his dark brows.

'You wished to speak with me?'

To her great discomfort Tallie felt a blush rising. It was one thing to storm out of her cousin's boudoir, declaring she would soon clear up this whole silly mistake, and quite another to confront this immaculate, gravely polite aristocrat with a wholly impossible tale.

'Laetitia seems to be under the impression…?' he prompted.

Tallie felt her blush intensify. The whole thing was too ridiculous. She had to escape. She could not ask this man whether there was any truth in the rumour that he wished to marry her. It was obviously a mistake. She knew she was being cowardly, but she could not imagine this coldly serious creature considering her—even for a jest—as an eligible bride. On the other hand, Tallie would not put it past her cousin to set her up for a humiliating fall. In fact, it would be very like her…

Tallie could just imagine Laetitia entertaining her London friends with the joke… *Imagine, that plain, foolish lump of a girl actually believing that Magnus wanted to marry her! When he has the pick of the* ton *at his fingertips! Oh, my dears, I laughed until the tears ran down my cheeks! But there, 'tis not kind to laugh at one's inferiors…but really, if you could have seen Magnus's face when the girl confronted him, Lord, he thought he was being pursued by a lunatic!* And gales of laughter would follow.

'Er…Cousin Laetitia was under the impression…' Tallie's eye fell on the newspaper '…that the maids might have forgotten to press the paper for you, but I see they have, so I

will go at once and tell her that everything is…organised.'
She stood up to leave. Lord d'Arenville rose also.

Heavens! He was looming again, standing so close she
could just smell the faint tang of a masculine cologne. Tallie
took a step backwards and stumbled against the divan. A
strong hand shot out and caught her by the arm, holding her
until she steadied, then releasing her.

'Thank you… So clumsy…' she muttered, flustered, and
annoyed with herself for being so.

'Stay a moment, Miss Robinson. I wish to speak to you.'
His hand touched her arm again, a light touch this time, not
the firm, warm grip of before.

Tallie looked up, puzzled. A faint warning bell sounded in
her mind as she saw the purposeful look in his cold grey eyes,
but she quashed it immediately. No doubt he had some complaint about a servant, or a message he wished her to carry to
her cousin. Outwardly calm, she allowed herself to be seated
a second time, folded her hands demurely in her lap and
waited.

Magnus noted the quiet way she folded her hands. It seemed
to him a pleasantly womanly gesture. Her whole demeanour
pleased him. Clearly Laetitia had told her of his decision, and,
whilst he wished she had not, this girl's reactions bore out the
soundness of his choice. She was neither filled with vulgar
excitement nor coy flutterings. Yes, she would do nicely. He
took a deep breath, surprised at how unexpectedly nervous he
suddenly felt.

'You said you had spoken with Laetitia?'

The cold knot in the pit of Tallie's stomach grew. Wordlessly she nodded.

'Yes, I should have expected she could not keep it to herself.' Without waiting for her reply, Lord d'Arenville began
to explain. 'It would be best if the wedding took place almost
immediately—it takes three weeks for the banns to be called.
We would be married from this house and my cousin's husband George would give you away. I would prefer a small

affair, just my immediate family—Laetitia and her husband—
and of course any friends or relations you wish to invite…'

It could not be true. She was not sitting here listening to
this cold, proud man elaborate on the arrangements for his
wedding. *Her* wedding! His wedding to Tallie Robinson! A
girl to whom he had scarcely spoken two words.

But his cool, indifferent demeanour, his very seriousness
convinced her. It was not a joke, not a malicious trick to make
sport of the poor relation.

But he hadn't even *asked* her if she wanted to marry him!

After a time, Tallie's shock wore off, and she realised she
was furious. And utterly mortified. She had known the likelihood of her ever marrying was slim. Living in the country
as Laetitia's unpaid governess, she came into contact with few
eligible men, and with neither looks nor fortune to recommend
her, her prospects were few and far between. But it was one
thing to face the prospect of a lonely and loveless future, and
another to be so little regarded that she did not even merit the
appearance of a courtship. Were her feelings and desires of so
little significance to him?

Tallie stared down at her knees, flushed and fuming, biting
her lip to prevent her rage from spilling out. Her hands shook,
itching to slap the smug condescension off his face. She
clenched them into fists, dwelling on how pleasant it would
be to box his arrogant ears! She took in very little of what he
was saying!

Lord d'Arenville rose from his seat and paced up and down
before her, explaining the arrangements. He noted his bride's
delicate blush, her modestly bowed head, and congratulated
himself again on the excellent choice he had made. No pam-
pered miss, this. She sat there, meekly listening to his plans
for her future. Quiet, submissive, delightful!

How could he ever have been so foolish as to consider a
sophisticated woman of the *ton* as the mother of his children?
Laetitia's candidates had been self-centred, selfish, and far too
sure of themselves. Much better to have chosen this sweetly
shy girl with her modest, downcast eyes. Thalia Robinson

would be grateful for his offer—she had no worldly ambition, no highly strung temperament.

His eyes ran over her figure. It was difficult to tell in that frightful dress she wore, but she seemed sturdy—certainly robust enough to survive the rigours of childbirth. And this girl, he believed, had the capacity to love, and he needed that—for his children. He recalled the tender way her hands had caressed young Georgie. He wanted that for his child…yes, for his child…

Her hands were trembling, he realised. Magnus watched approvingly as she clenched her fingers tightly together in an effort to control her emotions. Excellent. Self-control was a good thing in a wife.

He gentled his voice. Doubtless such disparity in their respective stations in life made her a little nervous, a little eager to oblige. The thought did not displease Magnus. He intended to treat her kindly—her nervousness would pass with time and she would no doubt be grateful for his forbearance. It would be a start… She would find him a good husband, he hoped. He would look after her, protect her, take care of all her needs. He continued to pace the floor, describing d'Arenville, the family seat, and how much she would like living there.

Tallie fumed silently, letting his words wash over her. So *she* was to be his quiet, compliant little brood mare, was she? The wife he intended to keep immured in his beastly d'Arenville for ten years or more!

In a pig's eye she was!

The nerve, the arrogance, the presumption of the man! He must have decided a plain, poor woman would give him the least trouble, a woman without prospects but with the hips and teeth and bloodlines to bear his heirs! A *sturdy* woman!

She longed to leap up, to fling his proposal of mar… No— Tallie Robinson, poor relation, did not merit a *proposal,* for he had not even waited for her reply. He'd presented his prospective brood mare with an *assumption* of marriage!

Well, whichever it was, she would fling it in his teeth! That would bring a shocked look to that insufferably complacent face. And how she would enjoy snapping her fingers under that long, proud nose! She would wait until he had finished describing the wonderful treats that marriage to him would bring her! What was he talking about now? The view of the lake from the summerhouse at sunset? Hah!

I'm sooo sorry, Lord d'Arenville, she would tell him, *but even the delightful prospect of viewing the d'Arenville duck pond at dawn cannot tempt me to marry you. I would much prefer to remain unwed. Sooo sorry to disappoint you.* And she would sail out of the room, head held high, leaving him stunned, furious, gnashing his teeth with chagrin.

No, she decided. Too tame, too straightforward. He deserved a taste of his own medicine. He hadn't even bothered to speak to *her*! He'd merely informed Laetitia, no doubt offering to take a poor relation off her hands. Tallie had been scalded and abused and accused of outright immorality. And all because of his arrogance. He needed to be taken down a peg or two! Or three!

Tallie smiled to herself, planning her revenge—she'd keep him guessing. A man of his pride and consequence would loathe being kept waiting. Especially by a little nobody from nowhere! A *sturdy* little nobody at that!

Laetitia's guests obviously knew of Lord d'Arenville's choice. They would be waiting for the announcement. And Laetitia—what would it do to her pride to have the despised poor relation keeping the head of the family dangling?

The thought filled Tallie with glee—she would let them all wait...and wait...and wait. And they would marvel at her temerity in making her future husband wait, for of course it would never occur to any of *them* that she could be so foolish as to refuse such a prize!

A prize indeed, Tallie thought scornfully, glancing up at him from under her lashes. As if a handsome face and figure and a wealthy purse were everything!

Yes, she would make him, and everyone else, wait. And then, just when everyone was starting to wonder how much longer Lord d'Arenville's temper would stand it, Tallie would carelessly decline his offer. *That* would serve him right! How his pride would suffer—the great Lord d'Arenville, prize of the marriage mart, courted and pursued by every matchmaking mama in the country, rejected by the plain and insignificant poor relation!

'The banns would be called immediately and the wedding set for three weeks from now. Would that be enough time for you to organise your bride clothes?' said Lord d'Arenville.

Tallie blinked up at him in mocking surprise. Was that a *question* he was asking? Something he *didn't* know? An arrangement he hadn't made? Something for *her* to comment on? Amazing.

She stood up. 'Lord d'Arenville. I thank you for your very…surprising…offer of marriage. May I consider my reply?' Without waiting for his response, Tallie hurried on, 'Thank you. I will let you know my answer as soon as is convenient.'

Magnus's jaw dropped.

She walked to the door, opened it, paused, turned back to face him and smiled sweetly. 'Until then, may I suggest you make no irrevocable arrangements?'

Chapter Three

'Well, what did he say? It was a hum, was it not?' Laetitia dragged Tallie into a nearby anteroom.

'No, I am afraid it was not,' said Tallie reluctantly. 'You were perfectly correct, Cousin, he thought to marry me.'

Laetitia caught the tense Tallie used and pounced eagerly. 'But he has changed his mind?'

Tallie knew she had to choose her words carefully, so as not to exacerbate her cousin's volatile temper any further. She was skating on very thin ice as it was. 'No, not exactly.'

'I knew it!' Laetitia stamped her foot. 'He is such a selfish wretch! How could he put me in *such* a position? Each girl out there was in daily expectation of being made an offer!' She glared at Tallie. 'Each one a diamond of the first water, an heiress or a duke's relative—and he chooses *you*!'

Tallie nodded, ignoring the insult. She understood how foolish her cousin felt. She even felt some sympathy for her. Lord d'Arenville was an arrogant, selfish, thoughtless boor.

'It is all right, Cousin,' she said soothingly. 'I intend to refuse him.'

Laetitia froze. She stared, stupefied. Her face went white beneath the rouge. 'What did you say?' she whispered.

'I am going to refuse him.' Tallie smiled reassuringly.

'Refuse *Magnus*?'

Tallie nodded. 'Yes.'

'*You*—to refuse my cousin Magnus? Lord d'Arenville?'

Tallie nodded again. 'Absolutely. I have no wish to marry him, so there is nothing for you to be upset—'

'Of all the brazen effrontery! You arrogant little bitch!'

Tallie took a step backwards, unnerved by the fury she saw in her cousin's face.

'Who do you think *you* are to refuse *my cousin Magnus*? You—a complete nonentity! A mere *Robinson*! Why, he is so far above the likes of you that he is the sun to your, your…' Laetitia waved her hand in frustration, unable to find a suitable comparison to convey to Tallie just how far beneath him she was. 'How *dare* you think to humiliate me in this fashion?'

'But, Cousin, how does my refusing Lord d'Arenville humiliate you?' interrupted Tallie, confused by her cousin's abrupt volte-face. 'I can see how choosing me instead of your—'

'Do not for one minute dare to gloat, you insolent hussy!'

'I am *not* gloating,' said Tallie indignantly. 'But I don't understand. Surely if I refuse him it saves you the embarrassment of people knowing he preferred me to your friends? We can say that your guests misunderstood.'

Laetitia threw up her hands. 'She even has the brass to boast of her conquest!' she muttered. 'Mortifying enough that my cousin chooses a shabby little nobody over my friends, but for the nobody to *refuse* him! No. No! It is too much!'

She turned to face Tallie, hands on hips. 'Little did I think when I accepted you into my household that it would come to this. You will pack your bags and be out of here within the hour. John Coachman will take you back to the village where you lived before you insinuated yourself into my home.' Laetitia's voice was low, furious and vengeful, her expression implacable.

Tallie stared at her, shocked. There was no hysteria in her cousin's manner now. 'You…you cannot mean it, surely, Cousin?'

Laetitia sniffed and turned her face away.

Tallie tried again. 'Please, Cousin, reconsider. There is

nothing for me in the village. The school closed down when Miss Fisher died. And…you know I have no money.'

'You should have considered that before you set your cap at my cousin.'

'I did *not* set my cap at him. I never even spoke to him! It was Lord d'Arenville who—'

'I am not interested in your excuses. You have one hour.' Laetitia was adamant.

Tallie's mouth was dry. 'You cannot mean it, surely, Cousin?' she began. 'I have nowhere to go, no one to turn to.'

'And whose fault is that, pray? Had I known before what an ungrateful, scheming jade you were, I would never have taken you into my home. The subject is closed. One hour.' Laetitia swept towards the door.

'Cousin!' called Tallie. Laetitia paused and glanced disdainfully back. Tallie swallowed. She had been about to beg, but she could see from her cousin's expression that her cousin was hoping for just that. No, she would not beg. In her current mood Laetitia would enjoy seeing her grovel, and it would do no good; Tallie could see that now.

'Will you write me a letter of recommendation so that I may at least seek work as a governess?'

'You have a nerve!' spat Laetitia. 'No, I will not!'

Magnus strode through the damp grass, snapping his whip angrily against his booted leg. He'd planned to go for a long ride, but had found himself too impatient to wait for a groom to saddle his horse so he'd gone for a walk instead. The gardens were looking quite pretty for the time of year. He stopped and stared at a clump of snowdrops, their heads nodding gently in the faint breeze.

He recalled the way she'd sat there, listening to his words with downcast eyes, all soft and submissive, her pale nape exposed, vulnerable and appealing. Her hair was not plain brown after all, but a soft honey colour, with a tendency to curl. And when she'd looked up at him at the end he'd realised that she had rather pretty eyes, a kind of deep amber, with long dark lashes. And her skin looked smooth and soft.

Yes, he'd been pleased with his choice. Right up until the moment she'd spoken and revealed that flash of...temper? Pique?

Magnus lashed at the nodding snowdrops with his whip, sending them flying. He stared unseeing at the carnage.

The chit was playing games with him! *Make no irrevocable arrangements.* There'd been a malicious kind of pleasure in the way she'd said it, sweet smile notwithstanding. He strode on, frowning.

For almost the whole of the house party the girl had been quiet, docile and obedient. He was convinced it was her usual state—it must be—how else had she survived living with Laetitia? And she lived here with the children all year round without complaint.

No. He must have imagined her anger. He'd taken her by surprise, that was all. He should have given her a little more warning of his intentions. And perhaps he'd been a little clumsy—he had never before offered marriage, and his unexpected nervousness had thrown him a little off balance.

He should have made a flowery speech and then a formal offer, instead of rushing into his plans. Females set store by that kind of thing. She was quite right to put him off for a time. It was what every young girl was schooled to do, pretending to think it over, as a true lady should.

His mouth twitched as he remembered the way she'd held her chin so high. For all the world as if she might refuse. Cheeky little miss! The small flash of spirit did not displease him. A spirited dam usually threw spirited foals, and he wouldn't want his children to be dull. Not at all. And he'd seen the mettle in her when she'd flown to little Georgie's side, like a young lioness defending her cub.

And spirited defiance was permissible, even desirable in the defence of children. It was a little disconcerting for it to be directed against himself, perhaps, but he was *not* displeased, he told himself again.

So why could he not shake the feeling that he'd reached to pluck a daisy and had grasped a nettle instead? He savagely beheaded another clump of his cousin's flowers and strode on, indifferent to the damage the wet grass was doing to the shine on his boots.

'Magnus, what on earth are you doing to my garden?'

Laetitia's voice jerked Magnus out of his reverie. He glanced back the way he'd come and flinched when he realised the havoc his whip had wrought.

'Sorry, Tish. I didn't realise—'

'Oh, never mind that. I need to talk to you at once, but do come away from that wet grass; it will ruin my slippers. Here, into the summerhouse, where we can be quite private.'

Laetitia settled herself on a bench and regarded her cousin severely. 'How *could* you, Magnus? In front of all my guests! I could just kill you! You have been extremely foolish, but I think we can pass it off as a jest—not in the best taste, of course, but a jest all the same. In any case, I have got rid of the girl—for which, I may add, you owe me your undying gratitude. Although, knowing you, you will be odiously indifferent as you always—'

Magnus cut to the heart of the rambling speech. 'What do you mean, "got rid of the girl"? You cannot mean Miss Robinson, surely?'

'Miss Robinson indeed!' Laetitia sniffed. 'She is lucky I even acknowledged her as cousin. Well, that is all at an end now. She will be gone within the hour!'

'Gone? Where to?'

'The village she grew up in. I forget its name.'

Magnus frowned. 'What? Is there some family emergency? I understood she was an orphan.'

'Oh, she is. Not a living soul left, except for me, and that's at an end after her base ingratitude and presumption.'

'Then why is she going to this village?'

Laetitia wrinkled her nose. 'I believe she spent virtually all her life in some stuffy little school there. Her father was in the diplomatic service, you know, and travelled a great deal.'

Poor little girl, thought Magnus. He knew what it was like to be sent away, unwanted, at a young age. 'And she wishes to visit this school? I suppose she must have friends there whom she would wish to ask to her wedding. I did not realise.'

'Magnus, what is *wrong* with you? What does it *matter* where the wretched girl goes?'

'Tish, of course it matters. Do you not realise I asked Miss Robinson to be my bride?'

'Of course I do, and it will be a long time before I will forgive you for making such a fool of me, Magnus! But that wretched little nobody plans to make a fool of us both, and *that* I will not allow!'

Magnus frowned. The uneasy feeling he'd had ever since he'd spoken to Miss Robinson intensified. His whip tapped a sharp and fast tattoo against his boot. 'What do you mean, "a fool of us both"?'

'She plans to refuse you!'

'*What?*' The instant surge of temper caught Magnus unaware. He reined it in. 'How can you know such a thing, Tish?'

'She told me to my head, not fifteen minutes ago. *Boasted* of it!' Laetitia noted his stupefaction, nodded smugly and laid a compelling hand on his arm. 'You see now why she must be got away from here at once. I will not have a *Robinson* crow to the world that my cousin, Lord d'Arenville, was not good enough for her!'

'Are you sure?' Magnus was flabbergasted. He had not expected any girl to refuse his offer...but a penniless orphan? Boasting? If it was true, it was more than a slap in the face.

'She actually said so? In so many words?'

'Yes, Magnus, in just so many words. First she *gloated* of her success in cutting all my friends out to snare you, and then she *boasted* of how foolish we would all look when she refused you. The ungrateful trollop! I would have her *drowned* if I could!'

Magnus stood up and took a few jerky paces back and forth across the small summerhouse, his whip slapping hard and fast

against his boot. 'I…I must consider this. Until I speak to you
again, do nothing,' he said, and stalked off into the garden,
destroying the herbaceous border as he passed.

*No, no, dearest Tallie, you cannot leave us…it was a foolish
misunderstanding… What would we do without you? What
would the children do? And George and I—oh, please do not
let my wretched cousin Magnus come between us—he is nothing but a cold, proud Icicle! You are family, dearest Tallie,
and you belong here! Oh, do not leave us, we need you too
much…*

'I…I've been sent up to make sure you're packed, miss.'
The maidservant hovered uncomfortably, wringing her hands
in distress. 'And John Coachman has been told to ready himself and the horses for a long journey… I'm that sorry, Miss.'

'It's all right, Lucy,' said Tallie shakily. Reality crashed
around her. Laetitia had not changed her mind. Tallie truly
was being thrown out of her cousin's house.

She got off the bed where she'd been huddled and tried to
pull herself together, surreptitiously wiping her eyes. 'There's
a bag on top of that wardrobe—if you could put my clothing
in that… I…I must see to other matters.' She rushed out, her
brimming eyes averted from the maid's sympathetic gaze.

Moments later she slipped out of the side door, across the
south lawn and into the garden maze. Tallie knew the con-
voluted paths by heart, and unerringly made her way towards
the centre. It was a favourite spot. No one could see over the
high, clipped hedges, and if anyone entered it she would have
plenty of warning. She reached the heart of the maze, hurled
herself down on the wrought-iron seat and burst into tears.

She had lost everything—her home, the children. She was
about to become a pauper. She'd always been one, she supposed, but now she would truly be destitute. Homeless. Taken
out and dumped like an unwanted cat.

She sobbed until there were no more tears, until her sobs
became hard, dry lumps stuck in her chest, shuddering silently
out of her with every breath she drew. Eventually they sub-

sided, only coming every minute or so, in an echo of the distress she could bear no more of.

What would she do? This very night, unless some miracle intervened, she would find herself deposited in the village square. Where would she go? Where would she sleep? Unconsciously her hand crept to her mouth and she began to nibble at her nails. No one in the village would remember her. The vicar? No, she recalled—he'd died shortly after she'd left. A churchgoer might recall her face amongst the dozens of schoolgirls who'd filed dutifully into St Stephen's each Sunday, but it was unlikely. It was two years ago—vague recognition was the best she could expect from anyone in the village. And no one would be likely to take her in.

There was not a soul in the world she could turn to.

The sharp, clean scent of the close-trimmed cypress hedges was fresh in the damp, cool air. Tallie drew her knees up against her chest and hugged them to her. In the distance she could hear the haunting cry of a curlew. It sounded as lost and alone as she felt.

She'd been happy at Laetitia's, but her happiness had been founded on a lie. She had deluded herself that she was part of a family—the family she had always yearned for. In fact she was little better than a servant. Worse—a servant was paid, at least. If Tallie had been paid she would have had the wherewithal to pay for a night's lodging or two. As it was, she had nothing.

Enough of self-pity, she decided at last. There was a way out of this mess. It was the only possible solution. She knew it, had known it all along; she'd just been unable to face the thought until she'd explored every other option. But there were no other options. She would have to marry Lord d'Arenville.

Lord d'Arenville. Cold-eyed, cold-voiced, handsome Lord d'Arenville. A cold proud Icicle, who simply wanted a brood mare for his heirs. Not a wife. Not a loving companion. A vessel for his children. A *sturdy* vessel! Tallie's mouth quivered and she bit down hard on her nails to stop herself weeping again.

There would be no love for Tallie now—the love she'd dreamed of all her life. But there would be security. And with the thought of sleeping in the village churchyard that night, security was suddenly more important than love—or, if not more important, certainly of more immediate significance.

No, there would be no Prince Charming for Tallie, no Black Knight galloping to her rescue, not even a dear, kind gentleman who was no one in particular. Nobody for Tallie to love, nobody who would love her in return. There was only Lord d'Arenville. Was it possible to love a statue? An Icicle?

Oh, there would be children, God willing, but children were different. You couldn't help but love children. And they couldn't help but love you back. Children were like puppies, loving, mischievous and endlessly thirsting for love.

Tallie knew. She'd thirsted all her life, ever since she'd turned six and had been sent away to school.

That was one thing she'd have to make clear to Lord d'Arenville from the start. She wouldn't allow him to send *her* children away to school. Not until they were quite old—fourteen, fifteen, something like that. And she would write to them *every* week, and send them special treats sometimes to share with their chums. And they would come home for every holiday and term break. And bring any of their schoolfriends who couldn't go to their own families. None of *her* children's friends would spend Christmas after Christmas alone in an empty school, with no one but an elderly headmistress to keep her company.

Her children would know they were *loved*, know they were *wanted*, know that their mother, at least, cared about them.

And the love of her children would have to be enough for her, she decided. It was only the lucky ones, the golden ones of this world, who were loved for themselves, after all. Who found a partner to share secret dreams and foolish ideas with. Who found a man to cherish them. *Cherish.* Such a beautiful, magical word.

Tallie took a long, shaky breath, a sob catching in her throat as she did so. Such dreams were for silly girls. She scrubbed at her swollen eyes with a handkerchief. It was time to put her dreams and her girlhood away.

It was time to go to Lord d'Arenville and tell him she would marry him.

It was a chilly, withdrawn and much chagrined Lord d'Arenville who returned from the garden half an hour after he'd spoken with Laetitia. The house party had been an unmitigated disaster. And now his ego was severely dented by the news that a penniless girl could not bear the thought of marrying him. Part of him concurred with his cousin that he would like to drown Miss Thalia Robinson. Or strangle her slowly, taking her soft, creamy throat between his bare hands... But an innate sense of fair play told him it would be a gross miscarriage of justice if he allowed his cousin to turn Thalia Robinson out on the streets merely because she didn't wish to wed him.

And he had been uncannily disturbed by the sound of someone weeping in the maze. Weeping as if their heart would break. Magnus *hated* it when women wept!

He'd taken a few steps into the maze and hovered there for some time, clenching and unclenching his fists, listening helplessly. Not knowing what to do. Knowing who it was, sobbing so piteously. Thalia Robinson.

He had told himself she'd brought it on herself, boasting to Laetitia of how she would spurn his offer. He'd told himself she deserved to be miserable, that the girl must be a coldhearted little bitch. He'd made her an honourable offer—there was no need for her to publicly humiliate him. He, who had long been regarded as the finest prize on the marriage mart, hunted by matchmaking mamas and their daughters alike! Most girls would have been grateful for an offer from him, but not Miss Thalia Robinson. No. She planned to humiliate him—and so she was reaping what she had sown. Her regrets had come too late.

Magnus had told himself all these things, but they hadn't helped—he just couldn't bear the sound of a woman sobbing.

The part of him that didn't want to strangle her had wanted
to go into the maze and speak to her—and what a stupid idea
that would have been! As if women ever made any sense when
they were weeping. And as if he would know what to do
anyway. He'd always managed to stop them crying by giving
them some bauble or other, but then all the women he'd ever
known had cried *at* him, not taken themselves into the middle
of a maze on a damned cold day and sobbed their little hearts
out in absolute solitude.

Magnus was sure he wouldn't know how to deal with someone who wept like that.

'Tish, I intend to withdraw my offer. She cannot refuse me
if there is no offer, so you need not worry about any insult to
the family pride. No one will know of it. I will speak to the
girl before any irrevoc—' He faltered for a moment, recalling
those cheeky last words: *make no irrevocable arrangements.*
Thalia Robinson had not realised she was sounding her own
doom. 'Before any irrevocable steps have been taken. Have
her sent to me at once, if you please.'

'But, Magnus—'

'At once, Tish.'

'Oh, very well. But it will make no diff—'

But Magnus had left. Laetitia pulled the bell cord to summon Brooks.

Magnus decided to receive Miss Robinson in the library. He
would speak kindly to her, show her he bore her no grudge
for her poor judgement. She would have no idea that she had,
somehow, got under his skin. He would be casual, relaxed,
indifferent. He would not receive her in formal dress, as a
gentleman would normally do when receiving a lady's answer
to his proposal of marriage. His offhand manner would be
conveyed by the silent message of his riding buckskins. It
would appear to be a spur of the moment chat, the outcome
of which held only lukewarm interest for him.

His brow furrowed as he tried to recall every detail of their
previous conversation. A cold smile grew on his face as he

realised he had not actually *asked* her to marry him. Not in so
many words. He had spoken of an intention to organise a
ceremony. Had used the conditional tense. Thank heavens. He
might be able to fudge it. He would make Miss Robinson
understand she was mistaken, that he'd made her no actual
offer.

It was not an honourable solution, but it should smooth
things over with Laetitia—enough to stop her throwing the
wretched girl into the streets. And then he would get the hell
out of this appalling house party and never have to set eyes
on the blasted girl or his blasted cousin ever again!

He leant against a high, leather-covered writing desk, one
leg crossed casually over the other, awaiting her entrance with
an expression of bored indifference on his face. The whip
snapped fast and furious against the glossy leather of his boot.

'Lord d'Arenville?'

She'd entered the room so silently that Magnus was caught
unaware. He stared, mesmerised, at the red-rimmed eyes
which failed to meet his, the drooping mouth and the woe-
begone little face, and it was as if he could hear every choking
sob again. With an effort, he gathered himself and began to
speak, feeling dishonest and uncomfortable as he did so.

'Miss Robinson, I gather from my cousin that you are under
the mistaken impression that I off—'

'Lord d'Arenville, I accept your offer of marriage,' she said
at the same time.

There was a long, tense moment of silence in the room.

What happens now? wondered Magnus. In all honour, he
could not continue with his reluctant pretence that he had
made no offer. There was no need—she had accepted him. So
that was it. An offer had been made and was accepted. The
rest was inevitable. Irrevocable. Ironic, that. *She* could call the
wedding off, but there was no question that he could do the
same. Lord d'Arenville was to wed Miss Thalia Robinson.
Thalia Robinson, who looked more like a martyr going to the
stake than a blushing bride.

The realisation was like a kick in the teeth. Until this moment he'd half believed that Laetitia was mistaken in saying the girl was going to refuse him. But this miserably bleak acceptance of his offer had convinced him as a thousand explanations could not.

It could not be said that Thalia Robinson actually *preferred* poverty to himself, but it would be clear to a blind man that it was a damned close race. The girl might be going to her execution, the face she was wearing. Magnus stared at the downcast face, the red-tipped nose, the resolute chin and the trembling lips and felt his anger rising. It had clearly taken a great deal of anguish and resolution for her to decide between abject poverty—or marriage to Lord d'Arenville.

Starvation and misery—or Lord d'Arenville!

The gutter—or Lord d'Arenville!

And finally, by a nose, or a whisker, or a hair's breadth, Lord d'Arenville had won. Lucky Lord d'Arenville!

Lord d'Arenville was furious. He could not trust himself to speak another word to her. He bowed stiffly, turned and stalked out of the room. Tallie watched him leave, blinking in surprise.

'Magnus, what—?' Laetitia was standing in the hallway, speaking to the vicar. Her voice died as she saw the look on his face.

'You may wish me happy!' he snapped.

'What?'

'She has accepted me.' He broke his whip in half and flung the pieces into a corner.

'Oh, Magnus, how dreadf—'

'I am *ecstatic*!' he snarled. 'The wedding will be in three weeks' time. Make all the arrangements. Spare no expense.' He laughed, a harsh, dry laugh. '*Nothing* is too good for my bride!' He noticed the vicar, standing there, jaw agape and added, 'You, there—Parson. Call the banns, if you please. I will return in three weeks for the ceremony.'

He stormed out of the door and headed for the stables. Laetitia trailed after him, pleading with him to slow down, to explain, but to no avail. Lord d'Arenville mounted his horse, and with no warning, no preparations and no baggage, set off for d'Arenville Hall, a good two days' journey away.

Chapter Four

'Blast and bother!' Tallie glared at her reflection. She'd brought a mirror up from one of the salons and propped it against the wall. It told her what she had already suspected—that she was the worst seamstress in the world and that her wedding dress looked like a dog's breakfast.

She tugged at the recalcitrant sleeves, pulling them this way and that in an effort to make them appear balanced. It was hopeless. One sleeve puffed beautifully whilst the other, which *should* have been an exact twin, sagged and drooped. She'd put the sleeve in and taken it out a half-dozen times and still it looked uneven—and slightly grubby from all the handling.

Tallie had no idea what arrangements had been made for her wedding. She'd tried several times to speak to her cousin, but Laetitia was still furious and had ordered Tallie to keep out of her sight or she would not be answerable for the consequences.

No one, not the servants, Laetitia nor Lord d'Arenville, had seemed to recall that the bride had not a penny to her name. Hopefully someone would remember the bride needed a suitable gown, but as the dreaded day grew closer Tallie decided she had better make alternative arrangements—just in case.

The attics contained dozens of trunks and bandboxes, filled with old dresses and ballgowns, relegated there over the years. She and the children had rummaged through them frequently, searching for dress-up materials. Tallie had found a lovely pale amber silk ballgown, hopelessly outmoded, with wide panniers and yards of ruching, but with enough good material left, when it was unpicked, to make a wedding frock. Using one of her old dresses as a pattern, she had cut and sewn it laboriously, wishing she had been more diligent in Miss Fisher's sewing class.

In another trunk she had found an almost new pair of blue kid slippers, which only pinched her feet a little, and a stained pair of long white satin gloves. The stains were impossible to remove, so she'd dipped the gloves in coffee until they almost exactly matched the amber silk.

She smiled at her reflection and pirouetted several times. It was not so bad after all. Oh, the neckline was a trifle crooked, to be sure, but Tallie was convinced only the most critical would notice it. And if the gathers she had made at the back were slightly uneven, what did that signify? It was only obvious when she was motionless, so she would be sure to keep moving, and if she had to stand still for any reason she would keep her back to a wall.

She examined her reflection in the mirror again as she tugged on the long satin gloves. She had never worn anything so fine in her life. She frowned at the sleeves... A shawl! she realised in a sudden flash of brilliance. Laetitia's spangled gauze scarf would hide the sleeves! It was not precisely a bridal mode, but perhaps observers would think it a new fashion. After all, she was wedding a man well-known for his elegance. Tallie's mouth grew dry as she stared at her reflection.

She was not just wedding a man...she was wedding The Icicle. Tomorrow morning. And afterwards he would take her away from the children she loved so much—the only living creatures in the world who loved her. Tomorrow she would belong only to him, swear before God and witnesses to love, honour and obey him. A man she barely knew and certainly didn't like. A cold man, who was famed for caring nothing for the feelings of others. Who wanted a wife he need not

dance attendance on, a wife he could get with child and then
abandon in rural fastness while he enjoyed himself in London,
awaiting the birth of his heir...

Tallie shivered. What did it mean, *get with child*? She knew
women bore children, of course, but how it came about she
had no idea. She'd lived virtually her entire life in Miss
Fisher's Seminary for the Daughters of Gentlemen, and the
subject had certainly never been on that prim spinster's curriculum.

It had, however, been a subject of much speculation and
whispering in the dormitories. But none of the various theories
put forward by the Daughters of Gentlemen had convinced
Tallie that any of her schoolfellows were more enlightened
than she on the subject. Some had insisted that women carried
a baby around in their stomach, for instance. Well, if that was
so—how did they get the baby out? Cut it out? Vomit it?

In any case, how did a baby get in there in the first place?
The man planted a seed in the woman? *A seed?* Babies didn't
grow from seeds! They did, Amanda Forrest had said. Her
mother had told her so. Well, how did they plant the seed—
swallow it? Tallie suspected it was an old wives' tale—like
that which said if you swallowed pumpkin seeds, pumpkin
vines would grow out of your ears. Tallie had proven *that* one
wrong by eating more than twenty pumpkin seeds—no hint of
a vine had appeared from her ears, though she'd been a little
anxious for a week or two!

No, Amanda hadn't been sure how the seed was planted,
but it was much the same as animals did, she believed. Tallie
had scoffed at that one—animals planting seeds? Ridiculous.

One girl, Emmaline Pearce, had spoken ghoulishly of wedding nights and blood and screaming, but everyone had known
Emmaline Pearce was a shockingly untruthful girl who made
up all sorts of deliciously scary tales. Miss Fisher had forever
been punishing her for it.

Get with child. Surely she had the right to be told how it
was done. Had her mother lived, she could have explained,
but all Tallie's mother had left her was a few letters. And

possibly— But there was no time to think on that… She had a wedding night to worry about first.

Tallie decided to ask Mrs Wilmot. She sought her out in the linen room and, with much beating around the bush, blurted out her question.

'Lord love you, Miss Tallie.' The housekeeper blushed. 'I'm not the one you should ask about such matters. I've never been wed, my dear.'

'But—'

'All housekeepers are called Missus, dearie, whether they're wed or not. But Wilmot is my maiden name.' She patted Tallie on the hand. 'You go ask your cousin, miss. She'll set you right.' The kindness shone so warmly from the elderly house-keeper's face that Tallie didn't have the heart to explain how very hostile Laetitia was.

Then she thought of the scullery maid, Maud, who was, according to rumour, *no better than she ought to be*. Surely Maud would know. But when Tallie asked her, Maud shrieked with laughter, tossed her apron over her face and ran from the room giggling, leaving Tallie red to the ears.

Finally she decided to approach her cousin about it.

Laetitia took one look at Tallie's blushing embarrassment, and snapped impatiently, 'Oh, God deliver me from puling virgins! Don't look so mealy-mouthed, girl—I'll tell you all you need to know about your wedding night.' She pulled Tallie down beside her and whispered detailed instructions in her ear. After a moment she sat back and pushed Tallie away.

Horrified, but too mortified to ask questions, Tallie turned to leave, but as she reached the door Laetitia hissed after her, 'Be sure you do not disgrace my cousin or your family. Remember, a lady endures it *in silence—without moving or flinching*. Do you hear me, girl?' She turned back to her mirror, a knowing smile on her face.

They were the last words Laetitia spoke to her, and the more she thought about them, the more nervous Tallie became. *Endure it?* What was *it*? Endurance sounded most unpleasant… And in *silence*? Why would she wish to cry out? Or flinch…

It sounded painful. She thought briefly of Emmaline Pearce, then shook her head.

'Miss, miss, he's arrived!' Lucy, the maid, put her head around the door, her face lit with excitement. 'Your betrothed, miss—Lord d'Arenville—he's here!'

Tallie's heart seemed to stop for a moment, and then began to beat in double time. He was here. She would be able to speak to him, then—about Italy—before the wedding. It was what she had been hoping for. In the three weeks since he had galloped off so intemperately, she'd kicked herself often for not having sorted out everything to her satisfaction. She had to speak with him, get the whole thing settled before the wedding, for afterwards there would be little likelihood of him agreeing to the demands of a woman who'd sworn in church to obey him.

'I must see him at once.' Tallie started towards the door.

'Oh, miss, miss, you can't! It's bad luck, no matter how eager you are to see your handsome gentleman again!' Lucy beamed in fond indulgence. The entire household had reacted to the news of Tallie's wedding as if it was a fairy tale come true for her, and Tallie found she didn't have the heart to disillusion them.

'Bad luck? Why?'

Lucy gestured to Tallie's gown. 'For the groom to see the bride in her wedding dress, a'course.' She looked more closely at the wedding dress, and, frowning, reached out to tug one sleeve into place. 'Are you sure this—?'

'Oh, never mind that,' said Tallie. 'I'll change my dress, Lucy, since you say it's so important, but will you please take a message to Lord d'Arenville and tell him I must speak to him as soon as possible? In private.'

Realising she was to be Cupid's Messenger, Lucy beamed and said dramatically, 'Of course I will, Miss Tallie. I'll go straight away, and before you know it you'll be reunited once more with Your Beloved.' She sailed from the room.

Tallie giggled. Her Beloved? She giggled again, trying to

imagine The Icicle involved in anything so human as a romantic assignation. It was simply not possible.

Having told the irritatingly coy maidservant he would meet Miss Robinson in the summerhouse in twenty minutes, Magnus found himself wondering why the girl wanted to speak to him so urgently. Something to do with her wedding finery, no doubt. He allowed himself a faint, cynical smile and felt in his pocket for the long oblong package. He was well ahead of her.

Magnus had ridden away from his last interview with his bride-to-be in a white-hot rage. He was still angry, but his rage had cooled to an icy implacability. Thalia Robinson would have to learn her place. If she wanted to be treated as a bride would wish to be treated she had better tread very lightly around him until she'd earned his forgiveness. He frowned and felt the package. He must make his motives for this gift very clear to her. He would not wish her to misunderstand him.

It had occurred to him a week before that she would very likely not possess any adequate jewellery. It was unthinkable that his bride wear cheap or shoddy jewellery at her wedding, so Magnus had looked through his late mother's jewel case until he had found a very pretty rope of matched pearls, earrings, and a bracelet—just right for a young bride. Simple enough to look modest and maidenly, yet the rope was very long and the pearls priceless. They were the perfect betrothal gift—and would be bound to go with whatever she had decided to wear.

From the little he had seen of her clothing, Miss Robinson preferred an odd style of garment, but Laetitia's taste was exquisite, and she would have ensured that his bride would not wear anything outrageous. And after they were married he'd supervise her wardrobe himself. The rest of his mother's jewels he would present to her as and when she deserved it.

'Lord d'Arenville?'

Magnus rose and turned quickly. He bowed slightly. 'Miss

Robinson.' His eyes were cold, his patrician features impassive.

Tallie closed the door to the summerhouse behind her. Her heart was pounding as if she had been running and her hands felt clammy. She curtsied automatically, trying not to stare. Gracious, she'd forgotten how very handsome he was. It made it so much harder to remember how cold he was.

'I was under the impression that you wished to converse with me, but perhaps you merely wished to see for yourself that I had returned.' His tone was blighting.

'Oh, no,' Tallie responded instantly. 'I believed Lucy when she told me you'd arrived. Lucy is a very truthful girl.'

He missed her irony. 'Lucy?'

'The maid.' Tallie seated herself on a bench beside a wall.

Lord d'Arenville folded his arms, leaned against the wall and regarded her sardonically. He was looming again, Tallie thought resentfully, and obviously had no intention of making this any easier.

'I wished to see you in private because there are things we need to have clear before the wedding,' she said in a rush.

Have clear? His eyes narrowed. 'Are there indeed?'

'Yes. You left so suddenly I had no chance to talk to you about them.'

'Well, I am here now,' Magnus drawled.

'Th…they are very important to me, and I could not agree to marry you unless we do so.'

'I was under the impression that you had already agreed to marry me, madam,' he said silkily.

'Well, I did, yes, but we had not finished our discussion when you rushed out, and I only discovered later that you had gone to d'Arn…d'Anvil…' She stumbled over the word in her nervousness.

'D'Arenville Hall, madam. You had best learn the name, as it will be your home for the rest of your life.'

This veiled allusion to the rural imprisonment he planned for her threw Tallie into a temper. He did not know she had overheard him in the library that night, telling his cousin his plans for a bride and an heir. She recognised his threat.

'It is *not* my home yet.' Tallie bared her teeth in what she hoped would look like a smile. 'And there are issues to resolve before I agree to make it so—several conditions, in fact.'

Conditions! Magnus was outraged. The chit was trying to blackmail him. Threatening to jilt him unless he agreed to her demands. The day before the wedding, when guests would be arriving at any moment. By God she had a cheek!

With difficulty he held onto his temper, kept his face impassive. He would wait until he had heard her 'conditions'— then he'd show her who was master here! He'd march her to the church and marry her out of hand, and then set about teaching Miss Thalia Robinson a lesson she'd never forget! Gritting his teeth, he coolly inclined his head, inviting her to continue.

Tallie regarded him nervously. He was leaning casually against the wall, seemingly relaxed and at ease, but his jaw was clenched tight, and there was a most disturbing look in his eyes. She should not have spoken of conditions, should have put it more tactfully. He was annoyed. Still, this was her only opportunity to ensure that not all her dreams ended in the dust. A betrothed female still had some power—a wife had none.

'There are a number of cond—matters that we need to agree on. The first concerns children.'

He stared at her and his frown darkened. 'Go on.'

'I…I know you want children…but I must tell you that I will not…' Tallie gulped at the black look on his face, but forced herself to continue. 'I will *not* allow you to send them away to school.'

Magnus blinked. Her statement had taken him unawares. He'd thought she was going to refuse to bear his children, refuse to share his bed. Not send them to school? Did she think it a threat? 'And why should our children not be sent to school? Do you wish them to grow up ignorant and uneducated?'

'Of course not,' she flashed indignantly. 'They shall be taught at home, of course, by the very best and kindest governesses and tutors. I am not saying they shall *never* go to school, only *not* when they are still babies. When they are eleven or twelve, perhaps, but no younger than that.'

Magnus opened his mouth to agree to this extraordinary request, but was cut off.

'No, you need not argue—I am absolutely adamant on this point. I won't have my children sent off to be reared by strangers. Not until they are old enough. And *I* will decide when that is.'

She clenched her fists and glared at him defiantly, a mulish set to her jaw, and continued, 'Oh, you need not think I wish to tie them to my apron strings—I value strength and independence, and will nourish these qualities in my children— but you can have no idea the damage it does to very young children to be away from all that is familiar and those who love them, and I will *not* have my children feeling unloved and unwanted.' Her voice quavered with emotion and she stopped to catch her breath.

Magnus stared. He recalled the devastating loneliness he had first felt when sent off to school himself at the age of six. A lump in his chest made it difficult to breathe. 'I accept,' he said coldly.

Tallie blinked in surprise and relaxed slightly. The first hurdle had been unexpectedly easy. No argument at all. She supposed he didn't particularly care what happened to the children, as long as he had an heir. The next would be a little more difficult, for she could not let on she had overheard his infamous plan to immure her at d'Arenville Hall for ten years.

'You said I would be living at d'Arenville Hall for the rest of my life…'

He nodded curtly.

'Well, I wish to come up to London for a short visit once a year—no more than two or three weeks,' she added hurriedly. The black frown was back again. 'I realise you'd prefer me to stay at d'Arenville Hall, and for the most part I will, but I have never been to London and would very much like to visit it.'

He said nothing. He was going to refuse; Tallie could sense it. She hurried on, 'Your children's mother should not be totally ignorant of the world they will move in.'

Magnus was puzzled. On the contrary, he expected his children's mother to learn the ways of the polite world as soon as possible. Why would he wish her ignorant? He didn't see her point. It had something to do with visiting London. For a few weeks only. Was she trying to tell him she didn't wish to go out in society? The chit made no sense. Well, he would not take no for an answer on this one—he had every intention of taking her to London immediately, to order her new clothing, introduce her to society and teach her how his Countess should conduct herself. And the sooner Miss Thalia Robinson accepted that, the better. He did not want society to think the mother of his children was an obscure, ignorant rag-bag. He knew full well the gossip that had already arisen about his bride as a result of the house party.

'If you lock me away, people will gossip, and I would not want my children to discover that people think their mother is strange or odd or even mad,' concluded Tallie desperately.

Lock her away? Did the silly chit think he had a dungeon at d'Arenville Hall? Her eyes were fixed anxiously on his face. She looked rather appealing. Magnus frowned. 'I have every intention of taking you to London. I have no desire to have my wife thought an eccentric social recluse, madam, and the sooner you realise that the better.'

Tallie was amazed. Somewhere along the line he must have changed his mind about keeping her at d'Arenville Hall for ten years—or perhaps he planned to change his mind back again after the wedding. 'Do I have your word on it, sir?'

Magnus stiffened. He was not accustomed to having his word questioned. By anyone. And certainly not by an ill-dressed poor relation attempting to blackmail him.

'You do, madam,' he grated.

'Good.' Tallie smiled triumphantly. His anger at her question had confirmed her suspicions. He *had* planned to change his mind, but she'd been too clever for him. She'd gained his agreement to the most important things—now there was just the matter of the bride trip. It would be the most difficult, she knew. 'Now, my next request you may find a little unusual… and possibly a trifle expensive,' she said.

Magnus mentally braced himself. The last two 'requests' had, as he'd expected, been mere bagatelles, intended to soften him up. This one would be the cruncher.

'I have always wished to travel,' Tallie began, 'and I was hoping that you would agree that on the honey…on my bride trip we could visit some of the places I have always dreamed of seeing.' She clasped her hands in unconscious supplication. 'On the Continent.'

Magnus relaxed. So that was it. The girl wished to go to Paris. Not surprising. Every woman he'd ever known preferred French gowns, French hats and French perfumes. And the war was over… He shrugged mentally. It would be no hardship to take her to Paris and purchase her new wardrobe there. It might even be a good thing—allow her to acquire a touch of town bronze in Parisian society before she made her entrance in London.

He shrugged indifferently. 'All right. If you wish to brave the Channel crossing, we shall.'

Tallie was incredulous. 'You do not mind?'

Magnus shrugged again. 'Not at all.' He wondered what her final request would be. He shifted, and felt the bump of the jewel case in his pocket.

'The trip will take some time,' said Tallie. 'You may not care for the inconvenience. You are sure?'

The chit was questioning his word again, damn her! 'You have my word on it, Miss Robinson,' he snapped.

Tallie beamed. 'Then may I prepare an itinerary?'

Magnus inclined his head.

'I can speak several languages, you know,' she said confidingly. 'French, of course, and Italian, but also German and a little Dutch, for there was a girl from the Low Countries at school, and she taught me some Dutch and some Flemish, too.'

'What the devil are you talking about? You won't need all those languages in Paris.'

Tallie laughed. 'Not in Paris—for Italy—and elsewhere, of course. I won't need an interpreter in Paris. I told you—I speak French fluently. And Italian.'

'Do you mean to tell me you wish to travel to *Italy*?'

Tallie nodded. 'Yes…and Germany, Switzerland, and perhaps we can visit the Low Countries on our way back to England.' *Anywhere, as long as we go to Italy, where poor Mama died. And then, perhaps, I will be able to find out—for certain—if…*

'That is The Grand Tour,' said Magnus, in a forbidding tone.

'Yes. I have wanted to take it for years.'

'Quite impossible! And too dangerous—Europe is still at sixes and sevens because of the war.'

'Nonsense. It is perfectly safe since the Peace Treaty was signed at Amiens,' retorted Tallie triumphantly. 'Several of my cousin's acquaintances departed for Paris even before it was signed, and they are all surviving nicely.'

Magnus glared at her. Ladies were supposed to know nothing of political matters. She ought not to question his judgement.

'And if it is so terribly dangerous, why did you agree to take me to Paris?' she added.

'Paris is one thing—The Grand Tour another. Ladies do not take The Grand Tour,' he stated coldly.

'They do,' Tallie contradicted him. 'I know of several.'

Magnus stared down his nose at her. 'Perhaps you are speaking of females,' he said. 'I was referring to *ladies*.'

'Well, so was I!' retorted Tallie. 'Lady Mary Wortley Montagu, Lady Fetherstonhaugh, and…and Mrs Ann Radcliffe, who embarked on The Grand Tour with her husband, in the very year that Robespierre was guillotined—the same year her *Mysteries of Udolfo* was published, I believe.'

Magnus was exasperated. 'That damned silly book—'

'It is not a silly book! It is utterly thrilling, as anyone who did not have ice-water in his veins—'

'We are not speaking of Lady Mary Montagu or Lady Fetherstonhaugh or Mrs Radcliffe. We are speaking of *my wife*.'

'I am not your wife yet!' Tallie interrupted him. 'And you gave your word!'

'I gave my word to take you to Paris, but no further.'

'I never mentioned Paris, and neither did you,' argued Tallie. 'Not until *after* you gave your word.'

Magnus thought back. Damn it—the chit was right!

'The rigours and difficulties of The Grand Tour make it too exhausting and dangerous for females to attempt.' His voice brooked no argument.

'Nonsense. I have read *Letters From Italy*, and—'

'Hah!' Magnus snorted. 'Anne Miller's book was written thirty years ago and more.'

Tallie bridled. 'I know, for my mother read it on *her* Grand Tour, when she married my father. And it was *much* more dangerous in those days. Now that The Terror is over, all of England is flocking to the continent. People of the utmost respectability.' Her eyes dared him to contradict her.

There was a short silence. 'It will be extremely uncomfortable. You will be miserable with the appalling accommodation,' stated Magnus. 'I know because I have travelled on the Continent. You cannot imagine the state of the roads—if roads they can be held to be. And as for the wretched inns—if inn you can find—on several occasions I had to sleep in a barn! With the animals!'

Tallie shrugged, unconcerned. 'It does not seem to have done you any harm. And if it is me you are concerned about, then let me remind you that I have spent most of my life in a seminary for young ladies—'

Despite his anger, Magnus's lips twitched. 'Are you suggesting that a seminary for young ladies is worse than a barn full of animals?'

Tallie laughed. 'Well, there were a couple of absolute

cow—' She blushed, and caught herself up. 'No, of course
not, but it was a very Spartan place, and I am tougher than I
look.' She fixed him with her most determined expression. A
few weeks ago he'd called her *sturdy*. Now, to save himself
inconvenience, he was pretending she was too delicate. Lord
d'Arenville would find he could not have it both ways. 'And
anyway, you *promised*.'

Magnus swore under his breath. He was trapped and he
knew it. The wretched girl was not going to give in on this—
he could tell from her mulish expression. And he had promised, even if he hadn't meant what she said he'd meant. But
he was damned if he was going to give in tamely. He cast
around for a way out and had a sudden thought.

'Travel is very dangerous for ladies who are *in a delicate
state*,' he stated. Let her try to refute that one.

Tallie looked puzzled. 'But I just told you I was stronger
than I look. I am not the slightest bit delicate.'

He stared down into her innocent face and cursed silently.
'But you may be *in a delicate state* soon after your wedding,'
he said. 'And many ladies become quite ill.'

'But why, when I am strong now? A little thing like a wedding isn't going to weaken me…' Suddenly Tallie paled, realising what he meant. He was talking about *it*. And he expected
her to be *ill* after she had *endured it*. It was worse, then, than
she had thought. It was not just that she must not move or cry
out while she endured it, she could be sick for some time
afterwards. Gracious—it must be very dreadful.

'If I were *in a delicate state*, and I am ill, would it last long,
do you think?' she whispered.

Magnus was torn between concern at her sudden extreme
pallor and embarrassment at discussing pregnancy with such
an innocent. At least she *was* an innocent, he thought, and she
should be discussing pregnancy with Laetitia, not her prospective bridegroom. But he had clearly frightened her by raising the question and was obligated to respond. 'I am not sure
but…I, er…I believe many women feel ill for the first few
months.'

Months! It must be appalling, Tallie thought. No wonder people did not inform girls about such things—they would never agree to marry. But surely it got better, otherwise why would women wish their daughters to be married?

'And after that?'

'After that, I believe they usually feel quite well until they are brought to bed.' Magnus drew out a handkerchief to wipe his brow. His betrothed was clearly shaken. Obviously it had not occurred to her that she might begin breeding while she was on the Continent. Strike while the iron is hot, he decided.

'So we are agreed—if you find yourself *in a delicate condition* the Tour will be called off and we will return to England at once.'

Tallie chewed her lip. She was strong. Her mother had managed it. So could she. And if she really was ill, she supposed there would be no point in travelling.

'Very well,' she agreed grudgingly.

Magnus refrained from rubbing his hands in triumph. He had every intention of getting her with child before there was any question of travelling beyond Paris. He would take her to Paris, show her the sights, purchase gowns and hats and perfumes and all manner of feminine fripperies, then whisk her home to d'Arenville Hall to await the birth of their child.

Their child. He could not wait. But first he had to get the wedding over with.

'And what is your next "condition", may I ask?' he said.

'Next condition? There are none. You have agreed to everything, more or less.' Tallie was still worrying about the wedding night.

Magnus was stunned, and vaguely suspicious. He'd been certain that she was building up to something truly outrageous.

Tallie stood up to leave. 'Thank you for agreeing to speak to me. You have relieved my mind…about some things.' *And frightened me to pieces about others.* She opened the door.

Magnus recalled the jewel case in his pocket. 'Miss Robinson, a moment longer, if you please.'

'Yes?' She turned back and looked at him, wide-eyed and pale.

'You may wish to wear these at your wedding. They belonged to my mother.' He held out the box.

Tallie opened it. 'Pearls, how pretty,' she said dully. 'Thank you very much. I shall wear them tomorrow, since you ask.'

She shut the box and left the summerhouse. Magnus stood watching her cross the lawn and enter the house, frowning. He'd never had a woman accept jewellery in quite that manner. There'd been no squeals of joy, no excited hugs or kisses, no play-acting and flirtation. Not that he wanted that sort of response from the woman he would take to wife, Magnus told himself. Not at all.

He should be happy to discover his intended bride wasn't greedy or grasping. He *was* happy. Her cool acceptance was well-bred and ladylike… It was, in fact, exactly how his mother had accepted jewels from his father.

And why did that thought annoy him so much?

Nonsense! He was *not* annoyed. There was no reason to be annoyed. She'd answered him perfectly politely.

Too politely.

She'd accepted his gift of priceless pearls like a child accepting an apple, with polite, mechanical thanks, quite as if she was thinking about something else.

Damn it all, but this girl was an enigma to him. Magnus didn't like enigmas. And he was *very* annoyed.

Chapter Five

*O*ld Mr Penworthy, the organist, plays the opening chord, so softly that at first the congregation is barely aware of it. Gradually the music swells, filling the ancient and beautiful church with a glorious torrent of sound. The bride has arrived.

The pews are crowded to bursting point, mostly with friends of the bride, well-wishers from the village and from much farther afield. There are foreign dignitaries, resplendent in silk hats, glittering with medals and imperial orders—men who knew the bride's father abroad, who come to her wedding representing princes, dukes—even an emperor.

Outside in the churchyard, tall, handsome men watch from a distance, loitering palely, some gnashing their teeth, others silent and crushed with despair—their hopes and hearts dashed for ever by the bride's acceptance of another.

In the lane beyond the churchyard wall sit two elegant carriages. Rumour has it each carriage contains an aristocratic lady, each one an heiress and a diamond of the first water. Screened from the stares of the vulgar by delicate black netting, the ladies weep. Their beauty, their riches and their rank serve them naught, for the groom has chosen his bride, and she is no famous beauty, nor even rich or aristocratic. But she offers him a prize he values beyond earthly riches—her heart. And he gives her his in return.

The first chord draws to a close and the bride steps into the *centre aisle. The congregation turns to look and a sigh whispers around the church. From where she stands, the bride can hear only fragments of what they say... 'Lovely gown...' 'A beautiful bride...'*

The music swells again and she begins her slow walk down the aisle. Her beloved awaits her. His eyes feast on her. He makes a small move towards her, as if he cannot wait for her to reach him but must rush up the aisle and take her in his arms. She almost weeps with joy at his loving impatience; she, too, wants to run down the aisle towards him and fling herself into his arms. Instead she walks in proud and happy dignity, her head held high, feeling, as she always does when he looks at her, beautiful.

Mr Penworthy times it perfectly; as she reaches the altar, the music soars to its final crescendo. The last notes echo around the ancient oaken rafters and her beloved takes her hand in his, murmuring, 'Tallie, my own true love, you make me the happiest man on earth.' He lifts her gloved hand to his mouth, and...

'Ouch! Bloody h—what the dev—er, deuce do you think you're doing?' exclaimed Lord d'Arenville angrily, one hand clamped over his nose—the nose that Tallie's gloved hand had forcibly collided with. His eyes were watering from the impact. He blinked down at her, then took her hand, which still hovered dangerously close to his face. A faint cloud of aromatic brown dust rose from her glove.

He stared down at her hands, raised one cautiously to his nose and tentatively sniffed. 'Good God! They reek of coffee!'

Tallie didn't respond. She just stared up at him, the last remnants of her dream shattering around her feet. For one heart-stopping moment, when he had lifted her hand to his face again, she'd thought he was going to kiss it. But it was not to be. The Icicle was incapable of a romantic gesture like that. He was merely inspecting her gloves.

His grip on her hand tightened and he thrust it down between them. He nodded at the vicar. The vicar stood staring at Tallie, bemused.

'Get on with it, man,' said Lord d'Arenville curtly.

'Er, of course,' the vicar muttered, then announced in ringing, mellifluous tones, 'Dearly beloved, we are gathered…'

Dazed, Tallie stood there, listening to herself being married
to The Icicle. And a very bad-tempered Icicle he was, too. He
was positively glaring at her. Of course, he did have reason
to be a little cross, but it wasn't as if she had meant to hit him
on the nose, after all.

Mind you, she thought dejectedly, he seemed always to be
furious about something—mainly with her. Towards others he
invariably remained cool, polite and, in a chilly sort of fashion,
charming. But not with Tallie… It didn't augur at all well for
the future.

Still, Tallie rallied her spirits, this was her wedding day,
and she'd made up her mind to enjoy every moment of it. She
began to mentally tick off her blessings: the weather was almost sunny, and the wind not too cold at all. And her frock
had turned out quite well—the lovely amber material was absolutely perfect for her colouring, and she was sure no one
would notice the one or two little mistakes she'd made. The
music had been absolutely glorious—Mr Penworthy had truly
outdone himself—and her cousin's husband George had escorted her down the aisle looking every inch a gentleman. He
wasn't even very drunk, as far as she could tell.

And if she wasn't the most ecstatic bride in the world, she
was determined no one else would notice. All brides were
happy and joyful—she didn't want her friends and relations
upset by her own misgivings. That was why she'd invoked
her fantasy—it was one of her favourites—and because of it
she'd been able to act like a radiant bride should. She hoped
everyone had been taken in by her performance—she didn't
want to disappoint them.

She wondered where they were sitting—she'd been too involved in her fantasy to notice. She turned her head to take a
quick glance at the pews behind her, searching for Brooks,
Mrs Wilmot and the children…

'Thalia!' Lord d'Arenville's hand jerked her back to face the altar.

Tallie blinked at it for a moment. She felt dizzy, bereft, disorientated. She looked helplessly up at Lord d'Arenville. He stared back, his brow furrowed, his cold grey eyes intense. One hand held hers. His other arm slid around her and tightened around her waist. For a moment it seemed to Tallie that he could see into her very soul. She quivered under the hard gaze and closed her eyes—the intrusion was too painful. For a moment or two she was aware of nothing but the cold chill of the church and the pressure of his arm supporting her. His arm felt warm, but the grey eyes watching her looked angry. In the distance she could hear the vicar mumbling something. She closed her eyes harder, wishing with all her heart she could invoke her fantasy back to deal with this. She heard the vicar mumbling again. Lord d'Arenville gave her a little squeeze and Tallie opened her eyes.

'Do you, Thalia Louise Robinson take this man…?' intoned the vicar forcefully, his manner conveying to Tallie that he was repeating the question, and not for the first time.

Embarrassed, Tallie mumbled, 'I do,' and hurriedly repeated after him the words about loving, honouring and obeying Lord d'Arenville. She shivered.

She was bound for life to Magnus Philip Audley St Clair, Seventh Earl of d'Arenville. A surge of deepest misery washed over her. Her wedding was so very different from what she had hoped for, dreamed of. And she didn't mean all that nonsense about rejected suitors and important guests and beautiful gowns—that silliness had nothing to do with her true dreams.

All she truly wanted was to be loved.

The other had been mere play-acting, an attempt to distract herself, to get through the day with some semblance of good spirits in order not to disappoint her friends. But there hadn't been much point…

Dully, she felt her glove being tugged off.

'With this ring I thee wed, with my body I thee worship…' His voice was deep, harsh.

The ring was cold as it slid onto her finger.

She was married.

Tallie glanced up at her husband. He was staring down at her small hand, still resting in his large one. She followed his gaze and saw the faint brown stains on her fingers from the dye she had used on her gloves and lace. And at the end of each grubby hand was a chewed and ugly fingernail. That was what her new husband was staring at—her dirty hands and horrible bitten nails.

He put back her veil and kissed her, a hard, brief pressure on her mouth, then straightened, having done his duty. A lump rose in her throat and she bit her lip to stop it trembling. Such a cold, hollow sham of a wedding.

It was her own fault, she knew. She had stupidly allowed herself to dream of how it would be, and so of course she was disappointed. She invariably was. Life was always a disappointment when compared with her dreams. So the dreaming would have to stop...

But, oh, she'd never felt so miserable or alone in her life. Tallie felt a tear roll down her cheek, then another. She surreptitiously wiped them away. She straightened, preparing herself for the walk back down the aisle. She looked at the sparse, silent congregation and cast a quick glance up at the grim face of her new husband.

A straggle of the poorer villagers were watching from the very back of the church—come, possibly, with the expectation of largesse from the rich and happy groom. Tallie sighed. The villagers were, like everyone else, doomed to disappointment in her wedding, for the veriest blind man could see that her groom was not happy. There would be no largesse.

Magnus was indeed not happy. He was furious. Had been from the moment his cousin Laetitia, swooning artistically, had claimed she could not move another step that morning, that her head was positively shattered and the pain simply too, too much for a lady to bear. She had collapsed onto a Grecian sofa, reviving sufficiently to forbid that the children be taken to the church, claiming they were sickening for something, a mother always knew. It would be the basest cruelty to tear her beloved ones away from their mama when she was in such agony. A frail wisp of lace had been delicately brandished and applied to dry eyes. A battalion of small crystal bottles had been hastily arranged on a small table nearby—smelling salts, a vinaigrette, cologne water, feathers to burn...

Magnus had been helpless in the face of this determined barrage of feminine sensibility. The children had looked perfectly healthy to him. Nor had he missed their disappointed little faces when they'd come downstairs dressed in their best and their mother's decision had been announced.

Then Laetitia had insisted that she could not possibly spare Mrs Wilmot—no one's hands were as gentle and healing when it came to the headache. And, of course, Brooks would have to remain at the house—someone had to run the household while its mistress was indisposed.

Magnus had seen that Brooks and Mrs Wilmot had also been crushed with disappointment. They too had been dressed in their Sunday best—Mrs Wilmot in a large flowered hat, with a bunch of violets pinned to her bosom. For a moment he'd half expected her to argue with Laetitia. But they were elderly servants, entirely dependent on Laetitia's good will and with an uncertain old age facing them. Like the children, they had had no choice but to obey.

Magnus had fumed impotently. He could not veto the orders of a woman in her own house, particularly when those orders concerned her own children and servants.

But when Laetitia had claimed, in a failing thread of a voice, that she could not do without the comfort of her husband's presence in this, her hour of infirmity, Magnus had intervened. He had practically frogmarched George into the carriage, turning a deaf ear to Laetitia's wailing and George's blustering. The short trip to church had been accomplished in a mood of grim silence.

Alighting from the carriage, Magnus had looked around, frowning. There had been suspiciously few carriages. He'd told Laetitia to arrange a small wedding—meaning he didn't want a huge noisy crowd. But this…

He'd entered the church in a mood of black foreboding. His suspicions had been confirmed. The only people seated had been the two or three people he'd invited himself—none of them particularly close.

Not that he had many close friends—he would have liked Freddie to stand up with him, but Freddie had sent word that there was an outbreak of typhus in the village and he could not leave his wife and children, nor his parish, at such a time. Nor would he wish to risk conveying the disease to Magnus and his new bride.

So the only people seated in the church had been a couple of chaps from his club, a fellow he'd known at Oxford, who lived locally, and Magnus's valet, his groom and his tiger. A congregation of six—three of them servants and all male.

Magnus had cursed long and silently. Better to have no one at all than to humiliate his little bride with such a poor showing. For himself, he cared not a jot—marriage was a business transaction, and required the bare minimum of fuss. He was acquiring a wife who, with God's blessing, would give him children, and she was acquiring wealth, a title, and security for her lifetime.

But women set great store in weddings.

The bigger the better. With hordes of people. Expensive gowns and jewels. Flowers. Champagne. Happy throngs of celebrating guests! That was what women liked—he was sure of it. And little Thalia Robinson would be no exception; he was sure of that, too.

So where the hell was everyone?

And what the hell was he going to do?

What the devil had Laetitia been up to? He'd *told* her to organise everything, damn it! And it wasn't as if she'd indicated it would be any sort of imposition—far from it.

Women *liked* organising these affairs—look at how Laetitia had jumped at arranging that blasted house party with all those simpering debutantes. She'd organised that at a moment's notice. She'd had weeks to arrange his wedding. Three whole weeks. And a day or two to spare. He'd given her *carte blanche* with the arrangements. And the costs. And had sent her a stunning emerald necklace.

So where were all the happy blasted guests?

The organist had played the opening chords and Magnus had turned to see Miss Thalia Robinson, his bride, standing at the entrance of the church. Smiling blissfully. Beatifically. For a moment he'd frozen, staring, riveted by her smile—dazzling, even from behind the lace veil she was wearing. Her smile had driven every angry thought from his head. Every thought.

She had looked radiant. Beautiful. And utterly happy.

Was this the same girl he'd overheard sobbing? Alone and forlorn on a cold afternoon in her cousin's garden maze. Sobbing as if her heart would break—because Lord d'Arenville had offered her marriage.

The girl who, with reddened eyes and blotchy skin, had accepted his offer in a bleak little voice laced with defeat?

The girl who'd cold-bloodedly laid down her set of conditions only days before the wedding?

But today she was smiling…

Music had filled the church, soaring up amongst the blackened oak rafters as she had stepped out onto the strip of red matting which ran down the centre of the aisle. Her movement had jolted him out of his daze, and as he had watched her walking slowly towards him, floating proudly to the music, he'd gradually become aware of what she was wearing. And his frown had slowly returned.

Magnus was no great follower of feminine fashions, but he knew when something looked right. Or, in this case, when it looked wrong. Though exactly what it was he hadn't quite been able to put his finger on. The pale shimmering amber colour was not particularly fashionable, but it suited her. The fabric seemed rather too stiff for the soft, gauzy look which was so *à la mode* today, but that was not the problem…

His eyes had been drawn to the neckline, and for a moment he hadn't believed his eyes. It was *crooked*. Distinctly crooked. And so, now he had come to notice it, were her sleeves—or at least one of them was. And the gown hung all wrong. She had a nice little figure, he had realised suddenly, but this gown was utterly atrocious.

His temper had grown. How the devil had Laetitia allowed Thalia Robinson to go to her wedding dressed in a gown like that? Women always strove to look their best, but the most important time of all, the day when every woman expected to look beautiful, was on her wedding day. It was another thing Magnus understood about women. Which was why he'd specifically told his cousin to spare no expense in fitting out his bride. So why was she not wearing the finest gown a London modiste could provide? Good God, she looked for all the world as if her gown had been made by some half-wit in the village!

The closer his bride had come, the more he had noticed. Stains on the gloves, inadequately removed. A darn in the lace of her veil. A crooked hem. Uneven stitching…the list had grown.

And through it all Thalia Robinson had smiled, as if this truly was the happiest day of her life. As if she was not dressed in a frightful travesty of a wedding dress. As if the church was not virtually empty of well-wishers. As if Magnus was the man she loved…

He'd stared, angry, bemused, dazzled…

And then she'd cracked him on the nose so hard that tears had come into his eye and he'd been embarrassed, and growled out something which had caused the smile to drop from her face and the joy to seep out of her body. He'd watched it happen before his very eyes—one moment she had been joyous and radiant, the next miserable.

So then Magnus had really been furious. With himself.

He'd tried to keep her from noticing how few people there were in the church. He was sure she hadn't yet seen who was or wasn't there—her eyes hadn't left his on her proud, triumphal march down the aisle; she'd been smiling at him and only him.

But he hadn't succeeded. He knew to the second the moment she had realised there was no one on her side of the church. That no one had come to see Thalia Robinson married. The small gloved hand lying so limply in his had suddenly gripped him, tightening convulsively around his fingers. She had made no other sign, had stood straight and slender, looking ahead at the stained glass window above the altar, but Magnus had felt her trembling. Beneath the darned veil he had seen her biting her lip, struggling to maintain her composure. He had slid his arm around her, and unknowingly she had clutched onto him, tighter than ever, hanging onto his hand as if it was all she had to hold her up.

That pathetic, wounded look she'd given him had pierced him to the core. He would never forget it.

She had expected well-wishers—the children, the housekeeper and the butler at least. And was reeling under the cruel impact of the empty pews. And Magnus had been able to do nothing about it. Except become even more furious.

Then he'd tugged off her glove—her attention had been elsewhere at the time—and slipped his ring on her finger. She'd repeated her vows in a wooden little voice, and as he'd listened he had stared down at his ring, gleaming on the small, stained paw with the childishly chewed nails. And had wondered what the hell he was doing, marrying this little orphaned stranger, so very much out of her depth in his cynical, sophisticated world.

And so very innocent and vulnerable and alone.

The coach swayed and bounded along the road at a breakneck pace. Tallie had been proudly informed by Lord d'Arenville's coachman that the vehicle was the latest design, built for speedy modern travel and sprung to ensure the smoothest ride. She hung onto the travelling straps like grim death, wedged into the corner of the coach as tightly as she could to prevent herself being thrown off the seat again. Tallie was feeling rather queasy. She had travelled very little in her adult life—only from Miss Fisher's seminary to her cousin's house. If this was what travelling entailed... And this was England, where the roads were said to be the best in the world...

Her mother must have been stronger than she'd realised. Lord d'Arenville had not exaggerated when he had said that travel was difficult for a lady to endure— But of course! That was it! The realisation hit Tallie like a bolt of lightning. That was the reason for this dreadful journey—undertaken in such a rush and at the last minute! Departing in the late afternoon, when nobody ever travelled in the dark unless they could help it! Pretending he had quarrelled with Laetitia and would stay not a moment longer in her house. Bundling Tallie into his coach on her wedding day, tossing her embarrassingly small bundle of belongings after her and riding off on his own horse as if the hounds of hell were in pursuit. What nonsense!

As if Lord d'Arenville—The Icicle—ever dashed about the country in a rage. The man was a positive by-word for cold self-control. He must be trying to frighten her, to get her to change her mind about foreign travel. The day before, he'd made no secret of his opposition to it. Hah! Lord d'Arenville would find his bride was not so simple—she was awake to his dastardly machinations! She *would* have her Grand Tour. He'd *promised*!

Tallie sat up, her queasiness forgotten in the light of her discovery. For some reason she felt immensely cheered. She'd had some slight suspicion that she'd been, in some unknown way, the cause of his quarrel with her cousin.

The moment they had arrived back from the church he'd sent her upstairs with a maid to refresh herself while he spoke to Laetitia. Tallie, annoyed to be dismissed like a child, had crept back down the stairs to listen at the door, but had heard frustratingly few actual words—only the sound of their voices. His voice had been icy-cold, cutting, as if flaying her cousin with sarcasm, but Tallie could not see why *he* should have been so cross.

She had a right to be upset—a tearful Mrs Wilmot had explained how Laetitia had prevented herself, Brooks and the children from coming to the wedding. But *he* would care little about that; he'd wanted a small wedding—she'd heard him say so. And look at how few people he'd invited!

Pressing an ear to the thick wooden door panel, Tallie had been sure she'd heard something about a dress. Her dress? She'd pressed her ear harder to the door. But then he had said something about a village half-wit, so that couldn't be it. And Laetitia had denied any responsibility for it and burst into noisy tears. It had all been very peculiar, and Tallie had been most intrigued, but then she'd heard his footsteps coming towards the door and she'd fled up the stairs.

So, it was all a hum—Tallie was convinced of it. And she was going to teach her husband a lesson about attempting to trick women out of their promised rights. She pulled open the shutters which covered the coach window. The sound of the pounding hooves and the creaking springs was almost deafening. Holding the leather straps tightly, Tallie knelt on her seat and peered out of the window.

It was very dark. Clouds moved across the sky, obscuring the moonlight intermittently. Wind whipped at her hair, tiny pellets of rain stung her cheeks and dark shadows whooshed past the window at an incredible rate. Goodness knew how fast they were travelling—Tallie had heard some gentlemen kept teams of horses that could travel at twelve, even fifteen miles an hour. The speed was a little scary, but also very exciting.

Tallie took several deep breaths. The fresh night air was most exhilarating, and she felt a thrill of naughtiness as she breathed it in—Miss Fisher had maintained the night air contained evil humours. Her pupils had been strictly forbidden to breathe it. Tallie wound the straps around her wrists more securely and leaned farther out, inhaling blissfully. Her husband was out there somewhere ahead, riding his own horse—not for him a stuffy ride in a horrid jolting coach. The coach lanterns provided some light, by which she could see the outline of the two rear horses, but there was no sign of Lord d'Arenville. He was probably a long way ahead of them.

'What the devil do you think you're doing?' a voice suddenly roared in her ear, giving Tallie such a fright that she almost let go of her straps.

She turned her head and saw her husband had come up close beside the carriage, so close she could almost reach out and touch him. Her mouth dropped open. She stared, wide-eyed, suddenly oblivious of the lurching of the coach. This was her husband? This creature of speed and power, shadows and moonlight—this was The Icicle?

He rode as if born to the saddle. Tallie had heard the expression before but had never been able to imagine it. She stared, half fearfully, at the superb black beast beneath him, gleaming with sweat in the moonlight. She noted its strong arched neck, the powerful hindquarters, the steam coming from its nostrils, the slight flecks of foam at its mouth. It seemed enormous, and very fierce, its hooves pounding through the night. And yet her husband dominated this huge, powerful beast effortlessly. Tallie had never ridden a horse—it had not been on Miss Fisher's curriculum...but ancient myths and legends had.

Suddenly Tallie knew exactly what a centaur looked like.

She had always imagined them to be rather ridiculous creatures—but this... He was...magnificent.

She stared at horse and man, pounding along in the intermittent darkness, now a mysterious black creature of the night, now a gleaming silver knight, kissed by moonlight. He rode bare-headed, and wet locks of dark hair clung romantically to his brow. How he could ride his horse so perilously close to a racing, bouncing carriage was more than Tallie could understand—it looked frightfully dangerous.

And then she suddenly remembered—he was probably trying to scare her. She turned a blinding smile on him, freed one hand and waved.

He moved even closer. 'Is something wrong?' he shouted.

Hah! thought Tallie. You hope in vain, my lord. 'Not...in the least,' she shrieked back at him, her hair whipping about her face. 'In fact…it is monstr—' The coach lurched and she nearly fell off her seat again.

'What did you say?' he yelled. 'Are you all right?'

Tallie plastered her smile back in place. 'I am per—perfectly well, my lord,' she shouted as she jounced around on the leather cushions. 'This tr—trip is…most delightful! I am having—' She hauled herself back from the edge of the seat again and clamped her fingers onto the window frame. 'I am having…a won—wonderful time. It…is monstrous exciting!' She directed the biggest smile she could muster out into the darkness. That should do it, she thought.

'We'll stop in an hour or so.' Lord d'Arenville rode even closer to her window. 'You can rest and recover yourself then. We shall sleep the night at an inn.' He galloped off into the darkness.

Sleep the night! Tallie gulped. She had forgotten—it was her wedding night. And at some time tonight, in some unknown inn, Lord d'Arenville would *know* her, and she would become, in truth, his wife. Her mouth was suddenly dry.

Chapter Six

The inn was small and ancient, with exposed black beams and a sagging roof. Lamps spilled warm puddles of golden light across the wet cobblestones. The coach stood in the courtyard, the horses weary, their breath smoky against the shadows.

The rain had intensified in the last hour. Lord d'Arenville waited to hand Tallie down. She emerged stiffly and stumbled as she landed on the wet and slippery cobbles, but a cold, strong hand caught her and she was safe. Her husband pulled her hard against his body and allowed his greatcoat to drop over her, shielding her from the rain.

The sensation was overwhelming. His body radiated warmth and strength and power. And an odour—not at all unpleasant, she decided—of horse, damp wool, leather and fresh male sweat. Tallie allowed her body to lean against his, knowing her behaviour was indecorous and that there were grooms and other people watching. She was too cold to argue, too tired to pull away—and in any case his arm was wrapped around her like a warm steel band, and she could not have moved away if she'd tried. She had never been so close to a man before and was entirely taken up with the sensations it produced in her. Odd, fluttery sensations. And a sort of breathlessness.

Nerves, she decided. Bridal nerves…

'Landlord!' Lord d'Arenville shouted, hustling her inside.

'A private parlour, and refreshments for my wife!' He handed her over to the care of a large clucking woman, the landlord's wife. She ushered Tallie to a small, cosy sitting room with a fire crackling in the grate.

Shivering with cold, Tallie stood as close to the fire as she dared. Lord d'Arenville's coach contained several warm fur rugs, which she had used, but they hadn't prevented a chill from seeping into her bones, a chill she knew stemmed as much from nerves as from cold.

Tallie looked around her. The inn might be old, but it was clean and warm. There was a knock on the door and the landlord's wife bustled back in, bobbed an awkward curtsy and set down a tray containing a large steaming jug, some cut lemons, a small brown pot and several pewter mugs. An enticing aroma of wine, spices and citrus fruit came from the jug.

''Ere you are, milady. 'Is lordship bespoke some mulled wine, and says you're to take some immediate and not to wait for 'im to arrive. 'E's seeing to the 'orses, makin' all right and tight.' She chuckled. 'There be no need to worry. Our Jem reckons it's Christmas—such prime bits o' blood 'is lordship's 'orses are.'

She poured some steaming liquid into a mug and handed it to Tallie, beaming. 'Drink it down now, milady. It'll warm your blood proper.'

It was very strange, Tallie thought, to be addressed as milady, but she supposed she would become accustomed to it. She took a cautious sip of the steaming drink, then smiled at the hovering woman. 'It's very good,' she said softly, and sipped again.

The woman beamed. 'Good of you to say so, milady, but there's more lemons if you want them, and honey, too, if it be too sour for you.'

'No, no, it's very good just as it is,' Tallie assured her, taking a large swallow of the hot drink and feeling the tangy warmth of it curl around her empty insides. 'Thank you.'

The landlord's wife seemed to swell with delight. 'A pleasure to be serving such a kind-spoken lady. The Quality ain't so easy to please in general. Now, I'll be off to the kitchen, milady, but I'll be back in a trice with dinner for 'is lordship and yourself. I've got a couple o' fat hens a-roasting, and a stewed pig's ear and faggots, as tender and sweet as you could wish for. And mutton pie, if 'is lordship fancies it.' She frowned and hesitated. 'I—er—I didn't 'ave much warning of your arrival, milady, so I'm afraid I ain't got no jellies or…or delicacies what a lady might—'

'Please don't worry, Mrs…?' Tallie reached for the jug, refilled her mug, added honey, and sat on a plush-covered chair.

'Mrs Farrow, milady. Farrow, my 'usband, be the landlor—'

'Mrs Farrow, you must not worry about any lack of ladylike delicacies. I am hungry enough to eat whatever you can provide, and I am sure Lord d'Arenville is too. And if he is not,' Tallie added, with a gleam of mischief, 'he has only himself to blame, does he not?' She took another mouthful of mulled wine. 'He did not, after all, give you sufficient notice of his arrival.'

The landlord's wife, appalled at being implicated in any criticism of a lord, uttered a series of embarrassed disclaimers and hurriedly curtsied herself out.

Tallie reached forward and refilled her mug. She sat back in her chair, snuggling against the warm plush, remembering Miss Fisher's high, adenoidal voice—'A lady never allows her spine to contact the back of a chair.' She took another sip of mulled wine. It really was a most deliciously warming and relaxing concoction. She had tasted wine before, and had found it rather nasty, but this—the lemons, honey and cinnamon—made such a delightful difference.

She kicked off her slippers and tucked her stockinged feet under her—another of Miss Fisher's solecisms—and basked in the warmth provided by the fire and the mulled wine. The scent of roasting meat tantalised her tastebuds. She leaned her head on the back of the chair. So nice not to be bouncing and jolting around… Such an interesting journey… She closed her eyes…

*The dashing highwayman thundered along the road in dare-
devil pursuit of the runaway coach. The coach lurched and
swayed perilously, but the kidnapped princess remained calm,
knowing her beloved was riding* ventre à terre *to rescue her.*

*Desperately she battered at the shutters which the evil Count
had nailed over the coach windows, but they were too strong
for her. Then, suddenly, crash! With a splintering of wood the
shutters were wrenched away from without. Laughing with joy,
the lost princess leaned out, her long dark tresses tossing romantically in the wind.*

*'Beloved,' he called in his deep and manly voice. 'I am here.
Hold out your arms.' Smiling into the darkness, the princess
trustfully held out her arms. Hooves pounded, wind whipped
at her hair, and then out of the inky depths of the night rode
the highwayman, moving as one with his magnificent jet-black
steed. He rode perilously close to the razor-sharp wheels of
the coach. The treacherous coachman turned his gun and
fired. She gasped, filled with horror.*

*But the highwayman's gleaming white teeth glinted in the
moonlight and she heard his soft laugh. Suddenly she was
seized in a strong, secure grip and lifted by powerful arms
onto the back of his gallant steed. 'Cold, my little love?' he
murmured, his breath warm against her ear, and he wrapped
his black velvet cloak around her shivering body and drew her
close.*

*His strength supported her and his body warmed her, smell-
ing of leather, wet wool and fresh male sweat. 'You belong to
me now, Tallie, my dearest one,' he said, 'and I belong to
you.' And, holding her safe against his heart, he galloped into
the night...*

Magnus, stripping a sodden pair of leather gloves from his
hands, had to duck his head under the low, smoke-stained
portal as he entered the private parlour. His riding buckskins
and his high leather boots were spattered with mud.

He straightened, sniffing appreciatively. 'Ahh, mulled—'
He stopped, seeing his bride of ten hours curled up in a chair

like a kitten, her slippers kicked carelessly off, sound asleep. He stood looking down at her. Her hair tumbled about her shoulders; damp wispy curls clung to her pale forehead and clustered around her neck. Long dark lashes fanned her cheeks, which were flushed from the heat of the fire. Or maybe not, he thought wryly, as he bent down and removed the pewter mug which dangled precariously from one hand.

He put a hand on her shoulder. 'Thalia,' he said, then, 'Thalia,' more loudly. She didn't stir. He decided to let her sleep until dinner arrived.

He poured himself a mug of mulled wine and drained it quickly, shuddering pleasurably as the warm spicy liquid flowed down his throat. He poured himself another, then set it down pensively, his eyes on the sleeping girl. She looked exhausted. Magnus watched the gentle rise and fall of her chest and regretted the rough haste of the journey. He should not have inflicted such a long trip on his gently bred bride, especially on her wedding day. Not that little Thalia Robins— no, Thalia St Clair she was now—was particularly gently bred.

He shook his head, recalling the way the little hoyden had hung out the window of the coach, pert little nose in the air, her hair whipping around her face, her eyes huge and dark in the pallor of her face. Her skin had been damp with rain, glowing softly in the moonlight as she had shrieked some nonsense about how much she was enjoying the journey. Monstrous exciting, indeed! His lips twitched. She'd looked frightened half out of her wits.

Magnus sipped the mulled wine and watched his bride sleep. He noticed the faint sprinkling of freckles over the bridge of her tip-tilted nose. Freckles were generally held to be a flaw, but hers were oddly appealing. It was almost impossible to believe that he'd married this little scrap of humanity. He didn't feel married. And he had so little in common with her. His wife. His new Countess. His impulsive choice of her was most unlike him.

He would have to train her, he supposed, train her until she resembled the wives… He frowned, considering the way he'd become acquainted with most of those wives... No, he didn't want her to be a typical society wife at all. He'd be damned if he'd let her cuckold him. This Lady d'Arenville would not stray from her marital bed; he'd make sure of that!

He took another sip of wine and pulled a face. It was almost cold. He leant over towards the fireplace and pushed the blackened poker into the coals. Thalia, he pondered, watching the flames flicker and dance. Peculiar name. It didn't suit her at all. He wouldn't saddle a child of his with a name like that...a child of his... With any luck she could conceive this very night...

The poker soon began to glow red-hot, and he pulled it out, shook the ash from it, then plunged it into the jug of spiced wine. It sizzled briefly, and aromatic steam filled the air. He tossed the poker back onto the hearth, poured the heated mixture back into his mug and drank deeply.

The innkeeper, Farrow, entered with a tray of steaming dishes. Magnus silently indicated his sleeping wife. Farrow and several creeping minions set out cutlery, glasses and dishes with muted clatters and clinks, Farrow issuing instructions in a hoarse whisper that could probably be heard in the next room. The new Lady d'Arenville slept on, serenely oblivious.

When the innkeeper had left, Magnus touched her shoulder. 'Thalia, our dinner has arrived.' She didn't move. He shook her gently and she stirred, but did not awaken. He stood for a moment, oddly unsure of himself. She probably was hungry—there had been no proper wedding breakfast after all—she had eaten nothing for hours. But women seemed to eat almost nothing anyway, and she did seem to be very tired. Perhaps it would be better to let her sleep through dinner and then wake her when it was time to go up to bed.

Yes, that was the better plan. He would wake her then, for he had every intention of consummating his marriage tonight. The sooner he got her with child the sooner she would forget about this Grand Tour nonsense.

* * *

Magnus twirled a glass of port in his hand, admiring the flickering flames of the fire through its ruby glow and berating himself for his uncharacteristic state of indecision. After a hearty dinner and several glasses of good claret he was now perfectly ready to undertake his duties as a bridegroom. But she was still asleep. Frowning, he set his glass down and walked towards his wife. He shook her shoulder again. She did not move, did not so much as flicker an eyelid. He bent over, slid his hands under her and lifted. She stirred, muttered, and snuggled her cheek against his chest. Her arms and legs dangled bonelessly. Curse the girl—she slept like the dead.

Grunting slightly, he managed to open the door. He carried her up the narrow steps, taking care not to bump her against the walls—although why he should bother he did not know. Very likely a stampede of elephants would not wake her. He had bespoken only one private bedchamber—it was a small inn, after all. The bedclothes were turned back, and with a sigh of relief he laid her on the bed and regarded her with a jaundiced eye.

His bride was dead to the world. Magnus glared at her, aggrieved. He had not particularly looked forward to his wedding night—he'd never taken a virgin before, had restricted his carnal dealings to experienced women of the world, and the thought of causing pain instead of giving pleasure had caused him to view the coming night with a certain amount of trepidation. But now, having steeled himself to do the deed, his bride was proving most uncooperative.

Furthermore, having departed on his honeymoon in a state of pique, he had failed to provide her with a maidservant. He probably ought to call for the landlord's wife to undress her. And so he would—damn it—if he wanted all and sundry to know how he'd passed his wedding night. No, he had the choice—leave her to sleep in her clothes and emerge as an even more bedraggled bride in the morning, or prepare her for bed himself.

Swearing under his breath, Magnus undid the buttons of her shabby pelisse. He slipped it off and hung it on a hook. He had to grope for the fastenings of her dress, and called down a silent curse on dressmakers when he finally discovered them under her arms. He slipped the dress off her shoulders and tugged it down over her hips, then hung it on the same hook.

Feeling cross and impatient, Magnus turned back to his bride and froze, staring. She lay on his bed, soft and sweet and vulnerable. Her hair was tumbled in an unruly mass, spread out against the white sheets, glinting gold and brown and cinnamon, like strands of honey. Her skin glowed golden-rose in the flickering candlelight.

Magnus's mouth dried as he gazed at her sleeping form. This was his wife, he told himself…but he felt like a thief in the night, standing over her, gazing like this, with her all innocent and unknowing.

But he could not stop himself staring…at the rosy arms flung out high on the pillows, at her long, smooth legs, gently parted and disappearing beneath her petticoat, her breasts rising creamy and rounded from the neck of her chemise…

He reached for the tapes which fastened her petticoat and noticed wryly that his hands were shaking. He wrestled for a moment with the knots, then, losing patience, took out his knife. He cut the remaining tapes and, holding his breath, gently eased the petticoat from her body.

Bloody hell, he thought, staring at her legs, at her thighs hidden beneath the uneven hem of her chemise. His heart was pounding. The chemise was a simple affair, sleeveless, with an adjustable drawstring neckline. It strained across her chest and hips, as if made for a smaller person. Idly his fingers reached out and pulled lightly at one of the ends of the small bow which fastened the drawstring. The bow fell apart and the neckline loosened under his gaze.

By all that was decent he ought to leave her to sleep in her chemise at least. She was a virgin, modest and maidenly. A gentleman should show proper respect for his wife, only raising the hem of her nightgown during their conjugal meetings. It was what he'd expected, planned to do, after all. And she was asleep. Only a cad would bare her naked to his eyes like this on her wedding night. Without her knowledge or consent. Yes, in all decency he should allow her to sleep in her chemise, not stand here staring at his wife as if she were a twopenny peepshow...

She stirred, rolling her face to one side, and flung an arm over her head. Her movement sent the drawstring neckline gaping even wider. Magnus held his breath. Was she about to waken? Candlelight danced over the creamy expanse of skin.

Without further thought Magnus cut through the tapes fastening her chemise and with bated breath tugged the garment down. Her breasts spilled out, creamy and lush, and under his fascinated stare two rosy nipples lifted and hardened in the cold night air. He tugged it further, over her hips and down her legs. Dry-mouthed and aching with desire, he examined the rest of her, her slender waist, her appealingly curved little belly, the flaring hips and the gold-brown triangle of curls at the apex of her rounded, satiny thighs.

Bloody hell, thought Magnus again, dazedly. She was beautiful. Under all those appalling garments she wore, she was beautiful. Soft, lovely and utterly desirable. And she was his wife.

And, the devil confound it, she was absolutely sound asleep, and there was no way in the world that he could avail himself of her beautiful body. He groaned, feeling the painful intensity of his arousal, knowing he would have to wait.

He bent over her, inhaling the scent of her body, and closed his eyes for a moment, savouring it. She smelled unique, in his experience. Most women he knew drowned themselves in strong perfumes. Not his bride. She smelled of soap and nothing else—just herself. Of innocence. She was his lawful wife, wedded to him in the eyes of God and society, he told himself.

Magnus took a deep breath. 'Thalia,' he said urgently, in a loud voice. She did not stir. He cupped her shoulders in moist palms and shook her. The creamy breasts bounced and quivered. Magnus moaned as he watched. But she did not awaken. Instead, she wriggled a little—causing his tongue to cleave to the roof of his mouth—then turned on her side, cuddling into the pillows, curling up her legs and presenting him with a view of a delectable peachy backside. His arousal was rock-hard, and aching like the very devil.

It was no good, he thought frustratedly, Thalia Robinson could sleep through an earthquake. He lifted the bedclothes over her and watched sourly as she snuggled into their warmth. Thalia—God how he disliked that name. It hadn't suited the ill-clad little urchin he'd married and it certainly didn't suit the siren he'd discovered under the dreadful clothes. Perhaps he'd call her by her second name—what was it? Lucy? Louise? He grimaced. No, that didn't suit her either.

Forcing himself to turn away from the temptation in his bed, Magnus bent to pick up the undergarments he'd dropped. He started to hang them on the hook behind the door, then paused, truly noticing them for the first time. Holding them in a clenched fist, he moved closer to the branch of candles burning near the bedside. A surge of anger rippled through him.

The stockings were darned in several places. Both chemise and petticoat contained numerous patches and inserts of different material. Though spotlessly clean, and soft with many washings, they were made of coarse linen, old and well-worn. Not a scrap of lace or a frill enlivened either garment. And these were the delicate ladies unmentionables that Lord d'Arenville's bride had worn on her wedding day! Could Laetitia not even have seen to that? He bunched the offending garments in his fist and hurled them at the far wall.

He stormed towards the door, then paused. He glanced back at the underclothes in the corner. He'd rendered them unusable, cutting through the tapes like that. What would she think when she awoke? Cursing under his breath, he scooped them off the floor and stuffed them into his pocket.

He left the room, slamming the door behind him, and stomped downstairs, his high boots echoing on the wooden steps. Rousing the innkeeper, he called for a bottle of the best brandy and retired to the private parlour to brood on his inexplicable marriage and the debacle of his wedding night.

* * *

'Oh, I am utterly ravenous this morning,' exclaimed Tallie, reaching for a slice of fresh crusty bread and buttering it lavishly. She took a mouthful of coffee and closed her eyes, savouring it, then bit into the bread with evident relish.

Magnus watched her sourly. His head ached from the brandy. The fire in the small parlour had smoked, and the landlord's excuses about the unreliability of chimneys when the wind blew from the northwest had not impressed him a bit.

'Can I not tempt you to a slice of this excellent bread and butter, my lord?' said Tallie. She glanced at the tankard by his elbow doubtfully. 'I cannot think it healthful for you to break your fast with nothing but ale.'

Magnus snorted and raised the tankard to his lips.

Tallie glanced guiltily at the empty platter on her left. 'I am sure Mrs Farrow would be delighted to cook more bacon and eggs—I did not mean to consume it all—it was just that I found myself so extremely hungry when I awoke.'

Magnus closed his eyes for a moment, unable to endure even the thought of greasy eggs and bacon.

Tallie reached for the pot of honey. She dipped in a spoon and wound it deftly, then drizzled honey all over her bread and butter. The sight recalled to Magnus the look of her hair on the pillow, gleaming in the candlelight. He glowered silently.

'Mrs Farrow says there is cold pork, fowl, or some mutton pie still remaining from last night's dinner, if you should prefer that—I know many gentlemen prefer meat at breakfast,' persisted Tallie.

Magnus rolled his eyes and took another mouthful of dark, bitter ale.

'I must say,' she continued, 'dinner last night sounded quite delicious. Why did you not awaken me? I was extremely hungry, you know. It was most unkind of you to forget me!' she finished indignantly, licking honey off her fingers.

Forget her? Magnus stared at her in stupefaction. He opened his mouth to respond, but she hadn't finished.

'I would very much have preferred to be woken. So in the future, if you please, remember to do so, should I happen to take a little nap before dinner.' Tallie smiled to soften the impact of her demand, resolving to be more tactful with him, especially in the morning. He seemed to be one of those people whose tempers did not appreciate conversation in the morning.

It occurred to her that he might not have slept very well last night. 'Did you not sleep well, my lord?' She smiled sympathetically at him. 'Some people do not sleep soundly, I believe, if they are in a strange bed. I do not myself. I remember when I first came to my cousin's house it was days before I could accustom myself to the new bed. Was your bed not sufficiently comfortable, my lord?'

Magnus could barely speak. Indignation and outrage choked him. He searched his mind for something sufficiently pithy and cutting to say. A drop of honey quivered on the corner of her mouth and the sight of it distracted him considerably.

She continued. 'Mine was quite comfortable, although I woke up a little cold.' She blushed, and did not meet his eyes. 'I gather Mrs Farrow put me to bed. I must thank her, though I don't understand how she could have missed my night-gown—it was on the top of my valise. And she must have taken my—er—some things to wash, because I could not find them anywhere.'

Magnus's ears turned slightly pink. He walked over to the fire and kicked some of the burning logs with his boot. Smoke gushed into the room.

'My lord—'

'Oh, for God's sake let us have done with all this "my lord" nonsense!' Magnus exclaimed. 'You are my wife. You may call me Magnus and I will call you Thalia. Agreed?'

Tallie wrinkled her nose. 'I would prefer not to be called Thalia.'

'What else should I call you? Lady d'Arenville, perhaps?'

'Good gracious, no,' she said, vigorously scrubbing the

honey off her lips with a napkin. 'I should never remember to answer to that.'

Magnus frowned. 'Never remember to answer to your title?' He was stunned. He'd expected the title to be the very first thing his wife would learn to use. That and his wealth.

Tallie perceived she had mortally offended him and smiled placatingly. 'I suppose it is all still so new to me. I cannot seem to think of myself as a countess yet.' She smiled brilliantly, with false confidence. 'I am sure I shall soon grow accustomed to it.'

'But in the meantime I am not to address you as Thalia. You would prefer Miss Robinson, perhaps?' he finished acidly.

'Of course not. It is just that I have always disliked the name Thalia.'

'Well, there we are agreed—it is an appalling name to inflict on someone.'

Tallie suddenly found herself annoyed. It was one thing for her not to like her own name; it was quite another to have him criticising it with such enthusiasm. 'Well, at least I am not called Euphrosyne or Aglaia!' she snapped.

Magnus blinked. 'Why on earth should you be?'

'Euphrosyne and Aglaia were Graces.'

'Good for them. But I don't see—'

'And Thalia was a Grace, too.'

'Grace is a perfectly unexceptionable name.' He shrugged. 'I have no objection to calling you Grace.'

'But I don't wish you to call me Grace!'

'Well, what the devil do you want me to call you? Euphro-what or Agalia?'

Tallie's lips twitched. 'Thalia, Euphro*syne* and Ag*laia* were the three Graces—the daughters of Zeus and servants to the other deities,' she explained severely. 'My mother thought it romantic to name me after one of them.'

'Romantic! She must have been a hen-wit,' he said frankly. 'I suppose she wanted more daughters to complete the set. You must thank your lucky stars you were born first.'

Tallie giggled.

He smiled down at her, feeling more in charity with her. 'So, if you do not wish me to call you Thalia, what is my alternative—Lucy?' he said, pleased with himself for recalling her second name.

Tallie pulled another face and shook her head. 'No, I don't like *Louise* either.' She hesitated. 'My friends from school and my cousin's children call me Tallie, so you could call me that—if you wish it.'

'Tallie…Tallie,' he said thoughtfully, then nodded. 'Yes, it suits you. So, you shall call me Magnus and I call you Tallie—agreed?'

'Agreed, my lor—Magnus.' She found her hand enveloped in his and looked up at him, smiling shyly.

He looked down into her shining amber eyes and his hand tightened its grip. 'Come then, Tallie, for we depart within the half-hour.'

'Where to, my lor—Magnus?' she asked breathlessly.

He couldn't help but smile at her excitement. 'Paris!'

Chapter Seven

'What is that most uncommon smell, my lor—Magnus?'
Tallie called from the window of the coach.

They had come to a steep hill. The horses slowed to a walk,
and, for the first time in several hours, Magnus was close
enough for conversation.

Magnus frowned, inhaled and shook his head. 'I smell nothing untoward.'

'Oh, you must,' she said, sniffing the air vigorously. 'It
is…it is… Oh, I cannot explain it, for I have smelled nothing
like it before…' She sniffed again. 'It is a little…tart, but
vastly refreshing.'

Magnus inhaled and shook his head again. 'I can smell
nothing—the wretched sea drowns all other smells.'

'The sea?' Tallie exclaimed. 'It is the sea I can smell? Oh,
how very exciting. I have never seen the sea and have always
longed to do so.' She bounced up on the carriage seat and
craned her neck as far as she could out of the window.

Magnus regarded her thoughtfully for a moment.

She turned her head. 'Pray tell me, my lor—I mean Magnus,
in which direction is the sea?'

'You cannot see it yet,' he said, 'but once we are over this
hill you should be able to catch a glimpse of it.'

Tallie's eyes avidly scanned the approaching horizon. Sure

enough, within a few moments she saw a sparkling blue line stretching between the dip of green hills. 'Ohhh,' she breathed.

She fastened her gaze on the horizon for the next forty minutes, catching tantalising glimpses of blue and silver, until the coach breached the final crest and the English Channel lay spread out before her in an endless gleaming expanse.

'Ohhhhh.'

Amused by her naive enthralment, Magnus signalled the coach driver to stop. He himself dismounted and opened Tallie's door.

'Come,' he said, holding out a hand. 'Alight for a moment or two and gaze your fill.'

Eyes shining, she hastened to do his bidding, almost tumbling into the road as she did so. She hurried up a small rise and stood there, drinking in the incredible sight.

'It is not the true sea, you understand. This is just the Channel.'

She turned to stare at him in amazement. 'Truly? But it is enormous. I cannot see to the other side at all.'

He shrugged. 'Nevertheless…'

She turned back and gazed in silence for several minutes, her hands clasped to her bosom. 'The English Channel…' she breathed reverently. 'It is so much bigger than the maps would have you believe… And just over there is Europe.' She clapped her hands. 'Oh, I cannot wait! Come! Let us delay no further.'

She hurried back to the coach and scrambled back up the let-down steps, oblivious of the groom waiting to assist her.

Magnus sighed and made a mental note to find someone to teach his wife how a lady should step into and descend from a carriage.

The town of Dover was not particularly prepossessing, in Magnus's opinion, consisting, as it did, largely of cheap, unsavoury taverns and inns kept by retired rum-soaked sailors for the benefit and entertainment of other rum-soaked sailors. There were but two decent hostelries in which a gentleman could safely repose his bride—the Ship Inn and the King's Head. The Ship Inn being the more fashionable of the two, it was there that Magnus naturally made his way.

To his annoyance, however, the inn was full. The landlord explained. It seemed there had been no wind, not even a breeze for days. The Channel lay smooth and glassy and the boats' sails limp, and so the inn—the whole town, in fact—was crowded with people waiting to leave for France. The landlord was extremely apologetic, but every single room was taken.

'Check again,' said Lord d'Arenville, laying several shining coins on the counter. The landlord regretfully shook his head. Lord d'Arenville added several more to the pile.

Lord d'Arenville's name was not unknown. Nor was it The Ship's practice to turn away titled gentlemen. The landlord hesitated a moment, then leaned forward. 'All I can offer your lordship is accommodation to share, I'm afraid—for a small consideration, of course. There are several young gentlemen who would be pleased to accommodate your lordship for a reduction in their tariff, and your lady wife would, I am sure, be welcome to sleep with Mrs Entwhistle, an elderly widow of the utmost respectability.' His fingers crept towards the money.

'Share?' exclaimed Lord d'Arenville, outraged, sweeping up the coins. His wife to share with some old woman—a cit, no doubt! The notion was preposterous. His countess did not share her bed with strange old women! She shared it with him—or she would as soon as he could manage it. He had waited quite long enough as it was.

The memory of her naked softness had stayed with him the whole day, and each sight of her, each movement, had caused him the sort of discomfort he had not had to endure since he was a green youth. It was a ridiculous situation for a man of his age and experience, and he was determined to remedy it immediately—all he needed was a bed and his bride.

The landlord spread his hands in a gesture of helplessness and shrugged. ''Tis all I can offer you, my lord. Without the wind, the ships can't leave, and until they do we must all make the best of things.'

'Well, then,' said Lord d'Arenville coldly, 'be so good as to recommend some respectable private accommodation where my wife and I can stay.'

The landlord shook his head. 'Nothing left, I'm afraid, my lord. The ships have been stuck here for six days already, and the whole town is full up—as tight as a tick, if you'll forgive the expression.' He paused, then added doubtfully, 'You might find something in one of the taverns near the waterfront, but I'd not wish a lady there, myself.'

'Quite!' said Lord d'Arenville crisply. He pondered the situation. It was far too late to retrace their steps and find some other town. His bride was waiting in the carriage, tired and no doubt hungry, though she had not complained. Repressing his frustration, he accepted the landlord's terms, hiding his chagrin behind an icy demeanour.

Mrs Entwhistle was, as Magnus had feared, a cit. A wealthy widow, she currently owned several large woollen mills and manufactories—a fact of which she did not hesitate to inform them, much to his disgust. She spoke with an assumed air of 'refainment,' which intensified when she found the exalted company in which she was to mix. She was also garrulous to the point of strangulation. Magnus was in her company no more than ten minutes before he had formed an understanding of why all three of her husbands had died young—seeking the peace and quiet of the grave. She was, however, intensely respectable, and only too delighted to share her chamber with a youthful countess, so Magnus was able to leave his bride to dine on a tray in the woman's chamber with no doubts about her safety.

He himself passed a most frustrating night. It took him hours to get to sleep, images of his naked wife being the chief cause. Then, when he finally fell into a fitful sleep, the young blades with whom he shared the room stumbled in, foxed to the eyeballs and talking at the tops of their voices. He bore it as long as he could, then sat up in bed.

'If you young gentlemen do not put yourselves to bed with the utmost speed—and silence—I will be forced to get out of this bed,' he said, in a voice which froze the young men in their tracks. 'I do not believe you would enjoy the consequences.'

After that, the only noise in the room was furtive breathing.

Magnus lay wide awake, wondering what malignant twist of fate had caused him to end up sharing a room with three drunken sots while his wife was curled up in bed with a vulgar old woman. He had never been so uncomfortable—nor so frustrated—in his life. Except for his wedding night.

Nothing had gone right for him since he'd offered for the girl, he thought sourly. Why had he ever been so foolish as to consider marriage? It was all Freddie's fault...

One of the young blades started to snore. Magnus turned over in bed, attempting to block out the sound. A second set of snores joined the first, then a third, making a loud and inharmonious din. Magnus pulled the pillow over his head.

Lord d'Arenville was far from his best when he entered the inn's crowded public dining room to join his bride for breakfast. He had passed a most indifferent night—again—and even the expedience of tossing the noisiest of his companions out of bed had failed to quell the vile nocturnal sounds.

Further, he'd had to shave and dress himself without his valet. Again. He was forced to acknowledge he missed the man's skills—Magnus had detected a hair on his coat when it had been returned to him, his cravats were insufficiently starched and, worst of all, the inn's bootblack had left a thumb-print on his hessians!

'Good morning, my lord.' Tallie greeted him with a sunny smile. 'Did you sleep better last night?'

Magnus gave her a baleful glance and sat down. He ordered kidneys, bacon and a tankard of ale. His wife applied herself vigorously to a plate of kippers.

'I gather you slept well. Again,' he added, noting her bright-eyed demeanour and her clear, smooth skin.

She shook her head, glanced furtively around the room, then leaned forward and whispered, 'No, not at all, for—you will not credit it—Mrs Entwhistle *snores*!'

Magnus let out a surprised snort of laughter.

'Oh, but it is perfectly true,' Tallie whispered, and rolled her eyes. 'It was dreadfully loud.' She glanced around the room again and added, her eyes brimming with mischief, 'It seems she cannot bear to be silent—even in sleep!'

Despite his bad mood, Magnus found himself smiling back at her. 'So, too, did my companions.'

'Oh, then you understand. I do so dislike the sound. And it goes on and on, doesn't it? Until you feel as though you wish to smother the person who is doing it.' She took another forkful of kipper and chewed it meditatively, regarding him with a speculative expression. 'Do you—? I mean…no.'

'Do I what?' said Magnus.

She blushed. 'I have forgot what I was going to say. Er, do you think the wind will be in the right quarter today, my lor—Magnus? For the packet to depart, I mean. It is beautifully sunny, at any rate. If we cannot depart today, do you think we might walk up to the Western Heights? I have heard that the view is most spectacular and the walk very invigorating.'

Magnus frowned. What had she been about to ask him? Something that caused her to blush. Had she been going to ask him whether he snored? He opened his mouth to reassure her…then shut it, disconcerted. He had no idea whether he snored or not.

Certainly no one had ever told him he did—but then he rarely slept with the women he'd been involved with. Pleasured them, yes, and gained his own pleasure. But he generally departed their beds after the event and returned to his own. He was fastidious in that.

Perhaps he did snore. Would his bride wish to smother *him* in his sleep? It was a most unsettling notion. Magnus finished his breakfast in silence.

After breakfast he accompanied Tallie in an exploration of the town and the waterfront, which, to his surprise, she seemed to find fascinating, despite the smells. They climbed the Western Heights, where his wife waxed rapturous about the view. And that, as far as Lord d'Arenville was concerned, was the sum total of entertainment to be found in the dreary little town of Dover.

But the more time he spent in his wife's company the more his thwarted desire grew. She was such a contrast to the bored, world-weary women he knew. She seemed to find unselfconscious pleasure in the smallest things, and he could not help but wonder if she would react with equal delight to the pleasures he planned to introduce her to—as soon as he found the privacy in which to do so. In the meantime, the mere sight of her pressing a shell to her ear to listen to the sea, or clambering over a stile, or running down a hill shrieking with glee was enough to have him almost moan aloud. He attempted to control his response to her, but the very impossibility of it unsettled him and made him, on reflection, furious.

He had never expected to *desire* his wife. He felt it was both unseemly and foolish for a man to do so... He had seen other men in thrall to the charms of their wives—his father, for one—and Magnus had observed that it gave the wife an unwholesome influence over their husband. No woman had ever possessed the slightest control over Magnus, and nothing was going to change that. No, this unaccountable penchant he had for his wife was merely a whim of the moment, a result of a recent lack of female companionship. It would pass as soon as the marriage was consummated—if it ever was!

Damn it! He had never been so desirous of coupling with a woman and so utterly unable to find an opportunity to do so. With any other woman he would have dealt with the matter by hiring a room at some low tavern, or, if the worst came to the worst, there had always been the coach. But Tallie was both a virgin and his wife. He owed it to her to carry out the deed in an atmosphere of respectability, at least.

Lord d'Arenville prayed for wind.

The Channel remained smooth and still.

* * *

Her husband might have been acting like a bear with a sore head, but Tallie did not repine. He was clearly a difficult man to please, but she had known that from the start. In fact, marriage to Lord d'Arenville was turning out vastly better than she had expected. Despite his general air of bad temper, she had discovered several unexpected aspects of his character which she found rather endearing—unexpected flashes of kindness, for instance, like stopping the coach so she could look at the sea. She had half expected him to laugh at her ignorance—but he hadn't. And he'd made no demur about escorting her along the waterfront—a place she had seen perfectly well he disliked, wrinkling his long, patrician nose as he steered her around a puddle of fish guts or a basket of live crabs.

Yes, Tallie thought, it felt wonderful to be strolling about the town on the arm of such a handsome gentleman—it was still almost impossible to believe such a magnificent-looking man was actually her husband. The feeling of warmth that glowed within her as she laid her hand on his arm, the occasional bumping of their bodies as they walked—it was most agreeable. And when he smiled, as he had once or twice, and those long, harsh lines down his cheeks deepened, and his sea-grey eyes gleamed, she would look at him and feel her breath catch in her throat…

She could not help but enjoy all sorts of little things he did. Like the way he placed himself protectively between her and the roadway as they walked. And helped her over stiles as if she were some sort of fragile, helpless creature, which heaven knew she wasn't, but still…it was nice to be thought so, at times. And even nicer to reflect that perhaps he didn't think of her as sturdy any more…

Of course, it was probably only good manners. No doubt he would do exactly the same for Mrs Entwhistle—if she ever stopped talking, that was. He had beautiful manners—when he chose to employ them.

Tallie sighed. There were times when she felt as though she and her new husband could come to some understanding, when she felt that she could find some degree of happiness with him after all. But then, for no reason she could see, he would suddenly turn back into The Icicle, and any attempt of hers to thaw him out only seemed to make him snappish as a wolf.

Then Tallie would recall she was not a beloved bride on her honeymoon, but an inconvenient necessity who was putting him to a great deal of trouble instead of quietly retiring to d'Arenville Hall to bear his heirs. Well, she would go into rural seclusion—eventually—but she had made up her mind to enjoy every moment of her bride trip, and enjoy it she would!

So, she told herself, rallying, Dover was a fascinating place, and she had much better things to do than fret herself to flinders over her husband's disposition. There was nothing she could do about that, after all. She was foolish to wish for anything more—she was nothing but a brood mare to him— he had said as much to her cousin, that night in the library. And, though he'd had enough of exploring the town, she had not.

Each morning Tallie slipped away from the Ship Inn to visit the waterfront, secure in her husband's belief that she was with Mrs Entwhistle. He himself could not bear the woman's inane chatter without coldly excusing himself after a few moments, and so Tallie used his ill-concealed antipathy to her own advantage.

She was intensely curious about every aspect of marine life. She marvelled at the way gnarled and twisted fishermen's hands could knot fine and delicate nets. She learned to identify brigantines, sloops and schooners, and was most excited to have the Revenue cutters pointed out to her. The fishermen filled her head with thrilling tales of smugglers, shipwrecks and storms.

One morning a friendly seaman even offered to row her out and show her over one of the ships. Delighted, Tallie accepted, and was deeply impressed to discover the ingenious manner in which its interior was fitted out. The seaman was rowing her back to shore when she noticed the irate figure of her husband awaiting her. His arms were folded, his legs braced, and his head was thrown back in a manner which told her he was not pleased.

When their little boat reached the shore, he hauled her grimly ashore. 'What the *deuce* do you think you are doing, madam?' he said as he escorted her away from the waterfront in such a rush that she would have slipped on the wet cobblestones had he not been clasping her arm so tightly.

'Exploring that big ship out there,' she panted. 'It was really most interest—'

'How dare you leave the inn unescorted?' he raged in an undertone, propelling her onwards at a great rate. 'Have you *no* idea of how to behave? No idea of the sort of villains and ruffians who frequent places of this sort?'

Villains and ruffians indeed, thought Tallie crossly. As if she did not know very well how to tell whether a person was trustworthy or not. And, since he was so obviously bored by her fascination with things nautical, what alternative did she have but to go by herself? She was now a married woman, after all, and had much more licence than an unwed girl to go where she pleased. It was just that he had these stuffy ideas about her behaving more 'suitably', more like a countess. Well, it was not possible to go from being an unwanted poor relation to feeling like a countess in a few days. Particularly when he kept reminding her of her unsuitability!

'Oh, pooh!' she retorted. 'They are most of them very nice.' She smiled and waved at an old woman who sat smoking a pipe outside a tavern, knowing it would annoy her husband. 'Hello, Nell!'

The woman took the pipe out of her mouth and raised it in a salute, baring blackened stumps in a wide grin. 'Ar, Miz Tallie.'

Magnus swore and lengthened his stride, forcing Tallie to hop and skip to keep up with him. He stormed up the stairs of the Ship Inn and flung open the door to Tallie's chamber.

'Oh, there you are, my dears—' began Mrs Entwhistle.

Magnus bowed, slammed the door, and strode off along the corridor and up the next flight of stairs to his own room, dragging Tallie with him. He threw open the door to his own room and was about to usher Tallie in when he halted abruptly, swearing. Tallie peered around her husband's body. A half-dozen young sprigs of fashion were sprawled about, smoking, drinking and playing cards.

'Come in, d'Arenville, ol' chap,' called one young fellow, flushed with drink. 'An' bring that pretty li'l filly with you.'

Magnus seemed to harden with icy rage. 'You refer, sir, to my wife!' he said in a soft, savage tone. It quite quelled the young gentlemen, Tallie thought. He pushed her away from the door and shut it. Towing her behind him, Magnus stalked downstairs and coldly summoned the landlord.

'Kindly direct me to a private room immediately—one in which I can speak to my wife without interruption.'

'Regrettably,' said the landlord, 'not a one is to be had, my lord. People are even sleeping in the public rooms tonight.'

The reply fanned Magnus's temper to flames. 'Then summon my carriage!' he snapped.

The carriage was duly brought round, and no sooner were they seated and the driver directed to 'Drive, damn it!' than Magnus began a tirade which blistered Tallie's ears.

He began with her iniquity in sneaking out of the inn behind his back and her perfidy in using a garrulous bloody cit as a smokescreen! He condemned her lack of decorum in venturing out alone and unescorted in such a filthy little town. He was scathing about her foolhardiness in entering into conversations with the most unsuitable people—villainous cut-throats, verminous old women dressed in rags, smoking God knows what in evil-smelling pipes!

Tallie sat, her hands folded submissively in her lap, listening with downcast eyes to all he had to say.

'...and as for the utter folly of venturing aboard a strange ship in the company of...of some tattooed ruffian with gold rings in his ears—why, anything may have befallen you! You

could have been kidnapped—or worse. A villain like that
would slit your throat as soon as look at you!'

Tallie looked up at this. 'Oh, no, my lord, Jack may look a
little rough, but truly he is a decent fellow under all those
tattoos. His wife in Jamaica gave him the earring—'

Magnus rolled his eyes and ground his teeth. 'He could have
stolen you away on that boat—'

'Ship. A boat is much small—'

'Will you *listen* to me, you foolish chit?' Magnus slammed
his fist onto the leather squabs. 'He could have drugged you,
stolen you away and sold you as a white slave in some foreign
port!'

Tallie stared at him. She had heard of white slaves, of
course. The girls had talked of such things after dark in the
dormitory. But she had been in no such danger. Everyone on
the waterfront had known where she had gone. 'But how could
he, my lord—?' she began.

'Quite easi—'

'For there is no wind to enable the ship to sail away,' she
finished. 'That is why we are not yet in France. Have you
forgot?'

Magnus glared at her, stumped for a response.

The coach rattled onwards. Tallie glanced out of the window. They were well out of town by now, green hedges and
trees whipping past in a blur. It was remarkable how accustomed she had become to the speed of coach travel. For a girl
who'd never been anywhere, she was fast becoming a sea-
soned traveller.

She looked back at her husband. He was staring out of the
window, a black frown on his face. He obviously still hadn't
got over his crotchets. She sighed. One would expect such a
handsome man to have a more agreeable temperament, but the
least little thing seemed to set him off. Still, anyone who had
been reared in Miss Fisher's Seminary for the Daughters of
Gentlemen knew all about bad tempers. She sighed again.

The sound made Magnus turn to look at her. She cocked
her head and smiled enquiringly at him.

It was the smile that did it, Magnus told himself later. Quite obviously she *still* had no idea of the imprudence of her actions, of the danger she'd been in. Her countenance showed not the slightest sign of contrition. His temper, held rigidly in check, burst its bounds again.

'And what if that damned filthy ruffian had decided to ravish you out there on that boat?' he snarled. 'What then, eh? You could have done *nothing*! Nothing to save yourself! Did you think of that, madam, eh? No, I am very sure you did not. You did not think of anything at all, did you?'

'Oh, he would have done nothing of the sort,' retorted Tallie crossly. 'And if he had—' she glared at him defiantly '—I know very well how to deal with such matters.'

'What?'

'Well—' she began, but her words froze in her throat as Magnus launched himself at her, lunging across the carriage to grab her arms. In seconds he had her hands pinioned behind her back and she was thrust back along the wide seat of the coach, legs flailing, his muscular body pressed heavily on top of hers. She stared up at him, struggling, her eyes wide with surprise.

'What if he'd had you like this?' Magnus growled. 'Your body vulnerable under his. Accessible to his every desire.' He pressed himself against her, his eyes devouring her face.

Tallie felt something hard pressing into her stomach. She tried to wriggle away. Her husband's face loomed dark and angry over hers, his flinty grey eyes boring into her. She could feel his breath warm on her skin. Ignoring her struggles with ease, he gathered both her wrists into one hand, leaving the other free.

'And what if he had wanted to do this to you? What would you have done then, eh?' His hand moved slowly over her breast, stroking and squeezing.

Tallie gasped in amazement. What on earth was he doing? To take such liberties with her person… She knew about men taking liberties with a girl's person from Miss Fisher—she had just never known what exactly 'liberties' were. And she knew very well what the correct response for a genteel young lady was in this situation—she just wasn't sure she wanted to make it—just yet. These liberties felt remarkably pleasant, and she didn't want to stop him…yet.

The big warm hand exploring her breast caused all sorts of wondrous shivery responses in her body. Particularly when he touched her…like that. Ohhh! Like ripples in a pond, the feelings started from her chest and shimmered deliciously outward. And downward. She lay there, entranced, staring up at her husband's dark visage, lost in the sensations his caresses were producing.

'And what if he'd done this?' muttered her husband thickly, and pressed his mouth hard over hers.

Tallie closed her eyes. Her husband's mouth crushed hers for a moment, then softened. His lips explored hers slowly, gently, and she gave herself up to the sensations. His mouth was so tender and warm as it moved caressingly over hers. And he wasn't merely pressing his lips against hers; he seemed to be nibbling and sucking and…licking. She shivered pleasurably and pressed closer to him.

Even his body pressing so heavily on top of hers felt interestingly… Gracious! His tongue was pushing between her lips! Running along between her teeth and her lips…very peculiar…yet…utterly…thrilling. Sensation vibrated through her body from his, and she felt her body softening and melting with the pleasure of it…and yet an odd sort of tension seemed to be rising within her.

His tongue plunged again into her mouth, sweeping in slow, sensual arcs, stroking the roof of her mouth, curling around her own tongue. Tallie shuddered rapturously as wondrous sensations flooded her. His powerful thighs imprisoned her, and he pressed against her, in deliberate, rhythmic movements, his body moving in time with his tongue. Tallie felt languid, thrilled and apprehensive—all at the same time.

His hand had left her breasts, she realised suddenly. It was sliding up her legs, over her stockings… It was past her knee and touching bare flesh! The hand moved higher and she tried to wriggle away from it, at the same time straining to press herself more closely against him. He moaned, caressing her eyelids with his mouth and tongue, nuzzling her throat and stroking the skin of her thighs with warm, strong fingers. Tallie's legs quivered in response, then fell apart, trembling. His hand moved higher, circling, stroking, pressing.

Suddenly the coach lurched, and Tallie abruptly became aware of what she was doing. And where his hands were! She stiffened in shock. These were indeed liberties! And Tallie knew her duty.

'Ohhhh,' she gasped loudly, and collapsed dramatically back against the seat cushions, her body loose and boneless.

'Tallie? What is it?' Magnus pulled his mouth from hers and blinked dazedly down at his bride. Oh, Lord! He'd let himself get carried away. The slightest touch of his lips to hers and the passion he'd tried so hard to repress had flared uncontrollably. Lord help him, he'd been about to ravish his innocent virgin bride in a carriage in the middle of the countryside! And frightened her half to death by the look of things!

'Tallie, are you all right?' He picked up one hand and began to chafe it frenziedly. He patted her cheeks and took her chin in his hand, searching in vain for signs of animation. Her head lolled in his hands. Oh, Lord, what if she were ill?

Thoroughly alarmed, Magnus sat up and ran his hands through his hair, wondering what the devil one did with swooning females. A vinaigrette, that was what he needed. He searched every cranny of the coach, as if one would magically be found to contain a bottle of smelling salts, but no.

What else? Burnt feathers? He'd seen women revived when burnt feathers were held under their noses—but he had no feathers to burn. What else? he thought in desperation. Cold water? Yes, there was bound to be some lying around outside—a stream or a pond or even a puddle. He shouted at the coachman to stop the coach, and as it slowed he flung open the door.

A noise from his beloved bride halted him in his tracks. He could not believe his ears. The sound came again. Magnus turned in dark suspicion and looked at her. Sure enough, her body was convulsed—in not quite silent giggles.

'You little witch!' Magnus exclaimed wrathfully. 'You were faking it!'

Tallie sat up, groping for her reticule to find a handkerchief to wipe her streaming eyes.

Magnus stared, outraged, incredulous! She was laughing? At *him*? He had been lost in the heights of passion…and she'd faked a swoon…and was *laughing*! He opened his mouth to deliver a blistering tirade to end all blistering tirades.

'You see, my lord, I was in no danger.' Her voice was a little shaky, but she seemed in full control of her faculties.

No danger? Magnus's eyes narrowed into glacial slits. 'Danger of what?' Right now the little baggage was in danger of being throttled! By her brand-new husband!

'From that sailor, of course,' Tallie responded as brightly as she could, given the fact that her body still trembled with the aftermath of his passion. She had reacted automatically, feigning the swoon, but all the time she had lain there with her eyes closed she had been reliving his caresses. She'd felt like bursting into tears when he had sat up, releasing her from his embrace, and begun chafing her hands. She'd been shaken, in turmoil, wondering what to do, but then laughter had bubbled up from nowhere, and she'd let it come…

She continued, 'If he had done what you said he might— what you did to me just now—I would have pretended to swoon, just like I did. Then, while he was wondering what to do, I would have escaped.'

She smiled triumphantly at him and straightened her skirts, hoping he would not notice her trembling hands. She had never known a kiss could be like that, but she could never let him see how strongly it had affected her. She did not wish to disgust him, after all.

She felt quite proud of herself, of her apparent self-possession, as she said, 'Now, shall we return to town?'

He was still looking murderous, so she said earnestly, 'You really have no need to worry about my safety, my lord, for truly there is no need, as you saw. I learned how to deal with unwanted liberties when I was at school, you know. Miss Fisher considered it very important.' She added confidingly, 'Of course, this is the first time I have ever actually *needed* to do so, but I think it worked splendidly, don't you agree?'

'*Splendidly.*' Lord d'Arenville glared balefully at his bride of only a few days. *Unwanted liberties?* Hell and the devil roast it, but he'd teach her to want those liberties from him— if he died in the attempt!

Chapter Eight

The handsome pirate bent over her, and a lock of crisp dark hair fell over his brow. His sea-grey eyes darkened with passion as he lowered his mouth to hers…

'Ohhhh,' Tallie moaned.

…his arms drew her closer and she felt as if there was no other place on earth she wished to be. He smiled, the long, vertical grooves in his cheeks deepening, and kissed her again.

Tallie groaned.

'Fear not, my love,' the pirate murmured. *'No one can catch us. No one will ever take you away from me. For the wind is blowing swift and strong…'*

Tallie moaned again. It wasn't fair. She loved the sea.

'…and my ship is fleet and sure…'

'Ohhhh!' Tallie whimpered. She loved ships, too.

'…and she rides the waves like a dolphin…up and down.'

'Oh, no, no—no more…' Tallie muttered woefully. She was betrayed—by the ship, by the sea!

'Here, take this.' Lord d'Arenville's eyes were sea-dark with concern as he leaned over her. He held out a basin and Tallie clutched it gratefully, closing her eyes again to shut out the sight of the lantern swinging with the motion of the ship.

She bent over the basin for a long, painful interval, then felt it removed from her grasp. A cool, damp cloth gently wiped her mouth and she felt hands tucking the blanket more se-

curely around her shivering body. Warm, strong arms gathered
her close and she sighed in relief. She felt herself lifted up
and her eyes flew open again in alarm.

'It's all right. I'm taking you up on deck,' Magnus murmured as she clutched his neck in distress.

'No, no.'

'Trust me, you will feel better in the fresh air,' he said, and
carried her out of the small, gloomy cabin.

Tallie was certain she would die if she had to go up to the
pitching, rolling deck, but she was too miserable and exhausted to argue. She would die soon in any case. Why had
no one told her sailing was like this? She felt the ship lurch
and shudder, heard the frightful creak and groan of straining
timber, and clutched her husband tighter, finding comfort in
his warmth and strength. And courage. For he seemed not the
least distressed by this dreadful storm which would surely kill
them all.

On deck the wind was brisk and cold. Magnus carried her
over to the railings and found a place to sit, still holding her
in his arms. Splashes of sea spray cooled her clammy skin.
Magnus wiped it with his handkerchief. Wind whipped at her
hair and tugged at her skirts. He smoothed her hair back and
tucked the blanket more securely around her.

'Feeling better?' he said after a while.

Tallie shivered and leaned against his chest. She did feel a
little better. The fresh sea air was helping her head to clear—
if not her stomach, which was aching dreadfully from all that
she had lost from it. She would never eat kippers again.

'It's perfect weather for sailing,' he said.

She stared at him incredulously. Perfect weather? Surely it
was a storm! Those white-capped waves were enormous, and
the way they dipped and swelled and crashed against the sides
of the ship was terrifying.

'According to the captain, this wind will have us in France
in under five hours,' he continued. He glanced down at her
and smiled slightly. 'That's a little under two hours from now.'

'Two hours,' Tallie groaned.

He laughed—rather heartlessly, Tallie thought.

'Here, this will help settle your stomach.' He pulled out a flat silver flask, unscrewed the top and held it to her lips.

'No,' she muttered, turning her lips away. She couldn't bear to eat or drink anything, knowing she would only lose it in a few minutes.

'Trust me.' He grasped her chin in his hand and tipped what seemed like half the contents of the flask down her throat.

Tallie shuddered as it burnt its way down her throat, then coughed as it hit the pit of her empty stomach, depriving her of all ability to breathe for a moment or two. 'What—?' she spluttered indignantly.

'Brandy.'

She subsided, gasping against his chest, and closed her eyes, waiting to die, but after a few minutes she found a warmth stealing into her body which seemed to banish the dreadful queasiness. Wearily she laid her face against his throat, taking comfort in the scent of his cologne water and his skin. She felt the faint prickle of whiskers against her cheek and rubbed against them, enjoying the sensation.

He had been so very kind to her, she thought drowsily. The last thing she would have expected of Lord d'Arenville was that he would prove so gentle and sympathetic in the sickroom. He was such a fastidious person. She would have expected him to be revolted by her illness…gentlemen were, she'd understood.

But instead he had cared for her with a quiet competence that, now she thought about it, made her almost want to weep… She could not remember when anyone had cared whether Tallie Robinson was well or ill, if she lived or died. And now, this—this so-called Icicle had tended to her needs with a careful tenderness that nearly broke her heart. It was wicked for people to call him The Icicle. He wasn't at all. He was…

'You're so kind,' she mumbled into his skin, feeling tears prickling, hot against her eyelids.

Kind? Had she said he was *kind*? Magnus was stunned. He

must have misheard her. No one had ever called him kind before. Any one of his acquaintances would laugh at the notion. He shifted his hold on her slightly, tucking her more securely into the curve of his body, savouring the relaxed weight of her, the feel of her soft cheek against his skin. Errant tendrils of her hair tickled his chin, and he inhaled the scent of it, soap and sea and the faint sour remnants of her recent illness.

Poor little mite. Her seasickness had come as such a shock to her. A blind man would have seen how thrilled she'd been when they had finally embarked, her eyes sparkling with excitement. And not a half hour later she had been drooping, green and wan, over a basin, retching her little heart out, a picture of misery.

And she thought him kind... It wasn't kindness that caused him to look after her, he reflected ruefully. He'd had no choice—there was no one else... And besides, she belonged to him now. He had a duty to her. He was her husband.

He felt her body relax against him, felt her breathing slow to an even rhythm. She was asleep. In his arms. His wife.

Magnus watched the waves, enjoying the brisk salt spray which blew occasionally against his face. He pulled the blanket up to protect her from the wet. It had been nothing like he'd expected, this business of marriage. Lord, what a simpleton he'd been, thinking to get himself a wife in order to get children. He'd thought about the children only; he'd barely considered the wife, except to find a healthy woman who would disturb his life as little as possible. He laughed silently. What a gudgeon, to think a woman would not disturb his life.

Perhaps if he'd married one of Laetitia's candidates... Ironic to think he'd picked Tallie because she'd have so few expectations. She was simply bursting with expectations; that was the trouble. She had a thirst for life that amazed him.

If he'd chosen one of Laetitia's girls he'd have had a conventional bride trip—to Brighton or Bath, perhaps, or even to his country home. Then a season in London, by which time she'd have been pregnant and would have retired gracefully to the country to give birth. And when she'd been ill she would have had her mama and a dozen attendants to care for her. And after the birth she would have returned to London and they would have resumed their separate lives in the normal civilised fashion of the *ton*.

But instead of a cool sophisticate who understood her duty he'd chosen this naive little creature, who'd thrown his life into chaos. He'd not realised just how alone in the world she was— Lord, she didn't even have a maid. He hadn't even arranged to get one for her—he'd just assumed one of Laetitia's maids would accompany her. His cousin had refused, of course.

And so, because of Laetitia's spite and his own lack of forethought, he'd had to be maid, groom, sickroom attendant and protector to his wife. Everything except husband. And because of crowded inns, stinking waterfronts, vulgar cits— not to mention his delayed wedding night—he'd been bad-tempered and unpleasant a good deal of the time.

And yet she called him kind…

He wasn't, of course. Magnus knew that. Along with the knowledge of his duty to his lineage, his lands, and his family name, his father had drummed into him a rigid sense of responsibility for those who were dependent on him. And there was no doubt in Magnus's mind that his bride was more dependent on him than anyone had ever been in his life. *Kind?* She just didn't understand *noblesse oblige*.

But he did enjoy the warm weight of her in his arms.

By the time they reached Calais, she had almost fully recovered from her seasickness. 'France!' she announced in relief as they headed towards the customs house.

The French officials examined their passports with an insulting attitude of suspicion and searched their baggage with greedy hands. One turned to examine Tallie's clothing—while she was wearing it—and Magnus stepped forward with a warning growl. There was a short muttered exchange, gold passed from English to French hands, and they were allowed

to leave. John Black, Magnus's coachman and general facto-
tum, remained behind to supervise the luggage.

With every step on firm, dry land, Tallie gathered animation. Her eyes darted everywhere, drinking in the sights and
sounds and smells of her first foreign country. A foreign country, moreover, which only a short time ago had experienced
bloodthirsty revolution and war—and murdered almost all of
its aristocrats. She was now an aristocrat by marriage. Tallie
pressed close to her husband, thrilled by the sense of danger,
secure in his presence.

And what sights there were too, for almost every man had
savage black whiskers and gold earrings, and wore a cocked
hat with a red, white and blue cockade pinned to it—the *tri-
colore*. Some grenadiers marched past, looking very daunting
and military, with prodigious moustaches and an erect, menacing gait.

The girls, *grisettes*, were very smartly dressed too, adorned
with sparkling crosses, necklaces, earrings—all kinds of glittering decoration—and pretty starched white caps close upon
their heads.

The sounds of French surrounded them, and Tallie frowned
as she listened. These people spoke very differently from Mademoiselle, who had taught French at Miss Fisher's, and Tallie
could only understand a word here and there.

She was surprised at how cheerful and friendly people
seemed, but the Peace of Amiens had been signed almost a
year before and things had obviously settled. She had half
expected them to be rude, or hostile, but nothing could have
been farther from the truth—particularly when the landlord
bustled out of the Lion d'Argent, bowing and smiling, welcoming *Milord Anglais et la belle milady* with genuine pleasure.

'I…I do not think I am very hungry,' said Tallie as they
entered the private dining parlour. Her stomach had settled a
good deal, but it was still feeling a little peculiar.

Magnus frowned. 'You will feel more the thing with some
good hot food inside you.' He summoned a thin, lugubrious

garçon and ordered coffee, eggs, steak and ale for both of them. The *garçon* gave a Gallic shrug and pointed out that they were not in England now, and decent Frenchmen did not drink ale. Magnus gave an English shrug in response and said nothing.

Tallie waited until the *garçon* left. 'I have no wish for food, thank you. I am not at all hungry.'

'Nonsense,' Magnus said bracingly. 'You will eat, and that's the end of it.'

The *garçon* returned in a few moments and placed a plate of poached eggs in front of her. Magnus addressed himself to a large, rare steak. Tallie glared at him mutinously and pushed her eggs away. How could she have thought her husband was kind? She was very sure she had not a trace of her insides left. No man with an ounce of sensitivity would expect her to eat runny eggs—or watch him devour a greasy steak—when she was still feeling so delicate. She averted her eyes from the disgusting sight and stared out of the window, where two men dressed in ragged finery played republican tunes on an organ and tambourine.

Magnus signalled to the *garçon*. A moment later he brought in a large cup of steaming, fragrant coffee and a dish of rolls and placed them on the table. Tallie watched Magnus break open the rolls. Wisps of steam escaped as the golden crust broke. The scent was heavenly. He buttered a piece with pale butter and, before she knew what he was about, popped it in her mouth. Reluctantly she chewed and swallowed. It was delicious.

Clearly he was not going to allow her to refuse to eat. Grudgingly she reached out, buttered the next piece herself and ate it cautiously. Next she took a sip of coffee. It was wonderful—hot and strong, milky and sweet. She drained the cup, then looked up to see her husband watching her, a faintly quizzical look on his face. As their eyes met, the long grooves down his cheeks deepened and the grey eyes almost twinkled.

Wryly she smiled, feeling a little foolish. 'Very well, it is delicious. I do feel better.'

He nodded. 'Food is the best thing after a bout of seasickness. Will you have the eggs now?'

Tallie glanced at the orange yolks and shuddered. 'No, I thank you. I will be content with these rolls and some more of this lovely coffee. It is different from English coffee, is it not? And then I would like to wash and to change my clothes.'

'Make haste, then, for we do not stay the night here,' said Magnus. Tallie looked up in surprise.

'We made good time in the ship,' he said, 'but it will not be long before this town is as crowded as Dover was. I have every intention of beginning the journey to Paris as soon as possible and avoid the inconvenience of over-full inns.' He added, 'We shall stop in Boulogne, which is some hours' travel from here. I understand there are several decent inns where we can repose ourselves for the night.'

Tallie nodded and wiped her mouth with a napkin. 'Very well. I shall postpone my bath until just before I retire for the night.'

Magnus met her eyes in an oddly searing glance for a moment, then stared at his plate, 'John Black is, at this minute, arranging transportation with the postmaster. We shall depart as soon as he has hired a post-chaise and four.'

The trip along the post-road from Calais to Boulogne delighted Tallie, the faint aroma of onions that lingered in the hired vehicle notwithstanding. 'One would think that farms would be farms and fields the same the world over, but it is not so at all, is it?' she commented to Magnus. 'Even the people in France look different.'

He nodded, never having given the matter any thought. He'd decided not to ride, the horses for hire being decidedly inferior in his opinion, so he was sprawled lazily in the corner of the chaise, observing his bride's fascination with the passing scenery. Her ability to be pleased by the smallest things struck him again, and it occurred to him that, had he wed one of Laetitia's collection, he would, no doubt, be having to exert himself to entertain her. Tallie was young, he realised, but she had never yet bored him as Laetitia's friends had.

The late afternoon sun was sparkling on the Channel when they reached Boulogne. They found the inn the landlord of the Lion d'Argent had recommended. Magnus engaged a suite of rooms, bespoke an early supper, then went for a stroll while a *bonne* ushered Tallie up to a large chamber and then went to arrange for her bath to be drawn.

Tallie explored. Her chamber was spacious, with a small dressing room attached. It was comfortable, rather than elegant, and contained an enormous bed with a heavenly feather mattress. On top of the bed were several quite peculiar pillows—long, round and narrow—more like bolsters than pillows. She wondered if Magnus's bed had proper pillows and decided, if it did, she would borrow one of his.

Connecting doors led to a private parlour and a narrow balcony overlooked the sea. Tallie passed several enjoyable minutes observing the scenery until the *bonne* returned with a pile of soft towels. Behind her trooped footmen, carrying an enamelled hip bath and numerous buckets of steaming hot water.

Tallie bounced into the wonderfully soft bed and snuggled down under the thick down quilt that the inn provided instead of blankets. It was very light, and quite insubstantial compared with the thick woollen bedclothes she was used to, but it seemed warm enough.

Her first day in France. It had been very exciting, for Magnus had taken her for a stroll through the town before they had sat down to an utterly delicious supper. She had heard about French cooking, and now she knew! Even quite ordinary vegetables took on a new splendour in the hands of a French cook, with delectable subtle sauces and interesting combinations. And the variety of dishes…wonderful. Tallie sighed in pleasure and leaned over to blow out her bedside candle. Before she could do so, however, she heard a knock on the door. She sat up in bed, clutching the down quilt to her chest.

'Who…? Er…*qui est-ce*—?' she called hesitantly.

'It is I,' said the deep voice of her husband.

'C…come in.'

Magnus entered, shutting and locking the door behind him.
Tallie pulled the quilt more tightly around her.

'Was there something you wanted, my lor—er, Magnus?'

He looked down at her enigmatically for a moment. 'This
is my room, too.'

Tallie blinked. 'But there's only one bed.'

He smiled slowly. 'I know.'

'But…'

'We are married, Tallie. Married couples share a bed.'

Tallie's mouth opened in surprise. It wasn't true. Her cousin
Laetitia had her own bed, and most of her married visitors had
separate chambers, too—Tallie knew because she'd been the
one who had usually arranged the accommodation for guests.
The only time they ever shared a bedchamber was when there
were too many people for separate ones… Maybe this inn was
crowded too.

'Oh,' she said, and swallowed.

'I'll disrobe in here, shall I?' Magnus entered the small
dressing room, pulling the door after him.

Tallie sat in the bed, wondering what to do. There was a
look in his eye that she had seen before—in the coach in
Dover, when he had kissed her in that extraordinary way.

She'd thought about the kiss a lot since it had happened.
She knew people didn't usually kiss like that, with their tongue
inside your mouth, and wondered if that was how a man put
a baby inside a woman. Amanda Forrest had said her mother
said it happened when a man put himself inside a woman, and
he had certainly put himself inside her then. She shivered deliciously, remembering the bold sweep of his tongue over hers.

Did she have a baby inside her yet? Probably not, after all
that vomiting on the ship, so perhaps he was going to kiss her
in that special way again. She wouldn't mind it at all. It had
been quite wonderful… She hadn't felt the need to flinch or
anything, as her cousin had said she would.

The dressing room door opened and Magnus emerged, dressed in a heavily embroidered dark silk dressing gown, tied at the waist with a sash. He walked over to the bed and smiled. 'Move over,' he said softly, and with a small, nervous smile Tallie wriggled over to her side of the bed. He sat down on the edge of the bed and slowly undid the sash, watching her all the time. He peeled off the dressing gown and Tallie gasped and averted her eyes.

He was naked! Completely naked. No nightshirt at all!

He stood and, naked, walked a few steps to a chair, over which he neatly draped his dressing gown. Tallie shot a quick, furtive glance at him. She had never seen a naked man before. Aside from the powerful muscles across his shoulders and back, and the long, hairy limbs, men weren't all that different from women, she decided. They were just bigger and stronger and hairier. Then he turned, and Tallie's eyes almost popped out of her head. There was something *very* different about men…and her husband looked *nothing* like little Georgie in the bath!

Tallie suddenly realised he'd caught her peeking, and she hurriedly turned her head away, closing her eyes for good measure. He laughed, and said, 'It's all right to look, you know.'

Tallie didn't reply. She lay down in the bed, her eyes shut tight, and felt the bed sag as he climbed into it. His body was very close to hers—she could feel the warmth radiating from him, even though he was naked and should be cold.

'Will you blow out the candle, please?' she said after a moment.

'Not yet,' said a deep voice beside her ear. 'I think it's my turn to look, don't you?'

Tallie's eyes flew open and she clutched the comforter to her chin. 'Y…your turn?' she quavered.

'My turn,' he confirmed. 'It's what married people do.' He reached out, gently tugged the comforter from her nerveless grasp and pushed it down to her lap. Slowly he began to un-button her nightgown…one button…two…three…until it was

undone almost to her waist. She was shaking by the time he'd
finished and her eyes were screwed shut.

'Don't be frightened,' he said softly, and began to stroke
her cheek. He moved closer, and she could feel the solid heat
of his body lying all along hers. He bent over her and kissed
her lightly on the mouth, then kissed her again, moving his
lips softly over her, small, tiny kisses, feathering them over
her mouth, her eyelids, her cheeks. Tallie relaxed a little.

His hands caressed her, stroking her cheek, her throat, down
her arms, then back up to her throat. He touched her breasts
through the cotton of her nightgown, moving back and forth
in the softest, lightest touch. Tallie felt a faint quiver pass
through her every time he did so. He kissed her deeply, then
touched his tongue to the hollow at the base of her throat and
kissed her again. Slowly, slowly the kisses moved lower, and
she felt the faint abrasion of his chin as he nudged her nightgown apart.

She felt the moist, warm trail of his kisses down in the
valley between her breasts, then his hand slipped in and eased
her gown aside. He sat up on one elbow for a moment, staring.

'Beautiful.'

Tallie's eyes opened for a fleeting, stunned glance. Beautiful? He thought her beautiful?

He cupped first one breast then the other, in a warm, strong
hand, then rubbed his thumbs gently back and forth across
their tips. Tallie felt them harden, and shivers of pleasure
coursed through her. She watched, trembling, as his dark head
bent and he suddenly buried his face in her breasts and made
a low, deep sound in his throat. She had never before felt so
close to another human being. She wanted to put her arms
around him, to cradle his head against her. Her hands rose,
hovered, and then dropped uncertainly.

'Let's get rid of this thing,' he said, sitting up. He reached
under the bedclothes, took the hem of her nightgown and began to pull it upwards, over her legs.

Tallie tried to stop him. 'I…no… But it's cold…and this
comforter is extremely light.'

'I'll keep you warm.' He tugged at the hem. 'Lift your bottom.'

Mindful of her wedding vows, Tallie obeyed, and in seconds she was lying in bed with her husband, not a stitch of clothing between them. He pulled the comforter down and gazed at her body with possessive, heavy-lidded grey eyes which seemed to burn into her skin. Tallie tried to shield herself from his stare, but he lifted her hands away, saying, 'I am your husband, Tallie. You don't have to hide yourself from me.'

He lowered his mouth to her breast again, and Tallie almost leapt out of her skin as red-hot spears of pleasure pierced her. He muttered inaudibly, caressing her with hands, mouth and tongue. Sensations spiralled through her and she found herself shuddering convulsively. What magic was he performing to make her feel this way? She wanted to take his head in her hands and press him tighter against her breasts, wanted to touch him as he was touching her. She pressed a small, shy kiss on his hair instead.

He caressed her softly, tenderly, and so slowly... It was... lovely... At one point he slowed, and seemed to hesitate, and Tallie opened her eyes. He, too, had his eyes closed. He was breathing heavily and gritting his teeth. She wondered for a fleeting second if he was in pain. But she soon forgot that thought because—ohhh... The feeling of his warm strong hands caressing, smoothing, shaping her body, learning it. She knew now why some people called this possessing—Magnus was possessing her. And it was wonderful.

She tentatively laid her hands on his shoulders and, light as thistledown, stroked his skin. He felt warm, slightly damp with sweat, and very, very good. His skin smelt of the cologne water he usually wore, and some darker, musky scent that she knew was him. He didn't react, didn't tell her to stop. Feeling braver, Tallie stroked the wide muscular shoulders and the crisp dark hair on his arms, exulting in the feel of his strength. Such a powerful man, and yet so tender with it.

He rubbed his hands down over her stomach and hips, and

the slightly roughened skin of his palms set up a delicious friction on her soft skin, then dipped between her thighs. Quivers ran through her, and without conscious volition her legs fell open. He cupped her between her legs and began small circular motions that soon had her gasping with excitement. She felt his fingers moving intimately in the folds of her flesh, and she parted her legs further, writhing in pleasure at the sensations coursing through her body.

Groaning, he pushed her legs wider and settled himself between them, his hands stroking, caressing, probing and teasing, his mouth hot and hard on hers. She felt something hard and blunt nudging her between her legs, and she stiffened.

He paused, looking deep into her eyes. 'I don't want to hurt you, but the first time, I fear, it is inevitable.'

Suddenly Tallie recalled her cousin's instructions. She closed her eyes and grabbed the bottom sheet tight in her fists. He pushed, and she wanted to wriggle away, but she remembered the bit about not flinching and braced herself instead. He pushed harder, groaning, and Tallie gasped. She wondered if it was hurting him as much as it was hurting her, and then she stopped wondering as a sharp pain lanced through her and she forced herself to remain motionless.

He hesitated. 'It's done now,' he murmured, and caressed her cheek for a second. Tallie, panting, was relieved, and waited for him to remove himself, and the thing that was stretching her and stinging so dreadfully. Instead he started to move inside her, moving back and forth, slowly at first and then faster and faster. His mouth came back over hers, and she realised his tongue was moving at the same pace, creating those amazing sensations in her again.

She was not hurting so much now, but still an unbearable feeling of tightness was growing inside her, until she thought she must burst. She wanted to writhe and squirm and scratch, but she knew she could not move, nor flinch or cry out or otherwise disgrace herself. Or him.

This was her husband, and she was now truly his wife, and this was what husbands did to get their wives with child. But, oh—she wanted to take hold of him and hold herself hard against him while he was doing this to her. But she couldn't.

She loved him, she realised suddenly. Against all her expectations she'd fallen in love with this cold, kind, abrupt, gentle man. She wanted to cry out and cover his face with kisses, but she owed it to him to lie here without flinching, without crying out.

He mightn't love her, but she wanted him to be proud of her...

His movements built to a rapid crescendo, and she found herself panting shallowly in time with them, feeling as though something was about to happen...as though she was being swept away by some tide... She forced herself to lie still. Finally, with a loud, unintelligible groan, her husband gave one last heavy thrust, arching his body over her, his head thrown back in pain—or exultation—she wasn't sure which—and subsided heavily on top of her. They lay, unmoving, panting, their bodies beginning to cool.

He was still inside her, she could feel him, though it was not so uncomfortable now. He lay heavily on top of her and she could hardly breathe, but Tallie decided she liked the feeling of being surrounded by his strength and his warmth. His head was buried in the hollow of her throat. Tentatively she lifted her hand and stroked the short crisp curls on his head. They were damp. She trailed her fingers down the side of his neck and across his shoulders. His skin was moist and warm. He sighed and shuddered under her hand, and then moved away from her. She felt his withdrawal and felt a momentary sense of loss. The candle was still burning, and she felt him watching her in the flickering golden light.

He smoothed back a damp curl from her face. 'Are you all right?' he asked softly.

She couldn't look at him, felt too full of emotion, so she just nodded.

He slipped out of bed and disappeared into the dressing room. She watched him leave and felt like bursting into tears. He was going to dress and return to his own room.

He came back, still naked, carrying a cloth. She wanted to look at him properly, to see exactly how he was made and how it all worked now that she knew how he felt. But she was too shy to do more than cast a quick flicker in his direction, then look away.

He came back to the bed and reached for her thighs.

'Again?' Tallie jumped, disconcerted.

He smiled ruefully. 'No, not tonight.'

She sat back, relieved, then stiffened in shock as he parted her thighs and began to wipe her with a damp cloth. She was sticky and sore there, but for him to be doing such a thing! Her face burned with embarrassment and she tried to stop him, but he took no notice. Finally he finished, and stood up. She glanced at the cloth and saw to her amazement that there were streaks of red on it.

Emmaline Pearce had been right, thought Tallie as her husband moved around inside the dressing room. All those punishments from Miss Fisher for telling lies—and Emmaline had been right all along. There *was* blood, and there certainly could have been screaming had Laetitia not warned her it was not allowed.

Magnus returned and slipped into bed beside her, pulling the cover up around them both. 'And now we sleep,' he said, blowing out the candle and turning on his side. He pulled her against him, holding her around the waist.

Despite her recent experience, and the knowledge that she loved him, Tallie still felt odd, being naked in bed with him—with all that bare skin. 'Shouldn't I put on my nightgown?'

He pulled her tighter against him and stroked a hand up over her hip, briefly cupping her breast. 'You won't get cold,' he murmured, his breath warm against her ear. 'Now hush, and try to sleep.'

Tallie closed her eyes, and soon she heard the slow, deep breathing that told her Magnus was asleep. She sighed, feeling unaccountably miserable all of a sudden. A slow, solitary tear slipped down her cheek, then another.

Chapter Nine

'Six months?' Tallie's voice rose with surprise. 'In Paris?'

Magnus nodded. 'Unless, of course, you find yourself in a delicate condition before then.'

Tallie blushed. She knew now what he meant by 'a delicate condition'. The possibility she might be carrying his child made her heart beat faster. But it also made things even more urgent. She *had* to get to Italy before she became *enceinte*.

'I don't want to spend six months in Paris.'

Magnus pokered up and looked down his nose, the way he usually did when she questioned his decisions. 'I think you'll find six months is not long enough—or is that what you mean?'

'No, not at all,' Tallie said. 'Six months is far too long. If we stay in Paris for such a long time, it will be near winter, and we shan't be able to cross the Alps into Italy until next year.'

'Cross the Alps?' His dark brows rose.

She nodded vigorously. 'Yes. I have heard so many tales of crossing the Alps. It sounds monstrous exciting and I am most eager to do it. And to reach Italy...' Her voice tailed off and she diffidently twirled the wine glass in front of her. 'My parents' graves are in Italy,' she said, not looking at him.

Magnus stared at her for a moment. It was the first time she'd mentioned her parents.

'How old were you when they died?'

'Eleven, almost twelve.'

'And how did they die?'

She hesitated for a long moment, toying with the apricot pastry in front of her. 'I am not entirely sure,' she said at last. 'I think there was a coach accident.'

He frowned. 'You think?'

She nodded, pressed a crumb of sweet pastry onto her finger and transferred it to her mouth. 'The stories conflict. The official notification said their coach overturned and both my parents died immediately, but then I received a letter from someone who knew Mama which suggested that Mama died before Papa...and not from her injuries in the accident...' Tallie licked the grains of sugar which clung to her fingertips.

'What do you mean?' Magnus frowned, watching her.

She shrugged. 'I know no more than that. But it is why I wish so much to go to Italy. I would like to see their graves.' There was a lot more to it, but she did not wish to explain it to him. Not with him being so cool, and frowning as he was. As he had been since they had left Boulogne. Tallie sighed.

It had been almost a sennight since that momentous night, and he had been so cold and distant and abrupt with her that she could almost believe it had been a dream. Except that her body told her it wasn't. Despite the initial soreness and stiffness, her body still sang with the memory of how it had felt to have him hold her and caress her and possess her. She knew the difference now between dreams and reality...

But he had not shared her bed since. Nor had he so much as touched her, except to help her into the coach and such things, and even then he drew back his hand afterwards, as if she was hot metal... And when he spoke to her it was in such a formal manner he might well have been addressing the House of Lords, she thought despairingly.

She had, indeed, married an Icicle.

Magnus watched the changing expressions flit over her countenance and frowned again. It was not going at all as he had planned. His desire for his wife's body had not been slaked by that one night in Boulogne—it had only whetted his appetite for more. He'd watched her licking the sugar off her small pink fingers and felt more than ever like a rampant green youth.

But it was not to be thought of, he told himself sternly. She'd been an untried innocent and was not yet healed—he could tell by the way she tensed up when he came close to her. He would wait until they reached Paris before he shared her bed again. It was the only decent thing to do.

And besides, he had no intention of allowing himself to fall in thrall to a woman's charms. Down that path lay disaster. He'd seen it before—his father and a dozen others, dancing to a woman's tune, helpless in the face of feminine betrayal…

A few sparkling grains of sugar clung to her lips. Magnus refused to notice them.

'We shall reach Paris on the morrow,' he announced, rising from the table. 'We shall depart this inn at first light, so you had best retire early. I bid you goodnight, madam.' He bowed.

Madam. Tallie rose, a lump in her throat at his cool indifference. In a husky voice she murmured goodnight and left the private parlour.

'Tallie.'

She turned on the stairs, a tiny surge of hope rising in her at his voice.

'You will like Paris, I know,' said Magnus from the doorway. 'For a start, you will have a great many fine new gowns and hats and so on. Neither the Terror nor the war has managed to extinguish Paris's reputation for modishness.'

'Oh. Yes,' she murmured dully. 'I suppose not.'

'Think of it—gowns of silk, satin and lace—day gowns, evening gowns—the finest that money can buy.'

She stared down at him in silence.

'And gloves, slippers, French perfume. And balls and routs and glittering assemblies—you will enjoy it very much,' he insisted, frowning.

'Yes, my lord, if you say so.' She turned and mounted the stairs to her chamber.

Curse the woman! What was the matter with her? Magnus watched her go, watched the sway of her hips under the dreary gown she wore. She was dressed like the veriest drab and he had promised her the finest gowns money could buy. So why could she not offer him at least a smile? Any one of the mistresses he had kept in the past would have shrieked with delight and flung her arms around his neck at such an offer. She—his wife—had responded with a dutiful murmur of obedience!

Damn it! He would never understand women! Here he was, allowing himself to be dragged off to foreign parts for her benefit, enduring bad roads, poor accommodation and hard-mouthed horses for her benefit, opening his purse for her benefit and—not least of all—restraining his desires for her benefit!

And was she grateful? Not in the least! Swearing, Magnus took himself off to his cold, empty chamber and his cold, empty bed. He brooded on his wife's unnatural behaviour as he disrobed. He'd wanted a plain, convenient, grateful wife! Hah! He shrugged himself out of his tight coat and tossed it on the bed. She was none of those.

Plain! Even the dowdy gowns she wore hadn't been able to disguise her attractions—not since his so-called wedding night, when he'd put her to bed. He ripped off his cravat and shirt and flung them on a chair.

And as for convenient—why, that was sheer bloody fustian! He sat down on the bed. She was putting him to a vast deal of blasted inconvenience, he thought, tugging furiously at his long boots. He'd even had to do without his valet because of her passion to go to France—the fool had been too frightened to return to his native country, having escaped Madame Guillotine once already! With some difficulty Magnus managed to drag his boots off. And all the time, he thought, in spite of his own desires and frustrations, he had treated her with unfailing politeness and consideration.

But did she show the slightest bit of gratitude for her husband's generosity and forbearance? No! Not she! Magnus hurled his boots across the room. She had taken herself off to bed without a murmur, completely unmoved by the delights he had offered her! Even now she was disrobing, preparing herself for bed, only too happy to snuggle into bed alone. She would have removed that dull stuff gown, rolled her stockings down over those smooth calves and dainty ankles, discarded her petticoat and chemise and was probably—even now— standing naked, warm and pink and glowing, preparing to don that hideous voluminous monstrosity she called a nightgown!

Well, he would not stand for it! She was his wife. A husband had rights! She had no business making him wait until Paris! He snatched his dressing gown from the end of the bed, threw it on, and in bare feet crossed the hall from his chamber to hers, barely remembering to knock as he flung open her door.

'Oh! Magnus! Is there something wrong?'

'Why is your door not locked?' he snapped, staring at her, outraged. She was bent over a dish of water, up to her elbows in soap, clad in that dreadful nightgown and an even worse dressing gown. With not an inch of skin to be seen.

'Oh, I must have forgotten it.'

'See you do not forget it in future. Anyone could have just walked in.'

She looked at him for a long moment and a tiny smile appeared on her face. 'Someone just did.'

'Who the *devil* was it?' he thundered, glaring round the room.

Tallie giggled and bit her lip. 'You, my lord.'

Magnus stared at her for a moment. The tips of his ears turned faintly pink. 'Ah, yes...well...hrmph,' he said, and strolled around her chamber, glaring at the neat, untouched bed, her clothes hanging tidily on the hooks behind the door.

Tallie resumed her washing. The motion drew his attention. 'What are you doing?'

She blushed. 'Just rinsing out a few things.'

He strode over and stared at the basin. 'What the deuce are

you doing that for? There are maids for that sort of thing. My wife does not wash clothes!'

'It's nothing, just a few bits and pieces,' she said, trying unsuccessfully to hide them from his sight. They were her underclothes, he realised—he recognised the patches. He had a set just like them in his valise, with the tapes cut.

'I don't care what they are—get the maid to do it.'

'But I don't want the maid to see—' She broke off, her cheeks rosy with embarrassment.

'See what?' he said, puzzled. A thought occurred to him. 'You're not…is it your time of month?'

Tallie's face flamed. 'No!' she gasped, horrified. She had not known men even knew of such things.

Magnus indulgently observed her flaming cheeks. His innocent little wife was easily flustered. He rather enjoyed it, found it surprisingly arousing, though he did not intend she should realise it. He shrugged. 'Then what do you not wish the maid to see?'

Tallie was infuriated by the cool enquiry. 'It is nothing to do with you. I will do as I like in my own bedchamber. There is no one to see me—you need not worry about what people will think!'

'You will do as I tell—'

'I am your wife, not a slave—'

'Exactly! And I will *not* have my countess washing clothes!'

Magnus stared at her, baffled by her intransigence over such a trivial matter. What the devil was wrong with the wench? Most women who'd had a life like hers would lap up the luxury of having unpleasant little tasks done by a servant. Why would she want to wash her own underclothes? And what did she not wish the maids to see? As if the maids had not seen underclothes before—and a damned sight better—

The truth suddenly hit him with the force of a blow to the midriff. She was embarrassed. Not because her unmentionables needed washing, but because they were in such appalling condition—patched and darned and ill-fitting. She had pride, his little wife, too much pride to have a maid pity her for her lack of adequate clothing. Again he called down silent curses on his cousin's head for her lack of care for Tallie. He vowed his wife would never again have cause to be embarrassed by her clothing. The moment they arrived in Paris he would procure her the finest garments that money could buy. From the skin out.

He shrugged nonchalantly. 'Very well, then, I will tolerate it this time. But once we reach Paris, mind, you shall leave all tasks of that nature to the servants.' He strolled over and sat on the bed.

Tallie stared at him a moment, stunned by his abrupt *volte face*. Then a fresh thought hit her. He had come to her bed-chamber. He was sitting on her bed. In his dressing gown.

He was going to lie with her again.

With shaking hands she hurriedly finished rinsing out her petticoat and chemise, anticipation and excitement rising within her. She darted quick little glances at him as she worked. His large, strong hands fiddled with items on the bed-side table. Tallie shivered with pleasure, imagining the way those hands would soon move across her skin, knowing her, possessing her.

He wanted her again. The thought thrilled her. Quickly she wrung out the clothes and laid them over the back of a wooden chair, out of his sight, then moved shyly towards the bed.

Blushing, she slipped out of her dressing gown and climbed into the high bed beside him. 'M…Magnus…' she whispered.

He turned towards her, cupped her chin in his hand and gazed deep into her eyes.

'It is not too soon? You do not mind?' His breath caressed her skin. His voice was low and deep and resonated through her bones like music.

She blushed, shook her head, and raised her face for his kiss.

Tallie learnt two new things about the marriage act that night. First, that it didn't hurt the second time—not one little bit. And, second, that it was very much more difficult for her to remain still and dignified while her husband's ministrations evoked all sorts of wondrous and thrilling feelings. It took all her will-power, every bit of concentration and determination she possessed, to lie passively under him, making no sound or movement, as her cousin had warned her to.

But she managed it.

The very most she allowed herself was to press several soft, moist kisses on his chest and jaw—and that was only after he had fallen asleep. He could not be disgusted by what he did not know she did. And he could not know the intense pleasure she gained from snuggling up to his warm, relaxed, naked body while he slept.

She was very proud of her efforts, too. She wanted so much to be a good wife to Magnus, wanted so much for him to be proud of her, to respect her—even, perhaps, to learn to love her, just a little. He wanted a child, that much she knew…perhaps he would come to care for her if she gave him one.

She lay in the dark, enjoying the feel of her husband's arm draped heavily across her, his chest and torso pressed against her back, one long, hairy leg thrust between hers. Sleepily she wondered whether she was increasing, and, if so, how she would know.

The princess gazed out through her prison bars, straining for a sight, a sound to indicate that someone was coming to rescue her. But all she could see or hear were the happy celebrations of the townspeople far below her. There would be no rescue today for the princess. She would have to remain here, in the highest turret of the Callous Count's castle. But wait, what was that scraping sound? She turned again to the high, barred window. A muscular hand reached out and effortlessly plucked the bars, one, two, three, from the window. 'Tallie, my love,' a thrillingly deep masculine voice called. She ran to the window and looked out. There, clinging to a rope, was her handsome outlaw prince, his dark hair blowing in the breeze, his grey eyes glinting… No! Not grey! Blue eyes, perhaps, or brown or green—anything except grey! People with grey eyes were selfish. And disobliging. And horrid!

Tallie sat fuming in a chair by the window of her *hôtel* room, glaring out. Outside were people and noise and activity such as she'd never seen or heard before in her life. She shifted restlessly in her seat and punched a cushion into a more comfortable shape.

Outside was a thrilling concoction of smells and sights and sounds that shrieked *Paris!* She bounced up and paced angrily around the room.

Outside was a huge, exotic city, and she'd never in her life been in a city. And where was she? Stuck inside a stuffy parlour, that was where, under orders from her stuffy husband not to venture out until he gave her leave! And where was *he*?

Outside, that was where! Exploring this wondrously exciting city. For the last four hours! While *she* was forced to wait.

It wasn't fair. He'd muttered something about preparations to make before she was ready for Paris and gone out into the city himself, needing, apparently, no preparations for his magnificent self! Leaving her with nothing better to do than study Sinderby. A guidebook. When the real thing was just outside her door! She snatched up the cushion and hurled it at the door in frustration.

'Oops! Sorry,' she gasped as the object of her fury ducked, regarded her with a raised eyebrow and then closed the door carefully behind him. His face was utterly impassive and Tallie's spirits sank. He was The Icicle once more. Ignoring the cushion at his feet, Magnus came forward and presented her with a large brown paper parcel, tied with string.

'A modiste will be here within the hour to fit you out with some decent clothes. You will need to don these before she arrives.' He strolled over to the window, glanced out into the street, then opened up a news sheet and began reading it, quite as if he had nothing more to say to her.

Tallie, clutching the parcel to her bosom, stared at him, suddenly confused. Part of her wanted to rail at him for leaving her for such a long time with nothing to do, but the large, squashy parcel in her arms intrigued her. A gift? She could not remember the last time anyone had given her a gift. Only her wedding pearls. And now, a gift for no reason… With trembling fingers she unknotted the string and spread open the wrapping. Soft, silken things dripped from her fingers and slithered to the floor.

'Ohhh,' she gasped, enchanted. She bent and lifted them. A chemise—no, six, in soft, silky material. And petticoats, in fine lawn and muslin, trimmed with lace. Silk stockings, dozens of them—*silk*! And six finely embroidered nightgowns, so thin and fine and delicate you could almost see through them. She had never seen the like, except once, on a friend of her cousin's. And…good gracious!

She picked the last few items up and frowned in confusion. These were surely not for her… But they, too, were made of the finest, most delicate lawn…pink lawn. Tallie fingered the garments, stunned. They could not possibly be for her husband, for they had lace on them, and besides, they were too small for him. But she had never worn such things…never heard of such things, except in a scandalised whisper. Not even Laetitia wore garments like these.

'I cannot wear these,' she whispered.

Magnus did not turn his head. 'Of course you can. You will oblige me by retiring to your chamber and donning them immediately, madam. The modiste is coming.'

Madam. Tallie gathered up the clothing and left the room, feeling mutinous. The first true gift she had received in years and was she allowed to be excited about it? No, she must be silent and obedient and don them 'immediately, *madam*,' for we would not wish to inconvenience an unknown French modiste, would we? *Madam.*

In her chamber, she stripped off her clothes and quickly slipped into one of the new chemises and a petticoat, savouring the cool, silken feel of them against her skin. The chemise was close-fitting, with gussets under the arms and side gussets to accommodate the flare of her hips. The neckline was extremely low and edged with a tiny frill of lace. The petticoat was long and straight, made of fine, sheer muslin. It was almost like wearing nothing at all. She felt very daring and sophisticated.

She glanced at the other garments on the bed. Drawers! For a woman! Pink ones, with fine French lace around each knee. She had never seen anything so scandalous in her life. Drawers were male attire. For a female to wear them would be truly shocking. Miss Fisher would have fainted at the very notion. Tallie picked up the drawers and held them against her. She ought not to…but her husband had instructed her to wear them.

Quickly she bent, and with some difficulty she pulled on the drawers. They felt very peculiar. She had never felt her bottom and legs so enclosed, so restricted… It was indeed very shocking. Tallie rather liked the feeling.

But however would she manage when she had to…? She pulled the drawers away from her body and peered down inside them. Good heavens! There was a slit. How very shocking! But practical, she supposed.

A knock on the door made her dart behind the screen in a panic. *'Qui est-ce-que—?'*

The door opened. It was her husband.

'I came to see whether the…er…things fitted.'

Tallie, blushing, nodded from behind the safety of her screen. 'Yes, thank you. They do.'

'Well, let me see them,' he said a little impatiently.

Blushing furiously, Tallie took a deep breath and stepped out from behind the screen.

Magnus's eyes narrowed as he took in the picture of his bride dressed in nothing but fine undergarments. His mouth dried as he noted the way the fine silk of the chemise did nothing to hide the creamy swell of her breasts or the faint dark pink of her small thrusting nipples. He dropped his gaze to her hips and frowned in surprise, as he saw what appeared to be pink drawers under her petticoat.

He had not actually selected the garments himself, had simply given the manageress of the establishment an order for the finest, most fashionable underclothes Paris could provide. So the drawers were a shock. He had heard that some women were wearing them, not just women of the *demi-mondaine*—ladies, too, but these were the first he had seen.

'Take off your petticoat,' he said in a deep, husky voice.

Tallie undid the tapes, took a deep breath, closed her eyes and dropped the petticoat. It pooled in a whisper around her feet.

Magnus felt all the breath leave his body at the sight of his wife dressed in intimate male attire. A feminised version of male attire, to be sure, but...no male had ever looked like that... He had never seen anything so erotic in his life. The drawers were gathered at her knees and he wondered how far he could run his hands up inside them. The delicate material hugged her thighs and her skin glowed beneath the fine weave. The drawers bunched slightly at the apex of her thighs over a shadowy, unmistakably feminine vee shape, and then pulled tighter against the slight swell of her stomach.

'Turn around,' he said huskily.

Slowly she turned, her eyes still clenched shut.

Magnus stared. The drawers hugged her rounded bottom and hips and suddenly he longed to see her bending over. 'You have dropped your new petticoat on the floor,' he said hoarsely, and she bent to gather it up. The material pulled tight across her bottom and Magnus could stand no more. He embraced her from behind, running caressing hands up over her body, cupping her breasts, moulding them, seeking out the hardening nipples.

'Magnus!' Tallie squeaked in surprise. 'It is the daytime.'

Ignoring that, he turned her in his arms and lifted her onto the bed, his hands feverishly exploring her scandalously clothed body. He ran his palms up under the knees and gloried in the smooth, satiny feel of her thighs. He bent down and suckled her hard pink nipples through the silk of the chemise and felt her shudder beneath him. He ran his hands down over her backside and up between her legs. 'Aha!' he exclaimed triumphantly as he found the slit. His hands caressed her and he frowned as he felt her stiffen.

'But you said the modiste was coming soon,' said his wife through gritted teeth.

'Damn the modiste!' He caressed her more gently, determined she would, this time, participate in his passion.

'But—'

'The modiste can wait!' he growled, annoyed with her hesitation. He continued to stroke and caress her with one hand, fumbling with his own clothes until he was free of their restraint, and then passion overcame his control and he surged into her and was lost.

Tallie clenched her teeth and hung on, determined she would not disgrace him by moving or calling out. It was getting harder and harder for her to behave as she knew she should. Her husband's desire for her thrilled her, and she probably would have wept with joy—if only she didn't have to concentrate so hard on controlling her own recalcitrant body. But it was so very exciting…

Tallie locked her legs into a stiff line and repeated the usual words over and over in her head. It was the only way she could concentrate on her duty to him.

The rest of the day passed in a whirl. The modiste, Mademoiselle Célestine, arrived—luckily a little late—with an entourage of assistants who draped, pinned, snipped and pulled as they discussed, with much hand-waving and Gallic imprecation, exactly how milady should be attired. Tallie was utterly scandalised by the new French fashions. They seemed to her to consist of nothing but a few wisps of gauze or muslin, and she felt almost naked wearing them. But the modiste and her assistants laughed and assured her everything was perfectly *comme il faut*, and milady didn't wish to appear dowdy, did she?

Tallie looked doubtfully down at her almost naked chest and the transparent veil of embroidered muslin covering the rest of her and thought that milady might indeed prefer to be dowdy if that was the only alternative. It was one thing to appear almost naked in front of her husband—she was becoming accustomed to that—but she could not imagine wearing these…these little wispy things out in public. But she was assured she must, *absolument*, and she supposed when in Rome…or Paris…

However, at that point Magnus entered the room. 'Just thought I'd see how—' He came to an abrupt halt, took one long, burning look at Tallie's flimsy new gown and snapped, 'No! It will not do. Not at all.'

'Oh, but, milor—' began Mademoiselle Célestine.

He strode forward and felt the fine embroidered muslin in long, disdainful fingers. 'Too thin, too flimsy. Shoddy goods.'

'*Mais, non, milor',*' gasped Mademoiselle Célestine, horrified. 'It is of the very finest—'

'No matter.' He brushed off her explanations. 'I should have made my requirements clearer. My wife requires much thicker clothing than this.' He flicked the material scornfully. 'You would not think it to look at her, but she has a very delicate constitution—'

Tallie gasped in indignation.

'She catches cold at the slightest draught and I will not allow her to risk her health for the sake of mere *à la modalité*. No, *mademoiselle* I wish Lady d'Arenville to be warmly and decently clothed, with high-necked gowns in thick, warm fabric.'

And he marched out, leaving Tallie fuming. A sickly constitution indeed! This from the man who'd called her sturdy! And how dared he criticise all her old clothes and then give the modiste orders to ensure she looked just as dowdy in her new ones? Suddenly Tallie felt perfectly comfortable with the new French fashions, flimsy or not.

'You will ignore my husband, if you please, Mademoiselle Célestine. Men do not have the least idea of fashion,' she said firmly. 'The gowns will be as we agreed.'

Mademoiselle Célestine smiled knowingly. 'Ah, but you play with fire, milady. *Alors.* Perhaps we make the necklines a little higher, *hein*? And then we take a slip, like so.' She took out an opaque underdress and held it up. 'Many women wear flesh-coloured stockings also. And of course there are your beautiful pink drawers, quite warm enough for the most fragile constitution, and yet, when the gentlemen look, they see only the colour of flesh…and they wonder…ah, *oui*, they wonder…' She laughed and pulled a very expressive face. '*Très chic* and yet *très respectable*, so your so-jealous husband is almost—but not quite—happy. Husbands must be taught their place, *non*?' She and her assistants laughed again.

Tallie smiled vaguely, distracted by the modiste's words. Her *jealous* husband? That could not be right, surely… Still, he had told all those dreadful lies about her delicate constitution. She felt a small glow in the region of her heart. It was a start, perhaps…

By the time the modiste and her chattering assistants finally left, promising to have a beautiful gown ready for her by the morning, and many more *au plus tôt*, Tallie felt exhausted.

However, her husband had not simply arranged a modiste but also a hairdresser, Monsieur Raymondo, a small, dapper man with an elegant waxed moustache. He prowled around her shrinking form a dozen times, muttering under his breath, bunching her hair this way and that and exclaiming in raptures over its texture and natural curl. Magnus ventured into the room just as the hairdresser picked up his scissors. 'Don't you dare shear off all that beautiful hair!' he roared, and Monsieur Raymondo dropped his scissors in fright. A long discussion ensued over exactly how much Magnus would tolerate being cut off.

Tallie took no part in it; she was in a small, happy daze of her own. *Beautiful hair!* He had lied about her fragility, now this, about her very ordinary hair.

In the end Magnus and Monsieur Raymondo reached a compromise. Short, feathery curls would cluster around her face, while the rest remained quite long. It would please her husband, yet still have the required classical look about it—the new fashions, like the new French Republic, paid homage to the Ancient Greek and Roman ideals.

Tallie could hardly believe the reflection which stared back at her from the mirror when Monsieur Raymondo had finished. Her face seemed quite a different shape; she looked elegant…almost pretty. Her eyes seemed larger, her horrid nose not so pointy, and curly wisps of hair caressed her cheeks and highlighted her cheekbones.

Monsieur Raymondo showed Tallie several ways to arrange her hair. She could put it up and hold it with a crescent, like the goddess Diana. She could wind a spangled scarf around her head, wear it in long, snaky ringlets *à la Sappho* or in the unique style Monsieur Raymondo had invented for her. Milady was now completely *à la mode*. Tallie expressed some concern that she would not be able to manage the new hairstyles, but her husband called a smartly attired young woman into the room and introduced her as Monique, Tallie's new maidservant and dresser. Tallie's mouth fell open. She had never in her life had someone dress her.

But she didn't have time to question anything, for then a shoemaker arrived. He measured her feet, produced a pair of jean half-boots and two pairs of smart kid slippers for immediate wear, and promised to send a dozen new pairs within the week.

Finally, Magnus announced that if the dressmaker delivered as she had promised, Monique could take Tallie shopping on the morrow, so that she could be fitted out with all the other falderals women found so indispensable. Tallie's head was aching by this time and she took umbrage at his tone.

'I do not wish to go shopping tomorrow,' she announced. 'I have done without falderals quite happily—well, almost happily,' she amended honestly, 'for all my life.' She took a deep breath and faced him, her hands clasped to her chest. 'I do not wish to sound ungrateful, indeed I am truly very grateful for all these beautiful things you have bought for me—'

Magnus stiffened uncomfortably. So much for wishing for

a grateful wife. He found he did not want gratitude from her at all.

'It must have cost you a tremendous—' She flushed suddenly and muttered, 'I am sorry. I know it is vulgar to refer to money. But I *do* thank you for all the purchases you have made on my behalf…I cannot remember when anyone gave me…' She broke off and scuffed her foot against the Turkish rug on the floor. Her eyes were bright with unshed tears, Magnus noticed, before she ducked her head down to hide them from him. There was a short pause before she resumed.

'It is only…I do not want to waste any more time in shopping for…for *things*. I want…I want so much to see Paris. Already I have been here a full day and a night, and I have seen nothing except this room. Could we not…?' Her eyes fixed on his, wide with entreaty. 'If I wore a cloak, no one could see my clothes and you need not mind…'

Magnus stood up, affronted. She thought he was ashamed of her clothes, ashamed to be seen in her company. She thought he had hidden her away until she was fit to be seen. To his chagrin, he found there was an element of truth in the unspoken accusation. Though he was *not* ashamed of her—he just wished her to feel equal to those clothed in the very finest.

'It is too warm to wear a cloak,' he said, 'but if you wish it, there is still time for us to see something of the city.'

'Now?' she blurted, surprised.

'Yes, immediately. If you are not too tired.'

'Oh, no, I am not,' she said, her eyes shining. 'Oh, Magnus, thank you. I will just fetch my hat.' She hurried from the room and returned in a moment, fitting an old-fashioned bonnet to her head. He watched her tie its strings.

'I wished only to please you,' he said stiffly. 'I did not think of how you must feel, cooped up in here all day, when you have looked forward so eagerly to our arrival.'

Her face fell. 'Oh, no, I did not mean to criticise—'

He interrupted her. 'Shall we?' he said, presenting his arm.

Tallie was enchanted with Paris. She loved the narrow streets and the incredibly tall stone houses—some as many as seven storeys high. She admired the public buildings with the slogans of *Liberté, Egalité, Fraternité* and *Indivisibilité* written on every one. She especially loved the wide, elegant boulevards, so thickly planted with trees the branches almost met in a cool green arch. And under those branches there seemed to be a constant scene of festivity. Parisians did much of their socialising out of doors, and Tallie adored the outdoor cafés, where it seemed a thousand happy people sat, quaffing lemonade, wine, cider, beer or coffee. They strolled through parks where she was delighted by the 'Theatres for the People' as they were called—outdoor booths with conjurers, puppet shows, menageries and music, always music playing somewhere, on an organ, fiddle, harmonica, tambourine or flute.

And when, finally, night fell, and she thought they must return to the *hôtel*, Magnus took her to a place where a thousand lamps sparkled like fireflies in the branches of the trees, and a hundred flickering candles lit tiny intimate tables. There he ordered champagne and a meal, and Tallie ate her first dinner in Paris out of doors, totally enraptured. The food was delicious, but she could not recall afterwards what it was, for she was entranced by the sights and sounds of Paris all around her, and by the sight of her handsome, silent, considerate husband, who had so splendidly made amends for his earlier ineptitude.

And afterwards they strolled back to their hotel.

And Magnus came to her room.

Chapter Ten

Tallie braced herself and gritted her teeth. The tension was unbearable. She couldn't stand much more. Her body was sheened in sweat. She clutched the sheets on either side of her stiffened body and imagined them shredding under the pressure. She knew exactly how they felt—if sheets could feel, that was.

'Oh, for heaven's sake get it over with,' she gasped. 'I can't take much more of this!'

Magnus, naked and sweating from his labours, froze. He stared at his bride of two weeks, outraged. Never, *never* had any female dared to suggest he was less than adequate in the bedchamber! And this chit, barely out of her virginity, was daring to criticise! He swung himself away from her body, and she gathered the sheet against her to cover her nakedness.

Tallie stared at his furious face, appalled at her own lack of tact. She hadn't meant to say it—it had just slipped out.

'I'm sorr—' she began.

'So I should think!' he rapped. 'I've never been so insulted in my life.'

'Well, but—'

'Do you think it is easy for me, making love every night to a bride as cold and unmoving as a corpse?'

'I have no idea, never having considered the matter, although it seems to me you do not exactly dislike the procedure. In any case, it is very difficult for me, too!' Tallie was incensed by his criticism. 'You have no idea how difficult. It is pure torture!'

'Torture?' Magnus's grey eyes glittered with rage. 'Torture, is it?' He was mortified. Furious. He had half a mind to storm out of the bedchamber and abandon her then and there. He glared down at her. It would serve her right if he throttled her where she lay, clutching that sheet so inadequately, provoking a response from his body despite his fury. He wanted to rip the sheet away and tumble her until she cried for mercy!

Except that she already had!

He was her husband, for God's sake! And she was his wife! His wife! He had every right to take her when and how he liked! And besides, she owed him children.

'Well, madam wife,' he said stiffly, 'I am afraid you must endure more of that torture until you are with child.'

'I know it!' she retorted. 'And if you care to recall, I did not tell you to stop. I said to hurry up and get it over with. The sooner I am with child, the better, I say.'

'Very well, then,' he muttered grimly, and, ripping the sheet from her clutches, he returned to his labours. By God, he would wring a response out of her if it killed him!

He used every skill and technique in his repertoire, stroking, caressing, teasing, his hands and mouth fully occupied.

'Enough!' she shrieked, pushing him off her at last. 'I can do it no more.'

'Do what?' he snarled, frustrated. 'You're doing nothing.'

'Well, of course I am doing nothing—what else would I do? And it takes every bit of concentration I have. Why can you not simply get on with it? Why must it take so much time?'

Concentration? Magnus swore. And was she complaining about the amount of time he took? If so, she was the first woman in his experience ever to complain of *that*. He started to pull on his clothes. He had no intention of staying in a room with her any longer, otherwise he might find himself strangling her. And it was simply not done to murder brides on their bride trip. Not in his family, at any rate.

'I understand now what my cousin meant. It is inhuman to expect women to endure that night after night,' said Tallie rebelliously, wrapping the sheet tightly around her.

Magnus paused, one leg sliding into his trousers. 'What do you mean—what your cousin meant?'

'My cousin warned me that my marital duties would prove to be difficult and painful.'

He frowned. 'Painful? I am causing you pain?'

'No…not pain, precisely. It…it is just…unbearable.'

She continued muttering angrily into the pillow while he finished dressing. Magnus attempted to block out her ugly words. So his lovemaking was unbearable to her, was it? Then his ears picked up one sentence and he was riveted.

'…to be forced to lie there night after night, not moving or uttering a sound, while a husband creates wondrously plea-surable sensations…'

Wondrously pleasurable sensations? Magnus dropped his shirt. 'What did you say just now?' he demanded, his voice harsh.

She blinked up at him. There were tears in her eyes.

'You said, "wondrously pleasurable sensations".'

Tallie sniffed and dropped her head. 'Yes, well…' She turned a deep, fiery pink.

Magnus stared down at her with narrowed eyes. Part of him wanted to storm out and give vent to his injured masculine pride. The rest of him wanted to solve the mystery. It seemed to hinge on one point—*my cousin warned me*.

He sat down on the bed. 'Tell me, Tallie. What exactly did our dear cousin Laetitia tell you about your marital duties?'

With much blushing and hesitation Tallie attempted to explain what her cousin had told her concerning her marital duties. 'And I have tried to remain still and dignified, truly I have…' She hung her head. 'I am sorry I have found it so difficult, but the…the things you do to me…well…'

Wide amber eyes, awash with tears, met his in a quick,

fugitive glance, and she dashed a small hand across her wet cheeks. Her nails were chewed to the quick. Magnus felt as if someone had reached into his chest and squeezed his heart until it hurt.

'Please, my lor—Magnus, let us try again. I promise I will behave better this time. I have found that saying my multiplication tables can be helpful…'

Magnus could not believe his ears. 'Saying *what* is helpful?'

She hung her head lower. Tawny locks tumbled around her face, hiding it from him and exposing her delicate, creamy nape. He longed to plant a kiss on it, but was too distracted by her incredible words.

'You have been saying your multiplication tables while I make love to you?'

'Yes,' she whispered.

'So that you will not be distracted by my lovemaking?'

A tiny sob came from beneath the mop of hair as she nodded.

'And you think that this will please me?'

She nodded again.

'Because my cousin told you I would have no respect for you if you responded? And that you would shame your family and mine if you did anything other than lie as still as a corpse?'

'Yes,' she snuffled.

Magnus did not know whether to laugh or explode with rage. Rage won.

'Bitch!' he swore violently.

Tallie flinched. Magnus saw it and swore again. 'I didn't mean you, my dear.' He reached out and laid his hand on her shoulder. He felt her tense, and his heart clenched in his chest again. So small and naive and vulnerable…and his—all his—despite his bitch of a cousin and her malicious attempt to ruin his marriage.

'Come here, sweetheart,' he murmured. 'I'm not angry. Not with you. Come, there is no need to be upset anymore.' Gently he slid an arm around her resisting body and pulled her against his side. She still wouldn't look at him. He could feel repressed sobs convulsing through her.

'My cousin is a spiteful, malicious bitch,' he said softly, 'and the advice she gave you was completely and utterly wrong.'

The sobs suddenly stopped on a long, shuddering gasp.

Magnus continued, stroking her soft, smooth skin as he spoke. 'She did it to cause trouble between us.' He paused, and tightened his arm around her. 'But she hasn't succeeded, has she? Because I'm not angry with you; I'm angry with her.'

Tallie let out a long, quavery sigh and at last he felt her relax against him. Something unwound inside Magnus.

'Come, Tallie, look at me,' he murmured, putting a gentle finger under her chin. Slowly she looked up at him, her woe-begone, tear-drowned face pale, her uptilted nose damp and rosy.

'You're not angry with me?' she whispered.

He shook his head. 'No. Are you angry with me?'

She stared at him, surprised, and suddenly tears began to well up in her eyes again. 'No, of course not,' she muttered, and with a tiny choke of relief fell into his arms. 'I love you, Magnus,' she wailed, and, completely overwrought, she burst into tears against his bare chest. Magnus gathered her close and held her tight, feeling as if the very foundations of his life had just been shattered.

I love you, Magnus.

Her head was tucked into the curve between his shoulder and his throat and he could feel the warmth and dampness of her tears as she sobbed, clutching him as if she'd never let him go. His cheek rested against her hair and he closed his eyes and held her and wondered what had become of him. Never in his life had he felt like this—so attached, so linked, so committed to another soul—and with absolutely no idea of what to do about it.

He was all at sea in a storm, with no anchor and no rudder and no one and nothing to guide him...except his heart...a heart which, in all his twenty-nine years, had neither given nor received love…

I love you, Magnus.

Oh, God. He groaned in despair and tightened his hold on her.

He did not know how much time passed, but eventually she left his arms and went behind the screen to wash her face. He lay on the bed, listening to the sounds of splashing water, imagining her movements. He felt exhausted, and for one cowardly moment thought of sneaking off to his own chamber before she returned. That way he could take the night to decide how best to deal with the situation. He had just eased himself upright and was preparing to slip off the bed when she returned, clad in a fresh nightgown. The look of soft expectancy in her eyes sent his spirits plummeting. She climbed onto the high bed and settled herself beside him.

'So…' She blushed rosily, unable to meet his eyes. 'If Laetitia was wrong…' She ran her finger back and forth along the hem of the sheet. 'How…? I mean, what should I…? How do you wish me to behave when we…you know?'

Magnus felt his throat tighten. He felt trapped, panic-stricken. What the devil should he say? Visions of the various women he had known flitted through his mind. Courtesans, sophisticated married women, widows—with painted faces, vulgar minds and quick, clever fingers. World-weary women, skilled in pleasing a man, who could calculate a man's needs and desires as quickly and efficiently as they calculated his income.

He did not want to teach his wife the tricks of their trade. He could not bear to imagine his innocent little Tallie earnestly and diligently learning how best to please him in bed as those women had. But he had to say something, offer her some guidance to replace Laetitia's poisonous advice… Only what? How? His mind was a complete blank.

'Magnus?' she prompted.

'Just…' He wiped a hand over his suddenly damp brow. Lord, who'd have thought marriage would be such a quagmire? It had seemed so simple and straightforward just a few weeks ago.

'Just be yourself,' he heard himself saying.

'But…'

'All I want from you are your honest reactions.'

She looked back at him, clear-eyed and doubtful, waiting for him to explain further.

'Don't hide anything,' he said, feeling suddenly as though he had stepped onto even more dangerous ground. 'Do and say exactly what you wish to. Honesty. That's all I require.'

'Honesty?' she said hesitantly. 'That's all you want from me?'

He nodded.

She beamed at him, and it was like the sun breaking through the morning mist. 'Then that will be easy.'

He stared back at her, uneasy at her apparent confidence. If she could be honest with him, then she would do more than any other woman in his life had done, his mother included.

'Easy?' He raised his eyebrows in doubt.

'Very easy,' she said, smiling radiantly and wriggling her fingers into his warm grip. 'A great deal easier than the multiplication tables, I can tell you. I am always making mistakes—especially with the eights.'

Magnus blinked for a moment, then from somewhere deep inside him he felt laughter begin to well up. 'The eights?' he gasped, grabbing her around the waist and pulling her down to the bed with him. His laughter echoed around the room and she rolled with him, clutching him and laughing with him. After a few minutes the deep chuckles slowed. He lifted his head and looked at her again, shaking his head. 'The eights?' he repeated.

'Utterly impossible,' she giggled.

His eyes darkened and became intent. 'Then from now on,' he said in a deep, slow voice, 'I suggest you concentrate on nothing but addition, starting from one plus one.' And he lowered his mouth to hers.

* * *

Tallie awoke very late next morning. Sunlight streamed through the open curtains and lay in slabs of gold across the floor of her chamber. She stretched and watched the dancing dust motes, feeling dreamy, pleasantly lazy and filled with contentment. She was alone in bed, but she did not feel lonely. Her husband had woken her at dawn and made love to her again. And then he'd kissed her and told her to go back to sleep and he'd gone out.

She had learnt many more things about the marriage act that night. The most important by far was that once she stopped fighting her own reactions it was utterly, thrillingly, splendid. She knew now why the vicar had said marriage was a holy estate, for there had been times, when her husband was making love to her, Tallie had known there could be no more wonderful feeling in heaven or on earth. And afterwards, when she had lain silently in her husband's warm strong arms, his hand caressing her hair while she listened to the beat of his heart slowly returning to normal, it had felt as if she was floating on a cloud, like the angels did.

She had been a little frightened at first about the extremity of her reactions, but Magnus had reassured her and encouraged her and continued that marvellous caressing and stroking. And then he had become rather extreme himself, she reflected, smiling a secret feminine smile. It was very exciting to think that a magnificent being like Magnus could be brought to such a state by ordinary little Tallie Robinson, she thought, snuggling into the pillows. She could still smell his scent on them, and if she shut her eyes she could imagine he was still here in bed with her.

'Milady?'

Tallie opened her eyes. Her new maid, Monique, stood there.

'Milady, your breakfast awaits you.' Monique indicated a tray containing Tallie's favourite French breakfast—sweet, flaky pastries and a large pot of hot milky chocolate. Reluctantly she sat up, then, blushing, clutched the sheet to her, recalling her nakedness. Monique showed no surprise, but came forward with a wrapper. '*Votre peignoir*, Milady.'

Tallie supposed that a dresser was used to seeing people without a stitch of clothing; it was she who had to get used to being seen. She was a long way now from Miss Fisher's establishment, where pupils had dressed and undressed beneath their voluminous nightgowns behind curtained screens. Married women had no privacy at all.

'Milor' d'Arenville said you are to go shopping after breakfast, Milady. I have ordered the bath, and laid out a gown for you. I thought per'aps we go first to the milliner, and then later to the glover, and after that…'

'After that we shall see,' said Tallie, deciding she needed to be firm about this shopping business. It was all very well to shop, but she wanted to see more of Paris, too. She wanted to experience as much as she could before they left for Italy.

'Where is my husband, do you know?' she asked, picking up a pastry.

''E 'as gone out, milady. 'E say to tell you 'e will back in time to escort you to dinner.'

Dinner? She was to wait until dinner to see him? Tallie was crushed. She did so want to see him now, after all they had shared during the night.

'Oh, but—'

We 'ave Claude, the footman, to escort us, milady,' Monique assured her. 'Milor' d'Arenville 'as left instructions that you are always to 'ave 'im as your escort, so you need not worry. All 'as been arranged by milor'.'

So it seems, thought Tallie, disappointed. Escort indeed! A paltry footman instead of her magnificent husband. She did not want to explore Paris with a maid and a footman—she wanted Magnus.

'Very well, then, I suppose we will have to waste the whole day shopping,' she said dolefully. 'Perhaps if we hurry we can get it all finished and out of the way today.'

Monique gave her an odd look, which Tallie ignored. She finished her pastries and the chocolate, had her bath, got dressed and went downstairs. Her new personal footman, Claude, awaited her in the hall. She blinked in surprise.

Claude was a most unlikely-looking footman. He was short, with a barrel chest and long arms which hung down like a gorilla. His face, too, had a simian quality; most of his teeth were missing and his skin was badly pitted with the pox. He was quite the ugliest man Tallie had ever seen in her life.

Wondering what on earth had possessed her husband to hire such an odd-looking footman, Tallie allowed herself to be escorted off in search of feminine falderals, Monique tripping beside her, Claude trudging heavily in the rear.

Hoofbeats pounded over the cold ground, echoing in the dim silence of the Bois de Boulogne. The hooves of the sweating horse tossed up clumps of grass and damp earth. Branches swatted its sides. But the rider held his mount with a firm hand and pressed on, faster, harder, as if to outride the devil himself.

But it was not possible to outride one's own thoughts and fears, thought Magnus, even as he spurred his horse to greater speed. He was on the brink. She'd driven him to it. He rode onwards, oblivious of his surroundings.

Was this how it had started with his father, too? With a declaration of love from an innocent bride? A lifetime of control, shattered in an instant…

He pulled up his sweating horse, dismounted and led it to a stream. The horse drank thirstily. Magnus leaned against the warm, heaving flank and stared into the fast-flowing water, listening to the burble of clear water over smooth round stones. Her eyes were like that, he thought—dappled with colour, clear and bright and glowing with life.

He groaned. Had his father also felt this aching chasm open up in him? This void, this abyss…of need. Was this how it had begun for him?

He knew how it had ended—a slow, inevitable descent into hell… A strong man of honour and dignity reduced to…what? A beggar at his wife's gate. A slavish worshipper, whose happiness, well-being and position—whose very honour—depended, in the end, entirely on his wife. A wife who cared for nothing but riches and the pleasures of the flesh—with whomever her roving eye descended on.

Magnus could not remember a time when his parents had not fought, lavishly and long. The bitter recriminations and violent rages. And each time ending with his mother giving his father that sultry come-hither smile, the smile which had invited him to her bed once again. And his father gratefully accepting—honour, dignity and self-respect forgotten—until the next time he discovered her with a handsome footman, a good-looking stableboy, one of his friends or even a passing gypsy.

Magnus had grown up swearing he would never let a woman make a fool of him that way. He'd resolved never to marry, never to allow a woman close enough to cause such damage. He'd thought it no hardship…until he'd held a sleeping toddler in his arms and realised he was depriving himself of children… And so he'd married. Thinking he could handle it. Believing he could keep his wife in her proper place—at arm's length.

But he'd chosen Tallie, naive, innocent Tallie, who needed a protector more than any female he knew. Who'd undermined his defences from the moment he married her. No, from even before that—he would never forget the sound of her sobbing in the maze that day. He should have walked away then…only he hadn't been able to leave her alone and unprotected, to fend for herself in the world.

Bedraggled little orphan that she was then, he'd never suspected how much he would come to desire her. Magnus closed his eyes in despair. He had never desired a woman so much in his life. And that had been prior to last night…last night, when she'd accepted his embrace with a joy and a sweet, loving passion that had left him shaking inside. And even now, hours later…

He'd thought he could slake his desire for her…he only craved her more…

Man of the world that he was, thinking he'd experienced everything a man and woman could do together—he'd never known it could be like that, two coming together as one, an explosion of sensation and emotion filling a void inside him he had never known existed.

When one blurted, tearful declaration of love had shattered a lifetime's resolution and sent him spinning towards the abyss.

I love you, Magnus.

Magnus remounted his horse and spurred it onwards.

He returned in the evening. Tallie was overjoyed to see him, and hurried forward for his kiss, but he turned away to remove his coat and hat. When he turned back to face her his visage was impassive and coolly polite. 'Did you have a good day?' he said, walking past her to a sideboard and pouring himself a drink.

'I…all right,' she faltered, a little thrown by his coolness.

'Enjoy the shopping?'

'N… I…er, yes, I suppose so. We did a lot of it. Monique insisted.'

'Very good. It is almost time for dinner, so I suggest you make yourself ready. We have been invited to dine with friends of Laetitia who are also visiting Paris—Lady Pamela Horton and her husband Lord Jasper. Shall we say one hour?' And with that he laid his glass aside, stood up and left the room, leaving Tallie staring after him.

What had happened? Was he angry with her for some reason? Why was he treating her as a polite stranger would? Where was her husband of last night? The man who'd called her sweetheart—twice—and held her tenderly in his arms while she wept? And then made magnificent, glorious love to her—not once, but three times in one night. Four, if you counted the wondrous morning episode.

Hurt and confused, Tallie allowed herself to be dressed in her new finery. As Monique added the final touches to her hair Tallie stared at herself in the mirror and ordered herself to stop moping. She should be thrilled—she was going to dine out with her husband and his friends. In Paris—the most romantic and exciting city in the world. And she was wearing the finest and most fashionable clothes she had ever worn in her life.

But she didn't feel thrilled at all... All she could do was wonder what had gone wrong, why Magnus was acting so distant and cold towards her when only that morning he had made love to her and kissed her goodbye so tenderly...

Oh! It was foolish to repine, Tallie told herself sternly.

It wasn't his fault if he did not love her—it was a marriage of convenience, after all. He hadn't been cruel—not even cross or irritable. Only reserved and distant. And very polite. It would be foolish in the extreme if she allowed herself to fall into a fit of the dismals merely because her husband was *polite* to her.

On that bracing thought Tallie left her chamber and joined her husband in the entrance hall.

'Lord and Lady d'Arenville.' The footman's announcement caused a small stir in the spacious and elegant salon. Lady Pamela, a tall, elegant woman dressed in a ravishing green dress, came forward and greeted Magnus warmly.

'Magnus, you wicked man, you're late. And this is your little wife. How do you do, my dear?' She cast a quick, indifferent glance over Tallie, who at once felt small and plain, despite her fashionable dress.

'Now, Magnus, there are a dozen people who wish to renew acquaintance with you. Oh, and here is Jasper. Take care of Lady d'Arenville, my dear.' And, slipping her arm through Magnus's, she led him away to join the throng.

Tallie watched with dismay, then recalled it was not *comme il faut* for a wife to dwell in her husband's pocket. She didn't wish to embarrass him, particularly on this, their first social engagement as a married couple. She turned to smile at Lord Jasper.

'Champagne, Lady d'Arenville?' he said, and without wait-

ing for her reply he beckoned a footman over and handed her
a glass.

'That'll do the trick, my dear. Now, who do you wish to
meet? Anyone you know?'

Tallie shook her head.

'Ah, well,' said Lord Jasper and shepherded her over to a
small knot of people. He quickly introduced her and a moment
later left. Tallie gripped her glass and did her best to join in
the conversation, much of which concerned people she didn't
know and places she hadn't been to. It was very difficult when
one had spent most of one's life in Miss Fisher's, where pupils
had been expected to be silent except when laboriously prac-
tising *conversazione* once a month over weak tea and stale
cakes. Miss Fisher's *conversazione* had been nothing like this.

It seemed an age before dinner was finally announced. Tallie was heartily glad of it—Magnus would come to take her
in to dinner and she could relax for a time. And besides, she
was ravenously hungry.

Tallie dipped her spoon in the lemon sorbet and tried not
to stare down the long table to where her husband was sitting.
With Lady Pamela. Talking and smiling and showing every
sign of enjoying himself. Sighing, she turned her head and
shouted once more at her neighbour. He was an elderly general, and deaf as a post. His deafness, however, did not prevent
him from firing question after question at her, obliging her to
shout responses into his ear trumpet. She glanced at her other
neighbour, a tall, thin, depressed-looking Polish man, who
spoke no English, very bad French and had the appetite—and
the table manners—of a starved gannet. His dinner was the
only company he required.

On the other side of the table a lively middle-aged Frenchwoman flirted light-heartedly with her neighbours. She caught
Tallie's eye several times and smiled in a friendly fashion.
Tallie smiled back shyly, wishing it was possible to join in,
but it would be dreadfully bad manners if she tried to talk

across the table. No, she was stuck with the General and the Gannet.

She glanced up to the head of the table. Lady Pamela had her hand on Magnus's sleeve, whispering in his ear. Tallie sighed, and shouted once more into the general's ear trumpet.

At long last the ladies retired, to leave the gentlemen to their port, but by that time Tallie's throat was quite sore from all her shouting. In any case, almost nobody spoke to her. The friendly Frenchwoman had left early and everybody else seemed to have known each other almost from the cradle.

She might as well be a Hottentot for all she had in common with these people, she thought, sipping her tea. Lady Pamela was just like Laetitia—all she did was talk about people who weren't there, and the nastier the story the more everybody laughed. Tallie sat with a teacup on her lap and smiled and tried to look interested and smiled some more, feeling as if her jaw would crack if she had to go on smiling much longer.

The Hottentot princess sat chained to the chair of the foreign invaders. She was hostage for the good behaviour of her husband, the Prince of all the Hottentots, but her spirit was not daunted and she did not feel betrayed by her husband's absence. These were her enemies, these foolish, arrogant people who spoke so freely in front of her. The Hottentot princess smiled at her enemies, but it was the smile of a sleeping tiger. Little did they realise she understood every word they said.

Very soon her dashing husband would come to rescue her. 'Tallie, my dearest love,' he would say. 'Let me rescue you from these evil ones whose tongues wag like chattering monkeys. You mean more to me than any kingdom or throne. I will take you to a place far away from here, where we can be alone.' The beautiful grey eyes of the Prince of all the Hottentots would darken, and he would bend and add, in that wonderfully deep voice which never failed to send shivers of delight through her, 'And then, my beloved Tallie, we will make love all night long, and again in the morning, too…'

But at the end of a very long evening, Magnus brought her

home, wished her goodnight, perfectly politely, and went to his own chamber.

Miserably, Tallie curled up into a small huddle in the middle of the large bed. It had become plain during the course of the evening that Magnus *was* angry with her. She had displeased him in some way. Some dreadfully significant way. Several times during the evening she had caught him staring at her, and the expression in his eyes had sent an icy chill down her spine.

It was if she had betrayed him in some way…almost as if he hated her. Tallie had obviously failed him…but she could not imagine how. True, she hadn't been very successful at the dinner, but she had tried…and he knew she'd mixed little in society. And besides, he'd been cold and distant to her before that.

But how could a man spend all night making passionate, tender love to his wife, and in the morning kiss her and call her sweetheart, and then return in the afternoon acting as if she had tried to destroy him?

When all she had done was love him?

Over and over in her brain, Tallie's thoughts churned, until she felt quite sick with misery.

The next day, when she awoke, Monique brought her the news that her husband had gone to stay with friends near Versailles. He would return in a week. Or two.

The first night Magnus was away Tallie cried herself to sleep. She had visited an art gallery during the day. The second night he was away she cried herself to sleep again. But during the day she had attended an outdoor puppet show, and gone for a promenade with Monique and Claude in the park. She might be unhappy, and upset with her husband, but she didn't want the world to know it.

The next morning Tallie had a visitor: the French lady she'd seen at Lady Pamela's—Madame Girodoux. Tallie was feeling utterly blue-devilled, but didn't have the heart to say she was not at home. Besides, she was lonely. Company might cheer her up.

Madame Girodoux swept into the room. She was a widow in her forties, very thin, very fashionable and very sophisticated, but there was kindness in her narrow, sloe-dark eyes. She seated herself beside Tallie on the chaise longue and chatted for a short time, but in the middle of a story she suddenly broke off, took Tallie's hand in hers and said, 'You must forgive my forwardness, my dear, but I was an unhappy young bride once, and I recognise the symptoms.'

At her words Tallie burst into tears.

'Now, *chérie*,' said Madame Girodoux some time later, 'it seems to me as though your young man 'as bitten off more than 'e can chew.'

Tallie blinked. 'What do you mean?'

'It was a *mariage de convenance, n'est-ce-pas*?'

Tallie nodded.

'But you 'ave fallen in love, *oui*?'

Tallie nodded again. Madame Girodoux smiled. 'I think per'aps you are not the only one.'

Tallie blinked again.

'I have noticed your 'usband watching you—it is not the look of a man who is indifferent.'

'No, he… I think he dislikes—'

'Nonsense! I have 'eard of your 'usband before this. They call him The Icicle, *non*?'

Tallie nodded.

'Well, I see no ice in 'im when 'e looks at you, my dear. I see fire.'

'Fire?'

'*Oui*. Fire, to be sure. *Absolument*. And when ice meets fire, something must crack—and it is not the fire, believe me. Your 'usband is afraid, but 'e will return and the ice will disappear.' She patted Tallie's hand. ''E will not be able to stay away from you for long, *petite*—'e will be back soon. That will make you 'appy, *non*?' She eyed Tallie shrewdly. 'Your bed is lonely, *non*?'

Tallie felt a fiery blush flood her face.

Madame Girodoux chuckled. 'Yes, I thought so. The bed has a way of melting ice. May I give you some advice? I 'ave been married twice, you know, both times very 'appily—though the first one started badly.'

Tallie nodded, a little embarrassed at the other woman's frankness, but eager to hear her advice.

'No doubt when your 'usband returns you will be ready to do anything to please him. Per'aps entice 'im to your bed again.'

Tallie blushed rosily once more.

Madame Girodoux chuckled. 'No shame in that, *chérie*, but women need to use their brains as well as their bodies when it comes to marriage. It does an 'usband no harm to be kept a little uncertain at times—remember that when your man comes back to you. Men respond to the uncertainty of the chase.'

Tallie blinked. Magnus was not chasing her—on the contrary; he was running away. But she nodded, pretending to understand.

Madame Girodoux stood up. 'Now, my dear, run upstairs and wash your face. My nephew, Fabrice, will be 'ere in thirty minutes to take us to a concert. When your 'usband returns to Paris you will not wish him to know you 'ave been pining for 'im. I 'ave many social engagements planned for you—and it will do you good to go about more in society, *non*?'

Tallie's head was spinning, but she knew a lifeline when she saw it. She blinked back tears. 'You have been so very kind to me, *madame*, and I am no one—a stranger. How can I thank—?'

'*Ah, non.*' Madame Girodoux brushed Tallie's thanks aside gruffly. 'We are all strangers at first—*oui*—but 'ow else can we make new friends, eh? Now, run upstairs, child, and wash your face. Fabrice will be here any moment.'

True to her word, Madame Girodoux arranged all of Tallie's entertainment over the next ten days. With the willing escort of her nephew Fabrice, an elegant young fop, she showed Tallie a new side of Paris. Tallie made morning calls, attended concerts, routs and soirées. She still missed Magnus desperately, still felt as though she had failed him in some indefinable way, but now, with Madame Girodoux's assistance, she was learning to cope with the public aspects of her new life, at least.

But after a week had passed without a single word from Magnus, Tallie had begun to feel aggrieved. It was not right that he had left her to sink or swim in a foreign city. He was careless and thoughtless and cold-hearted. Obviously their night of passion meant absolutely nothing to him. The most wonderful night of her entire life and the very next day he'd gone off to some horrid hunting lodge. He didn't even seem to care whether she loved him or not, for how could he abandon her like this if he did?

And the worst thing was she still loved him—cold-hearted Icicle that he was!

Chapter Eleven

Two days later, in the evening, Magnus returned. Tallie was in the hall, about to leave for a concert. Mindful of Madame Girodoux's advice, Tallie greeted him coolly. He responded with equal politeness, quite as if he'd been away for an hour or two instead of abandoning her for days on end. He offered no word of explanation for his absence. That omission gave Tallie the courage she needed. She wished him a polite 'Good evening,' and sailed out of the *hôtel* to attend the concert.

Stunned, furious, Magnus watched her blithely step into a strange carriage. He'd spent the last two weeks missing her, fighting his desire to return to Paris immediately and take her straight to bed. He'd told himself he could handle it, handle her, that he would not fall in thrall to her like his father had to his mother. He'd kept himself busy during the day, riding, hunting, playing cards and drinking. But at night all he'd been able to think of was the sweet, loving way she'd responded to his caresses, and her words—*I love you, Magnus.*

The abyss had beckoned blackly. But the craving to hear those words again had grown within him until he'd been well-nigh unable to think of anything else, and so, with distracted words of thanks and farewell to his hosts, he'd ridden back, all the way to Paris, imagining her falling into his arms the moment he walked in the door.

He'd pictured it a thousand times, her start of surprise, pleasure and welcome. He would carefully remove his hat and coat, careful not to show her how much power she had over him. She would be waiting anxiously, that sweet look of anticipation and desire in her clear amber eyes, her tender body swaying gently towards him. He'd force himself to wait…and dinner would be spiced with anticipation and desire.

And at the end of dinner she would look at him, that wide-eyed look which never failed to move him, and he would wait no more. He would lay his table napkin down, push back his chair, walk around the table and hold out his hand. She would place her small, trembling hand in his and he'd raise her to her feet and escort her to his bedchamber. And then…

Instead, damn it, she'd greeted him politely, chatted for five minutes about how busy she had been while he was away and gone out to a concert with some damned French female! And an elegant blasted French fop!

'Where the *devil* have you been, madam?' demanded Magnus as he followed her into the breakfast parlour next morning. 'And who was that puppy who handed you out of his carriage just now?' It was the same fellow who'd escorted her last night. The fellow who'd be dead by now had Magnus not heard her return the previous night at about eleven. He'd also heard her lock her door, which had infuriated him, but he'd decided to deal with that in the morning. But when he'd awoken this morning, and found a spare key, he'd entered her chamber only to find her gone. And his rage had grown.

Tallie pulled up short at his accusatory tone. Where the devil had *she* been? *Madam!* When *he* had been absent for two long weeks! 'I told you about it last night,' she said indignantly.

He glared. 'I don't remember any arrangement about you leaving here at some ungodly hour of the morning. Where in Hades did you get to? And with whom?'

Tallie remembered Madame Girodoux's advice about quarrels and tried to quell her shaking insides. She carefully removed her hat and laid it on the side-table. Glancing in a gilt-framed looking glass, she took her time tidying her still-damp hair, well aware that her husband was glowering at her back.

He would have to learn she did not care to be spoken to in this tone before breakfast, particularly when she knew perfectly well she had done nothing wrong. He might well have forgotten where she'd said she was going, but he should know she never took a step outside without Claude, his tame gorilla, in tow. And *he* was the one who'd taught her that husbands and wives did not live in each other's pockets. Sauce for the gander and all that.

Finding her hair sufficiently tidy, she went to the sideboard and selected warm rolls, scrambled eggs and kedgeree, then seated herself at the table.

'Mmm, this kedgeree smells delicious. Have you tried it, my lord?' If I am to be 'madam' then he can be 'my lord', she thought rebelliously.

He slammed his fist down on the table. 'Damn it, Tallie, where the devil did you get to? You weren't in your bed when I woke.'

Tallie's annoyance dissipated in a rush of warmth. He had wanted her when he woke. He had missed her. Frustration— that was why he was so cross. Good. She hid a tiny smile and took a bite of eggs.

'Do you not recall, my lord?' she said when she had swallowed. 'I had an engagement to visit a bathing establishment with Madame Girodoux.'

'At half past seven in the morning?'

Tallie nodded, her mouth full of kedgeree. 'Yes,' she said eventually, 'but it was worth it. Do you know? They scent the bath water with any perfume you wish—eau de cologne, rosewater, lavender—even salt water if you want, which I believe is frightfully healthful. The *parfumier* even offered to create a scent especially for me.' Tallie blushed, remembering how the dapper *parfumier* had kissed her hand and called her *la belle Milady Anglaise*.

Magnus watched the pretty colour rising in her cheeks. He frowned. His desire for her was well-nigh unbearable.

'But I asked for lily-of-the-valley instead.' She raised her wrist to her nose and sniffed. 'Mmm, lovely, don't you think? It was the most wonderful place. Each bath is large, and so deep you can have hot water almost to your neck, and you just sit there in this deliciously scented water and look out onto an exquisite little garden simply filled with red roses—quite private, of course. I've never seen anything so lovely or exotic.' She blushed again, recalling how she had wallowed for over an hour in the deepest bath, dreaming of how Magnus would take one whiff of her, sweep her into his arms and make violent, passionate love to her.

Magnus's frown darkened. Her words painted a very vivid picture—one he could imagine only too well. His wife, pink and naked in her bath, her skin slick with water and scented oils, fragrant clouds of steam swirling around her, and outside a flower garden, giving the illusion of being out in the open. It sounded as if the bath would have been large enough for two. He swallowed, his mouth suddenly dry, his body throbbing, painfully aroused.

'And that damned French puppy?' he growled.

She made a moue of irritation. 'He is not a puppy, but a very pleasant and gentlemanly young man, my lord. Fabrice Dubout—Madame Girodoux's nephew. I...I took a little longer than expected in the bath, and Madame Girodoux had another engagement, so she asked Fabrice to escort me home.' Tallie bit into a roll.

'And on the strength of this brief acquaintance you call him Fabrice?' he grated.

Tallie glared across the table at her husband and set down her cup with a snap. 'Yes!'

Oh! He was infuriating. He could go off to who knew where, doing who knew what, leaving her behind, hurt, confused and lonely, and then return, growling and snarling like a suspicious wolf! Pretending to believe she would behave immorally. As if she would.

He knew perfectly well that she loved him—she'd told him so. And even if she hadn't fallen in love with a horrid, suspicious man, she had taken vows of fidelity and she would *never* break them, no matter how fashionable it was. And even if she *did* wish to betray him, how could she, when she was accompanied everywhere by the ubiquitous Claude?

No, Magnus was just being disagreeable because when he had returned she hadn't behaved as he'd expected her to, and when he'd awoken she hadn't been where he'd expected her to be. Madame Girodoux was right—a little uncertainty *was* good for a husband.

'I am invited to a *thé* this morning, my lord. Do you care to accompany me?'

'A what?' The frown had not left his face, but she refused to give in and explain herself.

'A *thé*.' Tallie smiled. 'Being English, we are known to adore tea—'

'Can't stand the stuff, myself.'

'I know, and though the French firmly believe their *thés* are English through and through, any resemblance to an English tea party is purely coincidental, I promise you.' Tallie smiled reminiscently, recalling her first *thé*.

It was not the consumption of alcohol as well as tea, and the combination of children's games and gambling which had surprised Tallie at first—it was the French ladies' tea gowns.

Parisian women seemed to cover themselves more with cosmetics than clothing. To English eyes, their gowns left the ladies almost in a state of nature, being so light and almost transparent, and having *no* sleeves and baring the *whole* of the neck. It was a little disconcerting to address oneself to an elderly dowager attired as flimsily and inadequately as one of the statues in the Louvre—Tallie hadn't known where to look. She smiled again, imagining her husband's face when she appeared in her own French tea gown, only half as daring.

'And I suppose if I do not escort you to this blasted *thé*, that damned puppy will.' His voice bristled with dark suspicion.

'Yes, Fabrice will escort me…if I ask him.' She met her husband's gaze in a direct challenge.

'Hrmph!' Magnus fiddled with his coffee cup for a moment. 'It might be interesting to see how the French botch a simple tea party,' he said at last.

Tallie hid a smile. 'In that case, I must rush and change, for we leave at ten.'

Magnus watched her hurry from the room, noting the enticing sway of her hips and the damp wispy curls that tumbled around the nape of her neck. A faint trace of lily-of-the-valley hung in the air. It took all his resolution not to follow her up to her bedchamber.

Damn and blast it all. He was getting deeper and deeper into her toils. It had shocked him to realise how bereft he had felt when he'd looked for her that morning and found her gone. For one wild moment he'd thought she'd left him, and the feeling of abandonment and devastation still haunted him. He'd imagined all sorts of things, and when he'd seen her being handed down from a strange carriage by a mincing, hand-kissing Frenchman he'd been filled with a mixture of relief and rage.

She was picking up female tricks, he realised. Getting herself a damned Froggy *cicisbeo*. And when he'd challenged her about it, had she acted guilty or distressed? No! She had stared at him with those big amber eyes and got him all hot and bothered talking about a bath big enough for two.

It had been a mistake to leave her in Paris on her own. And perhaps she was a little annoyed with him—yes, that was it. She *wasn't* like his mother—not really. He was a fool even to consider it…

Dark uncertainty gnawed at him.

Damn it! If tea was what it took to keep his wife where she belonged, then he would drink gallons of the filthy stuff.

'Madame Girodoux has invited me to go vagabondising this evening,' said Tallie as they returned home. Her husband glowered silently from the corner of the carriage. He had not said a word since she had removed her cloak on arrival at the *thé*. Revealing her new pale gold French tea gown.

It was perfectly respectable—compared with most of the other ladies' gowns. But after his first stunned glance his eyes had narrowed to icy chips, and an even blacker frown had descended on his face.

He'd said not a word to a soul all afternoon. And to think she had once thought his manners were beautiful. He hadn't taken his eyes off her for an instant. Tallie had found that dark, icy glare decidedly unnerving, but her courage had been bolstered by Madame Girodoux's smiles and nods of approval.

And so Tallie had mentioned the vagabondising excursion, knowing full well Magnus would disapprove.

Magnus snorted wrathfully. 'Madame Girodoux and her simpering blasted nephew, I suppose.'

Tallie shrugged. '*Madame* did not mention who else was in the party, but it would not surprise me if Fabrice were included. She is very fond of him.'

Magnus grunted. 'What exactly does "vagabondising" mean?'

'I'm not entirely certain, but I think it means exploring the less respectable parts of Paris by night. It sounds utterly thrilling, does it not?' Still a little nervous about these tactics, Tallie forced herself to smile sunnily at him. She wished she had not to resort to stratagems to gain his attention… It would be wonderful if he craved her company as much as she craved his…but she was learning to cut her coat to suit her cloth. And if stratagems were what it took, then so be it. And he *had* responded to her gown in a wonderfully jealous manner.

Magnus glowered at her. 'I think I know as much about the night life of Paris as *madame* or her precious nephew. Would you object if I escorted you on my own private tour?'

'Oh, Magnus, it would be utterly splendid!' Tallie exclaimed and, jumping up, she flung her arms around him and pressed a fervent kiss on his mouth.

Taken by surprise, Magnus hesitated for a moment. Tallie started to draw back, but before she could he gathered her into a hungry embrace and was kissing her with unrestrained passion. He drew her onto his lap, kissing her hard, his mouth devouring her, one large, warm hand cupping her head in a firm, tender hold, the other possessively roaming her body, caressing, seeking, bringing her to the brink of pleasure.

'Oh, Magnus,' she gasped, overwhelmed by his unexpected move. She kissed him back with all the love in her heart, her anger forgotten. She slipped her hand into his shirt and rubbed the palm of her hand over his chest in a way she knew he liked. She felt a glow of feminine satisfaction, feeling him shudder beneath her fingers.

The carriage rumbled to a halt and they fell apart as the door was pulled open by a footman. Magnus stepped out and held out his hand to help her down, his eyes burning into hers. Blushing, she descended the steps and entered the house with her hand still clasped firmly in his.

As the front door closed behind them he swung her into his arms and took the stairs, two at a time, seeming not even to notice her weight. She clung to his neck, delighted with his passionate impetuosity, so unlike her Icicle. He kicked open the door of his bedchamber, stepped inside, kicked it shut and laid her carefully on his bed.

He took the neckline of her gown in his long, strong fingers, saying, 'You'll not wear this blasted thing in public again,' and ripped it open in one dramatic move. Tallie was utterly thrilled. His eyes darkened as they moved over her partially revealed body. He wrenched off his beautifully arranged neckcloth and flung his shirt away. 'I think, madam wife, any engagements you have made for this afternoon will have to remain unfulfilled.'

Tallie smiled naughtily up at him. 'Yes, but I doubt whether I will.'

He looked startled for a moment, and then eyed her hungrily. 'Nor will I, my dear. Nor will I,' he muttered hoarsely, and lowered his mouth to hers.

That night, Magnus took her out vagabondising—after ensuring she was muffled to the ears and buttoned to the neck. He directed the carriage to a part of the city Tallie had never seen, where the streets were narrow and dark and vaguely threatening. They were, nonetheless, full of people dressed in all sorts of costumes: gaudy women with painted faces, beggars and cripples, elegantly dressed gentlemen, shopkeepers, soldiers… Tallie almost slipped on the oily cobblestones, and Magnus held her clamped tight to his side. Claude loomed in the gloom several paces behind them, and for once Tallie was glad of his fearsome visage.

'After you, my dear,' said Magnus, stopping at a doorway lit by painted lanterns. He ushered her down the stairs into a dark and mysterious place called a cabaret. They found a table and called for drinks. Tallie's was bright green. She eyed it with suspicion.

'Does it not meet with my lady's favour?' Magnus said, quirking an eyebrow.

On her mettle, Tallie sipped it cautiously, then smiled. 'It tastes of peppermint.'

Magnus's white teeth glinted in the candlelight.

Setting down her glass, Tallie looked around her. All sorts of people of all walks of life rubbed elbows and mingled in the smoky gloom. Grimy crimson curtains hung across a small stage.

'What do the curtains conceal?' she asked.

'Wait and see.'

After a few moments a dwarf came forward, dressed as a Turk, with a red fez. With a shout of something unintelligible, he pulled aside the curtains and scattered applause filled the room as a sultry, exotic-looking woman came forward. She was dressed, quite indecently, in red satin and black lace. She sang several songs which had all the gentlemen chuckling, including Magnus.

'She has a lovely voice,' whispered Tallie, 'but I can hardly understand a word. Will you tell me what the songs are about?'

Magnus looked at her, a faint smile on his face, then shook his head. Tallie opened her mouth to argue, but suddenly a group of scantily clad dancers whooped onto the dance floor, twirling glittering scarves and performing some exotic dance to the rhythm of drums and wailing music. Their movements left Tallie in no doubt of what the dance, at least, was about. She stared, wide-eyed, feeling her cheeks warming. Magnus stood up, frowning, and said brusquely, 'It's time we moved on, I think.'

Tallie's face fell. 'Oh, no, it cannot be time to go home already, can it?'

He looked down at her and his frown softened. 'No, there's plenty more to see, little vagabond. Only not here, I think.'

'Oh, I suppose you are right,' said Tallie reluctantly. 'Those dances are vastly improper, aren't they?'

Her husband gave a choke of laughter and took her arm. 'Outside,' he said. 'Now.'

They took a carriage to a place beside the Seine, where a crowd of people were gathered in a large circle, watching. Magnus, keeping Tallie safe in the circle of his arm, shouldered his way to a place where she could see. Tallie felt as if there were just herself and Magnus in the world, as if everything else was just a magical many-splendoured rhapsody whirling around then, binding them together in a spell of enchantment.

Acrobats dressed in glittering finery leapt and tumbled on a tattered cloth of red and gold, while a one-legged man played merry tunes on an organ. Then a pair of young girls came out, looking as innocent as schoolgirls. They twirled and tossed burning brands, leaving trails of fire hanging in the dark night air. And finally, to the gasps of the crowd, they swallowed the fire, then spat out whooshing bursts of flame, bowing and smiling afterwards, apparently quite unhurt. Tallie clapped her hands until they hurt.

Then there was a puppet show about a young girl lost in the forest, and a dragon and a brave bold knight, and Tallie's heart was in her mouth. She knew they were just puppets, but she clasped Magnus tight even so and was glad of his warmth.

They watched until there was no more to see, then strolled on beside the silently flowing Seine. They ate hot nuts cooked on a brazier before their eyes, and Magnus had to lend Tallie his handkerchief to wipe her greasy fingers. And he kissed her in the darkness and tasted salt on her lips.

Later, following the sound of music down a dark lane, they came to a small, open courtyard, where gypsies sang and leapt and gyrated under flaming torches, their heels tapping out a frenzied tattoo, their guitars and throats sobbing with tragic passion. Tallie found them very moving, even though she could understand none of the words, and she clutched her husband's arm and watched the gypsies with tears in her eyes.

And Magnus dried Tallie's eyes and took her home and made love to her, first with an urgency and passion that left her gasping with ecstasy, then later with such tenderness she found herself weeping again. Only this time he did not dry her tears, but kissed them away, and held her in his arms until they both fell asleep.

The next evening they went to the Théâtre Français to see Fleury, the most famous actor in all France. It was Tallie's first visit to a theatre, and though it was hot, stuffy and crowded, she found it quite wondrous and fantastical. Her husband found he could barely take his eyes off her enraptured face, and when he brought her home that night he made slow, sensual love to her, marvelling at her passionate response, fearing and hungering for her to say it again. *I love you, Magnus.*

But she didn't say it.

Magnus accompanied her everywhere. He took her to the new Palais Royale, which contained libraries, gambling houses, coffee houses, pawnbrokers, jewellers, ice shops, exhibition rooms, theatres and even a chess club. They attended balls and masquerades. And each night they made magical, tender love.

And she seemed happy, Magnus thought. She told him once in sweet exhaustion that she imagined two people could feel no closer than when making love. He wanted to tell her it could also be the loneliest feeling in the world, that it had been for him—until her. But he couldn't.

And she never again said the words he both craved and dreaded. *I love you, Magnus.*

'Milady,' said Monique one morning while she was arranging Tallie's hair. 'When do you think your baby will be born?'

Tallie stared in surprise at the reflection of her maid in the looking glass. 'Baby? What do you mean, Monique?'

'*Oui*, you are *enceinte*, are you not, milady?'

'*Enceinte?* I have no idea.'

The maid frowned. 'But, milady, I 'ave been with you more than seven weeks now.'

'Yes, it would be about that. But what does that signify?'

'In all that time you 'ave not 'ad your monthly courses.'

Tallie's eyes widened. 'No, that's right,' she said slowly. 'How clever of you to notice. But what has that to do with a baby?'

Monique explained.

'Really?' exclaimed Tallie. 'So that's how one knows... And you really think I am increasing?'

'*Oui*, milady. Unless your courses are always irregular?'

Tallie shook her head. 'No, never. I just thought I had missed them because of being married or travelling or something.' She felt a quiver of excitement ripple through her. A baby. How wonderful.

Monique smiled at her mistress. 'Lord d'Arenville will be very pleased, yes?'

Tallie froze. Once her husband discovered she was increasing, he would want to take her home to England and d'Arenville Hall. He had said so in no uncertain terms.

And then she'd never get to Italy.

And getting to Italy was almost as important to Tallie as her baby was. She had delayed too long in Paris as it was. There was something much more important at stake here than mere pleasure. She had been selfish and thoughtless and had allowed herself to be seduced by pleasures and entertainments.

'No, Monique,' she slowly. 'I will not tell my husband just yet. It will be our little secret, agreed?'

Monique looked troubled. 'If you say so, milady.'

'I do,' said Tallie firmly. 'And now, if you please, we must make preparations to leave Paris.'

'Leave Paris?' gasped Monique.

'Yes, in three days, I think,' said Tallie firmly. 'You will come with us, will you not? To Italy?'

Marie shrugged. 'Of course, milady. Why not? I 'ave never been to Italy. But milor'—will 'e wish to go so suddenly?'

Tallie smiled. 'You may leave milor' to me.'

Chapter Twelve

'Oh,' said Tallie, stretching luxuriously in her canvas seat and gazing contentedly at the passing scenery. They had left Paris three days before by coach, but had transferred to a barge that morning. 'This is indeed much more agreeable than I had expected it to be. How pretty those fields and vineyards are. And how smooth the water slipping by.'

Magnus smiled. The barge trip had been suggested by Luigi Maguire, the major-domo hired to make arrangements for the journey, a Frenchman with an Italian mother and an Irish father. Maguire was already proving his worth.

'I did tell you it would be easier on the bones than a carriage, but you wouldn't have it, would you? Now confess—you thought you would get seasick, didn't you?'

Tallie nodded. 'You are right, as usual. Oh, the Rhone is such a pretty river. How long do you think it will take before we reach Italy?'

Magnus frowned. There was something peculiar about her sudden rush to get to Italy. Of course, she had told him once that she wished to go there—to visit her parents' graves, or some such thing—but he'd thought she'd forgotten about it. Certainly one would have thought the delights of Paris would more than compensate for what could only be a duty visit, after all. But she was adamant, and he was finding it more and more difficult to refuse his wife anything these days. He pushed aside the unwelcome thought…

But if they wanted to get to Italy, they had to cross over the Mount Cenis Pass. Magnus repressed a shudder. He hated heights, and would infinitely have preferred to go by ship, but with his wife's tendency to seasickness there was no question of it. It had been difficult enough to persuade her to travel down the Rhone in a flat-bottomed boat. Besides, there was always the danger of pirates in the Mediterranean.

'According to Maguire, we will remain on this barge for at least five days,' he said. 'Until we reach Avignon. And I thought we could rest there for a week or so. You will want to visit the Palais des Papes, and several other sights.'

'Oh, no, I do not think that would interest me very much,' responded Tallie mendaciously. 'I have seen a great many palaces now, and one more, even if it belonged to a pope, is no great thing. I am not greatly interested in popes.'

Magnus regarded her thoughtfully. 'I did hear,' he said casually, 'that some people prefer to view the Palace des Papes by moonlight…'

'Moonlight?' Her eyes lit up, as he had known they would. Tallie thought for a moment. 'Perhaps if we stay in Avignon for just a day or two, then.'

Magnus repressed a smile. It was becoming easier to calculate his wife's tastes. He watched her as she turned her head back towards the riverbanks. He had found so much of his life dull and tedious before his marriage. But Tallie's open fascination with all sorts of things had opened his eyes to a host of small pleasures and interests and he was beginning to see the world differently. It was probably a sign of weakness, he knew, but there seemed nothing he could do about it.

After Avignon, they returned to their coach, which had also been transported on the barge. The roads were a little rough, and Magnus had been worried his wife would be sickened by the incessant jolting. Instead, she spent most of the journey peering out of the window and deriving great enjoyment from the way the postilions leaped out of their enormous jackboots at every stop, leaving the boots in the stirrups until a new man came out and leapt into the same boots.

Finally the roads narrowed and their pace slowed as they climbed higher into the foothills of the Alps. Tallie called to Magnus, who was riding. 'Magnus, I don't think these poor horses can pull us any more. It's getting terribly steep. Whatever shall we do?' She stared up into the mountains. 'They cannot possibly pull us over those mountains.'

'We stop at the next village,' he called back. 'The coach will be dismantled and mules and men will carry it, and us, over the pass.'

'Carry the coach?' she squeaked in amazement. 'Are you hoaxing me?'

He grinned. 'Wait and see.'

They stopped for the night at the next village, and in the morning Tallie saw the coach had been dismantled and bound with rope into a number of huge packages. A dozen men and as many mules were assembled outside the tiny inn. There was much shouting and discussion as the packages was strapped to the mules under the supervision of Maguire. John Black, Magnus's coachman, watched with phlegmatic English disapproval.

'Oh, the poor things,' Tallie said, clutching Magnus's sleeve in distress. 'Those bundles are far too big and heavy for such dear little animals.'

'The porters know what they are about, my dear. Do not concern yourself, they've all—men and mules—done this trip many a time before today.'

Tallie looked around. 'And how do we travel?'

'By mule, I believe,' he replied.

Tallie looked aghast. 'I cannot ride a mule.'

Magnus frowned. 'You have no choice. There are no horses.'

'It would make no difference if there were. I cannot ride. I have never been on the back of an animal in my life.'

Magnus was stumped. He had never heard of such a thing. Everyone he knew rode; even the females. 'What, never?'

She shook her head and bit her lip worriedly.

Magnus walked over to Maguire and the head porter and a brief discussion ensued. Maguire called out an order and a young boy emerged from a nearby barn, carrying a large, odd-shaped wicker basket. He began to strap it to the back of a mule.

Tallie observed the preparations with deep mistrust.

Magnus's lips twitched.

'I am not going over the Alps in that!' she muttered mutinously.

'Then there is no point in continuing. We shall return to Paris at once,' responded Magnus.

She flung him a black look, then stalked over to the mule and waited to be helped into the basket. One of the porters reached towards her to do it, but Magnus was there before him. He swung his wife into his arms and set her sideways in the basket. 'There you are,' he said, tucking a thick bearskin around her to protect her from the cold. It emitted a pungent odour uncomfortably reminiscent of its original unfortunate inhabitant. Tallie wrinkled her nose. Magnus bent forward and kissed her lightly on it. 'As snug as a bug in a rug.'

She gave him a baleful look. 'I feel very silly. Why can I not walk, like those men?'

He didn't respond, but glanced over to where Monique, with shrieks and giggles, was being installed likewise on another mule.

'Oh, very well,' said Tallie crossly. 'I shall behave myself—but I feel ridiculous.'

'Sometimes we must sacrifice dignity for expediency,' said Magnus austerely, and walked away.

The ascent was slow and tortuous, the pathway narrowing visibly until it seemed to Tallie's eyes no more than a few inches wide. It was amazing how the porters even knew which was the path, for there were goat tracks leading off it at almost every turn. The men took it in turns to carry the huge packs of their belongings. Tallie thought of all the shopping she had done and felt guilty.

However, she soon cheered up, because the scenery was magnificent: enormous jagged peaks and rough crags, the occasional twisted tree, gnarled and bent by the harsh weather. And the higher they climbed the colder it became, even though it was summer.

The track was narrow and tortuous, but Tallie had no time to be concerned. The most splendid, awe-inspiring vistas lay all around her, and fresh delights were revealed with each turn of the track and each minor peak accomplished. She had never seen anything like it in her life—only imagined it from books like Mrs Radcliffe's.

And silence seemed to hang in the air all around them. She could see some bird of prey, a falcon or a hawk, perhaps, circling with grim patience over a crag in the distance. She watched it bank and soar effortlessly, then suddenly dive out of sight, and she shivered, imagining some poor tiny creature caught in its talons. The air was cold and crisp and so pure that she felt almost dizzy breathing it. All she could hear was the stomping of the heavy boots of the men walking close to her and the occasional musical ringing of a mule's horseshoes on a stone. The sound carried in the still, crystal air, rebounding and repeating from the jagged peaks.

Tallie had never heard such a superb echo. She could not resist it.

'Helloooo,' she called. The echo came back to her from a dozen distant crags. Ahead of her Magnus turned on his mule and looked back, as if concerned. She waved. 'Hellooo, echo,' she called again and, 'Echo-echo-echo,' her words came back to her.

One of the porters grinned at her delighted face and began to sing. In seconds others joined in, strong male voices, deep and true, ringing through the mountains with the joy of being young and strong and alive. Someone up ahead began a harmony and another man joined him, then another. An older man

with a thick white beard began a third line of harmony, a deep
bass, and more voices joined him. The mountains threw back
the sound, magnifying it and leaving a trail of echoes to mingle with the harmonies. It was better by far than any choir
Tallie had heard. It had none of the solemnity and restraint of
a choir. There was something special about a score or more
lusty male voices, ringing in the open air, echoing with the
confidence of strength and vigour as their heavy boots
pounded out the rhythm. Music rolled and swirled and echoed
around the mountains.

Tallie was enchanted. She sat spellbound, drinking in the
wonder of what was happening. Here was plain, ordinary Tallie Robinson—who had once thought she would never go anywhere—and now look at her! Almost at the very top of the
world, gazing at what was surely one of the most utterly splen-
diferous sights imaginable. And listening to the most glorious
music in the world. And up ahead rode her handsome, magnificent husband. And she was almost in Italy, where she
should be able to discover the truth about her mother's death.
And she was going to have a baby. The cold mountain air
prickled at her eyes and she had to grope for a handkerchief
to wipe her eyes. It was odd how easily she cried these days,
she reflected, when really she had nothing to cry about.

She finished wiping her eyes, then, noticing one of the porters watching her, began to clap her cold hands in time to the
music, humming along to the tune. With the singing, the time
passed more quickly, until at last the porters stopped and Magnus came to lift her out of the basket.

'Could you hear the singing from up ahead? Wasn't it utterly wonderful?' she said, stretching her cramped limbs.

'Very nice,' he responded. 'Are you warm enough?' He
took her small cold hands in his and began to chafe them
gently. His hands were not exactly warm themselves, and she
became concerned when she saw he looked rather heavy-eyed
and preoccupied.

'Are you all right?' she asked.

He shrugged. 'Picked up a bit of a chill, I suspect. Nothing to worry about. Now, I think those fellows have brandy, or some such local brew. I want you to have a little—keep the cold out.'

She looked around. 'Magnus, what are they doing?'

The porters were unloading the mules. Magnus went to discuss it with them. He came back, a faint grin on his face.

'This is as far as the mules go. And now, my dear, you will have to resign yourself to being carried.'

Sure enough, the men had brought out some rough-looking woven wicker litters attached to crude poles. They gestured to Magnus, and Tallie went forward reluctantly.

In minutes she was installed in a litter, tied down—for safety, they said—and packed in straw, as well as bearskins, for warmth. 'I feel ridiculous,' she said. Magnus chuckled and wound a thick woollen shawl around her face.

'You look quite delightful, my dear.'

Tallie could hardly move, so she directed an almost invisible glare at him.

'Monsieur?' said a porter. Magnus turned. The porter gestured to another litter, sitting beside Tallie's. 'Please, *monsieur*, we must hurry.'

'What? I don't need a blasted litter!' said Magnus, outraged.

The porter shrugged. 'It is the only way, *monsieur*. The way we move, no one who was not born in these mountains can keep up with us. You must go in the chair.'

A muffled giggle came from the bundle that was Tallie. Magnus hesitated, stiff with annoyance.

'An inexperienced person will slow us down. And there are wolves, *monsieur*, and bears.'

Magnus didn't budge.

'And *madame*, she is getting cold, *monsieur*.'

'Oh, very well—damn your eyes!' said Magnus, and allowed himself to be strapped into the litter. Tallie watched in glee as her immaculate, elegant husband was bundled into a litter and wrapped until he looked like a pile of old washing. Two porters hoisted his litter onto their shoulders with a jolt. They moved forward.

'Oh, Magnus?' called Tallie as he came alongside her. The porters paused.

Magnus glared across at her. 'What?' he snapped.

'Sometimes we must sacrifice dignity for expediency, my dear,' she said solemnly.

Magnus swore and ordered the porters to move on.

'Don't worry, my dear,' she called. 'You look delightful in your litter, too.'

He swore again, and her laughter followed him up the steep pathway.

The porters must be part mountain goat, Tallie decided breathlessly after an hour of climbing. There were four for each litter and they leaped up impossibly steep slopes at a pace which Tallie doubted she could maintain on flat ground for more than a minute.

On one side, the narrow, winding path dropped away to a bottomless precipice, on the other were violently soaring peaks and huge vertical slabs of rock. There was no room to manoeuvre; the slightest misstep would have them plunging hundreds of feet over the precipice, to perish on the ragged rocks below. The porters didn't even pause or blink when Tallie heard what she was sure were wolves howling in the not very far distance. She hardly dared to breathe.

Tallie heaved a sigh of relief when they came to the top of the pass and stopped for a break of perhaps a minute or two. The view was superb. In every direction lay mountain peaks— some glittering with snow—sharp against the crisp vivid blue of the sky. On one side of them was France, down there somewhere below was Italy, and across in the distance were the peaks of Switzerland. It was a moment to remember, she thought excitedly, a moment to tell her children. She laid her hand on her flat stomach, marvelling, still unable to believe that there was a baby growing inside her.

With a sudden jolt, she found herself on the move again, this time at a breathtaking pace. The bearers ran, rather than walked, taking tiny little steps where the path was most perilous and great bounding strides when it levelled out or widened. Tallie clung on like grim death, bouncing and swaying.

Finally they came to a tiny village, which clung to the side of the mountains in apparent impossibility. The panting porters set down the litters and one of them came forward to lift her out. She looked for her husband. He was still in his litter. She hurried over on stiff legs.

'Magnus was that not the most terrifyingly thril—? Magnus, are you all right?'

His face was death-pale, his eyes closed. He did not move.

She pulled her gloves off and felt his forehead with her hand. Despite the chill in the air, his forehead was hot and clammy. 'Magnus!'

Slowly he opened his eyes. 'Oh, there you are,' he said, and fumbled to get out of the litter. She helped him out, but when he tried to stand he reeled, and would have fallen if one of the porters had not grabbed him. Tallie was greatly alarmed.

'He's ill! Is there a physician nearby? Maguire!'

Maguire and the head porter came over and there was a brief discussion.

'He's ill,' Tallie repeated. 'He needs a physician. Can we take him to an inn or somewhere?'

The porter shook his head and glanced significantly around. Tallie followed his gaze. The village consisted of a half-dozen tiny cottages. Certainly there would be no doctor here. Anxiety gripped her throat.

'I must get him to the nearest physician,' she insisted.

'I'm all right,' muttered Magnus thickly. 'Just a bit woozy, that's all.'

Tallie ignored him and fixed the head porter with a determined stare. 'Please transport us with all haste to the nearest place where I can get help for my husband,' she said firmly. 'At once, if you please!'

The porter nodded, then smiled and patted her on the shoulder, saying something in a dialect that Tallie could not understand. He called out to the others, and to her relief they soon had a vaguely protesting Magnus safely stowed back in his litter and were moving off down the mountain. This time Tallie saw nothing amusing in the sight. 'Hurry,' she urged the bearers.

The trip down the mountainside was a nightmare to Tallie. She wished she could see how her husband was faring, but the path was still too steep and narrow for them to go in anything except single file.

They passed several more tiny hamlets, but Tallie didn't even consider them. She had to get to the nearest town big enough to support a proper physician. Whenever they slowed, even for a moment, she urged them on. 'Hurry, oh, please hurry!'

Finally one of the porters pointed and mumbled something. Tallie followed the direction of his arm. Far, far below, she could see a town, a tiny sea of terracotta rooftops and the spire of a church. Her heart leapt. It was still a long distance away. She nodded. 'Doctor?'

The man nodded back. *'Dottore.'*

Tallie caught her breath. 'Oh, thank the Lord. Now, please hurry.'

The men jogged onwards. Tallie noticed nothing of the scenery; her eyes went from the bundle that was her husband, then down to the town, then back again.

Suddenly shots rang out. Tallie was jerked to a sudden halt. She blinked, and was almost thrown out of her litter as her bearers dropped it. They had stopped on a corner. Above them on both sides were steep rocks. She could see nothing ahead, nothing behind. All around her was sudden silence.

'What is it?' she called. 'Pray, what is the matter? And why have we stopped?'

'No questions,' an unfamiliar voice shouted in rough Italian above her. She looked up and saw a tall, dark-haired man with a large moustache pointing a gleaming silver pistol in her direction. He was thin, but broad-shouldered, and dressed in a ragged uniform; there were battered traces of dull yellow embroidery on his jacket, which she supposed might once have looked gold. Was he a soldier? But the war was over, surely.

There was a sudden flurry ahead and a single shot rang out.
Tallie's heart almost stopped. Magnus! But she could hear or
see nothing. The man above called something to someone unseen and then nimbly leaped down onto the path ahead, bringing a scattering of small rocks down with him. Immediately a
dozen more men appeared, all dressed in some sort of uniform,
one in braided trousers, another in a waistcoat, all ragged, none
of them matching. Each one of them brandished a knife or a
pistol or both.

'What is it? Who are they?' Tallie whispered to the porter
standing nearest her.

He turned to look at her, his eyes sombre. *'Banditti,'* he
said.

Chapter Thirteen

'*Banditti?*' gasped Tallie.

The porter jerked his head significantly up to the left. 'Bad men. Live up there.' His lip curled and he spat in scorn. 'Not our people.'

More orders rang out in dialect and the porters moved slowly forward. The ragged collection of armed *banditti* watched every move from their lofty positions on the rocks above. The party reached a small clearing, bordered on three sides by rock walls and on the fourth by a plunging precipice along which the narrow track passed. It would be impossible to escape; only one person at a time could move along that path. This was obviously a well-planned ambush.

The bandits had already disarmed the guards and Tallie could see that two porters were injured, although it didn't seem as if they were badly hurt; they could still walk, though with some difficulty. The hired guards, luckily, seemed untouched.

The tall dark man in the ragged gold braid uttered a sharp order and two bandits with pistols shepherded the porters and guards to a shallow cave in the rock, and forced them to sit, hands on heads. Tallie breathed a sigh of relief. The bandits did not mean to kill anyone—yet.

Several ruffians hovered over the prisoners still in their litters, a variety of firearms and gleaming knives and stilettos pointed menacingly, while the rest fell upon the bundles of baggage, emptying their belongings onto the mountainside with careless greed. They removed everything of value, even Magnus's fine leather boots.

Bundled in her litter, Tallie waited helplessly. The bindings that had been for her security now kept her imprisoned. She wondered how Magnus was faring, and struggled inconspicuously to escape her bonds.

The bandit leader thrust his silver duelling pistol through his belt and swaggered towards them. 'Aha, what have we here?' he said in oddly accented but surprisingly urbane Italian. 'A lady—no, two ladies,' he added, lifting a rug to discover Monique cowering underneath. 'And four gentlemen.' He glanced at the litters containing Magnus, Maguire, John Black, and Guillaume, Magnus's valet. 'Which one is the English milord?' His vivid green eyes examined each man narrowly.

The English milord? How did he know one of the travellers was an English milord? wondered Tallie anxiously. Their major-domo, Luigi Maguire, had stressed that they should appear as ordinary travellers. 'Naturally, while no foreign traveller is precisely poor,' he had said in his unique accent, 'it is not a good idea to advertise wealth, so if you will accept my advice, Lord d'Arenville, you will travel as plain Mr d'Arenville. Or even Mr Smith, if you like. And in your plainest coat and boots. Your good lady, too, in her plainest, most serviceable gown and cloak.'

And they *had* taken his eminently sensible advice. So how did this bandit know there was an English lord in the party?

'Come, gentlemen, I know one of you is an English milord, and a fine fat pigeon for my plucking.'

No one said a word.

The bandit leader strode forward, and with a rough oath he dragged first Maguire, then Guillaume, then John Black from their litters. He examined each man briefly, then thrust them towards his men, who stripped them of any valuables they found.

Behind her Tallie heard Monique shrieking as she was

robbed of her finery. A slap rang out and a bandit laughed.
John Black swore in a litany of solid English curses and surged
forward. A scuffle broke out. There was a loud crack and John
Black fell to the ground, groaning and clutching his head.
Guillaume and Maguire did not stir. Guillaume looked terrified. Maguire seemed unmoved. After a moment, to Tallie's
relief, John Black struggled to his feet, shaken but apparently
still in one piece. A bandit tied his hands.

The bandit leader turned and dragged Magnus from his litter.

'Leggo of me, damn y'r eyes!' muttered Magnus, swaying
as he stood, trying to fend off the bandit.

'Aha, our arrogant English milord, I presume,' said the bandit leader in excellent French, and he bowed mockingly as he
drew the money belt from Magnus's waist.

Tallie's eyes widened. This ragged villain was no simple
peasant.

Magnus swayed again, and the bandit grabbed him by the
coat, laughing. 'Is it drunk you are, my fine English milord?
Or are you a coward, like the rest of your kind?'

'He's nothing of the sort! He's ill,' shouted Tallie furiously,
struggling to clamber out of her litter. She freed herself, scrambled out and rushed over to her husband, thrusting her body
between him and the bandit. 'Leave him alone. He's ill. Can't
you see?'

The bandit snorted. His green eyes narrowed.

'He is, otherwise he would have shot you dead, you villain!'
Tallie said fiercely, wedging her shoulder under Magnus's to
support his swaying form.

The bandit looked at Magnus again and spat on the ground.
'Pah, look at him! He's shaking with fright!'

'He's shaking with *fever*,' Tallie retorted angrily, wiping her
husband's brow with her handkerchief.

The bandit leader snorted disbelievingly. He reached out a
surprisingly clean hand and took her ear between his fingers.
Tallie froze as he carefully removed her gold studs. Then he

reached for her neck, slipping his fingers inside the neck of her gown, and she recoiled.

'Take y'r filthy hands off my wife, you ruffian!' Magnus lurched forward, his arm shooting out in a clumsy, but well-aimed punch. The bandit reeled back and stood clutching his chin, while Tallie struggled to help Magnus regain his balance. Her gold necklace lay broken on the ground.

The bandit stood silently for a moment, then shrugged. 'We'll take him anyway.' He bent and scooped up Tallie's necklace.

'What do you mean, take him? Take who? My husband?'

'*Si,*' said the bandit, reverting to Italian. He called two of his henchmen over. They grabbed Magnus by the arms and started to march him away.

'No, stop!' cried Tallie. 'What are you going to do with him?'

The bandit leader turned back and regarded her impassively for a moment, then shrugged again. 'He is a fine English milord. Someone will pay gold for his safe return, *si*?'

'Ransom?' gasped Tallie. 'But you can't take him. He's too ill! He needs a physician immediately.'

The bandit shrugged and turned away.

'No!' shouted Tallie angrily. 'I will not allow it!'

The bandit turned and regarded her in faint surprise. He grinned, and a gold tooth glinted in the sunlight. '*You* will not allow it?'

'No, I won't,' she retorted defiantly, and moved to rejoin her husband. 'You will have to kill me before I allow you to kidnap my husband!'

'Be quiet, woman. Stay out of this,' Magnus mumbled angrily. His skin looked white and papery, but there was a hectic flush across his cheekbones.

'I will do no such thing. You are in no condition to be dragged off to some horrid bandit lair in the mountains, and even if you were, I still wouldn't allow it!'

Magnus staggered and swore, dashing his hand impatiently

across his brow, as if wiping off sweat. 'Hold your tongue and wait with John Black and Maguire.'

'I have no wish to wait with John Black and Maguire. My place is beside my husband.' And, with that, Tallie pushed one of the bandits aside and took Magnus's arm. She glared defiantly, first at her husband, who was ineffectively trying to detach her from his arm, and then at the bandit leader, who watched them both in amusement. He chuckled, then, sobering, reached out and effortlessly hauled Tallie to his side. Magnus lunged out to save her, but missed. Another ragged robber came and held him back.

'R'lease my wife, damn you,' slurred Magnus, swaying. 'Harm a hair on her head and I'll kill you.'

The bandit leader's brilliant green eyes narrowed, and his grip tightened on Tallie.

'Oho, so the English milord cares for his wife, does he? And she for him? Good. A loving wife will ensure her husband's ransom is paid quickly and without fuss.'

'You shall *not* take—'

The bandit clapped a hand over Tallie's mouth. 'Take him,' he ordered.

Tallie wrenched herself free with a cry. 'No! He is sick! He will *die* if you take him,' she said desperately. 'Then how would you get your precious ransom?'

The bandit shrugged indifferently. 'It is a risk we will take.'

'It is not your risk! I will not allow it!'

The bandit grinned. 'How will you prevent us, little English milady?'

Tallie fumed impotently. She could not stop them; she knew it. But Magnus was swaying and shivering in the cold, and unless she did something, he would die. And that she could not bear. She had to do something!

'Take me instead,' she said.

'Damn it woman, hold your—' Magnus's angry bellow was cut short as a rag was stuffed in his mouth. Another man came to assist the two who were already holding him.

'Take you?' said the leader, surprised. His green eyes narrowed. 'What game are you playing now?' He glanced at Maguire, who said nothing.

'No game,' said Tallie. 'You clearly will not leave without a hostage. My husband is too ill to go with you, but I am not. It is a perfectly sensible arrangement.'

A muffled roar came from Magnus. His eyes glared at her over the gag, charcoal pools of rage and frantic worry in an unnaturally pale face.

'Take a woman hostage?' The bandit regarded her suspiciously, smoothing a finger over his thick, dark moustache. 'Is this one of your immoral English games, milady? You think it will be romantic to dally with a handsome bandit in the mountains, eh?'

Tallie was outraged. 'No, of course not!' she spluttered indignantly. 'How dare you suggest such a wicked thing? I wouldn't walk two steps with you if I had any choice in the matter, but I will *not* let you take my husband when he is ill!'

'But if he was well…?'

'Hah!' Tallie snorted. 'If he was well you would never have taken us prisoner in the first place!' She cast a look of magnificent scorn at Maguire, and the silent gaggle of guards he had hired to protect them. 'My husband would never have surrendered without a proper fight!'

To her astonishment the bandit leader winked at Maguire.

'All right, then,' the bandit said, 'we take you with us and leave your loving husband to arrange the ransom.'

Magnus surged furiously, but was held down by his captors.

Tallie swallowed, her mouth suddenly dry. She had not truly thought the bandits would agree to take her, and she was suddenly terrified. But she had offered herself, and there was really no choice after all, she told herself. And the sooner they left, the sooner the others could get Magnus to a physician. She squared her shoulders and stepped forward to speak with her husband, whose eyes glowered over his gag, angry, desperate and fevered.

'It's all right, Magnus. I am happy to do this.' She swallowed again. There seemed to be a large dry lump in her throat. 'Please try not be angry with me. I could see no other way… And if…if I…' She swallowed again. 'If I should not see you again—'

Magnus shook his head, furiously chafing at his bindings.

'Please, my love, I…I do not want what may be our last moments… Oh, please, do not be angry with me.' Tears filled her eyes as she laid her hand on his cheek. He stilled, his eyes boring into hers in a silent, frustrated message. She tried to tug his gag away, but it would not budge, and the bandit beside him growled an incoherent warning, so with trembling lips she reached up and kissed him fervently on an ice-cold cheek. 'I love you, Magnus,' she whispered, and clung tightly to his body, as if she would never let him go.

'Enough,' said the bandit, and with another kiss Tallie released Magnus, tears spilling down her cheek.

The bandit regarded Magnus for a brief, solemn moment. 'She will not be harmed,' he said at last. 'We are bandits, *si*, but we do not harm women.' He took Tallie by the arm and led her away.

'*Mais, non, non.* You cannot take milady into the mountains,' cried Monique, suddenly aware of what was happening.

The bandit ignored her and kept walking.

'*Elle est enceinte!*' shrieked Monique in desperation.

The bandit froze. He glanced at Tallie's face, down at her stomach, then at her face again. She was gazing at her husband, her eyes filled with a mixture of joy, anxiety and entreaty. The bandit did not need to ask; her stomach might be flat, but confirmation of her maid's story was there in her eyes, for all the world to see.

He swore long and violently, released Tallie's arm in disgust and stamped across to Maguire. An argument ensued, in a language Tallie had heard somewhere before. She stared at the arguing men and the truth suddenly dawned. It was Gaelic. A maidservant at Miss Fisher's had been Irish, and had taught Tallie a few words.

'*You* betrayed us, Maguire,' she cried.

Maguire started, looked across the small rocky clearing at

her, and shrugged in a manner which uncannily echoed the
bandit's.

Tallie noted the way the two men were standing and her
eyes widened in sudden suspicion. 'He…he's your *brother*,'
she accused. 'He has the same long, thin face and the same
nose…and your eyes are green, too, only not so…' Her voice
tailed off.

The bandit turned and grinned, his gold tooth glinting in
the light. 'Correct, milady,' he said in perfect lilting English.
'The Maguire brothers at your service. I am Antonio.' He
bowed. 'And my little brother, Luigi.'

Tallie ignored him. She turned to the erstwhile major-domo.
'Why, Maguire? Why did you do it?'

Maguire sneered and shrugged. 'The wars are over and a
man must earn his living somehow. And we have no love for
English lords. It was an English lord who hanged our father
and grandfather, an English lord who drove us from our homeland—'

His bandit brother interrupted, 'And English lords who have
provided us with a steady income since we took to living in
the mountains like our mother's people.' He glanced from Tallie back to Magnus. 'But it seems we will get only the pickings
of the baggage this time, for it is one thing to hold a man to
ransom, but if an English lord died on us we would have the
authorities hounding our every footstep. And I do not kidnap
pregnant women.'

He turned and shouted orders, and the clearing suddenly
became a hive of activity as the bandits packed up every por-
table item that could possibly be of any value.

'*Adieu*, milord,' said Maguire the bandit. 'I envy you your
wife—she is your real treasure. *Au revoir, bella donna.*' He
took Tallie's hand and kissed it lingeringly, quite as if he was
a gentleman born and not a ragged mountain robber. In moments the *banditti* were gone, Maguire the younger and his
false guards with them. The others watched them go until no
echo of their leaving remained in the cold mountain air.

Tallie rushed to relieve Magnus of his dirty gag and bindings. He spat the gag out, gasping for breath, and tried to say something, but his knees buckled beneath him and he sank to the ground, clutching at Tallie as he did so.

'Oh, help me, please,' she cried to the porters. 'Let us be gone from this dreadful place immediately. I must get my husband to a physician at once. Quickly, we must go!' She turned to beckon to one of the men but found her wrist caught in a hard, feverish grip.

'Don't…leave…me,' Magnus grated hoarsely, fixing her with a wild, agonised stare. 'Not…leave… Not—' He collapsed, insensible.

'*Signora*, the fever has broken.' The dapper silver-haired physician bent over Tallie, speaking in a gentle voice.

Tallie stared up at him dazed, blank incomprehension in her face.

'It means your husband is over the worst,' the physician explained. 'He will be well soon. A week, perhaps, before he can get up. He needs to rest.' He looked at her and his face softened. 'And so do you, *signora*. You are exhausted.'

Tallie blinked at him as his words slowly sank into her tired brain. Magnus was going to get better. He would live. Tears flooded her eyes as she turned back to the still figure on the bed beside her. Magnus was breathing more easily now, and his skin was drenched with sweat. Beautiful, healing sweat. A sob escaped her.

'Come now,' said the doctor. 'Carlotta and the good John Black will stay here with your husband and your maid will put you to bed. You must sleep. You have slept little the last three days, *si*?'

Tallie nodded. Was it really only three days since they had arrived in the town of Susa? It seemed so much longer… A nightmare journey down from the mountains with Magnus strapped onto a mule, unconscious, his head swaying and bouncing with every bump so that she was terrified he would break his neck. But he hadn't. And then the fruitless, interminable search for a place which would house a stranger with no money and a fever.

Thank God for Carlotta, who was some sort of relative by marriage to one of the porters. She had glanced indifferently at Magnus bundled on his mule and begun to argue with the porter in a thick dialect Tallie hadn't been able to follow. Tallie had been terrified that Carlotta, like all the others, would shut the door in their faces. She'd pushed past the porter and, summoning up her best schoolgirl Italian, had begged Carlotta to help her husband. Carlotta, a large, flamboyant-looking woman with improbably brilliant rust-coloured hair, had taken one look at Tallie's youthful, tear-stained face and flung the door wide.

Within moments she'd sent a boy running to fetch the *dottore*, called for wine and refreshments for Tallie and the others, and loudly supervised the men carrying Magnus up to a bedroom. She had stripped Magnus's shivering body with firm, motherly hands and had him sponged down and in her dead husband's best linen nightshirt by the time the physician had arrived.

He'd examined the patient carefully. To Tallie's relief he had announced that the patient was unfit for cupping—she hated seeing people being bled. But then, to her horror, he had produced from his bag a small box containing a half-dozen leeches, which he had applied to Magnus's skin with deft fingers. She'd watched, appalled, as the leeches swelled and grew fatter, until at last, shiny and bloated, they'd fallen off, leaving a trickle of blood behind them. Tallie had felt ill just watching, but she hadn't been able to leave.

The doctor had carefully collected the gross leeches and replaced them in the box. He'd then shaken out a mysterious-looking powder, mixed it with wine, added several drops from a thick greenish bottle and administered the mixture through a funnel forced between Magnus's clenched teeth. 'Laudanum. He will sleep now,' he had said to Tallie in careful French. He'd given Carlotta more instructions in rapid Italian and left.

And that had only been three days ago, Tallie thought in-

credulously. It was all a blur to her now...days and nights
spent at Magnus's bedside, watching him toss and turn and
mutter unintelligibly, sponging him down when he was hot,
rugging him up when he was cold...and all the time praying
that he would live.

'Come, *signora*, it is time you slept. Your husband is safe
now,' the doctor said again.

Tallie nodded, and winced as she gently prised her husband's fingers apart. She stood up stiffly, tried to flex her fingers and winced again.

The doctor made a low exclamation and, frowning, bent to
look closer. Tallie hurriedly thrust her hand in a fold of her
skirts.

'*Signora*, you permit?' Tallie shook her head and moved to
step back, but the doctor ignored her. He reached down, gently
brought her hand from its hiding place, and examined it. He
swore softly in Italian. 'Why did you not say something?' he
said in a low, angry voice.

Tallie shook her head, embarrassed. 'It's nothing—a bit
stiff, that's all.'

Carlotta came up behind him and peered curiously over his
shoulder. She gasped. Tallie's left hand was black and blue
with bruises, where her husband had gripped it in his fever.
Several fingers were swollen. She could hardly move them.

'Ice for the *signora's* hand, immediately,' the doctor
snapped. Carlotta ushered Tallie from the room in a tender
rush, scolding her gently in Italian, interspersing her comments
with shrill calls to the servant to hurry up with the ice.

Tallie had no choice but to be swept away in the motherly
embrace. It was strange, but oddly comforting to have someone fussing over her, even for such a trivial matter. No one
had ever done it before, not even when she had been ill at
school. She couldn't recall her mother very well, but perhaps
her mother had fussed over her like this when she was a baby.
Tallie laid her good hand on her belly, feeling the faint swelling beneath it. One day she, too, would fuss over this child
the way that Carlotta was fussing over her. It was a wonderful

thought. A tear trickled down her cheeks. Oh, heavens, she was more tired than she realised.

Her hand was plunged into a bowl of ice-water, and after the first excruciating pain there was a blessed numbness. After a while the feeling started to come back. It throbbed, but not as badly as before. Carlotta smoothed on some foul-smelling ointment and wrapped the hand lightly in a cloth, then bustled her into a huge warm nightgown and tucked her into bed.

'*Signora*…Carlotta, I must thank you—' Tallie began, but Carlotta shushed her and pressed her gently back on the pillows, smoothing her hair with a gentle rhythmic touch. She started humming—a lullaby, Tallie supposed—and a faint smile crossed her lips as she recognised that she was indeed being mothered like a small child. It was foolish, for she was a grown, married woman, and not a child at all…but it was very comforting… She closed her eyes and slept.

'Magnus, you must stay in bed! The physician said—'
'Damn that blasted leech. I have no intention of idling—'
'But you are not yet strong enou—'
Magnus flung back the covers and swung his legs to the edge of the bed. He sat there a moment, then shakily stood up, gripping the carved wooden bedhead for support.

Tallie, despite her anxiety, found herself smiling. Carlotta's late husband had evidently been much shorter than Magnus, for his nightshirt dangled well above Magnus's knees. The length of hard, hairy leg looked incongruous beneath the embroidered linen. She bit her lip and tried to look cross. 'You are not supposed to be up this soon,' she said severely.

'Nonsense. I feel perfectly well. And besides I am bored—'
'But—'
'And damnably lonely,' he finished, giving her a heated look.

Tallie blushed. This time she could not stop the smile which quivered on her lips. She, too, had been lonely in the bed next door. It was amazing how quickly one could become accustomed to sharing a bed. Only a few months ago she had been unable to imagine it as anything but an intrusion, an inconvenience, an invasion of her privacy…but now she would not wish to fall asleep anywhere except in her husband's warm, strong arms. She'd missed his warmth, missed the wonderful feeling of belonging, the feeling of safety she felt when she fell asleep in his embrace. She loved waking up in the night and finding his long hairy leg wrapped around hers, loved resting her cheek on his smooth, hard chest and hearing his heart thudding steadily under her ear, loved the way he sometimes woke her in the morning… *'Morning, sweetheart…'* knowing that it was the prelude to a splendid bout of lovemaking.

She loved those mornings best, watching his sleepy eyes focus, then darken into that brooding, storm-cloud grey that meant he wanted to make love to her. The look never failed to thrill her… And the feel of his unshaven jaw scraping sensuously against the softness of her skin… A pleasurable shudder passed through her. Yes, she had been lonely in her bed, too.

'Fetch me that robe, would you?' Magnus said. 'It's chilly.'

The man was impossibly stubborn! She didn't want to assist him, but he was clearly going to get up whether or not she agreed, and it *was* cold. Reluctantly she went to do his bidding, but before she reached the hook where the robe was hanging he took a few steps and wavered dangerously. She raced back to his swaying form.

'I told you it was too early to venture out of bed,' she scolded. 'The physician said you must rest for another few days and regain your strength before you try to move. If you try too soon, you could have a relapse.'

'Damned quack!'

'He saved your life.'

'What would a blasted village leech know?'

Tallie, incensed by his stubbornness, abruptly let him go and stood back. Magnus swayed. His knees started to buckle. She gave him a tiny push and he collapsed onto the bed, swearing.

Hiding a triumphant smile, she bent to lift his legs back into
the bed, but with a jerk Magnus pulled her on top of him.
'That's more like it,' he growled in soft satisfaction, and
planted his mouth on hers.

Tallie gave up the struggle. It was bliss to be back in his
arms again, and a kiss wouldn't tax his strength too much,
surely. She kissed him back with all the fervour in her heart.
Oh, she loved this stubborn man so much. His kiss deepened,
and hazily she felt his hands seeking to undo the fastenings
of her gown.

'*Madonna mia!* Stop that at once! It is not the time!' It was
Carlotta in the doorway.

Magnus swore. Tallie tried to pull back from his embrace,
but he refused to let her go. Trust his strength to come back
now, she thought, embarrassed.

'Signora Thalia, Signor Magnus, you must stop it now!
Basta! Enough!'

'Out, damn it, *signora*! Now!' snapped Magnus. 'A man
and his wife are entitled to…to— Confound it, Tallie, what's
the Italian for privacy?'

Carlotta ignored him. She hurried over to the bed, scolding
in an undervoice, and tugged Tallie off. 'Quick!' she whispered. 'Fasten your gown. And as for you, Signor Magnus—'
She broke off and began to smooth the covers over him.

'Blast you, woman—'

'Hush!' Carlotta snapped. 'It is the Father.'

'What father? I haven't got a father,' retorted Magnus angrily. 'Damn it, woman, what the devil do you think you are
doing?' He tried to fend off the hands that were busily but-
toning his nightshirt to the neck, but Carlotta would have none
of it.

'It is *the Father*!' she hissed. Footsteps sounded on the landing outside and she turned, smoothed her dress with quick,
anxious hands and waited, a deferential smile on her lips.

'Hell and the devil confound you, woman, I told you I
haven't got a fath—'

The door opened and an elderly priest in a long black robe

entered. He paused on the threshold, took out a small vial and sprinkled a few drops of liquid around the room, murmuring in Latin.

'Holy water,' whispered Carlotta, crossing herself.

Magnus closed his eyes in resignation and Tallie stifled a giggle. What if the priest had just walked in on them? Thank heavens Carlotta had come in first. But what was he doing here anyway?

'How do you do?' the priest said in slow, rusty English. 'I am Father Astuto. Carlotta tell me you make the difficult...' he frowned, then his brow cleared '...convalescence.' He bowed, clearly delighted at having remembered such a complicated word. 'I come to entertain you with English conversation. I speak the English well, no? So we shall converse.'

He placed his vial of holy water on the bedside stand, pulled up a chair and sat facing Magnus with such a look of pleased and proud expectancy that Tallie was hard put to it to maintain a straight face. Magnus groaned and rolled his eyes.

'You are in pain, my son.' Father Astuto laid a thin, veined hand on Magnus's brow. 'Do not try to talk. Repose yourself and I will talk to you of my life and my travels. It will be of great interest to an Englishman. I was born in the small village of—'

A smothered choke of laughter escaped Tallie. Magnus opened one eye and glared balefully at her. Clapping a hand over her mouth, she hurried from the room. Behind her, Father Astuto's voice droned on.

'Coffee, Signora Thalia?' said Carlotta, following her down the stairs. 'The Father, he will stay at least three hours.'

'Th...three hours?' quavered Tallie.

Carlotta nodded. 'Three, possibly four.' She gave Tallie a sly glance. 'That will keep your husband quiet, no?'

Tallie's jaw dropped. She stared at her hostess incredulously. 'You mean—?'

'*Il Dottore* said he must stay in bed, yes? And who better to keep him there than Father Astuto? He loves to practise his English. He will come every morning for the rest of the week.'

Carlotta winked. 'And if your husband doesn't sleep for the rest of the afternoon, then Father Astuto is losing his touch.'

'Carlotta, you are brilliant!' Tallie exclaimed. 'I couldn't keep him from over-exerting himself, but Magnus is too polite to argue with a priest…especially such a sweet old man. How splendidly devious!' And she laughed until tears ran down her cheeks.

Finally she sat drinking Carlotta's strong, milky coffee. Magnus was recuperating safely and she had no need to worry about him anymore. And with Carlotta and Father Astuto's help he would be out of the way for at least a week. This was the opportunity she hoped she might get. A chance to trace the last footsteps of her mother.

'Signora Carlotta,' she said slowly. 'My parents are both dead.'

'Ahh, you poor child—' Carlotta began, her broad face crumpling in sympathy.

'They died in Italy,' Tallie interrupted the flow.

'What? In Italia? No.'

'Yes, somewhere between Turin and the mountains.'

'Eh? Near Torino, you say?'

Tallie nodded. 'Yes, but I'm not sure where, exactly. Near some small village. There was a coach accident. It was about seven years ago. Did you hear of anything like that happening around here?'

Carlotta frowned. 'You say your *mamma* and your *papà* died in this accident?' She shook her head slowly. 'I do remember something about an Englishman's coach… It was near the village where my husband's sister-in-law's uncle lives, but I do not remember anything about an English lady in the coach. And I would know, yes, for English ladies are not common in these hills.' She patted Tallie's hand sympathetically. 'I am sorry, child.'

Tallie felt the excitement inside her grow. It was as the letter had said. Her mother had not died in the coach accident with her father. 'But you do remember a coach accident where an Englishman was killed? About seven years ago?'

Carlotta nodded.

Tallie took a deep breath. 'Carlotta, can I trust you?'

Carlotta frowned, and drew herself up as if insulted. 'But of course—'

'No one, not even my husband, knows this secret,' Tallie said hastily. 'Especially not my husband.'

Carlotta's eyes gleamed. 'I swear by the robe of the Holy Virgin, I keep your secret to the grave,' she said, crossing her breast quickly. She spat into her palm and offered it to Tallie, who shook it gingerly.

'I thought my parents died together in the coach accident, but a few years ago I received a letter which said that my father was killed but my mother died a week before, in a small village.'

Carlotta frowned. 'I have not heard of this.'

Tallie continued in a rush. 'The letter said she died giving birth…to a little boy. It said that my father believed my mother had been unfaithful and that he would have no for-eigner's bastard foisted onto him.' She fixed her eyes on Car-lotta. 'The letter said he left the baby behind in the village where my mother was buried.'

Carlotta looked stunned. She shook her head in disbelief at such goings-on.

'Carlotta, don't you realise? All my life I have been without a family, with no one in the world who belongs to me. No one who loves me.'

'But your husb—'

Tallie waved that aside. She didn't need to burden Carlotta with the knowledge that while Magnus might act possessively towards his wife he did not love her. 'It's not the same. But perhaps, in some small village not far from here, there is a small boy who also believes he belongs to no one. But if the letter is right, and there is such a boy, he has a sister—a sister who wants him, who will love him.' Her eyes sheened with tears. 'I want to search for him, Carlotta, and I need your help.'

'But why not wait until your husband is well?'

'He mustn't know.'

'But why, *cara*?'

'I know we told you that we were Signor and Signora d'Arenville, but the truth is, in England, my husband is a great lord, from a proud and ancient family. It was bad enough that he chose a nobody for his wife, but what do you think his feelings would be if the nobody wanted to search for her bastard half brother?' Tallie shook her head. She loved her husband, but she was not blind. He had chosen a nobody because she would cause him the least amount of bother.

And the only child Magnus was interested in was an heir to carry on his family name. Certainly he would have no interest in a bastard child of unknown parentage, possibly half-foreign and raised in a small and probably dirty peasant village. She could just imagine what he—and everybody else— would say. But if she found her brother first… Magnus was not the only one who could be stubborn.

'Do you honestly think my husband would help me? Or would he hurry me back to England and thus prevent a scandal?'

Carlotta's eyes were sombre. She nodded. 'I will help you, *cara*. I know of these great proud lords. If we can, we will find your little brother. But are you sure Signor Magnus would deny him shelter?'

'Shelter, no,' said Tallie with feeling. 'In an orphanage or school, perhaps. Or he might pay a tenant to keep him. But if I do have a little brother, I want more for him. I never had a home of my own, but I will do everything in my power to ensure my brother has one. And if my husband doesn't like it…' Her eyes filled with tears. 'I do not know what I will do—but I will *not* give up on my brother—bastard or not.'

Chapter Fourteen

'So, John Black and Monique and Carlotta's nephews and I will travel to Turin with your letters of credit and introduction, and you'll stay here with Carlotta.' Tallie patted the reticule containing the letters. She was dressed for immediate travel.

'But—' Magnus glowered at her from the bed. He was not at all happy about her travelling without him. But Tallie was determined.

'Magnus, you know it is the only possible thing to do. We cannot all go, for then Carlotta will think we mean to run out on her, when she has already been to so much trouble and expense on our behalf. And besides, I'll be perfectly safe with Carlotta's nephews and John Black—and if you cannot trust him, who can you trust?'

'Yes, but—'

'Would you prefer I stay behind, then—by myself? While you risk your health and possibly your life? Or perhaps it suits you to continue to allow a lone widow to support us and our servants. To be sure, she has not yet begun to dun us, so perhaps—'

Magnus looked frustrated. 'No, of course I do not wish it. It galls me past bearing, but—'

'Very well, it is agreed,' Tallie said decisively. 'You need not worry, Magnus. I am not at all tempted to take your purse and continue my journey. I have no intention of abandoning you.'

The look of blank shock on his face told her he had not even considered such a thing. But now he was, if the black frown was any indicator. Tallie hid a smile.

'And you could not possibly be lonely, with dear Father Astuto visiting you so often. I wonder if he could visit more frequently while I am away?'

A low growl erupted from the bed. 'Saddle me with any more of that blasted priest, madam, and you will rue the day you wed me.'

'Will I? And are you so sure I do not do so already?' she said lightly, and, planting a quick kiss on his mouth, she hurried from the room, leaving Magnus frustrated and uneasy.

Curse it, but there was a vast deal of decision about his wife these days. What the devil had happened to the dependent little creature he had married? He missed her. She was fast turning into an impertinent baggage. He swung his legs out of bed and tried to rise. Blast—he was still as weak as a kitten. He had to get his strength back quickly, or the way things were going his wife would consider it was she who wore the pantaloons in this family... She was already wearing the drawers.

He felt his body stir as he recalled the sight of her in those damned alluring pink drawers. He settled back into bed, prepared to indulge himself in a fantasy where his wife was standing over him, clad in nothing but her pink drawers, her hair tumbled around her pert, naked breasts...

'Ah, Signor d'Arenville, you are awake, I see.'

'Father Astuto,' groaned Magnus.

'Repose yourself, my son, and I will tell you of the Holy City and my audience with His Eminence,' said the priest with a gentle, reminiscent smile. 'It was a cold, wet day...'

Magnus closed his eyes and tried to recapture his fantasy about his wife in the pink drawers with their very erotic slit...

'I was wearing a new cassock—that is the correct term, yes?—which I had purchased especially for the audience...'

It was no good. It was simply not possible to indulge oneself with an erotic fantasy when one was entrapped by an elderly, unworldly, celibate, stupefyingly dull priest.

Magnus closed his eyes and prayed that sleep would come soon.

'And of course I had prepared a small speech to make to the Holy Father. To this day, I still remember—it went like this…'

Magnus hunched down in his bed, trying to block out the priest's rambling. But sleep eluded him. He was kept awake by his wife's last comment.

Did she rue the day she had wed him? It was an unsettling thought. She seemed to him to be quite happy…but you never could tell with women. Women were natural actresses, in his experience. They never said what they meant… Although his wife was not like most women… She was different…but how different? Could she feign happiness so consistently? He pondered the notion. Now he thought about it, there were times he had caught her looking at him as if… Damn it, what was that look she got sometimes? Sad? Wistful? Pensive?

This wretched weakness of his—he *hated* the idea of her heading off to Turin alone, with none but John Black and a gaggle of Carlotta's nephews to protect her. What if there were more *banditti* on the road? They would not be so gallant as that blasted Irishman. Magnus snorted… A bandit who kissed women's hands! And who did that fellow think he was—rot him—to compliment Magnus on his wife? None of his business what sort of wife Magnus had. Shouldn't even be looking at another fellow's wife, blasted bandit. Blasted green-eyed bandit.

Magnus closed his eyes, reliving the moment when he had realised that the bandit was taking Tallie up into the mountains to hold her hostage. It still haunted him. He had never in his life felt so furious…or so terrified…or so helpless.

If he lived to be a hundred years old he would never forget that brave little smile she'd given him as she kissed him good-bye. *I love you, Magnus.* And then she'd hugged him as if he was the most precious thing in the world.

She'd *offered* to go. To take his place as hostage. Like a heroine in a Greek drama. Because she'd thought if they took him he would die of his fever in the mountains. And she would have gone, too, quite happily…if that maid of hers hadn't said what she'd said.

Pregnant. Every time he thought of it, he felt… He didn't know what he felt. Breathless? Joyful? Proud? Obviously. Then why did it feel so much like terror? Lord, what was the matter with him these days? He should be over the moon—after all, a child of his own was the reason he'd decided to take a wife. He tried to envisage a child, a child of Tallie's. A little girl with glossy honey-coloured curls and big amber eyes. A miniature tip-tilted nose and teeth like tiny pearls, one of them endearingly crooked… But all he could think of was that women died in childbirth all the time… He broke out in a cold sweat just thinking about it. *Pregnant.* Oh, Lord.

He thought of her playful threat to abandon him. After the first shock, he hadn't actually believed it for a moment. Of course she wouldn't leave him. He knew it as well as he knew himself. She'd do exactly what she'd said she would—go straight to Turin, get the money and return to him immediately. With a start, it occurred to Magnus that he trusted her; he actually trusted a woman.

No—he didn't just trust a woman—he trusted Tallie.

Good God! When had that happened? When she had offered to take his place? No. He thought back. He couldn't pin a time on it, but it had started well before then… *He trusted her.* The realisation was shattering. His heart thudded faster in his chest and he shivered, feeling suddenly exposed and vulnerable. What if she—? No, he wouldn't think about that. There was no point in dredging up the past—she was different; his wife was different. Somehow, by some incredible, wonderful stroke of luck, he'd got himself a wife who was different from any other woman he had known… And he was overwhelmingly grateful for it.

He trusted his wife.

And she was increasing. But, oh, Lord…what if he lost her?

The priest's voice droned on in the background. Magnus wrestled with his demons, plunging from exhilaration, to doubt, to despair, then back to exhilaration, until at last, in the middle of a description of the vestments worn by a bishop at a mass Father Astuto had attended forty years before, Magnus finally dozed off.

'What the *devil* do you mean, the mistress isn't with you? Where the hell is she, then? Don't tell me you left her on her own in Turin—you know better than that, John!' Magnus stared at his coachman, baffled and not a little worried. Of course he didn't believe for a moment that his wife had gone off and left him…but where the hell was she?

John Black shifted uncomfortably. For the first time in twelve years he failed to look his master in the eye. Magnus felt a cold hand steal around his heart. She couldn't possibly have left him. She couldn't. She wouldn't. But where was she? He braced himself.

'Out with it, man, where is she?'

'The mistress never went to Turin,' said John Black at last.

'Never went to Turin? What do you mean? I saw her leave.'

John Black nodded. 'Went with me a dozen miles or so, then turned up into the mountains.'

Magnus felt as if he'd been hit in the chest with a hammer. That damned green-eyed, hand-kissing bastard!

'And you just let her go? By herself?' It was more than a week ago. He'd never be able to catch her now. His insides felt hollow.

'No, my lord, of course not,' said John Black indignantly. 'I hope I know better than that. She had that French wench with her, and a half-dozen of the Italian widder-woman's relatives, including one old woman.'

'*What?*' Magnus stared at his coachman. Something eased slightly in his chest. It was one thing to suspect his wife had run off with some damned good-looking bandit, but quite another to imagine her taking her maid, an old Italian lady and half a dozen relatives of the eminently respectable Carlotta with her. It was not the usual way of elopements. But then his wife was not the usual sort of wife.

'If she was escorted by the widow's relatives, the widow will no doubt be able to cast some light on the matter.' Magnus strode to the door and flung it open. 'Carlotta,' he roared.

She came immediately.

'What the devil have you done with my wife?'

Carlotta looked at him for a moment and smiled. 'Do not worry Signor d'Arenville, your wife is perfectly safe. She has gone on a visit with the wife of my husband's oldest brother. She wished to visit her uncle, you understand.'

'Her uncle?' Magnus was dumbfounded. 'She never she told me she had an uncle living in Italy.'

Carlotta laughed. 'Not your wife's uncle, *signor*. The uncle of my husband's sister-in-law.'

'The uncle of your sister-in-law's husband? But why on earth—?'

Carlotta laughed again. 'No, not the uncle of my sister-in-law's husband—he lives in Chiomonte—he is the stonemason, you understand? No, your wife has gone to visit the uncle of my husband's sister-in-law. The uncle of my sister-in-law's husband is a very unpleasant man. The uncle of my husband's sister-in-law is—'

'I don't give a hell's bloody damn about your blasted relatives, madam. *I want my wife.*'

Carlotta drew herself up and gave him a look of magnificent Italian scorn. 'I do not care for cursing in my house, *signor*. No matter if you are a great lord in England.' She sniffed, turned her back, and with immense dignity began to depart.

Magnus groaned. 'Carlotta.' He laid a hand on her shoulder. It remained stiff and averted. Magnus took a deep breath and counted to ten. '*Signora*—Carlotta.' He forced himself to use a much softer voice. 'I apologise for cursing in your house.'

The shoulder twitched huffily.

'And I apologise for any offence I may have made concerning your relatives. I am sure they are very worthy and respectable people.' He would have them all hanged if harm came to Tallie.

The shoulder twitched again.

'Please forgive me. I did not mean to upset you, *signora*, but I am extremely worried about my wife.'

Carlotta turned and said stiffly, 'She is with my relatives, *signor*. No harm will come to her, I assure you.'

Blast the woman's touchy Italian soul. He should give up this soft-soaping and just choke the truth out of her. Magnus made one more effort. 'I know,' he said. 'It is just that I am very anxious about her. She…she is increasing, you know.'

Carlotta frowned in puzzlement. 'Increasing?' Then her face lit up. 'You mean a baby?'

Magnus nodded, wishing he knew whether he was telling the truth or not.

'Oh, *signor*, that is wonderful. No wonder you are anxious about the *signora*. But how happy you must be. A baby.'

Magnus nodded, and managed what he hoped looked like a joyful smile. But he was too damned worried to waste much more time grinning at some woman whose blasted relatives had carted Tallie off into some godforsaken mountain village. 'So, would you tell me now, please, where is my wife?' He managed a reasonably polite tone.

'But I told you, *signor*, she is in the village of my sister-in—'

Magnus held up his hand. 'No more relatives, I beg of you.'

Carlotta sighed and said simply, 'She has gone to find the place where her mother died.'

The breath left Magnus in a great gush. So that green-eyed scoundrel hadn't got her after all. He closed his eyes in relief. The place where her mother died. Of course. She'd mentioned it before. It was very important to her, he remembered. The main reason she'd wanted to come to Italy.

But why had she not waited until he was well enough to escort her? He would have gone with her. No question about it. In fact, now he came to think of it, he damn well *wanted* to go with her. She needed him—not just as an escort, but to support her in her grief. She would need support; his wife was a very emotional little creature.

So why the deuce had she not waited? And why sneak off as she had, pretending she was going to Turin? As if there was something havey-cavey about visiting her mother's grave. There was no need for secrecy and deception for such a visit. So what was she about, creeping off behind his back? He frowned. Carlotta shifted uncomfortably under his stare. She averted her eyes and gazed with sudden interest at the ornately carved settee beneath the window.

His suspicion deepened. There was funny business going on, or Magnus was a Dutchman. And he wasn't. He was English to the core, as far back as the Conqueror. And beyond.

So what was his wife up to, the deceitful little baggage?

Tallie stood and stared desolated at the tumbledown cottage. The whitewash was ancient, dirty, and falling off in great flakes. The uneven shingled roof had holes visible from the narrow track below. A door swung drunkenly on one leather hinge and the wind rattled broken-slatted shutters and whipped at tattered remnants of oilcloth. It was a ruin. Nobody could possibly live here.

Her heart sank. She turned to their guide. 'I thought you said a man and woman lived here. With a little boy.'

The man shrugged and mumbled something in an incomprehensible dialect. One of Carlotta's nephews translated. 'He says they used to live up here but he hasn't visited for a year or so. He doesn't know what's happened to them. He's been living in Torino.'

'Well, what about one of the people in the village down there? Would any of them know?' Tallie said.

'Perhaps.'

They retraced their steps down to the village, about five minutes' walk from the ruined house. They knocked at door after door, but no one wished to answer questions posed by a strange young female, a foreign English female at that. But Tallie insisted they try every house in the village. She had not come this far to give up merely because people were suspicious of foreigners. Finally they came to a house where, after some dialogue between a nephew and the householder, a connection was established; it seemed to involve a great many cousins and in-laws.

Tallie was ushered into a small, neat room which seemed to fulfil the function of kitchen, sitting room and bedroom. A fire crackled and a pot of something pungent and aromatic was bubbling over it. Fat brown sausages, flitches of ham and plaited strings of garlic, onions and herbs hung in the rafters. The room was warm and cosy, with colourful hand-woven rugs on the floor and the bed. Tallie sat on a crude wooden bench. The woman of the house offered her an earthenware bowl filled to the brim with creamy milk. She drank it thirstily.

'Thank you very much, *signora*, that was delicious,' she said gratefully, wiping a rim of cream from her upper lip. The woman smiled and bobbed her head in shy acknowledgement. Then, with the nephews translating, Tallie began her questioning.

'*Si*, Marta, who lived in the cottage up the hill, is dead.'

'No, he was not her husband; he was her brother. Her husband died a long time ago—four years, maybe five. Her brother? He went away. Nobody knows for certain. Maybe he went to be a soldier.'

'A little boy? *Si*, there was a little boy. Her *miracolo bambino*, she called him. She was nine years barren, then, *presto*, one day she comes home from church with a little baby.'

'*Si*, it would be about seven years ago.'

'No, the baby had blond hair. Marta was dark.'

'No, the little boy did not die. Where? Who knows, *signora*? Not anyone around here.'

'With the brother? No, he did not like the child. Called him little foreign bastard. Said he was no relative of his.'

'God only knows, *signora*. In times like these, many children lose their parents. Some run wild in the hills—those who have no relatives, of course. *Si*, it is a tragedy, but what can one do? One has enough trouble feeding one's own without looking for more.'

'What sort of boy, *signora*? A bad boy, to be sure. Bad? Eh, steal my apples, ride my goats—*Madonna mia*! But always merry, you understand—whistling, laughing. *Si, signora*—a bad, merry little boy.'

'*Si*, of course. If I hear anything… It has been a long time now…but, *si*, I will ask.'

'No, no, you are welcome, *signora*. God go with you.'

'They come, *signor*. Your wife and my nephews, they come—see?' Carlotta gestured triumphantly.

Magnus strode to the window and stared out, breathing heavily. It had been four days since he had discovered Tallie had not gone to Turin. Four days of ever-increasing anxiety. Four days in which he had discovered that his wife was indeed a liar.

'Yes, I can see her,' he growled. He had barely slept the past few nights, and now, to see her coming down the street unharmed and apparently perfectly content… He'd begun to believe he would never see her again, and now…

Relief, after days and nights of the most intense anxiety, turned to rage. How dared she arrive as if nothing in the world were wrong? As if she hadn't just run off, willy-nilly, with a bunch of foreigners, leaving her sick husband with a demented old priest? Pretending she'd gone to visit her mother's grave. Then just to bounce casually in, for all the world as if she'd been off on a picnic! He'd teach her a lesson. One she'd never forget.

He stalked to a window facing the opposite side of the house and glowered out of it, at the mountains in the distance. She wasn't going to think he'd be waiting for her, arms outstretched. Behind him the door opened. Magnus didn't move; he gazed out of the window. There was a short silence.

'M…Magnus?' she said tremulously.

'Madam?' he said coldly, turning at last to face her. 'Did you find what you were looking for?'

She opened her mouth to answer him, but not a sound came out. Her lower lip quivered, then suddenly her face crumpled. 'Oh, Magnus,' she wailed, and ran across the room and hurled herself into his open arms.

He gathered her to him—hard—a dry lump working in his throat. She clung to him—hard—as she had when she'd been about to be taken away by the bandits, as if she would never let him go. Her head was buried in the hollow between his shoulder and his jaw. He could feel the chill on her skin from the biting wind outside, smell the faint tang of woodsmoke in her hair and the lingering fragrance of the lavender soap that Carlotta had given her. He laid his face against her hair and inhaled deeply, tightening his hold around her quivering body. She was weeping; he could feel the damp warmth of her tears on his skin. After a moment he became aware of Carlotta beaming benevolently upon them, and with a silent oath he swung his wife into his arms and carried her up to the bedroom.

He wanted to drop her onto the bed and fling himself down beside her and tumble her until she knew where she belonged, who she belonged with. He forced himself to set her carefully on her feet, then released her and stepped back. Her face was awash with tears.

Magnus groped in his pocket and handed her a handkerchief. He wanted to dry her tears himself or, better still, kiss them away, but he could not let himself move a single step towards her. If he did, he would be lost for ever, that much he knew. As it was, he was in the grip of an emotional turmoil he had never dreamt was possible. He could not believe how weak and irresolute he felt, how strong was the impulse just to take her in his arms and forget the past week. Forgive and forget. Like his father. Forgive the fact that she had lied to him. Forget that she had gone off into the mountains without his knowledge or permission. No, he was weak, but he would make himself strong. He would neither forgive nor forget.

He paced over to the window and stood, coolly looking out, staring at the mountains into which she had disappeared, forcing down the overwhelming feelings of hurt, humiliation and betrayal, replacing them with cold anger. He waited until the sobbing had stopped, then turned and repeated his question in a bitter, icy voice.

'Well, madam, I asked you before and I will repeat the question. Did you find what you were looking for? Did you find your mother's grave?'

She looked up at him with drenched, bewildered eyes and nodded. 'Yes,' she whispered.

'And once you found it, you came straight back here?'

She hesitated, paled, scrubbed at her face, dropped her lashes and nodded.

'Liar!' he roared, slamming his fist against the wall.

She flinched, and regarded him with huge, wary eyes.

'You found your mother's grave eight days ago! I saw her grave myself and spoke to the priest about you. Eight days, madam! Eight days! And what did you do in those eight days, eh?'

She opened her mouth, then shut it again, biting nervously on her lower lip in a manner that drove him wild. He slammed his fist against the wall again and swore. 'Shall I tell you what you did in those eight days—shall I? You betrayed me, madam. Betrayed the name you took on the day we were wed. Broke the vows you made before God and man.'

She flinched again. 'B…betrayed your name? So…so you know? Carlotta told you?'

He snorted. 'No, to be sure she did not. You women stick together in your deceptions.'

'So how—?'

'Do you think I am a fool, madam? I worked it out for myself.'

She frowned, puzzled. 'But how could you?'

He snorted again. 'Betrayal is something I have been acquainted with all my life. I believe I am an expert on it.'

'Betrayal…I was worried you might see it in those terms.' She sighed, and sat on the bed.

'Worried I might see it in those terms?' he repeated incred-

ulously. 'Pray, how else would I see it?' He paced furiously
around the room.

'I thought…hoped you might be different…only—'

'And I hoped…believed you were different, madam,' he
said bitterly. 'But now I see you are just like all the rest.'

'All the rest of whom?' She stared at him, apparently bewildered.

And he had convinced himself she was no actress! Hah!
'Well, I hope you learnt your lesson. So, did he weary of your
charms after only a week?'

'Weary of my charms? What charms? Who are you talking
about?'

Her wide-eyed look of confusion and innocence enraged
him. He strode to the bed, grabbed her by the shoulders,
yanked her upright and shook her in fury. 'That blasted green-
eyed Irishman, of course! Do you take me for a complete
fool?' He glared down at her, his rage compounded by the
knowledge that he still desired her.

There was a long pause as they stared at each other, then
suddenly her face flooded with dawning comprehension. Her
mouth dropped open.

'You think I betrayed you…with that bandit?' she gasped.

'I know it,' he responded coldly.

They stared into each other's eyes for a long moment.
Abruptly she flung her arms up, breaking his grip on her shoulders. She thrust at his chest—hard—pushing him away, and
stepped back, panting, hurt, shock and anger in her eyes.

'You think I betrayed you!' She side-stepped him and
marched to the other side of the room. Her hands shaking, she
picked up an ornament on the shelf and stared blankly at it
for a moment, her mouth working. Setting the ornament down
with a snap, she turned. 'How dare you? Oh, how *dare* you
say such a thing!' Her chest was heaving as she fought to
control herself. 'As if I would ever, ever betray you with another man!'

She took several deep, shuddery breaths. 'Oh! I cannot believe you could think such a thing of me!' She began to pace around the room.

Magnus watched suspiciously. Was this another very good act? It didn't feel like it.

She continued her pacing, then suddenly whirled on him. 'And with that…that *bandit*! Ooh!' she raged.

'So you deny it?' he said coldly.

'Deny it? Deny it?' She snatched the ornament off the shelf and hurled it at him. He ducked, and it shattered against the wall behind him. 'No, I don't deny it—I don't have to deny anything—there is nothing to deny!' she stormed. 'I cannot believe you would even *think* such a thing.'

His eyes narrowed. 'So you did not go to meet that bandit?' He ducked as another ornament was hurled at his head.

Magnus suddenly felt very uncertain of his ground. He'd never seen her like this before. He could not believe it was an act. The cold knot that had lodged in his chest slowly started to loosen.

'So where did you get to in those eight days?' he said slowly.

'None of your business,' she snapped.

'It is my business. I am your husband. Where you go concerns me.'

'Oh, does it indeed? And you wish me to account for every moment, do you? Well, I am sorry to disoblige you, but I will not explain my every movement to a horrid, suspicious beast who believes I am…I am…' She sniffed, and blew her nose defiantly into his handkerchief. 'Well, from now on, if you cannot find me you will just have to assume I am off cavorting with a lover, preferably some unshaven criminal.' Her voice quivered with hurt and outrage.

Magnus stared at her. He could not bring himself to believe that she was not completely and utterly genuine. She had not betrayed him. No one could be that skilled an actress. Relief swamped him. He took several steps towards her. She snatched another ornament off the shelf and held it up in an unmistakable threat.

'I believe Carlotta's late husband gave that to her on their last wedding anniversary,' he murmured mendaciously.

She glanced at it in sudden shock and guiltily bit her lip. Hesitantly she put the ornament down. He took another step towards her and she moved instantly away.

'Don't come near me, Magnus,' she warned. She was like a wary woodland creature, mistrustful, poised to run.

Magnus took a deep breath. There was no alternative. He would have to do what he had sworn he would never do. Break the rule of a lifetime.

'I thought… I was—' He dashed his hand through his hair and took another deep breath. 'I was worried about you, and then when I went to that church and found you had been there days before…' He found it hard to meet her eyes and had to force himself to look at her. 'I didn't know where you were. I only knew you weren't with me—where you belong.'

He walked over to the window and stood there, fiddling with a fringed curtain. He turned and met her eyes, his face sombre and vulnerable. 'I was…I was jealous. I was wrong. I'm sorry. Please forgive me.'

Tallie's lip quivered. Her eyes fixed him with painful intensity, searching for the truth in his face.

The moment stretched, interminably. Magnus could hear nothing but the thudding of the heart in his chest and the thin, high cry of some far-off bird soaring on the wind. He had accused her of the vilest conduct. Would she, could she forgive him? Or forget? He thought he might be able to forgive her, in similar circumstances, but doubted whether he could ever forget. Trust, once shattered, was not easily mended. Who understood that better than he?

'You were jealous?' she whispered at last.

He nodded.

'Oh, Magnus,' she cried, and flung herself into his arms.

Chapter Fifteen

After a time Magnus woke. The late afternoon sun streamed through the open shutters, spreading golden oblongs of warmth over the walls and the bed. He lay there, savouring the moment. His wife lay warm and relaxed against his chest, her body curled against him like a small, sensuous cat. He reached down and gently lifted one of her hands and examined it. Four smooth ovals, just one slightly ragged end—her little finger. He laid the ragged nail gently against his mouth.

She stirred. 'Magnus?' she said sleepily, and smiled. 'Love you.' Still with her eyes closed she turned her cheek and began planting small sleepy kisses over his chest. Magnus closed his eyes, as if in pain. It all came so easily to her. It was these times when he felt the most vulnerable and uncertain. Bed sports he understood—he was experienced, in control; he knew what to do, how to give pleasure and how to gain it.

But this…this intimacy…when affection simply poured from her, and small clumsy kisses filled him with a piercing sweetness… He felt on the edge of…what? The abyss?

It terrified him, yet filled him with a ravenous hunger.

She'd said it again. *I love you, Magnus.*

They were only words, he told himself. Women used them all the time. It seemed to come easily to them, too easily. He recalled the times she'd said it; the first time, when she'd still hardly known him, after their marriage had been consummated.

And though he'd waited for her to say it again every night since, dreading it, but waiting for the words with a hunger that had frightened him, she hadn't.

Not until she'd been about to be taken from him, by that bandit. When he'd been furious, and terrified for her safety. She had whispered it then, as she'd kissed him goodbye. *I love you, Magnus.*

And now, a third time.

Again, after a quarrel…

He still didn't know where she'd been for those eight days. The question burned into him…but he didn't want to ask. He'd become a coward, too, just like his father. But as long as she was here, with him, he could tell himself it didn't matter.

Her hands caressed him and he felt his body stir in response. Yes, he could find oblivion there, sweet oblivion. He rolled over, taking her with him, and raised himself over her pliant body. She smiled and stroked his cheek, then lifted her head and kissed him. He tasted the tender passion in her and groaned. She wriggled under him, smiling into his eyes, and thrust her body eagerly against him. Magnus needed no further prompting. He surged into her, and found his sweet oblivion.

'Signor d'Arenville, Signora Thalia, wake up!' Carlotta banged furiously on the door.

Magnus swore. 'Wait, I will be with you in a few moments.'

'No, it is urgent, *signor*, very urgent! Please, *signor*, open the door!'

Cursing, Magnus threw on a robe, stalked to the door and flung it open. 'What the devil is all this noise about, Carlotta?'

Carlotta glanced past him to where Tallie sat in bed, the downy quilt tucked around her naked body. '*Signor*, *signora*, I am so sorry to disturb you but there is news, terrible news.'

Tallie sat up straighter. 'You mean about——?'

'No, no, *signora*. Sorry, but no news about him yet.'

Magnus frowned. *Him?*

Carlotta continued. 'No, this is important news just arrived from Torino. I heard it from my—'

Magnus held up a hand. 'Let me guess. Your cousin's uncle's brother-in-law's niece's great-aunt's nephew.'

Carlotta shot him a look of blank surprise. 'No, *signor*, I heard it from my neighbour who just got back from Torino.'

Magnus rolled his eyes. Tallie giggled.

'It is war, *signor*,' Carlotta said.

'What?' Magnus was dumbfounded. 'War? Are you certain.'

'Very certain, *signor*. My neighbour said in Torino the streets are full of soldiers. England and France are once again at war. And we are at war, too. Napoleon's troops are all over the Piedmonte.' She glanced from him to Tallie and back again. 'You must flee at once, *signor*. The soldiers are taking foreigners for questioning.'

Magnus swore again.

'He said he passed a troop of soldiers on the road. They will be here in two hours. They are searching houses on the way. They will most certainly come here.' Carlotta added, a little shamefacedly, 'All of Susa knows of my English visitors.'

'We will leave at once,' Magnus assured her. 'You have been exceedingly good to us, Carlotta. We would not wish to cause you trouble.'

Carlotta laid an anxious hand on his arm. 'Oh, no, Signor Magnus, it is not myself I am concerned for. I would not like to see you and Signora Thalia taken by soldiers.' She glanced at Tallie, who had already slipped out of bed and was dressing quietly. 'Especially with the baby coming. You must hide in the hills until dusk. It is too dangerous to try for the coast from here—Napoleon has soldiers all over Piedmonte. And you cannot go back through France. My nephews will take you into Switzerland. It is arranged.'

She turned to leave. Magnus stopped her with a hand on her arm. *'Signora*...Carlotta,' he said. 'You are a...a queen among women.' He took her hand and, bowing, kissed it lightly.

'Oh, *signor*.' She blushed, flustered. 'One does what one can. Now, I make food for you to take. Pack only what you can carry. My nephews will you meet after dark, so that no one will see you leave.' She shrugged apologetically. 'Some of my neighbours have no honour. If they do not see, they cannot tell which way you went. Most will expect you to go south, to the coast—there are too many soldiers that way, but they do not know it.'

'We will be ready within the hour,' Magnus said.

Carlotta turned to leave, then hesitated and turned back, a tiny smile on her face. 'My neighbour said in Torino all is confusion. English ladies are fainting; the men are in panic.' She regarded Magnus and Tallie proudly. 'Not *my* English visitors.'

Less than two hours later, Magnus and Tallie were sitting on a bundle of straw in a small shed a mile or so out of town. It belonged to Carlotta's uncle. They were waiting for John Black, Monique and the nephews to meet them in the shed after dark. Then they would make their way to Switzerland. Tallie had bidden Carlotta a tearful farewell. The two women had embraced, Carlotta whispering assurances in Tallie's ear that she would keep an ear out for news of her little brother.

Tallie sat chewing a piece of straw. Magnus glanced down at her worriedly. She had said very little since they left. 'Don't worry. I won't let any harm come to you,' he said softly.

She smiled up at him. 'I know,' she said simply. 'I was not worrying about that.'

The heavy feeling came into his chest again. She was so trusting and certain… He wished he could be as certain.

'You never did find out what I was doing when I didn't come back for those eight days, did you?' she said at last.

Magnus felt as if a fist had slammed him in the chest. He didn't want to know—what the hell was she doing, deciding to confess now? He wanted to get up, to pace around the tiny shed, to change the subject. He knew from her face it was something dreadful—it had clearly been weighing on her conscience since she'd arrived back from her mysterious journey. But he'd already decided he could live with whatever she'd done—as long as she stayed with him from now on. 'No, but it doesn't matt—'

'I was looking for my brother.'

'Your brother?' he said, stunned. *Brother?* It was the last thing he'd expected. 'I never knew you had a brother.'

'Neither did I, until some years ago—well, actually, I wasn't absolutely sure of it until a few days ago.' She leaned against him and sighed, and without conscious volition he put his arm around her. Quietly, without looking at him, she told her story.

'...and I wasn't sure whether to believe the letter or not—it was so incredible—but I couldn't get it out of my mind, and so when we came here....' She told how she had found her mother's grave, and met a young priest who had not known her mother but who had recalled the story. He believed the orphan child had been given to a woman who was childless—a good woman, a true daughter of the church.

'But the woman's husband died and she went to live with her brother, who hated the little boy. And then she died and the brother just went away and left him.' Tears sparkled on the ends of Tallie's lashes. 'Left a little boy of only seven years to fend for himself.'

Magnus pulled her into his arms and held her tight against his heart. 'The boy died?' he asked gently.

She shook her head. 'No, not that anyone knows of.' She looked at him in distress. 'Oh, Magnus, apparently there are children living wild in the mountains since the war, because no one will take them in. People are too poor to worry about somebody else's child.' She hugged him convulsively. 'It is so utterly dreadful. I wish I could do something, but now here we are, fleeing from the French and in no position to do anything. I did so much want to stay and search for my brother.' Tears ran down her cheeks and he kissed them softly away.

'We have to leave, my dear. You know that.'

She was silent.

'If not for our own safety, then for this child.' He laid his hand on her stomach and felt the now familiar surge of joy— and of terror. As far back as he could remember, from the time he was a little boy, he had always felt alone. Alone in a bleak, cold world. With only a bleak, cold future ahead of him.

But now there were two people who belonged to him, two people to care for—and to protect. He had never dreamed it could happen to him, never dreamed he would be so fortunate. And so grateful. He would protect her and her unborn child with his life. He drew her head down, laid his cheek against her hair and simply held her. His throat was full.

Half an hour later they were joined by John Black, and a few moments afterwards Monique arrived, a handsome young nephew with her. Then the rest of the nephews slipped in under cover of darkness, carrying baggage and bringing mules.

They set off in the moonlight, towards the far mountains glistening with snow.

'The captain says we shall reach England tomorrow,' announced Magnus joining his wife at the ship's rail. 'He plans to land at the nearest port—some problem with the mast, I gather.'

Tallie nodded but did not reply.

'It is a glorious night, is it not?' he said, looking out at the moon-tossed waves.

'Mmm.' His wife nodded. Magnus's arm closed protectively around her, bracing her against the slight rolling of the ship. They had made it. He had brought them to safety. But it seemed that was not enough.

'Look, there are traces of fire glittering in the water.' He pointed as he spoke.

'Yes.'

'It's caused by the movement of the ship.'

Tallie nodded again.

'Can you see the luminescent bubbles trailing in our wake?'

'Yes,' she murmured. 'Very pretty.'

Magnus tried again. 'And all the stars are out, so clear and bright. Nearly as clear as they were in the mountains…but not as close. I do not think we have ever been as close to the stars as we were in the mountains. Do you remember when you said it was as if you could truly just reach out and touch them?'

Tallie did not reply. Magnus tightened his grip around her, silently willing the return of his eager, excited bride. It was the sort of night which would have had her in raptures just a short time ago…

Tallie sighed. 'It is difficult to believe so much time has passed… Sometimes it feels like it was just a week or so, and at others…a lifetime.'

'It's just over two months,' murmured Magnus.

'But it feels like less, doesn't it?'

Magnus slipped his free hand under her cloak, laying it on the rounded curve of her belly. 'It feels like more to me.'

Tallie smiled and leaned her head against him.

'You've coped magnificently, my dear.' Magnus pulled her closer. There had been times he'd thought he'd never get her home safely.

The journey had taken much longer than anticipated, and had been much more arduous. For when they had reached the Swiss border they had discovered that Napoleon had invaded Switzerland as well. There had been no alternative but to head into Lombardy, and then east, towards the Austrian border. Numerous times they'd had to scramble off the road and hide from French soldiers.

Once over the border, they'd made their way towards Vienna. From there they had travelled to Prague, on to Dresden, and thence to Berlin. From Berlin they had headed towards the coast, and finally, at Husum, in Schleswig-Holstein, they'd managed to secure passage on the packet *Lark*, which was crowded with other fugitives—not only Englishmen and women, but others hostile to Napoleon's conquests.

They had boarded the boat with great relief, only to spend the next two anxious weeks at anchor, waiting for a favourable wind. Magnus had chafed at the delay. But now, finally, after six days and nights of sailing, England lay ahead.

'You have become a much better sailor, have you not?' Magnus was determined to cheer her. He hated to see her so low in spirits.

She shrugged. 'I suppose it has something to do with my condition.'

Magnus trailed his knuckles down her cool cheek in a gentle caress. 'Are you not enjoying this beautiful night, my dear? You are cold, perhaps? Would you like to return to your cabin?'

'No, not at all. You are right, my love—it is a lovely night,' said Tallie sadly. 'On such a night one finds it almost impossible to imagine that there is such ugliness in this world as war…'

But she knew there was, because lashed to the deck in front of her, secured in oilskin bags, were all the important papers on board—passports, regimentals, letters and dispatches. The captain of the *Lark* had ordered them secured out in the open—ready to be tossed overboard should the ship be boarded by the French. It was no idle threat, because for two days their ship had been pursued by French cruisers. On the third night the *Lark* had managed to slip away.

And so she was safe…but her little brother was still in danger. Her unknown little brother, so much more real to her now than he had been when first she had decided to search for him. *A bad, merry little boy*…alone in the mountains. She hoped there were plenty of apples for him to steal…but winter was drawing nearer.

'Oh, I do hope he will be all right.'

Magnus frowned. He knew full well who *he* was. She'd spoken of him almost every day since they had left Carlotta's, just like this—out of the blue—indicating how constantly he was in her thoughts.

He wished there was something he could do about it, but

there was nothing. He'd racked his brains, over and over. It was his unexpressed opinion that the boy was probably dead, but he would rather cut off his hand than say so and distress her further. But he could not bear to see his vivacious little bride so wan, and his inability to do anything about it chafed him unbearably.

'No doubt one of Carlotta's relatives will find him,' he said bracingly. 'They do turn up in the most unexpected places.'

He inclined his head towards the couple standing at the rail near the bow of the ship. Monique and Gino—the handsome young nephew who had followed them to Switzerland and then Austria. Finally, in Berlin, he had convinced Monique to marry him.

'I hope I won't be obliged to provide homes and jobs for all of Carlotta's relatives,' Magnus murmured jokingly in her ear. 'I doubt even d'Arenville Hall is big enough for them all.'

Tallie smiled, but it was still a trifle too wistful for his liking. Damn it, he wished he could do *something*.

It was almost an anticlimax to land at the placid English town of Southwold, with its small fleet of sailing boats and its line of little bathing boxes arrayed along the beach.

They found an inn, and Magnus and Tallie entered while John Black went to hire a coach and horses. The smell of new-baked bread and roasting beef informed them dinner was almost ready. Tallie's stomach rumbled as they sat down to table in a private dining room. Magnus smiled. 'It smells very good, does it not, my dear? At last—fresh bread and good honest English beef with no fancy sauces. And plain baked potatoes and boiled vegetables.' He rubbed his hands. 'A real pleasure after all that foreign food and our recent rations of pickled pork and ship's biscuits.'

Tallie cast him a look of burning reproach. 'At least *we* always had plenty to eat. *We* were never in danger of starving.'

Magnus gritted his teeth. It was not his fault they had not been able to stay and search for her brother, blast it! And he was getting fed up with feeling guilty about it. He had his wife to protect—and her unborn child! What did she expect him to do? Take a pregnant wife on a wild-goose chase, searching for a child who'd been abandoned in the mountains God only knew how long ago! No child would have survived that. Even without the added danger of the war, it would have been an exercise in heartbreak—and he knew whose heart would break. And he was *damned* if he'd allow it!

'You cannot prevent your brother starving by starving yourself,' he said bluntly. 'And besides, you have another child to consider.'

'Oh, yes, I am well aware of that!' she retorted, suddenly angry with the way he kept trying to divert her from speaking of her brother. 'A more important child—*your* child, the heir to the great d'Arenville name. Not some poor little lost, half-foreign bastard—' She stopped, clapping her hand to her mouth, horrified by what she'd suddenly blurted out.

'A bastard?' said Magnus, frowning. 'Your brother is a bastard? He is only a half brother, then?'

'No, he is *my brother*!' she insisted angrily. 'I do not care what Mama may have done, or who his father may have been. I do not care a rush for what anyone may say—he is my brother!'

'But—'

She pushed her chair back from the table and said bitterly. 'I planned never to tell you. I knew how it would be. The noble family of d'Arenville must never be tainted with such as he.'

She glared at him. 'Oh, do not bother to deny it, Magnus, I can see from the look on your face what you think. That is why I never told you why it was so important to me to find my mother's grave, why I went off into the mountains to search for him without your permission. I knew what you would say, knew you would find some way to prevent me finding him.'

'I was not responsible for the blasted war breaking out again!'

She waved his objection away. 'I know that! But even without it you would not have taken me into the hills to search, would you?'

He met her level gaze. 'No, I probably would not have allowed my pregnant wife to drag herself around the mountains on some wild-goose chase—'

'Exactly! And if I had found him, what then?'

Magnus hesitated.

'You would have considered him an embarrassment, wouldn't you?' She nodded, as if she had read confirmation in his eyes. 'I thought as much. You would have sent him away to be hidden from the eyes of the world, wouldn't you? Farmed him out with a tenant—the more obscure and distant the better, no doubt.' She sniffed. 'And you wonder why I did not tell you.'

She seemed to have it all worked out, he thought dully.

She thumped her fist on the table. 'Well, I won't have it. Do you hear me, Magnus? As soon as this frightful war is over I will go back there myself and search until I have found him. Do you understand? And I will bring him home and we will be a family. I do love you, Magnus, but if you do not like it, you can…you can *disown* me!' She burst into tears and fled the room.

Magnus sat there, unmoving, his face stiff and hard. So that was what she thought of him, was it? That he would be so shocked by a bastard half brother…an unknown bastard half brother who meant more to her than…and that he valued his family name more than…

You can disown me. The choice she expected him to make.

Yes, her news had come as a surprise to him. What man would not be shocked? But he had said nothing…nothing to make her think…

She certainly seemed to feel she understood him well enough to predict his reaction… She'd been judge, jury and executioner.

Would he have predicted her reaction with such complete and utter certainty? Yes, he realised ruefully. His wife was nothing if not predictable. She was loyal…and loving. It was not in her to turn her back on anyone who needed her—not a bastard half brother. Not even a cold-hearted earl…

She still claimed to love him. He still found the notion ter-rifying…even though he had come to depend on it utterly for his happiness. Happiness. Six months ago happiness had been a foreign concept to Lord d'Arenville of d'Arenville Hall. As had love…

He loved his wife. He recognised the truth of it now. He loved her, loved Tallie, with an intensity that rocked him to his soul. And he had no way, no words with which to tell her.

The words sounded easy enough, simple enough to say.

The words came to others so easily—a lie to smooth a path, to get a diamond necklace, to flatter, to deceive. He had never been able to utter the lie before. Had never expected to wish to.

But now he loved her.

And he could not say the words.

She wouldn't believe him anyway, he decided. Not after what she had just revealed. She thought him a cold, proud man, who cared only for his family name. Her reading of his character had shocked him, hurt him… Because there was an element of truth…

She expected him to disown her bastard half brother and to force her to do the same. And six months ago, before he had met her, he might have. Six months ago he would have had every expectation that a wife of his would no more acknowl-edge a foreign-born bastard half brother than walk naked down St James's Street. But that was six months ago.

A great deal had changed in six months—not the least Lord d'Arenville. Magnus drained the tankard of ale at his elbow and called for another. He knew what he had to do.

'That is d'Arenville Hall?' Tallie peered out of the coach window, looking up at the imposing edifice with some trepi-dation. It was enormous. A great grey building, heavy with carved, ancient stonework, glittering mullioned windows the only sign of life.

'Your future home, my lady,' murmured Magnus behind her.

Tallie blinked. She could not imagine herself as mistress of such an impressive establishment. And as for a small boy who'd been raised by Italian peasants...

'It...it's very grand,' she said at last, casting him a quick glance. He still had that...that stony look on his face. He hadn't forgiven her for her outburst yet.

He seemed deeply offended by her desire to provide a home for her brother. It upset Tallie to think of it, and she was distressed by his coldness towards her, but she had resolved not to give in to him on this. Her husband would have to learn to accept that at times she could be just as stubborn as he.

And if she couldn't go into raptures about his home she was sorry. It was very difficult to manufacture delight she didn't feel, especially difficult when he kept looking at her like that.

It was her fault, she knew. She had annoyed him with her defiance, and he was punishing her with his stiff and starchy manner. But now that they'd finally arrived at her husband's home she would have the opportunity to mend their differences. Hopefully they would share a bed once more. Their differences had a better chance of being sorted out there, in her experience...

Tallie sighed. It had been a long time... She'd had to share her ship's cabin with three other ladies. She missed him in her bed most dreadfully...missed the comfort of waking in the night, feeling his warm body beside hers, hearing his deep, even breathing. It was lonely in bed without him. And since their quarrel she felt lonelier than ever.

The coach drew up on the curved, immaculately raked gravel drive and a string of servants poured from the house and lined up.

'The butler's name is Harris and Mrs Cobb is the housekeeper. They will take their instructions from you,' said Magnus gravely. He moved solemnly forward, introducing this servant or that. It was all horribly formal, Tallie thought, as she received yet another bow and curtsy. She walked into the huge marble entry hall. Her steps echoed and she shivered.

'Are you cold?' Magnus enquired with cool solicitude. 'Harris, please show Lady d'Arenville into the Brown Room. I presume you've lit a fire?'

Harris bowed. 'Yes, of course, my lord. This way, my lady.'

Tallie was ushered to the Brown Room. It was enormous and gloomy, for the windows were shrouded with heavy brown velvet curtains. The room was stuffed with large, ornate, heavy items of furniture. Tallie wrinkled her nose. Everything upholstered in the same horrid dark brown. She wandered over to the fire, having to step around no fewer than three occasional tables, two embroidered firescreens and a settee. The room was immaculately clean, but she felt stifled. She thought instantly of the little peasant cottage in the mountains of Piedmonte and its cosy simplicity. She pushed the thought out of her mind with a pang of regret. There was no use in her worrying about her brother just now. This was her new home and she needed to accustom herself to the fact. Besides, she had fences to mend with her husband.

A few minutes later Magnus entered, followed by Mrs Cobb, the housekeeper. 'Are you warm now?' he asked. Tallie nodded.

'Then Mrs Cobb will show you to your room. You will wish to rest. I've ordered a tray sent up for your dinner,' he informed her.

No, Tallie wanted to cry, I do not wish to rest. I want you to show me your home and introduce me to all your favourite haunts. I want you to tell me stories of when you were a little boy growing up here, so that I may learn to love this hideous mausoleum. I want things to be normal between us again.

But she could not bring herself to say it. This Magnus was not her beloved Magnus; this was Lord d'Arenville of d'Arenville Hall, very cold and formal, and she did not yet know how to deal with him. Tallie followed the housekeeper dolefully. She did not like the sound of *your room*. She hoped she had misheard Magnus; she hoped she was being taken to *our* room.

But she was not. It was clearly a woman's room, fussy and expensive and elegant. The chairs were tiny, dainty, with delicate twisted flutes for legs. They matched the dressing table. The windowframes and bed were painted white and draped with gold silk. Large gilt looking-glasses were on every wall and Tallie could see herself reflected no matter where she stood in the room. White fur rugs lay scattered on the floor. Tallie hated the room on sight. It had an atmosphere, a hardness she did not like. She could not feel comfortable sleeping in here.

'Whose was this room?' she asked Mrs Cobb tentatively.

'His lordship's mother's, my lady.'

'Oh,' said Tallie. Magnus had never spoken to her of his mother. Perhaps he found it too painful to talk of her. It was hard, losing someone you truly loved, and a mother was special. 'What was she like?'

Mrs Cobb pursed her lips oddly, then shook her head. 'More'n my job's worth to say, my lady, begging your pardon.'

Tallie stared at her, astonished. 'I didn't mean you to *gossip* about M—Lord d'Arenville's mother. Just to tell me what sort of a person she was.'

Mrs Cobb shrugged. 'Can't do one without doing t'other,' she said. 'Best not enquire too closely about the past. Only one Lady d'Arenville is important now—best you forget about what's gone and get on with your life, begging your pardon, my lady.' She eyed Tallie's waist shrewdly. 'I hope you don't think me impertinent, my lady, but would you be expecting an interesting event in the not too distant future?'

Tallie blushed and laid her hand on her belly. 'You mean the baby?'

Mrs Cobb beamed and nodded. 'Thought as much. Good news for d'Arenville, my lady. His lordship's pleased, I expect. May I tell the other servants?'

Tallie nodded. 'I do not see why not. They will all be able to see for themselves before too long. I am getting so fat!'

'Fat? What nonsense! Bloom about you. A joy to behold.' Mrs Cobb nodded again. 'Good news you bring us, to be sure. 'Tis too long since there was a child at d'Arenville.'

'Were you here when Magn—his lordship was a boy?' Tallie asked eagerly.

'Not really,' Mrs Cobb said. 'I've been here just over a score of years, come Michaelmas.'

Tallie frowned in puzzlement. 'Twenty years? But my husband is only nine and twenty. You must have known him as a boy.'

Mrs Cobb looked at her a moment, then shook her head. 'He were off at school years before I started here.'

Sent to school at the age of six or seven, poor little boy, Tallie thought. She touched her stomach protectively. If this child was a boy he wasn't going to be parcelled off to school at a young age like his father. 'But in the holidays—'

Mrs Cobb shook her head sorrowfully. 'He weren't often asked home in the holidays.'

Asked home? As if he were a *guest*? 'Not asked home in the holidays?' repeated Tallie, appalled. 'But why not?'

Mrs Cobb pursed her lips, shook her head, opened her mouth then closed it. After a moment she said, 'You never heard this from me, mind, but word was in servants' hall his ma couldn't abide him. And his ma's word was law to his old lordship. Despite her immoral ways.'

Tallie could hardly believe her ears. His mother hadn't been able to abide him? And so Magnus hadn't often been asked home in the holidays? She had never heard of anything so shockingly selfish and callous in her life. Oh, to be sure Tallie had spent her own childhood in a school, but that had been because her parents had been forever travelling, not because they hadn't been able to abide her. She had a packet of letters from her mother, tied with a ribbon, to prove it. But poor Magnus. Poor little boy. What sort of a woman would do that to her own child?

A horrid, cruel woman, and Tallie knew she would sleep not a wink under her vile gold silk canopies. 'I won't sleep here,' she said decisively. 'Please find me another bedchamber.'

'But his lordship said—'

'You may inform his lordship that I did not wish to sleep in his mother's old room and that I chose another.'

'But—'

'That will be all, Mrs Cobb,' said Tallie firmly, feeling bold and autocratic. She had learned a thing or two since she was insignificant Tallie Robinson, and one was how to avoid an argument—with servants, at any rate. Her husband was a different matter.

Chapter Sixteen

Tallie looked around the breakfast room in surprise. She turned to the butler. 'Has his lordship not yet come down?'

'Yes, m'lady, he broke his fast early.' Harris pulled a chair back and waited.

Tallie sat, feeling quite despondent. It was her own fault— she had stayed awake late last night, hoping he would come to her, and then overslept this morning. 'I suppose I shall see him later, then.'

Harris, in the process of serving her with scrambled eggs, hesitated. 'He had urgent business to attend to, m'lady.'

Tallie ate her eggs slowly. She had no idea what to do with herself. The previous day Magnus had made it plain that he wished her to take up the reins as mistress of this establishment. Thanks to Laetitia's habit of delegation, Tallie was not without some experience in running a household. But this house was at once bigger and much grander than anything she had ever seen before. At Manningham she'd been her cousin's dogsbody, an errand-runner rather than mistress. Here she'd be expected to know everything.

Tallie glanced around the breakfast room with a critical eye. The room had a pleasant prospect, facing east, receiving morning sunlight. And the windows would have let in plenty of sunlight, had not they, like every other window here, been shrouded in heavy drapery. It was all so gloomy.

She wondered how Magnus would respond if she asked his permission to make a few changes. In her admittedly limited experience, men didn't like changes to their homes. Her cousin's husband George had complained incessantly when Laetitia redecorated their country home. He hadn't minded her turning the London house upside down with 'fancified nonsense', but his boyhood home had been another matter. On the other hand, according to Mrs Cobb, Magnus had not spent much of his boyhood here at all, so…

No, Tallie decided, she'd speak to him about it at dinner. And in the meantime she'd ask Mrs Cobb for a tour of the Hall.

By the end of the day Tallie was tired and dusty, but faintly satisfied. She'd been through the pantries, the linen presses and the storerooms, and examined the house from attic to basement. Many of her tentatively offered suggestions had been roundly approved by Mrs Cobb, and she now felt more confident about discussing changes to the house with Magnus. It was barely half an hour until dinner, so she hurried upstairs to bathe and to change her gown. Magnus had seen her rumpled and untidy enough times, and hadn't seemed to mind, but that had been when they were travelling. This was different. Tonight they dined at home together for the first time in their married life and she wanted to look her best. She had a quarrel to mend.

She hurried through her preparations and sat impatiently in front of the looking-glass while Monique did her hair, scanning her reflection intently, hoping her looks would please Magnus.

The gown she had finally chosen was one he'd bought her in Vienna. It had become a little limp during their travels, but now, in a big house with skilled laundrywomen, it looked almost as good as new. The fabric was fine and delicate. It clung to her breasts and swirled around her hips. It looked a lot like her golden Paris tea gown that Magnus had ruined so dramatically.

Her eyes misted reminiscently as she recalled how he'd

swept her into his arms and ascended the stairs two by two.
Could this gown, too, cause a wondrous, utterly splendid night
of passion? And put an end to a distressing period of coldness.

Tallie gazed at the gown in the looking-glass. She was
counting on that reaction tonight. It was the only way she
could think of to break down the icy barrier that had arisen
between them. Talking would do no good, for she was determined not to give in to him and she could not imagine him
giving in to her. No, this was the only way. And maybe then
he would be able to forgive her intransigence.

She fastened a string of pearls around her neck. Her breasts,
slightly enlarged with pregnancy, swelled above the low-cut
gown most satisfactorily. Her skin, with a light dusting of rice-
powder to disguise the dozen or so freckles, looked pale and
smooth. Tallie frowned critically at her image, then tugged the
neckline a little lower. She had no intention of being sent to
her room tonight, alone with a supper tray, like a naughty child
to contemplate her sins. No, her husband might be displeased
with her defiance on the matter of her brother, but she had
every intention of seducing him back into her bed. Tonight.

His urgent business, whatever it was, had kept him away
from the house all day. She had imagined her first day at
d'Arenville Hall—Magnus would show her around, telling her
tales of this and that as he introduced her to her new home,
her arm on his, or, better still, his arm around her. Today Mrs
Cobb had shown her the house, not Magnus, but Tallie was
determined Magnus would show her the rest. And then, perhaps, she would come to understand the man she loved—to
discover the boy and learn what had made him the man he
was.

Urgent business or not. She could wait for urgent business,
but she would wait *with* him, not for him. And when it was
finished, she had urgent business of her own... Tugging her
gown a little lower, Tallie stood up, took a deep breath and
left her chamber.

*The pale young princess descended the curving marble
stairway slowly. Her enchanted silken gown clung to her fig-*

ure, whispering softly with every movement. Below her, a statue of a handsome, dark-haired prince awaited her, his marble features cold and unmoving, his eyes blind and unforgiving, trapped in a spell by an evil Ice-Witch. Candlelight gleamed on his frozen features.

The princess came closer. With each whisper of the magic gown, each flicker of golden candle-flame the statue seemed to warm. The eyes flickered and darkened from a pale ice-grey to a stormy sea-dark colour. The blindness lifted from him and marble melted into flesh. Slowly he moved towards her, first one step then another, then he was leaping up the stairs towards her, two, three steps at a time. He swept the princess into his arms. 'Tallie, my dearest love, forgive me my coldness. I need your warmth, your love.' And his mouth descended on hers and the evil spell was broken...

But there was no Magnus waiting for her at the foot of the stairs. There was only Harris, the butler. Magnus must already be in the dining room. She was a little late from fussing about her appearance. He must have become impatient.

'Good evening, Harris.' Tallie smiled. 'I am looking forward to dinner. The aromas coming from the kitchen earlier were delicious, and I must confess I am extremely hungry.' She hurried towards the dining room.

But when she entered, she came to a sudden, shocked halt. The long, gleaming table was set for only one person. He could not, surely, still be attending to his business?

'M'lady,' murmured Harris. Hiding her anxiety, Tallie allowed him to seat her.

'Is my husband not joining me?'

A footman entered with soup, and Harris waited until she had been served and the footman had gone before answering. 'I told you this morning, m'lady. He left on urgent business.'

'But his business surely cannot last all night,' she said. 'Lord d'Arenville must eat, must he not?'

Harris looked awkward. 'M'lord left d'Arenville this morning. He did not say when he would return.'

Left d'Arenville? Tallie stared at the butler in confusion, a
cold thread of dread winding around her heart. 'I assumed you
meant he'd left the house.'

'No, m'lady. He left.' The butler looked at her in concern.
Left? Left for where? Tallie tried to keep her features even.
'Did you not know about it, m'lady?'

Tallie attempted a smile. 'Yes...yes, of course I did, but I
did not realise he meant to leave today. I thought he was going
to...to...' She felt her lips quivering and hastily touched a
starched linen napkin to them to hide her distress. 'A foolish
misunderstanding, that is all,' she mumbled, and lowered her
head as if to say a silent grace.

*Where had he gone? And for how long? All day and night,
obviously. But without a word to her?* She spooned up some
steaming substance and conveyed it to her mouth. Her hands
were shaking. She laid the spoon down with a clatter, hoping
the butler hadn't noticed.

There was a short silence. She wondered whether Harris
could hear her heart pounding. It sounded terribly loud to her.

After a time he cleared his throat and said, 'Lord
d'Arenville left a letter for you, m'lady. Did you not receive
it?'

Tallie stared. 'A letter?'

'Yes, m'lady. I shall fetch it immediately,' said Harris,
sweeping from the room. He returned in a moment, bearing a
sealed letter on a silver salver. He placed it beside her, hesitated, then bowed and left the room.

Heart pounding, Tallie watched him leave. Her first letter
from Magnus. She broke open the wafer and began to read.

My dear Lady d'Arenville,

Lady d'Arenville. Not Tallie. Her heart sank.

*You were sound asleep when I came to your room and
I did not wish to disturb your rest. I know how much you
need it.*

Not as much as she needed him. Why could he not have woken her?

I have important business to transact and must leave for London first thing this morning. I am unsure of when I shall return, but be assured I will do so as soon as my business allows it.

London? The letter dropped from Tallie's nerveless fingers and fluttered onto the table. *Gone to London?* He had just gone off to London? Without explaining or saying goodbye? With shaking fingers she picked up the letter and continued to read, her numb brain hardly able to take it in.

You will have plenty to occupy you in settling in to the Hall and making preparations for the nursery. I noticed you did not sleep in the chamber allotted you. You have my full permission to make any changes you wish and draw on any sums you think necessary. My man of business, Jefferies, has been informed thus.

Full permission to make any changes she wanted? Draw on any sums she thought necessary? How long was he expecting to be gone to make arrangements like that? Informing his man of business?

In addition, you will need to order a new wardrobe.

Tallie glanced down at her golden tea gown. It probably was a little shabby, she reflected sadly. Despite the miracle wrought by the maids. And it was growing a trifle tight. Yes, she supposed she would need a new wardrobe...

You will not lack for either advice or masculine support during my absence, for I offered my oldest friend,

> *Freddie Winstanley, the living at d'Arenville and he*
> *moved into the vicarage last month. You may repose com-*
> *plete confidence in both Freddie and his wife,* ~~Joan Janet~~
> *Jenny. You will like them.*

Was that an opinion of her taste in people or an order to
like his friends? It was hard to know. But why was he not
here to introduce her to them? How long did he plan to stay
away? Tallie read the last lines with great trepidation.

> *I will make every effort to return before you are*
> *brought to bed of a child, but if not my thoughts will be*
> *with you. Take care, my dear.*
> *Yr affectionate husband,*

She could just make out the scrawl at the bottom—*d'Arenville*.
Tallie crushed the letter slowly to her breast and stared
blankly out of the window. She had no idea how long she sat
there staring, but she was vaguely aware of Harris coming in
at some stage and silently removing the dish of cold soup.

He brought a plate of roast beef, fresh and hot, but she took
one look at it and pushed it away. She felt sick.

I will make every effort to return before you are brought to
bed of a child, but if not my thoughts will be with you.

She could think of nothing, no business, however important
that could keep him away for such a long time...

Harris took away the second untouched plate and returned
with Mrs Cobb and Monique. Tallie was vaguely aware of
some whispering behind her, but she could take in nothing...nothing but the fact that Magnus had brought her here
to d'Arenville Hall and left her the very next morning. Leaving
a coldly formal letter explaining he might possibly find the
time to return after his heir had been born.

He had abandoned her. The truth pounded in her brain like
a hammer against an anvil, but she could not take it in...

It was as she had heard him say to Laetitia all those months ago... He wanted a plain, convenient wife whom he would get with child and live in the country...

But he *couldn't* have just left her. Not Magnus. Surely he wouldn't...not without even saying goodbye...

Unless he really *had* abandoned her... He would have found it difficult to face her, knowing what he planned...maybe too difficult...

A new thought occurred to her. Perhaps his coldness towards her after their difference of opinion about her little brother had been feigned...or at least exaggerated. Perhaps even then he had been preparing to leave her here...alone...

She shivered, suddenly feeling very cold.

'Milady,' said Monique at her elbow. 'Are you all right?'

Tallie did not answer.

'Feeling a bit poorly, the wee mite,' said Mrs Cobb gruffly. She picked up the linen napkin and gently blotted Tallie's face with it. The napkin came away damp, and Tallie stared at it, dimly puzzled. She lifted a trembling hand to her cheeks and found tears. She'd been crying without knowing it.

Shakily she stood up.

'I want to go to bed, please. I don't feel very well.'

On trembling legs Tallie approached the staircase she had floated down so hopefully only a short time before. It loomed before her now, an almost impossible climb. Doggedly she took one step, then another, then another.

'Tallie, my dear, forgive me for calling unannounced—'

Hurriedly Tallie sat up, surreptitiously wiping her eyes before turning to face the minister's wife, Janey Winstanley, who had become a good friend over the last few months.

Janey stopped in midsentence. Her face crumpled with concern as she took in Tallie's woebegone face and reddened eyelids. 'Oh, my dear—' she began.

Tallie interrupted. 'All these dratted changes to the house have stirred up so much dust and I am forever catching it in my eye.' She rubbed her handkerchief over it, blinked carefully, and then said with a bright, false smile, 'See, it is out now. Shall I ring for tea?'

Janey looked at her in dismay. 'My dear, you don't have to pretend with me. It is monstrous crue—'

Tallie cut her off. 'Yes, tea, I think, and shall we take it in the new Blue Room? I am anxious for your opinion.' She took her friend by the arm and led her towards the new blue salon.

Janey allowed herself to be taken, a troubled frown on her face. She stood in the doorway, admiring the newly refurbished room. 'I cannot believe what a change you have wrought in this house, Tallie,' she said. 'I never did like— I mean, this house was always very grand and impressive, but—'

Tallie smiled. 'I didn't like it much either.'

Janey smiled back. 'Forgive me, I didn't mean to be rude. But you've made such a difference. It is so light and…so pleasant and welcoming. How did you manage, in your condition?'

Tallie shrugged. 'It was not difficult. My husband gave me *carte blanche* to do as I wished with the house, and all I had to do was decide what changes to make.'

Tallie made light of her achievements, a little embarrassed to receive praise for something done in a surge of anger. During the first shock of Magnus's abandonment she'd blamed the house itself for her predicament—the house where the boy Magnus had not been welcome, where the man Magnus could dump his unwanted bride.

If he'd had a home instead of an ancient showplace Magnus might have been a different man, a man who could let himself care, even a little, for his wife. So she'd attacked it with a vengeance, changing everything she could, forcing the past into obscurity, removing all reminders, all echoes of his forebears. It might not ever be a home for Magnus, but she was determined it would become a home for her children. And for herself.

'I cannot believe what you have done,' added Janey.

Tallie looked at her new friend with faint trepidation. She

had done what she'd set out to do—made Magnus's boyhood home unrecognisable. Men hated change. He would probably be furious with her. Good. She was utterly furious with him—she told herself so a hundred times a day so she would not forget.

'You have turned a mausoleum into a home.'

Tallie smiled politely, but she knew Janey's words were not true. The house was more pleasant, but it was not yet a home. A home needed love to warm it…and children. She felt her eyes mist and laid her hand on her stomach.

Janey's eyes followed her movement. 'It won't be long now, my dear. Do…have you had any word from your husband?'

Tallie rubbed a hand over her swollen belly and gazed out into the garden. She turned to her companion and smiled brightly, but without a great deal of conviction. 'Oh, no. But then he is extremely busy. Urgent business, you know.'

Janey snorted. 'In all these months?'

'Well, men do not enjoy writing letters, I believe. In any case, they say no news is good news,' said Tallie with a pathetic attempt at cheeriness. The two women fell silent for a while.

'I cannot believe he—' began Janey.

Tallie laid a hand on her friend's knee. 'Don't, please.' She bit her lip and Janey subsided.

'I am sorry to distress you. It is just I cannot bear to see you so unhappy.'

'Unhappy?' said Tallie tremulously. 'How could I be unhappy? I have a lovely house, a secure home, wealth to spend as I like… You forget I was little better than a pauper before I married.'

'As if that—'

'But I explained it to you before, Janey. I knew what I was doing when I married Magnus. I knew then he planned this, planned to leave me here as soon as I began increasing.'

'It is just so cruelly unjust—'

'No! It is all my own fault. It is just… I have a foolish

tendency to indulge in silly, childish daydreams, and in my foolishness I read something more into Magnus's behaviour towards me, that is all. But he never said anything to make me believe he…he lo— He never lied to me. It is just…I misunderstood…he has…he has beautiful manners…that is the trouble.' Tallie pulled out a damp and crumpled handkerchief and blew noisily into it. 'This dust is shocking, is it not?' she added, blinking her lashes furiously.

There was a long pause as Tallie dabbed at her eyes. At last Janey spoke. 'You know you do not need to face this alone, my dear. I will—'

'It is very good of you, but I will not be alone, thank you, Janey. My husband said he will come, if he can. This child means a great deal to him, you know.' Tallie added wistfully, 'He needs an heir. The d'Arenvilles are a frightfully ancient family.'

Janey patted her hand. 'Well, just in case, be sure to send for me the minute you experience the slightest twinge.'

'There is plenty of time. Monique says it will be several weeks yet,' said Tallie. Poor Monique, Tallie thought. She, too, had been unlucky in love.

'Um…Freddie wrote to Magnus, you know.'

'Does *Freddie* know where he is?' Tallie turned a look of painful intensity on her friend.

Janey shook her head, regretting her impulse. 'No, he sent it to Magnus's lawyers to pass on. It was just about…about parish matters,' she lied.

'Oh.' Tallie nodded dully. 'Parish matters. Of course.'

'I must go now,' said Janey. 'Sorry I cannot spend more time—'

Tallie forced herself to brighten. 'No, no, of course you must go. I cannot keep you from your dear husband and your two lovely children. It must be wonderf— It was very good of you to visit me, Janey. I find it hard to walk far these days; my ankles swell so if I overdo it.' She levered herself out of the chair.

Janey bent to kiss her on the cheek. 'Take care, my dear,' she said, and left.

Take care, my dear. Magnus's last words; his last written instructions to her. Tallie closed her eyes. It was dreadful how shockingly weepy her condition caused her to be. It would pass soon, she told herself. That and the dull aching pain of knowing she was not loved, not valued at all, except as a brood mare.

It was her own fault, she told herself firmly. She had deceived herself. He had *never* said he loved her.

And it wasn't as if she had anything to cry about. Others had much more serious problems—her little brother, for instan— No. The thought of a small boy facing the winter alone was too distressing even to contemplate.

It was just her condition that made her feel a touch melancholy. And it wasn't as if she didn't have *hundreds* of moments of happiness to look back on...

Tallie gasped suddenly as a tiny fist or foot thumped her from within. It was a timely reminder... She should stop fretting over the past and think only of the future, for soon she would have a dear little baby to love.

The pain would pass.

Everybody said it would.

Although they were only talking about the pain of childbirth.

Chapter Seventeen

Tallie sat on the terrace enjoying the winter sunshine. She had several shawls tucked about her, for it was very cold. It would have been sensible to go inside, but she did not feel inclined to be sensible. She felt both lethargic and oddly restless.

Idly she watched a coach bowling along the road bordering the estate. She knew most of her neighbours' conveyances and she did not recognise this one. A passing stranger?

She sat up straight as it turned in at the gateway. Miles Fairbrother, the gatekeeper, came out to speak to the driver. Then he opened the gate and the coach drove through. Whoever it was must have legitimate business, for Miles did not grant entry lightly.

For one terrifying, ecstatic moment it occurred to Tallie that it might be Magnus, returning for the birth of the child, but this coach was plainly not her husband's. It was small, outmoded and shabby, and the horses were not at all the sort of cattle her husband would own. The horses seemed tired. Whoever it was had travelled a long way.

Tallie pushed herself out of her chair and walked around the house towards the front. Harris had also seen the visitors, for the front door was wide open and he stood there, waiting.

'Do you know who it can be?' she asked him.

'No, m'lady. I've never seen that coach before. I hope Fairbrother knows what he's doing. Would you care to wait inside the house, m'lady?'

'No. I know it is not the thing for me to wait here like this, but I'm curious,' answered Tallie. 'I'm sure it will be all right.'

The coach came rapidly up the drive and halted. The driver, an unshaven ruffian in a frieze coat and red muffler, climbed down. Tallie frowned. He reminded her of Gino, but he turned to let down the coach steps and she could see his face no longer.

Tallie stood watching. A frisson of tension passed through her and a hand crept to her throat. A tall man stepped down from the shabby coach, a tall, weary-looking man, with over-long dark hair and—she knew without seeing them—grey eyes.

'Magnus!' She hurried down the steps and ran awkwardly towards him, then recalled herself and stopped short, hesitating, suddenly afraid. By the very manner of his leaving he had made it abundantly clear he did not want her love. So how was she to respond to his return? All she wanted was to be in his arms. But what did he want?

He took several steps towards her, then stopped and stared.

Tallie ran a hand self-consciously over her stomach, but she did not take her eyes off Magnus. His skin was uncharacteristically bronzed, but under that he looked exhausted. He had not shaved in several days and his eyes had dark shadows beneath them. His face was thinner, too, almost gaunt. A tattered greatcoat was draped around his shoulders. He lifted a hand in an awkward, half-hearted greeting, and the coat slipped from his shoulders. His arm was in some sort of sling, she realised.

'Magnus, you are hurt,' she cried, and hurried across the gravel towards him, her misgivings forgotten in her concern. But just as she was about to reach him he turned away from her. She stopped, unbearably wounded.

He said something she didn't catch to a person inside the coach. Tallie waited, struggling for composure. He had brought a guest.

A small figure scrambled out of the coach and stood behind Magnus, as if hiding. The coach rumbled away, leaving the three of them standing on the gravel drive. Magnus reached behind him to pull the small person out, but he or she resisted.

Magnus said something. In Italian.

Italian? Tallie's heart was in her mouth.

A thin, sharp, not very clean little face peered out at her, frowning, then ducked back behind Magnus. Tallie could hardly breathe. The face peered out at her again, examining her intently. Tallie didn't move. After a moment he stepped out, a skinny little boy, dressed in clothes too big for him. A boy with ragged, curly, light brown hair, streaked with sun. A boy with a scattering of freckles over the bridge of his nose. A boy about seven years old.

'My dear,' said Magnus, 'I have brought you your brother. Richard, this is your sister.'

'No Richard—*Ricardo*,' the little boy muttered fiercely, but he did not take his wary brown eyes off Tallie.

'Of course, Ricardo,' said Tallie, smiling through her tears. She held out her arms. The boy looked up at Magnus, who nodded. The child shrank back a little. Magnus gave him a gentle push towards Tallie. The little boy came towards her slowly, suspiciously, glancing frequently back at Magnus, as if fearing he would disappear. Magnus nodded encouragingly. The child allowed himself to be embraced, standing rigid in her arms for a moment or two, like a small, stiff block of wood. It seemed to Tallie she could feel almost every bone in his body, even through the layers of ill-fitting clothing. Poor little lad. As soon as she loosened her hold he wriggled out of it and scurried back towards Magnus, gripping Magnus's sleeve firmly in his grubby little hand. It was plain her little brother trusted only one person.

Magnus laid a gentle hand on the child's shoulder. 'He has had a hard time of it, my dear,' he said softly. 'You must not take it to heart.'

Tallie shook her head, smiling, her heart too full to speak.

Tears streamed down her cheeks, but they were tears of joy, not sorrow.

Magnus, his intense gaze boring into her, stepped forward, took out a large handkerchief and carefully dried her face, cupping her chin in a large warm hand. She stood motionless, drinking in the beloved Magnus smell of him, the tender motion of his hands on her skin, his warm, ragged breath on her face. She had yearned for this so often during the last months she was almost afraid it was yet another dream.

Shakily she lifted a hand to his thin, lined cheek and traced the long groove that bisected it. Whiskers rasped beneath her fingers. He was real. Magnus had come back to her.

'Oh, Magnus,' she whispered tremulously, and lifted her face blindly up to his. With a hoarse groan he drew her against him and lowered his mouth to hers.

He kissed her hungrily, as if unable to get enough of her, his tongue moving ravenously, possessively, slaking a desperate need, arousing desperate desires. He pressed burning kisses on her mouth, her nose, her throat, her wet eyelids, her mouth again, holding her hard against him, smoothing her body against his, remembering, reclaiming.

She kissed him back fervently, feverishly, with equal passion, burning away the lost months of loneliness, the anger, the distress and the fear. She only knew he was here, with her, and that the part of her that had wanted to die was vibrantly, joyously alive. Her arms clasped him around the neck, pulling him closer, and she pressed herself against him, hard. She ran one hand through his long thick hair, glorying in the cool texture of it and the bony, beloved shape of his skull. She slipped her other hand into the opening of his shirt, longing to feel his skin against hers once more. There was a sharp thud.

'What was that?' Magnus pulled back suddenly and looked at her, shocked.

Tallie smiled mistily. She took his hand and laid it gently on her stomach. 'That was your son.'

He stared at her, then jumped as he felt another little kick.

His eyes fixed on the swell under his hand for a long moment, then his eyes met hers in a look of dazed wonder. The baby kicked again, and again Magnus started.

'Does it happen often?' he whispered.

Tallie nodded.

Magnus blinked. 'Does it hurt?'

She shook her head. 'Not at all.'

'Oh, Lord,' he groaned, and drew her into his arms again and buried his face in her hair. They stood there a long time in silence, feeling the baby kick occasionally.

After a few minutes Tallie felt a movement at her elbow. She glanced down. A small grubby face scowled up at her, then tentatively pushed closer to Magnus. Gently she reached down to draw him in to their embrace. His body was stiff and resistant, like a wild animal, and he gripped hold of Magnus's shirt possessively. Gently she touched his hair. She felt him flinch, but he didn't move away.

She started to stroke the tangled honey-coloured curls, so like her own, and he let her, still poised like a wary creature, to flee or to fight. She continued stroking his hair, lightly at first, then more confidently as she felt him start to relax. It was the last thing she would have expected to do with her brother, tame him like a little wildcat. Her heart bled at the thought of the life he must have led, the life which made him so wary and mistrustful.

After a time she felt him thrust himself between her and Magnus and she dropped her hand away in disappointment. It would take time for her to earn his trust, she told herself. He turned his head to glare at her again, then looked away. Slowly, without looking at her, he reached down and took her hand, then placed it back on his head. Tallie felt a surge of joy as she began stroking him again, and she felt him lean imperceptibly into her caress. He was hungry for love, she realised.

He was not the only one.

She looked up at her husband and saw with amazement a sheen of tears in his sea-grey eyes as he gazed at her.

'Shall we go inside?' he said huskily.

She nodded, her heart once again too full for words.

She moved to step away, but he pulled her back, his good arm holding her hard against his side. A small bony body burrowed defiantly between them and Magnus smiled and loosened his hold on her, making room for the little boy. 'I see I'm going to have to learn to share you,' he murmured.

Tallie smiled tremulously back. 'Me, too,' she said, and then, with not a sliver of the dying evening light showing between their bodies, the little family moved slowly towards the house.

'Gino and I took a shorter version of the route we left by,' said Magnus, sipping a glass of burgundy with pleasure. 'Into Holland, then Westphalia and so on, travelling overland, mainly by night.'

Tallie listened in silence, her eyes wide. Travelling across miles and miles of enemy territory in the middle of a war, and by night. It sounded terribly dangerous, yet he spoke of his journey as if it were nothing. 'Have some more roast beef,' she urged him.

His eyes travelled to Tallie's brother, who was ploughing happily through a second plate heaped with food. He smiled. 'I think young Richard is proving himself the better trencherman here.'

The boy looked up frowning, his mouth full. 'No Richard— *Ricardo!*'

Magnus shook his head. 'He will soon accustom himself to his English name.'

'Ricardo,' came a mutter from the other side of the table.

Tallie intervened. 'And then where did you go?'

'Back through Venice and thence to Piedmonte. Carlotta sends her love, by the way.'

Tallie smiled and nodded, but she was not going to be sidetracked. 'Wasn't it terribly dangerous to travel all that way?'

Magnus shrugged. 'Oh, we ran into a French patrol here and there, but honestly, my dear, if you'd seen them—more than half of Napoleon's recruits are beardless boys, dragged off their farms. And the officers are not gentlemen, as ours are. I was in no great danger.'

He was lying, thought Tallie. She had heard Freddie discussing the war. There might be a lot of young lads in Napoleon's army, but there were also a lot of strong men. And if his officers were not gently born, it seemed to her they would be even rougher with an Englishman caught in the wrong place.

'It took some time, but in the end I found him—and half a dozen other young orphans.' He darted an odd look at her. 'You'll never believe who was keeping an eye on them, making sure the children didn't starve. That bandit fellow.'

'Maguire?' Tallie was astounded. And intrigued.

Magnus nodded. 'Hard to believe, but it's true. In fact he brought me to the little chap...after he'd bound my wound up.'

'*Maguire* bound your wound?' Tallie squeaked. Then she frowned in dire suspicion. 'He didn't cause it, did he?'

Magnus shook his head, smiling. 'No, it was a French bullet. The bandit dragged me to safety.'

'Oh, I knew he was a noble fellow!' Tallie clasped her hands in thankfulness.

'Odd you should say that,' Magnus drawled. 'He claims to be Irish nobility—well, they all say that, of course. But still, he's got a look about him. I sent him back to Ireland.'

Tallie sat up, alarmed. 'But won't they hang him? He said—'

Magnus snorted. 'I'd like to see them try! No, I've appointed him manager of my Irish properties—for his lifetime.'

Tallie's jaw dropped.

'Fellow might be a damned blackguard, but he's got a good heart,' said Magnus gruffly. 'Those children would have perished without him. And he did save my life.'

'Yes, of course, and I think it's a wonderful idea,' exclaimed Tallie warmly. 'And what did you do with the other children?'

Magnus regarded her oddly a moment. Naturally his wife would expect him to take care of any other orphans he came across. 'They are in the very best of care.'

'With whom? Maguire?'

Magnus grinned. It had been a tempting thought, to saddle the green-eyed rogue with a pack of children, but he hadn't done it. 'No, I thought they were better off in the care of a good woman.'

'What good woman?'

'Guess.'

Tallie thought for a moment. 'Carlotta! Of course! What a splendid idea, Magnus.'

He nodded. 'I left her with five hungry little urchins, cooking up an enormous batch of pasta and mothering them to her heart's content. I settled money on her, of course, to help with the cost, although she was damned stiff-necked about it.'

Tallie regarded her husband in amazement. She could still hardly believe it; not only had her husband *not* abandoned her, he had risked his life a hundred times over, so that she could be united with her brother. Her bastard, half-foreign brother... *And* he'd given a childless widow five needy children to care for. He'd even removed Maguire from his life of crime and given him a position of respect in his homeland.

The very contemplation of his noble deeds threatened to overwhelm her. She watched the small boy as he mopped up gravy with a piece of bread, then lifted the plate to lick it clean. Out of the corner of her eye she saw Magnus frown and open his mouth. She laid her hand on his arm. 'There is plenty of time to teach him his manners.' Magnus relaxed.

The door flew open and Harris entered, carrying a trifle—a staggering confection of cake and cream and jelly that had young Richard-Ricardo's eyes popping. The very thing to appeal to a young boy, thought Tallie delightedly, making a mental note to thank Cook for her thoughtfulness later.

'M'lord's favourite,' Harris announced. 'Cook prepared it especially.'

Tallie glanced at her husband. He looked almost as pleased

as Ricardo, though he was trying not to show it. She hid a smile. All these months and she hadn't realised he had a secret sweet tooth.

There was a long break in the conversation as the trifle was treated with the respect it deserved. Tallie, whose own sweet tooth had disappeared during her pregnancy, watched her husband and her brother attack the towering confection with gusto. She was hard put to it to decide which one of them enjoyed it the most, but she could see which of the two had never tasted trifle before.

Her little brother was still dressed in his ill-fitting clothes. There would be time enough tomorrow to find more suitable attire. But he looked a great deal cleaner in the face and the hands, at any rate. Tallie smiled as she observed the ecstatic expression that passed over the thin, vivid face with each sweet, gooey mouthful.

He looked so much like her, she mused. There could be no doubt in the world that they were brother and sister. It was an utterly wonderful thought—people would look at them and know they belonged to each other. But it was such a peculiar feeling, to be looking across a table at someone and seeing a miniature version of oneself. The same curly hair in a dozen tawny shades. The same freckled, pointy nose—only his didn't turn up, like hers. And the same eyes. *The same eyes!* The thought hit Tallie like a bombshell. *Ricardo and she had the same eyes.* And she had Papa's eyes. And Papa's curly streaky hair. And Papa's nose. And so did Ricardo.

Ricardo was Papa's son!

Papa had been wrong. Her brother was her true brother. He wasn't a bastard. Relief and joy poured into her. Bastardy would have made no difference to her, nor, apparently to Magnus, but it was a huge handicap in the eyes of the world. It would have affected his acceptance in society, his chance of making a good marriage, of making his way in the world. Her little brother had had a difficult enough beginning; she was glad, so very glad, the rest of his life would not be so hard.

She could not keep the wonderful news to herself. 'Magnus!' she said in a low, excited voice.

He turned to her.

'Ricardo looks exactly like me, does he not?'

Magnus glanced from the boy back to her, and nodded. 'But you are prettier.'

She blushed with pleasure. 'Thank you, but that is not the point. I am held to be the image of my father!'

He made the connection instantly. 'So your father was wrong. Delighted to hear it.' He reached out and lifted her hand to kiss it. 'Excellent news for all concern—' He broke off with an oath, staring at her hand.

'Why the devil have you been chewing at your nails again?'

Tallie flushed with embarrassment. She tried to tug her hand from his grip. 'I'm sorry.'

His eyes scanned her face intently. 'Has something been upsetting you? Or someone? Tell me instantly and I will see to the matter.'

Tallie blinked and stared at him in disbelief.

'Tell me at once, Tallie. There is no point in hiding it.' He brandished her ragged nails in her face and ran his thumb over them. 'These are testament enough. If someone has been upsetting you I intend to get the matter sorted out immediately. I do not like you to be upset. Did you not speak to Freddie about it—surely he could have sorted the matter out for you?'

Tallie tugged on her hand, feeling no small degree of irritation. Who did the stupid man *think* had upset her—the cook or the butler? Did he think he could just disappear from her life with a cold, horrid formal note and *not* upset her? She wrenched her hand from his and stood up.

'It is time to get that boy into a proper bath and then to bed,' she said.

'Do not change the subject, wife,' growled Magnus in a low voice.

'There is a time and place for everything,' she retorted, 'and this is neither. Now, Harris, could you arrange hot water for his lordship, and also for young Master Ricardo's bath?'

Ricardo looked up, grinning, recognising nothing in the speech except his name. *'Si, Ricardo.'* He gave Magnus a triumphant look. 'No Richard,' he repeated, and allowed Tallie to take him by the hand and lead him from the room.

'He is asleep.' Magnus stood at the doorway of Tallie's bedchamber.

Tallie nodded. 'Good,' she whispered. *And you?* she thought. *Where are you going to sleep?*

'You were right; the puppy did the trick. They're both tucked up in bed together.'

Tallie nodded again.

'Good idea that.' He stood in the doorway, staring at her, the burning heat of his gaze at odds with the casual diffidence of his voice. 'Um…I like what you've done to this room.'

Tallie nodded again. There was a lump in her throat, making it difficult to talk. Chit-chat, like one had with a guest or a stranger, not a husband.

'Like a garden in the bottom of the sea,' he said. 'Very light and airy, all that green…muslin, is it? Nice.' He gestured to the gauzy window drapes and then to the curtains surrounding her bed. He strode across the room and caught a bunch of the fine soft fabric in a fist. He stood there, running it through his fingers for a moment, and then said diffidently, 'I thought to sleep in here with you tonight. Do you mind?'

Tallie stared at her husband. *Did she mind?* Was the man totally blind to her feelings for him? She supposed she had not been as blatant as she'd thought. But how often did one need to tell a man you loved him before he took notice?

'I mean—' he said awkwardly. 'Er…I know we can't… You can't… Oh, Hell!' He dashed his hands through his hair and said in a rush, 'I know we cannot make love, but if you do not mind, I want very much to hold you tonight.'

If I do not mind? She couldn't answer, just shook her head dumbly and held out her arms to him. He reached her in two strides and pulled her into his arms. His mouth came down on hers…tenderness…leashed hunger…possession.

After a while he lifted her onto the bed and sat down. He sat there looking at her, devouring her with his eyes. He reached up to smooth her tumbled curls away from her face, delicately, clumsily, his big hands trembling slightly.

'There were times when I thought I would never do this again, never see—' His voice cracked and he pulled her tight against his chest.

'Me, too,' she whispered, rubbing her face against his freshly shaven chin.

He pulled his head back and stared at her in surprise. 'You thought *you'd* never see me again? But you didn't know where I was.'

'No, I didn't.'

'Then how—?' He frowned. 'Why on earth would you think I wouldn't return? You weren't to know I'd gone back to Italy, that I was behind enemy lines. I distinctly told you I'd gone to London on business.'

Tallie scanned his puzzled face in utter disbelief. 'I *know* what you told me,' she said, unable to disguise the edge in her voice. She knew his horrid letter off by heart.

'So then…?'

She stared at him. He seemed genuinely confused.

Magnus stared back at her. 'You sound upset.'

'Of course I am upset!' she snapped. 'How did you expect me to feel when I got that letter?'

'I didn't want to worry you, so—'

'Didn't want to worry me! Didn't want to *worry* me!' Her voice rose in indignation. 'You great mutton-headed man! You dumped me here like an unwanted cat and slipped away in the night like a criminal, leaving me a note that said you had important business elsewhere and that I was to get on with my life! How did you expect me to feel?'

Magnus's mouth gaped open. A frown furrowed his brow. 'But it wasn't like that at all,' he said slowly.

'It was *exactly* like that!' Tears quivered on her eyelashes and she groped for a handkerchief. 'Oh, drat it. This always happens,' she mumbled, and reached for one of the muslin bed curtains to dry her eyes.

He lifted her trembling hands from her face, holding them gently in his, and gazed into her swimming eyes. 'You thought I had abandoned you?' he said slowly.

Tallie nodded.

'That I didn't care?'

She nodded again.

His grip shifted and he lifted her hands, the ragged nails showing stark and ugly between his fingers. 'Then these…' he stroked them with his large tanned thumbs '…are all my fault.'

Tallie said nothing. She bit on her lip.

'Oh, God,' Magnus groaned. 'I never dreamed you would take it like that.'

'What did you expect?' she whispered. 'I told you I loved you.'

'But—'

'But what?

'Women say that sort of thing all the time,' Magnus said after a moment. 'I was not sure you really meant it.'

Tallie closed her eyes, unbearably hurt. After a time she managed to say, 'Well, I did. I'm sorry if you don't—'

'Hush!' he murmured, and drew her into his arms. A long silence passed with only the sound of two heartbeats to fill it.

'I have heard more "I love you"s than I care to remember. Starting with my mother,' he began in a low, roughened voice.

Tallie drew back a little, regarding him with heavy eyes. 'But I thought—'

Magnus gave a hard little laugh. 'Only in company, of course. Then she pretended to dote on me. As for the rest… She couldn't bear the sight of me.'

'But why?'

'God knows. I started by ruining her figure; I remember that accusation.' He shrugged carelessly, but Tallie could sense the ancient wounds in him. They had cut very deep. She stroked his cheek.

'Oh, it's all water under the bridge now,' he said, 'but I

suppose it made me hesitate to…to trust a woman. I have known a number of women,' he continued. 'Birds of paradise, cyprians, that sort of thing. Each one told me they loved me.' He shrugged. 'Always when they wanted something—a bauble of some sort, usually… Although sometimes it was because they had betrayed me and were trying to placate me with their lies…'

Tallie continued stroking his cheek, loving the faint rasp of whiskers beneath her skin. He was telling her he could never love her. She could deal with that, she thought sadly, as long as he continued to hold her, as long as he let her love him.

'And then I married you,' he said softly, and his voice changed. 'I hadn't planned to. I'd planned to ask one of Laetitia's girls.'

'Why did you change your mind?' whispered Tallie, wondering if he'd tell her the truth, as she'd overheard him tell Laetitia that night in the library.

'I think it was the puppy.'

Tallie pulled away to stare at him. 'The *puppy*?' She felt vaguely offended.

He drew her back into his arms and tucked her head under his chin. 'I saw a small boy whose puppy had got them both into trouble. The puppy was to be destroyed as a punishment for the child's disobedience.'

Tallie sighed, remembering.

'I knew exactly what it was like to be that little boy. My father destroyed a number of my own pets for the same reason—in our family it is called "making a man of the boy",' he added bitterly. 'I watched that boy, knowing grief was inevitable.'

He hugged her tighter and rubbed his jaw against her hair. 'And then out from nowhere sprang a young lioness to defend the cub, a lioness who risked her own insecure position in the household to save a boy-cub who was not even her own.' He planted a kiss on her ear. 'She even saved the puppy…'

Tallie lay against his chest, her eyes wet once again at the thought of the boy Magnus and how little he had known of love and joy.

'I wanted that young lioness for my own children,' he said at last. 'I knew it was too late for me, but my children would grow up knowing what it was like to be...to be...' His voice shattered into dry splinters.

'To be loved, Magnus. *Loved*.'

He nodded, overcome.

'And they will be, I promise you,' Tallie whispered, placing both their hands on her belly. 'This one already is.' She cupped his face with her hands. 'And so are you, Magnus. It isn't too late for you at all. I love you.'

She gazed into his tormented eyes and said softly, 'I love you so much, you have no idea. You are everything I've ever dreamed of, you know.' She smoothed his hair and said again, 'I *love* you, Magnus. Even when I was so hurt when you left, and so angry with you, I still loved you. I think I will always love you. It doesn't matter if you don't love me back; I've enough love for both of us.'

'But—'

'Hush, it doesn't matter,' she said, and kissed him.

He kissed her back, ravenously, but after a moment he drew back with a groan. 'But it does matter—'

'No—'

'Let me finish,' he said, kissing her again, a brief, hard kiss. 'I...I never expected marriage to be like this... I thought...I thought I could just pick a suitable woman and continue my life, almost unchanged. It was the children I was thinking of.'

'An heir.' She nodded.

'No, *not* an heir. Children. If we only had one little girl, I would be happy. If we had a string of little girls I would be just as happy.'

'Do...do you not want a boy, then?' she asked worriedly.

'A boy would make me very happy, too,' he assured her. 'A boy, not an heir. I want a *child*. The sex is immaterial.'

She smiled, not entirely sure she understood, but reassured just the same.

'My father had me thrashed every morning from the age of

five,' he said bluntly. 'It was the time-honoured way to ensure the heirs of d'Arenville became strong enough for the position.'

'But that is appalling,' she gasped. 'In that case I am glad you were sent away to school so young. Such a thing is utterly barbarous.'

He smiled, a smile of cold reminiscence that made Tallie shudder. 'Oh, he had me thrashed at school, too. Every morning at eight o'clock sharp, except for Sundays. Until my eighteenth birthday.'

'Oh, Magnus, that is…' Words failed her. She could only hug him tight and press kisses on whatever part of him she could find.

'You understand now why I do not want a d'Arenville heir?'

Tallie hugged him tighter and kissed his ear. 'I love you, Magnus, I love you,' was all she could think of to say.

He rolled her back on the bed and kissed her, covering her face, her neck, her breast with his kisses. He cupped her breasts gently. 'They are bigger,' he murmured, lavishing kisses on them. He ran a hand down to caress her swollen belly. 'I want to see you—all of you.'

Tallie blushed. 'But I look—'

'You look beautiful, and I want to see you,' he repeated, and reached for the hem of her nightgown. Slowly he drew it up, over the long slender legs, up to the thatch of tawny curls at their junction and up over the smooth, tight mound of her belly. He lifted it over the creamy swelling breasts and over the tumbled honey-streaked curls. He tossed the gown to the foot of the bed and knelt above her. And then he just stared, his eyes moving over her, absorbing every change, every nuance of her body.

Tallie's embarrassment died away.

His storm-dark eyes caressed her, bathing her in a warm radiance. She had never felt so beautiful in her life. Obscure little Tallie Robinson, plain and ordinary, swollen and ungainly with pregnancy, feeling so utterly beautiful when this man looked at her.

'I love you, Magnus,' she said softly, reaching for him.

'I wish I had been here to see all these changes,' he murmured, stroking her body, learning it anew.

'Thank you for bringing me my brother.' She arched against his hand like a cat. 'I don't think I said it before. I don't understand why you wanted to, but it has made me very happy.'

His hand stilled. 'I had to.' His voice was husky and deep.

'Had to? But why?' She reached up and began to undo his shirt.

'To…to show you.'

'Show me what?' Her hands finally undid his shirt and she reached for the buttons on his pantaloons. His hand stopped her.

'Don't you see?' He gripped her hands tightly. 'I couldn't *say* it—the words mean…meant nothing to me. I couldn't say it, so I had to…to show you.'

'Show me what?' she said softly.

'That I—' He stopped. 'Damn it, you know what I am trying to tell you.'

She shook her head gently. 'No, Magnus, I don't know.'

'That I… I… Oh, curse it, that I love you, of course!' he said gruffly.

Tallie scrambled up on the bed and knelt facing him. 'Oh, Magnus! Oh, Magnus!' And she flung herself into his arms.

After some time he said, 'I know we cannot make love at this stage of your confinement, but…do you think…? I want to touch you here.' His hand cupped the curly thatch at the base of her stomach.

Tallie blushed and shook her head happily. 'I'm sure it will be all right…if you want to.'

His eyes darkened into the brooding sea-grey darkness she had never thought to see again. 'I do want to.' He lowered his head to the curls.

Tallie's jaw dropped. 'Magnus, what are you—?' She gasped. Then she gasped again. Then she gave a little wriggle, an ecstatic little wriggle. 'Ohhh…Magnus…'

Epilogue

A lady sits gazing out over the rolling fields of green to the deep, dark woods beyond. Her smooth, pale unfreckled brow is wrinkled with worry...nay, more than worry; it is fear she feels, fear for her loved ones. For in that dark and dangerous forest lurk a hundred unknown hazards—raging torrents, fierce beasts and dreadful monsters. And her loved ones are there, on a Quest. All for the sake of her unworthy self. The Lady hangs her head.

A faint, plaintive cry causes her to raise her head like a startled doe. She lays a hand on the innocent babe slumb'ring at her elbow and whispers, 'Fear not, my darling. Our brave and gallant knights will return unharmed from their Quest, I am sure of it.

'My Knight has been on a Quest before, you know—a terrible, long, dangerous Quest—with danger at every turn—bold, green-eyed banditti, ungentlemanly enemy soldiers and slavering wolves. But my Knight returned, triumphant and unharmed, or only a little harmed—just a flesh wound which healed very quickly. And he was most dreadfully thin and gaunt...but still, he was unharmed, so, you see, you need not fear for him, my precious, for he is strong and brave.'

The baby gurgles again and the Lady bends to her. 'It was the most wonderful Quest in the world, you see, for he did it *to win his Lady. Only the Lady was already his, heart and soul.*

'But his Quest was for you as well, my darling, did you know that? For do you know what my Brave and Gallant Knight brought back from the wilds of the terrible Alps? He brought our own little knight, your uncle Ricardo, rescued him from Durance Vile. Wasn't that a wonderful Quest to make— better than finding a silly old Grail, don't you agree?'

The Lady turns her head and stares at the darkening woods. It is getting very late and she wishes her Knight would return from his latest Quest soon. And when he does he will stride up to her on his long, handsome legs and bend over her and kiss her, saying, 'Oh, my beloved one, I have returned to you. Tallie, my dearest love...'

'Tallie, we're back, sweetheart,' said Magnus. 'Were you asleep?'

'No, I—'

'Look, Tallie, I catch you three enormous fish—three!' Ricardo shouted excitedly. 'And this one on the very first cast. Magnus never catch not even one. Me—I catch everything! All by myself. Look!' He brandished three large, glistening, very dead fish in her face. Their eyes stared glassily at her, their innards gaped hollowly.

Tallie shuddered. 'How absolutely clever of you, Ricardo. Now take them around to Cook at once.'

'Cook!' exclaimed Ricardo scornfully. 'Cook does not know how to cook Carlotta's fish stew! Cook just boil fish in salt water and call it cooking.' He snorted with fine Italian contempt. 'Gino, he has garlic and herbs and oil and wine— Gino will make it just how you remember it—only better, he says.'

Tallie nodded, wishing she had never mentioned how she would love to taste Carlotta's fish stew just once more. 'Then take it away to Gino at once, my love, I beg of you, or you will be dripping water on your little niece.'

'She doesn't mind, do you, *cara*?' said Ricardo, pushing aside Magnus, who was tickling the baby's chin. 'You named her after the water, no? Little Marina, the water baby.' He bent over the baby and whispered to her in Italian, then announced, 'I will teach her to fish and swim next year, when she is older.'

'Oh, but—' began Tallie.

'Whatever you like, Richard, but take those fish to Gino now!' interrupted Magnus.

'Not Richard—Ricardo,' retorted Ricardo automatically, and grinned at Magnus cheekily. But he took the fish off, whistling. In the six months since he had been in England he had become a new boy, filling out and shooting up like a healthy young weed. And without a trace of the fear and suspicion he had brought with him. Tallie watched him go, her heart full. His adoptive mother must have loved him, too, or he would not have recovered so quickly from his ordeals. He was her bad, merry boy again.

'I should have fed that boy to the wolves when I had the chance,' said Magnus gruffly.

'Oh, no, how can you say it?' said Tallie reproachfully. 'What has he done to annoy you now? Oh, I cannot like his plan to teach Marina how to swim—it is not at all proper for a little girl—but—'

Magnus covered her mouth with his own. 'He kept me from doing this,' he said, and kissed her again. He lifted her out of her seat and sat down again, with her resting in his lap. 'I come home from a day's fishing with a chattering bagpipe of a boy and find my beautiful wife dreaming in the sunshine. What were you dreaming of, my love?'

Tallie smiled blissfully at him. 'Of my brave and gallant Knight, of course.'

Magnus sat up straight, almost tipping her from his lap. 'What knight?' he said ominously. 'I didn't know you knew any knights. Who the devil is this blasted knight?'

'My very own Sir Galahad,' she said softly, caressing his cheek. 'A dear, brave, wonderful, occasionally mutton-headed Knight. I sometimes call him Magnus.' She lifted her mouth and he devoured it in a way that sent shivers of delight through her body. The hunger was never far away for either of them.

'I've got news for you, my love,' said Magnus after a time. 'It may come as a shock to you.' His voice was deadly serious.

'What is it?' She scanned his face anxiously.

'I'm not your Knight, you know.'

'Yes, you are my Knight,' she reassured him.

'I am not,' he growled, his grey eyes dancing wickedly. 'I'm your Earl.' And he planted his mouth on hers.

*   *   *   *   *

THE PROPERTY OF
A GENTLEMAN
by
Helen Dickson

Helen Dickson was born and still lives in South Yorkshire with her husband, on a busy arable farm where she combines writing with keeping a chaotic farmhouse. An incurable romantic, she writes for pleasure, owing much of her inspiration to the beauty of the surrounding countryside. She enjoys reading and music. History has always captivated her, and she likes travel and visiting ancient buildings.

Also by Helen Dickson
in Mills & Boon Historical Romance™:

LORD FOX'S PLEASURE
JEWEL OF THE NIGHT
HIGHWAYMAN HUSBAND
(within Mother's Day volume 2003)

Look for:

THE PIRATE'S DAUGHTER
Out now

Chapter One

1800

Born into the private establishment of privilege and exclusivity, Eve Somerville was every bit as beautiful as she was rich.

She was passionate and feckless and subject to all the moods and contradictions of a high-spirited girl. The only daughter of parents who adored her and cosseted and indulged her every whim, she knew exactly what the future would be. She would marry well and be happy and secure for the rest of her life.

But when she was seventeen years old she discovered that nothing is that certain, for when her mother died from consumption, her father was also struck down by a terrible illness—the doctors he consulted telling him he could not hope to live beyond the next three years. Sadly, he did not even have that because he was killed in a carriage accident shortly after Eve's twentieth birthday.

The funeral of Sir John Somerville was attended by a few distant relatives, friends and acquaintances, having come from north and south, east and west to the steadily thriving, coal-mining market town of Atwood in the West Riding of Yorkshire, a manor in the ancient and extensive parish of Leeds. It was attractively situated in an area of contrasts, with beautiful hills and valleys lying between Atwood and the pleasant and equally prosperous market town of Netherley five miles to the north.

The narrow, tree-shaded lane from Burntwood Hall to the church, set away from the town and adjacent to the grounds of the great house, with its beautiful slender cream spire soaring high above the trees, was fringed with a silent line of estate workers and coal miners alike—men and women who, like their ancestors before them, had helped make the Somervilles what they were today.

The estate, which, unfortunately for Eve, was entailed in default of male heirs—the next in line being a cousin of her father's, Gerald Somerville—was causing some speculation as to what would happen to it when the new owner took up residence, and to Eve, although it was certain she would be well taken care of.

The cortège was quite magnificent: the elegant carriages carrying the many mourners leaving Burntwood Hall, the splendour of the black hearse which was drawn by six plumed black horses with their coats highly polished, carrying Sir John Somerville's coffin, depicting everything he had attained in life.

Shrouded in black silk with a black lace veil attached to her bonnet and covering her pale face, Eve sat beside her maternal grandmother, the formidable Lady Abigail Pemberton, both in the carriage and in the church, taking strength from the older woman's stiff, straightbacked figure, whose gloved hand clutched the gold knob of her walking cane so hard that her knuckles stood out sharply.

Her face behind her veil was grim, her thin mouth pressed in a hard line as she looked straight ahead, giving no indication of her thoughts or emotions, for she had been brought up in an age and society that had taught her it was not done to show one's feelings in public, not even grief for the death of a dear son-in-law. Eve accepted the condolences of those who came to pay their respects graciously, sadly contemplating on what her future would be like without her father.

When the funeral was over they returned to Burntwood Hall, a large, stately Tudor manor house set in a wooded hamlet on the south side of Atwood, a prosperous and populous township where the Somervilles had lived from the sixteenth century. The mining of coal was anciently established in the area, the Somervilles one of several families dominating its production.

Apart from Mr Alex Soames, Eve's father's lawyer, sitting at the big, highly polished table, his elderly grey head bowed over her father's last will and testament, few people were present for the reading, just a few important members of the household, Gerald Somerville, her grandmother and herself—and Mr Marcus Fitzalan from Netherley.

Marcus Fitzalan was tall and lean with strong muscled shoulders. His sharp, distinguished good looks and bearing demanded a second look—and, indeed, with his reputation for being an astute businessman with an inbred iron toughness, he was not a man who could be ignored. There was an authoritative, brisk, no-nonsense air about him and he had an easy, confident way of moving and a haughty way of holding his head. His hair, thick and jet black, was brushed back from his forehead, his cheek bones high and angular, making his face look severe.

Thirty years old, he was a striking-looking man with an enormous presence—a man Eve had met three years ago and had not seen since. It was an encounter which had been most unpleasant, one she did not wish to recall, for anger and the humiliation she had suffered at his hands still festered like a raw wound deep inside her. It was an encounter that had left a stain on her reputation and lost her the man she might have married.

From the moment Eve had seen Marcus Fitzalan in the church she had been unprepared for the uncontrollable tremor that shot through her. During the three years since she had last laid eyes on him, she thought she had remembered exactly what he looked like, but now she realised she was mistaken as her eyes refused to tear themselves away from the sheer male beauty of him.

He seemed to radiate a compelling magnetism, everything about him exuding a ruthless sensuality. He had a straight, aquiline nose which suggested arrogance, and his firm lips, which she knew to her cost, could be cynical or sensuous. His stark black brows were slashed across his forehead and his eyes were compelling, pale blue and clear. Hidden deep in their depths was humour, but also a watchfulness that made one wary. Eve found it hard to believe this was the same man who had kissed her so seductively and passionately three years ago.

When he had taken his seat across from her at the other side of the church in one of the tall box pews, he seemed to sense her watching him and had turned slowly. As their eyes met his dark brows lifted in bland enquiry. Eve caught her breath and felt heat scorch through her body before hastily looking away, ashamed that his look made her legs begin to quake and her treacherous heart to race, as it had on that other occasion when he had kissed her so devastatingly and sent her young, innocent heart soaring heavenwards.

His presence made her feel uneasy and she did her best to evade him, having no desire to come face to face with the man for whom she felt resentment heavy in her breast.

But her grandmother, always keen to meet the local gentry and, unlike her granddaughter, impressed by Mr Fitzalan's importance and air of distinction, lost no time in acquainting herself once they were back at the house. She made sure that her granddaughter was introduced afterwards, ignorant of the fact that he was the man responsible for her ruin and disgrace, even though her father had packed Eve off to Cumbria to stay with her immediately after the unfortunate affair, the explanation being that a visit to her grandmother was long overdue.

Fortunately, her reputation had not been ruined beyond recall, the incident had soon passed over and she had returned home, but Marcus Fitzalan's conduct towards her had left her with a deep sense of loathing and bitter humiliation.

He had left for a lengthy stay in London the following day, blissfully unaware of the furore he had left behind, thinking her nothing more than a promiscuous little flirt whom he had taught a harsh, yet valuable, lesson in life, and she had been too proud to let him think anything else—and it was that same pride that refused to let him see how deeply his callous behaviour towards her had hurt her.

'Let me take you over to meet Mr Fitzalan, Eve. I find it difficult to believe you have never been properly introduced, considering he and your father were such good friends and partners in several business concerns,' said her grandmother.

Panic gripped Eve as her grandmother began steering her in Mr Fitzalan's direction. 'I would really rather not, Grandmother. Besides—see—he is engaged in conversation with Mr and Mrs Lister. I would not wish to interrupt.'

Unfortunately, her grandmother was not to be put off. 'Nonsense, Eve. Come along. Mr Fitzalan will not eat you, you know.'

Marcus turned as they approached, Mr and Mrs Lister moving on to speak to someone else. With Eve's veil turned back over her bonnet, Marcus was able to look down into her white face, framed by hair of sable blackness, and their eyes met, frozen by time and memory. He thought how young she looked, more beautiful than he remembered, and he noticed how her soft lips trembled as she tilted her head back a little to look up at him.

With a warmth flooding and throbbing through his veins he remembered how it had felt to hold her, how soft and yielding her lips had been when she had kissed him with such tender passion, and how her body had moulded itself innocently into his own. He was seized by the same uncontrollable compulsion to repeat the pleasurable incident that had left a deep and lasting impression on him three years ago when she had sought him out at Atwood Fair.

A poignant memory came back to him of that time, of a bewitchingly beautiful young girl who had brazenly approached him and foolishly made an immature and improper attempt to seduce him—he later discovered for some mischievous prank concocted by her and her friends for their own amusement. But it was unfortunate that the man she had hoped to marry had found out about her indiscretion and spurned her because of it.

At the time he had regarded the incident with amusement, remembering how surprised she had been when he had turned the tables on her with an expert subtlety and started to play her at her own game. Because of her inexperience and ignorance of the rules of nature he had soon had her at his mercy. In no time at all she had been unable to prevent herself from becoming his victim—and he retained a poignant memory of how willingly she had melted in his arms.

But the incident had not turned out as either of them had intended, for he had continued to think of her. For a long time afterwards he had been unable to get her out of his mind. She had done something to him, aroused feelings he had not experienced before.

'Mr Fitzalan, I would like to introduce you to my granddaughter, Eve Somerville—although I have just been saying to her how odd it is that the two of you have not been formaly introduced before, considering your close friendship with Sir John.'

Bowing his dark head slightly, Marcus looked at Eve with a gaze that seemed to look straight into her heart, seeing that her lovely eyes were shuttered, giving no insight as to what her feelings might be. With the exception of a muscle that tightened at the corner of his mouth his expression was impassive, his voice coolly polite when he spoke.

'On the contrary, Lady Pemberton, we have met briefly, several years ago—although we were not properly introduced at the time,' he said, without any hint of implications, for he was gravely conscious of the solemnity of the occasion and had no wish to embarrass Eve or cause any constraint between them. But Eve knew exactly to what he was referring. It was a meeting she would prefer to forget and she was angry that he had the audacity to allude to it now.

'It's a pleasure to meet you again, Miss Somerville,' he continued. 'However, had it not been for your father's untimely death, I believe he was about to bring you over to Brooklands shortly,' he told her, referring to his home. Taking her hand, he felt it tremble slightly. 'May I offer you my condolences. What happened to your father was a tragedy. He will be sadly missed.'

With cool disdain she lifted her chin and smiled politely, trying to ignore the tightness at the base of her throat. 'Thank you.'

'Your grandmother has only recently returned from London, I believe,' he said by way of conversation, as the aforesaid lady turned to speak to an acquaintance.

'Yes,' she replied stiffly, wishing he would go away and speak to someone else—anyone, just so long as she did not have to suffer his odious presence. 'She has been visiting my Aunt Shona—my mother's sister who lives in Bloomsbury with her family. She is travelling back to her home in Cumbria and thought she would break her journey to spend some time with me and my father here at Burntwood Hall. Sadly, it has not turned out as she expected. I am only thankful she arrived to see my father before the terrible accident happened.'

'I am surprised you did not travel with her to London to visit your aunt.'

'Had my father been in better health I might have—but as it was I did not wish to be away from home in—in case…'

'I understand,' he said quietly when she faltered, her tight façade of dignity slipping slightly, and for a brief moment she looked like a forlorn child. 'Your father spoke of you often. Indeed, he told me so much about you that I feel I have known you all my life.'

'Really!' she retorted crisply, the shutters up once more. 'You surprise me, Mr Fitzalan. So much of my father's time was spent away from home, despite his illness, that I am flattered to learn he could find the time even to think of me, let alone to discuss me with a total stranger.'

'Your father and I were hardly strangers, Miss Somerville. And,' he said with a gentle lift to his eyebrows, holding her gaze steadily, 'neither are we, come to think of it.'

'Despite what took place between us on our previous encounter you are to me,' Eve replied directly, her voice cool, finding it difficult to conceal her dislike. 'However, when he was at home it may interest you to know that he always spoke of you a great deal, too, Mr Fitzalan,' she said pointedly. 'In fact, there was never a day went by when he did not sing your praises.' Her voice held a faint trace of sarcasm and was cold, which she knew was reflected in her eyes.

'I myself would hardly deem our meeting a pleasure,' she continued, the impressionable, ignorant girl she had been when he had last seen her having fled away, although the remembrance of their encounter and the resulting chaos knifed through her as it had then.

Marcus frowned. 'What happened between us was a long time ago. Surely now—especially at this time with your father so recently laid to rest—we can at least be friends.'

'I doubt we can be friends now or in the future, Mr Fitzalan. After today it is most unlikely that our paths will cross again.'

His eyes became probing, penetrating hers like dagger thrusts, his face a hard, expressionless mask. 'Don't be too sure about that, Miss Somerville,' he said quietly. 'Atwood and Netherley are not so far apart—and your father and I were business partners as well as friends. I would say it is inevitable that we meet at some social event or other.'

'We do not mix in the same society, Mr Fitzalan, but if we do chance to meet you will forgive me if I seem to avoid you.'

'Come now, you were not so ill disposed towards me the last time we met,' he said, his tone silky, easy, his eyes regarding her with fascinated amusement. 'In fact, you were rather amiable, as I remember.'

'You remember too much,' Eve snapped, two sparks of anger showing briefly beneath her lowered lids. 'It was an incident which I have had cause to reproach myself for many times.'

Undeterred by her show of anger Marcus chuckled softly, a glint of white teeth showing from between his parted lips. 'I recall how you went off in an extremely disagreeable mood.'

'I am still disagreeable and will remain so while ever I am in your company, Mr Fitzalan. Now you must excuse me. There are several people I must speak to before they depart.'

Before Marcus could reply and uncaring that her words might have given offence, Eve turned from him, seeing her friend Emma Parkinson moving towards her. Quickly she moved on, leaving her grandmother to carry on the conversation, determined not to give Mr Fitzalan another thought.

But it was not possible for her to dismiss a man of Marcus Fitzalan's calibre from her mind—in fact, she thought with bitter irony, she doubted that anyone would be able to. Once met, he was not the kind of man who could be forgotten. When he had taken her hand he had kept it far too long in his hard grasp for her liking, and the fact that she had to look up at him had annoyed her, causing fresh resentment to flare up inside her, but she had been unable to take her eyes off his handsome features, which had caused him to arch his clearly defined eyebrows and a half-smile to curve his infuriatingly arrogant lips.

When he spoke, his voice was of a depth and timbre that was like a caress, causing a faint stroke of colour to sweep over her creamy skin, bringing a smile to his lips, for he knew exactly the effect he was having on her.

Despite the solemnity of the occasion, as she moved among the mourners who congregated at Burntwood Hall after the funeral, she was conscious of Marcus Fitzalan's presence throughout, becoming annoyed with herself as she found her eyes unconsciously seeking him out, and she would find herself studying him when she thought he was not looking. But several times their eyes would meet and he made no attempt to hide the gleam of interest that entered his eyes as she felt herself undergoing the selfsame scrutiny.

Eve was not used to men of the world like Marcus Fitzalan, and for the first time in her life realised she was in danger of stepping out of her depth. He had a reputation as being one for the ladies, although he was always discreet in his affairs. By all accounts he was arrogant, conceited and ruthless—in fact, he was everything Eve hated. She had every reason to dislike him and, seeing him again for the first time in three years, she was determined that nothing would sway her from her opinion.

Waiting for Mr Soames to begin reading the will, Eve could feel Marcus's eyes on her yet again, vibrant, alarmingly alive, assessing her in a way she found offensive as he stood by the window, looking for all the world as if he owned the place.

He was a neighbour and an associate in several of her father's business concerns, a man her father had been extremely fond of, as well as being a wealthy land and mine owner in his own right, so there was nothing unusual about his presence for the reading of the will.

The Fitzalans had had to struggle to achieve prosperity as opposed to the Somervilles, who were rich not only in wealth but also in lineage. Marcus's grandfather had been an astute, self-made man, seizing on the opportunities to be achieved by the mining of coal, knowing it was fuel for a whole range of industrial processes and for the new generation of industrial workers—and also knowing there was no shortage of it beneath the soil of Britain.

Reaching some degree of financial ability, he had bought

fifty acres of land adjacent to the Somerville estate and opened his own mine—Atwood Mine. Coal had enabled him to sink more mines and given him the means to build Brooklands— a house to be envied and admired—but after a series of serious mishaps Atwood Mine had fallen into the hands of John Somerville.

Marcus's handsome eyes raked the face of the girl sitting primly at the table across the room without her bonnet. His eyes dwelt on her hair, as ebony black and shiny like his own, her eyebrows arched and sleek, her neck rising graceful and swanlike from her slender shoulders. There was a creamy smoothness to her skin with a soft blush on her angular cheeks, giving a slant to her large and mysterious violet-coloured eyes that held his like magnets. Her lips were luscious, her chin pert with a stubborn thrust, and all these attractive features were encompassed in a perfect, heart-shaped face.

She was beautiful, slim and vibrant, the gentle curve of her young breasts straining beneath the bodice of her black dress. She still had the looks of a child, but there was something bold and defiant in the way her eyes locked on to his, which told him she was no innocent and that she possessed a spirit as strong and rebellious as his own, giving him the feeling that in this seemingly fragile girl he might have met his match.

After Mr Soames had read out the generous bequests Sir John Somerville had made to his loyal retainers and they had quietly left the room, everyone waited for him to continue as he licked his lips nervously, focusing his gaze on Eve.

With growing impatience Gerald Somerville was sitting with bated breath for Sir John's will to be read out, finding it difficult to control his excitement. It was like finding a treasure chest just waiting to be opened. His hooded eyes were transfixed on Mr Soames, knowing he was about to inherit the title and complete control over his cousin's property, which would elevate him at last from the penury and insecurity that had bedevilled him for far too long. It was a moment he had waited for, a moment which had come sooner rather than later owing to the tragic, but fortuitous, carriage accident which had killed Sir John.

Always the poor relation, all his life Gerald had hated poverty and dreamed of being rich and enjoying all that money could buy. He had loathed his respectable home and his parents' dull existence. Aware that he was heir to Sir John's estate he was impatient, knowing that it could be years before he came into his inheritance, but on learning of his cousin's increasing ill health he had quietly rubbed his hands with hopeful anticipation, suspecting he would not have too long to wait after all. He bided his time, enjoying the adventures and excitement in the gaming rooms of London, which had become his haunts on the death of his parents, seeing gambling as a chance to become rich and powerful, which he craved.

'What I am about to disclose will come as something of a shock, Eve, and you must understand that the will was written at a very difficult time of your father's life,' said Mr Soames gently, looking at her in a kind and sympathetic way, having known her from birth.

Her parents had spoilt and cosseted her to excess from the moment she was born, sheltering and allowing her to go her own wilful way—until three years ago, when, by her own foolishness, she had suffered a lapse from grace and her mother had died, causing her much grief. Her sorrow had increased in intensity when Sir John had become ill soon afterwards with a cancer that had slowly begun to eat its way through his wretched body.

Sitting perched on the edge of her seat as if her backbone was made of hard steel, Eve tried to fight off her growing alarm. Until now she had believed that the reading of the will was to be a mere formality, confident that she knew exactly what it contained and having no reason to be concerned—that even though the estate was in entailment and that no part of it could be sold to provide for her, her father would have seen to it that she would be well taken care of.

But suddenly she felt herself grow tense and anxious, sensing instinctively by the tone of Mr Soames's voice that all was not as it should be. Her throat went dry and she spoke with difficulty.

'A shock? But why should it be a shock? What precisely do you mean, Mr Soames? My father has left me well taken care of, hasn't he?'

'Yes—that is so, but it may not be what you are expecting.' He focused his eyes on Gerald, who was watching him intently, every muscle in his face tense. 'The entire estate—that is, the land, the house and other properties—both here and in London, are to go to you, sir.'

Eve waited, going colder by the second, trying not to look at Gerald as he tried to conceal his triumph, knowing there was little left to come her way but expecting her father to have made a substantial sum over to her.

'You, Eve,' Mr Soames went on, shifting his gaze once more to her, 'are to receive an annuity in the sum of two thousand pounds a year.'

When he fell silent she waited in expectant anticipation, expecting him to continue, to tell her there was more, until she realised there was nothing more. Her heart rose up to choke her and she stared at him in absolute confusion and astonishment.

'But—but that's not possible. There must be some mistake. There has to be. My father's assets—he—he was an extremely wealthy man. It has to be more than this.'

'There is no mistake,' he said quietly, his voice penetrating the mist of Eve's bemused senses. 'His main assets are private matters and have nothing to do with the estate—namely, his shares in several coal mines and interests in various industrial concerns and so forth, several of them in which he and Mr Fitzalan were partners and which he made over to him before he died.'

All the colour drained out of Eve's face and her hand rose and clasped the collar of her black mourning dress. She was stunned, unable to believe what he had told her. A silence fell upon the room which seemed to last an age, the small assembly around her becoming shadowy, faceless figures, all staring at her, until Gerald, acknowledging his good fortune in inheriting the estate—and yet beginning to feel a trifle perplexed that not all Sir John's property had passed on to him as he had expected it would—began talking animatedly to Mr Soames about what it would mean to him, with little regard for the pain and disappointment that was tearing Eve apart.

The still, quiet figure of Lady Pemberton sat rigidly on her chair towards the back of the room, neither shock nor surprise disturbing the marble severity of her face, but her eyes and ears missed nothing. Only the hand cupping the gold knob of her cane gave any indication of the way she felt, for it gripped the knob hard, so hard that her knuckle bones nearly punctured the thin white skin covering them.

Only Marcus seemed to be aware of the pain Eve was suffering. She was young and unable to deal with the dilemma in which she found herself. As he looked at her his gaze was secretive and seemed to probe beneath the surface, but he could see by the terror in her eyes, how her face had become drained of blood and the way her fingers clutched her throat, that this unexpected blow from her father had hit her hard.

From what Sir John had told him he knew she was a strong-minded girl who would know how to take care of herself well enough, but it was only a girl who was behind the artificial ageing of bereavement, and it would not be easy for her to get over something like this.

Something in the region of his heart softened and he wanted to go to her and offer some words of comfort, wishing he could erase the sad, stricken look from her face, but he knew by the cold hostility she had not attempted to conceal when they had been introduced after the funeral, and in her eyes when she looked at him, that by his own fault she would not welcome his sympathy.

'Is that it? Am I to get nothing else?' she asked, her voice surprisingly calm, but so quiet Mr Soames had difficulty hear-

ing her. 'With all his wealth, did my father make no other
financial provision for me? Am I to be reduced to such dire
straits that I must starve?'

Mr Soames was beginning to feel distinctly uncomfortable
before Eve's hard gaze and his eyes wavered as he looked
down at the papers in front of him, coughing nervously. 'No—
it is not quite as bad as that.'

'Then please tell me. And where am I to live?'

'Perhaps when I have explained everything to you it will
be much clearer. Your father did not leave you as destitute as
it would seem—for, as you know, he always had your best
interests at heart. But there are certain conditions to be adhered
to—certain clauses that may seem strange to you.'

'Conditions? What kind of conditions?'

'That you and Mr Marcus Fitzalan marry within six months
of his death.'

Eve was so stunned she was unable to speak.

'Should this be agreeable to you both,' Mr Soames went on
hurriedly, wanting to get this unpleasant part of reading the
will over and done with as quickly as possible, 'Atwood
Mine—of which your father was the sole owner—will become
yours jointly.'

The words came as a shattering blow to Gerald, whose face
became as white as his frothing lace cravat, bringing an angry
exclamation to his lips and jolting him to his feet, causing all
heads to turn in his direction. 'No, sir. It will not do. This I
cannot accept. Atwood Mine is Sir John's main asset and is
surely entailed with the rest of his estate.'

'That is not the case. Sir John purchased the lease, not the
land. As everyone is aware Atwood Mine—which is the larg-
est and most profitable mine in the area—was sunk by Mr
Fitzalan's grandfather and the lease sold by Mrs Fitzalan to
Sir John privately on the death of her husband. The lease has
another fifteen years to run—with the rent arranged annually
on a scale related to the amount of coal mined. You are correct
in saying it was Sir John's greatest asset, and it was his wish

that the lease be returned to the Fitzalan family—providing
Mr Marcus Fitzalan marries his daughter Eve.'

Eve looked at Gerald properly for the first time that day.
Both his parents were dead, and his home, where his younger
brother Matthew—a quiet, gentle young man whom she knew
well and had a strong liking for—still lived, was three miles
from Burntwood Hall, but for most of the time he resided in
London and she had not seen him for several months.

He had been a frequent visitor to Burntwood Hall in the
past, and both she and her father had shared a very low opinion of him. On his last visit she noticed how changed he was
towards her, as if he noticed for the first time that she was no
longer a child but a young woman. She hadn't liked the way
he looked at her—too long and too hard, and not in the least
like a relation who should know better than to lust after his
cousin's daughter.

Seeing him now, she liked him even less. At one time she
had thought him to be as handsome as a Greek god, with hair
the colour of spun gold and looks that made every woman he
came into contact with swoon and fall at his feet. He was more
corpulent than when she had last seen him, but he was a handsome figure still, though soft living and overindulgence had
blurred him somewhat and there was a seediness creeping
through.

At twenty-eight he had been spoilt by an adoring mother
and fawned over and adored by countless women. He thought
he had only to wink an eye to have any one of them tumble
into his bed; if all the stories about him were to be believed,
then there was an army of women he had enjoyed and then
grown tired of, casting them aside as one would discard a
worn-out toy. In the past he had been involved in one scandal
after another, causing her father acute embarrassment.

As her gaze focused on his face she saw his expression was
closed as he watched, his brown eyes, glittering with menace,
darting from her to Marcus Fitzalan. They were filled with
such hatred that her heart skipped a beat. His slack lips were

set in a slight smile that was not pleasant; in fact, there was
something about him that reminded her of something sinister
and evil.

Her eyes shifted from Gerald and travelled across the room
to meet the cold, pale-blue implacable stare of Marcus
Fitzalan, where he still stood with what she could only describe as lounging insolence. He seemed so cool, so self-
assured, while she felt as if she were falling apart.

Chapter Two

Marcus Fitzalan's expression was unreadable, but Eve suspected he must be feeling every bit as shocked and horrified as she was. Or was he? she asked herself. It was no secret that her father had been an ill man, whose health had deteriorated rapidly over the last few months. The doctor had given him another twelve months to live at the most, and being such close friends, was it possible that this had been contrived by Mr Fitzalan in order to get his hands on Atwood Mine? After all, there wasn't a man or woman in the whole of Atwood or Netherley who didn't know how much he wanted it returned once more to his family. A wave of sick disgust swept over her.

'Did you know about this?' she demanded, having to fight to keep her anger in check, the horror of that first dreadful shock having left her eyes. 'Did my father discuss this with you?'

'No, he did not,' he said crisply, giving no indication of the initial rush of gratitude that had washed over him towards Sir John for making it possible for him to own his father's mine once more, for sentimental reasons rather than profit—the enormous wealth he accumulated from his other mines and business ventures provided him with more than adequate profit to enable him to maintain Brooklands and live comfortably.

The condition that he marry Sir John's daughter did not pose a problem—providing she was agreeable. He was confident that despite the hostility she so clearly felt towards him she could be persuaded, for he seemed to have a power over women that often puzzled him. They had a way of retaining him in their minds and once met he was never forgotten, but no woman had ever managed to push him over the edge and into marriage—the love of his life being his work. But with Atwood Mine being offered to him he was prepared to adhere to any conditions Sir John had made.

Eve stared at him with angry, bewildered eyes. This was too much. Her father should have called Marcus Fitzalan out and shot him over his disgraceful behaviour towards her, after he had degraded and humiliated her so shockingly. How could he have been so audacious as to arrange a marriage for her with him when he had almost ruined her? The very idea was unthinkable—impossible.

'I cannot possibly agree to this,' she said furiously, beginning to lose control of her precariously held temper. 'What can my father have been thinking of to ask this of me? He should not have done it. Why did he not tell me what he intended?'

'Perhaps he would have—but for the accident,' said Mr Soames. 'It was very sudden.'

'Nevertheless it is quite preposterous. Let me make it quite plain here and now that I will *never* agree to conditions such as these.'

Marcus remained silent, but roused from his complacent stance by the window he moved towards the table.

'Shouldn't you at least consider it?' said Mr Soames. 'When you get over the shock and weigh up what it will mean to you both—is it really so preposterous as all that?'

'Yes, it is—to me. It was quite outrageous of my father to expect me to marry on these terms. I have been troublesome in the past, I know, but I have done nothing to contribute to his decision to treat me so shockingly. Clearly he was sick in mind as well as body—or it was done for some malicious reason of his own. He seems to have thought of everything.'

Marcus shot her an angry look. 'Hasn't he just. But your father was not insane and nor was he a malicious man, Miss Somerville—and you do him a grave injustice by accusing him of such. Being a man of honour and integrity, a man who considered the well being of others before his own throughout his life, I am sure he thought this over very carefully before laying down conditions that are clearly so abhorrent to you,' he said coolly, in defence of her father, fixing her with an icy, hard stare.

Eve's own eyes snapped back at him, angered that he of all people should have the temerity to reproach her like a naughty child, although she did regret using the word 'malicious', which was spoken unintentionally and in the heat of the moment. Mr Fitzalan was right. Her father had been a caring and gentle man and as honest as the day is long, and could not be accused of being 'malicious', but she did not need the likes of Marcus Fitzalan to tell her so.

'And you would know, wouldn't you, Mr Fitzalan?' she said heatedly, accusingly, blinded with wrath, standing up and lifting her head imperiously, meeting his gaze boldly and squaring her chin in her proud challenge to his authority.

'From the amount of time the two of you spent together you must have got to know my father very well. Knowing what little time he had left, was it your intention to wheedle your way into his good graces in an attempt to persuade him to transfer the lease of Atwood Mine back to you? After all, everyone knows how keen you are to get your hands on it once more.'

Her accusation bit deep, causing Marcus's own temper to rise. His lean face darkened and his metallic eyes narrowed furiously, warningly, and Eve felt the effort it was costing him to keep his rage under control.

'I refute that. I have been accused of many things, Miss Somerville, and have been the subject of much gossip and speculation over the years, but let me make it clear that, contrary to what you might think of me, it is not in my nature to stoop so low as to acquire anything by flattery or guile. I held your father in the highest regard and knew he was a very sick man—but not how sick. We were friends, good friends, and I thought—and hoped—him fit for a good many years to come.'

His lip curled scornfully across his even white teeth as he spoke softly and with a menacing calm. 'At any other time— and if you were a man—I would take you to task for such an insult, but this is neither the time nor the occasion for doing so.'

'That is extremely civil of you, Mr Fitzalan. But I do not retract what I said,' Eve retorted, trying to speak with the utmost composure while growing more and more angry by the second.

'That is your prerogative. I understand that you have justifiable reason to be shocked by the contents of your father's will and that you are naturally quite distraught by your tragic loss—which I shall put down to being the reason for your outburst—so I shall take no offence and will ignore the affront to my character.'

His voice sounded calm, giving everyone the impression that he was not in the least put out by her insulting remark, but Eve was not deceived for his mouth hardened and his eyes flared like molten quicksilver, daring her to say more. But she refused to cower before him. Her eyes flashed defiance and her face assumed an expression of hardened resentment.

She opened her mouth to challenge his statement but the expression in his eyes made her close it quickly. With her lips clamped together she averted her gaze, considering it prudent to let the matter rest—for now.

Everyone present had listened to the angry altercation between them in astonishment and silence, amazed that Eve could have been so outspoken and unable to think of anything that could justify such behaviour, but, like Marcus, they put it down to her being overwrought and her dispirited and anxious state of mind. Only Gerald remained watchful, a ruthless gleam lighting up his eyes.

Marcus chose to put the matter from his mind—hoping that everyone else would do the same—but it was not forgotten.

'What happens to the bequest if we do not marry?' he asked, prising his eyes away from Eve's stony expression and fixing them on Mr Soames, trying hard to ignore the burning hatred in Gerald Somerville's eyes as they bored into him. He knew how Gerald had coveted Atwood Mine and how cheated he must be feeling on discovering that the estate had been creamed of its most lucrative asset—an asset Gerald had been depending on to help clear an outstanding debt of thousands of pounds he had acquired through gambling, having borrowed the money to settle his debt from ruthless moneylenders who would stop at nothing until it was repaid with extortionate interest.

But Marcus also knew how hard Sir John had worked to achieve success where Atwood Mine was concerned, and how much he had wanted it kept out of the hands of his cousin, who would have little interest in the mine itself, only the wealth it would bring to him.

'You get nothing,' said Mr Soames in answer to his question.

'Nothing!' whispered Eve, deeply shocked, turning her attention to her father's lawyer. 'But what will I do? Where am I to live.'

'Should a marriage between you and Mr Fitzalan not take place you will get your annuity, of course, and he has made provisions for you to live with your grandmother in Cumbria.'

'And the mine?' asked Marcus abruptly.

'Will revert to Mr Gerald Somerville and his heirs until the lease has run out, at which time it will be up to you or your heir—should you not be alive at the time—to decide whether or not it is renewed.'

A cold and calculating gleam entered Gerald's eyes when he realised all might not be lost after all. It would appear that all he had to do was prevent Eve from entering into a marriage with Marcus Fitzalan, and if he wasn't mistaken that shouldn't prove too difficult—not when he observed that every time she looked at him or spoke to him, she did so with unconcealed hostility.

'I realise that no one can force you to marry,' Mr Soames went on, 'that is for you to choose—but I ask you to give very serious thought to the matter.'

Marcus nodded, his face grim. 'You can count on it.'

Eve scowled at him. 'The day I marry you, Mr Fitzalan, will be the day hell freezes over. We do not suit.' She returned her attention once more to Mr Soames, ignoring Marcus's black look. 'Did my father give no explanation when he laid down these conditions?'

'I'm afraid not. Whatever it was that prompted him to do it I cannot say—and indeed, we may never know. I think, perhaps, that if he had lived a little longer, he might have explained everything to you. As you know, your father and I were friends for a good many years, and I knew him well enough to know he would not have set down these conditions without good reason. Knowing his death was imminent sharpened his anxiety to procure a suitable match for you.'

'But what if Mr Fitzalan had decided to marry someone else before my father died?' asked Eve, wishing he had.

'Your father knew Mr Fitzalan had no one in mind—and, considering your father had only a few months left to live— a year at the most—he thought it unlikely that Mr Fitzalan would do so before his death.'

Eve looked at Marcus Fitzalan and could see that he was contemplating what the loss of the mine would mean to him— and to her. Then she saw herself living in the harsh, craggy wilderness of Cumbria with her grandmother, where everyday life can be particularly severe and so remote she would see no one from one day's end to the next. The thought was not pleasant.

Turning his gaze on Eve once more, Marcus's black brows

drew together in a deep frown. He seemed to sense what was going through her mind.

Feeling betrayed, abandoned and unable to think clearly because of the shock all this had been to her, Eve rose suddenly, clenching her fists in the folds of her dress to stop them from shaking.

'Please, excuse me,' she said, turning and crossing to the door with a quiet dignity, having no wish to stay and hear more, only a strong desire to be by herself.

Not wanting to leave the matter in suspension indefinitely—which, he suspected, was what Miss Somerville intended doing—with long strides Marcus followed her out of the room into the large dark panelled hall, closing the door behind them. Two sleek liver and white hounds lay curled up in front of a huge stone hearth where a fire burned bright in an iron grate, despite the heat of the summer's day. They stretched languidly, each cocking an uninterested eye in the direction of the intruders before resuming their doze in a state of blissful lassitude, ignoring the disturbance.

'Wait,' Marcus commanded. 'We cannot leave matters like this.'

Eve paused at the sound of his voice and turned and faced him, extremely conscious of his towering, masculine presence. The immaculate cut of his coat was without a crease, moulding his strong shoulders. As his ice blue eyes swept over her his expression was grim and Eve felt extremely uncomfortable at the way he was regarding her—no doubt assessing her suitability as a possible wife, she thought wryly.

Having recovered some of her self-possession, she threw back her shoulders and lifted her head, the action meaning to tell him she was in control of herself. He felt a stirring of admiration for the way in which she conducted herself, but looking into her lovely violet eyes he could see they were as turbulent as storm clouds and that she had withdrawn inside herself to a place where she could not be reached.

'This has come as a shock to you, I can see,' he said, glad to be out of earshot of the others.

'Yes. I am both shocked and disappointed. I cannot imagine what prompted my father to do this,' she said, trying to keep a stranglehold on her emotions, 'unless, of course, he had a momentary lapse of his senses when he saw fit to make these conditions in his will in the first place. But the last thing I want right now, Mr Fitzalan, is a husband—and when I do I would prefer to choose my own.'

Faced with her anger, Marcus paled and his eyes glittered like steel flints as he tried, with great difficulty, to keep his own anger in check, knowing exactly why she was doing her utmost to make matters as difficult as possible between them. She was still embittered by what had happened between them three years ago—although why she should continue to be so baffled him, for she had no one to blame but herself. Was it usual that the moment her will was crossed she started the sparks flying and spitting fire?

'And I have no more need of a wife than you a husband, Miss Somerville,' he replied, his voice carrying anger. 'However, if we want to hold on to the mine then we have no choice but to heed your father's wishes and make the best of it.'

'And how do you know that is what I want? How can you possibly know?' she said, her voice as cold as her face, whilst inside her stomach was churning. 'As far as I am concerned the mine is the last thing on my mind at this moment. Marriage to me is important and I am hardly likely to walk into it blindly with a man who has treated me so abominably—to put my trust and myself completely in your power for the whole of my life. Besides, it is hardly flattering to know you would only be marrying me for what I could bring, Mr Fitzalan.'

'The same could be said of yourself, Miss Somerville,' he replied coldly. He gave her a hard look, his mouth tightening as he stared down at her. 'Are you always so difficult?'

'I can be as impossible as I like when something—or some-one—upsets me,' she answered.

He arched an eyebrow. 'Really?'

'Yes.'

'Then I suppose that is something I shall have to get used to if we are to make anything of your father's will. Tell me, are you well acquainted with Gerald Somerville?'

'No. I believe he has been in London himself and has only returned to the north this last week. We have met frequently over the years, but I cannot say that I know him at all well. My grandmother does not hold him in high regard and saw nothing of him while she was in town.'

Marcus's lips twisted with slight scorn. 'How could she? The kind of world your father's cousin inhabits is a night-time world of gambling and high living. There is no polite way to describe him. He is a slippery character and he has only one motive in life: to serve himself. He'd be considered a joke if he were not so ruthless in everything he does. He is to be found anywhere the *beau monde* chooses to congregate, and has an inability to resist the gambling halls and social whirl of London.'

'That I am already aware of.'

'His own estate is falling apart and bankruptcy is staring him in the face. He has lived in penury for most of his life and Sir John's death has suddenly elevated him to an attainable position. I do not believe it will be too long before the estate shows signs of neglect as he uses it as a means to pay off his debts—which, I know for a fact, are astronomical.'

Wanting desperately to escape the threat she imagined this overbearing man suddenly posed to her life, Eve stepped back from him abruptly. 'Do you think I haven't worked that out for myself? It's what I have always known. But it would seem you know Gerald well, Mr Fitzalan. Perhaps he frequents the same seedy establishments as yourself—is that it?'

'I am very particular in choosing my friends, Miss Somerville,' Marcus replied scathingly, choosing to ignore her outspoken attack on his social habits. 'Your father's cousin has a reputation for spending far more than his own father could support when he was alive. It is my misfortune to be a member of the same club—White's in St James's—and I was witness to him squandering his entire fortune at the card tables at a single sitting.'

Eve stared at him in astonishment. 'Might I ask how much?'

'If you are interested. It was thirty-five thousand pounds.'

She was stunned, unable to believe anybody could lose so much money, although her Aunt Shona had told her on one of her visits to London, that the rattling of a dice box or ill luck at cards, could well result in many a gentleman's country estate being lost, and that as a result suicides were not uncommon.

'But that is an enormous sum of money.'

'Indeed it is. It is not something that can be dismissed with a flick of the wrist.'

'And what did he do? Could he pay?'

Marcus smiled indulgently at her naïvety. 'No. His estate was already mortgaged up to the hilt. Facing ruination, anyone else would have shot himself—but not Gerald Somerville. He took the only option and borrowed the money from unscrupulous moneylenders—who, on learning of your father's death and knowing Gerald was his heir, have called in the loan…with astronomical interest. These men are ruthless and show no mercy to those who cannot pay. I have heard that they are exerting enormous pressure on him, so I don't wonder at his anger on finding Atwood Mine is not his by right. He is in deep water. He needs it desperately to pay off his loan and get the these men off his back.'

Eve was astounded to learn all this. 'I—I had no idea Gerald's situation was so serious.'

'Yes, it is. Inheriting your father's estate will have come as a godsend to him—but your father has seen to it that he has not come into a fortune. Through his own hard work and good management the estate has never been so prosperous, and if Gerald is sensible and takes legal advice on how to settle his loan, then it will continue to be so—but if he does not mend his ways then I am afraid that in no time at all you will begin to see signs of its decline. Everything your father has worked so hard to achieve will be eradicated in one fell swoop.'

Eve winced, the very idea of her beloved home being mortgaged to pay off Gerald's gambling debts and falling into the greedy hands of moneylenders and suchlike angering her beyond words. But there was nothing she could do.

'Which is why your father made quite sure his financial affairs were put in order before he died.'

'It's a pity he did not consider putting me before his financial affairs,' Eve remarked bitterly. 'It seems to me that I was as much his property as Atwood Mine.'

'But a more desirable property,' Marcus smiled, his expression softening.

'Am I?' she remarked coldly. 'I'm glad you think so, Mr Fitzalan, but that does not alter the fact that you cannot have one without the other—or, at least, you cannot have the mine without me, whereas you would not have me without the mine by choice.'

Marcus frowned with annoyance. 'You do me an injustice, Miss Somerville. I am not nearly as mercenary as you make me out to be.'

'And I have every reason to think you are,' she shot back at him, referring to their encounter three years ago. 'But what if I do not agree to marry you? And if my father thought so highly of you, why did he not leave Atwood Mine to you outright, knowing how important it is to you? It would certainly have avoided all these complications and I would not be faced with the daunting prospect of marrying a man not of my choosing—a man I have every reason in the world to despise. I could as easily have gone to Cumbria to live with my grandmother—or to London to my Aunt Shona.'

'He knew that—just like he knew you would see the sense in what he was asking of you. I tend to share Mr Soames's view.'

'And that is?'

'That, if it were not for his untimely death, he would have explained it to you himself—and to me. He probably believed you would fall prey to all manner of fortune hunters if you were left alone.'

'What? Two thousand pounds is hardly a fortune, Mr Fitzalan.'

'Two thousand pounds is a great deal of money to men who have nothing, Miss Somerville. Perhaps the conditions he laid down were his way of making sure you would be taken care of. Do not forget that your father desired only your peace of mind and future happiness. You must believe that.'

'Which is why he has suggested making you my keeper, is that not so, Mr Fitzalan?' she said scathingly. 'However, I do not need you or anyone else to tell me what my own father desired for me,' she said, lowering her head so he would not see the tears collecting her eyes.

'Your husband—not your keeper,' Marcus contradicted in a low voice.

'Nevertheless, I confess I am bewildered by all this. It's a riddle I cannot begin to comprehend. I always believed I knew how his mind worked—but it seems I was wrong. I would like to know why, knowing how I feel about you, he has used what can only be described as emotional blackmail to virtually force me into marriage with you. If I decide not to abide by his wishes, and I am sorely tempted not to,' she said rebelliously, 'then Gerald will stand to benefit enormously.'

'That is true—and I implore you to consider his wishes seriously.'

Eve sighed deeply, so confused her head was spinning. Since her mother's death and the onset of her father's illness, she had stubbornly refused to consider the future and what it would mean to her when the inevitable happened, but now the future was with her and she was unprepared for the life that was being thrust at her. When she spoke a touch of anger had come to add to the bitterness of her disappointment.

'Oh, I shall. I always knew how much my father's work

meant to him—Atwood Mine and all his other concerns—but it did not occur to me until now that he would allow his loyalty to all that, and to you, to affect his dealings with me, his daughter. Please—you must excuse me,' she said quickly. 'All this has come as something of a shock. I need some time to myself.'

'Of course. I fully understand. I am leaving myself presently. I realise that you are your own mistress—but anger is a bad counsellor. Do not allow it to influence your decision, and do not foolishly refuse what is your due.' He sighed. 'We both have much to think about. I shall return to Burntwood Hall when you've had time to recover from today and we can talk seriously about what is to be done,' he said, standing aside to let her pass.

'Yes—thank you,' she said stiffly. 'Goodbye, Mr Fitzalan.'

Marcus watched her go, staring thoughtfully after her. Meeting Eve Somerville for the first time in three years had been like being a contestant in the first round of a boxing match. She was possessed of the most formidable temper he'd ever witnessed in a woman, having a tongue that could flay the meanest man, gladly stamping on his pieces of lacerated flesh before finally pulverising them into dust with the heel of her pretty foot.

He realised that the lady was a termagant, but he sensed she had a magic quality—if she chose to use it. Troubled, he turned to go back to Alex Soames, his expression tightening, his brows drawn together in an ominous black line when he continued to think of her.

He had felt a slight sense of shock the first time she had looked at him fully, when her grandmother had brought her to be introduced to him after the funeral. There was something in her eyes that set his pulse racing and he felt a great sense of excitement—as he had on that other occasion when he had had her at his mercy three years ago. She looked very young— almost a child—yet he already knew that behind the childlike exterior there was a ripe sensuality just bursting to be set free.

Instinctively, he knew that no matter how in control and
confident she might conceivably be, she had that bewitching
quality that could well captivate a man and enslave him for
life—a burgeoning femme fatale. Yet, when he recollected
how outspoken she had been at the reading of the will, of the
insult she had thrown at him and how quick she was to anger,
then he would make damned sure she curbed that temper of
hers if she became his wife; if she did not come to heel, she
would feel more than the length of his tongue.

When he entered the room once more, his eyes were cold
and without expression as he took stock of Gerald Somerville
and observed the unconcealed greed glittering in his eyes,
knowing it would be exceedingly profitable for him if Marcus
did not marry Eve. But there was something else lurking in
their depths, something unpleasantly sinister and unconcealed
as their eyes locked—a moment in which each of them knew
they were mortal enemies.

Marcus had meant what he said when he had told Eve that
Gerald Somerville was not unknown to him. He was a notorious rake about town, a man with a sordid reputation, and he
was well acquainted with his depraved and corrupt ways, that
differed greatly from the accepted standards of behaviour.

He remembered well the night Gerald had faced ruination,
and the card game which he himself had been privy to. He'd
been at White's, seen with his own eyes the money Gerald
had lost—and Gerald was aware that he knew and hated him
for knowing. He recalled seeing his fellow players sitting intently round the the table watching Gerald lose, and not even
wearing his loose frieze greatcoat inside out—which was often
the case by those hoping to win—had brought Gerald luck.

He'd heard it rumoured the following day that in desperation Gerald had borrowed the money to pay off his debt from
moneylenders—men without scruples who would resort to any
foul and violent means to reclaim loans—digging himself
deeper into the mire.

Gerald's expression became set and grim, his eyes shining with a deadly glitter as his gaze became fixed, his feelings for Marcus clearly beyond words. He was filled with an impotent, cold black fury on finding himself cheated by Marcus Fitzalan out of something that he coveted.

Gerald was the kind of man Marcus despised and went out of his way to avoid. Because he knew that nothing was beneath Gerald, that he might even attempt persuading—or, even worse, compromising—Eve into marrying him in order to revert Atwood Mine to him, Marcus was even more determined to return to Burntwood Hall very soon to save Eve from herself in securing her hand in marriage.

Later, slipping out of the house unseen by the few remaining mourners who still lingered on, content to partake of the late Sir John's liquor and to talk and rekindle old memories and dwell on times they had shared, in the falling dusk Eve took the path towards the church, glad there was no one about so that she could be alone, to pay one last visit to her parents' grave before the day that had heralded such a change to her life ended.

She opened the gate into the churchyard, which was enclosed by a high stone wall covered by a wild tangle of weeds and ivy. A mass of ancient yew trees, black in the gathering gloom, were in stark contrast to the creamy sandstone church. All around her was silence, a sudden stillness, as drifting clouds passed over the moon just beginning to appear.

The churchyard was a sad and sorrowful place and Eve moved along the paths in sympathy to nature's silence, the huge, cold grey gravestones covered in lichen and casting looming, grotesque shadows in the gathering gloom. Coming to a halt, she stood looking down at the mound of newly dug earth and clay strewn with flowers, noticing how they were already beginning to wilt and to lose all their frail beauty. Tomorrow they too would be dead. She felt a terrible pain wrench her heart when she contemplated the lifeless forms of her parents lying side by side beneath the soil.

Unlike their ancestors before them who had been interred inside the church, her parents had long since chosen to be buried side by side in the churchyard. Unable to contain the grief that had been accumulating in her heart since her father's accident, tears started in her eyes and streamed down her face.

She fell to her knees and bowed her head as she finally gave way under the long strain that possessed her. All her reserve was gone and she began to cry dementedly, her body shaking with an uncontrollable reservoir of grief, bewilderment and betrayal—unable to understand why her father, who had loved her, had treated her so harshly, unaware as she wept of the tall, silent figure that stood watching her from the gate.

Having taken longer to depart from Burntwood Hall than he had intended, Marcus had come to the churchyard to pay his final respects to the man who had become more than a friend to him over the few years he had known him, a man to whom he owed so much. He paused at the gate on seeing the kneeling, sorrowing figure beside the grave, only just able to make out in the dusk the profile of Eve Somerville, her slender form racked with grief.

His heart contracted with pain and pity, for never had he seen or heard so much desolation in anyone before. He took a step, intending to go to her, but checked himself, thinking it would be best to leave her, that it would do her good to cry, for he suspected there was no one in that great house to offer her comfort. He had to fight the urge to go to her, to take her in his arms and hold her, to caress the soft cloud of hair that had tumbled loose from its pins and fell in wanton disarray about her lovely face.

Aware of his own inadequacy he cursed softly, knowing that Eve Somerville had made a deep and lasting impression on him, penetrating his tough exterior and finding a way into his heart as no other woman had done before. It took all his willpower to tear his eyes from her forlorn figure, to turn and walk away—but it was a picture he knew would never leave him.

Chapter Three

Later, feeling drained of all emotion and extremely tired, Eve sought the sanctuary of her room, curling up in the large winged chair by the fire and closing her eyes, unable to cast Marcus Fitzalan from her mind. Falling into a fitful doze, she found her mind drifting back over the years to the time of Atwood Fair, when she had been seventeen years old, amazed that she should remember every detail and all the words he had said to her, which, because of the humiliation it never failed to evoke, she always refused to do.

She remembered that it had all begun as a silly, girlish prank on the day of the fair—although it could be said that the nature of the prank was not the kind any respectable, well brought-up young lady would have indulged in.

Knowing how much the townspeople looked forward to seeing them, normally her parents showed their faces for just a little while, allowing Eve to accompany them, but this time her mother was not feeling well so was unable to attend. However, knowing how much Eve loved the fair and not wishing to disappoint her, she allowed her to go in the company of Mrs Parkinson, a good friend and the wife of a reputable local squire, whose own daughter Emma was Eve's closest friend. She was confident that she would be well chaperoned and that Mrs Parkinson would see that she did not get up to any mischief.

Atwood Fair was a tremendous social event and the highlight of the year, when the close-knit families of Atwood and the surrounding countryside came together to enjoy and revel in the two days of festivities. It was also of economic importance, for livestock and farm produce were brought in from nearby farms and villages to be sold. Drovers also brought in flocks of sheep and cattle from considerable distances, and wandering gypsies came in gaily painted caravans, positioning them in fields adjacent to the fairground.

There was always so much variety, with so many delightful attractions such as puppet shows, waxworks, shooting galleries and bowling, but also what Eve considered the less attractive events, such as bear baitings, cockfights and prize fights, which always attracted large crowds but which she never went near, finding such spectacles quite revolting.

Traders and merchants had set up stalls to try to tempt visitors to part with their money, and children romped about while lovers strolled hand in hand among the many colourful booths. The appetising aroma of cooking food filled the air, and Eve's father always donated an ox to be roasted on a spit above an open fire, the fat sizzling noisily as it dripped into the hot charcoal embers.

It was mid-afternoon when Eve arrived with her friends Emma Parkinson and Angela Lambert. Eve and Emma were friends of long standing, but she had never got on really well with Angela, who rarely lost an opportunity to embarrass her. She was single minded and forever in pursuit of her own interests. Normally Eve would ignore her, although it did not occur to her that Angela might be jealous of her family's wealth and superior standing in the district, and envious of her popularity with the local young men, selfishly wanting all their attention focused on herself.

Angela and Emma were so very different. Emma was as slender as a wand and had nut-brown hair with eyes to match, and while she was of a gentle disposition with a placid indolence, Angela, with auburn hair and hazel eyes, was quite the opposite, being rather voluptuous, lively and full of energies she found hard to repress. There was also a jealous, malicious streak to her nature that often challenged Eve's own.

Sitting on the grass on the edge of the crowd beneath a warm July sun—where they were being watched over by a sharp-eyed Mrs Parkinson as she conversed with a group of ladies—they were discussing Eve's imminent betrothal to Leslie Stephenson, the good-looking eldest son of a baronet who lived in the area, who had taken little persuading to come to the fair, although he had soon taken himself off to watch the wrestling and boxing matches in progress.

Leslie seemed to find Eve quite enchanting and she couldn't believe her good fortune that she had made such a conquest, although he did seem to be taking an awfully long time in applying to her father for her hand in marriage, which was secretly beginning to worry and vex her.

Eve and Emma sat listening as Angela enthused at length about a young man from her home town of Little Bolton, which was situated halfway between Atwood and Netherley. She considered herself an authority on everything—especially men, positively thriving on their attentions; she was already an expert at knowing how to attract them.

'There are more important things in life,' Eve commented, bored by the fervour with which Angela insisted they know all about a young man they had not met.

Angela scowled crossly. 'You can say that when you're almost betrothed to one of the most eligible men in the north, Eve,' she said, reaching into a box of bonbons Leslie had brought them before disappearing.

'And you will find as big a catch one day, Angela. Men flock round you in droves. You know how to flirt, how to say what pleases them. You'll soon have yourself a husband—although if you carry on eating those bonbons like that you'll become so plump you'll put them off,' she said as Angela popped another into her mouth. She watched as Angela's soft pink lips closed around the sugary sweet, beginning to feel distinctly uneasy about the way Angela always attached herself to Leslie, who, to her anger and dismay, seemed flattered by it and not to mind in the slightest.

'If he's half as rich and good looking as Leslie, then I'll be well satisfied,' Angela replied, softly and serenely, licking each sticky finger, her mouth as pink as a rosebud and her eyes lighting with sudden interest when they came to rest on a man riding by on a powerfully built chestnut stallion, the man in the saddle exuding virility and a lazy confidence.

His head was bare, the sunlight shining on his hair, which was as black as ebony, his body in complete proportion as he moved as one with his horse. His shoulders and hips were firm, his booted legs long and his thighs powerful as they gripped his horse.

'Good Lord,' gasped Angela, agog with excitement. 'It's Marcus Fitzalan.'

As he rode past Angela and Emma stole long, lingering looks at him—but not so much Eve, who remained unimpressed. He was well-known and people moved out of the way to let him pass. Eve merely glanced at him with idle curiosity, because although they had never met—she had caught only a brief glimpse of him when he had called at Burntwood Hall once—she knew him to be a business associate and close friend of her father's.

He seemed oblivious to the mayhem he caused within the breasts of two of the young ladies, his mind being on other things, but on hearing Angela's unrestrained girlish giggles he condescended to look their way. The blast from his eyes acted like a douche of cold air as they swept over the group with little interest.

'Goodness! What a handsome man,' Emma exclaimed, sighing ecstatically as her eyes followed the delectable Mr Fitzalan, watching him become swallowed up by the crowd.

'And he knows it,' said Angela.

'I wonder what he's doing here.'

Eve shrugged. 'I really do not care,' she said, trying to sound indifferent, although the wave of excitement that had swept over her when she had watched him ride by told her she was not as indifferent to his masculine allure as she appeared.

'I wonder if he's staying for the dancing later,' said Emma.

'Maybe he will—although I'm sure he won't dance,' said Eve. 'He's far too superior—and I'm sure he wouldn't be seen dead dancing with any of the local girls.'

Angela's eyes narrowed, suddenly filling with mischief as an outlandish scheme came to mind. 'But we're not local girls, are we? At least not in the sense you mean, Eve—and I think we should have some fun with Mr Fitzalan—see if we can't melt that ice-sculptured exterior he's so fond of portraying to the world.'

'What do you suggest?'

'That one of us should ask him to dance.'

'Angela! That's quite outrageous,' gasped Emma.

'Yes—but it's fun—and I think it should be you, Eve,' she said decisively, her eyes coming to rest with a sly, faint challenge on her friend.

Eve sat up with a jolt and stared at her in disbelief. Normally nothing Angela suggested either shocked or amazed her, but this was something quite outrageous—even by Angela's standards.

'Oh, no. I couldn't,' she whispered. 'What you suggest is preposterous, Angela—and besides, if I am to dance at all— should Mrs Parkinson permit it—then I shall be dancing with Leslie.'

'That's if Leslie feels inclined to dance,' Angela commented flatly, piqued. On seeing Eve shoot her a cross look she sighed, not to be deterred. 'Oh, Eve—think about it. Leslie has paid you such scant attention today that I shall be surprised if he finds the time to seek you out at all—and he seems to be in no hurry to approach your father to ask his permission to marry you. He's been dithering for weeks and you know it.'

'That's not true, Angela,' Eve replied hotly, hating it when Angela took her to task over anything, but she could not deny that what she said was true. The manner in which he was dragging his feet in making any kind of commitment to her was being noticed by everyone.

'Just think, Eve,' Angela went on, smiling with enthusiasm, her eyes regarding her sardonically, 'if he sees a man of Mr Fitzalan's distinction paying you particular attention by asking you to dance, it's bound to make him jealous and increase his intention to marry you.'

'But if I am to do as you say, it will be *me* asking Mr Fitzalan to dance, not the other way round,' she said drily.

'Nevertheless, it could be just what Leslie needs to sharpen him up a bit. Mark my words, if he thinks Marcus Fitzalan is interested in you he'll insist on seeking your father out immediately to ask for your hand in marriage.'

Eve frowned, uncertain. 'Do you think so?'

'Of course he will.'

'But I could just as easily make him jealous by dancing with someone else. It doesn't have to be Mr Fitzalan,' she said, the very thought of approaching the formidable Mr Fitzalan making her stomach churn and her spirits sink.

'But that wouldn't have the same effect. Besides, everyone knows what good friends he and your father are. You're far more likely to succeed with him than Emma or I. Unless, of course, you don't think you can charm him into dancing with you—or anything else, for that matter,' she said, in a deceptively casual way, lying back on the grass and closing her eyes with a sigh, giving the impression that she wasn't really interested one way or the other.

But Eve was not deceived. The challenge had been tossed down and unless she wanted to look a fool she had no alternative but to take her up on it—but she had the uneasy sensation of being the victim of some secret plot. Goaded into action, she was determined to prove Angela wrong.

When a group of fiddlers started to play and the dancing began, that was the moment when Eve, having escaped the watchful eye of Mrs Parkinson, found herself walking in the direction of Marcus Fitzalan, unaware as she did so of the smug, self-satisfied smile curling Angela's lips, and the malicious, ruthless gleam in her slanting eyes as she watched her go—like a lamb to the slaughter.

Observing the scene with his brooding gaze, Mr Fitzalan stood where a large crowd of spectators gathered. Dressed all in black, apart from his startlingly white neckcloth, he reminded Eve of a predatory hawk. She stopped short, becoming nervous suddenly, for what had started out as a silly prank no longer seemed like fun and already she was beginning to regret her silly impulse to call Angela's bluff.

She was tempted to walk past Mr Fitzalan but, aware of Angela's watchful gaze and the challenge she had thrown down, her pride forbade it, despite being intensely conscious of the impropriety of her actions and that her parents would be furious and deeply shocked if they were to find out.

And so it was that against the dictates of her better judgement she hesitantly stepped into the arena, feeling rather like Daniel stepping into the lions' den, blessedly unaware as she did so that the situation she was about to get herself into would alter the entire course of her life.

She looked up at Mr Fitzalan with her heart in confusion, gazing into a pair of ice blue eyes, having no idea of the bright-eyed picture she presented to Marcus Fitzalan—a dainty, lovely image of fragility. He observed the healthy glow of her skin, how demure she looked in her high-waisted pale pink sprigged dress with its scoop neck, the delectable mounds of her young breasts peeping tantalisingly over the top.

He had seen her with her friends when he arrived, all of them in high spirits. Taking her for one of the country girls who had come to enjoy the fair—for no properly brought-up young lady would be seen watching what was about to take place—his eyes raked over her.

Eve looked up at him, taking the bull by the horns, for she would have to speak to him now. He would think it odd if she just walked away. 'Have you only just arrived at the fair, Mr Fitzalan?' she found herself asking.

He stared down at her in fascination, both repelled by the cool manner in which she had approached him and attracted by her physical beauty.

'Yes. And you? Are you enjoying the fair?' he asked politely.

She smiled. 'Very much, thank you.'

Marcus was the kind of man who understood flirting and always found it distasteful—except when it happened to be from the right woman. But this was not a woman, this was a girl, and if she had not chosen that moment to smile he would have moved on, but it melted his bones to water and he found himself wanting to know more about her and enjoy her company a little longer. He was intrigued. Perhaps a little dalliance wouldn't go amiss before he had to return to Netherley.

Eve felt herself begin to relax, turning to observe the event that was about to start. 'What is going to happen?' she asked innocently.

'Another prize fight,' he answered, his attention drawn to a brute of a man with a bare chest and massive shoulders prowling in the ring before them.

Eve paled suddenly when she realised she was close to the ring where pugilists were displaying their skills, accepting bets from amateurs who fancied their chances in fighting them. If she had known this was to be the attraction, she would have waited until Mr Fitzalan had moved away. Her eyes became riveted on the fighter awaiting another challenger. His fists were clenched and bloodied, his last challenger having retired with a broken jaw and bloody nose. He was powerfully built, rippling with muscles, his head covered with black patches to hide his scars.

Eve turned to speak to her companion, about to move further away, but the excited crowd closed in around them, forcing her to remain where she was, the roar that rose from a hundred throats as another challenger stepped into the ring rendering her speechless. She became dismayed and nauseated when she realised she would have to stay and watch the brutal slaughter.

Swallowing hard, she was determined not to waver, remembering Angela would be watching her mercilessly. 'Oh—on whom do you place your money, Mr Fitzalan?' she heard herself asking tentatively, wondering if he approved of this crude and violent sport. 'Will it be the reigning champion, do you think, whose last opponent looks to be in a sorry state,' she said, indicating the poor man holding his broken jaw and having a wound on his cheek sewn up at the ringside, 'or the challenger?'

'Neither. I'm not a gambling man. I would never bet on the obvious for I fear the challenger is destined to be the loser.'

'I disagree,' said Eve, studying the man who had stepped into the ring to try his luck. 'I suspect the challenger is about to make his reputation. The champion is strong and lithe, I grant you, while his opponent is stout and not so great in stature—but he is full of fire which will give him added strength.'

Marcus looked down at her with slight amusement. 'You speak like an expert. Do you enjoy prize fights?'

'No,' she replied, wincing, unable to hide her repugnance as the two men began hitting each other with their bare fists, a man holding a long staff standing by ready to separate them should blood flow. 'I confess it is the first time I have seen one at close range. It's horrible.'

'My feelings entirely. The public taste for violence always appals me. Come, we don't have to stay and watch two men knock the sense out of each other—if they had any in the first place for believing it wise to indulge in such brutality,' he said, taking her arm and drawing her back, the crowd parting to let them through. He paused where his horse was tethered to a tree, beginning to loosen the reins.

Free of the constriction of the crowd, Eve breathed a sigh of relief. 'Thank you. I don't believe I could have watched them fight to the bitter end. What a magnificent horse,' she said, her attention caught as always when she recognised good horseflesh, reaching up to slide her hand along its silken neck.

'Yes. He's very special. You like horses?'

She nodded, about to tell him her father had a stable full of superb horseflesh, but thought better of it. Better that he didn't know who she was. She became alarmed when she suspected he was about to leave.

'You—you're not leaving?'

'I must. It's a long ride back to Netherley.'

Panic washed over her as she turned briefly, seeing Angela with a smug expression on her face, watching her like a cat watches a mouse, reminding her what it was she had to do. 'Oh—but—but I...' she faltered, acutely embarrassed and unable to go on.

Marcus raised his eyebrows in question, waiting for her to continue, enjoying her confusion.

Eve looked towards the fiddlers and the laughing, dancing swirl of people, acutely conscience of Angela's challenge and knowing she would have to ask him now. 'I—I—thought you might like to dance.'

Unable to believe that she had said those words she watched him, unconscious that she was holding her breath or that her eyes were wide open as she waited expectantly for him to reply, seeing neither shock nor surprise register on his carefully schooled features at her bold request.

'No.'

'Oh—I see.'

Eve stepped back, ashamed and filled with mortification by his blunt rebuff, wanting to extricate herself from the awful embarrassment of the predicament she had created in the first place as quickly as possible, but she felt a stab of anger that he could have been so rude as to refuse her in such a brusque manner, and a dull ache of disappointment in her chest that Angela would crow with delight at her inability to tempt the high and mighty Mr Fitzalan to dance with her. Making a conscious effort to escape from the situation with as much dignity as she could muster, she stepped away from him.

'Very well, Mr Fitzalan. Since you seem averse to my company I will bid you good day. Please forgive me for troubling you.'

Marcus's hand shot out and gripped her arm. Out of the corner of his eye he saw her friends not twenty yards away watching expectantly, giggling and nudging each other in anticipation of what might happen next. His eyes narrowed and he nodded slightly, looking down at his delightful companion whose face was flushed with indignation.

He was no fool. He knew exactly what she was up to. For some reason known only to her and her friends she was playing some kind of game. He smiled slightly with bland amusement, determined to give little Miss Whoever-she-was a shade more than she had bargained for. But not here—he had no mind to be watched by two giggling girls.

'I did not say that. On the contrary, I find your presence pleasing. Come—it's just that I am not inclined to dance, I never do at these occasions. But perhaps you will take a walk with me along the path by the river?'

Eve stared at him, feeling her heart turn over at his unexpected request. His voice was incredibly seductive, his eyes smiling and compelling her to say yes. She felt a warmth creeping throughout her body which made her doubt her earlier conviction that she was not attracted by him. How could she not be when he looked at her like this? She was confused, the situation having become one she had not anticipated—one she was unsure how to deal with, not being experienced or worldly enough to grasp the type of man Marcus Fitzalan was.

'Why—I—I shouldn't—I…'

He smiled invitingly, his voice low and persuasive.

'Come—you must say yes. It's rather like the enticer becoming the enticed, is it not?' he said softly, lifting a knowing eyebrow.

Eve expelled her breath in a rush, her eyes registering shock, horror and disbelief, for his look told her that he knew exactly what she had been about. 'Oh—I wasn't—I mean—'

He laughed softly, his teeth gleaming white from between his parted lips. 'Does it matter?' and he sensed victory when she began to follow him as he led his horse along the path by the side of the river, long before she realised she had been defeated.

The fact that Eve's absence might have been noted by Mrs Parkinson, and that Leslie had returned to the group, was the last thing on her mind just then. As they walked the sun, warm and benign to lovers—and yet they weren't lovers—slanted through the trees that lined the river bank, showing them the way as Marcus drew her farther and farther away from her friends. The air was warm and sultry, with tiny insects darting along the surface of the water, the sound of revelry and music growing ever fainter.

They talked of inconsequential things, of Atwood and the people who lived there, until Eve realised how far they had walked and began to panic. Her behaviour was completely irrational and she wondered what her parents would say if they were to find out about this. Their code of behaviour was strict and must be adhered to. She should not be alone with a man who was not her betrothed—and certainly not walking alone along a river bank, half-hidden from everyone by a curtain of trees.

They paused and Marcus let go of the reins to allow his horse to drink from the river. Leaning negligently against a tree he folded his arms across his chest, watching Eve in speculative silence through narrowed eyes. He had removed his coat and loosened his neck cloth, and beneath the soft linen shirt his muscles flexed with any slight movement he made. He exuded a brute strength and posed with leashed sensuality, a hard set to his jaw and a cynicism in his ice-cold eyes. But then he smiled, lazily and devastatingly, his teeth as white as his neckcloth.

The breeze blew Eve's hair across her face and she reached up and absently drew it back, combing her fingers through it and sweeping it behind her ears, unconscious of how seductive the gesture was to Marcus. He stood absolutely still, watching her with a look that was possessive, and, looking at him, something in his expression made Eve flush and catch her breath, dropping her arm self-consciously. The moment was intimate, warm and vibrantly alive. His vitality at such close quarters alarmed her.

'I—I must go back,' she said, thrown into sudden panic, biting her lip nervously and keeping her face averted from his. She wanted to escape, to run away, and yet, at the same time, she could not move. 'My friends will be wondering what has become of me.'

Marcus reached out and placed his fingers under her chin and turned it round to face him.

'Look at me.'

She glanced up at him, breathing rapidly from between parted lips so moist, so soft, her wonderful liquid eyes wide and luminous, her small breasts thrusting against the bodice of her dress. She was the perfect picture of alluring innocence, but Marcus was not to be deceived. To a lustful man those magnificent eyes were proving to be far too alluring and inviting.

'You know it's wrong to be alone with me—that no decent young lady would dream of taking a walk with a total stranger. What makes you think you are safe?'

Eve flushed, her glorious violet eyes mist bright, knowing that now was the time she should tell him who she was, that she had never intended things to go this far, but somehow she couldn't. She found his presence vaguely threatening and just hoped he would allow her to leave and return to the others, and in so doing forget all about her. But his eyes had taken on a whole new look, one she neither recognised nor understood, one which seemed to scorch her with the intensity of his passion, making her wonder if she was strong enough to withstand him. They burned into her, stopping all motion.

'Clearly I am not one of the decent, well-bred young ladies you are acquainted with,' she said, her voice quavering. 'You already know by my forward behaviour when I asked you to dance that my knowledge of protocol is negligible. I—I assumed that because of who you are—your elevated position—I would be safe. This has all been a terrible mistake,' she said lamely, alarm bells beginning to scream through her head. 'I—I must return to my friends. I should never have come. I—I don't know why I did.'

Eve watched in wary alarm as Marcus moved closer, driven by an uncontrollable compulsion to possess her, her behaviour from the very start telling him that the last thing she wanted was to return to her friends just yet. 'Don't you? You're here with me because you want to be. You want what I want. Don't deny it because I will not believe you—and don't be too eager to run away back to your friends.'

Marcus should have seen the panic in her eyes, heard the slight catch in her voice, but all he could think of was her lips and how soft and inviting they looked. Sweeping the tangle of her hair from her face, he took it firmly in both his hands and lowered his head, feeling an explosion of passion the moment he touched her. His mouth clamped down on hers, snatching her breath from between her lips before she could protest, feeling the blood pounding through his veins with the scorching heat of desire.

Eve was too stunned to do anything except let him kiss her, but when he did not feel her respond he raised his head and frowned, puzzled, slipping his hands about her waist and pulling her close, their bodies touching full length.

'I want no chaste kiss, lady,' he said, his voice low and husky. 'I think you know how to do better than that.'

His hand slipped behind her neck as again he lowered his

head, and with tantalising slowness he caressed her lips with his own before kissing her deeply, surprising, but not shocking her. Naïve and inexperienced, she acted purely on instinct, responding naturally to his tender assault on her lips—and it was not just her lips that began to open and respond, but her whole body as they clung to each other, becoming caught up in a wave of pleasure.

Eve was seduced by his mouth, becoming captive to his touch, his caress and the promise of things to come, secret, mysterious things that set her body trembling. She didn't know what was happening to her. No one had told her what happened when men and women were intimate together. An inexperienced girl could not have imagined such a kiss. She had never been kissed by a man in her life, and to be kissed like this for the first time was devastating. The feelings he aroused in her, with his lips, his touch, his eyes, were irrational, nameless. But she was not so overcome with passion to know that what she was doing was wrong, very wrong, and she must put an end to it.

'Please—you must let me go,' she whispered, her lips against his. 'You must not do this.'

Marcus seemed not to hear her plea and continued to seek her lips, his inquisitive fingers caressing the soft swell of her breasts. She pushed her hands against his chest and stood back, breathless, gazing up at him in helpless appeal, while wanting what he had to offer with a physical intensity which was like no other need she had ever known or imagined.

'Please—this is not right—we shouldn't. If anyone should find out that I've been alone with you—the—the proprieties—the conventions…'

Jolted back to his senses, Marcus stared at her. 'What the devil are you talking about? Why should rules of social etiquette affect you—a doxy?'

Eve's cheeks burned at the insult. 'How dare you! I am no doxy.'

'You gave a pretty good imitation of one.'

'I am not,' she flared, trying to still the wild beating of her heart.

'Then who the devil are you?'

For a brief second Eve considered telling a small lie but thought better of it, knowing she would be found out—besides, she did not tell lies, preferring to tell the truth no matter what the situation. She turned as if to walk away but fury and dread at what she might tell him made him reach out and pull her round to face him. She tried to shrink away, but he held her firmly.

'Who are you?' he demanded coldly.

Taking a deep breath, Eve met his gaze squarely, all coquetry gone as her spirit rose to grapple with this unpleasant turn of events. The air between them had become tense and charged with an entirely new kind of emotion.

'I—I am Eve Somerville,' she whispered, forcing herself to look directly into his eyes. 'Sir John Somerville's daughter.'

Marcus stared down at her as though he had been felled. His jawline tightened, his eyes became steady and glacial, his face going as white as his neck cloth. 'Dear Lord! What folly is this? Is this true? Are you Eve Somerville?'

She nodded dumbly, lowering her gaze, flinching before the exasperation in his voice and the cold glitter in his ice blue eyes. Never had she felt such humiliation.

'Look at me,' he demanded.

Unwillingly Eve raised her head and met his eyes, defiance and perturbation on her face. He glared down at her, embracing her in a look that was ice cold.

'I never thought to meet Sir John's daughter in a mad escapade of this kind—but it seems I was wrong. Have you no sense?' he said, thrusting his face close to hers, the line of his mouth cruel. His hands shot out and clamped down hard on her shoulders and he shook her so forcefully that she thought her head would come off. 'Can't you see that it was the height of dangerous folly to embark on such a madcap scheme as this?' he admonished severely.

'It was a mistake,' she said desperately, wishing he would release his vicious hold on her.

'A mistake of your doing. The responsibility for your being here is your own. What made you seek me out?' he demanded. 'Come—don't keep me in suspense.' He fumed with growing impatience, thrusting her away from him and raking his hand in sheer frustration through his hair. 'Why did you not tell me who you were?'

Full of shame and mortification Eve wished the ground would open and swallow her up. Never had she felt so wretched. He watched her with a deadly calm.

'I—I meant to—but somehow—it—it was a hoax, a charade, that is all—my friends dared me to ask you to dance—'

Marcus looked at her as if she had taken leave of her senses. 'A hoax? Do you actually have the impertinence to tell me this was a hoax? My God, are you shameless? Can't you see? Has it not occurred to you that by your foolishness it is not only your own reputation that might be ruined, but also my own? And you are betrothed, are you not—or about to be—to Leslie Stephenson?'

'Yes,' she replied. His face was frightening, but feeling wrath and indignation rising inside her, she tossed back her head and glared at him defiantly.

'Then let us hope he does not hear of this, otherwise any expectations you might have of him asking for your hand in marriage will have been dashed. Now go home to your mother, Miss Somerville, she must be wondering where you are. If I were your father and I heard of this little episode—and you can be assured he will for I intend seeking him out at once— then you could be sure of a sound thrashing.'

His stern rebuke inflamed a smouldering resentment towards him inside Eve. 'Then I can only thank God that you are not my father,' she flared.

'You may, Miss Somerville. You may. In my opinion you are a self-indulgent, spoiled brat—the type I hold in contempt. You behaved like an accomplished flirt. You didn't know what

you were doing—what you were asking for when you so outrageously made sexual overtures to a gentleman of my years
and experience with women. Perhaps you will think twice the
next time you want to play games—and I strongly advise you
to learn the rules.'

Eve stared at him, her mind trying to adjust to his words.
No one had ever spoken to her like this before or insulted her
so severely. Fury blazed in his eyes as they locked relentlessly
on to hers, but she stood before him, full of youthful courage,
spirit and pride. Her mind was no longer in control and she
had no idea how adorable she looked with her face flushed
with ire and her eyes blazing furiously.

'And what of your own conduct? You should have known
better than to take advantage of me, regardless of who I might
be—unless this is how you normally behave,' she accused
him.

'I never take advantage of defenceless young ladies—but
you did not give me the impression of being defenceless. If
you, Miss Somerville, are under the impression that you may
sport with me in any manner you please, then let me tell you
that you do not know me.'

'And after your insulting attack on my person I have no
wish to know you. It would be interesting to know how much
of a gentleman you are, Mr Fitzalan—had you not found out
in time who I am.'

'Were I not a gentleman, Miss Somerville, it would not
matter a damn who you are. I would behave much worse and
take advantage of your delectable charms here and now. And
I know by your response that, if I had not released you when
I did, with a little gentle persuasion you would have yielded
to me completely, flinging all caution to the four winds with
no thought of the consequences. Let me tell you that I rarely
refuse that which is so flagrantly offered to me, but considering your age and that you are Sir John's daughter—who, as
you know, is an extremely good friend of mine—I must decline your offer.'

Eve was infuriated. 'Oh—how dare you speak to me like this? I know what you must think—'

'I don't think so, lady. If you did you'd turn and run,' he said with menacing, murderous fury. 'Now return to your friends before they send out a search party and accuse me of compromising you. Having met you, I cannot think of anything that would upset me more than your father insisting that I do the gentlemanly thing and marry you myself.'

Chapter Four

In disagreeable silence Eve turned from Marcus Fitzalan, her heart heavy with shame and helpless misery. Never had she been so shaken and humiliated in her seventeen years as she was then. Hurrying back along the path, she discovered to her mortification that her indiscretion had been witnessed not only by Angela but also by Leslie Stephenson, who was staring at her in absolute incredulity.

Unable to utter a word of explanation in her defence she hurried on, too ashamed, angry and humiliated to speak to anyone—but not before she had glimpsed, through the blur of tears that almost blinded her, Angela's look of triumph and barely concealed smile. Her features were stamped with smugness and a confidence which came from the knowledge that Eve's association with Leslie Stephenson lay in ruins.

Left alone, Marcus was angered beyond words that he had fallen into a pit of his own making. But she was right. Before he knew who she was he'd had every reason to believe by her actions and forward behaviour that she'd had lovers before, despite her youth, and something perverse inside him had refused to call a halt to his assault on what he believed to be a willing body.

He could be forgiven for thinking that her eagerness, her very willingness to have him kiss her, had confused him into believing she was experienced in the ways of seduction, but if this was her general pattern of behaviour when she was not under the watchful eye of her parents, then it was as well they knew about it, and soon.

Marcus Fitzalan did exactly as he said he would and had spoken to Eve's father immediately. Her parents' anger and disbelief at what she had done made the whole thing much worse. Her future looked bleak. Aware that Atwood society neither forgave nor forgot an indiscretion, and to avoid Eve becoming the object of derision, her parents sent her to Cumbria post haste to stay with her grandmother and did not allow her to return until the whole affair had died down.

But sadly Eve never saw her mother again, for she died before Eve returned to Atwood, leaving her with a well of grief and self-reproach. Blaming herself bitterly for not being there when her mother needed her, it was something she did not get over, and she spent her days in self-imposed isolation at Burntwood Hall, ignoring Emma's pleas to accompany her to the local assemblies and soirées in an attempt to cheer her, only venturing abroad for the odd visit to her Aunt Shona in London or her grandmother in Cumbria.

Mr Fitzalan, it would appear, was beyond reproach where her father was concerned. He held him in such high regard that he believed every word he said. It was not the first misdemeanour his high-spirited daughter was guilty of, and he had always said that one day she would go too far. Both he and his wife had been in agreement that her wild spirits were difficult to curb. But Eve was extremely angry that they chose to ignore Mr Fitzalan's part in the affair, making her suspect he might not have told them just how intimate their meeting had been at Atwood Fair.

And as for Leslie Stephenson, at the first whiff of a scandal he abruptly withdrew his suit and married Angela instead, just as she had contrived it.

The sheer malice of Angela's trickery had angered Eve beyond words—all because Angela coveted the man who was considering marriage to her. Angela had made sure Eve was seen with Mr Fitzalan, and was unable to believe her good fortune when he had declined Eve's request to dance and had disappeared into the bushes with her. When it had come out, Leslie had married Angela instead—only to die in a riding accident a year later, leaving Angela an extremely wealthy young widow.

Until that fateful night Eve had believed Angela to be her friend, and the pain of her betrayal hurt more than Leslie's rejection. She had not seen her since, but never would she forgive her unspeakable malice and deceit. She and Emma remained close, but Angela's name was never mentioned between them.

Eve was glad to put the whole sorry affair behind her, hoping she would never have the misfortune to set eyes on Marcus Fitzalan again. He had spared her nothing, making her see herself as fast, a flirt and a spoiled, overindulged, selfish child, but as she agonised over his cruel accusations, reluctantly she had to admit that they were close to the truth.

But no matter how resentful she felt towards him, he had awoken her desire, had left her with a strange ache rising inside her, and a sharp new hunger and need in her heart she could not explain. Looking back, she knew that that was the time when childhood had left her. She would never again be that same carefree, impulsive girl.

It was someone knocking on her door that woke Eve from her fitful sleep. With a deep sigh she opened her eyes, her mind still full of Marcus Fitzalan and that day three years ago as she rose and crossed wearily to the door, surprised to see her grandmother, who had come to speak to her before retiring for the night. Usually her presence had a daunting effect on Eve, but today too much had happened for her to feel intimidated by her grandmother. Whenever she came to visit them the house always became a different place, quiet and subdued, her presence invading every room from the attics to the cellars, and felt by everyone.

There were always the same questions and answers, the same stiff rules to be adhered to. She always demanded much of Eve's time, commanding her to read to her for hours, and she would sit with her to make sure she did her embroidery, a task Eve found tedious at the best of times. In the past her grandmother had constantly reproached her mother for allowing Eve too much freedom to do as she pleased, and the whole household would breathe a sigh of relief when she went back to Cumbria.

'Forgive me for disturbing you, Eve, but I must speak to you,' she said, stepping into the room and seating herself in an armchair by the fire, the very chair Eve herself had occupied until her grandmother had knocked on her door and roused her from her melancholy thoughts.

'Of course, Grandmother,' Eve replied quietly, giving no indication that this was a conversation she would have preferred to defer until another time, feeling in no mood to talk to anyone.

While she waited for her grandmother to speak she moved towards the window, pushing aside the heavy curtains and looking out, aware of a feeling of gloom and despondency. The night was dark now and beyond the church she could see the warm lights of Atwood glimmering in the distance, and also, some considerable distance away from the township, stood the tall, ghostly shape of the engine house of Atwood Mine and its surrounding spoil heaps, indicative of the area and so distinctive a feature of the landscape.

Her thoughts barely penetrated the fog that clouded her mind. She was numb in mind, body and soul, unable to comprehend all that had happened that day and what it would mean to her future. Her father's will had turned her life into an irretrievable disaster. How could he have done this to her— and why? How could he want her to marry Mr Fitzalan? The very idea horrified her.

But the thought of Atwood Mine falling into Gerald's hands brought a great emptiness of heart. He knew nothing about mining—and even though it would still be managed by competent men, if she let it happen he would be in absolute control. It would not be long before he spent the profits and it ran into difficulties. Everything her father had worked to achieve on the estate would be eradicated by Gerald, this she was certain of, and she would hate to see Atwood Mine go the same way.

Not until today had she realised how dear, how important the mine was to her, and she wondered what had possessed her to hold it so lightly all her life. Her father had been so proud of it, so proud of its efficiency, its worth—the lifeblood of the Somervilles, he often said. He had worked hard to make it what it was, and many were the times when he had been there from dawn until dark, causing her mother to gently taunt and tease him, telling him she would find it easier to accept another woman as a rival for his affections, but a coal mine was insupportable.

She sighed deeply. To leave Burntwood Hall would be like being uprooted, but to lose the mine completely and let Gerald have the run of it would tear her heart. She couldn't let it go. For his own reasons her father had bequeathed half of it to her—a half which would become a whole if she were to do as he asked and marry Mr Fitzalan—but that was the stumbling block. Marcus Fitzalan! There must be some other way of keeping the mine out of Gerald's hands other than that. There had to be. She couldn't let it go, she thought desperately. She just couldn't.

Of course Eve knew that as a married woman she couldn't actually be seen as the owner of the mine, in the eyes of the law, but whatever else Marcus Fitzalan was he was a man of his word. Eve felt certain he would stand by her father's legacy to her.

She had given the matter some considerable thought all day, trying to find some way to escape the impossible situation she found herself to be in, anything, so long as she need not marry Mr Fitzalan or go to live with her grandmother in a wild and unfrequented area of Cumbria.

But as her brain had gone round and round in ever confusing circles she could see no escape. If she wanted to hold on to a part of her past—to Atwood Mine, which she was fiercely determined not to let go—then she really had no choice but to marry Mr Fitzalan. But for now she would hold out against making that decision for as long as she could in the hope that a solution to her dilemma would present itself.

'This has all come as a terrible shock to you, Eve,' said her grandmother at length.

'Yes—it has, Grandmother. From my earliest memories my father's devotion was to be relied on unquestionably. I don't understand what has happened—why he has done this. Do you know? Did he discuss this with you? Mr Fitzalan has tried explaining it to me but still I fail to understand any of it.'

'Yes—your father did discuss the matter with me briefly when I visited you twelve months ago.' She looked away, awkward, suddenly.

'So you knew what he intended all along.'

'He wanted my opinion.'

'And you gave it. You approved of what he intended doing—that it would be in my best interests to marry Mr Fitzalan?'

'Yes, I did. I saw no reason not to. He is a good man and you know your father held him in the highest regard. He always admired a man who knew his own mind.'

She didn't tell her how deeply concerned her father had been by Leslie Stephenson's cruel rejection of her almost three years ago, or that it troubled him greatly to see that she showed no interest in marrying anyone since that time. But he loved her dearly and wanted to know she would be well taken care of after his death, and to his mind there was only one man worthy of his beautiful, spirited daughter, a man with a spirit to equal her own, and that man was Marcus Fitzalan.

He knew he had it within his power to bring the two of them together—that Atwood Mine would be used as the bait—and the idea of Eve being in the protective care of Mr Fitzalan when he was gone gave him a great deal of comfort.

'I know this isn't easy for you and you have every right to be angry, Eve. But what do you feel about Mr Fitzalan?' asked her grandmother directly. 'Will you marry him?'

'Oh, Grandmother—how can I? I hardly know him.'

'That will not be difficult to remedy. I would, of course, be happy to accommodate you in Cumbria, Eve, but for your own good I would advise you to accede to your father's wishes and stay here and marry.'

Eve turned slowly and looked at her grandmother, sensing by the tone of her voice and the manner in which she spoke that she didn't want her to go and live with her in Cumbria, which she considered strange, for she had never objected to her visits in the past—in fact, she had always encouraged them.

With her thin fingers coiled around the knob of her cane, her grandmother sat so straight and stiff she might have been armour plated. She was a woman of great dignity and had been beautiful in her time, and despite her grand age of sixty years the signs remained. But there was no emotion of any kind in her expression, no softness or gentle understanding, as she would have seen on her mother's face before her death.

Sensing what she was thinking, her grandmother looked at her severely. 'And you needn't look so put out, Eve. You know how much I look forward to your visits—but that's all they were. Cumbria's no place for a young girl with her whole life before her, and if you were to go and live with your Aunt Shona in London you know you would not endure it for long. After the first few weeks the excitement of city life would have worn off and you would be pining to be back in the West Riding. It always happens.'

Eve sighed. What her grandmother said was true. She always looked forward to visiting London and her Aunt Shona, but the excitement of the parties and balls her aunt and cousins were so fond of attending soon wore off and she could never wait to return home.

'But I don't want to marry Mr Fitzalan, Grandmother. He is practically a stranger to me—which I am sure you find surprising, considering the close friendship that existed between him and my father. From what I have heard of him I do not like him. Besides, he is so old.'

'Rubbish. Thirty is not old. My dear Eve,' her grandmother remonstrated with undue sharpness, 'you have to marry some time, so why not marry Mr Fitzalan? He may not have been blessed with noble blood, as you have fortunately been yourself, but there was nothing unsophisticated about him that I could see.

'Despite his humble origins, the fact remains that through his father's marriage to Mr Henry Woodrow's daughter, a gentleman and wealthy businessman over at Netherley, his present credentials are admirable. He is a man of power and influence, of considerable property and business—and owner of a fine house too, I have been told, built by his grandfather. It is reputed to be very grand indeed. I am sure life would be pleasant for you living there.'

'I dare say it would be—if I agree to marry him. Although it would appear that I am left with little choice, Grandmother,' she said, wondering what her grandmother would say if she knew of the close familiarity Eve and Mr Fitzalan had displayed towards each other three years ago at Atwood Fair.

She spoke harshly, more than was usual when she addressed her grandmother, causing the redoubtable lady to cast an imperious eye over her, but she did not reprimand her as she would have done at any other time, for she put Eve's irritability down to the trauma of the day.

'However, no one seems to have considered the idea that Mr Fitzalan might not want to marry me,' Eve said with an inappropriate lack of seriousness. 'He might surprise everyone and decide that the mine is not so very important to him after all—although, should that be the case, I doubt another will hurry to take his place. The reduced size of my inheritance is hardly large enough to tempt any other man in asking for me.'

'Nonsense. Two thousand pounds a year is a veritable fortune to some young men. And you forget that when I die, Eve, you will be comfortably well off—although not as well off as I should have liked to leave you, as I am the head of a large family and have other dependents scattered throughout the length and breadth of England. But that will not be for some considerable time because I fully intend living a good many years yet.

'But I would still advise you to seriously consider marrying Mr Fitzalan. Despite what you have just said, by all accounts he would dispose of everything he owns to bring Atwood Mine back into his family—so he will not take much persuading to marry you. I am sure if you put your mind to it and do not repeat the performance of this afternoon—when you forgot your manners and accused the poor man so shockingly of contriving to obtain the mine by devious means from your father—you will get on well enough.'

'I said nothing to Mr Fitzalan that he did not deserve.'

'Whatever your opinions might be, they are unjust and ill-founded, Eve. You really should know better than to listen to tittle-tattle. Your outburst was unpardonable and at any other time you could have been sure of my severest reproof.'

'But I don't love him—and I doubt I could ever love such a man as he has been painted,' and as I know him to be, she thought with secret shame.

Her grandmother stared at her askance. 'Love? What has love to do with anything? You are talking nonsense. If it's love you want then I dare say it will come with marriage. Young people of today enjoy a greater independence than was the case in my day, when marriages were arranged for the benefit of families. In situations such as ours it is expected to bring advantage, wealth and status to the prospective partners and their families. If this nation is to remain strong then it is important that distinguished families like our own continue to uphold that tradition.'

'But this is not your day, Grandmother,' cried Eve, unable to keep the bitterness and frustration from her voice, causing her grandmother to draw herself up and look at her severely.

'Maybe not—and I can see that things have not changed for the better. In cases such as this, take my advice and leave your emotions behind. Marriage is too crucial a matter to be determined on such frivolous considerations as romantic love. Call it old-fashioned if you must, but I am of the belief that children should defer to their parents regarding marriage. However, with marriage to Mr Fitzalan in mind, it's a pity your father did not think of introducing the two of you sooner.'

'But I had no wish to meet him.'

As if sensing her wretchedness, her grandmother's expression softened a little. 'Despite the fact that your parents allowed you to do very much as you pleased for most of the time, running about the countryside like a young hoyden, you're a good girl, Eve—and I am pleased to see you have become a sensible young lady at last, with far more about you than Shona's and Mary's girls,' she said, referring to her two remaining daughters, which caused Eve to look at her in surprise, for this was praise indeed coming from her grandmother.

'Listen, Eve,' she went on, leaning slightly forward in her chair and fixing her granddaughter with a hard stare. 'I know you think I am being hard—cruel, even, in asking you to think seriously about marriage to Mr Fitzalan—but like your father I want to see you well secured. If you stubbornly refuse, then apart from the annuity your father has left you—and your mother's jewellery and other possessions, which are already in your possession but not worth a fortune—you will lose everything to Gerald—and there's a wastrel if ever there was. You cannot turn your back on this chance of retaining something of your father's estate—which to my mind is the *best* thing he could have left you.

'Coming from Cumbria I have only a little knowledge of

the mining of coal, but I know enough to realise that it is the lifeblood of the people in this area and one of the most important, profitable commodities in England. Its potential and economic significance is immense. I have seen for myself that mines are being sunk all the way along Atwood Valley, and your father told me himself that Atwood Mine has no rival. Trade is increasing at a rapid rate and explorations have shown there are unexploited deep seams of coal reserves. My dear girl—you would be a fool to let it go.'

For the first time Eve felt a reluctant stirring of admiration for her grandmother. The intensity of feeling in her voice and her eyes told her that she cared, that it did matter to her what became of her, and she was grateful, but she could not suppress a deep sigh. 'You make it sound like an ultimatum, Grandmother—like some necessary evil.'

'I don't mean to—but you *must* think about it,' she said animatedly, thumping her stick, which she was never without, hard on the carpet. 'Let Gerald play at being Lord of the Manor all he likes—but you take control of the mine.'

'Me and Mr Fitzalan, of course.'

'Yes. You know your father would not have set down these conditions had he not your best interests at heart. He always wanted you and Mr Fitzalan to marry and this was his way of bringing it about. Take what is offered, Eve, and ask no questions. Had things been different he would have wanted you to marry a man of your own choosing, but knowing he would not be here to look after you, to protect you, he did what he thought was right and best for you.'

Eve's eyes remained doubtful, but on looking at the situation with cold logic, it was with reluctance that she recognised the sense of her grandmother's words. She was right. If she wanted to hold on to her pride and something she considered to be her birthright, then she really had no choice.

'I promise I shall give the matter serious thought, Grandmother. At this moment I cannot say more than that.'

Gerald left for his home on the day following the funeral,

leaving Eve with the knowledge that he would return to take up residence at Burntwood Hall just as soon as he had put his affairs in order.

She was alone in her father's study, writing letters to people who had been unable to travel to the funeral, when he entered to tell her of his departure and what he intended to do. She had no choice but to speak to him, to see the mockery in his eyes and hear the lust in his voice. She shuddered at the sight of him for she disliked him intensely. The mere thought of him had the power to make her draw her breath in sharply.

If he was aware of it he seemed unconcerned and chose to ignore it. He relaxed at the sight of her, a twisted smile curving his lips, and yet his expression remained hard, his eyes alert, boldly lingering appreciatively, greedily, on the soft swelling mounds of her breasts, insolently taking in every detail. Eve met his gaze coldly. She had known ever since his last visit to Burntwood Hall that he was attracted by her—known it by the way he looked at her—and she hated him—the smile on his slack lips, the glint in his dark eyes.

Sitting in a large winged chair beside the fire, he folded his hands casually across his rapidly expanding stomach and stretched his legs out in front of him with the lazy grace of a big cat, a cold, calculating gleam in his eyes as he looked at her sitting demurely at her father's desk.

'Do forgive me for intruding on your privacy, Eve, but I wanted to speak to you before returning to my home. I waited until I knew your grandmother would be resting, when I would be sure to find you alone. There is much to be done, you understand. Not wishing to appear uncharitable I just wanted to tell you that you must continue to look on Burntwood Hall as your home for just as long as you want to—that I have no intention of "turning you out", so to speak,' he said, with feigned sympathy and generosity in his eyes.

The truth of it was that Gerald had become aware of Eve as a woman several visits ago—an extremely beautiful and desirable woman, and extremely accessible while ever she continued to live at Burntwood Hall—but more importantly he also saw her as a means of retaining Atwood Mine, which would revert to him should she refuse to marry Marcus Fitzalan, and provide him with a much needed constant source of revenue for years to come.

But he was also in the devil of a fix. Having borrowed money after losing heavily at cards at his club in St James's, from men who knew he was Sir John Somerville's heir—a great deal of money, thirty-five thousand pounds to be exact, with an extortionate interest on the amount borrowed—there was no possible way he could repay the loan until he came into his inheritance. Before he left London the moneylenders, having heard of Sir John's death, had begun turning on the pressure for him to repay the loan with a terrible force. They were closing in on him, crushing him like a vice. He had to get the money. He was becoming desperate. The mere thought of what they would do to him if he didn't come up with it made sweat break out on the palms of his hands and his heart pound uncontrollably.

These men were experts at what they did, men who would not be crossed or defied. Gerald had soon learned from their dealings with others that beneath their elegant exteriors they possessed muscles of steel combined with a ruthlessness and cruelty that stopped at nothing—tactics he would not hesitate to employ himself on others to obtain the means to repay the loan and get these men off his back for good, and only the income from Atwood Mine would enable him to obtain the kind of money he needed to do that. Sir John's death had come as an enormous relief. He could not believe his good fortune—but without the mine his inheritance would not be enough to repay what he owed without selling off more land and property.

Everything hung on Eve's decision—on her not marrying Marcus Fitzalan. He was counting on her love for Burntwood Hall being greater than her obligation to her father and his wish that she marry Fitzalan. And if not, then there were other

ways of preventing a marriage from taking place between
them. So desperate and determined was he to have the mine
reverted to him that he would go to any lengths to do so. By
fair means or foul—it didn't matter to him. He would win in
the end.

'That is extremely generous of you, Gerald,' Eve said stiffly
in answer to his offer, breaking in on his thoughts, putting
down her pen and folding hands in her lap, the loss of
everything that was familiar to her suddenly becoming more
bitter as she looked at him coldly and in silence, calmly and
warily waiting for him to continue, shuddering slightly as he
continued to watch her with the calculating eyes of a man
eager for conquest. Every nerve of her body was tense as she
waited for him to continue, fighting a creeping fear.

'I must tell you that I do not intend letting go of Atwood
Mine,' Gerald said, sounding very sure of himself. 'I assumed
that it would come as part and parcel of my inheritance.'

'My father—and Mr Fitzalan's father and grandfather before that—worked too hard to make it what it is today to be
foolish enough to leave it to someone who would not appreciate its worth, Gerald. You are renowned for spending money
faster than it can be earned—and I can only hope you appreciate and keep this house in better order than you have your
own, which, as I understand it, is soon to be auctioned off to
pay your creditors.'

Gerald's eyes narrowed and his voice was calm and full of
meaning when he spoke. 'Never fear, Eve—I shall appreciate
it and I know *exactly* what Atwood Mine is worth.'

'Yes, I'm sure you do—down to the last penny, I shouldn't
wonder. It is rumoured that you are heavily in debt—that you
need a great deal of money to pay off a massive loan for a
debt you incurred after an unsuccessful card game,' she said
scathingly.

He frowned crossly. 'How do you know about that?'

'I know a great many things about you.'

Gerald shrugged carelessly, his instinct telling him she had acquired this information from Marcus Fitzalan, damn the man. 'I don't deny it. Indeed, I have no reason to.'

Eve's lips curled with irony. 'No—somehow I didn't think you would.'

Gerald ignored her sarcasm, knowing nothing was to be gained by showing his anger at present. 'Tell me, Eve—have you decided whether or not to marry Fitzalan?'

'No, not yet. And when I do he will be the first to know.'

'You don't have to marry him, you know. I observed how angry you were yesterday when your father's will was being read—that you were not exactly enamoured by his suggestion that the two of you marry. I can understand the anger you must feel, when I remember how the man almost ruined you three years ago. Small wonder you are still at daggers drawn,' he drawled. 'Forgive me, Eve, but Marcus Fitzalan does seem a trifle dull and on the serious side for such a vivacious, beautiful creature as yourself. You have grown into an exceedingly lovely young woman.'

He rose and moved slowly towards where she was sitting. His lips slackened in a sensuous smile and a sudden fire leapt into his eyes as he devoured her, his eyes dwelling appreciatively on her lovely face.

Eve ignored the unwelcome compliment and stood up quickly, moving away instinctively to avoid getting too close, the thought of any contact with him revolting her. If only she could treat him with icy detachment and appear indifferent to him, but somehow he always managed to slip through her guard. His eyes fastened themselves on hers and he smiled thinly.

'There is an alternative, you know.'

'Oh? And what might that be?'

He shrugged, a callously hard malicious gleam entering his eyes. 'I merely thought you could stay here and take your mother's place.'

His insolent, smiling face angered Eve beyond words and a

wave of sick loathing swept over her. She favoured him with a glance of bitter contempt.

'What! Marry you?'

'Why not? You will find me more appreciative of your charms than Marcus Fitzalan, I do assure you.'

'You flatter yourself if you think that,' she replied drily, eyeing him with distaste, without flinching before his direct gaze, revulsion rising up inside her so that it almost choked her.

'Not only that—if you marry me, it would ensure Atwood Mine will remain in our possession, where it belongs.'

'If you recall the contents of my father's will, Gerald, you will know that it does not require marriage to me to have the mine reverted to you. I merely have to refuse to marry Mr Fitzalan, that is all.'

'*That* I am aware of—but I know Burntwood Hall means a great deal to you, and marriage to me would enable you to live here for the entirety of your life. Surely my suggestion is a far more agreeable prospect than marriage to Marcus Fitzalan. After all, we both stand to gain something—besides the pleasure it would accord me having you here,' he said, exhibiting an inordinate, lascivious interest in her body as his gaze swept over her.

Eve stared at him in stupefaction, rendered speechless by the content of his words and their implication, hearing him savour every word he spoke as he imagined how great his eventual triumph would be over Marcus Fitzalan if Atwood Mine was snatched from under his arrogant nose by her say so. She could not deny that the temptation to do so was great indeed, but fear prickled her spine and a small voice deep inside her told her not to underestimate Gerald. He could be dangerous, and if she chose to remain at Burntwood Hall as his wife feeling as she did about him, life would be one long agony. Her chin came up and she glared at him, quivering with a mixture of anger and fear.

'You are mistaken if you think that. I would not marry you if you were the last man on earth.'

Gerald sighed, pretending not to have noticed the force with which she spoke. 'Why you have such a low opinion of me baffles me, Eve.'

'My opinion of you was decided years ago.'

'Come now,' he coaxed, his voice persuasive and intimate. 'You know the situation and you have so much common sense, which is what I have always admired about you. It occurred to me that it is a solution to both our problems.'

'It is you who has the problem, Gerald. Not I.'

'Nevertheless, it is a generous gesture on my part.'

'Generous, you say!' exclaimed Eve forcefully. 'You have the most astonishing effrontery. Do you take me for a fool? You are only generous in the sense that your proposal of marriage to me is nothing more than a cunning ploy to prevent a marriage from taking place between myself and Mr Fitzalan. It is nothing more than that to get your hands on the mine.'

'I agree there is that, but where my proposal is concerned let me assure you that I am thinking only of you.'

He drew closer to her and took her hand between his, which she quickly snatched away, feeling as if she had been burned. Gerald's eyes narrowed menacingly.

'Don't touch me.' Eve flared with an anger that was all the more violent because it was born of fear. 'Don't touch me or I swear I shall scream for the servants—whatever the consequences. Now please go, Gerald.'

Gerald sighed and took a step back, speaking with a terrifying softness. 'What a little spitfire you are, Eve, but I like it in you. You are so fiery—so adorable. It suits you to be angry. It makes your eyes sparkle and your wonderful bosom to heave. You are like a horse that is unbroken—but one day I shall be the one to rectify that.'

It was not so much a threat as a statement of fact, which made Eve's blood run cold. She saw the fire leap in his eyes and heard the passion rising his voice, and she sensed danger.

'I think you have said quite enough, Gerald. Now please go.' She looked him straight in the face, her eyes blazing. He must have seen the hatred.

Gerald's eyes narrowed, and without warning his attitude changed. His expression convulsed and he seized Eve's wrist in a painful grasp, beginning to speak in a low, angry voice.

'I'll go, Eve, but I shall be back very soon to take your father's place in this house.'

'You! You are not half the man my father was,' Eve said scornfully.

'No, maybe not in your eyes. But know this, Eve,' he said, a warning underlying his words, which told Eve that he spoke in deadly seriousness, 'I am a man who must conquer—must win—whatever the odds against him, and I shall do all in my power to prevent you marrying Marcus Fitzalan in order to obtain the mine.'

'Even if you have to kill me first?' she hissed, wrenching her arm free of his grasp.

'Oh, yes. Even that if necessary. Nothing will stand in my way. I can be very ugly when crossed. You would do well in the future to remember it. So don't be foolish, Eve. Think about what I have said very carefully, because if you do not heed my words you will regret it.'

Eve's face turned ashen, sensing this was no idle threat spoken in the heat of the moment. 'You would not dare.'

Gerald shrugged. 'Why not? On the other hand, if you act sensibly, as I hope you will, then I can promise no harm will come to you.'

She glared at him with pure loathing. 'You are a scoundrel. I hate you.'

'Yes, I know. However, that does not disturb me. With some women, hatred has more allure than love.' He gave her a twisted smile. 'I shall have Atwood Mine, Eve. You can depend on it.'

Eve watched him go, sitting down to steady her nerves and trembling limbs, feeling an icy trickle of fear run down her spine, knowing she could expect no mercy and nothing but violence from him; and he would never be satisfied until he had Atwood Mine in his grasp.

But it was madness to think Gerald would harm her. He would never dare do that. She forced herself to believe this and cast such thoughts from her mind, but she was shaken to the core by what had just passed between them.

Chapter Five

For three weeks Marcus continued with the everyday mundane activities of his mines, the towering engine house at Atwood Mine in the distance a constant reminder of how close he was to owning it once more—providing he married Sir John's daughter. For sentimental reasons the mine was important to him, but he was a businessman and would be lying if he said he did not know of its potential, that it was a veritable gold mine compared to all the other mines in the area.

He continued to work the mines opened by his grandfather, who had speculated every penny to make them successful. As his own interests had expanded further, three years ago he had taken out a lease on a hundred acres of land on an adjacent estate for thirty years to come, for a substantial yearly rent on the two pits he had sunk; through his own determination and dedication, and the financial backing of his partners, they were rapidly increasing their output of coal.

But it was not enough to meet demand, which was why he was concentrating all his efforts on developing another, deeper mine, at Pendle Hill, three miles to the north of Atwood Mine.

He was fortunate to be situated within the marvellous new network of navigational canals that were being cut through the industrial regions. This expansion of inland waterways greatly eased the transportation problems, making it possible to expand into geographically larger markets.

Since the day of Sir John's funeral he was surprised that, hardened though he was, he was once again unable to cast Eve Somerville from his mind. He had made the occasional visit to Burntwood Hall in the past but, apart from their encounter at Atwood Fair, he had never had the pleasure of meeting her again—if it could be called a pleasure now that he had. She was always away staying with friends when he called or visiting her grandmother in Cumbria or her aunt in London.

On the day of the funeral he had watched her with a speculative gaze. Although she had sat docilely beside her grandmother throughout the day, drawing on an inner strength to see her through, he had sensed her restlessness, her impatience for it to be over. She had been like a young, leashed colt, eager to break free.

He admired the way she had conducted herself, sensing she wasn't the type to faint or weep in the company of others—a trait, he suspected, she'd inherited from her formidable grandmother—although witnessing her private grief, when she had thought herself to be alone at her father's graveside later, had touched a hidden chord deep inside him.

Constantly he found himself dwelling on her warm femininity, and for the first time—despite the strong liking and respect he had felt for Sir John and would always feel—anger welled up inside him against the man, and also against himself for being unable to turn his back on what he had offered, possibly at the price of his daughter's happiness.

He was touched by some private scruples. It really was shameful of him and utterly mercenary to consider using her so callously, to intend making her his wife merely to obtain the mine. But when he recollected how lovely and spirited she was, how young and vulnerable, despite her quality of mind to show self-possession, how ripe she was for being initiated along the secret, mysterious paths of womanhood, he smiled,

his instinct telling him that, given time, they would both be
well satisfied with the arrangement.

Curious to see for herself the object of her inheritance—
should she agree to marry Mr Fitzalan—and having cast her
meeting with Gerald to the back of her mind, Eve seized the
opportunity of doing so one fine, sunny morning four weeks
after her father's funeral, taking the road that led up to the
mine, accompanied by her grandmother's elderly maid, her
grandmother having declined her invitation to go with her.

But it was no easy matter trying to forget Gerald. Ever since
her conversation with him on the day after the funeral, when
he had reduced her to a frightening, trembling awareness of
him, she was determined to leave Burntwood Hall before he
returned to take up residence—and she would do everything
within her power to keep Atwood Mine out of his hands.

But no matter how hard she tried to dispel his threatening
image from her mind, there was an obscure menace about him
which unnerved her. He was reluctant to let the mine go, this
she knew, but to what desperate lengths would he go to hold
on to it? she asked herself, suddenly afraid for her own safety
as every sense she possessed screamed out a warning.

Her air of despondency began to recede the closer she got
to the mine. The hillside was covered with mounds of black
slag and slate, and a pond of thick, black slurry lay at the
bottom, still and unmoving and shining like black glass beneath the glare of the sun.

Atwood Mine rose above the dark, metallic line of the canal
which threaded its way along the valley bottom—an artificial
waterway which had been constructed by her father to cut the
cost of carrying coal by road to the larger Aire and Calder
Navigation's waterway.

On the other side of the canal stood the town of Atwood, a
conglomeration of shops and dwelling places, with a broad
main street going through the middle, and on the outskirts was
a huddle of colliers' cottages, principally for those colliers

employed by the Somervilles to work Atwood Mine and others in the area.

A pall of grey smoke hung over the village, which had begun as a small settlement and was steadily beginning to encroach insidiously on the township of Atwood, as more and more colliers and their families moved into the area to work with the rapid expansion of the coal industry. The mine, large in comparison with other mines in the area, was reached by a swing bridge over the canal.

The closer they got to the mine Eve could hear the clanking and groaning of the pumping engine drawing water up from the pit, the giant contraption nodding its great head like a tired-out old donkey over the cavernous opening of the shaft. She could see the wooden-constructed headgear, winding ropes and pulley wheels, which raised to the surface the cage holding the tubs of hand-hewn coal, operated in the shaft by a steam-driven winding engine.

The carriage pulled into the pit yard, which was bustling with activity. Youths pushed tubs of shining lumps of coal, which was moved from the surface by wagons pulled by sweating horses, down the track to the canal where it was loaded on to the waiting barges. The mine employed men, women and young boys, although the women were not employed to work underground and worked in the sheds with some of the younger boys.

The carriage and its occupants drew the attention of the workers as it pulled up beside a rather magnificent chestnut horse, tethered to a rail outside one of the sheds with a wooden awning, which was used as an office, where Eve hoped to find Gerald's brother, Matthew, the young man who had been employed by her father as one of the mine's agents.

Instructing her grandmother's maid to remain in the carriage, she stepped out just as a young clerk—in a state of nervous agitation owing to the unexpected arrival and importance of the visitor—emerged from the office.

Eve smiled at him. 'I'm here to see Mr Somerville. Would you kindly tell him I'm here?'

'I'm sorry, but both Mr Somerville and the manager are away today, Miss Somerville. They had some business to attend to in Netherley.'

'I see,' she said, feeling a rush of disappointment. 'Oh, well—it's my fault. I should have told him I intended paying him a visit.'

She turned back to the carriage, thinking to come back another time, when her eyes were drawn to a tall, black-suited gentleman who loomed out of the brick engine house. At first she was as startled as if she had seen a ghost, and her stomach did a little somersault when she recognised Marcus Fitzalan.

Immediately he saw her and smiled suavely, his white teeth gleaming startlingly as he walked briskly towards her, as though it were the most natural thing in the world that he should be there. He thought how fetching she looked, despite the sombre black morning dress and bonnet she wore.

'My dear Miss Somerville. You are the last person I expected to see here.'

Eve stiffened her spine and gave him a cold stare. 'I could say the same about you, Mr Fitzalan. Your visit is rather premature, isn't it? Wouldn't it be wiser to wait until you have my answer before eyeing up the merchandise—in a manner of speaking, of course?'

He grinned infuriatingly, giving a dismissive nod to the young clerk, who was glad to escape inside the office. 'I like to be prepared for every eventuality, Miss Somerville. And you? Are you interested in the workings of a coal mine?'

'If I am to become part-owner, Mr Fitzalan, then I intend learning as much as I can in order to understand and protect my inheritance. All I know about the coal industry I have learned from my father over the years—which is very little, considering a large part of my livelihood depends on it.'

'And you suddenly want to know more?'

'Yes, and being a woman will not make any difference. I

hope you do not share the common failing of most men, Mr
Fitzalan, and suffer from the masculine illusion that women
do not have heads for business, that they should bow and be
guided by the superior knowledge of men and have no opinions of their own—and, in particular, have no place at a coal
mine.'

'Heaven forbid I should think that,' he answered, his teeth
gleaming as his bold dark eyes laughed down into hers, 'and,
if I did, I would not dare say so. I like a woman who speaks
her mind, Miss Somerville, and I see you're not only beautiful
but courageous too.'

Eve flushed, so surprised by the compliment that she was
thrown off balance, but then she checked herself. 'Thank you.
A compliment from you of all people is to be appreciated,'
she said drily. 'But flattery will not get you the mine, Mr
Fitzalan. I do not weaken so easily.'

Marcus smiled and gave a sardonic lift to his brows. 'Come
now, don't be coy,' he said softly. 'I, more than anyone, know
how vulnerable you can be, just how weak you can be—how
easy it is to destroy your resistance with just a little tender
persuasion.'

He laughed freely, his black eyes dancing in merciless mer-
riment as he seemed to enjoy the confusion his words caused
her, seeing her cheeks flush crimson with furious embarrassment and shame at his reference to their amorous encounter
three years ago. But he took pity on her.

'Fear not,' he chuckled. 'Your secret is safe with me, and
I promise not to repeat my barbaric display to seduce you into
marriage.'

Roused to resentment, and conscious that they were being
observed by several pairs of curious eyes, Eve tried not to lose
her composure to anger, but she was highly incensed by the
ungentlemanly manner in which he spoke to her, lightly and
infuriatingly referring to matters he knew would cause her
embarrassment.

'Your reference to what took place between us three years

ago is highly offensive and insulting, Mr Fitzalan,' she said with deep indignation, trying to speak with composure. 'And nothing you can say can excuse your own contemptible conduct that day. However, you are mistaken if you think I am still the same green girl I was then. Things have changed. I have changed, and I am not so easily seduced by arrogant, self-opinionated men. Nothing *you* say will affect my decision about the mine and my own future.'

With a strong feeling of displeasure Eve saw that Marcus was watching her with an air which told her he was neither penitent about his previous behaviour towards her nor moved by any feeling of remorse.

'There is no need to be so impassioned,' he smiled infuriatingly. 'I believe you. Fortunately I have a sensitive heart and I am not unaware how difficult the decision is for you to make. But I ask you not to take too long in making up your mind.'

'You do not like being kept waiting, is that it, Mr Fitzalan?'

'It is indeed.'

'Then spare me your sensitive heart. I would find more compassion in a lump of coal,' she said coldly. 'Have you seen all you came to see of the mine?' she asked, turning and beginning to walk back to the carriage.

'No, far from it. Unfortunately the manager is absent.'

'Yes. He's gone into Netherley with Mr Somerville—Matthew, one of the mine's agents. Matthew is Gerald's younger brother,' she said, pausing and looking up at him, seeing him grimace. 'No matter what your opinion might be of Gerald, I have to tell you that Matthew is a fine young man, with a strong mind and good conscience. The only thing that can be said against him is that he is the younger son, which does not allow him to inherit the estate. You will be relieved to know he is not at all like Gerald,' she said, wondering how he would react if she told him what had passed between herself and Gerald on the day he had left Burntwood Hall—of the threats he had made, and how, on leaving, he had left her a trembling wreck.

'I'm glad to hear it. Another such as Gerald would be quite intolerable. Your father did mention him on occasion, but I cannot say that we have been introduced.'

'My father was extremely fond of Matthew. He has always shown an eager interest in mining and it was my father's intention to involve him more in the business,' Eve explained. 'He has already learned a great deal and, unlike Gerald, I know it would be safe in his hands. Gerald wouldn't want to soil his hand by getting physically involved in any industry—unless it is to sit back and cream off the profits, of course. I—I hear you are sinking a new shaft at Pendle Hill.'

Marcus's expression became serious, as it always did when he spoke of mining matters. 'Yes, and it is proving to be both expensive and time consuming. I don't mind admitting it is fraught with problems and is a drain on my resources.'

'But you must think it worthwhile to continue.'

'Very much so. The surveys and test bores I had done proved extremely favourable. It is a high-risk venture and will be very deep, but I, and my promoters, are well experienced in colliery matters and keen to proceed. I have two collieries nearing exhaustion, and the way the need for coal is increasing in the Aire and Calder valleys, if I do not speculate, the united output from the other mines will be insufficient to meet the demand.'

'Then I can see why acquiring Atwood Mine would be beneficial to you,' Eve said, with a trace of sarcasm.

Marcus's face hardened. 'My interest in Atwood Mine is more of a personal matter, Miss Somerville,' he answered sharply.

'And if it becomes yours once more, am I to understand that you would not make changes?'

'Yes, I would,' he replied without hesitation. 'The area is well proven and eventually I would sink a new shaft and extend in other directions, which would mean installing a new pumping engine to lift the water.'

'But what is wrong with the old one?'

'It's slow and outdated. I would have it replaced by one of Mr Boulton and Mr Watt's machines, which I am also having installed at Pendle Hill. The greater the power, the deeper the shaft—and because the stocks of shallow coal are running low, I do intend going much, much deeper, with a new engine lifting tons of water out of the mine with every stroke.'

Eve looked at him coolly, her instinct telling her he was man enough to do justice to what seemed to her to be a mammoth task. 'You are ambitious, Mr Fitzalan,' she stated calmly.

'Yes. I admit it. But with the expansion of Atwood Mine and the opening of Pendle Hill, it will attract more industry to the area—iron, brick and glass works and such like, providing employment for many.'

'But surely the deeper the shaft then the miners' work becomes more dangerous.'

'There are risks in any undertaking, but everything will be done to ensure their safety. We do our best to make them secure in their employment—and in the case of my own pits, we put the boys—none under the age of eight—to the easiest places below ground, although it is normal for them to learn their trade with their fathers or another relative.'

'But not all children are so fortunate, Mr Fitzalan. Some children have no family and I hear are treated quite abysmally.'

'Sadly, that is the case. However, I employ a number of children as bound apprentices from the Foundling Hospital at Netherley, and only in a very few instances are they treated so badly as to warrant a case to be brought before the Petty or Quarter Sessions. On the whole they are treated well and have little cause for complaint.'

'But disasters do occur. Atwood Mine has had its share of roof falls and floods over the years,' Eve said with a trace of sadness. 'And, as you will know, it is notorious for its outbursts of gas, resulting in dreadful explosions. Valuable though the coal is, often the colliers pay with their lives—and if not, they are horrendously injured, leaving them incapable of working and supporting their families for the rest of their lives.'

'Which is the case in almost every pit, and extremely tragic. We do our best to help such cases,' Marcus said. 'Like your father and other coalmasters, Miss Somerville, I subscribe to the General Infirmary at Leeds, which means that any bad accident cases from the collieries can be treated immediately.'

'And are women employed in your pits, Mr Fitzalan?'

He frowned, looking at her seriously. 'No—and never will be,' he replied firmly. 'As far as I am aware, there are no females employed below ground in any of the large West Riding collieries, and, personally, I find the very idea of them working alongside men in the kind of conditions that exist below ground quite abhorrent.'

Eve eyed him calmly. He had all her attention. His knowledge about mining she did not doubt, but his sincere concern for the people he employed made her look at him in a different light. His refusal to employ very small children and women down his mines—as was not the case with mine owners in other parts of the country—roused her grudging admiration.

She thought of his importance, of how much power he wielded over those who depended on him for their subsistence, making her realise that what he had just told her was making her think of him with a deeper sentiment than she ever had before. She turned and resumed her walk back to the carriage, just as the cage was bringing the colliers off their shift, their hours of work being from six in the morning until four in the afternoon. She paused and looked with pity at the men and boys clad in dirty rags, their bare legs exposed to above the knees.

Black and weary, they walked with their heads bent, looking neither right nor left, as if they had been driven to the limits of physical endurance. Some were permanently stooped from working in the dark passages below ground, where the roofs were supported by pillars of coal.

Along these passages, clouded with floating coal dust and

bad air, some so steep and others so narrow that the boys would have to crawl on their hands and knees, they would drag or push their laden baskets, filled by the hewers, to the bottom of the shaft where it would be raised to the surface— and there would be the devil to pay if the check weighman found they were not filled to capacity.

Many were aged prematurely with the dust, and older men could be seen with curved and worn backs, concave chests and sickly coughs and tight-lipped grey faces. Many of them found an early grave owing to lung disease or accidents.

'How do they stand it?' she murmured almost to herself.

'I often wonder that myself,' Marcus replied quietly, following her gaze.

'These men exist in a kind of world…living a life that is so far removed from my own that I cannot imagine it.'

'One cannot help but admire their stoic courage and their persistence to endure, for they get little in return for their toil. But mining is their livelihood. They know nothing else.'

Sighing deeply, Eve walked on. 'I wish you every success with Pendle Hill, Mr Fitzalan. What happens to this mine remains to be seen.'

'But it is not a matter to be dismissed lightly,' he said, following her and assisting her into the carriage, where her grandmother's maid was dozing lightly in a corner.

'No, indeed. I have told you that I shall give it my serious consideration. I just wish that in considering the mine I did not have to consider my relationship with you. Goodbye, Mr Fitzalan.'

With the great house around her still and silent, Eve felt nothing inside but a well of emptiness and a profound loneliness that stretched before her like a never-ending road. Anguish was not something she was accustomed to in her life, but now it washed over her like a tidal wave.

Feeling restless and wanting to clear her head early one fine, sunny morning when her grandmother had not yet risen, Eve had the groom saddle her favourite horse, and for the first time since her father's death she defied convention and cast decorum to the four winds as she cantered out towards the hills, curtly dismissing the groom when she saw he intended going with her, for she had a strong need to be by herself.

Besides, the grounds and surrounding hills where she would ride were familiar places where she had once ridden with her father. With long tendrils of early-morning mist curling along the ground and between the trees, which the hot sun would soon burn away, her ride took on a strong feeling of nostalgia when she thought this might be the last time she would be able to gallop over the estate she was loath to leave.

She rode her milk-white mare hard and as no lady should— in slim-fitting black breeches and astride, which had brought a frown of deep displeasure to the groom's features when he had seen her, and would have brought a stern reprimand from her grandmother if she knew she was riding about the countryside unaccompanied and dressed for all the world like a man, having temporarily cast off her black mourning dress.

Eve was unaware of the stir she had created in the stables, and would care little if she had—the need for privacy and to taste complete freedom for a little while so intense inside her that she refused to let anything get in the way of her ride, or to allow her mind to dwell on her inevitable future.

For an hour she rode along well-known tracks, weaving her way through the trees towering above her as she passed through woods which clothed the sides of the hills, giving her horse its head, exulting in its powerful force beneath her and its energy, pressing her heels in its flanks and urging it to greater exertion, before pausing on a grassy hill to admire and savour the view stretched out beneath her and to let her mare breathe. The day was hot and brilliant, the trees faded and limp with the heat and dusty with summer. With her long legs resting in the stirrups, she sat relaxed, feeling a welcome breeze waft over her flushed cheeks.

Resuming her ride, she headed for the towpath running

along the side of the canal, following it for some distance away from the village, passing barges laden with coal being drawn by tired horses, and seeing few people until she came to the Navigation Inn on the other side of the canal—not the most select establishment in the area, being a popular ale house for miners where they could slake their thirst after a hard day's toil down the mine. Finding the air heavy and humid by the water she turned back towards the hills.

So lost was she in her thoughts that she didn't realise until it was too late that she had ventured on to a neighbouring estate at Pendle Hill, where Marcus Fitzalan, having leased land from the landowner, was in the process of sinking a new shaft and having a new steam engine built and installed, the one he had told her about when they had met at Atwood Mine.

She paused in a clearing while her horse bent its neck and drank from a stream, having to squint, for the sunlight hurt her eyes as she looked at the untidy sprawl of newly erected pit buildings and the partly built engine house not fifty yards away, seeing several men hurrying quickly away from where the shaft was being sunk. She did not see Mr Fitzalan at first, for her eyes had not consciously sought his presence, but suddenly he was there, and she could not explain why her emotions became bemused or why her breath caught in her throat the way it did.

His breeches and white shirt were dirty and dishevelled from his labours, and he too was striding quickly away from the shaft and in the opposite direction from her, but, turning, as if he sensed her watching him, he saw her. She could not see the expression on his face but he halted in his tracks, as if amazed to see her there, but he made no move to approach her and carried on walking away. Relieved, Eve was about to turn and ride away, but too late.

Totally unprepared, suddenly she realised what was happening, why the men were hurrying away from the shaft, when the ground beneath her shuddered violently and the air became filled with a noise that almost blasted her out of the saddle, making her eardrums vibrate and jolting her senses.

With her knowledge of coal mines she knew the sinking of some shafts often proved to be more difficult than others, when thick beds of iron-stone more difficult to penetrate than flint were encountered and had to be blasted out. That this was in the process of being done occurred to her when, a split second later, the blast was followed by another, so earthshattering that she felt her brain knocking against the inside of her skull, the offending rock and stone being thrown high up into the air.

Immediately her terrified horse rolled its maddened eyes and screamed and reared, thrashing the air frantically with its hooves, and she was unable to prevent it from taking the bit in its teeth and bolting wildly. Being an expert rider, Eve fought to bring her mount under control as it went charging through the woods, knowing that in its maddened state it was useless trying to guide it with the bit, and sitting as balanced in the saddle as she could while she let it run blindly on, knowing it couldn't possibly keep up this pace for long and that it would have to slow down eventually.

But to her horror a fence suddenly loomed ahead of her, much too high for her mare to jump clear. Fearing the worst, the blood pounding in her throat, in desperation she applied her right heel firmly to her horse's side and the mare wheeled obediently to gallop at an angle. With enormous relief Eve felt her beginning to slow down, becoming aware for the first time of the hollow thunder of hooves behind her.

At last she brought her horse under control and managed to bring it to a shuddering halt. White-faced, she turned to see the man on the horse come thundering through the under-growth towards her, the two almost like one being. She knew immediately that it was Marcus Fitzalan, having recognised the tall chestnut stallion he rode.

He jerked on the reins, drawing his horse to a halt, which must have taken all his strength, for it was a huge beast and he had been riding at full gallop. Jumping down, he didn't hesitate to come to her and, as if to establish his supremacy, reached up and dragged her unceremoniously from the saddle.

Tearing herself from his arms, Eve was trembling with anger brought on by fear.

'Take your hands off me,' she flared indignantly, having had no time to recover her self-possession. She still felt unsteady with shock and the ragged thumping of her heart had not yet slowed to an even beat. Reaching out, she tried to calm her quivering mare with soothing words. She was lathered with sweat and foam dropped in frothy blobs from her bit. But the usually gentle horse picked up her anger and unease and continued to pull away from her.

In exasperation Marcus snatched the reins from her hands and tethered the horse to a sturdy tree before turning to her, his face white with rage, all his muscles tense, and a pulse throbbing at his temple.

'What in hell's name were you trying to do?' he blazed down at her, his eyes like molten ice. 'Kill yourself?'

'Me?' she broke out furiously. 'I thought it was you who was trying to do that? You saw me there. Why did you not warn me what was to happen—that you were blasting?'

'There was no time. I had to make sure the men close to the shaft were well out of the way before the explosion. You were far enough away not to be in any kind of danger.'

'Ha! Try telling *that* to my horse. Look at her. She's terrified.'

'Then you should know how to control your horse.'

'I am perfectly capable of handling my horse, Mr Fitzalan— as you must have judged for yourself, even though it would kill you to admit it,' Eve seethed, the force of his remark increasing her anger.

'Maybe you're right, but in the name of God I have never seen anything like this,' he said, suddenly appalled as he stepped back to take in her appearance, noticing for the first time that she was wearing breeches. 'Do you usually roam about the countryside unaccompanied, riding your horse astride and dressed in breeches?' he demanded.

Eve flung back her head rebelliously. 'No, not normally, but I felt like doing so today.'

'And you grandmother? Is she still staying with you at Burntwood Hall.'

'Yes. She will not be returning to Cumbria until my future is settled.'

'Very wise—taking into account your behaviour today, which is both reckless and irresponsible. Is she aware that you ride unaccompanied—and dressed as you are?'

'My grandmother is not even aware that I have left the house, and I am sure she would agree with you and be quite shocked by my appearance—but my clothes are the least of my worries just now. Besides—I like my freedom, Mr Fitzalan.'

'It would appear you have too much freedom, Miss Somerville,' he accused her harshly, while secretly thinking he had never seen her look more lovely—with her cheeks faintly flushed from the gallop, and some stray locks of glossy black hair that had escaped from its demure coil beneath her hat lying on the red silk collar of her blouse. After a long, hot ride he would have expected most ladies to appear drained and exhausted, whereas Eve radiated vitality, giving no hint of any discomfort she might have suffered when her horse bolted.

'Are you normally indiscreet?' he asked, giving no indication that he thought her a truly amazing young woman. She rode well and he admired the way she had handled her horse, having the presence of mind to bring it quickly under control the way she had.

'I do nothing I am ashamed of—and please do not think I rode this way so that I might chance to bump into you. It was not my intention to stray off Somerville land, and so if you don't mind I will return to it and continue with my ride.'

'Not until your horse—and yourself—have cooled down,'

Marcus said firmly, standing in front of her with his hands on his hips and preventing her from mounting her horse.

Stung to indignation, Eve was fuming. 'Then I shall walk her back.'

'Two miles?'

'Yes—if necessary.'

'Don't be a fool. Wait a while and then she'll be fit to ride.'

Enraged at finding herself held at bay, warm blood flooded her face. 'Do you mean to keep me here?'

'You can leave whenever you wish. You are not my prisoner.'

'Then have the goodness to move aside and let me pass.'

When he didn't do as she asked she eyed him warily, unsure what to do next. To pass him she would have to touch him, and after her last encounter on finding herself alone with him in a wood, she was determined to keep her distance.

'When I saw your horse bolt I came after you at once.'

'How dare you present yourself as my self-proclaimed champion. I'm glad you didn't rescue me, otherwise you would have placed me in the humiliating position of having to be grateful to you. You could have saved yourself the trouble and stayed at the mine—where I am sure your presence would be appreciated more,' replied Eve ungraciously. 'I managed to bring my mount under control myself.'

Marcus glared at her. 'You could easily have been thrown.'

'Well, I wasn't. Go back to your mine, Mr Fitzalan. I'm sure your men will be wondering where you've got to. Heaven help us should they come looking for you and find us alone like this. Imagine how people will talk,' she remarked with a strong hint of sarcasm.

'And that would bother you, would it?'

'No. Not in the slightest. But is it your intention to make me conspicuous—to ruin my reputation as you did once before—by keeping me here? Once is a scandal, but twice is not to be endured. Perhaps it is your belief that in doing so you will be able to force me into marriage—that by using your powers of persuasion you are hoping to rekindle the time you lured me into the woods three years ago?'

Marcus smiled crookedly, his anger of a moment earlier melting as he remembered the time she spoke of—when she had kissed him with such tender passion—with a great deal of pleasure. 'As to that, I was the one being compromised. I did not lure you. You came willingly, as I remember.'

'You remember too much,' she snapped.

'And you were tempted then.'

'I was very young and stupid.'

'And now you are wiser?'

'Yes, and no longer foolish enough to get carried away by you.'

'And despite your statement to the contrary the last time we met, you are sure of that, are you?' he asked, smiling, his eyes gleaming cruelly as he moved towards her.

Seething with anger, Eve tried to move further away. 'Don't you dare come near me. You're a monster, Marcus Fitzalan,' she flared.

'I'm happy to hear you address me in a more familiar manner, Miss Somerville. Marcus Fitzalan is an improvement on Mr Fitzalan.'

Eve ignored his gentle sarcasm. 'You're no better than those worthless fortune hunters my grandmother often refers to— except that with you it's a coal mine you have a mind to seduce from me.'

Marcus stopped then, his mocking smile widening. 'Half a coal mine,' he reminded her coldly.

'I don't care if a hundred coal mines are at stake. I have no intention of meekly accepting my fate. Believe me, Mr Fitzalan, marrying me would not be worth it.'

'Maybe you're right—but I shall never know unless I try it,' he said, as inch by terrifying inch he moved steadily closer until she was pressed up against a tree and there was nowhere she could go to escape him.

Chapter Six

Eve stood perfectly still, unable to look away, knowing that she was very much in danger of becoming overwhelmed by him, his lean, muscular body emanating raw power and his sternly handsome face hovering so very close.

Slowly his eyes moved down from her face and over the rippling silk of her red blouse tucked into her waistband, the sight of her long, slim legs and hips outlined beneath her close-fitting breeches causing a lazy, appreciative smile to twist his lips, and he found himself dwelling with a good deal of pleasure on the tantalising delights underneath.

'And I would be a fool if I thought marriage to you had nothing more to offer than a coal mine,' he murmured, meeting her gaze. Seeing shock mingle with fear in her wonderful eyes, he moved away a little, becoming less threatening to her sensibilities. He grinned infuriatingly. 'Just testing the water, so to speak,' he said softly, but his instinct told him she was no more immune to him now and her own vulnerability than she had been three years ago.

'Then don't venture too deep, Mr Fitzalan, otherwise you might find yourself out of your depth,' she retorted coldly.

His eyebrows arched and his pale blue eyes danced wickedly. 'There's little danger of that, Miss Somerville. I'm an extremely good swimmer. Now come along. If you insist on returning to Burntwood Hall, I'll ride part of the way back with you.'

'No. There's no need. I am perfectly capable of riding back myself.'

'I'm sure you are,' he said, moving towards her horse and making quite sure it was calm enough for her to mount once more, 'but they can do without me at the mine for a while and it will give me great pleasure to accompany you.'

Drawing a long breath Eve could tell he would not be dissuaded. 'Very well. If you insist.'

'I do.' He frowned crossly when she declined his gesture to help her mount, stubbornly preferring to do it herself—which she did, the agility of her movements as she swung one long leg easily over the saddle making his pulses quicken. 'Miss Somerville—Eve,' he said, his expression serious. 'Must there be enmity between us? Must you persist in getting on my wrong side all the time? Can't we call a truce and begin speaking to each other like adults?'

Unwillingly Eve looked down at him, meeting his gaze squarely, finding the warmth in his eyes far more disturbing and disarming than his anger, and making it extremely difficult to regard him as an enemy. She sighed, beginning to relax and soften towards him.

'Yes—you are right,' she conceded, 'and I suppose I should thank you for coming to my rescue so promptly. My horse could easily have thrown me. I do realise that.'

They rode in single file along a narrow track, which made conversation impossible between them for a while. Riding slowly ahead of Marcus, a curious dreaminess pervaded Eve as she let the sun's warmth seep into her. Time seemed to slow and everything around them was lulled in the shimmering heat. Tall grass and bracken grew along the banks on either side of the path, and the merry chirrup of birds in the trees, the buzz of an occasional bee and the snorting of their horses were all that disturbed the quiet. When the path opened out and they rode side by side, Marcus cast her an admiring glance.

'You know, you really should not ride alone,' he said quietly. 'All manner of folk roam these woods around Atwood.'

Lulled into a sense of calm by the gentle movement of the horse and the warm sun on her face, Eve glanced sideways at him, seeing he was in earnest. 'Why, Mr Fitzalan, you amaze me. Is it to protect me that you insisted on accompanying me?'

'Yes.'

She flashed him a bright smile. 'How gallant.'

He responded with a grin. 'There. Now you know I am not all bad, does that improve my character in your eyes?'

'It's too soon to say. There's still a great deal about you that I don't know. You are an opportunist, I believe.'

'If you mean I seize everything that comes my way, you are right. But I am not so mercenary as to do so without regard for principles or consequence.'

'And Atwood Mine? Does that mean more to you than personal relationships?'

'If you had asked me that before your father died I would have said yes. I always believed romantic relationships to be for dreamers and fools.'

'And now? What has changed?'

'You,' he replied bluntly.

Eve looked at him with a newly acquired wisdom, smiling wryly. 'I've already told you not to use false flattery on me, Mr Fitzalan. I am not deceived. I am no fool and know the mine's worth. Come, admit it. You want it badly enough to seduce me into marriage.'

He frowned crossly. 'If you want to know the truth, I'm beginning to curse the wretched mine. No matter what my feelings turn out to be regarding yourself, you will always have reason to be suspicious, to doubt them because of the mine. How much better it would be if I could pay court to you without you forever accusing me of having an ulterior motive.'

His words rendered Eve speechless, and she stared across at him, so surprised that for once she was unsure how to respond.

'You…have given some thought to the matter which is important to us both, I hope?' Marcus asked at length as they continued to amble in the direction of Burntwood Hall.

'Yes, I have—but the matter you speak of means more to you than it does to me, I think, Mr Fitzalan,' she said—which was not entirely true, but she would not give him the satisfaction of letting him know just how much Atwood Mine meant to her.

But Marcus was no fool. He knew by the fierce intensity he had seen in her eyes when Mr Soames had read out the conditions of her father's will exactly how much she wanted to hold on to it.

'You must understand that all this is very difficult for me,' she said.

'I realise that,' he replied, noticing that her tongue had lost none of its edge, despite her agreement to call a truce, 'but it has to be faced some time—and it's no use pretending I don't have a self-interest in the mine.'

'I know that. It's rather like myself. I took it for granted that more of my father's assets, as well as Atwood Mine, would be left to me, you see,' she said with marked irony which was not lost on Marcus.

He gave a wry smile. 'I learned long ago never to take anything for granted.'

Eve was beginning to feel a little uncomfortable and vaguely irritated by his close inspection as he turned his head towards her. She met his gaze, noticing how pale and blue his eyes were—as clear and sharp as the mountain streams that tumbled over the rocks and through the valleys in her grandmother's native Cumbria.

'How are you, really?' he asked, with a gentleness Eve would not have expected from him.

It was only a simple question, but there was so much sincerity in his voice that she looked at him with astonishment and studied him closely, his absolute masculinity stirring some hidden feminine instinct that her innocence and inexperience did not give her the liberty to recognise. She didn't know if it was the unblinking fascination of his eyes or the sensation his nearness evoked in her, but for a split second she was unable to stir, becoming mesmerised as she gazed at him. Then, with a shiver, she immediately looked away.

'I am as well as I can be—considering the unfortunate nature of the circumstances. Still, with time, I'm sure I'll get over it,' she answered with a forced lightness.

Her grieving was evident to Marcus, but he strongly suspected it was not just for her father that she mourned. 'It will be difficult for you, I'm sure, having to leave Burntwood Hall,' he said. 'It must mean a great deal to you.'

Eve's expression became curiously soft, with a yearning quality that touched Marcus. For a moment her face became unguarded and, for the first time in their acquaintance, it showed him something of the lost child behind the deliberately maintained façade of the woman. His heart contracted at the grief he saw etched on her lovely face, her violet eyes so dark with suffering they were almost black. It was clear that losing her father so tragically, plus the shock of his will, had done a great deal of emotional damage.

'Yes,' she confessed, in answer to his question, 'it will. I confess I hadn't thought how much it has come to mean to me until now. It saddens me to think how little Gerald will appreciate it. But it cannot be easy for you, either, knowing you could stand to lose the opportunity of owning Atwood Mine once more,' she remarked matter of factly as their horses fell into step beside each other, walking slowly along the paths that snaked along the hillside, neither of them feeling the need for haste as they conversed easily together for the first time.

'Only if you refuse to agree to become my wife.'

Eve's heart contracted at his words, for they told her that his mind was already made up.

'But I remember you telling me that you don't want a wife any more than I want a husband, Mr Fitzalan. Why—by your persistence, if I didn't know better, I would think that you find me completely irresistible and that you cannot live without me. I may not take kindly to having a coal mine as a rival for my husband's affections—if we marry, that is.'

'Nor I, Miss Somerville,' Marcus replied, smiling thinly and preferring to ignore her sarcasm, but a dangerous light gleamed in his eyes. 'I might say the same about you—seeing that we will be equal partners, don't forget.'

'Nevertheless, you must want it badly—enough to tie yourself down to a woman who is almost a stranger to you. Tell me why Atwood Mine is so important to you? By all accounts you already own several mines, have shares in others and invest your money wisely, enabling you to live like a prince for the rest of your life.'

'That's true, but Atwood Mine is important to me in the sense that it used to belong to my family. I know of its potential—that it's the most profitable mine in the area, with untapped coal reserves way beyond imagination. But it means more to me than that,' he said, speaking wistfully, a yearning, nostalgic quality entering his eyes which Eve saw and was surprised by, for it gave her an insight of the man who spoke, which she had glimpsed once before, when they had met and talked at Atwood Mine just a few days ago; for a moment, they seemed to be encapsulated by a quiet companionship.

'It was started by my grandfather and my own father died in that mine. I was at school at the time and was not aware that my mother—who hated everything to do with coal and felt unable to profit from something that had been the means of causing her untold misery—had sold the lease to your father until it was too late to do anything about it.'

'And if you had known, you would have stopped her?'

'Definitely.'

'I see,' she said, realising what a crushing blow it must have been for him to discover what his mother had done. It wasn't just a mine to him, it was much more than that. It represented everything his grandfather had fought so hard to achieve. It was a symbol of years of physically demanding toil. There was little wonder he wanted it back in his family. 'I knew nothing of this. And you felt no resentment towards my father for taking it from you?'

'Why should I? Apart from my own sense of loss there was nothing wrong with the transaction. He was a businessman and had done nothing wrong. As you know, your father and I became good friends and he was a tremendous help to me when I too went into the mining industry. He taught me a great deal about mining, for which I shall be eternally grateful. I admired him enormously and shall miss him in many ways.'

Eve knew by the depth of feeling with which he spoke those last words that he was speaking from the heart. The feeling between them had been mutual, their friendship firm and enduring, and a force entered Eve that made her own resentment and jealousy, which she had nurtured against Marcus Fitzalan for so long, seem petty in comparison.

She recollected the time when she had first begun to feel this way, when she had been a child and Marcus Fitzalan had started taking an interest in mining after his own father had died. Her father had recognised his natural aptitude for business and taken him under his wing. He had admired the way Marcus had set out to establish himself in the coal industry by being keen to learn and having ambition and drive, which had won admiration from friends and rivals alike.

Eve's resentment and bitterness stemmed from a time long before their encounter at Atwood Fair, when her father had come to look upon him almost as the son he'd never had, which had distanced him from her even further. Her father had talked of him often, constantly referring to things he had said and done, causing her to wonder if he ever spared a thought for anyone else…or for her.

'I regret we never met,' Marcus went on, smiling down at her, having no idea what was passing through her mind—he would have been shocked and surprised if he had. 'Perhaps we might have become friends before now.'

Eve was prompted to say she doubted it, but thought better of it.

'I did see you once—when you came to the house with my father. I was fourteen at the time. My friend Emma Parkinson and I were on the landing, looking down into the hall when you were leaving.'

'Oh!' he said, trying to imagine what she would have looked like then, as a child looking through the banisters. 'And what impression did I make?'

'You didn't,' she replied coldly, the peace of a moment before short-lived as she detected the mocking note in his voice. 'I remember telling Emma that I couldn't see what all the fuss was about. Your reputation for being one for the ladies had preceded you, you see.'

He smiled at that. 'My reputation?'

'Yes. It may surprise you to know that the odd bits of gossip about your liaisons and conquests have filtered through to Atwood from time to time.'

'So—you think you know all about me, do you? I am a notorious womaniser, gambler and anything else that defames my character—is that correct? Come,' he said when he saw her hesitate, one of his dark brows arched and his eyes gleaming with derisive humour, 'we must be frank with each other.'

'Very well—yes. I remember Emma thinking you were quite the handsomest thing on two legs.'

He laughed outright with unfeigned amusement. 'A lady after my own heart. I must remind you to introduce me to your friend Emma some time. And you?' he asked, watching her face closely. 'Tell me what you thought of me.'

She shrugged. 'I'm not as easily flustered as Emma. When she saw I wasn't impressed, she told me you would make a meal out of me in no time at all.'

'And what was your reply to that?'

'Only that I would give you indigestion,' she replied, regarding him with open candour.

Marcus's lips twitched at the corners as he tried to suppress a smile, thinking how very young she was. From his youth he had been favoured by women for his good looks and arrogant ways, and had been more than willing to sample their charms, but Eve Somerville was not at all like any of them, which he found a refreshing change.

'Yes, I think you are probably right,' he said softly, full of secret amusement as he raised his brows and let his eyes travel over her from head to toe, an assessment not devoid of insolence and appreciation, which caused a flush of embarrassment to spring to Eve's cheeks, 'but I think I would have to fatten you up a little first.'

All at once his expression became serious. 'You have made it plain that there is a great deal about me you do not like, but how this can be, when you really know nothing about me at all, leaves me feeling quite intrigued.'

'Why should it? By all accounts—'

'Gossip, you mean.'

'If you like. By all accounts, wherever you go, you have ladies dripping from your arms like bats in a belfry. To you love and relationships are a game, one that you are good at—used to winning and the world's worst loser. Forgive me if I appear outspoken, Mr Fitzalan,' she said in a matter-of-fact way when she saw his eyes open wide with surprise that she should speak with such candour, 'but you did ask that I should be frank—and, if we are to marry, then it's as well that I know all there is to know about you. Does it disappoint you to know what others say and think of you?'

He cocked a sleek black brow, speaking ironically. 'I long since ceased to worry about other people's opinions of me. However,' he said on a softer note, a warm intimacy creeping into his voice, and his incredible gaze passing over her in a manner which caused her stomach to quiver despite her resolve to stand firm against him, 'I am flattered to know I have kindled so much interest in you over the years.'

Eve flushed, bristling at his tone. 'Why—you conceited—'

'So others were fond of pointing out when I was a boy,' he said quickly, smiling infuriatingly and his eyes flashing wickedly.

'A trait which has continued.'

He was watching her, his expression unfathomable. 'So, you do not care for my arrogance and conceit?'

'No—not much.'

'But then—you know so little about me.'

'As much as I want to know. The knowledge I have of you does not inspire me to want to know more.'

'Pity. Only…a little knowledge can be dangerous,' he said softly, meaningfully.

'Oh, I'm perfectly capable of avoiding danger.'

'And you're sure of that, are you?'

'Naturally.'

Marcus smiled, mocking. 'Tell me, Miss Somerville, are you afraid to marry me?'

Looking into his intense, pale blue eyes Eve rose to the challenge. 'No, Mr Fitzalan. I'm afraid of no man.'

'You may protest all you like, but I get the distinct feeling that I unsettle you in some way.'

'You do not unsettle me in the slightest,' she replied with a slight quiver in her voice, beginning to feel exceedingly discomposed by the content of the conversation—and by his gaze and crooked smile which drenched her in its sensuality.

'Yes, I do. You're blushing.'

'No, I am not,' she protested, knowing she was and feeling the colour intensify under his frank scrutiny.

'Yes, you are. But don't worry, you look quite charming and your cheeks are as deliciously pink as those roses,' he said, indicating a wonderful array of dog roses rampantly blooming along the edge of the path, his voice stroking her like a caress.

Her gaze trapped in his, Eve regarded him in silence. He was riding far too close, she thought, and his potent maleness was making her feel too vulnerable by far.

Marcus smiled, his pale blue eyes dazzlingly clear and full of mischievous delight, well satisfied, knowing full well exactly how much havoc he was presenting to her sensibilities.

They paused for a moment, facing each other. Marcus looked into Eve's bold, fiery eyes, letting his gaze dwell appreciatively on her perfect features. He was a man of power and pride who always walked a straight line. He had always known what he wanted and usually got it—and he had already made up his mind that he wanted Eve Somerville…with or without the mine.

Given time he would cure her of her rebellious nature and mould her into the kind of woman he wanted his wife to be. A task he would enjoy. He intended to launch an assault on her that would have her weak at the knees and begging for him to make theirs a marriage in every sense of the word.

'Let me assure you that what you have just accused me of being—a philanderer of the worst possible kind, I believe—is exceedingly exaggerated. You really shouldn't listen to gossip. I am sorry to disappoint you and shatter the misguided illusion you appear to have of me, but I must tell you that it is with some regret that I find I have little time for the kind of pleasures you speak of. Much of my time is taken up with the more important matters of business.'

'And how can I be sure of that?'

'You'll have to take my word for it. But why it should appear to matter so much to you puzzles me.'

'It matters only in the sense that, if I agree to become your wife, I will be the butt of no one's joke.'

'And I would not have it so, Miss Somerville. However,' he said on a more serious note, 'this is a matter far too important for us to be sidetracked into light discussion. We have something much more important to occupy us. If we marry, we benefit considerably. If we don't, we stand to lose everything. It's a dilemma—don't you agree?'

'Yes.'

'I admit I have a lot to lose if we do not marry—and why shouldn't I avail myself of your father's generous offer in order to obtain the mine?'

'Half the mine,' Eve reminded him sharply.

Marcus bowed his head in acquiescence. Once again Eve met his glacier gaze. 'Of course. I stand corrected. Come, don't tell me you find the prospect of living in Cumbria with your grandmother appealing. Even marriage to me would be better than that.'

'Would it? I'm not so sure about that.' Eve sighed as they began to ride on, deflated, suddenly, for in truth she was unable to disagree with him. 'Nevertheless, you are right,' she conceded. 'My grandmother is not the easiest of women to get on with. She has ruled her family for many years, acting in accordance to the way she herself was brought up, and has little understanding for human frailties. The whole family stands in awe of her. My mother always became a different person in her presence. She always put off as long as she could Grandmother's visits.'

'And what is her opinion of all this? Is she in favour of a marriage taking place between us?'

'Yes. My grandmother is happy enough for me to marry you. She wants to see me settled. But she belongs to the old school, where a young lady should marry the man of her parents' choosing for advantage, wealth and title. Debilitating emotions such as romantic love she sees as a weakness which does not enter into the scheme of things.'

'And is that how you would like to enter marriage?'

'Of course,' she said frankly. 'What woman would not?'

He smiled. 'You make your grandmother sound like a tyrant—but I'm sure you exaggerate. Until the funeral we had not met, but I found her company pleasant enough.'

'She always gives that impression to strangers, but don't be fooled by it. If you become better acquainted with her, you'll soon share the opinion of everyone else.'

Marcus arched his black brows and looked down at her quizzically. 'Oh? And is there a chance of that—that we'll become better acquainted, I mean?'

'Why—I—I—'

'Come, now,' he said, smiling crookedly at her confusion. 'Am I to understand that you might agree to become my wife? Forgive me, but do you find me so repulsive?' he asked when he saw a look of distaste cross her face.

'I would prefer to choose my own husband—that is all.'

'Don't young ladies in your position usually have husbands found for them?'

'Yes—but not with conditions such as we have been presented with. The prospect my father has laid before me is one I feel loath to accept.'

'I can understand that. Is there anyone else you are contemplating marrying?'

Eve gave him a level gaze. 'No. But I think it is only fair to tell you that Gerald has asked me to marry him.'

Marcus looked at her in astonishment. His face became a stone mask, devoid of all expression. Gerald was a complication he could do without. 'He has what?' His voice was like ice, hard and implacable. The thought that Gerald Somerville would do his utmost to obtain the mine had crawled into his mind when he had been made aware of the conditions of Sir John's will, and it gave him no joy to discover that his worst fear had been realised.

'Gerald has asked me to—'

'I heard you the first time,' he exploded, causing Eve to start and tremble slightly at the anger her announcement had aroused in him. 'And what did you say?' he demanded. 'What was your answer? Because you know it was not what your father would have wished.'

'I said no,' she answered quietly. 'I do not reciprocate his attention.' She shuddered, recalling her last emotive encounter with Gerald, which still had the power to evoke fear and create unease within her. 'Nothing could ever tempt me to marry Gerald.'

Swamped with relief Marcus studied her thoughtfully, concerned to see how, when speaking, she avoided his eyes and how her voice trembled, which was suspicious in itself. He looked at her for a long moment, as if he debated some problem in his mind but could only determine an answer in the expression of her face.

'But it would appear I am a valuable commodity in the marriage market suddenly,' Eve continued quietly, 'and whoever I choose will profit enormously—except myself. But what of you? Is there no lady you would rather marry?'

'No,' he replied—too quickly, Eve thought, watching him closely. He radiated an unshakable calm and she was unable to read his well-schooled features, but her instinct told her he might not be telling her the truth. Did he want the mine so much that he was prepared to jeopardise a relationship he might already have with someone else? And, if so, was a man who would go to such drastic lengths to obtain what he wanted the kind of man she wanted to spend the rest of her life with?

'Let me make a suggestion—make it easier for you,' he went on. 'If you agree to become my wife, we will make it a marriage in name only—a marriage of convenience—until we want it otherwise. Come—what do you say?'

Eve looked at him sharply. 'A purely platonic relationship, you mean? A relationship in which we could each lead our own lives.'

'Up to a point.' He smiled slightly when he saw her relief.

'Do you mean it?' she asked. This was better than she had expected.

'Of course. But only until the time comes when there is better understanding between us—when we are no longer strangers. Could you agree to those terms?'

Their eyes met and held, and for some reason Eve could not explain, his words caused a faint stirring of disappointment inside her, causing her to question it and ask herself why this should be, unless it was that she wanted more of a commitment from him.

'It would be a private matter and would be between us and no one else. Let's face it,' he said, 'the situation is distasteful to us both, but whatever resentments we feel it is important to give the impression that all is well between us.'

'Pretend, you mean.'

'Precisely. We could announce our betrothal now and be married as soon as the required term of mourning for your father has been honoured—providing it is within the six months he stipulated in his will.'

'You do not waste much time, do you, Mr Fitzalan?' Eve said drily, having always hoped that when the time came for her to marry the moment of proposal would come from the heart, not as some cold and impersonal business proposition.

'Not when there's something I want.'

'And you want the mine—or half of it. Even if you have to take me as part of the package.'

'Yes. But it is a package I am not displeased with,' he replied softly, his eyes holding hers, causing a crimson flush to spring once more to her cheeks.

Marcus saw so many conflicting emotions chase across her face, which was far too expressive, and he realised she was not nearly as hard and in control as she would like him to think.

They had reached Burntwood Hall and to Eve's surprise Marcus dismounted, indicating that she should do the same. Taking her by the shoulders, he turned her towards him, his eyes serious and surprisingly understanding.

'Whatever your decision, Eve,' he said softly, speaking her name for the first time with an intimacy that already had them attached, his eyes penetrating as they held hers, 'I am on your side. Please believe that. No matter what harsh, misguided opinion you have of me—I am not your enemy. So what do you say? Will you consent to be my wife?'

As Eve returned his gaze, her expression was serious. The quality of his voice was smooth and it seemed to her that he had suddenly ironed all the difficulties facing them away—as if he had mesmerised them both by the quietness of his voice. The pressure of his fingers on her shoulders made her heart begin to beat in an unpredictable manner and his gaze held her spellbound, weaving some magic web around her from which there was no escape.

'I don't know. Every instinct is telling me I should know more about you, Mr Fitzalan, and your home and family, before I make up my mind.'

'Of course. That is what I would expect. Let me begin by telling you that my family consists of two brothers, both younger than myself, who have made their careers in the Navy. William, the middle one, is married with two children and lives in London—when not at sea, that is. Michael, who is just twenty, comes home to Brooklands when he can—which is where I live with my mother.'

'I see. And your mother? Will she accept me under these circumstances, do you think?'

'If she likes you and knows it is what I want, then she will not oppose you. I wonder—would you consider coming to Brooklands, to see for yourself what it's like? Take a look, see the house and find out all you need to know about me before you decide?'

Eve looked at him steadily. 'With no strings attached?'

'No strings.'

'Then—yes.' She smiled. 'I would like that.'

'Good. My mother is entertaining a few friends to dinner next Wednesday. Would you care to come along—if you have no other engagement, that is?'

'Yes, thank you,' she replied, relieved she would not be alone with him. 'I have no other engagement. But I cannot possibly come by myself.'

'I realise that. The invitation extends to your grandmother also. Do you have any objections to that?'

'No. I shall look forward to it.'

'Good. I shall look forward to showing you my home. Brooklands was built by my grandfather and may not be as old or as grand as Burntwood Hall, but it is lovely all the same. I am sure you will not be disappointed.'

He looked at her seriously for a long moment, reaching up and brushing her cheek slowly and gently with the back of his fingers, sending a disconcerting tremor of warm pleasure coursing through her and causing her heart to skip a beat, knowing full well that she was in danger of succumbing to his fatal charm—as no doubt he was certain she would.

Eve made no effort to move away, and as Marcus looked deeply into her eyes his own were tender, and she trembled once more, unable to control it. His fingers were warm, soft and strong, gently massaging her cheek, and she felt a sudden urge to turn her head and kiss the palm of his hand.

'You are under no obligation to marry me, Eve, but I sincerely hope you will. I want to marry you. I want to make you my wife. If you say yes, you will make me an extremely happy man. I believe I could make you love me.'

His voice was deep and incredibly sincere. Eve was deeply moved by his words, spoken seriously and without arrogance. His eyes continued to hold hers and his lips curved in a quiet smile. She gazed up at him, and a long moment passed before she replied.

'Yes,' she whispered. 'Perhaps you could.' She stepped back from him, afraid of the turmoil inside her, afraid of the weakening effect he was having on her emotions.

Marcus sensed what she was thinking. 'You are an extremely beautiful and desirable young woman—and please do not accuse me of flattering you in order to seduce you into marriage. The statement is completely true and spoken from the heart. Don't fight me, Eve. Don't be afraid to come close.'

'Afraid?'

'Yes. Because of the past you are wary and wish to avoid

being hurt. I don't blame you, but I assure you that the last thing I want to do is to hurt or distress you in any way.'

'You seem to know me well, Mr Fitzalan.'

'Well enough to deduce certain things, and well enough to know I want to marry you with or without your half of Atwood Mine.'

Eve stared at him—bemused and tranquillised by his soft words, knowing she was in danger of falling completely beneath his spell. In the past he had caused her nothing but grief. He had hurt her and aroused her resentment and jealousy by holding a special place in her father's affections—a place she had childishly wanted all to herself—and, knowing all this, still she was attracted to him. She didn't seem to be able to help it.

She took another step back, trying to shake off the effect he was having on her, knowing she should listen to the warning bell ringing inside her head—and yet why was she hoping...wanting him to kiss her?

'I—I must go,' she murmured, avoiding his penetrating gaze, unable to think clearly with him looking at her like that. 'Thank you for seeing me home.'

'The pleasure was all mine.'

It was as he was leaving, mounted on his horse in the driveway, that he paused and looked down at her. His expression was grave, his eyes still penetrating, but she could not see what lay behind them.

'The last thing I want to do is alarm you, but promise me you will take care.'

'Why? What are you saying?'

'It worries me that you are alone here—with Gerald in such close proximity. I am not unaware that he covets the mine, that he feels cheated. He is well aware that if we do not marry the mine will revert to him—and, from what I know of him, he is ruthless enough to try anything to hold on to it. He has already taken the first step by asking you to become his wife.

If he should approach you and threaten you in any way—you will let me know?'

Eve was touched by his concern. There was so much warmth and sincerity in his voice that she was quite disarmed. She smiled softly, giving him no indication that Gerald had already threatened her. Not wishing to cause trouble and hoping that Gerald's threats had been empty and that she would not have to face him in the future, she fully intended leaving Burntwood Hall before he arrived to take up residence.

'Yes. I will.'

Chapter Seven

Marcus left Eve an extremely confused young woman. That night, as sleep eluded her, she continued to think of the things he had said to her, things she could not believe he had said— especially the part when he had told her that he wanted to marry her with or without her half of Atwood Mine. That she found difficult to believe. It was too preposterous for words.

She had vowed never again to let him make her lose her composure as she had that time when he had made a fool of her in front of her friends, a time when he had got her so bewildered she hardly knew right from wrong—when his kisses had robbed her of the ability to think clearly.

She had been a silly, stupid girl, so inexperienced and un- qualified to deal with a man of the world like Marcus Fitzalan that she had been wide open to seduction. He had attempted to seduce her for his own amusement, his improper behaviour towards her both inexcusable and unforgivable, and she told herself that she must not allow herself to weaken, to give in to his forceful personality a second time.

But no matter how she railed against him, telling herself that she disliked him intensely, that she would rather be con- signed to hell than consider marriage to him, she could not deny that on finding herself alone with him once again, she had wanted him to repeat the same offence he had perpetrated against her person three years ago.

In fact, she was so confused she found it difficult—if not impossible—to analyse her feelings. There was that same fierce tug to her senses in being near him as there had been when he had drawn her away from her friends at Atwood Fair. For a long while after that encounter thoughts of him had persisted on intruding into her everyday life. In spite of her determination not to be similarly affected, she feared that resolve was lost, and found herself looking forward to her visit to Brooklands and to meeting his mother.

Eve's grandmother was delighted at the prospect of visiting Brooklands, and glad to see that Eve was being sensible at last now that the initial shock of the contents of her father's will had lessened slightly, after tilting her world sideways and flinging her life into total confusion. She suspected that her granddaughter's easy acceptance of the invitation to visit Brooklands and to meet Mrs Fitzalan was because she was softening towards Marcus Fitzalan, despite her earlier avowal to the contrary.

'I shall look forward to seeing Brooklands, Eve. I am honoured to have been invited—although you could hardly go without a chaperon,' she said as she walked slowly beside her granddaughter in the garden, enjoying the late afternoon sunshine. It was the day after Marcus had issued the invitation. Lady Pemberton cast Eve a shrewd glance. 'Does this mean that you are seriously considering marriage to Mr Fitzalan after all?'

'Yes,' Eve admitted. 'I realise that I must.'

'Good. I like him. He is a charming man and I am sure he is the one for you,' she said firmly. 'Although what a pity you're in mourning, Eve. It would have been so nice if you could have worn something of a more cheerful colour to make you look your best. I never did like black on young ladies. It's too severe for my liking.'

'I'm sure Mr Fitzalan will not notice what I'm wearing, Grandmother,' she smiled.

'Nevertheless, it's time you were introduced to his mother if you two are to marry.'

'Yes, I know. But I would also like to know Mr Fitzalan a little better before I decide.'

'That is sensible. You are bemused by him, I can see that—which is natural with a man of his character. But I know a good man when I see one. He will make a good husband.'

Eve stared at her grandmother, looking slightly forlorn. 'Will he? Do you really think so, Grandmother?'

Lady Pemberton reached out and patted her arm gently. 'Oh, yes.'

'But will a man who is respected, important, rich and powerful, owner of not one but several coal mines, and who lives in a splendid house, make a good husband in every other sense?'

Her grandmother smiled with understanding, remembering they'd had a similar conversation before. 'It helps. Money is an extremely useful commodity, Eve. As for the rest—the matters of the heart which I know are so important to you—they will come later. Now, stop frowning. It spoils your face. You must look forward to going to Brooklands and your meeting with Mrs Fitzalan.'

Ruth Fitzalan was the mother of three sons: Marcus, the eldest, because of his passion for mining and being his father's heir, was the only one left at home—unlike William and Michael, who had both sought careers in the Navy. Ruth was a tall, slender woman with a strong personality, not unlike Marcus in features, but, unlike him, her hair was light brown and liberally streaked with grey. She was a woman highly thought of and respected in the area, the only daughter of a man of considerable standing, socially and financially, and a leader in local government affairs.

She was proud of the way Marcus had taken over the reins

when her husband had died. Everywhere he went people courted his favour. Sir John Somerville had taught him how to select the right ventures in which to invest his money—and success had brought him notoriety and more wealth. But there was a price to pay—his right to privacy in Netherley—which was why he went further afield to partake of his pleasures—usually to London, where he combined business with pleasure.

But invariably he was seen and the lady on his arm at the time would be discussed at length by the gossips who longed to know more about him, until the affair had been grossly exaggerated, giving him the reputation of a rake. In and around Netherley he declined to accept invitations to balls and soirées, with matchmaking mothers trying to pair him off with their daughters, but he was aware of how they whispered and speculated among themselves.

Ruth was not at all enamoured over the affair between her son and Eve Somerville and had made her opinion known immediately she learned of the unusual conditions of John Somerville's will. Granted, the girl was eminently suitable to be Marcus's wife, and she had nothing against her or her family, for Sir John had been a good friend and business partner of both her late husband and Marcus, but—having no knowledge of what had happened between them at Atwood Fair three years earlier, the gossip it had created in Atwood at the time not having reached her ears—as far as she was aware, Marcus and Eve had not been introduced before the day of the funeral.

The haste and enthusiasm with which he wanted to marry Eve Somerville had come as a surprise and something of a shock to her, for until then Marcus had shown no sign of wanting to settle down, despite his amours in London and the eligible daughters of marriageable age of friends and acquaintance she had brought to the house and paraded before him in the hope that one of them would catch his eye.

And now, just when she thought she had found him the right girl in Angela Stephenson—a beautiful, strong-minded young widow who was the daughter of a close friend—he had casually shattered any expectations she had that the two of them would eventually marry.

Having spent some considerable time both in London and on her late husband's estate a little further north, which had been inherited by his brother after his death, Angela had recently come to spend some time with her parents at their home in Little Bolton, almost three miles from Netherley.

And who could blame her for beginning to hope for the match, for it had been plain for everyone to see that when they were in London Angela was strongly attracted by Marcus from the start, although it had not gone unnoticed by her keen eye that Marcus did not appear to be enthusiastic about forming a close relationship with Angela, and did not go out of his way to seek her company. She had thought that, when they returned to Netherley, something might develop between them and give both families reason to hope that a marriage just might be hovering blissfully on the horizon.

'I've invited Miss Somerville to Brooklands next Wednesday, Mother,' Marcus told her on returning from the mine, having returned there after his parting with Eve. He was still wearing his soiled and sweaty clothes, his black hair falling untidily over his handsome face as he strode into his mother's sitting room, where she was always to be found in the late afternoon, either reading or industriously employed at her needlework, seated before a long window where the light was good and where she could gaze out over the well laid-out rose gardens beyond.

Closing her book and placing it on an occasional table beside her chair, his mother looked up at him and her lips thinned, her grey eyes surveying her son reprovingly. 'But you can't have,' she said with a note of alarm. 'You know very well there will be quite a gathering here on Wednesday.'

'That is precisely the reason why I suggested that she come that particular day. She will be among people she knows and will not feel so uncomfortable. Her grandmother will be accompanying her.'

'But what about Angela?'

Marcus frowned with annoyance. 'Angela? What about Angela?'

'Marcus! You cannot have forgotten that she will be here with her parents.'

'No, I have not forgotten, but I fail to see why that should make any difference to my inviting Eve Somerville.' He sighed in exasperation, perfectly aware what was passing through his mother's mind. 'Mother—please. Will you stop trying to run my life?'

'Surely I am to be allowed to express an opinion.'

'Of course you are—but I have not made any commitment to Angela or given her any reason to think I am likely to, for that matter.'

'Nevertheless, there is an understanding—'

'No, Mother,' he said sharply. 'Only in your own mind.'

'Is it so unreasonable of me to want to see you settled with a wife—the *right* wife?' his mother said with slight emphasis on the last words.

'No. It is not unreasonable.'

'But Angela is so right for you,' she persisted fervently.

'No,' said Marcus sharply, trying to hold on to his patience. 'Angela is right for you, Mother. Angela Stephenson means absolutely nothing to me. I am always polite and courteous towards her because of the close friendship that exists between you and her mother. That is all. In fact, if you want the absolute truth, I do not care for her in the slightest. You must allow me to choose my own wife—to my own satisfaction.'

'Choose! If you are contemplating marrying Eve Somerville, then it is hardly by choice, is it? You would not give her a second glance if it were not for the mine,' she said crossly, observing the implacable lines of determination on her son's face, which told her he would not be dissuaded on this.

He was showing the same kind of stubborn resistance he'd shown ever since he was a little boy.

Fully aware of the conditions of Sir John's will, she had left Marcus in no doubt of her disapproval. It was not that she had anything against Eve Somerville—in fact, she had got to know Sir John quite well through the business transactions he and Marcus had made together over the years, coming to like and respect him for his integrity and sound common sense. It was Atwood Mine that was anathema to her, the mine she had sold to Sir John, the mine that had taken the life of her beloved husband. Because of that, she never wanted to see it back in her family again.

'You must want the mine pretty badly, Marcus, to consider marrying Eve Somerville in order to get it. Why—you had never met her until the day of the funeral. The next thing you'll be telling me is that you've named the day.'

'It's too soon for that. If she does agree to become my wife, we will become betrothed immediately. One of the conditions in Sir John's will is that we marry within six months.'

'When Atwood Mine will become yours,' Ruth said drily. 'I cannot help thinking that you will be marrying her for all the wrong reasons. But why is it so important to you? We are not paupers and certainly have no need of it. Do not forget it was in that mine that your father was killed.'

'I know that, Mother—but I also know how much Atwood Mine meant to him, and how hard my grandfather had to work to get it established, sinking every penny he had into making it succeed. That is the reason why I want it back in this family—where it belongs.'

'Despite the pain you know it will cause me?'

'Yes,' he replied gently. 'And for what it's worth, I'm sorry. I would not hurt you for the world, Mother, you know that— but this is something I must do.'

'And you are prepared to marry Eve Somerville to get it?'

'Yes. The lease has another fifteen years to run and I shudder to think what state it will be in by that time if it is handed over to Gerald Somerville.'

'I find it strange that Sir John did not leave you the mine outright without imposing these harsh conditions on you. Why did he not leave you the mine without you having to take his daughter? Good heavens, Marcus, what is wrong with the girl?'

'There is nothing wrong with her. In fact, she is extremely beautiful and quite charming. I think it was his way of making sure she would be well taken care of.'

'And you truly believe you can be happy within a marriage based on conditions such as these?'

'I see no reason why not. I know of marriages that have been made on rockier foundations and, given time, have turned out to the satisfaction of both parties. You must try to understand just how difficult all this is for Eve. She's had a lot to contend with, losing first her mother two years ago and now her father in such tragic circumstances. Please meet her—welcome her here. I know you'll like her. No one meeting her could fail to do that.'

His mother sighed, knowing by the tone of his voice and the look in his eye that he was determined to marry her regardless of anything she had to say. She looked at him, at his tall, lean figure, noticing how clear and compelling his pale blue eyes were as they gazed down into her own, and, as she never failed to do, she warmed to him, knowing as only a mother can how important it was for him to know he had her blessing and support on a matter such as this—regardless of any misgivings she might have.

As she relented, a softness entered her eyes as it never failed to do for, like his father before him, he always succeeded in breaking through her reserve. Marcus was a man of many complexities, who went through life with amusement and a cool recklessness, prepared to go along with most things providing none interfered with him. Sighing, she reached up and took his hand.

'Very well, Marcus. You need have no worries on my account. If she is all you say she is, then how can I fail to like her?'

'She is—and more besides. She has warm, velvety-soft violet eyes that would melt even the coldest stone,' he said with a teasing note to his voice, bending down and placing a kiss lightly on his mother's cheek, satisfied that she would come to terms, with no further argument, with what he intended doing.

'Dear me,' she murmured, receiving his kiss with a smile, 'if you begin speaking like this then I shall believe you are already halfway to being in love with her.'

'Yes—I believe I am. I have never met anyone quite like her. I am determined to marry her—and when I do, you may rest assured that it will be for all the right reasons,' Marcus smiled, straightening up and gently tweaking her cheek with his finger and thumb.

Eve was in no way disappointed when she saw Brooklands for the first time, which surprised her, for long ago, when she had made up her mind to dislike everything about Marcus Fitzalan, Brooklands had not been excluded.

The house, which was situated about a mile north of Netherley, nestled in a fold between the hills which protected it from wind and weather. There was something stately about the tall beeches that lined either side of the long winding drive leading to the house, their branches meeting overhead and virtually shutting out the sunlight.

Her first glimpse of the stately house, built of brick which had mellowed over the years, did not disappoint her in the least. It was a fine, long-fronted house with a columned porch and stables at the rear. Long French windows opened on to a rose-strewn balustraded terrace, overlooking well-maintained gardens and with lawns stretched out like thick velvet.

Eve was impressed and thought it quite remarkable that Marcus's grandfather had managed to make his way into the ranks of the landed gentry, buying land and building this great house, all from the production of coal.

The carriage came to a halt at the bottom of a short flight of steps and immediately, as if he had been waiting behind the door, Marcus came out of the house to meet them, his thick black hair glossy and brushed back from his face. He was immaculately dressed in a well-cut black suit. White silk stockings encased his muscular calves and a white cravat at his throat enhanced his dark good looks.

Stepping towards the carriage, he opened the door himself and reached inside, taking Eve's hand to help her alight after one of the servants had pulled down the steps. Despite the fact that she was in mourning she had taken particular care over her appearance, wanting so much to look her best when she was introduced to Mrs Fitzalan. Her black dress was made of silk gauze and was very simple, with a tight bodice and full skirt, the severity of it softened by a white lace collar at her throat.

On seeing her Marcus drew in a deep breath, his eyes glittering as they flicked over her with undisguised approval, from the tips of her pretty velvet slippers to her wealth of thick black hair coiled expertly about her head, making her appear older and more seductively alluring.

After greeting Lady Pemberton politely, sensing Eve's nervousness Marcus took hold of her hand, feeling her fingers tremble slightly.

'You look lovely,' he murmured in a gentle tone as he lifted her fingers to his lips, his gaze searching her face. 'I trust you suffered no ill effects from the other day when your horse bolted?'

'No. None, thank you. It would take more than that to unnerve me, Mr Fitzalan.' She smiled.

'Come and meet my mother. You can be assured of a welcome. She's looking forward to meeting you. Some of the other guests have arrived—some you are already acquainted with. Try not to be nervous.'

Eve quivered beneath his touch, thinking he looked breathtakingly handsome. She felt the force, the vital, physical power within him, and the warm grasp of his hand reassured her and she was strengthened by it. It was comforting to know there would be a large gathering. Glancing up at him, she saw he was smiling crookedly down at her.

Marcus conducted Eve and her grandmother into a large square hall with tall doorways and marble pillars. An elegant blue-carpeted staircase rose up from the centre to form a gallery. Eve's first impression of the house was one of elegance, but so intent was she on her meeting with Mrs Fitzalan that she paid little attention to her surroundings.

Mrs Fitzalan was happily conversing with her other guests but became silent when she saw Marcus. She glanced at the lovely young woman by his side and, after making a quick assessment, a feeling of relief washed over her. She liked what she saw and smiled, moving forward to welcome her and Lady Pemberton, determined they would feel in no way ill at ease during their visit to Brooklands.

'Mother, allow me to present Lady Pemberton and Miss Eve Somerville. Lady Pemberton, Miss Somerville, this is my mother.'

After her grandmother had been introduced, Eve smiled a little shyly at Marcus's mother. 'How do you do, Mrs Fitzalan,' she said politely, her first impression of Mrs Fitzalan was of her presence. Dressed in a wonderful shade of jade green, with diamonds at her throat and dripping from her ears, she looked younger than Eve had expected, a slim, elegant lady radiating calm and confidence who was completely at ease.

She had expected coldness and stiffness and was relieved to see there was neither—in fact, there were no reservations at all in the welcome. However, she did wonder how Mrs Fitzalan had reacted when her son had told her of the conditions of Eve's father's will.

'I am well, thank you, and happy to welcome you and Lady

Pemberton to Brooklands. I have heard so much about you, my dear—both from your father and Marcus—that I am glad to meet you at last. Your father was a frequent visitor—but, unfortunately, his visits were always on matters of business. Now you are here you must relax and enjoy yourself, but first you must meet our other guests, although some of them you will already know. As you see, we have quite a large gathering. After that, seeing that dinner will be a little late this evening, owing to some crisis or other in the kitchen which I hope Cook will sort out eventually—' she laughed '—I will show you the house.'

Eve and her grandmother were drawn forward and introduced to the other guests gathered in groups in the large pillared hall and in the adjacent drawing room, where servants flitted about balancing trays of drinks, offering them to the guests in order to make the time spent waiting for the meal to begin more pleasurable.

Immediately her grandmother was claimed by an acquaintance. Those unknown to Eve gave her a curious glance while others said how nice it was to see her, complimenting her on how well she looked. The fact that Marcus had casually informed them of her expected arrival earlier had already caused some arched eyebrows and given rise to speculation.

With a certain amount of indolence Marcus stood back while Eve was taken in hand by his mother. His pale blue eyes smiled as he observed, but his expression gave away nothing of his thoughts.

'You don't mind, do you, Marcus, if I take Miss Somerville away and show her the house—and perhaps take a quick look at the garden while there is still enough daylight left?'

'Of course not.' He smiled. 'Although I was hoping to do that myself.'

'Thank you. I would like that,' said Eve. 'But I should hate to take either of you away from your guests.'

'Don't worry about that,' smiled Mrs Fitzalan. 'The evening

is very informal. There are still one or two guests to arrive, but Marcus will receive them.'

Marcus raised his eyebrows, but before he could reply his mother said, 'Rest assured that I shall not neglect our other guests for too long. You can stay and entertain them, Marcus, while I get to know Miss Somerville a little better. We can gossip as we go along. No doubt the gentlemen will converse about that which is closest to their hearts—such as coal mines, how much coal they are producing and the latest in pumping engines—but I will not tolerate any discourse on the subject at the dinner table. By that time I hope it will have been exhausted and you can concentrate on more pleasant topics of conversation.'

'Very well, Mother,' Marcus said, knowing there was no irresistible argument he could raise that would have any effect on her and allow him to show Miss Somerville the house instead, 'but do not deprive us of your company for too long. All the guests have not yet arrived and I am sure they will want to be introduced to Miss Somerville before dinner.'

As Mrs Fitzalan gave her a quick tour of the house Eve took an interest in everything she saw, listening to her hostess as she chatted animatedly, clearly proud of the house her husband's father had built.

It lacked the feeling of antiquity and history that one was aware of when entering Burntwood Hall, but Brooklands had a wonderful, refreshing elegance in its modern furnishings. The decorations added lightness to the rooms—pastel shades, striped and floral wallpapers, with long windows and mirrors reflecting the light.

Eve admired the fine paintings that adorned the walls of every room, some being family portraits. She paused to examine one in particular that had pride of place on a long landing on the first floor. It was of a man in his prime, and not unlike Marcus in features.

Mrs Fitzalan paused beside her when she saw Eve's interest.

'The gentleman is my husband's father—Marcus's grandfather, founder of Atwood Mine.'

'Yes, I thought it might be. The resemblance to Mr Fitzalan is striking. What was he like, Mrs Fitzalan? Did you know him long?'

She smiled. 'Yes. He was an excellent man—of good character. He was respected by all who knew him and he worked hard all his life to achieve success, devoting all his time to his work and the affairs of the neighbourhood. When I married Marcus's father I lived here for a number of years before he died. We got on well—and I fell in love with Brooklands the minute I laid eyes on it.'

'Who would not? I think it's a wonderful house, Mrs Fitzalan. It's so different from Burntwood Hall, which is steeped in antiquity.'

'Ah—but no worse for that, my dear. A house as old as Burntwood Hall I am sure will have some fascinating stories to tell—they enrich a house, I always think, and make it much more interesting for the inhabitants. But I'm so glad you like Brooklands. Perhaps it will make your decision as to whether or not you marry Marcus a little easier.'

Eve flushed. 'Yes—perhaps.'

Eventually they came out on to the terrace where the seductive scent of roses wafted about them. Up until then their conversation had been of matters in general and about the house, but now Mrs Fitzalan looked at Eve intently, saying unexpectedly, 'Marcus has a habit of springing surprises on me, Miss Somerville—and I was never more surprised than when he told me of your father's will, of the conditions he imposed on you both. How do you feel about it?'

Eve was startled and unprepared for the question. 'Why, I confess I was as surprised as you, Mrs Fitzalan—at the time.'

'And have you had time to consider what you will do?' She smiled when she saw the confusion in Eve's eyes, for it was clear she had not expected her to broach the subject quite so soon, if at all. 'I'm sorry, my dear,' she said. 'You'd be quite within your rights to tell me to mind my own business. I do tend to let my tongue run away with me which frequently gets me into trouble. But it is a matter that is important to all of us.'

'Of—of course,' Eve found herself stammering. 'There's no need to apologise, Mrs Fitzalan.'

'It's just that Marcus can be so serious at times—and I see so little of him. I do try to keep abreast of what's going on, but it's so difficult. He's either supervising the running of the mines, away on some business or other, or dining with friends.'

'I do understand, but, in truth, neither of us has had the opportunity to discuss the matter properly. But we both agree that it would be as well to get to know each other a little better before we commit ourselves to anything. It might turn out that we are incompatible.'

'That's very sensible. But Atwood Mine is important to you, is it not?'

'Yes,' she replied, her eyes meeting those of the older woman's steadily. 'I would be lying if I said otherwise—and I know it means a great deal to Mr Fitzalan. He is loath to let the opportunity of being part-owner of his father's mine slip through his fingers—but I only hope he considers carefully what marriage to me will entail—should I agree to marry him, of course.'

'He does tend to let his enthusiasm run away with him— like his obsession for a new shaft he is sinking at the moment at Pendle Hill. He is trying to do it as quickly as possible in order to get the mine producing before two of the old pits are exhausted—which, I have to say, is proving extremely difficult and takes up nearly all his time. But he never does anything without careful thought.'

Mention of the new mine Marcus was sinking brought to mind the day she had witnessed just how difficult it was proving to be at first hand, causing her to remember the explosions as he was trying to blast his way through the rock and how terrified her horse had been, which had caused it to bolt. She also remembered their ride back to Burntwood Hall and their long conversation, which had enabled her to understand him a little better, and to make her think of him a little less severely, but she said none of this to Mrs Fitzalan.

'This matter between the two of you is important to him,' Mrs Fitzalan continued, 'but no matter how important Atwood Mine is to him—and I must tell you that he never forgave me for selling the lease to your father all those years ago after the death of my dear husband—I know he will put it aside while he thinks of that.'

'I sincerely hope so, Mrs Fitzalan.'

'Marcus is marked with the same proud arrogance and indomitable will as his father and grandfather before him. He is like a whirlwind, my dear. Anyone meeting him for the first time cannot help but be swept along with him—so, if you will allow me to give you some advice,' she said kindly and persuasively, 'do not let him pressure you into making a decision before you have thought it through very carefully, will you? This is not just about Atwood Mine. It's about you and Marcus—and your future happiness together. It is imperative to you both that you make the right decision.'

'I know and I don't intend to.'

'Good girl.'

At that moment one of the servants came out on to the terrace. Mrs Fitzalan had a quiet word with her before turning back to Eve, a look of exasperation on her face.

'You must excuse me, my dear. It would seem the crisis in the kitchen has yet to be resolved and needs my intervention. Would you like to return to the others?'

Eve smiled. 'No, not just yet. It's such a lovely evening I think I'll stay here for a while longer, if that's all right, Mrs Fitzalan, and probably take a walk in the garden.'

'Of course. I'll be back shortly.'

As Ruth Fitzalan went to sort out the domestic crisis in the kitchen she felt better for having met Eve Somerville and

could see why Marcus had spoken so highly of her. Any
doubts she had felt prior to meeting her had been quashed the
moment they had been introduced—and when she had seen
the way Marcus had looked at her. His eyes had held an open
admiration and something else, something she had never seen
in his eyes before, and it gladdened her heart. There was an
open honesty about Eve that she found refreshing and she
found herself intensely curious to know her better.

She appeared sensitive and reserved, and yet she suspected
Eve was no stupid innocent who would only open her mouth
to say yes and no. She recognised a strong will, someone who
would not be bullied—which would do Marcus good. Yes, she
approved, and if they decided to marry, then bringing Atwood
Mine back into the family was just something she would have
to come to terms with. However, there was still the problem
of Angela to be surmounted, she thought, having no idea that
the two were acquaintances of long standing.

Angela, who would no doubt have arrived by now with her
parents, was a young woman different in temperament to Eve.
It would be interesting to see what her reaction would be when
she was introduced to Miss Somerville and realised she had a
rival for her son's affections—not only in the shape of a lovely
young woman, she thought with considerable amusement, but
also a coal mine.

Eve watched Mrs Fitzalan go before perching on the edge
of the stone balustrade that fronted the terrace, sighing deeply
as she tried to picture herself living there, of being the wife
of Marcus Fitzalan. She tried to think of him dispassionately,
not to let her emotions become involved, because if she did
she was afraid she was in danger of being overwhelmed by
him. He had a way of intruding into her thoughts when for so
long her desire had been to keep him out.

He was different to any man she had ever met, and somehow the resentment she had built up against him over the years
no longer seemed important now that she had got to know him
a little. Despite their differences he had made a deep impres-

sion on her, this she could not deny, but she could not say that she really liked him—at least, not in the way one should when contemplating marriage. He was arrogant and accustomed to obedience from those about him, a man who set himself above others—all traits she did not admire.

But then, never had she met a man who was so alive, so full of confidence, a man who both stimulated and excited her, and he had a sensuous way of regarding her that made her physically aware of herself as a woman. He was certainly attractive, and seeing his home and meeting his mother presented some temptation.

With these thoughts occupying her mind, she breathed deeply of the sweet-scented air and let her eyes wander in the gathering dusk, looking with appreciation at the flower-filled gardens spread out before her, and a line of dark yews that marched down to the river beyond. The garden was laid out in formal flower beds forming a circle, the centre piece being a fountain where water spouted from a cornucopia held by three exquisitely carved cherubs, the fine mist of its spray drifting on the slight breeze.

She was about to step off the terrace into the garden when her attention was caught by a woman who emerged from a door of the house, trailing her shawl carelessly behind her as she walked aimlessly towards the fountain where she sat on its rim, gazing down and drawing her fingers over the surface of the water. She wore an oyster-coloured silk dress, and despite the chill of the evening her shoulders were bare, but she seemed oblivious to it.

Eve stood watching her in fascination, wondering who she could be, but then, as the woman turned slightly, she froze in recognition. It was Angela Stephenson. Her mouth went suddenly dry and clammy; sweat broke out on her brow on seeing Angela again after all this time, and the bitterness over the way Angela had tricked and deceived her, then claimed Leslie for herself, had not lessened and went searing through Eve like a knife.

Numb with shock, she watched as Angela threw back her head and looked up at the moon, closing her eyes, a beatific, dreaming smile on her face. Suddenly a man appeared out of the house and stood looking around the garden, as if he was searching for someone. He was about to turn and go back inside, but on seeing Angela he walked towards her.

Angela watched his approach without moving her position, and when he stood close, looking down into her upturned face, he smiled and sat beside her. The man was Marcus and Eve stared at them fixedly, feeling a searing stab of jealousy pierce her heart. She clenched her teeth and dug her fingernails into the palms of her hands to stop herself from crying out.

They seemed relaxed together, close, even, and when he rose he took her hand and she stood beside him, handing him her shawl which he slowly draped around her shoulders. They were in profile so Eve was unable to see the expressions on their faces, but she sensed it was intimate. With a familiarity that seemed to be born of long acquaintance, Angela tucked her hand possessively into the crook of Marcus's arm and the two strolled leisurely back towards the house, mounting a flight of stone steps and going inside.

But before they did so Angela seemed to sense Eve's gaze and turned her head to where Eve stood observing them. For a moment their eyes collided and they stared at each other, and then Eve saw her smile, not in the least put out about being observed, but there was something smug, almost a complacent self-satisfaction, in that smile, a smile that sent her a message of possession. She shivered suddenly, as if a cold hand had reached out and gripped her heart. Seeing Marcus and Angela together was like a stone being thrown into a quiet pool.

Chapter Eight

Just when Eve thought she was beginning to relax there was a tension inside her when she returned to the others and came face to face with Angela. She felt sick and trembling inside at the mere thought of confronting this woman who had caused her so much misery in the past. She had already decided to keep the fact that she had been a silent observer of the intimate little scene from Marcus, considering it had nothing to do with her and that she did not know him well enough to speculate on what his relationship with Angela might be.

Angela did not seem surprised to see her at Brooklands, giving Eve the distinct impression that she already knew all about the situation that existed between herself and Marcus. Her sharp, woman's instinct told her that she had a rival in her old adversary, which made her determined to be on her guard.

Close to, she saw Angela was still quite exquisite, her auburn hair arranged superbly in soft curls with ringlets on either side of her face, her mouth full and pouting, her cheek bones angular, causing her hazel eyes to slant a little. Eve could see that she was all woman and very much aware of the fact. Angela exuded a sultry sensuality that men would find impossible to resist—even Marcus Fitzalan, it would seem. She was very cool and fixed Eve with a hard stare, and then she smiled, a tight, carefully controlled smile, her eyes glittering, hard and ruthless as of old, and full of triumph.

Unaware that there was any animosity between them, Marcus introduced them, surprised to discover they already knew each other—he had taken little notice of Eve's companions on the day they had met at Atwood Fair and that Angela had been one of them. But it quickly became plain to him that the two were far from being friends when he heard the soft, sharp intake of Eve's breath and felt her stiffen beside him, and saw her fingers close tightly round her fan, her knuckles straining sharply beneath her white skin. The atmosphere between them was charged with something so palpable he could almost feel it, touch it, and he was at once puzzled by it and curious as to the reason. Seeing the initial look that passed between the two ladies, with the instinct of a seafaring man he feared a squall approaching, albeit a mild one.

Instead of turning her back and walking away, which was what Eve was tempted to do, courageously she stayed and faced Angela and forced a smile to her lips, giving no indication to either Marcus or Angela how painful this meeting was for her.

'Hello, Angela,' she said, her voice surprisingly level, telling herself she had nothing to fear from her, but her heart was palpitating nevertheless and she felt stifled. 'You are well, I hope.'

Angela inclined her head slightly and showed her pearl white teeth in a simulated smile, resentment and jealousy beginning to rise in her eyes which seemed to narrow a little, shining and as hard as a cat's, her look conveying to Eve that nothing was changed between them and that she was displeased by the attention Marcus was showing her.

'Perfectly. How long is it since we last saw each other? It must be ages,' she said, speaking in a cold and controlled voice—and lightly contemptuous, Eve's sharp ears detected, which made her hackles rise.

'Three years, I believe,' she answered, steeling herself,

equally as cold, feeling as though she were encased in ice, refusing to feel intimidated by Angela.

'Of course. It was on the day of Atwood Fair…if my memory serves me correctly.'

If Angela intended to embarrass Eve by referring to that day she was mistaken, for Eve did not look in the least put out. 'There was never anything wrong with your memory, as I remember, Angela,' she replied with a touch of humour. She turned to Marcus who was watching them in puzzlement. 'Angela and I were together at the fair that day—you remember, don't you, Mr Fitzalan? The day you so shamefully ruined my reputation,' she said pointedly, with a soft smile curving her lips.

With the eyes of both ladies upon him Marcus smiled down at Eve wickedly. 'How could I ever forget it? That day will remain imprinted on my mind for all time. But I do not remember seeing you there, Angela.'

'You wouldn't,' said Eve quickly on a teasing note, trying to make light of the humiliation she had felt three years ago, while trembling inside. 'It wasn't Angela who approached you.'

The byplay between Eve and Marcus caused Angela's eyes to flare with sudden anger. She lifted her chin a little in annoyance, trying not to show it as she gazed at Marcus. 'I was not acquainted with you at the time, Marcus,' she purred, her voice deep and provocative when she addressed him, throwing him a dazzlingly provocative smile.

'No,' Eve said, her beautiful brows rising slightly, the look she cast Angela making it clear that she remembered all Angela was guilty of where Eve was concerned that day, and that she was made of sterner stuff than Angela gave her credit for. 'We were just foolish young girls intent on mischief, as I remember, when the watchful eyes of our chaperon happened to wander for a while. But this is not the time to reminisce, Angela, and what occurred is ancient history now. Is that not so, Mr Fitzalan?'

Marcus's eyes twinkled and he smiled down at her with easy good humour. 'Oh—not all that ancient. I still reflect on what occurred with a certain amount of pleasure,' he murmured with a rueful, conspiratorial smile.

Sensing the tension inside Eve and feeling her tremble beside him, Marcus didn't need to be told that she and Angela were no longer friends; in fact, he was sure that if they were to find themselves together in an empty room their claws would come out and there would be all-out war. He knew Eve was finding it extremely difficult to maintain her calm demeanor and quickly rescued her from the situation.

'Please excuse us, Angela. I have to introduce Miss Somerville to one or two guests before we go into dinner.'

'Of course,' she replied, her voice stilted.

Eve shot Marcus a grateful smile when they moved on, ignoring the sudden noise of Angela's fan snapping shut behind them.

'You look pale—you were trembling,' he said softly when they were out of earshot and Angela had turned away, keeping his eyes on Eve with uncomfortable steadiness.

'Was I? I wasn't aware of it,' Eve replied, sounding terse, trying to hold on to her composure but her anger getting the better of her, making her want to lash out at someone, and pretending that she couldn't feel Marcus's eyes on her, querying, trying to probe, gently.

'I get the distinct impression that you and Angela are no longer the best of friends,' he said quietly lest they be overheard, steering her away from the groups of people gathered around, some sitting, some standing, conversing animatedly while waiting to be summoned into dinner, his mother flitting from group to group like a firefly, laughing and talking to friends of long standing.

'Friends? The fact of having lost the man I was to marry to a woman who contrived it to happen does not constitute the greatest bond of affection between us,' Eve confessed bitterly. 'Angela is adept at manipulating and controlling people—in fact, there is no one better, no one more subtle. People become like putty in her fingers. She tried very hard to destroy me, and almost succeeded. She was not my true friend. She never was—although she always pretended to be when it suited her. She betrayed me in the worst possible way.'

'By marrying Leslie Stephenson, the man you hoped to marry yourself?'

'Yes. And I don't think you need me to tell you how it came about,' she said cuttingly, accusingly, turning to look up at Marcus and fixing him with a hard stare, remembering the part he had played in her fall from grace. Her anger was now all aimed at him. 'Despite the lightness of my tone and touch of humour when I spoke to Angela, I hold you both equally responsible for what I suffered as a consequence of that day.'

Before Marcus could utter a word in his defence she had turned abruptly to speak to one of the guests, hearing him draw a sudden breath as she did so, knowing her thrust had gone home.

The dining room was elegantly furnished, lit by a huge crystal chandelier suspended above the exquisitely arrayed table that glittered and sparkled, the room becoming a kaleidoscope of colours when everyone was assembled. A variety of dishes of different flavours and delicacies was served, all equally delicious. Everyone seemed in high spirits, with laughter and conversation animated and of general topics of the day.

The meal passed pleasantly enough and Eve, still recovering from her confrontation with Angela, was relieved that she was seated at the opposite end of the long table, just far enough away to avoid any discourse. Although even when Angela wasn't looking at her, Eve felt herself undergoing her scrutiny, and when their eyes did meet Angela would flash one of her smug, knowing smiles, leaving Eve silently fuming.

She realised that getting angry accomplished nothing, and that was exactly what Angela had set out to do—and succeeded, she thought, reproaching herself when she recalled the harsh words she had directed at Marcus. She took several deep breaths in an attempt to calm her nerves, but there was no room for anything in her heart other than anger and a vast disappointment, for no matter how polite and persuasive Marcus might be towards her, she realised that she meant no more to him than a means to an end. When he had accompanied her on her ride he had told her that he would be happy to marry her without the mine—and fool that she had been to believe him.

Later, the gentlemen joined the ladies in the drawing room, having remained behind to partake of the customary after-dinner port and brandy. Every so often Marcus would meet Eve's gaze but he was in no hurry to speak to her as she mingled easily with the other guests, then sat for a while companionably with her grandmother, taking great care to avoid coming into contact with Angela again. He watched her absorb the atmosphere of the house, confident that she could not fail to be impressed by Brooklands—and by his mother who was, as always, charm and graciousness personified.

Eventually he managed to draw her away from the others, determined to speak to her alone, sensitive to the fact that she was still smarting over her meeting with Angela. They stood on the terrace—on the very spot where Eve had witnessed the intimate scene between himself and Angela earlier.

Eve was unable to cast thoughts of Angela from her mind, for she had acted like a pall on the whole evening. But she did experience a feeling of anticipation on finding herself alone with Marcus on the rose-scented terrace on a starlit night—alone, and yet not alone, for they were within sound of the others in the drawing room, their voices and the tinkling notes of the pianoforte in the background…and the image of Angela with her sly, insolent smile standing between them.

Marcus's manner was misleadingly indolent, his expression giving nothing away of his thoughts, but his eyes were questioning and forever watchful. Among so many people and seated apart at the dining table, they'd had no opportunity to converse, but his concentrated gaze had watched Eve carefully all evening, glad to see she looked relaxed, and that she showed no sign of the tension and anger created in her by her encounter with Angela earlier, but he was not deceived and knew it was still there, simmering away below the surface.

But whatever it was that caused so much animosity between Eve and Angela, Marcus did not feel as tolerant of Angela as he had. However, he was determined not to let it interfere with what was important to himself and Eve or allow either of them to forget the purpose of her visit to Brooklands this evening. He was impatient to have the matter that was uppermost in both their minds resolved between them, and seeing how perfectly she blended in with her surroundings, he was certain he almost had his quarry and was determined to pin her down before the evening was over.

Moving a little away from her, he leaned casually against the balustrade and looked to where she stood, her profile etched against the star-strewn sky, her face gleaming like alabaster in the white glow of the moon which bathed the garden in an incandescent light. She was proud and fine, and he wanted her. He suddenly realised that he wanted her more now than he had in the beginning. He wanted the challenge of her, to experience her goodness, and to see how she would come to terms with her passion when she was roused, to understand it.

He savoured the soft ivory tones of her face and the long gracious lines of her body, which were evident beneath the black silk of her dress. He liked the way her neck rose graceful and stem-like from her slender shoulders, and the way she moved, her steps light, with an unconscious swing to her body. Apart from her face and the white lace of the collar at her throat she was all black, as black as a blackthorn—and just as prickly if she was touched on the raw.

But beneath it all she was an innocent, which was such a rarity in the circles in which he moved when in London, where almost every woman of marriageable age he came into contact

with possessed the same grasping, immoral drive that moti-
vated women like Angela Stephenson, who, he was just beginning to realise, had all the trappings of a troublemaker.

Eve sighed and met the intensity of Marcus's wintry blue
gaze, beginning to relax as she became lulled by the quiet and
privacy of the terrace and the enveloping dim light, becoming
impelled by the sensations he roused in her, which became
stronger each time they met. She smiled softly.

'I feel that I must apologise for my harsh words earlier. I—
I did not intend allowing Angela to provoke me so easily. I
knew what she was like. I should be inured to her by now,
don't you think. I—it's just that I always swore that when we
met—which was inevitable that we would one day at just such
an occasion as this—I would never let her know how much
she hurt me when she married Leslie.'

'I understand,' Marcus murmured gently. 'Taking into account that I knew you hoped to marry him, and knowing that
Angela did become his wife—I confess that I did not know
the two of you were already acquainted. I realise now that I
should not have been so insensitive as to introduce you. Am
I forgiven?'

Eve smiled, beginning to melt beneath the warmth of his
gaze as he studied her closely. 'Of course.'

'Thank you. And so, Miss Somerville,' Marcus said, having
no desire to talk about Angela or Leslie Stephenson at this
moment, and wanting them both cast down into oblivion,
'what is your opinion of Brooklands? Is it to your liking?'

'Yes. I have to say it's a lovely house,' she replied, unable
to keep the admiration she felt for his home out of her voice,
while at the same time wanting so much to ask him about his
relationship with Angela, but was too proud to do so.

'I'm happy you think so,' he said, speaking softly, and looking at him Eve thought he sounded genuinely pleased.

'I remember you telling me you have two brothers,' she
said by way of conversation. 'I do not imagine they get home
very often if they are in the Navy.'

'No, which is unfortunate for my mother. She misses them both dreadfully.'

'Didn't either of them consider joining you in the mining industry?'

'No. They both take after my mother's family in that. Two of her uncles and one of her brothers were naval people.'

'And did the sea not appeal to you?'

A smile touched his lips. 'No. I take after my father and grandfather—which is fortunate, for I do have a position to uphold in the house.'

'And were you close to your father?'

'Very, until he was killed so tragically in Atwood Mine. But what of you, Miss Somerville? You were close to your father, were you not?'

A look of desolation entered Eve's eyes as she felt the pain of memory. 'Yes, I was.'

Marcus looked at her searchingly. 'He always spoke of you with affection.'

'Both my parents were exemplary. My only regret is that before my father died I saw so little of him. He chose to spend so much of his time away from home—as you will know, Mr Fitzalan,' she said with a faint hint of accusation, unable to conceal the bitterness she still felt, aware as she spoke that a constraint had come between them.

Marcus's eyes narrowed. 'Away from you, I think you mean,' he said quietly.

'Yes. That is what I mean,' she admitted, having subdued her feelings for so long that she was unable to prevent them bubbling to the surface. 'He was always at the mine—or with you. I missed so many precious weeks before he died—and when he did come home I would have to sit and listen to him talking about the mine, about you—of your attributes, of which there were so many—and I would feel such pain. Tell me, have you ever been jealous?' she asked softly.

'Jealous? No. I do not believe so.'

'Well, I was jealous of you. Silly, isn't it?' she said, giving a bitter, quivering little laugh. 'But I was. I was so jealous I wanted to scream every time my father spoke your name. He would listen to no wrong said about you—and even after that unfortunate incident at Atwood Fair you still remained above reproach in his eyes. He refused to consider defending my honour by insisting that you account for *your* actions. He said the fault was all mine.'

As she spoke, remembering, her eyes became stormy and malevolent. Her face was like an icon, her eyes luminous with unshed tears and exaggeratedly large in her heart-shaped face as she looked at him.

Marcus nodded slightly. So that was it. Now he understood the reason for her coldness, her hostility. It wasn't just the humiliation she had suffered at his hands on the day of Atwood Fair that had brought about her strong resentment. She had resented the time her father had spent with him.

'What can I say? Forgive me. I never knew.'

'Would it have made any difference if you had?'

'That I cannot answer.'

'I know. But how could you have known? Apart from the unfortunate circumstances of our first encounter you hardly knew I existed. And why should you?'

'But I did. I continued to think of you for a long time afterwards.'

'Really! You surprise me. After accusing me to my face of being an overindulged spoiled child—the type you hold in contempt, I believe you said—you cannot have thought of me with favour.'

'Forgive me. I was very angry.'

'Yes, you were—and with good reason,' she admitted on a sigh. 'You did not say anything I did not deserve.' She cast him a thin smile. 'My father would have agreed with you.'

'Perhaps—but it is clear to me that his absence from Burntwood Hall for the last months of his life continues to trouble you a great deal.'

She shook her head a little sadly, a whimsical smile breaking through. 'No. It did, but not any more. I learned to come to terms with it a long time ago.'

'Have you? Forgive me, but I am not convinced—and contrary to what you may believe, we were not always together. I have many business concerns which did not involve your father and which required a great deal of my time.'

'Yes—I know that now. I am being very foolish. I should not be speaking like this.'

Marcus sighed deeply, sorry for the anguish she must have felt for so long. 'You must have realised how difficult those last weeks were for your father—that his work kept him going, kept his mind occupied and off his illness. You, more than anyone, will know there were times when his pain was too hard for him to bear. He knew it could only get worse and that eventually he would become confined to his bed—something he looked on with absolute dread.'

'I know.'

'Do not blame him for paying too much attention to his work instead of remaining at home—he would have had too much time on his hands to brood about what was to happen to him. It was not intentional and was not done to hurt you. In fact—hard though it is to accept—perhaps the carriage accident was a blessing in disguise. It saved him a great deal of suffering.'

They both fell silent for several moments until Marcus said at length, determined to discuss the subject uppermost in his mind, 'Tell me, do you feel drawn to Brooklands—enough to make it your home?'

Eve hesitated, her expression becoming tight once more, for she realised he was about to ask her the question she had been dreading, but one she knew she must face sooner or later.

'I have already told you that I like it very much.'

'That is no answer. You are being evasive.'

'No. I know what you are suggesting,' she said coolly.

'Then what is your answer?'

Their eyes met and held and, for some reason Eve could

not explain, she knew she did not want to refuse. But then, how could she? she asked herself with bitter irony. What else could she do? What else was she fit for except going to live with her grandmother or her Aunt Shona? Whereas marriage to Marcus Fitzalan would ensure her a lifetime of security—and she would inherit half of Atwood Mine and in so doing hold on to a part of her past.

But she had no illusions. The kind of love that should exist between a husband and wife did not come into her decision, for it was the kind of love that had once existed between her parents—the kind of love she had never experienced and could never hope to if she was to enter into a cold and impersonal marriage of convenience with a man who would marry her for one reason only. Despite his words to the contrary when he had escorted her from Pendle Hill back to Burntwood Hall the previous week, Marcus Fitzalan had no more interest in her beyond the mine that marriage to her would bring him.

Eve looked at him, her face surprisingly calm as she prepared to tell him her decision, but her voice was strained, leaving Marcus in no doubt of the difficulty she had found in reaching her conclusion.

'It is a strange situation, is it not? We had only ever met once in our lives before the day of the funeral, and yet we find ourselves drawn together by my father. Normally I would scorn such a union and despise my father for placing the necessity before me.'

'Necessity?' Marcus asked suddenly.

'Yes. There is no other word for it. We each recognise the advantages of the conditions he laid down. We both want Atwood Mine. About that we are very definite. Short of marrying Gerald—which I have already told you is out of the question—the cards are stacked heavily against me. If I do not agree to marry you, you may not gain anything but you do not lose anything either, whereas I stand to lose a great deal. The way I see it, I really have no choice. I am between the devil and the deep blue sea. Beggars can't be choosers, Mr Fitzalan, so—what can I say other than, yes, I will marry you.'

In the dim light Marcus's face was suddenly grim, his dark eyebrows drawn together in a straight line.

'You are extremely forthright, Miss Somerville.'

'That is a natural characteristic of mine.'

'Do you always speak your mind?'

'Yes. Why? Does it offend you?'

'Not at all. Plain speaking is a quality I admire—providing it is tempered with tact and one knows when to keep one's opinions to oneself so as not to give offence.'

Eve looked at him sharply. 'Are you criticising me, Mr Fitzalan?'

Marcus's jaw tightened and his eyes glittered, his lips curving in slight scorn as he regarded her coolly, having hoped that when she finally agreed to become his wife she would have done so with a little more enthusiasm instead of the frigid politeness of a stranger.

'I would not presume. However, you are right—and I accept I have nothing to lose and much to gain. You are not obliged to marry me, so the choice is yours entirely. But I had hoped that, in making up your mind to become my wife, you would make your decision to do so sound less like you were going to your execution,' he said, his tone biting and angry.

'I cannot help how I feel,' she flared, an angry pink flush staining her cheeks. 'You can hardly expect me to be over the moon at the prospect. Dear Lord! I don't want to marry you. I don't want to marry anyone—but I am determined to make the best of it.'

'Then for *that* I suppose I must be thankful,' Marcus replied with cutting scorn. 'I know you must have tried to find a way out of this, but unless you are prepared to leave Atwood altogether and go and live in Cumbria, then there isn't one that I can see.'

'I know that. I have almost turned myself inside out trying to find some way of avoiding this, but it is truly impossible.'

'So it is settled, then?'

Eve took a deep, shuddering breath. 'Yes.'

'Then since we have reached an understanding we will announce our betrothal at once and be married just as soon as you are out of mourning.'

'Oh, no,' she said quickly. 'I do not wish to wait. The sooner the better.' She smiled with slight irony when she saw him arch his eyebrows in questionable surprise. 'Not because of any romantic inclinations I might feel towards yourself, you understand, but because I have no wish to be at Burntwood Hall when Gerald arrives to take up residence.'

This was better than Marcus had hoped for. 'And when do you expect him to arrive?'

'In about a month, I think.'

'Very well. We will be married within the month—just as soon as it can be arranged. However, no matter what our feelings are for each other, I must insist that we make it appear to the world that we live amicably together. Is that understood?'

There was a warning underlying the lightness to his words that Eve was fully aware of. 'Yes, I understand perfectly.'

'And you have no objections to this?'

'No. Providing you abide by the bargain we made.'

His eyes narrowed. 'Bargain? Please—refresh my memory. What bargain was that?'

'That ours will be a marriage in name only.'

'Yes, I remember saying that—and I meant it. But I will make it clear here and now, Eve, that it is not a situation I will allow to persist indefinitely. Do you really expect me to live with you in marriage and not complete our union?'

He rose from where he was sitting perched on the edge of the balustrade, intimidating Eve with his imposing height. His eyes glittered in the dim light like steel flints and she eyed him warily, aware of the tension between them.

'No—but—I—I hoped—'

'Then don't,' he said sharply. 'I shall keep the bargain I

made until there is better understanding between us—but it will be only a temporary situation of short duration; a situation, as your husband, I shall feel at liberty to remedy any time I choose, and there is not a law in the land that will say I do not have the right.'

His jibe, savage and taunting, flicked over Eve like a whip-lash, and his eyes glittered with a fire that burned her raw. For a moment she stared at him in horror and shrank back into the shadows, her eyes darkening, both frightened and fascinated by his anger, but then she seemed to burst into life as her chin came up and her lips tightened, her eyes blazing in defiance at what he implied.

'You mean you would force me?'

The smile that broke across his white teeth was infuriating. 'I have never forced my attentions on a woman who didn't want me—and I feel no temptation to do so now. Despite your hostile manner and waspish tongue—which, I might tell you, I will not endure when we are married—I have seen in your eyes and felt on your lips that which gives me hope for better things. I do not think, when you become my wife, I shall have too long to wait before things change.'

Temper flared in Eve's eyes as hot, angry words bubbled to her lips. 'Then I think I should make it plain here and now that I have no intention of changing—and if I do not live up to your expectations then you can go to the devil and be damned.'

She was so angry that she turned abruptly and moved across the terrace, intending to return to the drawing room, but before she realised what was happening Marcus had quickly crossed the short space that divided them with the speed of a cat and she found herself pinned against the cold stone wall of the house, his fingers biting cruelly into her shoulders, too tightly for either propriety or comfort.

For the first time sheer terror gripped Eve when she saw the blazing fury in his eyes. They were so compelling that she was unable to look away, and his face was so close to hers that she could smell the brandy on his breath, feel the heat of it wafting her flesh.

'Take your hands off me, you—you brute,' she hissed. 'If you don't I shall scream.'

He smiled, ignoring her plea, his eyes becoming focused on her lips as he lowered his mouth closer to hers. 'I don't think you'll do that,' he murmured, his lips finding hers at last, happy to discover they were every bit as soft and sweet as he remembered them to be, when he had first sampled their delights three years ago at Atwood Fair.

When he placed his mouth on hers Eve felt her stomach plunge. She panicked, raising her hand to push him away, but instead she found herself pushing herself closer, feeling the hardness of his body pressed close to hers. Suddenly his arms slackened a little and one hand began caressing the back of her neck, causing a strange, warm feeling to begin sweeping over her, a feeling that was new and exciting. His lips, which were hard and demanding at first, began to soften and he kissed her deeply, slowly and deliberately, and Eve felt fire shoot through her veins followed by a melting sweetness as her own lips began to respond and open under his, allowing him to drink his fill, satisfying the thirst that had tormented him for so long.

It was a kiss that seemed to last forever, and for one mad, glorious moment Eve wanted it to. For the first time in her life she felt an unknown joy awaking inside her as she was carried along on a wave of pleasure and exciting sensations began to stir inside her, sensations she had experienced only once before in her life, and he had been the one to bring them to her awareness then—so long ago, now it seemed. She felt bereft when his lips left hers, only to sigh with unbelievable bliss as they proceeded to travel ever so slowly down her neck, burying themselves in the soft curve of her throat where a pulse was beating just beneath the surface of her skin. Feeling his mouth pass over her naked flesh was like a flutter of wings, causing the blood to pound through her veins with the heat of desire.

Realising at last what was happening, that his tender assault on her body was succeeding in breaking down all her resistance, Eve was shocked to her core. She half-opened her eyes, as she forced herself out of her rapturous state, only to find his already fixed on hers.

'Please, Marcus—don't do this,' she begged softly, visibly shaken by what he had done.

But he ignored her plea and folded her in his arms once more, tasting her unresisting, willing lips, moist, fragrant, as sweet as honey, feeling her body pressed close to his, so firm, yet soft and yielding, her rounded breasts taut against him.

Eve purred like a kitten to his touch, which was incredibly sensual, feeling a quiver build up in the pit of her stomach, not knowing what she wanted from him, only that she was engulfed with an unfulfilled, aching need, having nothing but imaginings with which to compare the sweet agony of passion that rolled over her in huge waves.

When Marcus broke their embrace and lifted his head, his body throbbing uncontrollably, his senses reeling, he found himself wanting her with a fierceness that took his breath away. Never had he seen anyone so lovely.

'If I could have my way, I would take my pleasure of you here and now,' he murmured looking deep into her eyes, his lips hovering over hers, warm and dangerous, 'and awaken all the passion I sense you are capable of feeling.'

Still reeling from his devastating kiss, Eve stared up at him helplessly, wanting nothing more than for him to carry her away and make love to her, knowing the ecstasy of their union would bring her a wondering awe, but she was ashamed of her thoughts, ashamed that she was behaving in exactly the same manner as she had three years ago at Atwood Fair.

Looking down at her, Marcus saw how her lips suddenly trembled and that her face was chalk white beneath the mass of her black hair. Her eyes shone with bravely held tears, causing something inside him to melt. The sight of her aroused every protective instinct in him. She looked so young, so innocent, that it would be easy to take advantage of her, but he couldn't. He did not release her, but they stood and looked deep into each other's eyes, and for a moment something passed between them and each knew what the other was thinking.

Eve gazed up at him, mesmerised by his eyes that burned like twin, blue-white flames. She saw a softening in their depths as a solitary tear ran slowly down her cheek, which he wiped away gently with his finger.

'You are not as opposed to me as you would like me to believe,' he said, having read her response with his instinctive sensitivity, his smile one of satisfaction that he had just proved his point. 'However, I apologise, Eve. I did not mean this to happen. Please don't worry. I meant what I said and promise you will go unmolested after we are married, until the time comes when you want it otherwise.'

He let his hands fall to his sides and stepped back, leaving her trembling so badly she had to lean against the wall for support. Her heart was thumping so hard. The cold rationality in her head was telling her not to get involved with him, that it was sheer madness to marry a man who could render her so defenceless, and yet the emotional upheaval he had brought to her heart made her crave for more of what he wanted to give. Everything in her body had responded, shamelessly, wantonly.

'Please compose yourself. I think it is time we went back inside. I also think now is as good a time as any to announce our betrothal, don't you—after I have had a quiet word with my mother and your grandmother, of course. I will call on you at Burntwood Hall in a day or so to discuss the matter further.'

'I—I may not be there,' she said stiffly, still trembling slightly from what had happened between them.

'Oh?'

'I—I am going to stay with my friend Emma Parkinson—

she lives just outside Atwood on the Leeds road. Her mother has kindly invited me to stay with them for a few days. She thinks the change will be good for me.'

Marcus nodded. 'I'm sure she's right. I'll call on you there if need be,' he replied and, taking her arm, guided her into the drawing room.

Chapter Nine

Travelling back to Burntwood Hall, it was hard for Eve to think of herself as being betrothed to Marcus Fitzalan. The very idea of becoming his wife filled her with an excited dread. Whenever they met he made her feel defensive and there was a tension between them that was palpable. She was always in control when in the company of anyone else—but this was not the case when she was with him. She was far too aware of him and he disturbed her in a way she found uncomfortable and difficult to deal with. No one had ever had this effect on her before.

She told herself that marriage to him would be a disaster and it was not too late to call it off—to raise the drawbridge and exist in a state of siege, to retreat to the sanity she had known before she had been made aware of his existence—but remembering his kiss and the things he had said to her brought a wave of crimson to her cheeks.

Every nerve ending in her body had screamed out to her and all he had done was kiss her. What would it be like when he made love to her? This thought caused her heart to race and her eyes to open wide in alarm, realising that already she was thinking along those lines. He had told her he would not attempt to consummate their marriage until she was ready— but how long would she be able to hold out, seeing him day

after day and knowing he was sleeping close by night after
night. How long would she want to?

Sitting beside her grandmother—who was delighted with
the outcome of the evening—she felt peculiar, warm stirrings
deep inside her and her tongue passed over her lips. She could
still taste the brandy Marcus had been drinking earlier, and
they continued to tingle, feeling soft after his kiss. She drew
in a deep breath which she released as a shuddering sigh, causing her grandmother to turn and look at her curiously.

'Are you all right, Eve?'

'Yes—yes. Perfectly, thank you.' She smiled, laying her
head back on the upholstery and closing her eyes as so many
conflicting and chaotic emotions chased round and round inside her head—bewilderment, anger and humiliation, and yet
one thing rose clear and certain. She had not wanted Marcus
to stop kissing her. She could not begin to fathom what her
feelings were for him—but one thing she did know was that
she couldn't stop thinking about him.

All through the following day Eve reflected on her evening
at Brooklands—and not least on her meeting with Angela. She
recalled the moment when she had returned to the drawing
room with Marcus, when he had drawn her to his side and
announced that she had done him the honour of agreeing to
become his wife. Involuntarily her eyes had sought out
Angela, and apart from a narrowing of her eyes her expression
had not changed.

Their decision to marry was greeted with ill-disguised approval and they were showered with warm congratulations.

But just what did Angela mean to Marcus? She was puzzled
for there had been something contradictory in Marcus and
Angela's attitudes towards each other all evening.

Having observed them display a certain intimacy when they
had been together in the garden, and then seeing them in the
company of others when they rarely spoke or acknowledged
each other—which she thought might have been deliberate—

appeared strange to her and opened her mind to suspicion, which began making progress at a rapid pace the more she thought about it.

But why should it matter? she asked herself. Why did it rouse in her such a host of perplexing emotions that gave rise to so much confusion within herself? She had already made up her mind that she would marry Marcus Fitzalan for her own advantage, and had he not suggested that their marriage was to be a marriage in name only until they wanted it otherwise? A suggestion she had welcomed wholeheartedly until he had weakened her by kissing her so passionately, so deliberately, in an attempt to break down her resolve.

But this still did not change anything and she did not flatter herself that he felt any attachment to her. If there was something going on between himself and Mrs Stephenson, then he must want Atwood Mine very badly indeed to enter into such a marriage whilst being in love with another woman. But no matter how cold and impersonal an arrangement their marriage would be, she would not be made a fool of or humiliated, and would not take lightly to his carrying on an attachment under her very nose when she was his wife.

A few days after her visit to Brooklands, with her grandmother's permission—Lady Pemberton was to remain at Burntwood Hall until after Eve's wedding to Marcus—Eve went to stay with her close friend Emma Parkinson, who lived not far away in a fine manor house with her family. Her father was the local squire and, although the family did not possess a fortune, they were reasonably well off.

Eve and Emma had met as children and had been best friends ever since. The Parkinson household was such a contrast to her own; whereas she was an only child, Emma was the eldest of seven sisters and one brother, ranging from herself at nineteen to the twins at five years old.

Two days into her visit, they took a picnic to the river that flowed through the meadows half a mile from the house. It was a Sunday and the afternoon was hot and sultry, the children with their faces aglow playing happily and noisily on the river bank, with nursemaids and Nanny looking on from beneath the welcome shade of some trees, gossiping and industriously laying out the picnic on the grass.

With her feet bare after paddling in the cool, shallow water and hugging her knees in front of her, from where she sat beside Emma, who was half lying on the grass beside her, Eve looked on enviously, always happy to be a part of this charmed circle, content to watch and listen to the sound of the children's laughter.

'You're so lucky, Em,' she sighed wistfully, calling her by the shortened form of her name as she always did.

'Lucky?' said Emma squinting up at her, her fingers plucking idly at the grass.

'Mmm. To have a large family around you all the time. I'd give anything to have at least one brother or sister—but not to have any...'

'Don't go on,' laughed Emma lightly, glad that Eve had come to stay for a few days, and hoping that the summer activities they never failed to indulge in—picnics and riding and bathing in the river—might alleviate some of the sadness and grief that stared out of her eyes.

'There are times when they drive us to distraction. The twins are impossible and lead poor Nanny a merry dance. Mind you—Jonathan always winds them up and they are invariably punished for his misdeeds. He's a menace,' she said, smiling fondly as she watched her seven-year-old brother torment the twins unmercifully, with jovial, tousled-haired twenty-one-year-old Matthew Somerville, Gerald's younger brother, trying his best to maintain some semblance of order among the children, but with little success.

Matthew, of whom Eve's father had been extremely fond, did not resemble Gerald in any way, being of a gentle, often serious disposition. He was employed at Atwood Mine as an agent, responsible for the hiring of colliers, whilst learning as much about the mining industry as he could. It being Sunday and a day of rest, he had come along to share their picnic—although whether or not he would have done so had Emma not been present remained open to speculation.

'My parents tend to spoil Jonathan abominably,' Emma went on, 'because he's the only son and everyone thinks he's so special. But if you like children so much, Eve, you'll be able to have some of your own soon,' she said, rolling on to her stomach and resting her face on her hand, looking up at Eve sideways, her lips curling in a teasing smile, well aware that she was seriously considering marriage to the handsome and quite delectable Marcus Fitzalan. She knew of the conditions of her father's will and couldn't for the life of her think why Eve was being so reticent about it. Had it been her she would have jumped at it like a shot.

Eve flushed and bit her lip. 'I doubt it—at least not for a long time yet. Oh, Em,' she murmured, a yearning quality to her voice. 'I had long since made up my mind that I was going to meet the man of my dreams, fall in love and live happily ever after.'

'Sadly, life isn't like that.'

'I know. Marcus must think I'm awfully young—a child, even, in his eyes, but these last weeks have made me grow up very quickly. I feel as though I've aged twenty years and have a distinct feeling that I've been cheated somewhere along the way.'

'Cheated! I wouldn't say that. Not when you're about to marry the most eligible man in the West Riding. There are plenty of women who would give their eye teeth to be in your position—and you can count me as one of them.' She laughed lightly. 'You do intend marrying him, don't you?'

'I have told him I will. Although the fact of the matter is that I really have no choice,' she said with bitter regret.

'Well, my advice is not to change your mind. You must look on this as a golden opportunity. Don't let it slip through your fingers. If you do and you go to live with your grandmother with nothing to look at day in and day out but hills and sheep, then mark my words, you'll live to regret it.'

'It's just that I want to make quite sure I'm doing the right thing, Em. Now I am my own mistress I'm reluctant to change that. Why should I marry anyone if I don't want to? The truth is I'm frightened. I'm frightened of marrying this man and having him control my life. And that makes me angry.'

'If you don't marry Marcus Fitzalan then you're a fool,' Emma replied bluntly. 'Not only will you lose the opportunity of becoming the wife of the most handsome, sought-after bachelor in the district, but you'll also lose Atwood Mine— and considering all *that* entails, it is not something you should pass over lightly.'

'I don't have to marry him to retain Atwood Mine, Em,' she said quietly. 'I could remain at Burntwood Hall for the rest of my life if I so wished, and let the Somervilles keep the mine—at least for the remaining fifteen years of the lease—if I marry Gerald.'

Emma's eyes opened wide with astonishment. 'What?' she gasped. 'Eve—you wouldn't—you couldn't.'

Unsmiling, Eve shook her head. 'No—not in a million years. But he has asked me. I cannot say that I like Gerald very much, if at all. There's a side to him that's decidedly unpleasant. He—he frightens me sometimes. It's a pity Matthew wasn't the elder of the two.' She sighed. 'How much easier everything would be if he had inherited the estate instead of Gerald.'

Emma's eyes clouded over and her face became serious as she quietly contemplated Eve's words—and Eve would not have been surprised to know that Emma was saying a silent prayer of thankfulness that Matthew was not the elder of the two brothers, for she was well and truly smitten by him herself.

'Don't worry, Em—' Eve smiled reassuringly, having read her thoughts '—I know just how close you and Matthew have become of late. Anyone would have to be blind not to see.

But do you think obtaining Atwood Mine will make Marcus Fitzalan like me any better?' she asked, wistfully watching a small white butterfly as it flitted among a carpet of forget-me-nots close to the river bank. 'The seeds of discord have already been sown, Em—when I foolishly took up Angela's challenge that day at Atwood Fair.'

'That's rubbish, Eve,' Emma admonished forcefully. 'That's all forgotten now—over and done with. It must be, otherwise he would not be marrying you.' Sighing in exasperation at Eve's stubborn reluctance to fall victim to Mr Fitzalan's charms, Emma sat up, brushing pieces of dried grass from her skirts as she straightened them over her outstretched legs.

'Tell me, Eve. When you're with Mr Fitzalan, feeling like this, how do you manage to conceal your hostility? Does it not make him angry?'

'I'm sure it does—but I do find it difficult at times. He is so proud and arrogant—so full of his own importance.'

'It is scarcely to be wondered at. A man as rich as Mr Fitzalan, and with everything in his favour, can afford to be. I have heard that among his friends he is an agreeable, good-humoured man—but I have also heard he has the most violent temper. You would do well not to aggravate him before you are married, otherwise he might change his mind and marry someone else instead.'

Eve gave her a sharply suspicious look. 'I doubt it. Atwood Mine is too important for him to do that. But I dare say he would not be aware of my existence if my father had not made it over to the both of us on condition that we marry. But, Em,' she said, with slight reticence, knowing how her friend with her lively disposition loved to socialise—more often than not at the assembly rooms in both Atwood and Netherley, where she loved to gossip and contrived to learn what news she could about people in the area—and that if anyone knew anything about what was going on it was Emma, 'have you heard anything regarding Mr Fitzalan—gossip, I mean, and a certain person who is known to us both?'

Emma's eyes opened wide at the possibility of a scandal. 'No. Should I have?'

Eve shrugged. 'No. I don't suppose so. I—I just thought that—perhaps—seeing as you rarely miss any of the assemblies either in Atwood or Netherley, you might have heard something, that's all.'

'No, I can't say that I have. Mr Fitzalan's name frequently crops up in conversation, and everyone knows he has been romantically linked to several ladies in the past, but considering he has never shown the smallest interest in attending any of the local assemblies, nothing is known for certain. But what lady do you have in mind? Oh, Eve,' she begged when she saw Eve look away, as if she was reluctant to enlarge on what it was that had prompted her to ask the question in the first place. 'You have to tell me. What lady? What's her name?'

Sighing, Eve looked at her and said, 'Angela Lambert—or Stephenson, as she became after marrying Leslie.'

Emma was momentarily stunned. 'Angela? Angela and Mr Fitzalan? No—that is the most ridiculous thing I have heard in a long while. I do not believe it—and neither must you. What I do know about her is that, after Leslie died, by all accounts she did not resemble a grieving widow. She spent some considerable time in London where, according to Matthew, she became well acquainted with Gerald and his friends. She returned to the north four months ago. I cannot say that I have heard of her being involved in any way with Mr Fitzalan—not romantically, anyway, which is what I think you are implying. What gives you reason to think she is?'

'Oh—no reason, really,' Eve replied, forcing herself to smile. It came as no surprise that she was acquainted with Gerald, mixing as they did in the same social circles, both in the north and in London. 'Forget I said anything. I'm just being silly, that's all.'

Frowning, Emma cast her a serious glance, knowing Eve was not given to making idle statements without good reason, and that she had been deeply hurt by Angela's duplicity three years ago over the affair with Leslie Stephenson. She had every reason to be suspicious and on her guard where Angela was concerned.

'I'm sure you are, Eve. But why ask?'

'Only because I met her when I went to Brooklands. I—I chanced to see her in the garden with Marcus and they displayed a familiarity that gave me reason to suspect she might be more to him than a mere acquaintance. She—she made me feel like an intruder.'

'Well, if she did it was probably because she was jealous. We both know how malicious and conniving she can be when the mood takes her. Good heavens, it's you Mr Fitzalan's marrying, not her. If I were you I'd think no more about it.' Emma cocked her head sideways, looking at Eve with a gentle, teasing, whimsical smile. 'But if it concerns you so much, would I be right in thinking your feelings for Mr Fitzalan are not entirely hostile after all?'

Lowering her eyes Eve sighed deeply, the pink flush that suddenly sprung to her cheeks telling Emma all she needed to know. 'Yes, you would,' she admitted softly. 'He has a way of confusing me to such an extent that I do not know what I'm doing or saying half the time.' She looked up to find Emma watching her.

'It sounds to me as though you are already halfway to being in love with him,' she said softly.

'Yes,' she replied, meeting Emma's gaze, finding it impossible to give a different answer. 'It certainly looks that way. His treatment of me that day at Atwood Fair showed him to be a man without reserve or scruples, and I had every reason in the world to dislike him. I have always turned a deaf ear to those who esteemed and valued him, who spoke of him with affection and merit.'

'And now?'

'Now I am astonished and apprehensively perturbed that I no longer find it easy to discredit him. I have carried a strong prejudice against him for so long—but now I am getting to know him a little better, I am beginning to suspect I may have done him an injustice as I begin to see a different side to his nature, the side my father so admired. It would seem I might have to change my opinion of his worth.'

Emma smiled softly. 'Then I am glad to hear it. To begin a life together with so much bitterness and resentment between you would not make for a happy marriage. Now come along,' she said, getting to her feet. 'Nanny's beckoning to us. All the children are sitting down so I think it must be time to eat.'

Eve followed her, surprised by her revelation as to what her feelings were for Marcus, and how easy it had been to admit her true feelings to Emma. But having been the recipient of Angela's vindictiveness and knowing just what she was capable of, it was no easy matter dismissing her from her mind or the threat she posed to her future happiness with Marcus.

As Emma helped clear away the remains of the picnic, the children, along with Matthew and Eve, took to the river and in no time at all the voices of shrill childish laughter rose and fell in paroxysms of uncontrollable mirth as they splashed hilariously in the warm, shallow water, uncaring that their clothes were getting hopelessly wet as they tried to drench Matthew. He had a riotous sense of fun and they loved him unashamedly.

Having decided to ride over to the Parkinsons to see Eve, it was into this setting that Marcus headed, being drawn to it by the ringing tones of laughter. Just missing the playful interlude Eve and Matthew had been indulging in with the children, who had left them and scampered back to their nursemaids to be rubbed dry—an interlude which had left them happily exhausted—Marcus came quietly into the small clearing surrounded by trees, the thick, purple-shadowed undergrowth beyond consisting of blackberry and honeysuckle and a carpet of blue forget-me-nots. The trees were arranged in such a way as to allow the benign warmth of the sun to enter and become entrapped.

Marcus stared in astonishment to see Eve stretched out on the grassy bank. She lay quite still looking up at the small clouds that floated across the vast, untroubled sky, breathing deeply. He allowed his eyes to drink their fill. She looked as he imagined her namesake must have looked in the Garden of Eden—womanly, utterly female and at one with her surroundings, bewitching, completely unprepossessing and enchanting.

But he felt the joy of seeing her drain from him when his eyes strayed to the young man lying by her side. Panic and anger seized him. He told himself that the situation could not be as it looked, that this precious being he had only just found had been stolen from him before he'd had the chance to analyse the extent of the emotions she had aroused in him. But when his mind flashed back to the day he had first laid eyes on her three years ago, when he had accused her of being a promiscuous little flirt, perhaps he had not been so far from the truth after all.

When the lone horseman rode into the clearing, his horse's hooves muddying the crystal-clear water close to the bank, and his long shadow stretching menacingly over them both and blocking out the light of the sun, Matthew sat bolt upright, startled out of his reverie and frozen into stillness as he gaped wordlessly at the man who had come upon them so unexpectedly.

Marcus lounged indolently in the saddle while his large, sleek chestnut horse bent its head to drink the water. Matthew shrank visibly beneath his seniority and his withering glacier gaze, sensing his anger and deep displeasure. Having seen him on occasion when he had come to the mine to see Sir John, he knew him to be Eve's intended.

Aware of how the situation must look to Marcus—with Matthew's breeches wet and rolled up above his knees, his shirt hanging loose and his face flushed from his recent antics in the river as he had happily accompanied the children at their play—he wished he could disappear into thin air. His face became blood red with embarrassment.

Having had a moment to observe them, Marcus felt his stomach churn. Seeing Eve like this, dishevelled, with her rich curtain of hair, long and silky and glossy black, hanging loose, almost took his breath away and he could not take his eyes from her. She was magnificent. She held her head proudly, her violet eyes burning up into his, showing neither alarm at his appearance or caring much for modesty. He was disturbed by the sight of her, feeling a stirring of warmth in his loins.

She was laid out on the grass with her shoes and stockings strewn beside her, her face flushed from the sun's rays and her recent laughter, and the lower half of her legs exposed— long, white, slim and perfect—causing anger to shoot through Marcus like molten fire. How dare she let this callow youth see her like this, making no attempt to cover herself. Having seen the familiarity they displayed together a moment earlier caused his mouth to tighten ominously.

Matthew looked somewhat shamefaced and bemused but Eve, slowly sitting up, stared at her betrothed in defiance, in silent challenge to his authority, but his eyes were compelling and flashing with that particular pale blue that heralded trouble.

'I sincerely hope this is not how it looks,' said Marcus with an icy calm, his gaze, flicking from one to the other, coming to rest on Matthew, whom he vaguely recognised but could not place just then. 'I don't believe we've met. Be so good as to introduce us will you, Eve?'

'Gladly. Although considering you are already acquainted with his elder brother, I am surprised to find you have not met before. Matthew, may I present Mr Fitzalan. This is Matthew Somerville, Marcus. Gerald's brother. He is employed as an agent at Atwood Mine.'

Marcus's dark brows drew together in deep displeasure, certain that anyone who had the misfortune to be related to Gerald Somerville must be lacking in moral restraint.

Matthew scrambled to his feet, clearly flustered, having no idea of the deep hatred Mr Fitzalan felt for his elder brother.

'Yes—I—I know who you are, sir—you're—'

'Miss Somerville's betrothed,' Marcus said cuttingly. 'Is that not right, Eve?'

'Yes,' she replied, knowing by the cold severity on Marcus's handsome face that the fragile unity they had shared so briefly at Brooklands had begun to disappear.

'Then may I take this opportunity to congratulate you, sir,' said Matthew politely and hurriedly. Bending down he grasped his shoes, eager to extricate himself from the embarrassment of the unpleasant situation as quickly as possible. 'Excuse me. I must see what the children are up to.'

Coolly Marcus watched him go before fixing his hard gaze on Eve. Seeing his gaze flick coldly and contemptuously over the length of her body, and how his eyes came to rest on her bare legs, she modestly covered them with her skirts, but her toes peeped out in a continued act of defiance. The gesture angered him. It mattered not one jot to her that she had allowed the youth to look his fill while denying the same right to her betrothed. When they were married all that would change. He would show her from the start that she could not play the imperious young madam with him. Unflustered, she looked up at him boldly.

Marcus dismounted. His forbearance, never strong, was about to crack under her defiance. He stood looking down at her without speaking, but the tautness of his body, his brilliant eyes and the curl of his firm lips, told Eve everything she needed to know. He loomed over her like an angry, avenging god—but why he should be so incensed with anger baffled her. She sighed. Why couldn't it be someone like Matthew her father had left half of Atwood Mine to—someone she could relate to, someone uncomplicated? How much easier it would have been for her to decide.

With a sigh she got to her feet, trying to brush the creases out of her dress with her hands. 'I am surprised to see you, Marcus. I thought you were a busy man—too busy to ride about the countryside paying social calls.'

'Not too busy to call on my betrothed,' he replied coldly, ignoring her faint sarcasm.

'I am flattered. How did you know where to find me?'

'I did call at the house in the hope of seeing you,' he confessed. 'Mrs Parkinson told me where you could be found. It's fortunate I came when I did—otherwise there's no telling what you and Mr Somerville would have been up to. Have you nothing to say for yourself?'

'No. I don't feel that I have to defend myself to you,' she said looking at him calmly, ignoring the danger signals in his eyes, realising that the proud arrogance and indomitable will his mother had spoken of was set on a collision course with her own. 'I care nothing for your anger or your bullying. I do not fear you, Marcus.'

Marcus seethed inwardly, trying hard to control his anger. He took a menacing step towards her. 'The last thing I want is for you to fear me, Eve, but I am asking you to explain yourself. After all, there is only one thing that comes to mind when I see you behaving like a strumpet.'

Eve gasped with indignation. 'Don't be ridiculous. Because I was indiscreet once you think me capable of anything. Perhaps if you did not go creeping around and spying on me you would have seen the situation for what it was. You cannot possibly be angry at the friendly playfulness we were indulging in with the children a moment ago. It is commonplace when we are all together and, besides, Matthew and I have known each other from children.'

'Even children grow up,' Marcus said with scorn. 'Don't pretend to be so naïve. You know as well as I what must pass through his mind when you are alone together—and half undressed.'

Eve stared at him in defiance, enraged by the implication of his words. 'For heaven's sake, Marcus Fitzalan—you are behaving like a jealous husband already. I have only removed my shoes and stockings so that I might play in the river with the children—and do not judge everyone by your own questionable standards. I am sure that what you imply has never crossed Matthew's mind—and besides, Emma is the object of his affections, not I. Perhaps you object to people enjoying themselves, is that it?'

'Not at all. I like enjoying myself as much as the next man—but what I do object to is watching my future wife make a ridiculous spectacle of herself.'

'Oh! This is too much,' Eve expostulated. 'There is nothing ridiculous about playing with children.' She gave him a look of furious loathing. 'Perhaps you object to children, too.'

'I like children very much as it happens—and I intend filling the nursery at Brooklands with them in the not-too-distant future.'

'Don't you think you should consult me first?'

'Oh, I will. When the time is right. The kind of behaviour I found you indulging in today goes beyond the bounds of propriety, and when we are married I shall expect you to uphold the respectable position in society as befitting my wife. I shall feel happier when you concern yourself with your own household and children instead of other peoples'.'

'And I was brought up to understand that ladies are treated with courtesy and respect.'

Marcus smiled thinly. 'One must act like a lady if she wishes to be treated as such,' he said scathingly.

Eve flushed, lifting her head and glaring at him haughtily. 'I resent that. How dare you address me in this manner?'

Marcus stepped closer to her, feeling the blood pounding in his temples at her proud defiance to stand firm against him. 'Oh, I do dare—when I find the woman I am to marry carousing in the bushes unashamedly with an adolescent youth.'

'We were not carousing in the bushes and Matthew is not an adolescent youth. He is a responsible, caring adult, a relative and a man my father was extremely fond of. And what I do does not concern you,' she spat, her own eyes blazing as hot as his.

'Oh, yes it does, lady,' he snarled, his metallic eyes glittering with a fire that burned her raw. 'I will not stand by and be denied by my own wife that which she would give freely to another.'

Eve's own eyes narrowed furiously. 'I am not your wife yet, Marcus—and nor am I likely to be if you carry on in this aggressive manner. You told me you would not touch me until I was ready? Do you go back on your word so soon?'

'I never go back on my word. But you will not deny me indefinitely. I am not a patient man and abstinence is a heavy penance. However—I do not intend abstaining for life.'

'Then don't waste your time waiting for me.'

'I won't—but let it be understood that there will be no little amours behind my back. If you think you can carry on an affair, then you do not know me.'

'And if you can address me in this manner then let me tell you that I have no wish to know you,' Eve flared.

'Damn your insolence,' he hissed. .

'Then tell me, Marcus,' she said, throwing back her head, taunting him with her words, 'does what you have just said apply to you also?'

'What do you mean?'

'Angela Stephenson,' she said coldly, accusingly, her voice straining itself between her taut lips.

Amazement registered in Marcus's eyes and to her chagrin, instead of looking guilty or abashed, he threw back his head and laughed, a razor-edged laugh, the sound of it going soaring and ringing through the trees. Seeing red, Eve was infuriated—more with herself than she was with him, since she had not intended mentioning the incident she had witnessed in the gardens at Brooklands.

The last thing she wanted was to give him the satisfaction of knowing it troubled her, which would no doubt give rise to considerable amusement and give him reason to accuse her of jealousy. She wanted to lash out at him, to hurt him, and she glared up at him, her hair rippling in the soft breeze as their eyes became locked together.

'Angela!' he laughed, his eyes warm with his humour. 'That is ridiculous. Angela is a acquaintance and nothing more—and she is only that because her mother and my own happen to be close friends.' His smile suddenly broadened and his eyes narrowed suddenly. 'Oh! Jealous, are we?'

Eve's eyes snapped and her chin came up. 'No more than you were just now of Matthew,' she replied primly.

'Only because of the impropriety of the situation.'

'Come now—' she laughed, unable to resist a little sarcastic teasing '—you looked fit to throw him into the river—and don't deny it.'

'I don't. But believe me, Angela Stephenson is an acquaintance and nothing more.'

'After seeing the two you together in the garden at Brooklands, that is not the impression you gave me—and by her manner I suspect she is of the same opinion.'

Marcus's eyes narrowed and he became thoughtful as he tried to think what she could be referring to. 'I did meet Angela in the garden shortly after she arrived—quite by chance, I assure you. As a matter of fact, it may surprise you to know that I was looking for you at the time and was disappointed not to find you. I came upon Angela sitting by the fountain instead. That's all it was. But how you can accuse me of spying on *you* when you are guilty of the same offence, I confess puzzles me. If you were watching, then you should have made your presence known.'

Eve was seething and she found his mocking smile intolerable. How dared he put her in the wrong in this manner. 'It was way beyond me to interrupt such an intimate tête-à-tête. But I do not have to put up with this. It's not too late. I don't have to marry you,' she fumed, struggling to keep her voice under control.

'Oh, yes, you do,' he growled, his anger returning, the grinding resolve which always kept him in complete control with those with whom he dealt rising to the fore. 'If you want to hold on to Atwood Mine you do and you know it. You need me just as much as I need you and there's not a damned thing you can to about it. Now—put on your shoes and come and introduce me to your friends. The sooner that young pup realises you really are to be my wife the better I shall feel.'

'Put your stamp on me—is that what you mean?'

'If you like.'

'Then if you are to meet everyone I would be obliged if you would alter your expression.'

Marcus threw her a questioning look.

'You are likely to frighten the children,' she said tartly, tossing her hair out of her eyes and beginning to walk on ahead of him carrying her shoes and stockings, uncaring whether he followed her or not.

Marcus watched her go and then, grasping his horse's bridle, he chuckled softly to himself. With the flicker of a smile at the corners of his lips he began to follow, regarding her with admiration. Doubtless there would be many more skirmishes ahead he could look forward to.

Chapter Ten

If Eve thought Marcus would frighten the children he soon proved her wrong, and from the mischievous glances he kept throwing her way he seemed to delight in doing so. At first they were in awe of him, fixing him with dubious, uneasy glances, but he soon captivated their attention, possessing a natural ability to control them in a way that left their nurse-maids and Nanny more than a little amazed. They were enchanted.

Eve observed him with puzzlement, especially as she had just accused him of not liking children. He seemed to have a natural rapport with them and it was quite a novelty to see him in his shirt sleeves entertaining them, sending them into gales of laughter as they rolled about the grass.

'Well, who would have thought it?' said Emma, coming to sit beside Eve on the grass.

'Who indeed?' murmured Eve.

'Shall we rescue him, do you think?'

'No, let's leave him. It would be a shame to spoil his enjoyment.'

'Mr Fitzalan is so different from what I expected. I'm astonished. Clearly he has a fondness for children.'

'I'm as astonished as you are, Em. He is so much altered I hardly know him.'

'After your harsh description of him earlier he is not at all what I expected. There is nothing disagreeable about his character at all.'

Eve had to agree that Emma was right, but she suspected that it might just be a temporary measure to placate her for some mischievous reason of his own. Never had she seen him so unreserved, so eager to please as he sought to gain the good opinion of Emma and to put Matthew at his ease. The change in him was so great she could not restrain her amazement.

She looked at him as though for the first time and saw that with his hair lightly ruffled he looked much younger and less formidable, and for a moment she had the impression that he was little more than a boy himself. He did seem genuinely fond of children, and they of him. When she managed to catch his eye she saw so much laughter on his face that he seemed a long way removed from the proud, arrogant man she had come to know. It gave her an insight of a different side to him she was looking forward to knowing better.

After a while Marcus came to join Eve where she sat on the grass with her arms around her drawn-up knees watching him. Slipping into his coat, his black hair shining and falling over his brow, he sat beside her, and she felt a tingling of exhilaration, feeling drawn to him against her will by a compelling magnetism that radiated from his very presence.

'Really, Marcus, I am quite impressed. Never would I have believed you to be so good with children. I am pleased to see you do not view them as an encumbrance after all.'

'I told you, I like children.'

'You seem to be such an expert at controlling them that, should we have children in the future, I think we will be able to dispense with the services of a nanny.'

He smiled into her eyes. 'I'm not such an expert—or so patient.' He sighed, stretching out his long booted legs. Leaning on his elbow, he lay sideways looking up at her. 'I have yet to tell you the purpose for my coming here today.'

'Oh?'

'I have arranged for the wedding to take place at Atwood Church in just over three weeks' time—after the banns have been called. I hope that is agreeable to you.'

'Yes. I told you—the sooner the better. I have no wish to be at Burntwood Hall when Gerald arrives.'

On returning to Burntwood Hall after her visit to Emma, to her absolute dismay Eve found Gerald had arrived to take up residence. A terrible coldness gripped her as she entered the house. The violence of their last encounter, when he had uttered such menacing, ugly threats against her, leaving her in no doubt as to his determination to obtain Atwood Mine, crowded in on her mind. He had arrived unannounced, throwing the servants into utter confusion, and her grandmother was nowhere to be seen.

Steeling herself for her meeting with her father's cousin, she crossed the hall to the drawing room, finding not only Gerald but also Matthew, who looked awkward and apologetic as he watched Eve enter, aware of the dislike she felt for Gerald and how painful it was for her having to leave her home.

Having discarded his coat, carelessly at ease, Gerald was lounging in a large chair by the window, one of his elegantly shod feet resting on an upholstered foot stool. Already he had a proprietorial air about him. With a little shiver of dislike Eve was at once repelled, a pain in the region of her heart reminding her he was now the owner of Burntwood Hall, that she was the visitor, and there was not a thing she could do about it.

A decanter of claret stood on a green baize table beside him, and his slender hand idly turned his full glass to catch the light. He saw Eve come in but didn't bother to get up, his only movement being to raise a lazy eyebrow and throw her a mocking smile.

'Well, here's a strange turnout. I arrive to claim my inheritance and you were not here to welcome me, Eve. Imagine my disappointment.'

Mastering her surprise and disappointment, she said coldly, 'I'm sure you'll soon get over it, Gerald. Forgive me if I seem surprised. I did not expect you quite so soon.'

'Clearly,' he said, sipping at his claret and licking his lips, which made his mouth look like a vivid slash across his face.

'I—I hope you don't mind us being here,' said Matthew, stepping forward.

'Mind? Why should she mind?' Gerald expostulated before Eve could reply, momentarily roused out of quiet contemplation of his half-filled glass. 'A man does not need permission to enter his own home—is that not right, Eve?'

'Yes—of course,' she replied stiffly, trying hard to ignore his insolently smiling face. 'And will you be living here, Matthew?' she asked, favouring him with a warm smile, trying to put him at ease, for she knew how much Gerald's presence always intimidated him.

'Yes—I'm afraid so,' he said with a quick glance at his elder brother. 'It—it is necessary, you understand.'

Yes, Eve understood only too well. No doubt their own home would have to be sold to pay Gerald's creditors. How long would it be, she wondered sadly, before Burntwood Hall went down the same rotten, corrupt road now it was in his incapable hands?

'To be sure, you did not stay long at the Parkinsons,' Gerald commented.

'I did not wish to leave my grandmother alone for too long, that is why.'

'And when is the eminent lady to relieve us of her irksome presence?' he asked, speaking facetiously, for he had no liking for Lady Pemberton, but Eve paid no attention.

'Just as soon as I am married to Mr Fitzalan,' she replied coolly.

On hearing this Gerald's body became taut and he sat up in the chair, placing his glass beside the decanter on the table beside him. He was aware of this disagreeable fact, for it was common knowledge all over the West Riding that Eve had accepted Marcus Fitzalan's suit, and he did not approve. His eyes snapped open, alert, glittering with menace.

'So I hear,' he said, the quietness of his voice and the way his eyes fixed themselves on Eve's face having an unnerving effect. 'So—you have decided to marry our illustrious neighbour—a man without background or breeding, although I suppose his wealth can make amends for that.'

'It is no business of yours whom I marry—and insulting him will not help either. Mr Fitzalan is a gentleman and highly respected.'

'Then if the gossips were to be believed at the time, a true gentleman would not have taken advantage of your innocence and naïvety and attempted to seduce you before casting you aside so lightly—which, if my memory serves me correctly, is precisely what he did to you three years ago, and in so doing ruined any hopes you might have had of making a prestigious marriage.'

'As you say, that was a long time ago and best forgotten. I refuse to discuss the matter with you. All I ask is that you permit my grandmother and myself to remain here at Burntwood Hall until I marry Mr Fitzalan. It will only be for a matter of a few weeks. A month at the most.'

'I told you after your father's funeral that you don't have to leave. It is not unavoidable. I shall be happy to accommodate you for as long as you wish to stay. My offer of marriage still stands.'

'Which I still reject.'

'Come now, Eve, my offer is extremely generous. Marriage to me would not lack advantage. You would be mistress of this place—and wealthy beyond most people's imagination if we retain Atwood Mine. What more do you want?'

'What more indeed, Gerald?' she said scathingly. 'It is the choice of husband that is in question.'

All trace of blandness was wiped from Gerald's face and

Eve saw violence quiver in every inch of his frame. Two high spots of colour stained his cheeks and his mouth twisted in bitter scorn. 'Then you're a fool if you think you will be happy married to Marcus Fitzalan.'

'His intentions are honourable.'

'Pretentions, more like,' he sneered, his lips drawn back over his teeth. 'If I remember your words correctly when you first became aware of the terms of your father's will, you said that the day you marry Marcus Fitzalan will be the day when hell freezes over—that you would never agree to the conditions he laid down. The depth of your hatred and contempt for Fitzalan was plain for all to see. It's amazing to see how quickly he has brought you to heel.'

Eve's eyes glittered with rage. 'At the reading of my father's will I was upset and naturally angry when I discovered what he asked of me. But things change—I have changed, and after giving the matter of my future a great deal of consideration—and getting to know Mr Fitzalan better than I did—I know what I am doing is right. But whatever I do is not your concern, Gerald. It has nothing whatsoever to do with you.'

Gerald gave her a contemptuous smile. 'Perhaps not, but do not delude yourself into believing it's you he wants, Eve, because it isn't. It's the mine—but,' he said, being a consummate actor and looking completely at ease once more as he prepared to throw a spoke in the wheel, crossing one satin-clad leg over the other and regarding her with disdain, his devious mind reminding him that there was someone else who courted Fitzalan's favour, someone else who had her sights firmly set on becoming Mrs Fitzalan, 'I dare say that when the novelty of marriage to you wears off, the woman he might have married will continue to warm his bed as she has before.'

The remark was thrown carelessly, deliberately, causing Eve's eyes to flash with indignation and colour to flare in her face. 'I do not care for your words, Gerald. I have no idea what you're talking about—and nor do I care to. How dare you speak to me like this?'

He shrugged, his features marked by nonchalance. 'I merely state the obvious.' Suddenly Gerald's smile became one of malignant pleasure, knowing women and their eternal curiosity and was sure she wanted to know more, despite what she said.

'It's Angela Stephenson he's been carrying on an intrigue with, Angela whom he would prefer to marry him, but unfortunately she does not have the advantage of possessing a certain coal mine he is so desirous to obtain. He's probably with her this very minute.'

Gerald was taunting her, but Eve was determined not to let him get under her skin and arouse her to an expression of her personal feelings. Although she felt like she'd been felled and was frozen to a slender sliver of steel, she merely smiled and lifted her eyebrows in pretended surprise.

'Your sarcasm and cutting remarks are wasted, Gerald. They will neither destroy me or my intention to marry Mr Fitzalan, so you might as well save your breath. Besides, I do not believe you. But—if what you say is true—then I'm afraid Angela is going to be disappointed.' She smiled with irony. 'However, if she is so desirous to obtain another husband, she need not look very far. Perhaps with just a little persuasion she can be tempted to transfer her affections to you.

'After all, now you have come into your inheritance, women like Angela will find you an extremely desirable prospect. I know she was financially well taken care of when Leslie died, but his brother inherited his estate. No doubt she is looking for somewhere to settle, and who would be well pleased with all this.'

Gerald frowned, watching her closely. 'Angela and I are just good friends. I've told you,' he said, his eyes penetrating as he continued to watch her closely, 'she has other fish to fry in the form of Marcus Fitzalan. All men are lamentably weak, my dear, where women are concerned, and a woman as beautiful as Angela can exert an inordinate power over them.'

'Marcus cannot be accused of being weak, Gerald.'

'Don't be naïve,' he said sharply. 'He is marrying you to

get his hands on Atwood Mine and you're a fool if you think otherwise.'

Gerald's narrowed eyes conveyed a threat and he did not care that his tone was openly menacing. 'Angela is vengeful and you will do well not to underestimate her. As you know to your cost, my dear, she is no simple little sugar-mop who will stand by and watch you take what she wants without a fight.'

The colour had left Eve's face, having become white with anger. 'Is that a threat?'

'I would not presume. Say, rather, that I am warning you.'

Eve's hands clenched by her sides as she fought to retain her composure. 'Please excuse me, Gerald. I have no wish to stay and listen to this. I must go and see my grandmother.'

Trying to hold on to her dignity, she turned from him, moving towards the door.

'Oh—and by the way,' he said carelessly, halting her momentarily. 'I've invited some people to stay. There will be a large party arriving at the weekend. Instruct the servants to see that things are made ready. This place is like a mausoleum,' he commented, replenishing his empty glass. 'It could do with some life injected into it.'

Matthew followed Eve out of the room.

'Eve—please wait. I am so sorry about this. I tried to stop Gerald arriving unannounced, but you know what he's like. He just wouldn't listen.'

Eve smiled, swallowing back the lump that had risen in her throat. 'When did he ever?' She sighed when she saw the unhappiness on Matthew's face, feeling some sympathy for him. Gerald was hardly an ideal role model for a younger brother. 'But you need not apologise. It's not your fault, Matthew. But how much easier all this would be if you had been born before Gerald. Forgive me. I know he is your brother and that you are fond of him in your own way—but I have to say that he is the most unpleasant man I have ever come across.'

As she climbed the stairs to go in search of her grandmother, if she had looked back she would have seen, through
the open door of the drawing room, that Gerald's face was no
longer mocking, but had become purposeful. It was the face
of a man who has been struck a hard blow—and whose mind
was already reorganising and planning what steps to take next.
He was determined to obtain Atwood Mine, which was a sure
and continuous source of wealth, ensuring that once he had
settled his loan from the moneylenders, who were becoming
aggressively persistent, he could live in the lap of luxury for
at least fifteen years—and the only thing he had to do to obtain
it was to prevent a marriage from taking place between Eve
and Marcus Fitzalan.

Eve felt as if the breath had been knocked out of her after
her meeting with Gerald. She went to her own room to compose herself before presenting herself to her grandmother, extremely disturbed by what Gerald had told her about Marcus
and Angela. But it was a lie. It had to be a lie concocted by
Gerald with no other reason than to stop her marrying Marcus
and therefore prevent him from obtaining Atwood Mine.

It did not surprise her that women would find Marcus attractive. Who would not? He was so strikingly handsome. To
her cost, she already knew Angela was potential trouble. She
was beautiful, in a provocative sense, voluptuous and alluring—hardly the kind of woman any woman would like to find
interested in the man she was to marry.

But Marcus had denied there was anything of a romantic
nature between them, and she had believed him; having
learned to trust him after getting to know him better, she knew
him to be a man of truth and integrity, and that the use of any
form of deception was beneath him.

But she recalled Angela's past trickery and the barely concealed challenge she had seen in her eyes at Brooklands, and
the possessive manner with which she had clung to Marcus's
arm when they had left the garden together. She also recalled

the intimacy of the scene, the familiarity they had shown towards each other. If she had not known that Angela was aware of her watching them together from the terrace and had characteristically played on this—and if Marcus had not told her he had come out into the garden in search of her and to his disappointment had found Angela there instead—she would have reason to believe there just might be some element of truth in what Gerald had told her.

The house became a hive of industrious activity as rooms were got ready and the kitchen worked at full stretch to prepare food for Gerald's guests and accompanying servants. Knowing full well the sort of people they would be, for Gerald was not the type of person who would keep the company of anyone who did not share his own enthusiasm for high living, Eve was determined to keep a low profile during the visit.

The guests arrived in a succession of fine carriages, the wide driveway in front of the house a picture of gaiety and confusion as they alighted. They were flamboyant and colourful, a dozen in all, three of the gentlemen having brought their wives, who, to Eve's mind, were rather giddy, empty-headed creatures, with whom she had very little in common.

Gerald's friends could not be accused of being dull or dowdy, and she was quite certain her mother and father would not have approved. They belonged to London's social world, which Gerald enjoyed to excess. Having seen many like them on her trips to London, it took Eve no more than a quick glance to see that they were a raucous, disreputable bunch and completely superficial.

They were to stay a week before travelling on to Harrogate to partake of someone else's hospitality. Like Gerald, the gentlemen suffered from a surfeit of idleness. When they grew tired of London they visited friends in the provinces, expecting them to provide a multitude of diversions, with a continuous play of variety and amusement.

Eve made a great impression on them all—despite being

unable to say the same for them. The gentlemen looked at her with undisguised admiration, although there was something insolent and insulting in the way their eyes openly devoured her—especially one gentleman called Timothy Harding, who had a long, prominent nose and deep-set blue eyes. He was nearing thirty and his head and body seemed too large for his spindly legs. He made a great deal of being introduced to her, bowing and almost slobbering over her small hand, seeming not to notice how she flinched when his lips touched her fingers.

'This is a long-awaited pleasure, Miss Somerville,' he said in a curiously falsetto voice, which seemed incongruous to his heavy features. 'Gerald has told us so much about you and I am pleased to see his praise has not been exaggerated. I compliment you on your magnificent house. Gerald is indeed fortunate in his inheritance.'

'Thank you,' she said coolly, her eyes sweeping critically over his person, finding him extremely distasteful and becoming eager to make her escape, 'although Burntwood Hall is no longer my home. However, I am sure it will give Gerald great pleasure to show you around later.'

'I would much rather see it with you,' he said, smiling lewdly to reveal yellowing teeth, his voice low with seduction.

Eve winced, sharply indignant at his sheer effrontery. However, she forced herself to smile sweetly. 'I'm sure you would, but unfortunately I shall be otherwise engaged.'

When they had been shown into the drawing room and were taking refreshment, she left them to return to her grandmother, taking every eye with her as she swept out of the room. She paused as one paralysed outside the door on hearing one of the gentlemen make an unpleasant remark. Her body went tense, for it had to be herself they were talking about.

'My God—pretty little piece, isn't she?' Timothy Harding remarked. 'Plucky, too. Good thing you can't read my mind.'

'Maybe not,' said Gerald drolly, 'but you have a distorted

mind, Timothy, and, knowing you have the manners and behaviour of a sewer rat, I can well imagine.'

'Sight too prim and proper for me,' said another unattached
gentleman called David Blenkinsop.

'You lucky devil, Gerald. You always did have a penchant
for beautiful women. Does she come with your inheritance?'

Eve heard Gerald laugh lightly with salacious undertones.

'You've got the wrong idea about her, Timothy. David was
nearer the truth. Unlike the women you usually keep company
with, she will not be tempted by the lure of flattery—to the
regret of every red-blooded male in the West Riding.'

'My suspicion tells me she can be a spitfire when roused—
still waters and all that. I have a fancy to ask her for an assignation. You won't be offended, will you, Gerald?' Timothy
persisted. 'What I'd give to possess *her* maidenhead. And you
can't complain, old boy. I have it on good authority you were
lying with my latest whore while you were in London recently.
Unless you have a mind to lie with Miss Somerville yourself?'

Gerald laughed, and there was something horrible and malicious in its tone, but he was not to be so obliging to his
friend. 'There is a difference. Miss Somerville is not a whore,
Timothy, and I would be obliged if you would keep your
hands off her. I have my own plans for little Miss Somerville.'

This light-hearted conversation caused much amusement
among them all, but Eve did not find being the object of such
callous and open discussion at all amusing. They might be
aristocrats, but there was nothing distinguished about their behaviour. Their very crudeness offended her. With her cheeks
burning with anger and indignation she went to her room.

Gerald's guests spent the next two days riding, fishing and
shooting on the estate, taking advantage of all that was offered.
Eve painstakingly avoided them, but she could not ignore
them, and after much persuasion she did partake in the occasional game of cards after dinner.

On the third day it rained, forcing everyone to remain in-

doors. Tired of keeping to her room or keeping her grandmother company, Eve went downstairs to find a book to read
in the library. Familiar feminine laughter greeted her when she
reached the hall; peering into the drawing room, her stomach
plummeted on seeing Angela, her gold taffeta skirts rustling
like a gentle breeze as she swept among the company strewn
lazily about the room, pleased by the interest she had aroused
in the form of open admiration in the men and envy in the
plainer-looking ladies.

She was arrestingly beautiful, but her eyes became as hard
and ruthless as a cat's watching a mouse before it pounces as
she observed Eve from across the room, her gaze passing over
her with a sliding contempt.

Eve merely inclined her head politely in greeting, having
realised that because of her close friendship with Gerald
Angela was bound to turn up at Burntwood Hall sooner or
later, but having no wish to stay and have to speak to her she
turned and went into the library adjacent to the drawing room.
She was about to pick a book off the shelves and browse
through it, but at that moment Angela entered, leaving the door
slightly ajar behind her.

The two stood gazing at each other for a moment in silence
and then Angela gave Eve a smug, superior smile, her eyes
resting on her with a deadly coldness, but, unfazed, Eve sighed
and moved towards the window, knowing she hadn't come to
reconcile their differences.

'Please do not insult me with simpering compliments and
insincere smiles, Angela. If it won't pain you too much I
would be obliged if you would tell me why you have followed
me in here. I do not think you can have anything to say to me
that I want to listen to—unless, of course, it is to offer an
apology for your diabolical conduct towards me, which, I
might tell you, is three years too late.'

Angela's eyes glittered, growing steady with anger, taking
in every detail of Eve's face and perfect figure with a rage
born of jealousy. 'No, it won't pain me to tell you why I have

followed you in here, Eve—and it is not to offer you an apology since I do not consider I have anything to apologise for. Despite what happened between you and Marcus on the day of Atwood Fair, Leslie would have married me in the end. It is just that I should hate to see you get hurt a second time and thought to offer you a word of advice before you make a fool of yourself yet again.'

Eve's eyes opened wide in mock surprise. 'Excuse me if I seem surprised, Angela, but consideration for my well-being coming from you takes some believing. What are you talking about?'

Angela's lips curled. 'You know what I am talking about.'

Eve gave a delicate lift to her eyebrows. Her pride rose, ready to do combat. 'I'm afraid not. Please—enlighten me.'

'I hear you are to marry Marcus Fitzalan.'

'Yes. But I cannot for the life of me think what that has to do with you—unless, of course, you wish to congratulate me.'

'That I will never do. I've told you. I am here to try and stop you making a fool of yourself.'

Eve looked at her with distaste, wondering how she had ever been so stupid as to consider this malicious, vituperative woman her friend.

'And how am I likely to do that?'

Her hazel eyes gleaming with calculated malice, Angela studied her with unhidden scorn, and when she spoke her voice was low and intense. 'I think I know Marcus better than you do. How will you endure it being married to him, knowing it is me he loves—me he will always love?'

Eve raised her eyebrows in mock surprise. 'Love! You must know him well, Angela?'

'Yes. We became friends in London—*good friends*,' she informed her, placing strong emphasis on the last two words. 'Here—look at this,' she said, holding her fan out to her, a beautiful pale blue and silver fan inlaid with diamonds, which told Eve it was extremely valuable. 'This was Marcus's most recent gift. He gave it to me on my birthday—one of several gifts he bought me over the months since we were first introduced. He is always so thoughtful—so generous.'

Swallowing painfully Eve blanched, becoming prey to a gnawing uncertainty. Her heart wrenched. Oh, did ever a fool greater than herself draw breath, she chided herself, with anger and admonishment at her own stupidity. Angela had maliciously and wantonly deceived and betrayed her in the past by destroying any hope of happiness she might have had with Leslie—and, after doing it once, who was to say she would not do so a second time? Had she been duped yet again? She stared at the fan, unable to believe that such a little thing as this could be about to change her whole life.

'How do I know he gave you this?'

'Because he had it inscribed. See,' Angela said smugly, opening it and showing her the inscription.

The inscription was simple and Eve read 'With all my love. Happy Birthday. Marcus', but it left Eve in no doubt that Marcus had given it to her. Eve looked at her.

'You always were skilful at throwing fuel on the fire, weren't you, Angela?'

Angela's face was transfigured with a fearful joy as she took savage pleasure in flinging searing hurtful words in the teeth of her rival. Everything she uttered was calculated to provoke Eve's anger to greater heights, an anger she fondly hoped would provoke her into changing her mind about marrying Marcus.

'When I returned to the north he continued to see me. But for you and that wretched mine, it is me he would be marrying.'

Eve was looking at her with a repugnant horror, wanting to slap the sneering, triumphant smile from her lips, but she held on to her control.

Angela moved menacingly closer, snapping the offending fan shut, her whole body tense and purposeful. 'I know how persuasive Marcus can be when there is something he wants— and I do not doubt for one minute that he has used that same persuasion on you to tempt you into marriage, convincing you it is you he wants. But he is considering marriage to you with the same dispassionate logic with which he approaches his business transactions—and with Atwood Mine to mark his decision it is all the more exciting and challenging for him. Do you imagine for one minute it is you he wants?'

'I don't know, Angela. You tell me. I am not practised in the subtle arts of conniving and scheming the way you are.' Eve's lips curled with scorn, but she was stung by Angela's remark, particularly since she now knew it to be true. 'But I think I please Marcus as well as you—although my methods may not be quite the same. Tell me, Angela—do you always have to have that which is mine? Perhaps it gives it a special value. I think you are trying to tell me not to marry Marcus— am I right?'

Clearly angry, Angela turned from her sharply and moved quickly towards the door. 'Think what you like,' she flung the words back over her shoulder, 'but take care, Eve,' she said, turning back to her, her eyes narrowed and gleaming viciously. 'You're not married yet and I mean to have him. I intend to be his wife and I will not let you stand in my way.'

'And what will you do to achieve that short of killing me?' demanded Eve.

Angela smiled thinly, a vicious glitter in her eyes. 'Oh, I'll think of something, you can be sure of that. I can be a mighty dangerous enemy if I choose.'

When she had gone Eve was trembling with anger and apprehension, more disturbed by their conversation than she cared to admit. Angela might be beautiful, but she was also as venomous as sin, a woman who would use her feminine wiles like a weapon, selfishly and ruthlessly, to gain her own ends.

She would be a fool to deny that Angela posed a threat, and yet she felt more threatened by Gerald. But she did not trust either of them and between them they were proving to be a lethal combination.

* * *

From a distance Eve observed Angela with Gerald the following day when she called, having travelled in the carriage from her parents' home in Little Bolton. When they looked at her and each other there were secrets in their eyes, and she knew neither of them would have any compunction in destroying her.

Having seen the fan which Marcus had given Angela, having it flaunted before her very eyes, had upset her more than she realised, bringing tears of misery and disappointment to her eyes. She swallowed against the constriction in her throat and her heart twisted with pain as resentment against Angela tore through her, fighting with her rage and her jealousy. Just when she thought she and Marcus were becoming close, by knowing this, he had been removed to a great distance.

In the beginning, because their marriage was to be one of convenience, when emotions were not involved, she might have turned a blind eye to his transgressions—but even then she would have wanted it to be anyone rather than Angela he was involved with. Oh, yes, he would marry her, but he would never love her, not as she loved him, which, after looking into her heart and examining her thoughts and feelings, she had come to realise with astounding clarity—but he must never know.

Love had crept up on her—she had admitted as much to Emma. Her feelings and emotions when she was with Marcus were always so confused that she hadn't realised what was happening to her, and now it was too late. But she must never give in to her feelings—to the hopes and sentiments she had cherished and indulged since her visit to Brooklands. Ever since he had kissed her three years ago, no other man had been able to stir her heart the way he had—to anger and passion and every emotion known to man, which was the reason why she had lived in self-imposed isolation since.

It was ironic to know she was in love with a man she had unwillingly accepted to be her husband, and it would be no easy matter knowing that while he was marrying her he was thinking of someone else.

But, she thought bitterly, she knew the score, that she would not have his full attention. That would be elsewhere. She would be entering into the marriage with her eyes wide open, knowing what to expect, so why should she feel so disappointed and let down? If she went ahead knowing this, it was a situation she would have to learn to live with and make the best of.

Chapter Eleven

Later, just before everyone retired for the night, several of the gentlemen, having imbibed too much liquor, were behaving in a rowdy and unruly fashion. Returning from her grandmother's room where she had been to bid her goodnight, Eve encountered Gerald in the shadows on the top of the stairs, watching her. She had to pass him, and as she moved closer she saw there was something in his eyes which made her throat tighten and a thrill of fear to course through her veins.

It was plain that he had been drinking heavily but his gait was not unsteady. His eyes shone with an unusual glassy brilliance and his hair fell dishevelled over his forehead. His cravat was unfastened and hung untidily, and his white crumpled shirt was stained with wine and flopped open to reveal the upper part of his chest. He was terrifying when he was like this, his sneering, his sarcasm more cutting, more cruel, more precise. She was about to turn and go back to her room, but his voice halted her and he sauntered to where she stood.

'Where are you going?' he asked, his voice low, menacing.

'To my room,' she said, trying to still her wildly beating heart.

His hand shot out and gripped her arm as she was about to move away, which she tried to pull from his grasp, but without success.

'Will you not join us downstairs in a nightcap before you do? My friends—especially Timothy—are most offended that you have not allowed them to become better acquainted with you during their visit.'

Eve glared at him. 'If they are offended then they have only themselves to blame. Had they behaved more like gentlemen I might have been more amenable towards them. You're drunk. All of you. Now please let me go. Don't touch me, Gerald.'

'Why—it is not the first time you have been touched,' he drawled, undiscouraged by her anger. Bringing his evil, smiling face close to hers, his lust-filled eyes held a frightening glitter and travelled insolently over her body. Instinctively Eve tried to break free but he held her harder, hurting her. His other hand reached up and gripped her chin relentlessly, and he pulled her close, holding her captive body firmly against his. His breath was warm on her face, the heavy fumes of spirits making her stomach heave.

'I know a great deal about you, more than you think—about what happened between you and Marcus Fitzalan at Atwood Fair. How you threw yourself at him—and how it went a good deal further than a kiss, which he duped your father into believing was all that happened between you.'

'And I do not have to guess who told you this. Could it be Angela, I wonder?' She struggled within his grasp. 'Let me go, Gerald. Release me this instant.'

'And if I don't? What will you do?'

'I will see that Marcus hears of this.'

'But he is not here now to save you, is he?' said Gerald, who would not allow the close proximity of Marcus Fitzalan to deter his interest in Eve. 'And how do you think he will react when he realises I have dared lay hands on what he intends to be his? Somehow I do not think he will care about that, providing you bring him that which is dearer to his heart than any woman—Atwood Mine. So, if you thought to rekindle the liaison which took place between you three years ago—don't hold out too many hopes.'

'And isn't that the most important thing to you, also?'

'Yes. I admit it freely. But you would come as an added bonus. You attract me—your very resistance excites me to distraction.'

'If that is meant to be a compliment, then please save your breath. I hold you in contempt.'

'I care nothing for your opinion of me. I could break you if I so desired.' He laughed harshly, his eyes dilated and bloodshot as he thrust his face closer. 'What a firebrand you are. I'll conquer you—and the harder you fight the sweeter will be the ultimate pleasure. One day I shall have you at my mercy. I swear I shall.'

'Never. You will have to kill me first.'

'That I shall do, if necessary—especially if you do not heed my warning and call off your wedding to Marcus Fitzalan. I mean to have Atwood Mine, Eve, and I shall go to any lengths to do so.'

Eve was rendered speechless by the content of his words and listened with horror to the implication. His arms became slack and she thrust herself away, turning from him and going blindly back to her room, locking the door in her terror that he would come after her, shivering with a revulsion that rocked her whole body, her breath coming brokenly between her lips, unable to think of anything other than the man who had brought her to this state of weakness, a man whom she hated and feared.

That night she slept badly, nervously, her subconscious unusually active. She no longer felt safe at Burntwood Hall, but she had no choice but to endure the crisis until it went away. Gerald had threatened her, but she had no reason to believe he would make good his threats as long as she kept her distance.

But shortly after midnight a sudden sense of suffocating

danger brought her to a trembling awareness that something was about to happen when she heard a step outside her room. Moonlight streamed in through the half-open drapes and, rising, she went quickly to the door and stood there listening, straining her ears in the pregnant, terrifying silence that gripped the house, and then, starting with terror, she saw the handle slowly begin to turn. If she had not had the presence of mind to lock her door it would have opened—and she could not bear to dwell on what might have happened then.

She stood there, her heart thumping so badly she had to fight the inexplicable impulse to scream, certain that it was Gerald, and equally certain she could hear him breathing behind the door. Trembling violently, she did not move until she heard his footsteps die away. It was a long time before she crawled back to bed, taking long, steadying breaths to bring herself under control. Pulling the covers up under her chin, not even their soft warmth could still the chill in her trembling limbs, and try as she might, she could not sleep.

Staring blankly into the dark, her mind would give her no peace. It was in turmoil as she tried to forget about Gerald and think rationally about her relationship with Marcus. The problem Angela had presented her with would not go away. It was distasteful, which she would rather not confront, but she had no choice. She had truly wanted to make her ill-fated marriage to Marcus work, but with cold logic she knew she must reflect on her options yet again in the light of the problem Angela had presented her with, since she did not believe she would be able to deal with having a reluctant husband with equanimity.

Could she live with a man who was in love with another woman? she asked herself. No, she thought decisively, not even to hold on to Atwood Mine. Every time she looked into his eyes she would see him with Angela and torture herself when she imagined what they did together, what they talked about. But how could she bear to part from him now, loving him as she did? It would be like tearing the heart out of her breast, a heart on which he had put his hands and would never let go.

Suddenly she saw all her hopes and dreams begin to disintegrate before her eyes. An agonising, overwhelming awareness of what she must do brought a sudden deadening of her mind, a mind in which ardour and love for the man her father had wanted her to marry had been born, despite her antagonism towards him at the beginning. He was a man in possession of a steel-tempered strength, a man with an indomitable will who could not be manipulated, who had moved in on her, catching, twisting and moulding her into the shape of the woman he wanted his wife to be.

And now she was going to have to match his steel-tempered strength and prepare herself to face and absorb his anger when she told him she could not marry him, knowing his rage would be unconquerable when he discovered he was to be denied access to what had once been his family's dearest possession—Atwood Mine.

Having made her decision she felt empty and drained of life. Turning and burying her face in the pillow she wept hard, weeping until there were no more tears left in her.

When Marcus rode over to Burntwood Hall the afternoon after Gerald's assault on Eve, which had left her shaken and acutely afraid for her safety, he was surprised to see so much activity—and he was both horrified and alarmed for Eve's well-being when he saw Gerald had arrived to take up residence sooner than anyone had expected.

The large assembly of visitors had spent the morning riding about the estate and had just consumed a heavy luncheon when he was admitted to the house. They all turned simultaneously and watched as he walked purposefully into the centre of the room, his eye sweeping over them with disdain. He was coolly polite to Gerald, who regarded him with studied indifference, and he curtly acknowledged his disreputable bunch of friends before going out into the garden, where, on enquiring of one of the servants, he was told Eve could be found.

On seeing her he paused for a moment, his eyes held by her pale, graceful figure as she walked aimlessly along the paths in the formal garden that stretched down to a low stone wall, giving way to open fields and copses beyond. Her figure was slightly stooped and she looked so young, still very much a girl, her modest apparel and demure manner showing no resemblance to the fiery young woman he had encountered at the Parkinsons just a few days earlier.

He advanced towards her calmly, supremely unaware of the tumult raging within her breast or the clouds of apprehension hanging heavy on her shoulders. Beset by fear she was still deeply shaken by Gerald's violent assault of the previous evening, and certain he had been the one who had come to her room later.

Tired and bewildered, having fallen into a black hole of despondency and desolation that was so deep she felt she would never be able to clamber out and, having reached the painful decision that she could no longer consider herself betrothed to Marcus, sensing someone behind her she whirled round like a frightened rabbit.

A lock of hair had fallen over her face, and Marcus noticed how her hand trembled slightly when she smoothed it hastily into place. He saw that her face was very pale, her eyes wide and dark with a look of fear.

'Oh—Marcus! You gave me a frightful turn,' she gasped, having sought the quiet of the garden to escape the lewd and lustful, menacing eyes of Gerald and his male guests.

'And since when have you been the nervous type?' he murmured softly. 'Since Gerald arrived at Burntwood Hall with his associates, I don't doubt,' he said in answer to his own question, his expression grave and serious and at the same time enquiring. 'Why did you not inform me of his arrival?'

'Why—I—I saw no need,' she answered hesitantly, avoiding his direct, penetrating gaze, forcing herself to try and speak naturally, while part of her brain was agitated by what she had to tell him, knowing it could not be put off.

'And his friends. They have lost no time in paying him a visit.'

'It is no longer up to me to say who can and cannot stay at Burntwood Hall,' she said sharply.

'I realise that.' He frowned. 'Are they giving you a difficult time?'

'Nothing I cannot handle,' she replied, with far more conviction than she felt in her attempt to convince him that everything was all right, refusing to give in to the attraction that was making her heart race and her legs go weak.

Unconvinced by her statement Marcus frowned deeply and anger flared in his eyes. 'Eve, you are telling me the truth—because if Gerald has threatened you in any way, by God—I'll—'

'No—no,' she said quickly, lowering her eyes to cover her confusion, afraid that if he looked too close he would see she was lying. But his concern for her well-being warmed her heart.

'Nevertheless, there is quite a gathering. How long do they intend staying?'

'A week, I think. This is their fourth day.'

'Then let us hope they are not so overwhelmed by Gerald's generous hospitality that they decide to increase their length of stay. I must say he is looking rather smug and pleased with himself.'

'He has good reason—considering.'

'How is your grandmother?'

'Quite well—but she refuses to venture from her rooms at present.'

'I cannot say that I blame her,' he said, slowly walking beside her along the narrow paths that meandered between the blooming flower beds. 'Eve—I want you and your grandmother to come to Brooklands. The reason for my invitation is obvious. Besides, my mother would love to have you.

Naturally, she is eager to get to know you better and to discuss the wedding.'

He spoke quietly, but hearing the sound of laughter coming from the open windows of the house, Eve had the impression that he was alert and tense. There was no mistaking that he was in earnest and she felt a warmth in her heart for his consideration, tempted to accept his offer and go and live at Brooklands—to turn to him for the safety and security she craved.

Yet at that moment her conversation with Angela and his gift to her was still painfully clear in her mind, and she felt he was more dangerous to her than Gerald. She must have the courage to tell him that she had decided not to marry him after all and put an end to the whole sorry situation. She would rather get it over and done with than put it off and have the dread of doing it another time.

'That is very amiable of you, Marcus—but I must refuse.'

Pausing, he took her shoulders in his hands and forced her to look at him, the sweet, wild essence of her vulnerability staring out of her eyes. She was acting strangely, and he sensed something was wrong, very wrong. If only she would tell him what it was.

'Eve—why will you not let me help you? I am not blind. I can see how things are here. Do you feel yourself to be in any danger from Gerald?'

His eyes were warm with consideration and his voice was gentle, which surprised her, because whenever they met their conversation was like a fencing match. Feeling close to tears by the hopelessness of her situation, she swallowed down a hard lump that had risen in her throat, shaking her head slowly. 'No,' she lied, feeling the danger all around her, but her heart refusing to credit it while she was with Marcus. With him she was not afraid, thinking it was all a figment of her imagination and that Gerald would not harm her.

'Then will you promise me one thing?'

'What is it?'

'That if you are threatened or feel in any kind of danger—you will come to me at Brooklands—or send me word? I will come immediately.'

Taking the bit between her teeth, unable to go on pretending any longer, she took a step back from him, her face becoming hard, her expression closed, her violet eyes fixed steadily on his. Never had she felt more wretched, for what she was about to do was the worst thing she had ever had to do in her life.

'You may not want me at Brooklands when I tell you what I have been meaning to tell you ever since your arrival.'

He looked at her, his face impassive as he waited for her to continue. He did not have too much difficulty reading her expression and he could see her features were tense with some kind of emotional struggle.

'Marcus—I—I have decided not to marry you after all.'

His face changed as her words and their implication hit him, but if he was startled by her statement he did not show it. His eyes became fixed to her face and gleamed like molten fire. 'And may I ask what has brought about this decision?'

'I simply cannot go through with it. I have decided to go and live in Cumbria with my grandmother after all.'

Marcus's expression became pale with anger, which gradually became visible in every feature. He did not speak as he turned away from her, straight and proud, and Eve could almost feel the effort he was exerting to keep his anger under control.

'I see,' he said at length, turning suddenly to face her, with violence, on the verge of losing the struggle within himself. His pale blue eyes had gone hard between the narrowed lids, his face like granite, and he spoke with chill precision.

'And have you no sense of obligation—to me as well as to your father? We made a bargain, if you remember, and I fully intended keeping my side of that bargain.'

'Then I apologise for any inconvenience I may have caused you,' she said, trying to maintain the frozen stillness that held her in its grip. 'I know you will hate me for this, if you do not already, and I cannot blame you, but in all conscience I cannot marry you.'

'And the mine?'

'This is me I am talking about—not the mine,' she said quietly. 'The mine no longer seems important to me. I won't marry you, Marcus. I can't.'

There was so much finality in those two simple words that Marcus was momentarily at a loss to know what to say. He looked at her, thinking of arguments that might move her to reconsider. But he could see by the implacable set of her chin and the way her face was set against him, that this was not a decision she had taken lightly and he must respect that. But something had happened, something she was not telling him, and he strongly suspected it had something to do with Gerald's arrival.

His face hardened into an expressionless mask, his eyes probing hers like dagger thrusts, searching for answers as to why she was doing this. 'Don't you think you owe me an explanation?' he said tightly. 'Can't you tell me why, all of a sudden, I have become repugnant to you?'

'You—you haven't.'

'No? Then do you know what a man thinks when the woman he is betrothed to suddenly backs out of the agreement?'

Eve shook her head, quaking in front of his granite features.

'That perhaps there is someone else who has taken his place in her affections—if he was ever there in the first place,' he said with biting scorn. 'Who is it? Is it Gerald—or one of his dandified friends who has caught your eye?'

'Please, credit me with a little more taste. There is no one—and I have given you no reason to accuse me so abominably,' she flared, wanting to ask him about Angela, to beg him to tell her that what she had said were all lies, that he had never bought her gifts, and that nothing had ever happened between them—but her pride, and fearing he would confirm what Angela had so smugly told her was true, prevented her from doing so. Unable to look into his burning eyes she lowered her gaze, tears clogging in her throat. He might be a philanderer, but her heart refused to let go of the burning love it carried. 'I—I think you should leave.'

'No. I will not leave until this is settled between us.'

'It is settled. I am sorry. There is nothing else I can say.'

She tried to walk past him but his hand reached out and stopped her.

'Damn you—you cannot do this.'

'Yes, I can,' she replied wretchedly, trying not to look at him, at his blazing eyes. He was too powerful, too close and far too masculine. She was fighting tears, struggling to keep her voice under control, longing for him to take her in his arms, to feel his mouth on hers, setting her body on fire. But the image of Angela, with her sly, insolent smile, stood between them.

Their attention was caught by the clattering sound of horses' hooves and carriage wheels in the drive. Glancing towards it, Eve saw an elegant carriage drawn by a pair of sprightly white horses. It pulled up in front of the house and the lone occupant stepped out. Even from that distance she recognised Angela. As if recovering from a shock she experienced a fierce stab of jealousy and a coldness swept over her as she watched her walk towards the house, the sunlight catching the shining blue folds of her dress. She averted her face, having no wish to become embroiled in another argument with her.

'You have another guest, it seems,' said Marcus, with little interest, failing to recognise the carriage or its occupant, annoyed that it had arrived at that moment, diverting Eve's attention.

'No. It is Angela Stephenson,' she said with a brittle sound to her voice, her eyes glittering with hate. 'What an opportune moment for her to arrive. It is Gerald she has come to see— but I am sure she will be highly delighted to see you, and being aware of your interest for passionate affairs, Marcus, your delight will be just as great—and her presence will no doubt help soften the blow I have just dealt you,' she retorted with biting sarcasm, causing him to look at her sharply. Her anger on seeing Angela had revived her spirit. 'Please, excuse me,' she said quickly, her expression clouded, as though she were a thousand miles away. 'I must go and see if my grandmother is in need of anything.'

She turned from him but Marcus reached out and gripped her arm, moving closer, his mouth tightening as he stared at her gently heaving bosom and the tantalising mouth, determined not to let the matter end like this. He towered over her, his face dark and threatening, his overpowering physical presence and his intention catching Eve off guard. 'Before you go, tell me that this is what you really want—for our ways to part—never to see each other again?' he said, his voice softened to almost a whisper as he lowered his face to hers.

'Yes, it is,' she replied, her heart beginning to beat frantically as she tried avoiding his penetrating eyes.

'Then dare to look me in the eye and tell me,' he demanded, looking at her, the sunlight bathing her in light, her heavy mass of black hair surrounding her pale face accentuating its almost transparent whiteness.

'Yes,' she said at last, reluctantly. 'It is what I want.'

'And tell me that you don't want me to touch you, to kiss you. Despite the fact that you were raised to exhibit restraint and behave with proper decorum as befits a lady, I know how easy it is to make you forget all that, to make you behave with such wanton abandon.'

Before Eve, who was quite unprepared, could protest Marcus had hauled her against his chest, his hands unyielding as his mouth swooped down on hers. A fierce, silent, merciless struggle went on inside Eve as she fought to free herself, but Marcus was in full possession of his strength and she felt herself weakening slowly, knowing she could not hold out against him as a blaze of excitement leapt through her, her reaction a purely primitive one.

Avidly, like a man starving, Marcus crushed his lips over

hers, a kiss that devoured them, setting them both aflame, and he felt her trembling with innocence and helpless surrender against him, the heat from her scented body acting like a drug to his senses. He tasted her sweet breath, as her mouth responded, opening against his, and with a long, shuddering sigh their bodies became fused together as he determinedly pursued his course of sensual persuasion.

Eve could feel the heat and vibrancy of his body, with every sinew pressed against hers. She couldn't breathe and felt herself going soft, unable to resist temptation, forgetting everything as his hand left her waist to cup the gentle fullness of her breast, before rising and caressing the back of her neck, sweeping her whole body in one long, shuddering caress.

As quickly as Marcus had swept her into his arms just as quickly did he release her, thrusting her away from him with an abruptness that left her senses reeling. After their intimate contact he felt fire streaking through his loins and was almost overwhelmed with a mixture of pain and pleasure, finding her slender, supple young body more than capable of arousing him. His strategic attempt to weaken her into submission had rebounded with a vengeance. He had only succeeded in driving himself almost insane as he came close to losing the battle for control.

Wide-eyed and trembling with vulnerability Eve stared at him, so breathtakingly lovely he was almost blinded by the sight of her. Making a fierce effort to dominate and restrain himself his expression was grim, his eyebrows drawn together in anger as he glared at her, wanting her with a fierceness that left him breathless.

Dumbfounded, Eve stood there looking at him, shock holding her motionless. How weak she seemed suddenly, how helpless before him. She had not meant this to happen. It had only resulted in complicating matters further, making her love him all the more and regretting the decision she had made.

'I apologise for my barbaric behaviour, but when you remember during your long, lonely nights how it felt to have me hold you—to kiss you—and how willing your body was to respond, your desire will be sharpened with remorse. You may deny me until you are blue in the face, but the speed with which your body is aroused whenever I touch you proclaims stronger than any words how much you want to be with me.'

Helplessly Eve stared at him, her cheeks flushed and her lips soft and trembling, feeling an unfulfilled need inside her that made it impossible for her to deny that what he said was true.

'This is not the end, Eve,' Marcus went on, his voice low and soft in the silence that surrounded them. 'When you have calmed down we will discuss this further. You cannot put me from your life so easily. I shall not allow you to.'

'You must,' she whispered, her voice quivering slightly as she tried to bring her body under control. 'I have made up my mind. Please do not make it more difficult for me than it is already. There is nothing more to be said. Goodbye, Marcus.'

Dragging herself away she ran from him, entering the house through a side entrance, not wishing to come face to face with Angela. She was glad to escape Marcus's presence, glad she had told him, wanting nothing more at that moment than to soothe her head and compose her nerves that were in shreds after her meeting with him and the savagery of his kiss.

Marcus watched her go, bewildered and angry, trying to fathom out the reason for her change of heart; the only thing he could think of was that she had become infatuated by someone else. Despite her denial it was the only thing that made sense, but if this were the case then he doubted she would have yielded to his embrace quite so willingly. But when he thought this might indeed be so, he was unprepared for the searing pain of jealousy and hurt that overwhelmed him, which was beyond anything he had imagined existed.

In tight-lipped, rigid silence, biting back his fury and clamping his teeth together, he glared after her, tempted to go after her and demand an explanation to give him a chance to defend himself, but deciding against it. Setting his jaw he turned on his heel and stalked away. He'd be damned if he would plead with her further.

He intended to leave at once, knowing there was no longer any reason to remain, until he saw Angela walking towards him.

On reaching her room Eve swilled her burning cheeks with cold water, knowing Angela would have sought him out. Looking out of the window, which faced the gardens where she had left Marcus, she saw to her dismay that Angela had indeed found him and sauntered by his side.

Eve felt the world tremble beneath her and hot anger sear through her as she watched them together. Marcus gave the impression that nothing untoward had happened, seeming friendly towards Angela, gracious as he bowed his head and listened to what she had to say, considerately holding her arm when they descended a short flight of steps to prevent her from falling. With lingering looks—always a professional when it came to coquetry—Angela gazed up at him from beneath half-closed lids, laughter bubbling to her smiling lips at something he said.

Eve's grandmother was shocked and deeply disappointed by Eve's decision not to marry Marcus.

'You cannot mean this, Eve,' she said in disbelief.

'Yes, I do, Grandmother. I cannot marry him. I have told him so and there is an end to the matter.'

'How can it be an end? Too much is at stake.'

'No. Only Atwood Mine. As far as I am concerned Gerald can have it.'

'I can well imagine the extent of Mr Fitzalan's anger when you told him of this.'

'Yes, but his disappointment stems from losing the mine, not from any sentiments he might feel for myself. I was merely a means to an end, that is all—and I will not be a party to this any longer. I believe I have acted in a manner which will constitute my future happiness.'

Unconvinced, her grandmother looked at her closely, curious to know what had brought all this about. Her shrewd eyes observed her trembling lips and scanned the angry young face, seeing hurt and anguish mirrored in her lovely eyes.

'And might I ask what has happened to bring about this change of heart? I thought you and Mr Fitzalan were getting on rather well.'

'I thought so too. But it would seem Marcus has deceived us both. He has used me ill,' she said fiercely. 'He has been indulging in an affair with a woman I once deemed to call my friend, for some considerable time—a woman he would have married were it not for my father's will. The affair continues and will do so after we are married. I cannot accept that—and how do I know that if he tires of her he wouldn't soon be off on his next pursuit?

'Knowing your views on marriage, Grandmother, you probably think I am being very silly and foolish. But how dare he treat me so abominably? I will not be humiliated. I will not marry him simply to oblige my father, Marcus or you.'

'And has he told you he is in love with this other woman?'

'No. And he is not likely to. But I know it to be true. The woman in question has told me so herself—and so has Gerald.'

'I would take little notice of what he has to say, Eve, but it is evident you believe them—without giving Mr Fitzalan the chance to explain things to you himself. That's extremely harsh, don't you think?'

'Maybe. But I do believe them. I have every reason to after seeing them together with my own eyes, seen the beautiful gift he has given her—one of many, I was told. I will not be made a fool of.'

'I see. Then what can I say? I am deeply disappointed. I always thought Mr Fitzalan to be the one for you.'

Eve sighed. 'I'm sorry, Grandmother. Do not blame me for rejecting him.'

'I do not blame you. But what is to be done?'

'I shall return with you to Cumbria—if you will let me. And I would like to be out of this house as soon as possible. I cannot remain in it any longer now Gerald has arrived.'

'Very well. If you are resolved then we will not dwell on it. We will leave tomorrow—and I have to say I shall not be sorry to see the back of Gerald myself.'

Eve was desperately unhappy as she ordered her maid to begin packing her trunks for her departure for Cumbria. No matter how far away from Marcus she went, she would never forget him. Nothing would ever be the same again.

Chapter Twelve

On receiving a note from Eve informing her of her imminent departure, a stunned Emma came to say goodbye the following morning, believing Gerald to be the reason for her leaving.

'Oh, Eve!' she exclaimed on entering her room, staring in disbelief as her maid bustled about packing the trunks with her clothes and other possessions she was to take with her to Cumbria. 'Has Gerald made life so difficult for you that you have to leave? Well, you don't have to. You and your grandmother must come and stay with us until the wedding.'

'I cannot lie to you, Emma. Gerald is determined to obtain Atwood Mine and has issued savage threats against me concerning this. I have to admit that I am terrified and have reason to fear him—and it is one of the reasons why I am leaving Atwood.'

'Come and tell me,' said Emma, drawing her towards the bed where they sat facing each other. She was shocked to see how changed her friend was since the last time she had seen her on the day of the picnic. Then she had radiated vitality, but now her face was stricken and as white as the lace collar at her throat, and her dark circled eyes looked very tired.

'I am going to Cumbria with my grandmother.'

'But you can't. You are to be married in little more than two weeks. There is so much to do in preparation.'

'I won't be getting married, Emma,' Eve said quietly.

'But why? What has happened?'

'I am not marrying Marcus. I—I cannot.'

Seeing how distraught Eve was, Emma took her cold hand in her own. 'Tell me what's wrong. It's not just Gerald and his threats, is it? I can see that something else is wrong. Has something happened to Mr Fitzalan—is that it?' she asked, alarm entering her voice when she thought this might be the reason.

Eve shook her head sadly, haltingly relating the conversation she had had with Angela. Emma listened in stunned disbelief.

'I do not know when I have been more shocked,' she said when Eve fell silent. 'It is almost beyond belief that she would do it to you again. Who would think that so much wickedness could exist in one woman? And you believed her? Oh, Eve. We both know what Angela is capable of, but I strongly suspect she is just jealous of your relationship with Mr Fitzalan. If you run off to Cumbria now she will have triumphed over you yet again.'

'I have seen the proof of his affection for her, Em,' she said quietly.

'What kind of proof?'

'A fan, which Angela said was a gift from him. It was beautiful—pale blue and silver, and inlaid with diamonds. It was inscribed most lovingly, Em, and I saw his name with my own eyes. What more damning evidence could I have than that?'

Emma was shocked to hear this but, being acquainted with Angela's cunning and conniving ways, she was not utterly convinced and still thought Eve should give Marcus the benefit of the doubt.

Eve sighed, shaking her head in utter dejection. 'Oh, Em, I don't know anything any more. I told you on the day of the picnic that when they were together their behaviour was suspicious, leading me to believe their relationship was closer than that of mere acquaintance.'

'But you told me Mr Fitzalan denied it.'

'It is hardly something he would admit to. They have been very clever. I've been duped. Like Gerald, the mine is so important he will go to any lengths to obtain it.'

'It may not be as bad as it seems. Forgive me, Eve, but I cannot believe Mr Fitzalan would behave so dreadfully. In all fairness to him, you really ought to give him the benefit of the doubt until you have asked him outright as to the truth of it, instead of going off at half-cock.'

'I can't help it,' Eve said with angry confusion, trying desperately to keep her emotions under control. 'I could not bear to hear him lie to me again—but nor could I bear to hear him confirm what Angela told me to be the truth.'

'Then it is a dilemma that cannot be resolved unless you ask him outright. Do you intend to remain in ignorance?'

'Yes. I know the mine drew us together in the beginning, but Marcus has disappointed me. While he was paying court to me was it so very wrong of me to expect him to be faithful? Three years ago I was deeply hurt and humiliated by them both—equally. I will not go through all that again. I couldn't stand it, Em.'

Emma fell silent for a moment, studying her friend, touched by the grief she glimpsed there. She squeezed her hand in understanding, for what Eve said was true. She had been hurt, deeply. In fact it was a wonder she had managed to get over the indignities and ultimate heartbreak that had resulted from that silly, malicious challenge Angela had thrown down. It had been an affair in which Mr Fitzalan had been unfairly exonerated from all blame.

'As I recall, after confronting your father with his account of the affair—an account which I suspect did not cover the whole truth, otherwise he would not have been so lenient towards him and would have called him out and shot him at dawn—and after being absolved of any blame, he went di-

rectly to London for a considerable period of time. Maybe he
would be more concerned and understanding if he knew that
because of your encounter with him at Atwood Fair, it seriously damaged your reputation almost beyond recall. I doubt
he has any idea how much you suffered because of it—or that
it was contrived by Angela to secure Leslie Stephenson for
herself.'

'Perhaps you're right. But you know, Em, my mother spent
all the years of my life teaching me how to behave in a proper
and ladylike manner, but I flouted all the rules. I should not
have gone off alone with Marcus the way I did. After behaving
so outrageously, I suppose my parents' anger and the harsh
treatment I received from the people of Atwood was no less
than I deserved.'

'Nevertheless, Mr Fitzalan cannot be acquitted of blame.'

'I don't exonerate him—at least, not entirely.'

Emma sighed, looking compassionately into the pale, pensive face of her friend. 'You love him very much, don't you,
Eve?' she said quietly.

'Yes,' she whispered, blinking back her tears. 'I didn't realise just how much until today. But I stupidly forgot that his
interests went no further than Atwood Mine. I am a fool to
have let my feelings become involved—to dream dreams
which have no foundation in reality.'

Gerald found it almost impossible to hide his jubilation
when he knew Eve was to leave for Cumbria with her grandmother. After she had said goodbye to the servants, most of
whom would be staying on at Burntwood Hall when she had
gone, he managed to get her alone just before her departure.

'Running scared, Eve?' he taunted coldly.

'I do not run scared from you, Gerald.'

'Nevertheless, I am pleased to see you heeded my warning,'
he said softly. 'Am I to take it that you are not to wed our
illustrious neighbour after all?'

Eve looked at him with icy contempt, refusing to give him the satisfaction of knowing her decision. Let him speculate.

'Don't look so smug, Gerald. I am merely going to Cumbria for a short while. I have almost five months left in which to marry Mr Fitzalan, don't forget.'

And on that note Eve left Burntwood Hall, wondering if she would ever return.

On the journey to Cumbria with her grandmother, putting Gerald and his threats behind her, her spirits rose a little, but she was possessed of a curious apathy where Marcus was concerned. It had been hard for her to leave Burntwood Hall and Atwood, and her eyes were bleak with anguish, her heart numb with pain when she thought she might never see Marcus again. A man of his implacable character would never forgive her for the way she had rebuffed him. There would be no reconciliation, past differences forgotten.

It was the day after Eve had left for Cumbria with Lady Pemberton when Emma travelled to Brooklands to see Marcus. She could not have explained the impulse that made her act as she did, for she had no sympathy for him, considering him to be harsh, sardonic and pitiless. She only knew that she had to do something to help Eve.

She was not well acquainted with Marcus Fitzalan, only having spoken to him casually on the odd occasion. He was so formidable and excessively male, radiating a force and vitality that always made her feel shy and awkward when in his company. When she was shown into his presence she tried to focus her mind on how she had seen him at the picnic, because then he had not seemed quite so awe-inspiring as he had unashamedly amused the children; on doing so, her embarrassment and confusion began to fade.

On returning to Brooklands after leaving Burntwood Hall two days earlier, frustration was exploding inside Marcus as he tried to regain some semblance of control over his damaged pride and to marshal his scattered thoughts. He was both furious and confused by Eve's behaviour, craving an explanation to it all and having to suppress the urge to return and plead or persuade her to reconsider her decision, but his angry male pride prevented him from doing so.

Like a man possessed he threw himself into his busy work schedule to still his anger and frustration—anger that the mere thought of her left him throbbing for her like a lovesick youth. Only when night came did the terrible pain of her rejection, and what it would mean to his future to be without her, return, bringing with it an unthinkable, unbearable hurt.

At these times his mind gave way to long, slow thoughts of her, and he would dwell on how much she had come to mean to him, how much he had come to love her. He had known many women in the past—beautiful and amusing women, women he had loved and forgotten—but none of them touching his heart, not in the way Eve had done. It was as if his heart had been reserved for her and her alone, and even though she could drive him to the brink of anger and despair, nothing she could say or do would ever change that.

When Emma was shown into his study he rose from behind his desk, coming forward to offer her a seat, his face cold and indifferent and yet polite.

'Do sit down, Miss Parkinson. I have to say that I am surprised to see you here. Am I correct in thinking your visit is connected with Eve?'

'Yes,' she replied, sitting down while he remained standing. His tone was abrupt and stripped of compassion, and at any other time she would have turned and fled, for he bore no resemblance to the man who had amused her brother and sisters without restraint on the day of the picnic, but, nervous though she was, she faced him bravely. 'I—I came because I am worried about her. There are certain things I think you should know, Mr Fitzalan.'

'About Eve?'

'Yes.'

'Then why did she not come herself instead of sending her friend?' he asked sharply.

'She did not send me and would be extremely angry if she knew I had come here. However, I have to tell you that she has left Atwood and gone to Cumbria with her grandmother.'

Marcus froze, staring at her hard, and in that instant the austere control vanished from his sharp-edged, handsome face. Even though she had told him she would go with her grandmother to Cumbria, not for one moment had he believed she would leave, and not so soon. Renewed anger and a curious sense of desolation washed over him as he tried to keep his feelings under control.

'I see. When?'

'Yesterday.'

'Then what is the purpose of your visit? What have you to tell me that she did not see fit to tell me herself?'

'Have you really no idea why she told you she could not marry you, Mr Fitzalan?' Emma asked quietly, wishing he would sit down since his sheer height and forcefulness made her feel intimidated.

'No. I assumed that with the arrival of Gerald and his friends one of them had caught her eye. It's the only thing that makes sense.'

'Then you do her a grave injustice, sir,' said Emma sharply, ready to spring to Eve's defence, unwilling to hear any wrong said about her. 'Ever since you took advantage of her innocence three years ago—almost ruining her reputation beyond repair, there has been no other man in her life—and—after this, I doubt there ever will be unless it can be put right.'

'Ruin?' Marcus's lips tightened, then he gave a half-angry laugh. 'Miss Parkinson—what are you talking about?'

'That because of a silly, stupid prank that went terribly wrong, Eve has suffered because of it ever since. What happened between you and Eve soon became common knowledge. Angela Stephenson saw to that. But when you left for London the following day, had you no conscience?' she dared to say accusingly, for she too had been angered by the indifference and inconsideration he had shown towards Eve at the time.

'She was just seventeen years old, Mr Fitzalan, and her future looked bleak. To avoid her becoming an object of derision her parents sent her to Cumbria to stay with her grandmother—but the people of Atwood neither forgave not forgot her indiscretion. As you know, Leslie Stephenson withdrew his suit and married Angela—just as she had contrived it.'

'That I do know—and I remember Eve telling me that the whole thing was devised by Angela, but I regret to say I thought little of it at the time. I did not believe her to be capable of such vindictiveness.'

'Forgive me, Mr Fitzalan, but there appears to be a great deal you do not know about Angela,' Emma said with harsh criticism. 'Do you know that Eve did not return to Atwood for several months and never saw her mother again? She died of consumption—but, being a friend of Sir John Somerville, you will know that,' she said, with a trace of irony to her soft voice. 'Can you imagine how Eve has tortured herself over this? She should have been there. Her mother needed her and should not have died without seeing her.

'Eve never got over it and blamed herself. This tragedy kindled the sympathies of the people of Atwood and they welcomed Eve back. But the harm was done. Apart from visiting her Aunt Shona in London and her grandmother in Cumbria, she remained at Burntwood Hall in self-imposed seclusion.'

Marcus was clearly extremely shocked to hear this. 'Dear Lord—I knew nothing of this.'

'Of course not. Netherley is five miles from Atwood—but it might just as well be fifty. Eve told me of your anger on finding out who she was. Perhaps you thought to teach her a lesson—and you did—a harsh lesson, Mr Fitzalan. A lesson she did not deserve. It's rather cruel, don't you think, that whereas you treated the affair so lightly—and that you were beyond reproach where her father was concerned—Eve was treated so severely?'

Marcus did not move. He was like a cold, marble statue. Emma's revelations tore through him like a white-hot blade of anguish, searing and burning, unaware that he had inflicted so much pain, so much torment on Eve. He'd had no idea how much she had suffered because of his callous treatment of her. Sir John had never given him any indication of her distress, and he had been too thoughtless and too busy with other matters to enquire.

There had been no emotional ties between himself and Eve, and he had pompously believed he had taught her a harsh lesson in life, his only remembrance being when he left her of how it had felt to hold her supple young body close to his own, and how she had kissed him with such tender passion. He could not think without flinching of the things he had said to her—a flirt, promiscuous, a doxy—and how he had treated her. He now knew her to be none of these things.

He was choked with remorse. His conduct had been both wicked and unforgivable, and there was little wonder she had been hostile towards him when they'd met again at her father's funeral. He'd deserved all of it.

Anger and rage at his own blind stupidity overwhelmed him. How could he have treated someone as pure and sweet as she was so dastardly? Being a young, inexperienced girl, she'd had no defences against life to protect her. She had been the innocent victim of a prank that had gone hopelessly wrong—that had inadvertently placed her in the path of a man who could only be described as a libertine. There was no excuse for his conduct that day. Being an experienced man of the world he should have known better.

'What can I say? At the time I could not have foreseen the profound effect the incident—not nearly so insignificant as I had imagined it to be—would have on Eve's life…or my own. I knew she had gone to Cumbria and that Leslie Stephenson had dropped his suit and married Angela—and that her mother had died—but I was absent at the time and did not hear of it until I returned. Believe me when I say I had no idea Eve was not with her. But I still do not understand why she left—why she rejected me. Unless it was out of revenge for what I did to her.'

'Eve is not vengeful, Mr Fitzalan. She changed her mind about marrying you when Angela told her the two of you were in love and having an affair. Gerald lost no time, either, in confirming this.'

'Naturally! He would be only too happy to encourage a relationship between Angela and myself—for it would be to his advantage,' Marcus said fiercely.

'Perhaps if she had not fallen in love with you herself—and had it been anyone other that Angela,' Emma said quietly, 'it would not have hurt so much. Being the type of person she is, she was too proud to ask if this was true, too afraid that you would confirm what Angela had told her—especially when Angela flaunted a fan, a gift from you to her, under Eve's nose.'

Marcus stared at her in genuine astonishment. 'But that's ridiculous. A fan, you say? A gift from me to her?'

'Yes.'

'But I never gave Angela a gift.'

'That was not what Angela told Eve. Apparently if was affectionately inscribed.'

Becoming thoughtful, Marcus shook his head slowly. 'The only fan I have given to anyone was to my mother two years ago on her birthday—a very fine one of blue and silver, inlaid with diamonds.'

Emma sighed, beginning to see all too clearly what Angela had tried to do. 'That sounds like the one.'

'Then I can only surmise that my mother lent it to Angela or her mother on some occasion and they failed to return it. Please believe me when I tell you that Angela means nothing to me and never has—and I told Eve this when she broached the matter to me only last week. I had hoped I'd convinced her, but it seems I was wrong.'

'You did at the time, but when confronted by Angela—and when she produced such damning evidence—you cannot blame Eve for doubting you. When Angela called to see her at Burntwood Hall a few days ago, and after hearing what she had to say, Eve was not wholly convinced you were telling the truth—and Angela can be very convincing, Mr Fitzalan.'

'And what has Eve done to her to make her so vindictive towards her?'

'She has done nothing. Angela is of an extremely jealous disposition and it was enough when they were children that Eve's family were rich and titled—that she was beautiful and popular with everyone she came into contact with—and that she attracted the attention of Leslie Stephenson, which ultimately played on Angela's jealousy. She begrudged his attentions towards Eve. Her scheme was designed to alienate his affections away from Eve in the hope that he would turn to her. She was determined to secure him for herself whether she wanted him or not—merely to spite Eve.'

'And my arrival at Atwood Fair that day provided her with an opportunity to shame her, to manipulate her into a situation that would embarrass her.'

'Yes. The challenge was that Eve had to succeed in getting you to dance with her in the hope that Leslie would see you together and become jealous and increase his desire to marry her. He had been dithering for weeks about asking her father's consent to marry her, and Angela convinced her it was just what he needed to sharpen him up. When you disappeared into the trees with her it was more than Angela could have hoped for. She soon found Leslie and made quite sure he saw the two of you together.'

Marcus sighed when she fell silent. 'And I know the rest.'

Emma nodded. 'Being friends of long standing, I was well acquainted with Angela and her ways. I knew perfectly well what she was up to and tried reasoning with her when Eve had gone, but in moments like those she is deaf and blind to everything save her own satisfaction and needs. And despite what Eve told you, Gerald was making her life extremely unpleasant for her at Burntwood Hall—in a way that only Gerald can.'

Marcus paled visibly. 'My God, I should have known. I should have insisted she came here to Brooklands. But when she rejected me so firmly, I have to admit that I was so furious that all thoughts of Gerald went out of my head. What did he do to her?'

'He did not touch her, if that is what you mean,' Emma said quickly, wanting to reassure him of that. 'Eve knows that Gerald hides a streak of savagery that gives her reason to fear him. His rages are rare but dangerous. He has made it absolutely clear to her that he will go to any lengths to obtain Atwood Mine, and the threatening quality of his behaviour has terrified her. She is dreadfully afraid that if she were to go ahead and marry you, before the wedding could take place Gerald would contrive for her to meet with some well-organised accident, taking care that suspicions do not fall on him.'

A cold anger gleamed in Marcus's eyes. 'He would not dare.'

'I think he would, and Eve is right to fear him. She is afraid of both Gerald and Angela, Mr Fitzalan. Gerald wants the mine—Angela wants you. Together they could be a force to be reckoned with—a deadly combination, don't you agree?'

'Indeed.'

'However, Angela may be jealous and vindictive, but I do not believe she would do Eve any physical harm.'

'But knowing how spirited Eve is, I am surprised she gave in to Gerald's threats so submissively.'

'She would not have done once, but her fear finally obliterated her courage.' Emma rose and moved to stand close to Marcus, her face serious, the worry she so clearly felt for Eve mirrored in her eyes as she looked with gravity into his. 'I have spent three years picking up the pieces of my closest friend, Mr Fitzalan—and just when I thought she was beginning to put all the heartache and unpleasantness behind her, it starts up again. I doubt she can take much more.'

'But why did she not ask me about Angela? Why go to such extremes?'

'Both Lady Pemberton and myself tried persuading her to confront you with this, but she would not hear of it. She is so headstrong, like a wilful child at times. What will you do now?'

'You don't have to worry about Eve any longer, Miss Parkinson,' he said softly. 'I shall leave for Cumbria first thing in the morning—just as soon as I have paid a visit to Little Bolton to see Angela and put a few things straight. And then I think Eve and I must have a serious talk.'

'But what if she is too afraid of Gerald and his threats to risk returning?'

'I guarantee she will be safe with me. Once I have found her nothing—*no one*—will ever part me from her.'

Emma smiled, relieved. It was as though a great weight had been lifted from her mind. He spoke with such fervour that she was convinced he would take care of Eve and see she came to no harm.

'Forgive me, Mr Fitzalan, but I have to tell you that ever since that unfortunate day three years ago, I have silently wondered whether God was wise for placing you in her path. I see now that he was.'

Marcus looked at Emma, his face still. 'No one could have made me a more wonderful gift. I can't thank you enough for coming here today, Miss Parkinson. I owe you a great deal.'

'I did it for Eve, Mr Fitzalan. After all she has been through, her happiness is my sole concern. And if you can persuade her to reconsider her decision and to return to Atwood, then you must bring her to stay with us until the wedding. I can speak for my parents for they are extremely fond of her and love having her to stay. It's impossible for her to return to Burntwood Hall the way things are.'

Emma left after taking refreshment and having a friendly chat with Mrs Fitzalan, who confirmed that she had indeed lent Angela's mother her fan. It was on the night of the dinner party, when Eve had come to Brooklands with her grandmother. Mrs Lambert, having misplaced her own fan, had found the evening excessively warm and asked if she might borrow one of her own. Of course, she had been only too happy to oblige. No doubt she would return it when next she came.

Mrs Fitzalan knew of Eve's departure for Cumbria but had no idea she had ended her betrothal to Marcus, so Emma did not enlighten her. Not wishing to worry his mother unduly Marcus had not told her, hoping Eve would come to her senses and see the error of her decision.

Emma's coming to Brooklands had brought Marcus to a frame of mind which, if not exactly easy, was less tortured than before. He could think more calmly about Eve, realising how, with the malicious knowledge Angela had implanted in her mind, she had become swamped with doubt and mistrust.

He became filled with a dark rage when he thought of Angela, and that she had made Eve suffer untold misery for some spiteful reason of her own. He understood that what Angela had told her must have resurrected all the torments she had suffered three years ago, and that it had been the final blow that had broken her spirit so that she could no longer remain at Burntwood Hall. His attitude became sympathetic. After all, he could not blame her for acting as she had, and how could he possibly expect her to trust him after what he had done to her?

He would never know the depth of suspicion and hatred that had driven Eve to reject him and escape to Cumbria with her grandmother, but what he did know with absolute clarity was that he could not give her up. She was unlike any other

woman he had ever known and he could not face the pain of
losing her. He dwelt with something akin to wonder on what
Emma had told him—that Eve was in love with him—and he
wanted to know the extent of her love and when her feelings
had changed towards him.

Intent on paying Angela a visit, he had to resist the urge to
go to Eve at once, for more than anything else he wanted to
justify himself to her, for her to know she had been wrong to
believe Angela and her scheming lies. He was prepared to
expend all his patience in breaking down the barriers between
them, to bare his soul and hers, to tell her nothing in the world
mattered except her.

But one thing troubled him deeply. While ever Atwood
Mine remained at the centre of their marriage agreement it
would forever remain a barrier that separated them, and she
would always have an element of doubt about his love for her.
He wanted the mine, but not without Eve.

Angela's surprise on seeing Marcus was evident, for it was
the first time he had visited her parents' home, which was
modest compared to the magnificence of Brooklands and
Burntwood Hall, and had always been the cause of much of
her resentment towards Eve. This had increased a thousandfold
when she had become aware of Sir John Somerville's will—
that he wanted Eve to marry Marcus, the man she herself had
become infatuated with when they had been properly introduced by their mothers in London some months ago.

She had fawned and simpered before him to attract his attention, and he had always been polite and solicitous towards
her, but it rankled that he was no more attracted to her than
he was to all the other women who flocked around him, eager
for his attentions. Always used to having her own way in
everything, with men falling at her feet wherever she went, it
annoyed her when Marcus made it plain that he was quite
oblivious to her charms.

But already tired of being a widow, and desperate to marry

a man who would keep her in the style she had become accustomed to in the short time she had been married to Lesley—although not even the well-off Stephensons could compete with the wealth of Marcus Fitzalan—she was fiercely determined to capture him. She thought she might succeed when they returned to the West Riding, without the competition of other ambitious women flitting around him, and when they were in each other's company more—which proved to be often, their mothers being such close friends.

Then Sir John Somerville had died and laid down conditions in his will that threatened her own chances of marrying Marcus. This had infuriated her. Having set her own sights on him, she could not bear to be beaten and embarrassed by Eve. Her resentment against her was great indeed. Eve had always had too much, always been popular and sought after because of who she was, and in the past she, Angela, had pretended friendship, while secretly having no misgivings of wanting her downfall. It seemed that nothing else in her life had ever been so important. Any defeat of hers would give her immense satisfaction.

She received Marcus alone, becoming quietly alert and suspicious, noticing the obvious tension lining his sternly handsome features, knowing with a shattering certainty a moment later that he had been told of her conversation with Eve.

Marcus gave her an unsmiling nod, finding it virtually impossible to restrain his anger. 'This is not a social visit, Angela,' he said, the tone of his voice direct and as hard as steel, his expression the same. 'It is unappealing but necessary and I do not have much time. I am on my way to Cumbria to try and persuade Eve to return. You do know she has left Atwood, don't you?'

Angela blanched at the unwelcome news that he was to fetch her back but remained silent, waiting patiently for him to continue.

'What have you been saying to Eve?' he demanded harshly. 'What have you to say for yourself, Angela?'

'Me? Why—nothing that is not true, Marcus.'

'Don't insult my intelligence with your simpering denials. How dare you go to Burntwood Hall and pour your lies into Eve's ears—and in so threatening a manner?' he accused her angrily. 'And how dare you have the audacity to do something so base as to show her a fan you told her was a gift from me to you? You know perfectly well it was a gift from me to my mother, which she kindly let your own mother borrow on the night of the dinner party when you both came to Brooklands— the night when Eve was there also. Do you deny it?'

Angela allowed a scornful smile to play on her lips. 'No. The fan was an innocent fabrication on my part, I do confess, but what I told her were not lies. I told her nothing but the truth.'

'The truth? I never realised you could be so deceitful or conniving, or that you could be so talkative.' He moved to stand in front of her, looking down into her hazel eyes with a hard, murderous gleam, his lips curled over his teeth. 'How soft and persuasive you can be at times, Angela—how soothing and seductive your voice, but your caressing tones and beguiling smile do not cancel out the hard, calculating gleam in your eyes. Until now I did not guess what a weight of hatred and treachery you concealed, but at last I am beginning to understand you—and also to understand why, with such damning evidence, Eve believed your lies.'

Marcus's sharp tone stung Angela to awareness, and when she realised what he was saying her face became contorted with rage, her eyes as hard as ice and her fists clenched by her sides.

'You have deceived me into believing I was the one you cared for—the one whom you would marry,' she hissed.

'If that is what you think, you deceive yourself. I have never given you reason to believe that you are anything more than an acquaintance and you know it. I do not want you—not now—not ever. Is that clear? Eve was never your friend, was she? But what you have done to her—causing her unnecessary suffering—I cannot and shall not forget.'

'*You* are not entirely blameless,' Angela accused him scathingly.

'No, I am not, but I did not realise it until yesterday and will reproach myself for ever more.' His face was white with anger and his voice became icy calm as his eyes glittered and held hers. 'I love Eve—and I will say no more because I do not have to justify my feelings to you of all people. But I will say this—that you, Angela, are an evil-minded witch and the dirtiest fighter I have ever met…and believe me, I've met some dirty fighters in my time. You will stoop to any depths to get what you want.'

A deadly smile twisted Angela's distorted features and her voice became dangerously soft. 'You are right, Marcus. I do hate Eve. I hated her long before that day at Atwood Fair. But I won that time, and whether or not I do so again remains to be seen. I won't say I hope you'll be very happy together. We both know I would be lying.'

Marcus stared at her. Rarely had he seen such hatred in a human face. His anger was pitiless and so powerful he had to clench his hands by his sides to prevent them reaching out and throttling her for all the pain Eve had suffered because of her jealousy and hatred.

His eyes narrowed. 'For some malicious reason of your own, you are hellbent on destroying her, but I shall tell you this. Take care, for if any harm comes to Eve by your hand I shall have my revenge. There is no hole deep and dark enough for you to hide from me. I shall find you—that I swear.'

Marcus left Angela then, and if he had raised his voice or struck her she would have borne it better. Instead he kept his tone temperate, but his eyes were like slivers of ice, showing the depth of his anger. As Angela watched him go there was an all-too-evident hunger for revenge burning in her heart—but this time it was not only directed at Eve, but at Marcus also.

Chapter Thirteen

Eve's horse followed a grassy track almost of its own volition, where it stretched and wound on and upwards through a
cool forest, between tall trees—ancient English oaks and lofty
beeches, shivering aspen and silver birch, their leaves, soon to
cover the ground, shimmering and trembling in the slight
breeze that rustled through them, the green of their summer
glory giving way to the onset of autumn, turning them to bur-
nished copper, russet and gold. She rode slowly for almost an
hour, until she came out of the trees and paused on the summit
of a grassy hill.

Dismounting, she tethered her horse to a tree, where it began to graze while she sat on the grass in solitude, seeing once
again the familiar character of the pastoral landscape spread
out below her, beautiful and dramatic, and her heart was still.
All around her was loneliness and emptiness, the majesty of
the jagged expanse of the Cumbrian mountains separated by
high passes and deep lakes beyond her, fell and dale scenery
at its most impressive, the wind breathing low in the trees.

To the north she could see the dramatic Langdale Pikes, and
to the east she recognised the remote Dunnerdale village of
Seathwaite, and beyond that the grey slate houses of
Ambleside near the northern end of the silvery waters of Lake
Windermere. She allowed her eyes to drink their fill, the ap-

athy which had cloaked her since leaving Atwood beginning
to lift as her spirits rose.

For the first time since coming to Ruston House, her grandmother's Cumbrian home, three days ago, she allowed her
thoughts to turn wholly to Marcus. His betrayal with Angela
lived and breathed inside her mind, torturing her. Because he
had betrayed her love with the woman who had once pretended friendship while being bent on destroying her, it was
like a double profanation in itself. When he had left her, she
had thought her heart would break, crushed with despair, but
she had refused to give in to her anguish, unable to cry any
more tears, for they had all been shed before she had left
Burntwood Hall.

Already she missed him, missed the joy the sound of his
voice brought her, his nearness, for it seemed like a thousand
years since she had last laid eyes on his face, but she had to
go on, to survive. Her grandmother had told her that she
would, that time heals all things—but she knew it never
would. Nothing but death could take away the love she carried
within her heart. Nothing would ever heal the sense of desolation that covered her like a shroud. Her heart twisted with
anguish when she realised what she had done to him, knowing
how angry he must be and that he would never want to set
eyes on her again.

But at that moment, as Marcus rode up the steep path and
emerged into the open sunlight, she didn't know how far from
the truth that was. He paused, insensible to the wonderful
scenery all around him, every sense he possessed becoming
riveted on Eve's still figure. She was dressed in a sensible
black woollen skirt and crisp white blouse buttoned up to her
throat, having removed her jacket and bonnet and placed them
on the grass beside where she sat.

Her hair, coiled in the nape of her neck, shone and was as
smooth and black as a raven's wing, and her face was serene
and curiously soft, with a yearning, nostalgic quality as she
gazed at the fells laid out far below. It was as if she was stifled

by some emotion, as if her inner peace had been crushed and she had come to this peaceful hilltop to gain some quiet relief. Her expression was so calm, so open, that his breath almost ceased and his blood congealed, for it was as if her soul lay bare. Never had he seen her look more lovely, more desirable—darkly, beautifully perfect.

His love for her was more alive than he had imagined and his pulses leapt to the knowledge. It was so discernible that he could almost reach out and touch it, see it, and smell its sweet, intense aroma. Mesmerised, he became lost in thought as he silently watched the play of sunlight and shadow upon her lovely face, the rise and fall of her chest as she gently breathed, content to stand and gaze at her, but she turned her head, as if the compulsion of his intent gaze was strong enough to tell her he was there.

Eve stared at him, at his well-known features, so deeply buried in her heart. Her attention became riveted, a world of feelings for an instant flashing across her face, her eyes recognising his presence but her brain telling her he must be a figment of her imagination. For just a moment she thought she must be suffering from some kind of delusion, brought on by a wish of her own. She became still, her eyes brimming with love, disbelieving that he had come to her.

How long had he been standing there watching her? she asked herself, with his black hair blowing in the breeze, his bearing stamped with noble pride and emanating so much strength and naked power that he seemed as hard and invincible as Scafell and Langdale Pikes soaring in the distance.

Emotion rendered her speechless, her wide violet eyes imploring and devouring him all at once, and for one brief, marvellous moment her heart went soaring as high as the hills and she forgot everything save the immense joy that he had come to her after so much suffering.

She stood up and for a long moment they looked at each other with love and longing, until, relieved from the shock of his unexpected appearance, and unable to forget that she had broken their betrothal which was the reason why she had come to Cumbria, Eve managed to speak.

'Marcus! You! You here!'

He looked at her with inexpressible tenderness, moving towards her, his eyes narrowing in the bright sunshine, wanting to reach out and draw her into his arms, but all he could do was gaze at her.

'Did you honestly think I would dismiss you so lightly from my life? When we parted at Burntwood Hall I told you that I would not allow you to dismiss me so easily. I arrived at Ruston House shortly after you left on your ride. Your grandmother told you the direction you had taken.'

'Did she? I often come up here when I'm staying with her. The view is quite magnificent.'

Marcus frowned. 'Please—you might look pleased to see me.'

'I—I am so surprised,' she murmured, feeling her heart give a leap of consternation and, she had to admit, a certain excitement.

'I apologise if I frightened you.'

'You didn't frighten me. I—I cannot imagine why you have followed me here—after our conversation at Burntwood Hall,' she said, flushing as the memory of that day and the harsh words they had exchanged—and his savage kiss that had rendered her helpless—came flooding back to her, praying she would be strong enough to withstand the fatal attraction which never failed to draw her towards him, like metal filings to a magnet.

'When you rejected me so firmly—so decisively,' he reminded her, watching her closely. 'I haven't forgotten. But we have matters to discuss which are important to us both.'

'You could have written and saved yourself the journey,' Eve suggested.

'I daresay I could. But what I wanted to say could not be put down in a letter. I wanted to see you—to put things right between us, and persuade you to return with me.'

'That is not possible. Nothing you can say can possibly tempt me to return to Atwood.'

'No, not to Atwood. To Netherley—to Brooklands, as my wife.'

Eve stared at him aghast, unable to believe he had the effrontery to expect her to still marry him after all he was guilty of. All the hot, angry words that had festered inside her since she had last seen him bubbled to her lips, for no longer could she remain silent on his affair with Angela.

'Surely not even *you* would have the impudence to expect me to marry you while you are indulging in an affair with someone else? The fact that it is Angela—after all she is guilty of where I am concerned—is too much to be borne. Perhaps I should have been less eaten up with anger if it had been someone else.'

'Please—explain what you are talking about. I am quite astonished.'

'Are you? When you asked me why I had broken our betrothal I did not tell you the reason then—but now you have it. It needs no further explanation from me. I saw the proof of your feelings for Angela with my own eyes when she flaunted the fan you gave her before me—affectionately and so very touchingly inscribed by you. One of several gifts you have given her over the months of your acquaintance, she told me. I will not be played false, Marcus. And when she called at Burntwood Hall after I had left you that day, how dare you be so attentive towards her—almost loverlike—in front of me.'

Eve waited expectantly, watching him, wanting desperately for him to explain about his relationship with Angela—to set her mind at rest by reassuring her there was nothing to substantiate her jealous imaginings. But she was disappointed to see neither surprise or guilt register in his eyes; in fact, he remained infuriatingly cool and implacable.

'Was I? I was not aware that I was being,' he said at last, 'and I was certainly not being any more attentive towards Angela than I would have been had it been anyone else.'

'Angela is not just anyone else, Marcus,' Eve argued heatedly. 'You were being excessively attentive. I saw you. Are you her lover?'

He stared at her with some element of amusement, glad to see her spirit had not been defeated after all by Gerald's threatening behaviour.

'Are you?' she demanded.

A smile moved across Marcus's face, slowly, infuriatingly, his eyes becoming gently teasing as he moved closer, speaking softly. 'Well now, considering how matters stand between us—that you disapprove of me and have rejected me so completely—that is something I refuse to divulge.'

'Oh! You beast!'

'Am I?' He was mocking her with a wry sort of humour. 'I was wounded, Eve, deeply. Surely you cannot blame me for finding solace and forgetfulness in the arms of someone else.'

'There are other, worthier ways of finding solace and forgetfulness than to abandon yourself in the arms of another woman. But then, no doubt there have been many times in the past when you have sought pleasure in Angela's arms.'

'I find it strange that you should take me to task over this. After all—you can hardly blame me for seeking affection elsewhere when you rejected me so firmly now, can you?' His eyes darkened and he smiled slightly, mocking her, playing a subtle game with her emotions. 'Unless your excessive anger has been roused by my attentions towards Angela because you care a little after all.'

'Care? Care for you?' she flared furiously. 'You are arrogant in your assumptions.'

'I don't believe so. Perhaps you should look into your heart and ask yourself the reason for your anger. Has it taken the devotions I apparently show to another woman to make you aware of the true nature of your feelings?'

'No. I already know how I feel—I— Oh…' Flustered, Eve

turned from him sharply in embarrassment, having said too much.

Marcus smiled, lifting one eyebrow quizzically. 'Pray continue. You have my avid attention,' he murmured over her shoulder, so close that Eve could feel his warm breath caressing her ear, and the heat from his body. 'Don't stop now—not when you were about to divulge the depth of your feelings. Would I be correct in thinking that because you believe I am involved in an affair with Angela is why you called off our betrothal?'

Sighing dejectedly Eve nodded, turning to face him. 'Yes. It took me a long time to get over what happened between us that day at Atwood Fair—to put some semblance of order back into my life. I am not prepared to jeopardise that by entering into a marriage that cannot fail to end in tragedy because my husband is in love with another woman.'

Marcus's expression became serious, the gentle teasing he had indulged in disappearing from his eyes.

'But I am not. Eve—listen to me,' he said, taking her hand and drawing her towards him. 'I am not having—and never have had—an affair with Angela. I have never thought of her as anything other than an acquaintance. You have to believe that.'

'Then why did you have to be so attentive, so loverlike towards her? And how can you explain your gift to her? And you have just said—'

'Forget what I just said. I was teasing—which was cruel of me and I apologise. The fan can be explained quite simply. It was my mother's fan you saw—a fan I gave to her on her birthday two years ago. My mother lent it to Angela's mother on the night you came to Brooklands. It was a warm night, as you will remember, and Mrs Lambert had misplaced hers. She must have taken it home with her, and it is clear that for her own malicious reasons Angela set out to cause you further distress by pretending I had given it to her.'

Eve stared at him. His explanation was so simple that she

was beginning to feel very foolish. She remembered that the fan had been inscribed but it had not been dedicated to anyone in particular, so Angela had thought to use it out of sheer deviousness.

'I—I see,' she said softly. 'From past experience I should have seen through Angela's ploy—that it was just a typical touch of cruelty on her part to make me believe you saw marriage to me as nothing more than a business deal. In moments like those—when she sees something she wants being taken from her—she is deaf and blind to everything save her own hatred. But to go to such lengths—it is clear she must feel something for you, Marcus.'

'Perhaps—but it is entirely one-sided. You must believe that, Eve. The day you saw me strolling with her in the garden at Burntwood Hall—after you had so firmly rejected me—I behaved in a manner for which I am deeply ashamed. If I had known then the extent of Angela's malice towards you, how deeply her lies have hurt you, both now and in the past, I would not have been so attentive, but at the time I did it to goad you because you had driven me to such anger.

'I did it in an attempt to break through your indifference. I knew you were watching as we walked in the garden. I glimpsed you at the window of your room, and thought if I could raise your anger you would show some positive feeling—and I am pleased to see I succeeded.'

'You put on a good act,' Eve smiled, her lips trembling.

'I did, didn't I? But I'm tired of acting. I shall do what I should have done at the very beginning,' he murmured, moving closer, a slow smile curving his handsome lips as his smouldering gaze dropped to her breasts, softening, lingering, as if he could well imagine what lay beneath her high-necked blouse. 'You, my darling, are going to discover how dominant, how primitive a man I can be.'

'Am I?' Eve asked, feeling her cheeks burn crimson beneath his scorching look, that same arousing look she remembered from that fateful day three years ago, and the occasions after when he had kissed her, weakening her and arousing sensations and images that reminded her how quickly and wantonly she had yielded to him, how his arms had held her close, and how it had felt to have his mouth close over hers and to feel her body shuddering with awakened passion.

'Yes—and very soon. But for now I will have to content myself with a kiss.'

Drenched in the sun's warmth Marcus placed his hands on her shoulders and looked deep into her eyes, soft, swimming, velvety and glowing with an inner light. Eve trembled, unable to control it. His hands were strong and warm; lifting one of them up he caressed her cheek with a featherlight touch, and lowering his head he drew her against him and held her tightly, causing a ripple of intense pleasure to go soaring through her as she melted against him. Covering her mouth with his own, his parted lips were warm and moist, pressing, gently probing, firm and growing more and more insistent, his kiss long and urgent.

After a moment, with a sigh Marcus raised his head and looked down into Eve's upturned face, keeping her pressed close to him as he drank in her beauty, feeling the graceful swell of her breasts against his chest. He was unable to believe he was holding her in his arms when so recently she had told him she wanted nothing more to do with him. She was tantalising, bewitching him so that he thought she must be some kind of sorceress. Only a man with ice instead of blood in his veins could have resisted her looking as she did at that moment.

Lowering his head, with expert slowness he trailed his lips across her cheek, kissing and gently gnawing with his teeth at the soft, fleshy lobe of her ear, hearing her sharp intake of breath as he gently tugged. Raising his head he smiled slowly, but she moved away a little as his face descended to hers once more.

'Please do not try to distract my mind by trying to seduce me, Marcus,' Eve said breathlessly, while gazing up at him with silent yearning, wanting nothing more than to lie on the grass with him and let him make love to her. 'The time has come when there must be truth between us. We have still much to discuss. I have so much to tell you.'

Marcus pulled her back, this time circling her with his arms to prevent her escape, longing to repeat the kiss but having to content himself for now with holding her. 'I know all I need to know for now,' he murmured, his voice husky with seduction that both thrilled and excited her. 'Your dear friend Emma Parkinson saw to that.'

'Emma?'

'Yes. She came to see me when you left with your grand-mother—and I must say she can be quite forceful when she has a mind. I made no effort to defend myself when she accused me so severely of ungentlemanly conduct towards you three years ago at Atwood Fair—but did you know you made quite an impression on me that day? It certainly showed me you were no prim and proper cold-blooded female. I never forgot you.'

A thousand memories came flooding back to Eve of that day; in fact, they had never left her, but her foolish, wanton behaviour had made it impossible for her to look back with joy. She changed colour and brusquely pulled away from him, but secretly his words gave her reason to rejoice, for it was the closest he had come to saying he cared for her.

'Marcus,' she said quietly, 'please do not mention that day again. I have always retained a strange, unreal and at the same time uneasy memory of the time when I unashamedly threw myself at you. I cannot bear to think of it. I want to forget the whole of it.'

He smiled. 'My memory is not so accommodating—and nor do I want to forget how it was to kiss you, to feel your response, which makes me want to repeat the offence.'

He became serious. 'But I did exert unwarranted force on you. I was so full of my own conceit that in my arrogance I lost sight of what I might have done to you. I sincerely regret my actions, and I am truly sorry for any hurt and humiliation I may have caused you. I had no idea you suffered so much distress owing to my ignoble behaviour. How you must have hated me and blamed me for being the cause of your absence from Burntwood Hall when your mother died.'

Pain filled Eve's eyes and sadness wrenched her heart at the mention of her mother, for she still reproached herself for not being with her when she had needed her.

'I cannot deny that it was a terrible time and I deeply regret not being with her. But it would seem Emma has let her tongue run away with her. You must have had an extremely long and interesting conversation. What else did she tell you, Marcus?'

'She told me about Angela's visit to you at Burntwood Hall and her lies—and she also told me of your fear of Gerald and the threats he made, which he will answer for when I return to Netherley,' he said, his voice low with anger and his expression becoming grim.

'No,' said Eve quickly in alarm. 'I would rather you leave things as they are. He did me no physical harm so I would prefer to forget what he said. But tell me more about your relationship with Angela,' she said in an attempt to divert his thoughts from Gerald, not wishing to recall his menacing behaviour towards her or his threats, which worried her far more than she was prepared to admit.

Marcus sighed, his eyes fastening on the delectability of her soft lips. 'I am tired of talking about Angela.'

'Do not tell me you were blind to her charms, Marcus,' Eve breathed, trying to ignore the look in his eyes. 'Whatever else she is, Angela is an extremely beautiful woman,' she said, determined not to let him fudge and escape the issue. If she was to reassess her decision about marriage to him it was important to her that she knew everything there was to know.

'But not as beautiful as you,' Marcus murmured gallantly. 'You will be happy when I tell you that I have severed all connections with Angela. I have made plain what my feelings are for her and I doubt very much that she will bother us in the future.'

'You went to see her?'

'After Miss Parkinson's revelations, I could not ignore what she had done to you.'

'How long have you known Angela?'

'We met briefly in London, and when she returned to the West Riding she began calling at Brooklands with her parents—who, as you know, are friends of my mother.'

'Yes, I do know that. But did you not see the venom—the spite behind Angel's smile?'

'No. I confess I didn't.' He smiled. 'I never looked close enough for that. I have to say, my love, I was not as well acquainted with Angela as you—clearly an unfortunate acquaintance which has taught you to read her schemes and venomous insinuations.' He sighed, sitting down on the soft grass and drawing her down beside him.

'Caprice born of indifference and my mother's gentle coaxing drew us together and nothing more—and even if your father had not laid down conditions in his will, and if I had never met you, my darling,' he said, gathering her into his arms and planting a kiss on her lips, 'I could never have married Angela—not in a million years. What I felt for her was a poor emotion compared with the joy and blinding love I feel in just looking at you.'

He looked down at Eve's enchanting face, gazing at her with so much tenderness that happiness and joy went soaring through her and she allowed herself to hope in a way she never had before.

'There—now I've told you. Without realising it, you, my darling Eve, have become an immeasurably important part of my life. If you refuse to renew your promise to become my wife then I shall be the most miserable of men. I shall never be free of you. I would give you the world to make you happy.'

The quiet words did nothing to dispel the doubt hovering

at the back of Eve's mind that sprang cruelly to the fore to torment her, refusing to go away as she wanted it to—to enable her to drift along in the knowledge that he would be marrying her for no other reason than that he loved her.

She sighed. 'I will be more than happy to renew my promise to become your wife—but I don't want the world, Marcus. Titles and wealth mean nothing to me—and the one thing that seems to matter so much to you is no longer important to me.'

Marcus looked down at her, frowning. 'I take it that you are referring to Atwood Mine?'

'Yes,' she said quietly, averting her gaze.

Marcus was serious. 'Eve, look at me.'

Slowly she raised her eyes to his once more.

'Ever since your friend Miss Parkinson came to see me, I have given the matter a great deal of serious thought. What I have to suggest may shock and surprise you, but, with your agreement, I have decided to put the mine in trust for our children.'

Eve stared at him in disbelief, rendered speechless by his announcement, knowing just how much it had cost him to make that decision.

'If you are in agreement, that is what I will do.'

'Why—I—yes, yes, of course,' Eve uttered—what else could she say? She was extremely surprised by the unexpectedness of his suggestion and pleased. It was like being thrown a life line, something to cling on to. 'But—are you absolutely certain about this, Marcus?'

'I am as certain as I can be.'

'Then—then what can I say?' she stammered.

Marcus looked at her steadily, frowning a little. 'You seem a little confused.'

'No—no.' She smiled. 'I think it's a good idea. It's just that I do not want you to do something you will have cause to regret later.'

'I shan't regret it, and our children will benefit in the future—God grant we are so blessed.'

'And—and you will do this for me?' she asked quietly, genuinely moved by his decision, a decision which told her she meant more to him than she had ever dared to hope.

'For you, my darling, I would do anything.'

'But it doesn't seem fair. You are entitled to it. No one can question your right. Atwood Mine is what you've wanted for so long—to work it as your father did, and your grandfather before that. Consigning it to trustees will be painful for you, having to watch it being administered by others.'

Marcus smiled wryly. 'Sometimes getting what you want doesn't always seem fair, Eve. Owning Atwood Mine will always make you doubt my love—and that is the last thing I want. I do not want it. It would be the worst kind of punishment. I am doing the right thing. I am certain of it. Besides, I shall ensure that I have the utmost confidence in the trustees in whose care it is placed.'

With a rapidly beating heart, Eve was looking at him as she had never dared to look at him before, unable to believe he would do this enormous thing for her. He had abolished in one fell swoop any doubt she had that he loved her. His eyes burned down into hers with all the love and passion she had despaired of ever seeing there, and her own were brilliant with happiness.

'Then what can I say?'

'Only that you will renew your promise to become my wife.'

'Yes,' she whispered. 'There is nothing I want more than that.'

'When you left Burntwood Hall in such a hurry, Gerald must have questioned your reason for doing so. Did you by any chance tell him we were not to be married?'

'No.'

He smiled slowly, arching one sleek black brow, the teasing note returning to his voice. 'I see. Then that leaves me wondering that you may not have been so certain of your decision not to marry me after all.'

Eve looked up at him impishly. 'No. I know you would like me to admit that was the reason, but it wasn't. I merely wanted Gerald to sweat a little longer. Was that so very wrong of me?'

'Considering his harsh treatment of you—no, it was not. However, until we are married I would like you to come and live at Brooklands.'

'No—I think it would be best if I stayed with Emma, Marcus—until the wedding, that is.'

He frowned. 'I'd prefer having you at Brooklands where I can keep an eye on you.'

A cold hand seemed to clutch at Eve's heart, knowing what had prompted him to say this. 'Do you think Gerald will issue more threats, Marcus?'

Marcus thought Gerald was desperate and evil enough to go further than to utter threats against her, but kept his thoughts to himself, not wishing to worry her unduly.

'I sincerely hope not.'

'Then if you take me directly to Mr and Mrs Parkinson's, Gerald need not know I have returned until the wedding.'

Marcus frowned, uncomfortable about this, but he could see this was what she wanted. 'Very well. I have to go to Leeds as soon as we return, on business, and I shall also proceed with setting up the trust for the mine, which will be controlled by a board of trustees until one or more of our children are of an age to take control themselves.'

'But what if there are no children?' Eve asked, trying not to sound too pessimistic. 'It is not uncommon.'

'I know. If that is the case I shall see that my brothers' children benefit. But,' he said, looking deep into her eyes, 'I sincerely hope we have a nursery full of children, and,' he murmured, his voice thickened by desire, his lips nuzzling her cheek, so soft they were like wings on her flesh, 'I aim to set about making babies the moment we are married. I shall teach you how to make love, my darling, and I hope you will prove to be a willing and enthusiastic pupil.'

Eve gave him an incandescent smile. 'I really can't think of anything I would like doing better.' She sighed against him. 'I do love you, Marcus. I can't find the words to say how much.'

His arms tightened around her. 'I know. I love you in the same way. I want you to promise me you will not venture away from the Parkinsons' house while I am in Leeds—in case Gerald should discover where you are and come calling,' he said, his gaze once again becoming fastened to her lips as a soft breeze scented with pine caressed them. His eyes darkened. 'But at this moment I have no wish to discuss Gerald. I have other, much more important things on my mind to consider.'

'Oh? Such as?'

'Whether or not you will object if I kiss you again.'

'I did not object when you kissed me before.'

'Very well,' he murmured, proceeding to kiss her once more, unable to sit so close and not do so. He paused for a moment, fanning her lips with his warm breath. 'I can see you don't mind, but considering the bargain we made some time ago—that ours will be a marriage in name only until we want it otherwise—I shall abide by that and stop whenever you want me to.'

Eve sighed breathlessly against him as he tenderly assaulted her lips once more. She didn't want him to stop. She couldn't. She was powerless. She wanted him to go on and on.

'Do you mind if I break the bargain?' she breathed.

'No, I suppose not,' he smiled, smoothing a finger across her cheek. 'I welcome it. I am feeling extremely relieved to realise that Atwood Mine is no longer the most important thing in the world to me,' he said, 'now that I have been caught up in emotions over which I have no control.'

'No?' she whispered, placing small, tantalising kisses on his lips.

'No,' he admitted. 'It is now a close second—not the most important.'

'Then please tell me—what would be the first?'

'Do you really have to ask?'

'I think so.'

'Do I really have to show you?'

'Yes,' she sighed provocatively. 'It might be rather enlightening.'

'You are insatiable, Miss Somerville,' he said, his lips against hers, enchanted by her.

'If I am it is your fault,' she murmured, smiling in a tantalising way that swelled his heart.

And with that he proceeded to show her, laying her down on the grass and leaning over her.

Marcus's hands were gently caressing, arousing Eve to undreamed-of delights as he kissed her deeply, his breath fanning her lips warmly. She melted willingly in his arms, responding with such exquisite pleasure and causing Marcus to almost lose control. He was overcome with desire for her, and felt the heat rising inside him. His tender persuasiveness vanished, becoming replaced by a scorching demand, his hands clasping her face between them, his lips grinding on to hers, stifling her, but she welcomed his kiss and he felt her respond. Wrapping his arms about her, he crushed her as she moaned against him, filled with pleasure.

They were both far away, absorbed with each other, knowing now for certain that they loved each other desperately, that they had been created for each other through all time, and in their joy they forgot everything and everyone who had threatened to destroy their happiness.

When they could tear themselves apart and leave their pillow of grass, they rode at a leisurely pace back to Ruston House where Lady Pemberton was waiting with eager anticipation, knowing by the happiness she saw radiated on her granddaughter's face that all had been happily resolved between her and Mr Fitzalan.

Chapter Fourteen

Mr and Mrs Parkinson were delighted to have Eve stay with them until the wedding, and Eve was secure in the knowledge that her return to Atwood would remain unknown to Gerald until the wedding, a week hence, and despite the distinction of the two people involved, and the pomp and ceremony that would have accompanied such a wedding, it was to be the quietest wedding Atwood had seen for many a year.

But unbeknown to either Marcus or Eve, Angela saw them taking the road that bypassed Atwood and heading for the Parkinsons' house whilst she was out riding. On observing them together, jealousy and anger flared anew within her, reminding her of Marcus's angry and humiliating visit to her home, when he had rejected her and berated her so severely over her despicable treatment of Eve.

Determined to make things as unpleasant as possible between them, with a slow, malicious smile of triumph curving her lips, she turned her horse in the direction of Burntwood Hall, knowing she would experience a deep sense of satisfaction when Eve got her comeuppance.

After making sure she was settled with the Parkinsons, Marcus took his leave of her, an expression of immense concern clouding his face, for he was seriously anxious for her safety.

'Promise me not to venture out alone—that you will remain in the house and await my return from Leeds, when I shall fetch you over to Brooklands to see my mother. She is most anxious to discuss with you matters concerning the wedding and your position at Brooklands as my wife.'

Eve smiled up at him, strangely pleased by his solicitude. 'Of course I promise. I shall do exactly as you say.'

'Good,' he said, wanting to sweep her into his arms and kiss her full on her lips, but owing to the fact that there seemed to be a hundred pairs of smiling, inquisitive eyes observing his departure, it was with some annoyance that he had to content himself with giving her a light peck on the cheek.

Eve watched him go, exhilarated and deliriously happy in her love, his kiss still warm on her cheek as she impatiently began counting the days to their wedding, but the sweet drift of happiness was soon shattered when a letter was delivered to her from Burntwood Hall shortly after Marcus had left for Netherley.

Eve was in the parlour with Emma and she went cold on recognising Gerald's sprawling handwriting, staring at it with dread, reluctant to open it.

Seeing her dilemma and unease, Emma came to stand beside her. 'You'll have to open it, Eve—read what he has to say.'

Eve swallowed hard, a sudden fear clutching her heart. 'But how does he know I've returned to Atwood—and so soon? Someone must have seen me and told him. I must say he's lost no time in contacting me so the letter must have been written with some urgency.'

With trembling fingers she opened it, reading how he wished to apologise for his conduct before she had left Burntwood Hall and inviting her to dine with him the following day, stressing they had matters to discuss which were important to them both and could not be ignored.

Sensing her worry, Emma asked if she might read it, staring at Eve in incredulity when she had finished.

'Why, the man is impertinent,' she gasped. 'After all he is guilty of where you are concerned—threatening you so abominably, which was so upsetting to you at the time. You cannot go, Eve. You must show the letter to Mr Fitzalan and stay clear of Burntwood Hall—at least until after you are married. I fear Gerald is a reckless libertine with evil intent. He is known to be of an erratic temperament and I am sure you would not be safe.'

'Yes, you are right, Em. I shall answer his letter declining his invitation, of course, and let him know I do not welcome his attentions.'

Which she did. However, after Gerald's past, despicable conduct towards her, it came as no surprise that her refusal did not end his interest, for another letter arrived the following day repeating his invitation, which Eve ignored, although his audacity and persistence aroused all Emma's anger.

Eve tried to reassure her that she was not worried unduly by Gerald's behaviour, but deep inside she was terrified of him, becoming plagued by tension and impatient to see Marcus. Two days later when no further letter came from Gerald, her spirits were uplifted when another letter came, this time from Mrs Fitzalan, inviting her to Brooklands two days hence, by which time Marcus would have returned from Leeds. Eve began to feel much less alarmed, and being surrounded by boisterous children, it was hard not to feel light hearted.

The day before she was to go to Brooklands, Emma was to accompany her parents on a visit to friends on the other side of Atwood. They were to take the children, all except Jonathan, who hated visiting and declared he wasn't feeling very well. With some concern Mrs Parkinson felt his brow, but in the absence of a temperature she decided he was not so ill as to justify putting off her visit. However, she still thought it best to leave him at home where he must remain in bed until she returned. If he was no better she would send for the doctor.

Eve declined their offer that she accompany them, insisting

Emma went with them when she offered to remain at home with Eve for company.

'You're certain you don't mind me leaving you, Eve? I'll stay with you if you want me to.'

Eve smiled. 'I don't mind, Em—truly. I shall read a book to occupy my time, and have a look in at Jonathan later.'

'Are you sure you'll be all right?'

'What possible harm can come to me here?' she laughed.

They had not been gone an hour when the childrens' nurse-maid sought her out in the parlour where she was sitting on the window seat quietly reading a book. On looking up, she saw the young woman looked extremely worried and was wringing her hands in agitation.

'Why, what is it, Maggie?'

'It's Master Jonathan, miss. I left him sleeping—or so I thought at the time—but when I went to his room ten minutes since he wasn't there. His bed is empty and he's not in his room.'

'But I thought he wasn't feeling well.'

'So he said, miss. But Master Jonathan has a habit of putting it on when he wants to get out of things—and pretty good he is at it too. He's done it often enough in the past.'

'Well—have you searched the house?'

'Yes, miss, but he's not to be found anywhere. Nanny's searching the attics but he's not thought to be up there.'

Eve frowned. 'Oh, dear,' she said, putting her book down and getting up. 'We'd better look for him. He can't be far.'

'Yes, miss. He'll have gone off somewhere.'

At first Eve was unperturbed, but when Jonathan did not return after half an hour she grew alarmed and ordered what servants there were—six, all told—to extend their search be-yond the grounds, to divide and go off in separate ways. Watching them go, she turned to Maggie.

'Have you any idea where he might have gone, Maggie? Think very hard. Where does he like to go—to play? Does he have friends close by he might have gone to visit?'

'He does have friends at the Fairchilds who live close by—and there is a boy his age at the Simpsons down the road he visits now and then. He also likes to go fishing to the river or the pond—but he knows never to go alone.'

Eve went cold and felt dread quicken within her. The river! Why hadn't she thought of that? Jonathan loved to fish; in fact, it was his favourite pastime, but he never went to the river unless he was accompanied by his father or another adult member of the household. Besides, it was half a mile away and too close to the quarry for comfort. Surely he could not have gone there. The dangers were too great, and when she glanced out of the window and saw dark storm clouds gathering overhead, her alarm for Jonathan's safety grew.

'Dear Lord, Maggie—with the weather about to take a turn for the worse, let's hope he hasn't gone to the river. It's extremely naughty of him if he has. Run to the stables and instruct one of the grooms to enquire at any of the houses in the neighbourhood he might have gone to—the Fairchilds and the Simpsons in particular. Meanwhile I'll go to the river. When the others return—and if he still isn't found—have them follow me.'

Without thought for her own safety, and all the promises she had made to Marcus that she would not leave the house under any circumstances, thinking only of Jonathan, Eve immediately set off on foot in the direction of the river, unaware as she entered a wood some distance from the house that she was being followed. Eventually she came to a fork in the path, praying that Jonathan hadn't taken the steep path to the right, which was a shortcut past the deep, disused quarry to the river. The path was treacherous, especially after heavy rain, which made the edge crumble. One wrong foot could prove fatal.

Snagging her clothes on loose briars, she hurried along a twisting track, her heart hammering inside her chest. Emerging from the wood she breathed a huge sigh of relief on seeing the shining, tumbling water of the river ahead of her. It ran into a pond a quarter of a mile away, constructed to feed the canal further along. As she ran she tried to ignore the ever-darkening sky as her eyes scoured the river bank for Jonathan's small figure, fully expecting to see him sitting contentedly with his fishing rod dangling into the water, but as yet there was no sign of anyone.

Standing at the water's edge she stared in desolation at the water tumbling over its rocky bed, too shallow at this part to be of danger should Jonathan have found his way here and fallen in—but the pond was another matter. Quickly she ran towards it, knowing that if he wasn't there she would have to return by way of the quarry.

Hoping and praying nothing dreadful had befallen him, she was unable to believe her good fortune when she saw his golden head beneath some trees, where he sat on his bright red coat, just as she had imagined him, calmly placing something small and wriggling on to his fishing hook before casting his line into the water.

Eve's relief was enormous. She laughed out loud, calling his name as she lifted her skirts and ran towards him, not knowing whether to scold him or hug him with the sheer joy and relief she felt on finding him safe.

He looked up and grinned sheepishly at her when he saw her, but then his young face became transfigured with terror and he stood up quickly, screaming something at her and pointing at something behind her, as his fishing rod fell into the water and drifted away.

Instinctively Eve stopped, unable to hear what it was he screamed at her, and before she could turn and see what had so alarmed him, she felt her arms grasped roughly by hands from behind. Taken completely by surprise she struggled desperately to free herself, calling to Jonathan to run back to the house, but then she stumbled forward, uttering a cry of alarm as she plunged forward, hitting her head on something hard.

Her senses reeling, Eve was aware of two dark shapes bending over her. She wanted to call out to Jonathan, whom she could still hear screaming, to tell him again to run back to the house and fetch help, but as she felt herself seized by strong arms and brutally lifted off the ground, she was swallowed up by a suffocating darkness.

Quite by chance when Marcus was riding from one of his mines towards Netherley, he happened to run into Mr and Mrs Parkinson and almost their entire brood, travelling out to visit friends on the other side of Atwood. After pausing in the roadway to have a few words with them, a soft smile played on his lips as he watched them go on their way.

Having been told in a meaningful way by a smiling Emma that Eve had been left all alone in the house, he turned his horse round and spurred it on in the direction of Atwood, intending to surprise her. He was to collect her the following day to take her to Brooklands, but he hadn't seen her since his departure for Leeds four days ago and already he was missing her like hell.

Inside his pocket he had a gift for her, the first of many he hoped to give her throughout their lives together. It was an engagement ring, a cluster of rubies and diamonds he had purchased the day before in Leeds. It was the most expensive gift he had ever bought, but where Eve was concerned he would spare no expense.

As he rode up the drive towards the house he was aware of a strange quietness all around him, and he smiled, for with so many children normally running about the place it wouldn't always be as peaceful as this. Not until he dismounted did he become aware of the commotion coming from inside the house. Without waiting for someone to let him in he pushed the door open and stepped inside, seeing an extremely anxious-looking Matthew Somerville trying his best to calm the distraught servants.

There was an immediate, penetrating silence when they became aware of Marcus's tall, still figure observing them from the doorway, his presence dominating the scene. He stepped inside the hall, his eyes fixed on Matthew in stern enquiry, all his senses telling him something was very wrong.

'What is it? Has something happened?' Marcus demanded.

Relief that he had come flooded Matthew's eyes and he moved towards him. 'Thank God you're here, sir. I'm afraid something is wrong. I called on my way to the mine to see Emma, only to find the family are all away from home except Jonathan and Eve. According to the servants Jonathan—who had stayed home because he said he wasn't feeling well—went missing shortly after the family left the house, and Eve went to look for him.'

All Marcus's senses became alert. 'Where? Where did she go?'

'To the river. It was suspected that Jonathan might have gone fishing.'

'And what has been done? Has anyone gone after them?'

'Yes—but neither of them are to be found.'

'Then perhaps they are elsewhere.'

Matthew shook his head, reaching out and picking a small boy's red coat up out of a chair and a fishing rod. 'These are Jonathan's. The coat was found beside the river by two of the servants. The rod was found close by in the river where it had become snagged between the rocks. Unfortunately there was no sign of Jonathan or Eve.'

Marcus took the coat and fishing rod from him, holding them in his hands and looking at them hard, as if willing them to tell him what had happened, but he wasn't seeing anything. Something black and formless and terrifying in its secrecy had come alive inside him, almost stopping his breath and wrapping itself around his pounding heart.

'Who found them?' he demanded, looking round the circle of silent, anxious faces, his piercing, blazing eyes glaring at them one by one.

A groom and Maggie stepped forward. 'We did, sir,' said the groom. 'We searched all over for them—even down in the quarry to see if some mishap might have befallen them there—

but there was no sign of them or anyone else. There were signs on the ground close to where we found Master Jonathan's coat that there might have been a struggle, but it was hard to tell. I'm sorry but we had to come back. We didn't know what else to do.'

'You were right to come back. At least now we know where to begin looking. How long is it since Eve left the house?' he asked Matthew.

'Two hours ago.'

Marcus turned away towards the window, his eyes springing fiercely to life and his uncompromising jaw set as hard as granite as he looked in the direction of the river, seeing the first flash of lightning fork across the sky in the distance, followed by a hollow roll of thunder heralding the storm. He knew what had happened, knew without being told, and he became like a man in the grip of a nightmare, cursing himself for having let her out of his sight.

That Gerald had abducted Eve he did not doubt, and the thought of her, bewildered and terrified in the hands of a man who would go to any lengths to get his hands on a piece of property, caused a violent rage to fill his being, which increased with each passing moment. The cold look of black fury on his face when he turned rendered everyone mute.

'Two hours, you say.' His voice vibrated itself round the room, hurtling itself violently against the walls. 'It might just as well be two days. I told her not to leave the house—not to go wandering off by herself. I feared this might happen. I have every reason to believe she has been abducted.'

Ashen-faced, Matthew came to stand beside him. 'This has crossed my own mind but I can think of no reason why anyone would want to abduct Eve and Jonathan.'

Marcus's expression was hard, his eyes cold. 'Can't you? There is one person who springs to mind, Matthew. One person who wants Eve out of the way—one person who is desperate and demented enough—who will go to any lengths to prevent us marrying.'

Matthew blanched, swallowing hard, knowing after one devastating, heartstopping moment who he was referring to. But he could not accept it. 'You think it is Gerald, don't you?'

'Yes. I know it.'

'My brother may be accused of many things, Mr Fitzalan, but he would not resort to this.'

'Your loyalty to your brother is to be commended, Matthew, but he has made threats towards Eve several times since the death of her father. I firmly suspect he is behind this. However, the fact that he has Jonathan as well might save her.'

'Save her?' Matthew gasped, horrified by what he was implying. 'Surely you do not believe Gerald would harm her?'

'Yes. I have no doubt of it. Your brother is devious enough to resort to anything to prevent our marriage in order to retain Atwood Mine. He owes money hand over fist, and even though he is in possession of the estate, without the mine his situation remains desperate.' He looked at the groom. 'Come. We must hurry. Take me to the river where you found Jonathan's coat—and you, Matthew, ride into Atwood and get as many men as can be got to assist with the search. Mr and Mrs Parkinson must also be contacted at their friends' house and told to return at once.'

Matthew followed him out of the house just as the first heavy drops of rain began to fall.

'I do not believe Gerald will harm her, Mr Fitzalan,' he said, knowing better than anybody what his brother was capable of and trying to convince himself he would not stoop to murder.

Marcus looked at him and their eyes locked in fervent prayer to God that he was right.

When Eve regained consciousness she realised with a terrifying reality that her worst nightmare had come true—that Gerald's threats had become reality. She was stiff and sore and lying on a hard soil floor. Hearing a soft whimpering close to her she opened her eyes, looking around without moving her head, for it ached abominably.

Jonathan's white face and frightened eyes were the first things she saw. Crouching between herself and the wall he was like a captive bird, visibly trembling. His cheeks were wet with tears and his eyes filled with fear as, bending over her, he tried to shake her into wakefulness.

Despite her throbbing head and bruised and aching body, Eve set her teeth, determined not to give in to despair, and to thrust the growing, insidious fear away from her. She could not afford to weaken, to think of the dangers, not when she had Jonathan to protect. It was imperative that she kept a clear head and cool brain for when Gerald made his appearance—as he must some time.

Struggling to sit up, she leaned against the wall and gathered Jonathan to her. His body was cold but she was relieved to see there was no evidence that he had been physically abused. Taking comfort from the security of her arms, his trembling lessened.

'It's all right, Jonathan,' she whispered, her lips against his hair, wishing they had on more clothes to keep out the dank cold of the shed. 'Don't be frightened. No one is going to harm us.'

She could hear the storm raging with full force, with rain lashing through the trees, pounding against the walls of the building and on the ground outside. Quickly her eyes took in the comfortless dilapidation of their restricted domain, seeing they were in a small, disused shed, dirty and with huge cob-webs hanging from the walls, and with several broken implements and other useless objects scattered about the floor. A dim light filtered in through some rent sacking covering a small window high up in the wall, and through a hole in the roof where a slate was missing rain dripped through on to the floor.

The window was set too high in the wall for her to reach and there was nothing large enough for her to stand on to enable her to look out, and she knew without getting up and trying it that the stout door would be fastened securely to prevent their escape. On seeing there was no way out her spirits sank. There were so many worked-out pits in the area with disused buildings like this one that they could be almost anywhere.

She tried to remember what had happened. Someone had come at her and grasped her arms roughly from behind. Filled with alarm she had panicked and screamed to Jonathan to run, to go back to the house for help, but he had just stood there, too frightened to move. In a struggle to free herself from the vicious hold of her captor, she had stumbled and hit her head hard on a rock or something, but whatever it was the blow had been sufficient to render her senseless. Before she had lost consciousness she was sure she had seen two men. But what now? she wondered. What would happen next and how long would they have to remain in the shed?

Shuddering from the cold she drew her knees up, unable to believe this was happening to her. She thought it must be a dream and that she would wake up soon, but the damp permeating the walls of the shed and seeping through her clothes and into her body told her it was no dream.

She suspected the men who had brought her to this place—men who had been paid by Gerald—might still be outside somewhere, and if they weren't and she shouted no one would hear her. Anyone with any sense would not be out in this storm.

It wasn't until then that she realised how desperate, how determined Gerald was to obtain Atwood Mine, what lengths he would go to. She had no doubt he was prepared to kill her to do so, but she felt fury against him for daring to perpetrate such terror on a child.

'Jonathan, listen to me. Do you know where we are? Did you see where the men brought us?'

He shook his head, pressing his little body closer. 'No,' he whispered. 'They covered my eyes so I couldn't see.'

'Did you recognise them?'

'No.'

'How many men were there?'

'Two.'

'Did they hurt you?'

'No, but they frightened me.'

'How long do you think it was before we reached this shed?'

'Don't know. Not very long.'

'And did they have horses?'

'Yes. Two of them.'

So, thought Eve despairingly, if their persecutors had brought them here on horseback they could be further away from Atwood than she had at first thought. Closing her eyes, she tightened her arms around Jonathan. 'Don't worry. We'll get out of here. We'll have been missed by now and everyone will be searching for us.' She spoke with more confidence than she felt, but hearing Jonathan sigh she could sense she had won his trust.

Knowing they would have been missed and that everyone would be searching for them was the only thing she had to hold on to. Everyone would be so worried and Mr and Mrs Parkinson and Marcus would be informed immediately. He would suspect Gerald had abducted them and go to see him, forcing him to divulge where they were. He would come soon. He had to.

But suppose no one came? Suppose Gerald refused to disclose their whereabouts and denied all knowledge of their disappearance? She went to the door and hammered on the thick, unresisting wood in fear and frustration, calling for help, but the noise of the storm drowned the sound of her voice. After a while she stopped, knowing it was useless. It was stupid. No one would hear her.

Time dragged on and after what seemed to be an eternity she heard sounds of voices raised in anger outside the door, hearing something about a child and that everything had gone wrong. She sprang to her feet and clutched a terrified Jonathan to her, almost frightened out of her wits and having to suppress a scream when the door was suddenly thrown open and Gerald stepped inside, the two men she assumed had been involved in their abduction standing back. In the first wild, unreasoning panic, she almost threw herself at him, wanting to hurt him for causing herself and Jonathan so much distress.

Gerald stared around the shed, straining his eyes in the dim light, his face twisted by nervous spasms, his nostrils pinched as he realised his scheme had been botched by the two imbeciles he had hired to abduct Eve.

'So I was right,' Eve flared, unable to shake off the intense dislike she felt for this man that covered her like a foul odour. 'It was you who had us brought us here. How dare you? You are loathsome. How could you do such a wicked thing? Jonathan is a child and you have terrified him.'

Gerald's glance merely flicked over the small figure of the boy clinging to Eve's side. 'That part of your abduction was not intended. However, I intend doing all in my power to prevent your marriage to Marcus Fitzalan. When I have finished with you he will hardly appreciate being the recipient of spoiled goods. I doubt he will want a scandal, and I shouldn't think even he wants Atwood Mine so badly as to take you then.'

'Don't count on it, Gerald,' she scorned with an unmasked bitterness in her tone alongside an obvious contempt, unable to control the shaft of hatred that twisted through her, so savage that it must have been felt by Gerald himself. 'He will call you out—and I've heard he's a deadly duellist, with pistols or rapier.'

Gerald laughed, a cold unnatural sound, before his slack lips formed themselves into a malevolent smile. 'I'm a fair shot myself. But I doubt it will get that far. In his eyes you will be a shameless wanton, soiled, used and unfit to be his wife. It will take a miracle to survive the scandal.'

Eve went cold, for what he said was true. In no time at all

lurid versions of her involvement with Gerald would spread like wildfire throughout Atwood and Netherley, and the more people gossiped and speculated the whole sordid, damning episode would have been blown out of all proportion—just like it had been the last time, only then it had been Marcus her name had been linked to, not Gerald, and she would be too humiliated to protest her innocence. But she stood her ground, refusing to be cowed by him.

'And was it your intention to bring me here all along, to this shed, where you could carry out your wicked, sordid act?'

'Oh, no. Had we not been saddled with the boy I had somewhere much more pleasant than this in mind—a place where we would have been comfortable, to be seen enjoying each other's company enormously.'

'And you really expected me to be docile and go along with all this tomfoolery, did you?'

'There are methods I could have adopted to bring about your submission.'

'Drugs, you mean.'

'If necessary.'

Eve looked at him contemptuously, her voice trembling with unsuppressed hatred and anger when she spoke. 'What a loathsome, despicable creature you are, Gerald. I find it impossible to believe we are of the same blood. You are mad, for only a madman could have thought up this diabolical plan to abduct me in order to obtain the mine.'

Gerald's lips twisted in a cruel sneer. 'I am no more bad or loathsome than Fitzalan. And don't be fooled by his soft words, my dear, Eve. I have told you—it's the mine he wants. You come as an extra. Nothing more.'

'You are mistaken,' Eve retorted heatedly, determined to use all her wiles to try and bluff her way out of the ugly, desperate situation. 'I have to tell you, Gerald, that you really could have saved yourself the time and trouble of going to such extreme lengths as to have me abducted.'

His eyes narrowed, glittering like coals from between narrowed lids. 'What are you saying?'

Taking a deep breath Eve met his gaze, prepared to lie, to go to any lengths, to have him release them. Normally she could not get her tongue round a lie, but at this moment she had no such qualms in these desperate circumstances. But the way she felt left her in no doubt of her own uncertainty that she would succeed in what she was about to tell him.

'As you know, I have just returned from Cumbria where Marcus joined me. Perhaps you should ask yourself why.'

'No, but I will ask you—if it is important.'

'Oh, I think it is. You see, Marcus and I were married there.'

Gerald stared at her hard with eyes cold and lifeless. His face grew red and Eve felt herself begin to shake.

'You lie,' he hissed. 'You're trying to fool me. There was no time.'

'There is such a thing as a special licence,' Eve said with a touch of smugness, hoping and praying that she would succeed in convincing him that what she said was true. 'On our return Marcus went to Leeds. You see, Gerald, we intend putting Atwood Mine in trust for our children, and he thought it best to set the wheels in motion right away.'

Gerald was staring at her, his face no longer red but white and mute, and Eve had the satisfaction of seeing him tremble as realisation that what she said might be true sent him to the far reaches beyond his control. He looked like a man possessed of the devil. 'Is this true?' he demanded with a note of hysteria.

'Yes.'

He roared his anger, his frustration, madness filling his eyes as his arms thrust out and he grasped her shoulders in a ferocious grip, shaking her forcibly, savagely, snapping her head back and forth. Jonathan screamed in terror, his cry echoing about the shed as he continued to cling to Eve's skirts.

'You witch,' Gerald screamed, releasing her as suddenly as

he had grasped her, throwing her away from him where she fell against the wall, and, supporting herself, Eve watched him crumble. It was with immense satisfaction that she watched him suffer.

Beginning to realise that there might be some element of truth in what she had told him, that what he had wanted for so long had been finally and irretrievably snatched away, Gerald received it with pain and disbelief. It was too much to be borne. He moaned bestially and seemed to disintegrate into agonising torment before Eve's eyes. She knew she should feel sorry for him, but his menacing threats had instilled so much fear inside her, encapsulating her in an ice-cold, venomous rage that gave her no grounds for pity.

Gerald turned his wretched, demented face from her and moved to the door, breathing heavily.

'Where are you going?' she asked, moving forward in alarm. 'You cannot mean to leave us here.'

'You will remain here until I have decided what to do with you,' he hissed, turning his ravaged face to her once more. 'And don't look so smug. This is not over. You haven't won yet.'

'Come to your senses, Gerald,' she cried, beginning to panic. 'At least take Jonathan home. Have you thought what the consequences of your actions might be? Do you suppose no one will wonder where we are—that they will come look- ing for us?'

'They will never find you here,' he cried savagely. 'It will be hard to prove that I am involved in your disappearance— and should I think of disposing of you it will be no problem. It will be thought you wandered off in search of the boy. There are several uncapped mine shafts in the area and, as you know, accidents happen. At least if you are dead you will unable to accuse me of abduction.'

Eve began to panic as terror swept through her. He seemed to have thought of everything. 'Better that than to be accused of murder—which Marcus will prove. That you can be sure of.'

'Not even he will be clever enough to do that,' Gerald snapped, turning from her.

Alarmed that he was going to leave them there, Eve ran to him and appealed to him to let them go, but a ferocious glance and a violent shove that sent her crashing against the wall once more, showed her the futility of such arguments and he went out, making sure the door was well secured behind him. In desperation she sprang towards it, hammering on the solid wood with her fists, begging him to release them, but all she could hear was the still-driving rain and Gerald and his associates riding away from the shed.

Once again Eve found herself alone with Jonathan, who was whimpering softly with his face buried in her skirts. Utterly dejected and chilled to the bone she sat on the floor, pulling the terrified little boy down into her arms whilst trying to calm her own quivering nerves, her imagination beginning to work feverishly as their waiting began anew.

Chapter Fifteen

With almost the entire neighbourhood out searching for Eve and Jonathan, after making a fruitless search along the river and the pond, Marcus headed for Burntwood Hall, intent on confronting Gerald face to face.

He was shown into the drawing room where Gerald, reclining in front of a huge fire, was feeling utterly deflated in the light of what Eve had told him, his instinct—which was unreliable at the best of times—telling him she might not have been lying in an attempt to secure her release. After all, on recollection, he had thought it odd at the time that both she and Fitzalan had suddenly gone to Cumbria. Already he was bitterly regretting his actions and cursing himself for a fool. By abducting Eve he had seriously jeopardised his newly found status, and after much contemplation he could think of no honourable way of extricating himself without being arrested.

Opposite him sat Angela. For a long time she and Gerald had shared a dubious kind of friendship, being too much alike for it to be close—each holding a certain amount of mistrust for the other. But Angela knew from his past dealings with some of his associates that he could make a dangerous enemy and considered it to her disadvantage to have him as such. She had only just arrived at Burntwood Hall and was unaware that anything untoward had happened to Eve or the boy.

Surprise registered in Gerald's eyes when Marcus strode in, which, Marcus assumed, was feigned for his benefit, for he was certain he was expected. He also detected an underlying sense of nervousness and agitation behind Gerald's tense features.

Marcus was wet through, his clothes and coal-black hair clinging to his flesh, but there was no mistaking the imposing, angry man who glared at Gerald with fierce, pale blue eyes as cold as South Atlantic ice floes. His uncompromising face was set as hard as granite, his body powerful beneath his clothes, and it was all he could do to stop himself pouncing on Gerald and beating him to a bloody pulp but, not wishing to jeopardise either Eve's or Jonathan's safety, he behaved with ominous coolness.

Gerald watched him approach, making no attempt to hide his dislike. His tread had a measured, almost sinister steadiness. He rose casually and faced him. 'Why, Mr Fitzalan! To what do I owe this rather dubious pleasure?'

No matter how much he tried Marcus could not control his seething anger on meeting Gerald's insolent, somewhat smug stare. 'This is not a social call. Were it up to me I would never have set foot in this house again now Eve has left. You know why I am here so I shall be brief and to the point. You do not need me to tell you that Eve and the Parkinson boy have gone missing. I know you are responsible. Where are they? Where are you holding them?'

Gerald stiffened at the abruptness of the question and his eyes narrowed as they locked on those of his visitor. 'I don't know what you're talking about. The charge is ridiculous. Why should you think I am responsible for their disappearance?'

'We both know why.' Marcus pitched his voice low, the delivery of his words cold and lethal, his ice blue eyes gleaming with a deadly purpose. 'When it comes to the matter of

Atwood Mine, if you believe threats and bullying will achieve your purpose you are mistaken. Eve told me of your threats towards her, and when I would have come and confronted you she begged me not to. I now have good reason to regret not doing so.

'You made a serious error in threatening her, and you made an even more serious error when you chose to abduct her— which, I might remind you, is a serious criminal offence. You can be assured that the law will come down heavy on you and you will be committed to prison for a very long time—if they don't hang you.'

Sweat began to glisten on Gerald's forehead and he seemed to lose a little of his confidence as he shrank before the cold fury in Marcus's eyes. But with his own safety at stake he refused to surrender.

'I told you. I know nothing about her disappearance. Whatever she has told you was untrue—and if you believe I would harm a relative of mine you are mistaken,' Gerald lied, Eve's connection to him making no difference in his desire to gain Atwood Mine.

'So you would like me to believe. But you showed little sign of surprise when I told you she was missing. I feel sickened at the thought of someone as sweet and decent as Eve in your cruel and unscrupulous hands. You dared,' he said through clenched teeth, 'you dared to abduct her, thinking that by this means you would bring her to agree to cancel her marriage to me. Well, mark my words, I shall find her.'

Gerald shrugged, trying to look unconcerned while hanging on to Marcus's words in the sudden hope that Eve had been bluffing about a marriage taking place between them in Cumbria after all. His mind worked with sharp cunning, for there might still be a chance that he could succeed with his plan. If a marriage had not occurred between them then there was a possibility that he could still acquire the mine—if Eve were dead.

But to dispose of Eve he would have the unpleasant task of

disposing of the boy too. He would have to, otherwise Jonathan would condemn him, for he could not expect the boy to remain silent once he was set free. He cursed afresh the bungling idiots he had employed to abduct Eve. They should have separated the boy and Eve. He should never have let the boy see him. But it was too late now for self-recriminations

'I hope you do,' Gerald retorted coolly, speaking callously, 'and I hope she is not harmed and you do not find a corpse.'

'You would not dare,' growled Marcus, his expression murderous. His eyes flashed dangerously and he restrained himself with effort. With his fists clenched he held back and gained control of himself, and the hot rage that had possessed him since he had left the river where Eve had been abducted slowly cooled down to an icy anger. The air between them was charged with friction.

Gerald's smug expression began to disappear and he shifted with unease as the ice blue eyes continued to accuse. 'I've told you. Her disappearance has nothing to do with me.'

'And I've told you that I do not believe you. You are a scoundrel, Somerville, who can hold his own with the worst of them. I swear that if you harm one hair on Eve's head, or the boy's, there will be no hiding place safe enough to keep you from my vengeance. I shall settle my account the way you settle yours. You may be a Somerville and have inherited the title, but I am a powerful man and I have powerful friends, and I will destroy you if you so much as touch Eve. I swear by all that is holy that I will kill you with my own hands.'

'Even if you hang for it?'

'It will be a pleasure to pay the consequences afterwards to rid the earth of scum of your sort,' Marcus growled.

Angela stepped forward, and Marcus, having given her scant attention, acknowledged her presence with eyes that had never seen her before. His voice spoke to a stranger.

'As you will have gathered I am in no mood for social niceties, Angela. I am hardly surprised to see you here,' he mocked, casting a condescending, well-meaning glance over them both. 'Birds of a feather, and all that. It would not surprise me to learn that you are involved in this.'

Angela shivered beneath his cold, emotionless eyes, feeling slightly nonplussed. Having listened to the angry interchange between the two men she had gathered the gist of their conversation but, contrary to what Marcus might think, she had taken no part in Eve's abduction. Knowing Gerald's malice and determination to stop a marriage from taking place between Marcus and Eve—which had been as strong as her own but for different reasons—no matter what crime he was guilty of, if he went down she would make certain he did not drag her down with him.

'I know nothing about any of this. You must believe that.'

Strangely Marcus did. She might be guilty of malice and jealousy towards Eve, but he did not believe she would cause her any physical harm. 'Not only has Eve disappeared but also Jonathan Parkinson. His parents will be out of their minds with worry.' He looked at Gerald sharply. 'Where are they, damn you?' he demanded, his fists bunched by his sides as he restrained the urge to lash out at him, his patience almost worn out.

'I've told you, I do not know.' Gerald glowered at him. 'And now I suggest you leave quickly—before I summon the servants and have you thrown out.'

'I'm going, but this is not the end of the matter. I shall return with the law, Somerville, and then we'll see how eager you are to remain silent.'

When Marcus had walked out Gerald's face was as white as his shirt, for he knew with a shattering certainty that he had got himself into a situation from which he was beginning to see there was no way out. If he set off for the Kettlewell Mine now he would be followed, for he strongly suspected Marcus would be having his movements watched. Angela's eyes bored into his, seeing panic and a desperate fear staring out of their depths, knowing exactly what he was guilty of and eager to learn the whole of it.

'Dear Lord! It's incredible. You stupid, mindless fool,' she rasped. 'What have you done? Marcus was right. You will go to any lengths to obtain that damned mine. But no matter what you have in mind for Eve, you cannot harm the boy. Surely not even you would stoop so low as to hurt a child.'

Gerald began pacing up and down the room, becoming more agitated by the moment as he frantically tried to think of a way out. He stopped pacing long enough to look at Angela, suddenly thinking that she might be able to offer a solution to the dilemma he was in, although discretion was hardly her stock in trade.

'Very well—I admit it. I did have Eve abducted with the intention of compromising her sufficently so that she would have no choice but to marry me instead of Fitzalan. But it all went hopelessly wrong. Whatever I had planned for Eve, I had not bargained on the boy. He appeared when the men I employed were in the process of carrying her off, and they had no choice but to take him along.'

'Then where are they now?'

'If I tell you, can I rely on your entire confidence?'

'Only if you promise not to harm them.'

'I can't do that. Don't you see? I stand to lose everything.'

Angela moved closer, reaching out and grabbing his arm, her fingers clenching it so hard that he winced and tried to jerk away. She bent her face close to his, her eyes steadfastly burning into his own. 'You will lose everything anyway, Gerald. Marcus will find her—and when he does, if it is too late, you will hang. So, answer me. Where are they?'

Gerald seemed to sag, sensing all was lost. 'In one of the disused sheds at the worked-out Kettlewell Mine—a mile inland off the Leeds road.'

Angela stared at him for just a moment before turning and rushing out of the room, hoping she would be in time to catch Marcus before he left.

Having left the house, Marcus felt the dire need for fresh air to fill his lungs, to clear his head so that he might think, for his fruitless meeting with Gerald had affected him more than he realised. He paused to have a word with the groom who had taken charge of his horse, questioning him about the buildings in and on the estate, intending not to leave any stone unturned if he was to find Eve and the boy.

It came as a surprise when Angela appeared from the house, running quickly towards him, disregarding the rain as it soaked her clothes. Marcus looked at her coldly.

'Well?'

'You must believe that I had no part in this, Marcus. I can be accused of many things, but I am not a murderess. Gerald has told me that Eve is at the old Kettlewell Mine off the Leeds Road. Do you know how to get there?'

Marcus paled visibly. 'Yes. There isn't a mine in the area I don't know about—but I have reason to be alarmed that he has taken her there. The mine hasn't been worked for some time, but as yet I believe the shaft remains uncapped. I'll go directly. Have someone follow with a carriage and tell them to hurry. There's no telling what state they'll be in when I get there.'

Consumed with an acute sense of urgency, without wasting another moment Marcus had hoisted himself into the saddle and disappeared in a curtain of rain, unaware as he did so that Gerald, overcome with panic, and determined to make one last desperate attempt to save himself, had fled from the house by a back way, regretting having told Angela where Eve and the boy could be found. In no time at all he too was riding towards the Kettlewell Mine, hoping to get there before Marcus and remove any evidence of them having been there.

It would be growing dark soon and the very thought of spending the night in the shed horrified Eve. She was tired and exhausted by fear and anger, by despair that there was no reprieve—and even by hunger. She could not remember when they had last eaten. Jonathan, his tender lips set in a grim line and fear filling his eyes, was miserable and terrified and beginning to shiver in his damp clothes. It was turning extremely cold inside the shed, and she knew if they were there much longer he would catch a chill and could become very ill.

In sheer frustration and frozen to the marrow, after the first aftermath of shock wore off, rage began to burn inside Eve at Gerald's wickedness, growing so intense that she ceased to feel the cold. Her rage generated a peculiar kind of strength and she became infuriated that she might fail to escape. Never had she believe one person could be so evil—the evil side to his nature being robust, no doubt well developed by the wild and wicked ways he lived by whilst in London.

She was unprepared to sit and wait for Gerald to return, having decided their fate, without making some attempt to obtain their freedom. In the gloom she feverishly went and tried the door, seeing the wood was beginning to rot in places, but to her disappointment it wouldn't budge. No doubt it was chained and padlocked on the outside.

With a frenzied urgency she gathered everything she thought might be of use to try and prise the door from its rusty hinges—three in all—hoping the screws holding them in place might be forced out of the wooden jamb or that the hinges might break with some persuasion.

Taking an old broken pick she found on the floor of the shed along with other broken implements, she forced the long steel-curved head between the door and the jamb to use as a lever, grasping the broken shaft and gathering all her strength as she put her entire weight behind it, regardless of the damage the splintered shaft was doing to the tender palms of her hands. There was a slight splintering of the wood around the hinge but the door was stout and stubborn and resisted all her efforts.

Seeing what she was trying to do Jonathan willingly came to help, and together their strength—made five times greater by the spur of freedom—caused one of the hinges to snap. Jonathan gave a whoop of triumph, seeming to recover some of his spirits as he became eager to begin on the second hinge.

Eve's heart was beating wildly and her jaw was set as they

set about it, repeating the same process as for the first, pulling and pushing together, with Eve uttering gentle words of encouragement to Jonathan all the while. Concerned about his tender hands gripping the splintered shaft, she tore a strip of fabric from her dress and wrapped it round.

When the second hinge finally snapped, with freedom so close, sweating and gasping for breath, they lost no time in attacking the last hinge at the bottom of the door, such was their determination to be free of their prison before Gerald came back. Very slowly it yielded to the pressure, and using their last ounce of strength they pulled the door inwards and together stepped outside, their spirits soaring. They were free at last.

It was warmer outside than it had been inside the shed. The storm had passed and the rain had stopped and a cool, refreshing breeze stirred the shining, dripping trees around the disused mine. In the crystalline clarity that had been left in the storm's wake, Eve glanced at her surroundings, recognising the Kettlewell Mine, closed for the past eighteen months, its situation not so convenient and advantageous as the larger Atwood Mine. It was approximately two miles as the crow flies from the river where they had been abducted, and not a soul was about.

The mine had an air of neglect and abandonment, with a motley collection of sheds, all in an advanced state of dereliction except the one in which they had been imprisoned. Some old tubs were full of water and the ground was strewn with old haulage ropes and the remains of a rotting horse gin, gradually becoming buried beneath a wild tangle of ivy and weeds, the wood surrounding it encroaching on the pit yard. Her blood froze at the sight of the black gaping hole of the uncapped mine shaft, with nothing to protect the passer-by from falling into the gaping chasm but a crumbling, low stone wall surrounding it.

The area around Atwood had numerous exhausted pits, their shafts, under the conditions of the lease, carefully filled in and the ground left as it was before. Why this mine had been neglected she had no idea, but it was convenient for Gerald that it had been if he had a mind to dispose of her and Jonathan.

Eve paused for a moment, undecided which way to go, but then she took Jonathan's hand tightly in her own. 'Come along, Jonathan. It's growing dark so we must hurry. I know where we are, having ridden this way many times, so we won't get lost.'

Taking an old overgrown wagon track through the trees that led down a slight incline, they set off hopefully in the direction of Jonathan's home. Having taken a different route from Marcus to the Kettlewell Mine, Gerald was the first to arrive at the shed, becoming overcome with fury when he realised his prisoners had escaped. Aware that everything he had recently gained was about to be destroyed, he set off in pursuit like a man possessed, in the direction he knew they would be heading.

Marcus came upon the shed minutes later, but he feared they might have been taken elsewhere by men Gerald might have left to guard them. He paused, undecided which direction to take, but on seeing the muddy ground churned up by horses' hooves and human footprints, and seeing some of them belonged to a child, he realised they were heading in the direction of Atwood.

It was a relief when Eve saw the open fields and the river in the distance through a break in the trees, for the light was fading quickly and she had no wish to be in the woods after dark—the time when one's imagination began to play strange tricks, when everything became weird and uncanny, when the tall trees became awesome and took on the appearance of giants, and one imagined skulking figures could be seen in the shifting shadows among the undergrowth.

She shivered, hearing the yelp and bark of a dog in the distance, but so raw and tense were her nerves, and such was her sense of weariness, that she was convinced it was a wolf that would emerge from the dark, secret world of the undergrowth at any minute and set upon them both with teeth gleaming in a gaping mouth and claws bare.

Quickly she pulled herself together, rebuking herself severely, knowing nothing could be achieved by surrendering to her silly imaginings. Secure in the knowledge that they would soon be home, Eve and Jonathan were unprepared when suddenly a rider, mounted on a tall grey horse, came riding out of the trees like some kind of spectre, bearing down on them at a terrific speed. They became petrified, staring with terrified eyes as he came closer.

Eve recognised Gerald immediately. He was fearsome to look at, with something wild about him, in no way resembling the Gerald of old who was always calm and utterly in control. His face was ravaged by hatred and bitterness, and there was a cold, demonic look in his eyes, his lips drawn tight over his teeth as he bore down on them.

Quickly Eve recovered her presence of mind, and her instinct to protect Jonathan became paramount to all else. She pushed him behind her, unable to get out of the way of the oncoming threat. Knocked sideways by Gerald's horse they fell heavily to the ground, momentarily stunned by the shock of the fall rather than injury. Powerless, they could not move as Gerald began to bear down on them again.

It was the high-pitched scream of a woman that alerted Marcus to their whereabouts and he headed quickly towards the sound. In a few moments he burst upon the scene just as Gerald was about to dismount beside the huddled figures of Eve and Jonathan, but on seeing Marcus's powerful silhouette against the trees, Gerald let out a howl of outrage and frustration, resembling an enduring, hissing spirit of hatred, before digging his heels viciously into his horse's flanks and riding off at breakneck speed, as if all the demons in hell were chasing him.

Eve struggled to her feet, pulling Jonathan with her, and Marcus saw that she was barely able to stand. She had evidently reached the limits of her strength. Her face was as white as alabaster and pinched as if with cold, but her wonderful violet eyes shone with an unearthly brilliance and were fastened on his as she moved towards him. There was a trembling smile on her lips and her magnificent mane of black hair flowed about her shoulders.

'Marcus!' she said, speaking his name again as he seemed not to hear, dwelling on it with wonder, her legs taking on an added strength as she moved towards him, unable to believe he had come to her in time, saved her and Jonathan from the dreadful fate that Gerald had in store for them.

The palms of her hands were scraped raw and bleeding from her efforts to free herself and Jonathan, which she held out to him, tumbling headlong into his arms as they went around her, clasping her fiercely to him at last, where she immediately felt warm, secure and protected—at one with this man she loved above all else. It was as if she had come home.

At that moment Eve felt more tired than she had ever felt in her whole life. It was as if the last few hours had been days and had drained her of every particle of strength. For a long moment they clung to each other in silence, too relieved and deeply moved by the depth of their feelings for speech.

'Eve—my darling girl,' Marcus said at length. 'It's all right now. Everything is all right. You are safe,' he whispered, overcome with a profound relief that he had found them in time. 'What a time I have had trying to find you. That madman of a Somerville planned his stroke with evil cunning.'

'Yes,' Eve murmured against his neck, a great unbelievable joy overwhelming her. 'I'm safe—free. Oh, Marcus, I can't believe it's really you. Thank God you came in time.'

'When I think of you shut up in that place, knowing of your ordeal, of your terror—of the damage a man of Gerald's nature might have done to you—I could kill him.'

'Hush,' said Eve, raising her head and looking into his tormented eyes. 'I am all right, Marcus. Truly. He did not touch me in the way I know you mean, and for that I am thankful.'

'You look quite worn out. Are either of you hurt?' he asked, holding Eve at arm's length and looking with concern at them both. He was relieved to see that Jonathan looked surprisingly well as he looked up at him in wide-eyed wonder, but Marcus was alarmed when he saw a thin trickle of crusted blood on the side of Eve's face. Murderous fury filled his eyes and reaching up he touched it gently with the tips of his fingers, seeing her wince slightly. 'How did this happen?'

'I took a tumble—hitting my head when the men Gerald employed to abduct me came upon me unawares. But don't worry. I am exhausted but quite unharmed.'

Other people out searching for them, also having been alerted by Eve's scream, suddenly appeared on the scene, taking charge of Jonathan and allowing Marcus to go in pursuit of Gerald.

'Take them to the house,' he ordered. 'Quickly. I'll go after Gerald. If I don't go now it will soon be too dark.'

Eve looked at him in alarm as Jonathan was being lifted up on to a horse in front of one of the rescuers, his little face smiling now, for the whole thing had turned into one big adventure he couldn't wait to tell his sisters about.

'You will be careful, Marcus,' she begged as he swung himself effortlessly into the saddle. 'I couldn't bear it if anything should happen to you.'

Bending down he kissed her upturned lips. 'I will,' he said hoarsely. 'After what Gerald has done this day he has much to answer for. I do not intend letting him escape.'

Eve watched him go, and as she did so she glanced up automatically at the sky, seeing that all the stars were out, shining brightly in a clear, darkening sky, with no evidence of the storm that had raged throughout the day.

Chapter Sixteen

Losing no more time Marcus gave chase, relieved when he had Gerald within his sights once more, and as he gave his horse its head, plunging through the thick woods that cloaked the low hills, he was possessed of a grim determination not to let Gerald escape.

They were heading in the direction of Atwood, and it was a relief when he emerged from the trees and was able to see him clearly as he rode at breakneck speed towards the river, splashing through it and riding over ground that became uneven, broken and treacherous the closer he got to the quarry.

Aware that Marcus was in pursuit and gaining on him, without checking his horse's stride Gerald thrashed its sweating flanks hard with his whip. The terrified horse bolted from the pain cruelly inflicted on it, riding closer to the precarious, crumbling perimeter of the quarry, the recent rain having formed a pond at the bottom that was littered with piles of rocks and boulders which had become dislodged over the years.

Hawthorn and brambles grew thickly along the upper edge to deceive the eye, partly covering the slippery path which was in danger of crumbling down the steep precipice after the recent heavy rain. Marcus could see Gerald getting ever closer to the edge and shouted a warning, but he ignored Marcus. It wasn't until Gerald felt the ground beneath him shudder and he saw loosened earth and rocks tumbling down to the bottom of the quarry, that he tried to draw his horse away, but it was too late.

With a high-pitched, maddened squeal the horse reared up, losing its footing and thrashing its legs wildly at the empty air as it toppled over the edge. Gerald's face registered horror and surprise as he fought to regain control, but there was nothing he could do. Pulling his own horse to a halt, Marcus watched helplessly as horse and rider were somersaulted through the air, seeming to hover for a brief second like a bird, before becoming separated and bouncing off the rocky side of the quarry, finally reaching the bottom where they both lay still.

By this time some of the other riders out with the search party had caught up, and seeing what had happened immediately dismounted and accompanied Marcus down an overgrown track, once used by countless wagons and horses to shift the stone hewn out of the giant hole. Gerald was lying on his back, his limbs flung out grotesquely. His brown eyes were wide open and staring, a thin trickle of blood forming at his mouth. Marcus did not need to place his head on his chest to listen for a heartbeat that did not exist to know that Gerald was dead.

Relief was clearly felt in the Parkinson household when Eve and Jonathan returned, mercifully unharmed. Mrs Parkinson swept the little boy into her arms, refusing to let him out of her sight ever again. On hearing of the events leading up to their abduction, after scolding him severely for going off and causing so much trouble, she hugged him again.

After removing his clothes and placing him in a hot mustard bath, she put him to bed with a bowl of soup, where he was cosseted by all his sisters and his mother. Being a robust child he suffered no aftereffects from the ordeal, not even a chill after his soaking. But the story of how they had escaped from the shed would be an adventure he would never tire of telling.

* * *

The day of Eve's abduction and her imprisonment in the shed at the old Kettlewell Mine was like a grotesque nightmare in her memory. The hour was late but she refused to go to bed until she had seen Marcus. It was as though all the energy she had concentrated on getting out of that shed, of escaping Gerald's evil and protecting Jonathan, had drained out of her, and her spirits sank to such a low ebb that she almost ceased to function.

When she heard the news of Gerald's death in the quarry from one of the searchers, who called at the house with the news, she was overcome with shock—as was Matthew, who left immediately to go to him, even though it was too late.

When Gerald's body had been removed from the quarry, Marcus came straight to her. The house was quiet now, everyone having retired to their room after the worry and excitement of the day's events. Eve came down from her room where she had been resting, waiting for him to come to her.

As she came towards him, her hands outstretched, rage rose inside Marcus when he saw how deeply her ordeal at Gerald's hands had affected her. She was pitiful to look at. Her violet eyes were enormous in her pale face, the dark circles of pain and terror making them look even larger.

He opened his arms and she walked into them like a child seeking succour, but before she laid her head against his chest he saw her chin tremble and tears she could no longer hold back brimming in her eyes and spilling over.

'Oh, Marcus,' she wept, over and over again, with her face against his chest, letting the violence of all the raw emotions that would not come before now flow uncontrollably out of her. He held her a long time, rocking her and kissing her hair, murmuring sweet, gentle words of comfort while she sobbed, quietly and wretchedly, waiting patiently until she had mastered her tears, aching with a love for her that was like a deep, physical pain.

He cradled her in his arms, holding her close while she poured out all her anguish and misery. Everything that had happened to her that day came out in a torrent of words and he listened, knowing that it was good for her to talk like this, that it would help cleanse her of the evil Gerald had perpetrated against her, that it would help with the healing process later.

When Eve became still and quiet in his arms, feeling an unbelievable comfort of knowing he was holding her, that she was safe, she sighed, wiping her tears with her hands.

'My poor darling,' Marcus murmured, his lips against her hair. 'What has he done to you?'

'Nothing that won't heal,' she whispered bravely.

'How is the boy?'

'Jonathan is all right. He—he survived it well—better than I have myself, it would seem,' she said, smiling up at him through her wet lashes.

'Thank God.'

'We—we were told what happened to Gerald. Where is he?' she asked. 'Where has he been taken?'

'Burntwood Hall. It was his home,' he said gently. 'Matthew is there.'

'I know. He—he is taking it very badly. Did he suffer, Marcus?'

'I don't think so. I should think he died instantly. His neck was broken.'

Eve leaned back in his arms and looked up at him, her eyes luminous with tears. 'Gerald tried to destroy me, Marcus. If I hadn't got out of that shed I am certain he would have returned and killed me—and Jonathan, who just happened to be there when the men he paid to abduct me seized their chance by the river.'

Marcus's arms tightened around her. 'If he had then he would not have escaped with his life. I would have found him and exacted my revenge,' he said hoarsely, his voice shaking with angry emotion. 'Come,' he said, taking her hand and leading her into the empty parlour, where they sat close together on a high-backed settle beside the dying embers of the fire, Marcus's arm holding her close, reluctant to let her go ever again. 'How are you feeling now?'

'Overwhelmed by a turmoil of emotions. Oh—it's a combination of relief, gladness, and at the same time a feeling of horror, mingled with some element of surprise—knowing that the man who intended destroying my own life is dead himself. Oh, Marcus, I was so frightened.'

Marcus held her tighter. 'So was I. When Matthew told me you had disappeared, you have no idea how my thoughts tormented me—what I went through.' Sighing, he kissed the top of her head where it rested on his shoulder. 'When I imagined what he might be doing to you—that he might already have killed you—I went through hell. Dear God, how I wish I had never gone to Leeds—that I had insisted on you staying at Brooklands. If I had, none of this would have happened. I should have foreseen what he would do.'

'Don't blame yourself. It wasn't your fault. Neither of us were to know he would go to such drastic lengths.'

'You are very generous but I cannot be acquitted so lightly, my love.'

Eve stirred against him, raising her head and meeting his fierce gaze, seeing just how much he had suffered on her behalf. 'Yes, you can. When Gerald came to see me in the hut where he had Jonathan and me imprisoned, in my desperation I tried to bluff my way out by telling him we had been married by special licence in Cumbria, and that no matter what he did to me it was too late, that he could never get his hands on the mine.'

There was incredulity and admiration in Marcus's eyes. 'And he believed you?'

'At first he was suspicious and uncertain—but I tried to sound so convincing that I think he did in the end. He was so angry I wasn't certain what he would do. He became demented. I begged him to release us but he wouldn't listen. He left us there. I had no way of knowing what he would do next. By the way, there is one thing I do not understand. How did you know where to look for us? When you came upon us in the wood you were coming from the direction of the Kettlewell Mine. Someone must have told you we were there.'

Marcus smiled tenderly down at her. 'It will surprise you to learn that you have Angela to thank for that. She was the one who told me where I could find you.'

Eve stared at him aghast. 'Angela? Are you telling me that *she* had something to do with my abduction?'

'No. She knew nothing about it—not until I went to Burntwood Hall and confronted Gerald. She was there at the time and was clearly horrified that Gerald might be involved in some way. It would seem he told her where you could be found after I'd left, although I do not doubt she managed to force the truth out of him—by whatever means I know not, and nor do I wish to, but I'm grateful to her that she did. She may be jealous of you, my love, but I do not believe she would wish you any physical harm. I do not believe her to be vindictive enough for that.'

'I'm glad you think so,' Eve whispered, surprised by Angela's behaviour. 'Acting alone Gerald was bad enough—but Angela and Gerald together would have been a lethal combination. How he must have longed for you to confirm that what I had told him about a marriage taking place between us was true or false.'

'He couldn't very well ask me outright. If he had he would have been forced to confess his part in your abduction—and been too afraid of the consequences. I would have had no compunction about killing him.'

Eve drew back and looked up at him, shuddering slightly on observing his taut features and the steely gleam in his eyes, knowing he spoke the truth. 'You would have done that for me?' she asked.

'I would do anything for you, Eve' he said achingly, unable to restrain himself, pulling her back into his arms. 'Never doubt it. I love you and cannot imagine my life without you. I adore you and very soon the whole world will know it.'

'There is one thing that troubles me greatly, Marcus.'

'What is that?'

'These people Gerald owed money to. Are they likely to approach Matthew—being Gerald's brother?'

'I don't think so. If they try I doubt they will get anything. The loan had nothing to do with him. The people who lent Gerald the money are scoundrels of the worst kind. No doubt it's the unfortunate people in the future—people who find themselves in the same desperate situation as Gerald—who will end up paying. The interest on such loans is extortionate. Oh—I almost forgot,' he said, changing the subject. 'I bought you something in Leeds.'

Taking the ring he had bought for her out of his pocket, he placed it on her finger. Eve sighed, dazzled by its beauty, content to wallow in Marcus's doting gaze, having no doubts that he loved her—genuinely loved her—and that that love would grow with time and supplant everything else in importance. She could see that in his eyes and it made her ecstatically happy.

The following morning when Marcus was taking it into his own hands to see that the uncapped shaft at the Kettlewell Mine was securely sealed off, Matthew came to see Eve.

On seeing his deep distress over the death of his brother, her heart went out to him. He was distraught, almost demolished by it, knowing what it would mean to him and that drastic changes would take place and affect his life. He was panicked, and at one fell swoop his youthful air had vanished.

'You know what this means, don't you, Matthew?' Eve said when they were alone walking in the garden, feeling the sun cocooning them in its warmth. 'Gerald's death makes you the heir to the Somerville estate.'

'Yes, I know. But it is not the way I wished to inherit Burntwood Hall.'

'It is more than the truth when I say you are eminently

worthy of taking my father's place, Matthew. It makes me very happy to know the estate will be in capable hands.'

'Thank you, Eve. I shall do my best to always be worthy of it. I promise you that. But I never wanted this. I never thought I would inherit the estate at all. It was always Gerald's right, to pass on to his sons.'

'None of us could have foreseen this happening, Matthew,' Eve said sympathetically.

'I know. I knew what Gerald was—and I also knew he would never reform and give up his wild ways and settle down and take a sincere interest in the estate. But despite what he did to you, Eve—which was quite outrageous and unforgivable and has shocked me deeply—he was always civilised with me. Being so much younger than he was, he always looked out for me—especially after our parents died—and there were times when we were close.'

Eve let him talk, calmly listening to him defending the man who would have had no qualms in getting rid of her in order to retain Atwood Mine. She knew how difficult it had been for Matthew, growing up in Gerald's shadow, and she was sad for him, fighting the compassion welling up inside her, and the urge to argue and tell him he was a fool to be so generous towards a man whom she believed to have been capable of murder. She resisted the urge to vent her own bitterness, for all the raw emotions Gerald had awakened inside her were as strong as ever.

But she could not be so cruel. She would be immediately sorry. Let Matthew keep his illusions. In his own way he had loved Gerald, and Gerald had always treated Matthew well, regardless of what he was guilty of where everyone else was concerned. No matter how hard it was for her to come to terms with what Gerald had done to her, they had been brothers, and she must respect that.

'He wasn't really wicked,' Matthew went on, his eyes filled with pain and grief as he tried to make Eve see a side to his brother only he knew, one she had never seen and had no wish to. 'As a boy, and later as a youth, our mother and grand-mother doted on him, making him spoiled and unprincipled. He always had too much of everything and thought the world owed him obeisance. He was too good looking by far—more so than I was,' he said with admirable humility.

'You are generous towards your brother, Matthew. More than he deserves,' Eve said gently. 'Your loyalty is to be commended. But do not underestimate yourself. I cannot think kindly of Gerald, but I do understand that he was your brother and he did not deserve you. If he had been half the man you are, my father and I would have been content knowing the estate was to pass to him—but his character made that impossible.'

'I know, and I do understand, Eve. But,' he sighed, 'I am a simple man and life has suddenly become extremely complex.'

'I think you'll cope admirably,' she smiled, linking her arm through his as they continued to walk companionably around the garden. 'My father would have been a happy man, Matthew, knowing you were to move into Burntwood Hall—especially if Emma is to share it with you.'

Matthew stared at her in shocked amazement. 'Emma? Why—I—I had not thought—'

'You are going to marry her, aren't you, Matthew?'

'Why—yes,' he said, smiling with embarrassment, awkward suddenly. 'I suppose I am—if she will have me, of course. I haven't asked her.'

'Then when the time is right I think you should,' Eve said softly, teasingly, her eyes eloquent and her lips smiling encouragement. 'You are a good man, Matthew. No one knowing you could fail to love you. Whatever happens, no one can ever doubt you are worthy to fall into my father's footsteps.'

Eve returned to Burntwood Hall and the servants welcomed her back warmly and tearfully, knowing her return was only temporary and that she would leave very soon when she mar-

ried Mr Fitzalan. But they were happy knowing Matthew
Somerville was next in line and would shortly be taking up
residence.

Eve had them all assembled in the hall, telling them
Matthew would undoubtedly want them all to stay on, that he
would be depending on them, and she knew they would give
him all the help and consideration due to him.

Gerald's funeral was as small and quiet an affair as Eve's
marriage to Marcus one week later. Eve, having cast off the
gloom of mourning, was a vision of loveliness in a dress of
cream silk, as slender as a wand as she moved beside Marcus
Fitzalan, tall and powerful, looking extremely handsome in his
black suit beneath which he wore a white satin waistcoat, his
ebony hair brushed smoothly back from his brow.

The wedding was attended by just a few close friends, followed afterwards by a wedding breakfast at Burntwood Hall,
where the atmosphere was light-hearted, and Eve would catch
her husband's eye and a smile would move across his lean
face, his eyes becoming more vividly blue over the rim of his
champagne glass, silently informing her of his impatience for
the night to come.

'Marriage obviously agrees with you,' he told her softly
when he managed to get her to himself for a brief moment. 'I
have never seen you look more delectable than you do at this
moment.'

'Don't all brides?' she murmured.

'I only have eyes for the one,' he replied.

Emma was almost as radiant as the bride, losing no time in
telling Eve that there would be another wedding in the spring
of the following year, that Matthew had asked her to marry
him.

Eve hugged her happily. 'I am so thrilled for you, Em.
Things couldn't have turned out better.'

'I never thought this would happen to me. Can you imagine
it? Me! Lady Somerville! Oh—I'll never get used to it.'

'Yes, you will,' laughed Eve, 'and the title could not have

gone to a nicer person. Now I shall be able to come back to Burntwood Hall whenever I like.'

Emma became serious. 'We've both been fortunate, Eve—but Matthew is nervous about his inheritance. It's such an enormous responsibility.'

'He needn't be. He has you by his side and he is by far a worthier heir to the estate than Gerald ever was.'

Mr Soames was present for the wedding, clearly satisfied and highly delighted that things had been resolved between Eve and Marcus Fitzalan in the way her father would have wished. The love they felt for each other was plain to see; in fact, it was difficult to believe they were the same two people who had faced each other with so much rancour at the reading of Sir John's will.

'With Gerald dead and Matthew in charge of the estate, Eve,' he said when they were alone, 'your father would have been well pleased. His main reason for the conditions laid down in his will was to see you taken care of by someone he could trust. Knowing your reasons for doing so, I think you made a wise decision putting Atwood Mine in trust for your children. I know your father would not have objected to this.'

Eve had no regrets when she left Burntwood Hall with Marcus and his mother for her new home.

Ruth Fitzalan, who had been deeply upset by Eve's ordeal at the hands of her father's cousin, could not be happier at the way everything had turned out. She was also enormously relieved that both Eve and Marcus were in agreement about Atwood Mine, having put it in the hands of trustees until any children they might have came of age and were in a position themselves to decide what was to be done with it. Not wishing to be in the way at Brooklands, she had decided to travel to London the following day to stay with her son William, his wife Daisy and their two children.

'Please don't feel that you have to leave Brooklands,' said Eve, aware of her mother-in-law's intent.

'I don't, my dear,' she smiled. 'But it is important that you and Marcus should be alone. I want you to get to know each other and familiarise yourself with Brooklands without me breathing down your neck. I had hoped to travel to London with Angela, but I hear she left last week.'

Marcus and Eve exchanged knowing, secretive glances, having decided not to tell her of Angela's conniving and malicious behaviour towards Eve. It would solve no purpose and would sour the close friendship she had with Angela's parents—and besides, had it not been for Angela telling Marcus where Gerald had taken her, everything might have turned out much different.

'Now you're married, I am hoping to spend more time in London—visiting friends and so forth,' Ruth went on. 'And I am so looking forward to seeing William and Daisy and the children again. There is also a strong possibility that Michael may pay them a visit. His ship is due to dock at Plymouth shortly and he has written that he will try and get up to London.'

She looked fondly at her new daughter-in-law sitting close to Marcus, knowing that if she had not been present they would be in each other's arms. Never had she seen two people look more in love than these two and it gladdened her heart.

'I hope you will like living at Brooklands, Eve. I remember when I first came as a bride I was filled with trepidation—but I soon settled down and grew to love the place.'

'Then I am sure I shall,' Eve smiled.

Marcus looked at her, his eyes warm and full of affection. 'And she will love it all the more because I am there,' he teased softly. He arched a brow, amused when Eve gave him a feigned look of exasperation.

'Why, I see your conceit has not diminished now you are a married man, Marcus,' she chided playfully.

'You're not impressed?'

'Not in the least. You're a complete rogue.'

Marcus gazed at her, his eyes amused. 'I do not deny it. But it cannot bother you too much, otherwise you wouldn't have fallen so readily for my irresistible charm,' he teased and he smiled, the kind of smile that would melt any woman's heart.

Eve returned his smile a little shyly. 'I am beginning to see that I was a complete fool to get involved with you. You're quite outrageous.'

'Absolutely,' he grinned.

'He always was,' commented his mother in complete agreement, wishing the carriage would hurry and reach Brooklands so she could leave the two of them alone.

That night as they got to know each other, neither had any complaints. Marcus was a strong, superlatively aggressive, masterful lover, which was an aspect Eve had suspected of him, but he also knew when to be exquisitely tender and polite. How could either of them have believed that theirs could ever be a marriage of convenience? The attraction between them was too powerful, too consuming for either of them to resist.

On finding themselves alone in the room they were to share, unable to keep his hands off Eve a moment longer, Marcus had immediately encircled her with his arms.

'Have I told you you make the most beautiful bride?' he whispered, catching her ear lobe between his teeth and biting it gently before finding her lips, silently informing her of his love as she felt the hot breath in his throat, the hammering in his chest.

Eve smiled, loving him, wanting him. 'Several times,' she breathed, her lips close to his.

'And you look so delectable in your cream dress—but I am impatient to see what you're wearing under it. I suspect it conceals a body destined to stir the lusty instincts of any man.'

Eve laughed up into his face, flushing delightfully. 'Marcus Fitzalan, you are incorrigible. You will see soon enough,' she said, but she soon saw that all form of resistance was futile for already he was expertly fumbling with her buttons. She gasped. 'Marcus! This is not how a gentleman should behave. I have my maid to undress me.'

'And I have dismissed her. I can assure you I make a rather good lady's maid when the occasion requires it.'

'I am sure you do—but I would thank you not to regale me with the lurid details of your past amours. Kindly keep them to yourself,' she laughed breathlessly as he went on to remove her dress completely, leaving her standing before him in her white, soft shift, which was soon removed along with the rest of her clothes.

She stood tall and slender, lithe-limbed and graceful, watching him calmly as his eyes travelled from the top of her dark head to her slender feet, with incredulity and disbelief, before meeting her eyes. They looked at each other for a long moment that stretched into eternity.

'What can I say?' he murmured at length, moving to stand in front of her. 'You look quite incredible. Exquisite.'

Eve trembled, looking up into his blue, brooding eyes, her face full of passion and her moist lips parted and quivering, longing for the kiss she expected but did not come. Instead he brushed her lips with the tips of his fingers, sensing her mood.

'I intend to make love to you until you beg for mercy.' His lips curled into a smile at the warm glow that shone in her wonderful violet eyes, which told him he would be welcome.

Marcus proceeded to do what his fingers had ached to do all evening. Slowly and methodically he unbound her hair, spreading it like a soft, shimmering cloud over her gleaming shoulders before gathering her up into his arms and carrying her to the bed.

As he leant over her his warm, moist lips began to kiss every inch of her naked body and, touching, lingeringly tracing the line of her hip, her thigh, he felt the curl of her body towards his, the inevitable longing stirring his own. Overwhelmed by the intensity of his passion, Eve yielded herself to his soft, caressing touch willingly, clutching and clinging as he covered her quivering body with his own, and he felt her flow into him with a lavish generosity that left him astounded as they came together as easily as night follows day.

Afterwards Marcus gathered her into his arms and sighed, looking down at her upturned face. 'Happy?'

'Ecstatically.'

'You look wonderful. Your eyes are sparkling and your cheeks are pink. In fact, you look radiant and I cannot wait to make love to you again,' he murmured, his wonderful eyes devouring her, and then they were silent, each anticipating and savouring the sensations building up anew inside them.

'You are lovely, Eve—and you were lovely three years ago—the most captivating young lady I had ever seen. You were gentle, innocent, totally unaware of the effect you had on me.'

'And now?'

'Now you are even more beautiful.'

She smiled. 'I think you flatter me to tempt me, Mr Fitzalan,' she teased.

'You are quite right,' he murmured, his eyes glowing with love and adoration as he gazed down at her. 'Are you complaining, Mrs Fitzalan?' he asked, with his lips nuzzling her neck, persistent, soft, passionate.

'Not when I have such a passionate, attentive husband.'

'Then stop resisting and give in to the magic of the moment, my darling,' he murmured.

And she did as she was told, happy to do so now she was his wife, revelling in the sweet anticipation of the rest of the night—and the rest of their lives to come. They loved and slept and towards morning there was more love, and by the time the sun rose Marcus knew that the wonderful temptress who had tried to seduce him three years ago had returned to him. She had not vanished, after all. She was there, just waiting to be resurrected.

* * * * *

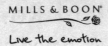

PENNINGTON

BOOK FOUR

Available from 3rd October 2003

*Available at most branches of WHSmith, Tesco, Martins, Borders,
Eason, Sainsbury's and most good paperback bookshops.*